PENGUIN CLAS

ANTON CHEKHOV
A LIFE IN LETTERS

ANTON PAVLOVICH CHEKHOV, the son of a former serf, was born in 1860 in Taganrog, a port on the Sea of Azov. He received a classical education at the Taganrog Gymnasium, then in 1879 went to Moscow, where he entered the medical faculty of the university, graduating in 1884. During his university years he supported his family by contributing humorous stories and sketches to magazines. He published his first volume of stories, *Motley Stories*, in 1886 and a year later his second volume, *In the Twilight*, for which he was awarded the Pushkin Prize. In 1887 his first full-length play, *Ivanov*, was produced in Moscow. For five years he lived on his small country estate near Moscow, practising medicine and writing many of his best stories, but when his health began to fail he moved to the Crimea. After 1900, the rest of his life was spent at Yalta, where he met Tolstoy and Gorky. He wrote his best-known plays in the last years of his life; in 1898 Stanislavsky produced *The Seagull* at his newly founded Moscow Art Theatre, and it was for him that Chekhov wrote *Uncle Vanya* (1900), *Three Sisters* (1901) and *The Cherry Orchard* (1903). In 1901 Chekhov married Olga Knipper, one of the Art Theatre's leading actresses. He died of consumption in 1904.

ROSAMUND BARTLETT lectures in Russian and music at the University of Durham. The author of *Wagner and Russia* (1995), *Literary Russia: A Guide* (with Anna Benn, 1997) and *Chekhov: Scenes from a Life* (2004), she has edited a collection of essays about Shostakovich and published numerous articles on aspects of Russian cultural history. She has also completed new translations of a selection of Chekhov's short stories: *About Love and Other Stories* (2004)

ANTHONY PHILLIPS learnt Russian in the Secret Classrooms of National Service in the 1950s and later at Oxford, where his tutor was the Chekhov specialist and biographer Ronald Hingley. The language continued to play an important part throughout his subsequent career in music administration, during which he became general manager of London's Royal Festival Hall. *Story of Friendship*, his translation of Dmitry Shostakovich's letters to Isaak Glikman, was published by Faber in 2000. He is now working on a version of Rachmaninov's letters.

ANTON CHEKHOV

A Life in Letters

Edited by ROSAMUND BARTLETT
Translated by ROSAMUND BARTLETT
and ANTHONY PHILLIPS

PENGUIN BOOKS

PENGUIN BOOKS

Published by the Penguin Group
Penguin Books Ltd, 80 Strand, London WC2R ORL, England
Penguin Group (USA), Inc., 375 Hudson Street, New York, New York 10014, USA
Penguin Books Australia Ltd, 250 Camberwell Road, Camberwell, Victoria 3124, Australia
Penguin Books Canada Ltd, 10 Alcorn Avenue, Toronto, Ontario, Canada M4V 3B2
Penguin Books India (P) Ltd, 11 Community Centre, Panchsheel Park, New Delhi – 110 017, India
Penguin Group (NZ) Ltd, cnr Airborne and Rosedale Roads, Albany, Auckland 1310, New Zealand
Penguin Books (South Africa) (Pty) Ltd, 24 Sturdee Avenue, Rosebank 2196, South Africa

Penguin Books Ltd, Registered Offices: 80 Strand, London WC2R ORL, England

www.penguin.com

First published 2004

025

Editorial material copyright © Rosamund Bartlett, 2004
Translation copyright © Rosamund Bartlett and Anthony Phillips, 2004
Chronology copyright © Ronald Wilks, 2004
All rights reserved

The moral rights of the editor and translators have been asserted

Set in 11.25/12.75 pt Monotype Fournier
Typeset by Rowland Phototypesetting Ltd, Bury St Edmunds, Suffolk

Printed and bound in Great Britain by Clays Ltd, Elcograf S.p.A.

www.greenpenguin.co.uk

MIX
Paper | Supporting
responsible forestry
FSC
www.fsc.org   FSC® C018179

Penguin Books is committed to a sustainable
future for our business, our readers and our planet.
This book is made from Forest Stewardship
Council™ certified paper.

Contents

Contents

Chronology

1836 Gogol's *The Government Inspector*

1852 Turgenev's *Sketches from a Hunter's Album*

1860 Dostoyevsky's *Notes from the House of the Dead* (1860–61)
    Anton Pavlovich Chekhov born on 17 January at Taganrog, a
port on the Sea of Azov, the third son of Pavel Egorovich Chekhov,
a grocer, and Evgenia Yakovlevna, née Morozova

1861 Emancipation of the serfs by Alexander II. Formation of revolutionary Land and Liberty Movement

1862 Turgenev's *Fathers and Sons*

1863–4 Polish revolt. Commencement of intensive industrialization;
spread of the railways; banks established; factories built. Elective
District Councils (*zemstvos*) set up; judicial reform
    Tolstoy's *The Cossacks* (1863)

1865 'Lady Macbeth of Mtsensk District' (1864) by Leskov, a writer
much admired by Chekhov

1866 Attempted assassination of Alexander II by Karakozov
    Dostoyevsky's *Crime and Punishment*

1867 Emile Zola's *Thérèse Raquin*

1868 Dostoyevsky's *The Idiot*
    Chekhov begins to attend Taganrog Gymnasium after wasted
year at a Greek school

1869 Tolstoy's *War and Peace*

1870 Municipal government reform

1870–71 Franco-Prussian War

1873 Tolstoy's *Anna Karenina* (1873–7)

Chekhov sees local productions of *Hamlet* and Gogol's *The Government Inspector*

1875 Chekhov writes and produces humorous magazine for his brothers in Moscow, *The Stammerer*, containing sketches of life in Taganrog

1876 Chekhov's father declared bankrupt and flees to Moscow, followed by all but Chekhov and his brother Ivan, who are left in Taganrog to complete schooling. Reads Buckle, Hugo and Schopenhauer

1877–8 War with Turkey

1877 Chekhov's first visit to Moscow; his family living in great hardship

1878 Chekhov writes dramatic juvenilia: full-length drama *Fatherlessness* (MS destroyed), comedy *Diamond Cut Diamond* and vaudeville *Why Hens Cluck* (none published)

1879 Dostoyevsky's *The Brothers Karamazov* (1879–80)

Tolstoy's *Confession* (1879–82)

Chekhov matriculates from Gymnasium with good grades. Wins scholarship to Moscow University to study medicine

Makes regular contributions to humorous magazine *Alarm Clock*

1880 General Loris-Melikov organizes struggle against terrorism

Guy de Maupassant's 'Boule de Suif'

Chekhov introduced by artist brother Nikolay to landscape painter Levitan, with whom has lifelong friendship

First short story, 'A Letter from the Don Landowner Vladimirovich N to His Learned Neighbour', published in humorous magazine *Dragonfly*. More stories published in *Dragonfly* under pseudonyms, chiefly Antosha Chekhonte

1881 Assassination of Alexander II; reactionary, stifling regime of Alexander III begins

Sarah Bernhardt visits Moscow (Chekhov calls her acting 'superficial')

Chekhov continues to write very large numbers of humorous sketches for weekly magazines (until 1883). Becomes regular contributor to Nikolay Leikin's *Fragments*, a St Petersburg weekly humorous magazine. Writes (1881–2) play now usually known as

Platonov (discovered 1923), rejected by Maly Theatre; tries to destroy manuscript

1882 Student riots at St Petersburg and Kazan universities. Increased discrimination against Jews

Chekhov is able to support the family with scholarship money and earnings from contributions to humorous weeklies

1883 Tolstoy's *What I Believe*

Chekhov gains practical experience at Chikino Rural Hospital

1884 Henrik Ibsen's *The Wild Duck*. J.-K. Huysmans' *A Rebours*

Chekhov graduates and becomes practising physician at Chikino. First signs of his tuberculosis in December

Six stories about the theatre published as *Tales of Melpomene*. His crime novel, *The Shooting Party*, serialized in *Daily News*

1885–6 Tolstoy's *The Death of Ivan Ilyich* (1886)

On first visit to St Petersburg, Chekhov begins friendship with Alexey Suvorin (1834–1912), very influential editor of the highly regarded daily newspaper *New Times*. Chekhov has relationships with Dunia Efros and Natalia Golden (later his sister-in-law). His TB is now unmistakable

Publishes more than 100 short stories. 'The Requiem' is the first story to appear under own name and his first in *New Times* (February 1886). First collection, *Motley Stories*

1887 Five students hanged for attempted assassination of Tsar; one is Lenin's brother

Tolstoy's drama *Power of Darkness* (first performed in Paris), for which he was called nihilist and blasphemer by Alexander III

Chekhov elected member of Literary Fund. Makes trip to Taganrog and Don steppes

Second book of collected short stories *In the Twilight*. *Ivanov* produced – a disaster

1888 Chekhov meets Stanislavsky. Attends many performances at Maly and Korsh theatres and becomes widely acquainted with actors, stage managers, etc. Meets Tchaikovsky

Completes 'The Steppe', which marks his 'entry' into serious literature. Wins Pushkin Prize for 'the best literary production distinguished by high artistic value' for *In the Twilight*, presented by literary division of Imperial Academy of Sciences. His one-act farces *The Bear* (highly praised by Tolstoy) and *The Proposal* extremely successful. Begins work on *The Wood Demon* (later *Uncle Vanya*). Radically revises *Ivanov* for St Petersburg performance

1889 Tolstoy's *The Kreutzer Sonata* (at first highly praised by Chekhov)

Chekhov meets Lidia Avilova, who later claims love affair with him. Tolstoy begins to take an interest in Chekhov, who is elected to Society of Lovers of Russian Literature

'A Dreary Story'. *The Wood Demon* a resounding failure

1890 Chekhov travels across Siberia by carriage and river boat to Sakhalin to investigate conditions at the penal colony (recorded in *The Island of Sakhalin*). After seven months returns to Moscow (via Hong Kong, Singapore and Ceylon (Sri Lanka)

Collection *Gloomy People* (dedicated to Tchaikovsky). Only two stories published – 'Gusev' and 'Thieves'. Immense amount of preparatory reading for *The Island of Sakhalin*

1891 Severe famine in Volga basin (Chekhov organizes relief)

Chekhov undertakes six-week tour of Western Europe with Suvorin. Relationship with Lika Mizinova deepens

Works on *The Island of Sakhalin*. *The Duel* published serially. Works on 'The Grasshopper'

1892 Chekhov buys small estate at Melikhovo, near Moscow; parents and sister live there with him. Gives free medical aid to peasants. Re-reads Turgenev; regards him as inferior to Tolstoy and very critical of his heroines

'Ward No. 6' and 'An Anonymous Story'

1893 *The Island of Sakhalin* completed and published serially

1894 Death of Alexander III; accession of Nicholas II (1,000 later trampled to death at Khodynka Field during coronation celebrations). Strikes in St Petersburg

Chekhov makes another trip to Western Europe

'The Student', 'Teacher of Literature', 'At a Country House' and 'The Black Monk'

1895 'Three Years'. Writes 'Ariadna', 'Murder' and 'Anna Round the Neck'. First draft of *The Seagull*

1896 Chekhov agitates personally for projects in rural education and transport; helps in building of village school at Talezh; makes large donation of books to Taganrog Public Library

'My Life' published in instalments. *The Seagull* meets with hostile reception at Alexandrinsky Theatre

1897 Chekhov works for national census; builds second rural school. Crisis in health with lung haemorrhage; convalesces in Nice

'Peasants' is strongly attacked by reactionary critics and mutilated by censors. Publishes *Uncle Vanya*, but refuses to allow Moscow performance (until 1899)

1898 Formation of Social Democrat Party. Dreyfus affair

Stanislavsky founds Moscow Art Theatre with Nemirovich-Danchenko

Chekhov indignant over Dreyfus affair and supports Zola; conflict with anti-Semitic Suvorin over this. Attracted to Olga Knipper at Moscow Art Theatre rehearsal of *The Seagull*, but leaves almost immediately for Yalta. His father dies. Friendly with Gorky and Bunin (both of whom left interesting memoirs of Chekhov)

Trilogy 'Man in a Case', 'Gooseberries' and 'About Love'. 'Ionych'. *The Seagull* has first performance at Moscow Art Theatre

1899 Widespread student riots

Tolstoy's *Resurrection* serialized

Chekhov has rift with Suvorin over student riots. Olga Knipper visits Melikhovo. He sells Melikhovo in June and moves with mother and sister into his new house at Yalta. Awarded Order of St Stanislav for educational work

'The Darling', 'The New Dacha' and 'On Official Business'. Signs highly unfavourable contract with A. F. Marx for complete edition of his works. Taxing and time-consuming work of compiling first two volumes. Moderate success of *Uncle Vanya* at Moscow Art Theatre. Publishes 'The Lady with the Little Dog'. Completes 'In the Ravine'

1900 Chekhov settles in the house built by him in Yalta. Actors from the Moscow Art Theatre visit Sevastopol and Yalta at his request. Low opinion of Ibsen. Begins serious work on *Three Sisters*; goes to Nice to revise last two acts

Sees *Uncle Vanya* for first time

1901 Formation of Socialist Revolutionary Party. Tolstoy excommunicated by Russian Orthodox Church

Chekhov marries Olga Knipper

Première of *Three Sisters* at Moscow Art Theatre, with Olga Knipper as Masha. Works on 'The Bishop'

1902 Sipyagin, Minister of Interior, assassinated. Gorky excluded from Academy of Sciences by Nicholas II

Gorky's *The Lower Depths* produced at Moscow Art Theatre

Chekhov resigns from Academy of Sciences together with Korolenko in protest at exclusion of Gorky. Awarded Griboyedov Prize by Society of Dramatic Writers and Opera Composers for *Three Sisters*

Completes 'The Bishop'. Begins 'The Bride', his last story. Begins *The Cherry Orchard*

1903 Completion of Trans-Siberian Railway. Massacre of Jews at Kishinev pogrom

Chekhov elected provisional president of Society of Lovers of Russian Literature

Completes 'The Bride' and the first draft of *The Cherry Orchard*. Arrives in Moscow for Art Theatre rehearsal of *The Cherry Orchard*; strong disagreement with Stanislavsky over its interpretation

1904 Assassination of Plehve, Minister of Interior, by Socialist revolutionaries. War with Japan

Chekhov dies of TB on 2(15) July at Badenweiler in the Black Forest (Germany)

Première of *The Cherry Orchard* at Moscow Art Theatre

Introduction

I'm getting to the end of the second volume of Chekhov's letters. They are such a joy to read! I can't put them down. What a delightful, clever man he was! A real charmeur! And what a pity that I have only got to know him properly after his death! Letter from Sergey Rachmaninov to Sofia Satina, 29 January 1933[1]

I
Chekhov and the Censors

Russian readers were astonished when they first started reading Chekhov's letters in the years following his death in 1904. They knew Chekhov as a short story writer and as a playwright, but they had no inkling of his brilliant epistolary legacy. Chekhov wrote a great many letters during his lifetime, and four and a half thousand of them have been saved for posterity and published in his collected works. Some of these letters are very brief and deal with business matters, and others, addressed to members of his family and his wife, are intensely personal, but a great number contain penetrating discussions of a wide array of topics and are of a literary quality on a par with his best prose. They are also sometimes extremely funny. Chekhov made jokes about everything – particularly about himself – and humour became his most efficient way of deflecting attention from the gravity of his physical condition when he became very ill. It was because Chekhov's letters were so exceptional that his correspondents began clamouring for them to be published almost immediately after his death: indeed, excerpts started appearing in newspaper tributes only months after he was buried in the cemetery of Moscow's Novodevichy Convent. But because of the deliberations of Chekhov's editors and censors, it has only become possible to read his letters exactly as he wrote them a hundred years after his death.

The first separate collection, containing seventy-two letters, was published in 1906, and it was with a view to publishing a fuller selection that Chekhov's sister Maria Pavlovna (Masha) launched an appeal in *The Russian Gazette* in 1910. She asked her brother's correspondents to send her letters they had received from him. Maria Pavlovna then became the editor of a six-volume edition of Chekhov's letters which was published between 1912 and 1916 – and her brother's first posthumous censor. For genuine reasons of propriety, the prim and upright Masha deleted words she considered indecent, but she also cut out references her brother had made in his letters to their awful childhood and tyrannical father, and derogatory comments about people who were still alive in 1912. Such sensitivity was no longer necessary when the Soviet government commissioned the first edition of Chekhov's collected works to commemorate the fiftieth anniversary of his death in 1944; eight scrupulously annotated volumes containing 4,195 letters were included in the first Soviet edition of Chekhov's collected works, published between 1944 and 1951. But because literary scholars were obliged to place haloes over the heads of ideologically acceptable writers in Stalinist and post-Stalinist Russia, they were therefore obliged for political reasons to purge the letters of anything which might potentially dent the official image of Chekhov as a saintly figure without a sex life, whose vocabulary was always without blemish. When Simon Karlinsky and Michael Henry Heim published their valuable selection of letters in English in 1973, they drew attention to the changing nature of Russian and Soviet censorship by commenting on the postscript to a letter Chekhov sent to his friend Ivan Leontiev-Shcheglov in May 1888 from his summer dacha.[2] 'There is no lavatory here,' Chekhov writes. 'You have to answer the call of nature in front of nature, in ravines and under bushes. My arse has been bitten all over by mosquitoes.'[3] Maria Chekhova censored the word 'arse' from her edition, but because Stalinist censors were even more prudish, the 1888 postscript was deleted entirely from the fourteenth volume of the

1944–51 edition, along with about five hundred other cuts. The smaller, twelve-volume, edition of Chekhov's complete works published after Stalin's death during the more liberal conditions of Khrushchev's 'thaw', restored the postscript but still omitted its last sentence. Such was the position when the Karlinsky and Heim selection of Chekhov's letters was published. Only in the 1974–83 Academy of Sciences edition does the postscript appear in all its unexpurgated glory; to this day the twelve volumes produced under its aegis and included as part of the *Complete Collected Works and Letters* remain definitive. But 'Complete Collected Works and Letters' is a misnomer, as many of the 4,468 letters in this edition remain censored. The postscript to Chekhov's 1888 letter may have been restored but plenty of other examples of his even more colourful use of language, as well as certain politically incorrect remarks, were still deemed by puritanical Soviet censors to be a little too indelicate for public consumption. In fact, the Soviet government was less concerned with sparing the feelings of its citizens, whom it treated in almost all other respects with complete contempt, than with concealing from the world the awful truth that the great Russian writers were also fallible (and in Chekhov's case often irreverent) human beings.

Until quite recently, therefore, our image of Chekhov as a letter writer has been quite distorted. With Gorbachev's introduction in the late 1980s of the policy of *glasnost*, which ushered in an era of unprecedented freedom of speech in Russia, the last obstacles to presenting an untarnished image of Chekhov were removed. In 1991 the distinguished Chekhov scholar Alexander Chudakov took advantage of the new openness in Soviet society to call for the letters to be published in full. In an article he published in *New Literary Review*, Russia's pre-eminent literary journal, he discussed the 'rude language' in Chekhov's letters in relation to the tricky question of the writer's official persona as a 'classic' writer in his native country. It was time, he argued, to expose the fraudulence of the hackneyed image of the 'decorous and refined gentleman with a stick, who never permitted himself to use racy language and who was rather pious and sickly, with little interest in women'.[4] Chudakov began that process by quoting liberally from some of the most notorious censored passages from the letters, in which Chekhov relates, for example, his colourful encounter with a Japanese prostitute in the Russian Far East (letter 116 in the present collection). Despite the publication of many valuable studies about Chekhov in Russia since the collapse of Communism, it has nevertheless been left to Western scholarship (most notably the publication of works such as Donald Rayfield's painstaking 1997 biography, *Anton Chekhov: A Life*) to produce the first comprehensive accounts of his life and times. The lingering avoidance of prurient topics in Russian literary scholarship, manifest in the continuing paucity of full-scale biographies of the great writers by native authors, is explained by the reverence with which writers are still regarded, despite the erosion of the authority of the nation's intelligentsia. Bearing in mind how alien to his nature was the whole notion of the writer as prophet (such had been so assiduously cultivated by writers like his antipode Dostoyevsky), such reverence is particularly ironic in Chekhov's case. It took the impending major event of the centenary of Chekhov's death in 2004 to provide the final impetus for an uncensored edition of his letters to be published in Russia. When literary scholars finally succeeded in gaining consent for the publication of a second, revised edition of the Academy of Sciences volumes, the impediments were merely of a commercial nature, the conditions of book publishing in post-Soviet Russia having unalterably changed in the intervening years.

II
Chekhov's Life in Letters

Chekhov grew up in a very close-knit merchant's family in the port of Taganrog in southern Russia. Born in 1860, he was the third of the seven children (one died in infancy) of Pavel Egorovich and Evgenia Yakovlevna Chekhov. The couple had married at the outset of the Crimean War in 1854 and were forced to flee their home temporarily when Taganrog came under attack from British gunboats; their first son, Alexander, was born the following year in a village in the middle of the steppe. Both Chekhov's parents came from humble peasant stock; although Evgenia Yakovlevna's father had bought his family's freedom before she was born, Pavel Egorovich remained a serf for the first seventeen years of his life. Paying the annual dues to win the right to engage in trade was one of the few means for freed peasants to better themselves socially, but the pious Pavel Chekhov was not a natural businessman. His attention was focused more on church services than on making the grocery store he opened profitable. His zealous observance of religious ritual, combined with his tyrannical behaviour, resulted in a great deal of unhappiness for his children, particularly his two eldest sons, Alexander and Nikolay (who later rebelled by leading irresponsible, dissolute lives). Pavel Egorovich's cruelty also left an indelible mark on Anton. 'I ask you to remember that your mother's youth was ruined by despotism and lies', he wrote to his brother Alexander in January 1889 (letter 76). 'Despotism and lies also destroyed our own childhood, so much so that we become sick and fearful when we remember it. Think back to the terror and disgust we used to feel whenever Father made a fuss at lunch about the soup having too much salt in it, or cursed Mother for being a fool. Now he cannot forgive himself for all those things . . .' In the patriarchal environment of the typical merchant home, the gentle Evgenia Yakovlevna's voice carried little weight: the Chekhov sons were forced to serve for long hours in their father's shop, sing in the church choirs their father conducted and endure being regularly beaten by him. The physical punishment inflicted on the young Anton instilled in him a lifelong hatred for violence in all its forms. For all his brutality, however, Pavel Egorovich gave his five sons a better education than he had ever received by paying for them to attend the Taganrog Gymnasium, a superior, highly disciplined state school based on the German model, in which there was a heavy bias towards the classics. This was a privilege of the merchant class; a Gymnasium education, in turn, paved the way for university entrance.

Pavel Chekhov bankrupted himself in 1876 and fled to Moscow to avoid his creditors, followed soon after by his wife and youngest two children. His eldest sons were already students in Moscow by this time, but his middle two sons, Anton and Ivan, were left behind in Taganrog to complete their schooling. Chekhov clearly started writing letters at some point when he was a schoolboy, but (with the exception of the postscript 'I wish *tibi optimum et maximum*' added to a letter written by his brother Nikolay in 1875) his first extant letter dates from 1876, when he was sixteen. It was sent from Taganrog to his brother Alexander in Moscow. Nearly all the letters Chekhov sent to his family in Moscow in his late teens disappeared as a result of his impoverished parents' constant moves from one damp flat to another. There are also very few letters from the time Chekhov was a medical student in Moscow in the early 1880s, but when one bears in mind the vicissitudes of Russian history in the early twentieth century – in which the country was ravaged first by World War I, then revolution and civil war – it is perhaps a miracle that so much has survived. Several of Chekhov's early letters were sent to his cousin Mikhail (Misha), who was working as an apprentice for Ivan Gavrilov, the wealthy Moscow merchant. It was Gavrilov who, in 1877, finally gave Chekhov's father a job at his haberdashery warehouse as a clerk. The letters to Misha show Chekhov to be a sincere if naive young man, his dutiful attitude to his parents balanced by an irrepressible zest for pranks. His fluently written and rather discursive Russian (he was already far more articulate than either of his parents) already reveals a keen enjoyment of the act of writing.

In the autumn of 1879, at the age of nineteen, Chekhov joined his family in Moscow when he became a student of the university's medical school. Pavel Egorovich was still working for Ivan Gavrilov and living mainly in work accommodation to save money (and relieve his family from his difficult character), but his meagre salary was still insufficient for his family to live on. Due to his family's financial misfortunes, Chekhov had been forced to develop a sense of responsibility from an early age, particularly when it became clear that his elder brothers could not be relied upon. Chekhov's younger brother Ivan became self-sufficient when he qualified as a schoolteacher in 1880, but Masha and his youngest brother Mikhail (Misha) were still too young to fend for themselves (in 1880 they were seventeen and fifteen respectively). Pavel Egorovich and Evgenia Yakovlevna therefore looked to their middle son Anton to help support the family, and he rapidly became the head of the family in practical terms. He was to care for and provide for his parents for the rest of his life, living under the same roof as his father for most of the 1890s (Pavel Egorovich died in 1898), and with his mother until his own death. It was Anton who brought in much-needed income in the 1880s by following his elder brothers' example and writing humorous little stories for the weekly comic journals sold on street corners. These journals had begun to spring up in increasing numbers for the rapidly growing population in Russia's cities and there was a constant demand for new material. With his medical studies to attend to as well, Chekhov was kept busy.

Chekhov's prodigious comic talent not only guaranteed a regular income, which enabled his family gradually to upgrade their rented accommodation from basement flats to apartments in more salubrious areas of Moscow; his stories soon brought him the attention of high-profile editors. In 1883, when he was twenty-three, Chekhov began contributing to *Fragments*, the most popular comic weekly in Russia, which was based in St Petersburg. Its editor, Nikolay Leikin, was a well-known writer and journalist himself and he became Chekhov's first most important correspondent. The letters Chekhov sent to Leikin in the early 1880s provide a vivid portrait of the young writer finding his voice. He was clearly flattered to be invited to write for *Fragments*, and to enter into correspondence with its august editor, and it was to Leikin that Chekhov initially wrote about literary matters. Although his initial impetus was to find a way of earning money, Chekhov showed an early interest in the craft of writing. Even the earliest letters to his cousin Misha, some of which seem to have been written almost for the sake of writing, demonstrate an enjoyment of the art of good expression, and Chekhov's precision and attention to detail stand out in his first letter to Leikin, in which he discusses the advantages and disadvantages of prescribed word limits (letter 10). As Leikin was Chekhov's main correspondent, he also received letters about his young contributor's medical activities. Chekhov qualified as a doctor in 1884, and he wrote to Leikin about a postmortem he assisted in that summer and the locum job he took on. He also confided in him about his own medical symptoms, which he typically made light of, all the while knowing how ominous they were. In December 1884 he had started to cough up blood, having had to work overtime in order to meet the deadlines for a series of court reports he had proposed to *The Petersburg Newspaper*, hoping he would receive further commissions and so climb another rung on the literary ladder.

With the Chekhov family's material situation eased somewhat, it became possible to escape from Moscow's sultry heat and rent a dacha in the summer months, and many of Chekhov's letters in the mid 1880s were sent from the Voskresensk area west of Moscow, where Ivan worked as a village schoolteacher. For three summers, Chekhov, his mother, Misha, Masha and sometimes his father and Nikolay lived in a dacha in the grounds of an elegant country estate in Babkino. It was here that Chekhov made his entrée into polite society, or at least into the world of the Russian intelligentsia (he never had the remotest inclination to move in aristocratic circles), by becoming friends with his landlords, the Kiselyovs. They were a cultured family and in 1885 Chekhov entered into a correspondence with Maria Kiselyova, who was a budding children's writer. Chekhov very quickly became her mentor, speaking authoritatively on points of literary craft. Some of Chekhov's most lyrical, dreamy letters were sent from the various dachas he rented for his family in the 1880s. Like his painter friend Levitan, he was profoundly inspired by the Russian landscape. He was also a keen fisherman and many of the sporadic letters he sent to his brothers Ivan and Misha (which are for the most part businesslike and relatively brief) are concerned with fishing tackle and traps.

In December 1885, after repeated invitations from Leikin, which he had been unable to take up through lack of funds, Chekhov finally made his first visit to St Petersburg. He was by now the star contributor to *Fragments*, and Leikin wanted to show off his protégé, but Chekhov was completely unprepared for the warmth of the reception he received in the capital. With Leikin's help he had started the previous summer to publish stories in *The Petersburg Newspaper*, which was a step up from *Fragments*, and he had begun to attract increasing interest in the city's publishing circles: people wanted to meet him. As was common for contributors to the lowbrow comic journals, Chekhov had started out by publishing under various pseudonyms, and had continued to sign his work as 'Antosha Chekhonte', hoping he might one day be able to use his real name for serious medical articles. With some justification he also feared that his professional reputation as a doctor might be jeopardized if people knew about his alter ego as a humorous writer for lowbrow journals. In fact, he was now beginning to take his writing seriously and having to write to tight deadlines with fixed word limits was becoming a burden. Chekhov was also beginning to tire of writing for laughs, and, indeed, many of the stories which were appearing in *The Petersburg Newspaper* had a wistful, elegiac quality to them. He needed to move on from *Fragments* and find a new outlet.

Leikin was responsible for launching Chekhov's early career, but he was a man of limited horizons and did not want to admit that his protégé had outgrown him. In January 1886, soon after he arrived back in Moscow, Chekhov received an invitation to contribute to *New Times*, Russia's biggest daily newspaper. The generous fee offered meant that he had more bargaining power with *Fragments* but he could not afford to stop writing for it yet. Chekhov's first letter to Alexey Suvorin, the proprietor of *New Times*, in which he thanked him for his editorial input (letter 25) shows how far he had come as a writer since his first modest publication in 1880. Suvorin was to become Chekhov's most important correspondent from the late 1880s onwards, particularly where literary matters were concerned; he was a man of great intelligence and refined literary tastes who was also a minor writer and dramatist in his own right. Although twice his age, Suvorin became Chekhov's closest friend between 1888 and 1898 and the person to whom he confided his most intimate thoughts, not just about writing but about life, love, the theatre and politics. It was Suvorin who insisted that Chekhov stop using a pseudonym, and who gave him the space to grow as a writer. Accordingly, Chekhov's hitherto voluminous output began to be drastically reduced and his popularity began to soar – although not yet among the high-minded St Petersburg intelligentsia who despised the pronounced right-wing bias of *New Times*, particularly in such a despondent political climate. Following the assassination of Alexander II in 1881 by political activists there was no question of Alexander III's continuing the progressive programme of social and political reform initiated by his father. Alexander III's reactionary policies, accompanied by a sharp increase in censorship and surveillance, produced an atmosphere of gloom among the educated population of Russia. Chekhov was certainly not oblivious of the risks to his reputation that association with *New Times* brought, but he was not a political animal and he still needed a regular income so as to be able to support his family and to pay the rent.

Another milestone in Chekhov's career as a writer came in 1886 when he received a letter from the sixty-four-year-old prose writer Dmitry Grigorovich, a distinguished figure in the St Petersburg literary fraternity, who had known Dostoyevsky and other luminaries from the older generation. Grigorovich had first noticed Chekhov's work when he had started publishing atmospheric stories in *The Petersburg Newspaper* and on 25 March wrote to him exhorting him to take his writing more seriously. Chekhov was thunderstruck, as can be ascertained from the reply he sent three days later (letter 26), and the touchingly boastful letter he wrote to his uncle (letter 28) in Taganrog soon after. Grigorovich's letter certainly had an effect on Chekhov's attitude to his writing, which, although it was perhaps not quite as casual as he made out in his reply, was still not particularly serious. The reverberations of Grigorovich's letter can also be felt in the extraordinary letter Chekhov sent to his elder brother Nikolay (letter 27), in which, while castigating him for his slovenly behaviour and lack of responsibility, he told him to respect his own talent. Chekhov was particularly close to his artist brother Nikolay, who showed abundant promise but who squandered his gifts on bohemian living. Chekhov's concern can be seen from the thoughtfulness of his admonitions, which are more the words of a father than of a younger brother. This letter (one of only two to Nikolay which have survived) was prompted partly by anger at having to pay off some of his brother's huge debts and partly by genuine fears for Nikolay's future.

Of all his brothers, Chekhov sustained the longest and the most literary correspondence with the eldest, Alexander, who had left Moscow after graduating from university in 1882. By the end of 1886 Alexander had settled permanently in St Petersburg with his family, taking a job as a journalist with *New Times*. Alexander was the most academically gifted member of his family (he had graduated from the

Taganrog Gymnasium with a silver medal), and he had ambitions of following a literary career, but he never fulfilled his potential and lacked his younger brother's raw talent. Partly for this reason, partly because Alexander's behaviour often left a lot to be desired – he was an alcoholic, like Nikolay, and in turn received a stern letter from Chekhov in January 1889 (letter 76) – and partly because Chekhov brazenly used Alexander as his chief literary factotum in the capital, their relationship was not without its tensions. Chekhov was far more open with Alexander than with most of his correspondents, and it was Alexander in whom he had confided in January 1887 about the tension in his relationship with Leikin (letter 35). By this stage, Chekhov was desperate to give up writing for *Fragments*, but still could not quite afford to. He was always short of money.

Chekhov continued to work part-time as a doctor throughout the 1880s but the income from his medical activities remained very small, and his literary 'mistress' (as he put it) had increasingly begun to take over from his medical 'wife' as the main focus of his attention, particularly when he also started to write plays. The theatre had interested Chekhov since his childhood (he had frequently gone to plays performed at the municipal theatre in Taganrog when he was a teenager) and in November 1887 he made his stage debut in Moscow with a play he had dashed off in just a couple of weeks. *Ivanov* created a furore, not least because the audience did not know how to react to a play whose characters were so ambiguous; it catapulted its author into the limelight of the Russian theatrical world. A few months later he published his first story in a prestigious literary journal (one of Russia's so-called 'thick' journals, which came out monthly). The appearance of 'The Steppe' in March 1888 in *The Northern Herald* marked the beginning of Chekhov's literary celebrity and his accept-ance by the Russian literary establishment. It also marked the formal end of his highly unusual literary apprenticeship, and he later joked that a statue ought to be put up to him for having paved the way for third-rate magazine writers to enter the literary firmament (letter 70). Chekhov knew from the beginning that he wanted to make his literary debut with a story about the steppe region in which he had grown up, and he had undertaken a momentous journey back to Taganrog in the spring of 1887 in order to find inspiration and to refresh his memories. The lengthy and evocative letters (letter 41 onwards) provided him with a convenient way of taking notes.

Alexey Pleshcheyev, Chekhov's editor at *The Northern Herald*, became an important new correspondent and friend. Like Grigorovich, also in his sixties, he was a well-regarded if undistinguished writer with (in contrast to Suvorin) pronounced left-wing views. He was most famous for being among the group of Petrashevsky circle members sentenced to death under Nicholas I for dabbling with socialist ideas, and, like Dostoyevsky, with whom he stood awaiting execution in 1849, he had won a last-minute reprieve. Chekhov's success with 'The Steppe' followed hard on the heels of the successful première of *Ivanov* at the Imperial Alexandrinsky Theatre in St Petersburg, Russia's most prestigious stage, and a miraculous year culminated in his being awarded the Pushkin Prize for literature by the Imperial Academy of Sciences and scoring a runaway hit with the Moscow production of his one-act farce *The Bear*. Chekhov was by now one of the most famous writers in Russia – and he was still only twenty-eight. From the beginning he had asserted his independence from groups and factions in the claustrophobic literary and theatrical communities in Moscow and St Petersburg and his need for personal freedom became ever more pronounced, as is clear from the letters he sent to the poet Yakov Polonsky in January 1888 (letter 53), to Pleshcheyev that October (letter 67) and to Suvorin the following January (letter 77). Chekhov was flattered by the attention he received and he quite enjoyed giving his opinion on the manuscripts he was now often sent by budding writers, but he quickly tired of being seen as a 'Famous Author', telling Suvorin in November 1888 (letter 75) how much he already longed to be treated as an ordinary human being.

If 1888 was a year of triumph, 1889 was, overall, a year of despondency and grief for Chekhov, despite the thrill of getting to know the composer Pyotr Tchaikovsky, whom he revered (letter 90). During the family's second summer spent at a dacha in an idyllic part of the Ukraine, his brother Nikolay died of tuberculosis at the age of thirty. Chekhov's characteristic stoicism led him to make light of his own tubercular symptoms when challenged (letter 73, to Suvorin), and it also explains his extreme reticence about the impact Nikolay's death had on him. Like the rest of his family, he was devastated. Prompted by the deep-seated malaise it induced, which was intensified by the Imperial Theatres' rejection of his next full-length play, *The Wood Demon*, Chekhov decided he needed to accomplish something extraordinary in his life before it was too late. His sense of duty towards his ageing parents no doubt partly prevented him from ever giving full rein to his love of travelling, but, by dreaming up a plan to travel overland across Siberia to the island of Sakhalin in order to write a book about its notorious penal colony, he deftly managed to devise a way of doing something of practical benefit that would also enable him to satisfy his wanderlust. He had also not forgotten his desire to produce a book of serious scholarly worth.

The evocative letters Chekhov sent home during his long journey (letter 103 onwards) convey a vivid impression of both the horrors and the delights of the trip. His demanding regimen interviewing convicts during the three months he spent on Sakhalin allowed no time for letters (his impressions were saved for his book, *The Island of Sakhalin*, published in 1893), and nor did he write letters during his exhilarating journey home by sea via Hong Kong, Singapore, Ceylon and the Suez Canal. The restlessness which soon descended upon him again when he returned to Moscow, having been away for eight months, led him to accept Suvorin's invitation to accompany him on a trip to Western Europe. The letters sent home from this journey (letter 134 onwards) convey Chekhov's infectious and naive enthusiasm for first Vienna and then Venice, before the novelty of traipsing from one museum to another and the luxury of his surroundings (the wealthy Suvorin liked to travel in style) began to pall. It was hard for Chekhov to be away from his family at Easter, which was always the most important Russian holiday: he went to the midnight service at the Embassy church in Paris (letter 145).

Upon his return to Moscow in the spring of 1891, Chekhov resolved to move out of the city. This he did the following spring when he and his parents relocated to the ramshackle country estate he bought, with the help of a mortgage, at Melikhovo, not far from Moscow. His sister Masha lived at Melikhovo at weekends and during holidays (she was now working as a schoolteacher in Moscow) and the other members of the family, plus numerous friends, made regular visits. The years Chekhov spent at Melikhovo were probably the happiest in his life. Apart from being able to live the life of a country squire (something he had always secretly coveted), he was able to start cultivating a garden for the first time and plant trees. Chekhov also enjoyed becoming the owner of two dachshund puppies, the generous gift of his old editor Leikin, with whom cordial relations had long ago been restored (letter 170). The dogs, Bromide and Quinine, initially created havoc in the flowerbeds, but quickly became adored members of the household. And Chekhov's parents no longer had to worry about living in rented accommodation: Pavel Egorovich had retired from his warehouse job and could now go to church as often as he liked, while Evgenia Yakovlevna enjoyed supervising activities in the kitchen.

Melikhovo also proved very conducive for literary work: it was here that Chekhov wrote *The Seagull* (1895) and *Uncle Vanya* (1896–7) as well as many of his best-loved stories, including 'The Black Monk' (1894), 'The House with the Mezzanine' (1896) and the trilogy which comprised 'Man in a Case', 'Gooseberries' and 'About Love' (1898). But he did not limit himself to writing. Chekhov continued to work as a doctor in the Melikhovo years, becoming a well-known and respected figure in the neighbouring villages; his sister Masha took charge of dispensing the medicaments prescribed by her brother to the numerous peasants who came to Melikhovo to seek treatment. Having the previous year helped with famine relief (letter 155), Chekhov's first summer on the estate was devoted to helping fight the cholera epidemic sweeping the country and he became very friendly with the public-spirited doctors who worked for the local government (the *zemstvo*). Chekhov also contributed substantially to funding and overseeing the building of three local schools (letter 187), and he took an active role in the national census in 1897, by supervising the fifteen enumerators in his area (letter 204).

Although Melikhovo conveniently removed the need for a summer dacha, Chekhov continued to travel from time to time. As well as the regular trips to Moscow and to St Petersburg, where he met up with Suvorin and discussed literary matters, in 1894 he made his second visit to the Crimean resort of Yalta (the first having taken place in 1889, shortly after Nikolay's death), and he also went abroad discreetly on his second trip to Western Europe, notifying few people of his whereabouts (letter 176). The following year he took the train to go to meet the sixty-seven-year-old Lev Tolstoy at his country estate of Yasnaya Polyana (letter 182). A warm friendship was struck up, although Tolstoy had no time for Chekhov's plays, which he roundly condemned, along with those of Shakespeare and other great dramatists. Although his literary career had mostly been based up until the early 1890s in St Petersburg, Chekhov began to develop close literary relationships with Moscow publishers during his Melikhovo years, in particular with Vukol Lavrov and Viktor Goltsev, the editors of the liberal monthly journal *Russian Thought*, with whom by now he had patched up his differences (letter 101). 'Ward No. 6' was the first story by Chekhov to appear in *Russian Thought*, in November 1892. He also became friends with Vasily Sobolevsky, the co-editor of the Moscow-based daily newspaper *The Russian Gazette*, which also began to publish some of his less trenchant stories, such as 'Rothschild's Violin' (1894) and 'On the Cart' (1897).

One of Chekhov's main motivations for moving out of Moscow was to remove himself from the public eye. In this he was only partially successful, as the family soon began receiving throngs of visitors – so many that, in 1895, Chekhov commissioned his architect friend Fyodor Shekhtel to build a small annexe in the garden to provide guest accommodation. Visitors were welcome when they were old friends like the landscape painter Levitan, who made an early visit in the spring of 1892 (letter 164), or Olga Kundasova, nicknamed 'the astronomer' (letter 167). A particularly welcome guest was the beautiful Lidia Mizinova, initially a friend of Masha's but who quickly became a friend of the whole family. Chekhov was very attracted to Lidia, or Lika, as she was more usually called. Although he had come close to marrying back in 1886 (letter 24), he had so far resisted the advances of the female admirers he always attracted (being tall, dark and handsome, talented and extremely engaging) – at least as far as forming a public relationship was concerned. Lika was one of the few women with whom Chekhov permitted himself to let down his guard (letters 148, 150–52, 171), but he was so secretive about his private life that his family learnt with surprise after his death that they had been romantically involved, and that he had ultimately spurned her. Stung by Chekhov's coldness, Lika formed an unhappy liaison with their mutual friend Ignaty Potapenko.

There were two major setbacks in the 1890s. The first was the disastrous opening production of *The Seagull* in St Petersburg in the autumn of 1896. Chekhov was well aware of the revolutionary nature of his play (letter 184). Through an unfortunate set of circumstances it was given its première in Russia's most conservative theatre (the Alexandrinsky), by a cast which barely understood the script and to a capacity audience which had bought tickets to a benefit night for a popular comic actress and was expecting to be entertained. Chekhov fled the first night in despair at seeing his play massacred, and he took a long time to recover from what had been a very humiliating ordeal for him (letter 194 onwards). The second major setback was the serious lung haemorrhage Chekhov suffered six months later while sitting down to dine in Moscow with Suvorin. Chekhov could no longer ignore the fact that he had tuberculosis and was forced to make a radical change in his lifestyle. In the autumn of 1897 he set off to spend his first winter in warmer climes, settling among the Russian community in Nice. During the eight months he was away from Russia, he bombarded his sister from the French Riviera with letters in which he asked her to perform various domestic errands, bravely concealing the extent of his illness and his terrible longing to be back in Russia. Masha had turned down suitors in the past in order to devote her life to her brother (whose behaviour in those situations had not always been wholly admirable), and he came increasingly to depend on her assistance in all sorts of ways. During his winter in Nice, Chekhov followed the notorious Dreyfus case closely, certain that the Jewish Captain Dreyfus had indeed been falsely accused of treason in 1894. He therefore sympathized strongly with Zola's moral stand, when the writer spoke out against the French authorities' anti-Semitism during renewed debate about the case, and was horrified by the virulent anti-Semitism of Suvorin's *New Times*. It led to his falling out, more or less permanently, with Suvorin.

The Melikhovo chapter in Chekhov's life came to an abrupt end at the beginning of his second temperate winter when his father died suddenly in October 1898. Chekhov's relationship with his father had changed considerably over the years. Pavel Egorovich still irritated everybody with his pompous ways and excessive religiosity, but he had mellowed as he grew older and no one could contemplate life at Melikhovo without him after his death. Chekhov had set off shortly before his father's death to spend the winter in Yalta, and he now decided to make it the permanent winter residence for himself and his family – along with hundreds of other tuberculosis sufferers. After impulsively buying a rather inaccessible little house on the coast (which was later sold), he commissioned an architect to build him a house on a hill just outside Yalta (letter 242). Shortly before Chekhov had left Melikhovo for Yalta that autumn, he had attended rehearsals in Moscow for the second staging of *The Seagull*. Understandably, he had misgivings after the traumatic experience with the first production but this time the circumstances were entirely different. The actors were part of a new company – the Moscow Art Theatre – whose whole approach to drama was forward-thinking, modern and in line with Chekhov's innovatory playwriting techniques. One member of the company in particular caught his eye: the actress Olga Knipper. A friendship developed between them the following summer when Chekhov came back to Moscow to sort out the sale of Melikhovo and to attend a private performance of *The Seagull* put on especially for his benefit. Olga Knipper now replaced Suvorin as Chekhov's main correspondent as the friendship quickly turned into a serious romance.

When Chekhov moved into his new house in Yalta in the autumn of 1899, his mother moved in with him, together with Maryusha, their old cook, who had long since become part of the family. His sister Masha also lived in Yalta part-time during school holidays. Chekhov had initially hoped he would only spend winters in the Crimea – he continually longed to be in Moscow – but his deteriorating health dictated that Yalta become his permanent home. For someone as restless as Chekhov was all his life, having to stay put for months at a time in a small seaside resort where he had few real friends was very difficult. He felt as if he was in exile and the loneliness he experienced was made worse by the intense interest the local population took in him. The people he found it hardest to turn away were the scores of poverty-stricken tuberculosis sufferers with nowhere to live who appealed to him for help (letter 264). It was Chekhov who, sick as he was, galvanized the local community into building a sanatorium for the poor.

Chekhov started cultivating a wonderful new garden, but there was only so much time he could spend poring over catalogues and pruning his roses, and even that eventually became physically difficult for him. Creative work was also demanding, but he nevertheless managed to write some of his most celebrated stories during his six desolate years in Yalta, including 'The Lady with the Little Dog' (1899) and 'The Bishop' (1902). During Chekhov's last years in Yalta he also wrote two of his greatest plays, *Three Sisters* (1901) and *The Cherry Orchard* (1904), and many of the letters he wrote during this time were addressed to Konstantin Alexeyev (Stanislavsky) and Vladimir Nemirovich-Danchenko, who directed the first productions at the Moscow Art Theatre. Letter-writing was one of Chekhov's main activities in Yalta. Revising his early work was another. In early 1899 (letter 248), Chekhov signed a deal with the St Petersburg publishing magnate Adolf Marx to bring out an edition of his collected works (ever the joker, he quipped that he had become a Marxist), and this involved a lot of laborious copy-editing and proof-reading. As a neat and supremely organized man, Chekhov wanted to put his affairs in order before he died, but he also had an eye on the royalties that his mother and sister would continue to receive after his death that would provide them with some income.

It is not surprising that death is what most preoccupied Chekhov during his last years but the epistolary romance that he entered into with Olga Knipper in the autumn of 1899 was a vital form of escapism for him and stimulated some of his most touching and witty letters. Some of these letters at the end of 1900 were sent from Nice, where Chekhov went to spend another six weeks living in the Pension Russe, and where he put the finishing touches to *Three Sisters*, just before its première a few weeks later in Moscow. In May 1901 he and Olga married secretly in an out-of-the-way church in Moscow. His mother was informed by telegram on the day of the wedding, when the couple were already safely en route for their honeymoon – not Paris or Rome, but a remote sanatorium in the Urals. News of Chekhov's marriage dashed the hopes of many young aspirants and makes a mockery of the letter Lidia Avilova claims to have resurrected from memory and incorporated in her memoir, *A. P. Chekhov in My Life*, published after her death in 1960 (letter 305), which in any case seems stylistically so un-Chekhovian. Avilova, who was married with children, was one of the many women besotted with Chekhov, but she went further than most in attempting to rewrite history by later alleging that she had been the love of his life. Chekhov's marriage also upset his sister, who felt betrayed and usurped (letter 307). Her previously friendly relationship with Olga now became one that was fraught with tension, and it remained that way until Chekhov's death, despite the fact that little in her brother's life changed outwardly. Chekhov was no doubt conscious that his relationship with Olga flourished precisely because he mostly lived in Yalta and she in Moscow, pursuing her busy career as an actress (after they were married they continued to live apart for a great deal of the time), but there were problems even so. In the spring of 1902 Chekhov had to confront the unpalatable thought that his wife had been unfaithful, when she arrived off the steamer in Yalta after suffering an ectopic pregnancy in Petersburg during a Moscow Art Theatre tour, and he was put in the awkward position of having to care for her for several months (letter 329). Masha was probably right in thinking that her brother's relationship with Olga drained his energy and hastened his end, but it is also probably true that Olga gave him something to live for in his lonely last years, when he was too ill to do much more than write brief letters in his tiny, neat script.

Chekhov visited Moscow as frequently as he could during his last years. In September 1901 he attended a performance of *Three Sisters*, and, although very sick, he attended the première of *The Cherry Orchard* in January 1904. A few months later he returned to Moscow, where he spent a month before leaving for the spa town of Badenweiler in Germany's Black Forest, upon the recommendation of his wife's German doctor. By this stage, Chekhov must have sensed he did not have long to live and may have even wished to die abroad to spare his mother and sister the unpleasantness of having to deal with his corpse. Olga accompanied him on his last journey, and he died on a warm summer's night on 15 July (2 July according to the old-style Russian calendar), having sent Masha a typically brave and upbeat letter a few days before.

III
Letters in Chekhov's Life

In some respects, Chekhov's letters are the autobiography he never wrote (professing himself stricken with an acute case of 'autobiographobia'). They are by far the best account of his life and times that we have, spanning the entire length of his literary career. Chekhov loved to write letters partly because he loved to receive them. In an age when telephones were still rare (talking to Tolstoy on the Ericsson telephone installed in his Yalta house was an event for Chekhov), and neither aeroplanes nor computers yet existed, correspondence was inevitably a favourite means of communication. The postal service, moreover, was prompt and efficient: letters Chekhov posted back to Russia when he was living in Nice took a mere four days, while there was guaranteed next-day delivery for letters sent between Moscow and St Petersburg. While letters were Chekhov's favoured form of communicating with his wide circle of family, friends, business acquaintance and fans, he was also aware of their greater value and significance even as he was writing and receiving them. In a letter to Pleshcheyev sent in May 1889, Chekhov declared that he was keeping the letters he received from him and Suvorin, with the intention of bequeathing them to his descendants. 'Let the sons of bitches read and find out about things which happened a long time ago . . .' he commented.[5] Chekhov left no specific instructions as to what should be done with his own letters after his death, but he obviously believed they would one day appear in print. He said as much in a letter of

December 1887 to Ivan Leontiev-Shcheglov, in which he asked his friend to insert into the letter some sayings and puns, since 'this letter will probably be printed in a collection of my letters after my death'.[6] He was joking – he had not even made his debut in a literary journal at this point – but clearly the thought had already crossed his mind. By the time he wrote a postscript to Dr Obolonsky, a family friend, in April 1889, however, the thought was firmly lodged in his mind. Chekhov gave Obolonsky permission to earn 500 roubles by publishing the letter in fifty years' time in *Russian Antiquity* (an historical journal which specialized in publishing documentary materials such as letters and memoirs).[7] He was quite vehement about the idea of publishing any of his letters during his lifetime, feeling it would severely cramp his style and make him feel permanently self-conscious when sitting pen in hand, but he clearly reconciled himself to the idea of posthumous publication quite early on. By about 1890, he had begun to be much more careful about what he wrote in most of his letters, far less self-revealing and altogether more guarded. The occasional obscenities soon disappeared altogether.

Something of Chekhov's attitude to letter-writing can also be gleaned from the way in which he treated the letters other people wrote to him. Even from a young age, he liked to keep the most interesting letters he received. At the end of the year he would choose the letters he liked best and put them into files, sewing them together and arranging them into alphabetical order. He had received 10,000 letters by the end of his life, so the annual task of sorting out his correspondence became more and more of a burden as time went on. Eventually Chekhov recruited his sister Masha to help. The meticulousness Chekhov showed with his letters was typical of a person who was always extremely neat and organized. Unfortunately, the same cannot be said of all of his correspondents. The discrepancy between the number of letters addressed to him and the ones he sent which have survived suggests that some of his correspondents were rather more careless – or at least did not have an eye on posterity, as Chekhov had. The artist Isaak Levitan, on the other hand, did not wish the letters he had received from Chekhov to be preserved precisely because he did have an eye on posterity. A great many of the letters found in Levitan's desk after his death in 1900 were from Chekhov, but the artist clearly felt it would be inappropriate for them to be published due to their personal nature. Levitan left a note with his letters requesting that they all be burned, and his brother Adolf complied. The absence of any letters from Chekhov to one of his closest and oldest friends – probably among the most unguarded he ever wrote – is a considerable loss. Another loss is the many letters Chekhov wrote during his bohemian student years to his cousin Georgy and his uncle Mitrofan, which were destroyed by a disapproving, priggish relative. Other letters, such as those to the actor and theatre director Vsevolod Meyerhold, perished due to an unfortunate set of circumstances. Meyerhold left the eight letters he received from Chekhov in a Petrograd museum for safe-keeping when he went to the Crimea during the Civil War in 1919, but discovered upon his return that the person he had entrusted the letters to had died, and that the letters had disappeared. He later complained that he had lost everything he had cherished, while everything else survived.[8]

The letters written by Chekhov that have survived reveal some clues to their author's character even in their physical details. The marked difference between the letters Chekhov wrote while he was still a schoolboy and those he wrote at the end of his life is manifest in the style of his handwriting. Chekhov did not develop his distinctive small, self-effacing script until he was in his mid twenties. To begin with, his writing was quite florid and full of extravagant flourishes and curlicues. Gradually these decorative elements were pared down, as was the effusive emotional content of his letters. But as his handwriting became smaller and smaller (he rebutted his wife Olga Knipper's complaint in 1901 that his letters were a bit short by reminding her that he had small handwriting),[9] the long descending squiggle at the end of his signature conversely became longer: in his typically self-deprecating, deadpan way, he compared it to a rat's tail. Chekhov's letters, like his prose and his drama, grew more and more pithy as time went on. The length of some of his more impassioned letters is thus all the more striking because of it, and provides justification enough for reproducing the contents of his letters in full – from the brief notes scribbled in pencil on postcards to the neatly penned letters copied out from drafts. As a man of simple tastes, Chekhov did not set great store by the paper he used to write on. His greatest thoughts were put down in black ink, on small, thin sheets of lined or squared notepaper; not on expensive watermarked vellum. They were usually plain white or cream, although more exotic colours such as mauve or pale green make an occasional appearance.

IV
Chekhov Revealed

Reserved and reticent in person, inscrutable in his stories and plays, Chekhov was often much more expansive when it came to wielding pen and paper in private, and the comparative openness which characterizes his letters is noticeable from a very early point, although this was a quality he reined in when he started to become famous. Even as a young man, Chekhov demonstrated a fierce independence; for example, belonging to a group or pledging allegiance to one kind of literary style was anathema to him and some of the most strident pages in his letters are taken up with an articulation of his need for freedom. He may have hidden himself in his literary works, leaving it up to his readers to puzzle out his point of view, and he may have had an aversion to talking about himself in public, but in his letters he could be surprisingly outspoken at times: the letter he wrote to Suvorin about the importance of studying Russia's penal institutions, and the vituperative letter he sent soon after to the journal editor Lavrov refuting the slur that he had no principles spring immediately to mind (letters 98 and 101). Chekhov's heartfelt outbursts about famine and cholera reveal him as a man with a deep social conscience. It was personal revelation which he had more qualms about. He clearly had a fear of exposing himself and making himself vulnerable, and he shrank in his life, as he shrank in his letters, from making grand gestures where his own persona was concerned. 'You won't like Melikhovo, at least not initially,' wrote Chekhov with apprehension to Alexey Suvorin in April 1892 (letter 163), soon after moving into his modest country estate south of Moscow, aware of his friend's luxurious lifestyle. 'Everything is in miniature,' he continued; 'there's a small avenue of lime trees, a pond the size of an aquarium, a small garden and park, and little trees, but when you have been round it a couple of times and really take it in, then the impression of smallness disappears. It is actually very extensive, despite the nearness of the trees.' This description could almost be a metaphor for Chekhov himself, who was defined as a miniaturist early on by critics whom he consistently confounded. Chekhov favoured small forms throughout his life, preferring to write stories rather than novels, understated, spare plays about small events rather than overblown dramas with earth-shattering dénouement, and letters which were usually quite short and to the point. But although Chekhov's writing appears at first glance to be as unassuming as his country estate, closer acquaintance reveals hidden depths. As Virginia Woolf once observed, the initial discomfort the reader feels at Chekhov's apparently random choice of incidents and endings ultimately gives way to a sense that the horizon is much wider from his point of view, so that we gain 'an astonishing sense of freedom'.[10] Chekhov's literary corpus is certainly small when compared to that of a giant like Tolstoy: thirty turquoise volumes set against ninety dark blue ones, which are also twice their size. His handwriting was small; his life and his literary career were short. But as in his literary works, not everything fits the picture: Chekhov was a tall man, contrary to popular belief, and he had a propensity for writing long, drawn-out sentences. He was also not immune to writing very long letters on the occasions when he felt particularly vehement about something. His deceptively compact legacy, moreover, proves upon closer inspection to be huge. Chekhov achieved an extraordinary amount over the course of his short life, which came to an end when he was only forty-four. In between working as a doctor, supporting his impecunious family, travelling the length and breadth of Russia, contributing to famine relief and the national census, building three schools, sending regular parcels of books to the library of his home town and planting trees, Chekhov managed to write a detailed and frank account of the lives of convicts on the island of Sakhalin (the most notorious penal colony in Siberia), nearly six hundred short stories and more than a dozen plays. He was also one of the world's great letter writers. It is no wonder he used to complain of his fingers permanently aching from all the writing he did.

Of all Russia's writers, it is perhaps Chekhov who is the best-loved. It is not hard to see why. The qualities which first endeared him to Russian readers back in the 1880s are the same ones which explain his appeal today. He wrote no vast novels in which he attempted to solve the problems of existence or fathom the forces of world history. He had no particular axe to grind about how people should live their lives, but, like the good doctor that he was, he had a superb ability to diagnose what it was that prevented people from finding happiness and fulfilment and a unique talent for pinpointing it in a clear-sighted way that was at the same time immensely gentle and compassionate. He also had an infectious sense of humour and an unerring sense of life's ironies, which prevented his writing from ever becoming too portentous or sentimental. Chekhov wrote stories and plays about characters whom people could relate to, and in whom they recognized themselves. They were not larger-than-life personalities confronting extreme situations but ordinary people with ordinary problems. And it is ordinary people who invariably take centre stage in his work and also in his letters, depicted by their author with unflinching honesty but abiding affection. To his compassion and understanding (partly the result of his coming into contact with an unusually wide cross-section of the population as both doctor and writer), Chekhov brought an uncommon artistic gift, and the result was fiction and drama which has moved readers and audiences for well over a century now. All these qualities are also abundantly manifest in his letters, which are often full of poetry. By the time Rachmaninov got to the fourth of the six volumes of Chekhov's correspondence that he had with him while he toured America as a concert pianist in the early 1930s, he was aghast that his 'communion' with Chekhov would soon cease.[11]

Part of Chekhov's appeal has to do with his lack of pretentiousness. As the son of a provincial shop-keeper, he never planned to become a famous writer: he had his sights set on a medical career. As he was invited to contribute to more prestigious publications, he began to take greater care with questions of form and structure, but the practical, down-to-earth objectivity Chekhov acquired in his medical training became a fundamental part of his literary style, which is distinguished by its precise, plain Russian lexicon, a lack of artifice and a remarkable even-handedness. 'I have no doubt that my involvement in medical science has had a strong influence on my literary activities,' he wrote towards the end of his life; 'it significantly enlarged the scope of my observations . . . My knowledge of the natural sciences and the scientific method always caused me to err on the side of caution, trying wherever possible to take scientific facts into consideration' (attachment to letter 261). Chekhov was just as straightforward and unbiased in his letter-writing as he was in his creative work.

Chekhov's contemporaries were rather bewildered by his plotless stories and plays with their inconclusive endings and their breach of literary and dramatic conventions. Nothing seemed clear-cut, but it was the very ambiguity in Chekhov's writing which most excited avant-garde writers like Virginia Woolf and Katherine Mansfield who recognized him as a master as soon as the first English translations appeared. Chekhov's themes of alienation and the absurdity and tragedy of human existence continue to have relevance, the random pathos and irony we find in his work indeed making him as much a twentieth-century modernist as a nineteenth-century realist. The ambivalence of Chekhov's creative work also finds its place in his letters. He did not shy away from the inherent contradictions of being on friendly terms, for example, with a diverse range of people, including right-wing newspaper publishers like Suvorin, passionate monarchists like Tchaikovsky, revolutionaries like Gorky and anarchists like Tolstoy. He was aware, moreover, of being both attracted and repelled by different qualities of the same person, and of the contradictions in his own behaviour and attitudes.

The sensitivity to the textures of prose we find in Chekhov's short stories is a quality of some of his best letters. While in the English-speaking world Chekhov is best known for his four last plays, which now occupy almost as hallowed a place in the repertoire as Shakespeare, Chekhov the prose writer remained for a long time the preserve of cognoscenti in the last century. The American writer Raymond Carver, who unequivocally called him the 'greatest short story writer who has ever lived', maintained that 'Chekhov's stories are as wonderful (and necessary) now as when they first appeared; it is not only the immense number of stories he wrote, for few, if any, writers have ever done more – it is the awesome frequency with which he produced masterpieces, stories that shrive us as well as delight and move us, that lay bare our emotions in ways only true art can accomplish'.[12] These words could be equally well applied to Chekhov's letters, which range in subject matter as widely as his stories, and are often deeply moving, particularly those written at the very end of his life. It is not without justification therefore that critics speak of his letters as being an intrinsic and important part of his literary legacy. Without them we would only have a very partial sense of Chekhov and the creative imagination out of which the stories and plays grew.

V
This Edition

The present volume includes the fullest collection of Chekhov's letters in English translation to date and is the first uncensored edition in any language. The texts of the 370 letters selected, many of which have not hitherto been translated, are reproduced in full.

The first collection of Chekhov's letters to appear in English translation was published in 1920 by Constance Garnett, the doyenne of Russian literary translation. She followed her first compendium, *Letters of Anton Tchehov to his Family and Friends*, with an edition of letters to his wife in 1926: *The Letters of Anton Pavlovitch Tchehov to Olga Leonardovna Knipper*. In 1924 Louis Friedland filleted the correspondence to publish *Letters on the Short Story, the Drama and Other Literary Topics by Anton Chekhov*, and a year later S. S. Koteliansky and Philip Tomlinson published *The Life and Letters of Anton Tchekhov*. While these early selections include letters from all periods of Chekhov's life, they all have the disadvantage of being drawn from the early six-volume Russian edition published by Maria Chekhova which contains less than half of the epistolary legacy that is now in the public domain. When, in 1955, Lilian Hellman edited and introduced *The*

Selected Letters of Anton Chekhov, published in Sidonie K. Lederer's translation, she was able to make her selection from the Soviet 1944–51 twenty-volume edition of Chekhov's collected works, which was fuller, but vitiated, for the reasons outlined above, by its swingeing cuts. Avrahm Yarmolinsky, Simon Karlinsky and Michael Henry Heim had the added advantage of being able to draw on the less severely censored 1963–4 edition for their respective selections, both published in 1973.[13]

In the useful overview of previous translations which Karlinsky and Heim provide in their foreword, they note how Garnett's prunings and abridgements 'frequently reduced the text to a mere skeleton of the original', how, in contrast to Garnett, the Koteliansky–Tomlinson translation 'misses the mark stylistically', while Louis Friedland's volume 'is a not very coherent patchwork of snippets accompanied by a regrettably uninformed commentary', and the 'Hellman–Lederer volume, which is widely quoted in studies of modern drama, abounds in mistranslations and arbitrary cuts of crucial passages'.[14] Mistranslations unfortunately also mar the most recent edition of Chekhov's correspondence to be published: Jean Benedetti's *Dear Writer, Dear Actress: The Love Letters of Olga Knipper and Anton Chekhov*, which appeared in 1996 (it is also hard to recognize the fastidious Chekhov in Benedetti's reference to his 'habitual untidiness, his unkempt state').[15] While many of Knipper's letters remain censored, this attractive volume of excerpted letters is nevertheless the first to follow the evolution of the couple's extraordinary and moving epistolary relationship in English translation. Like the Karlinsky and Heim selection, Gordon McVay's *Chekhov: A Life in Letters*, which appeared in 1994, stands out for its accuracy, but the sheer number of letters included (the first collection in English translation to be drawn from the definitive thirty-volume Academy of Sciences edition) precludes their being quoted in full; in many cases only one or two sentences are reproduced. The 185 letters in the Karlinsky and Heim edition are reproduced in full (unlike those in the Yarmolinsky edition), but the wealth of annotations and biographical material prevents the inclusion of a larger number of letters, and they are drawn from incomplete and not entirely accurate early editions.

The 370 letters included in this volume have been selected for the light they shed on Chekhov's biography. In putting together an English version of Chekhov's life in letters, the hardest task is to decide what to leave out, but the guiding principle has been to choose letters which convey as fully as possible the shape and texture of Chekhov's life in its different environments as he grew up as a young man in late nineteenth-century Russia: training as a doctor, slowly but steadily rescuing his family from penury, developing as a writer and playwright and interacting with the artistic community, engaging in practical philanthropic works, becoming a gardener, succumbing to illness and finally falling in love. One may gain a shrewd sense of Chekhov's position on various topics – including life, literature and love – by reading some of his more famous letters, which are often quoted. These include the letter of September 1888 to Suvorin ('Medicine is my lawful wedded wife, and literature my mistress', letter 65), the letter to Pleshcheyev of October 1888 ('My holy of holies is the human body, good health, intelligence, talent, inspiration, love and complete freedom', letter 67), the letter to Suvorin of March 1894 ('. . . there is more love for mankind in electricity and steam than there is in chastity and abstaining from meat', letter 173), the letter to Suvorin of March 1895 ('let me have a wife who, like the moon, will not appear in my sky every day', letter 180), the letter to Suvorin of February 1898 ('Even if Dreyfus is guilty, Zola is still right, because the writer's task is not to accuse or pursue . . .', letter 231) and the letter to Ivan Orlov of February 1899 ('I have no faith in our intelligentsia . . .', letter 250). To gain a rounded picture of Chekhov's life, however, it is necessary to read a sample of all the different kinds of letters he wrote, including some of the less significant ones. The fiery condemnations of Russia's flabby intelligentsia, invariably sent to his friend Suvorin, for example, need to be juxtaposed with the brief and tender notes addressed to his mother, the businesslike letters he sent to his sister Masha about domestic concerns (their dry manner masking an extremely deep emotional bond), and the ironic, playful communications penned to various friends, both male and female. In order to understand what really moved Chekhov, it is also vital to read a good selection of his very long letters inspired by his travels in the steppe and across Siberia, and to compare his ecstatic celebrations of their distinctive landscapes with the briefer letters he sent home from the French Riviera, whose flora and fauna left him completely cold. And a proper appreciation of Chekhov's multi-faceted personality as a writer can only be acquired by placing his sophisticated analyses of various aspects of literary craftsmanship in the context of the simple, affectionate letters he sent to his younger cousin Georgy in Taganrog. Chekhov was consistent in using plain, straightforward language in all his letters, as he was in his literary works, but each of his correspondents brought out different elements of his character. The inclusion of letters to a wide range of correspondents reveals how he carefully tailored his epistolary style on each occasion, just as he tailored his short stories according to which publication they were to appear in. We can also trace the whole history of certain relationships through his correspondence, such as the crucial friendship with Suvorin, who provoked some of Chekhov's most passionate confessions about life, literature, politics and relationships with women. Another important correspondent was his eldest brother Alexander, with whom he sustained a correspondence throughout his life, and a sometimes impenetrable language of bawdy private jokes and obscure references (particularly in the earlier years). Correspondence, of course, occupied a major role in Chekhov's love affair with Olga Knipper, who, though she became his wife for the last three years of his life, continued to live far away in Moscow. The flirtatious and increasingly affectionate letters Chekhov sent to Olga from Yalta reveal the warm, playful aspects of his personality that he rarely displayed in letters to anyone else. As well as appreciating the range of Chekhov's letters, it is also necessary to read the individual letters in full, since their varying lengths speak volumes about his preoccupations, and about his relationships with their addressees. The long and impassioned letters Chekhov sent to Suvorin about the horrors of the Russian penal system (March 1890, letter 98), to Vukol Lavrov about his alleged lack of principles (letter 101), to his family about the intoxicating beauty of the Siberian landscape (letter 113) and to Suvorin about the Dreyfus case (letter 231, cited above) make all the more impact through their contiguity with the much shorter letters he usually wrote.

Because the aim of this volume is to present a rounded picture of Chekhov's life and bring together all of his most interesting letters, not all of his correspondents are represented, nor does the selection of letters correspond proportionally to his epistolary legacy when viewed from the point of chronology. There are few extant letters from Chekhov's schooldays in Taganrog and student years in Moscow, and those that have survived often contain obscure allusions that are hard to decipher, but several have been included for the interesting light they nevertheless shed on him as an ebullient and surprisingly garrulous young man, full of curiosity. Conversely, comparatively few letters have been selected from the last six years of Chekhov's life, when he was living in Yalta, far removed from the literary scene in Moscow and increasingly frail. Although Chekhov wrote a great many letters during this time – almost half his entire epistolary legacy in fact was composed in Yalta – far fewer of these letters are as interesting as those he penned earlier, the letters to Olga Knipper and the young writer Maxim Gorky notwithstanding. With the demise of his once close friendship with Suvorin, Chekhov no longer had a sparring partner with whom to bandy ideas; nor did he have the physical vigour that accompanied his earlier robust letters about his attitude to, say, Tolstoyanism, Russian imperialism or the state of medicine. The letters of his last years are the letters of a dying man. Interwoven with his love letters to Olga Knipper are letters mostly concerned with practical matters such as the building of his house in Yalta and the negotiations he entered into with the publisher Adolf Marx.

Chekhov adopted a distinct literary style in his more important letters (such as those to Pleshcheyev and Suvorin) which corresponds closely to that of his short fiction, often employing paragraphs with long sentences, punctuated by numerous semi-colons, which sometimes end in ellipses. The aim in translating the letters selected for this volume has been to attain as much accuracy as possible, both in terms of vocabulary and style, while sacrificing as little as possible to fluency in English. All the letters included in this collection are printed in full and reproduce Chekhov's idiosyncratic use of punctuation.

What cannot be reproduced in English translation is the distinction between *vy* and *ty*, the Russian equivalent of the French *vous* and *tu*.

Part of the air of detachment which surrounds Chekhov may come from the fact that he retained his distance from most people, even his close friends, by continuing to address them as *vy*. Suvorin, who was twice his age, was always addressed by Chekhov as *vy*, for example, despite the intimacy of their friendship. Although Chekhov addressed his brothers and sister as *ty*, he wrote to both his parents respectfully as *vy*. The sudden switch from *vy* to *ty* in his letters to Olga Knipper, after a year and a half of correspondence, is dramatic, and clearly betokens a change in the nature of their relationship. But although Chekhov's natural reserve may have become more pronounced in later years, as first his literary, then his private persona came under increasing public scrutiny, his personality still stands out vividly in his letters. And whatever perception we may form of him early on, as a man who valued emotional control, is completely undone by the touching and intimate love letters he sent to his wife in his last years. As we follow Chekhov from day to day, week to week, from year to year in his letters, an impression of a complex but highly sympathetic human being emerges. Chekhov reveals himself as a man with an irrepressible zest for life, possessed of a deep sensitivity to nature and the environment in which he lived. Ebullient and gregarious one day, dispirited and lonely the next, he experienced the same setbacks that are faced by all human beings, but one cannot help but be impressed by his untiring efforts to exemplify the ideals he cherished, and which we learn were formulated early on in his life. It is hard not to warm to someone so lacking in hypocrisy and self-regard. Chekhov talked perceptively about the need for freedom, education and justice, but he also undertook discreet practical measures to advance these causes. An awareness of his artistic gifts deepened his sense of responsibility but never diminished his sense of humour.

NOTES

1. S. Rakhmaninov, *Literaturnoe nasledie*, ed. Z. Apetyan, rev. edn, vol. 2, Moscow, 1980, p. 345.
2. Simon Karlinsky, selection, commentary and introduction, trans. Michael

Henry Heim in collaboration with Simon Karlinsky, *Anton Chekhov's Life and Thought: Selected Letters and Commentary*, Berkeley, 1973, p. xxxi.

3. Letter to Ivan Leontiev-Shcheglov, 10 May 1888, *A. P. Chekhov. Polnoe sobranie sochinenii i pisem v tridtsati tomakh. Pis'ma v dvenadtsati tomakh*, ed. N. F. Belchikov et al., Moscow, 1974–83, vol. 2, p. 267.

4. A. Chudakov, '"Neprilichnye slova" i oblik klassika: o kupyurakh v izdaniyakh pisem Chekhova', *Novoe literaturnoe obozrenie*, 11, 1991, p. 54.

5. Letter to A. N. Pleshcheyev, 8 May 1889. *Polnoe sobranie sochinenii i pisem, Pis'ma*, vol. 3, p. 213.

6. Letter to Ivan Leontiev-Shcheglov, between 16 and 20 December 1887, *Polnoe sobranie sochinenii i pisem. Pis'ma*, vol. 2, p. 161.

7. Letter to Nikolay Obolonsky, 23 April 1889, *Polnoe sobranie sochinenii i pisem. Pis'ma*, vol. 3, p. 197.

8. L. M. Fridkes, E. A. Polotskaya, E. N. Konshina, 'O sud'be epistolyarnogo naslediya Chekhova', *Polnoe sobranie sochinenii i pisem. Pis'ma*, vol. 1, pp. 314–15.

9. Letter to Olga Knipper, 31 August 1901, *Polnoe sobranie sochinenii i pisem. Pis'ma*, vol. 10, p. 69.

10. Virginia Woolf, 'Tchekov's Questions', *The Essays of Virginia Woolf*, ed. Andrew McNeillie, 4 vols, London, 1987, vol. 2, p. 245.

11. *A. P. Chekhov v portretakh, illyustratsiyakh, dokumentakh*, ed. V. A. Manuilov, Leningrad, 1957, p. 317.

12. Raymond Carver, 'The Unknown Chekhov', in *No Heroics Please: Uncollected Writings*, New York, 1992, p. 146.

13. A. Yarmolinsky, selected and ed., *Letters of Anton Chekhov*, New York, 1973.

14. *Anton Chekhov's Life and Thought*, pp. ix–x.

15. Jean Benedetti, ed. and trans., *Dear Writer, Dear Actress: The Love Letters of Olga Knipper and Anton Chekhov*, London, 1996, p. x.

Further Reading

EDITIONS OF CHEKHOV'S LETTERS

Jean Benedetti, ed. and trans., *Dear Writer, Dear Actress: The Love Letters of Olga Knipper and Anton Chekhov*, London, 1996

Louis Friedland, ed. and trans., *Letters on the Short Story, the Drama and Other Literary Topics by Anton Chekhov*, London, 1924

Constance Garnett, ed. and trans., *Letters of Anton Tchehov to his Family and Friends*, 2 vols, London, 1920

—, *The Letters of Anton Pavlovitch Tchehov to Olga Leonardovna Knipper*, London, 1926

Lilian Hellman, ed. and introd., trans. Sidonie K. Lederer, *The Selected Letters of Anton Chekhov*, New York, 1955

Simon Karlinsky, ed. and intr., *Anton Chekhov's Life and Thought: Selected Letters and Commentary*, trans. Michael Henry Heim in collaboration with Simon Karlinsky, Berkeley, 1973

S. S. Koteliansky and Philip Tomlinson, ed. and trans., *The Life and Letters of Anton Tchekhov*, London, 1925

Gordon McVay, ed. and trans., *Chekhov: A Life in Letters*, London, 1994

A. Yarmolinsky, selected and ed., *Letters of Anton Chekhov*, New York 1973

BIOGRAPHY AND CRITICISM

Rosamund Bartlett, *Chekhov: Scenes from a Life*, London, 2004

Anton Chekhov, *A Journey to Sakhalin*, ed. and trans. Brian Reeve, Cambridge, 1993

J. Douglas Clayton, ed., *Chekhov Then and Now: The Reception of Chekhov in World Culture*, New York, 1997

Victor Emeljanow, ed., *Chekhov: The Critical Heritage*, London, 1981

Vera Gottlieb and Paul Allain, eds, *The Cambridge Companion to Chekhov*, Cambridge, 2000

Ronald Hingley, *A New Life of Anton Chekhov*, London, 1976

Robert Louis Jackson, ed., *Chekhov: A Collection of Critical Essays*, Englewood Cliffs, 1967

—, *Reading Chekhov's Text*, Evanston, 1993

Vladimir Kataev, *If Only We Could Know! An Interpretation of Chekhov*, trans. and ed. Harvey Pitcher, New York, 2002

Janet Malcolm, *Reading Chekhov*, New York, 2002

V. S. Pritchett, *Chekhov: A Spirit Set Free*, New York, 1988

Donald Rayfield, *Anton Chekhov: A Life*, London, 1997

—, *Understanding Chekhov*, London, 1998

Ernest J. Simmons, *Chekhov: A Biography*, Boston, 1962

René and Nonna D. Wellek, eds, *Chekhov: New Perspectives*, Englewood Cliffs, 1984

Nick Worrall, *File on Chekhov*, London, 1986

HISTORICAL BACKGROUND

Edward Acton, *Russia: The Tsarist and Soviet Legacy*, 2nd edition, London, 1986

Hans Rogger, *Russia in the Age of Modernisation and Revolution: 1881–1917*, London, 1983

David Saunders, *Russia in the Age of Reaction and Reform: 1801–1881*, London, 1992

Note on the Text

The main source for this translation is the twelve volumes of annotated letters included in the Academy of Sciences edition of Chekhov's collected works, A. P. Chekhov, *Polnoe sobranie sochinenii i pisem v tridtsati tomakh. Pis'ma v dvenadtsati tomakh*, ed. N. F. Belchikov et al., Moscow, 1974–83.

Some censored extracts have been taken from A. Chudakov's article ' "Neprilichnye slova" i oblik klassika', *Literaturnoe oboʒrenie*, 11 (1991), pp. 54–6:

Letter (75) to Alexey Suvorin, 24 or 25 November 1888
Letter (116) to Alexey Suvorin, 27 June 1890
Letter (124) to Alexey Suvorin, 9 December 1890.

Other censored extracts have been taken from Chekhov's original letters held in the Chekhov archive (fond 331) in the Manuscript Department of the Russian National Library, Moscow:

Letter (23) to Alexander Chekhov, 4 January 1886
Letter (27) to Nikolay Chekhov, March 1886
Letter (41) to Chekhov Family, 7 April 1887
Letter (45) to Nikolay Leikin, 14 May 1887
Letter (92) to Alexey Suvorin, 17 October 1889
Letter (116) to Alexey Suvorin, 27 June 1890.

Grateful thanks are expressed to Professor Vladimir Kataev and the Russian Academy of Sciences for supplying censored extracts from the following letters held in other archives in Moscow and St Petersburg in advance of the publication of the revised complete edition of Chekhov's letters in Russian:

Letter (9) to Alexander Chekhov, 8 November 1882
Letter (31) to Nikolay Leikin, 20 July 1886
Letter (51) to Chekhov Family, 3 December 1887
Letter (76) to Alexander Chekhov, 2 January 1889
Letter (99) to Ivan Leontiev-Shcheglov, 16 March 1890
Letter (103) to Chekhov Family, 23 April 1890.

TRANSLITERATION AND CONVENTIONS

A simplified form of transliteration has been used, preserving anomalies for well-known spellings such as 'Tchaikovsky' instead of 'Chaikovsky' and spelling names such as 'Kiselev', 'Orel' and 'Psel' as 'Kiselyov', 'Oryol' and 'Psyol', as they are pronounced. An exception has been made for 'Potyomkin', better known as 'Potemkin'.

The Julian calendar was used in pre-revolutionary Russia, which resulted in dates being twelve days behind the Western Gregorian calendar in the nineteenth century and thirteen days in the twentieth century. All dates cited here refer to the Julian calendar.

List of Correspondents

KONSTANTIN ALEXEYEV (stage-name STANISLAVSKY) (1863–1938) Actor and theatre director, founder of the Moscow Art Theatre, friend of Chekhov. Chekhov met Stanislavsky in 1888, but their close association began in 1898 when the Moscow Art Theatre staged *The Seagull*. They exchanged about fifty letters in the last five years of Chekhov's life.

ISAAK ALTSHULLER (1870–1943) *Zemstvo* doctor, tuberculosis specialist, friend of Chekhov. Another tuberculosis sufferer like Chekhov, Altschuller was resident in Yalta from 1898 and became his doctor.

LIDIA AVILOVA (1864–1943) Writer whose literary career began in 1890, a year after becoming acquainted with Chekhov in St Petersburg. Avilova, married with two children, later cast herself as the love of Chekhov's life, publishing a notorious memoir, *Chekhov in My Life*, and deluding herself that his story 'About Love' was about their thwarted relationship. Chekhov wrote her thirty-two letters.

KAZIMIR BARANTSEVICH (1851–1927) Writer associated with the Populist movement of the 1870s whose literary career began in 1878. Chekhov's acquaintance with Barantsevich lasted from 1887 until his death, during which time they corresponded only sporadically.

FYODOR BATYUSHKOV (1857–1920) Literary historian, critic and editor of the Russian section of the international magazine *Cosmopolis* from 1897 to 1898. Chekhov wrote approximately seventeen letters to him during the last years of his life.

VIKTOR BILIBIN (1859–1908) Comic writer who worked as an

official at the Post and Telegraph Department and contributed to a couple of St Petersburg newspapers and to *Fragments* (becoming its editor in 1906). Chekhov became acquainted with Bilibin during his first visit to St Petersburg in 1885 and corresponded occasionally with him until 1901, but a close friendship never developed.

ALEXANDER PAVLOVICH CHEKHOV (1855–1913) Chekhov's eldest brother, writer and journalist. Alexander Chekhov – Sasha – began contributing to comic journals in 1876, while studying at Moscow University. After graduation in 1882 he worked for the Taganrog, St Petersburg and then Novorossiisk customs, but at the end of 1886 he took a position with *New Times* in Petersburg. He also edited at different times various small journals (such as *The Fireman* and *The Herald of the Russian Society for the Protection of Animals*). Following the death in 1888 of his common-law wife (with whom he had a daughter who died in infancy and two sons, Nikolay, Anton), he married Natalya Golden the following year (their son Mikhail later achieved renown as an actor, and married Olga Knipper's niece). In addition to publishing a few books of his own in the 1890s, Alexander Chekhov wrote some important memoirs of his better-known brother after his death. Their correspondence began when Alexander moved to Moscow to go to university and lasted until Chekhov's death. Alexander wrote 381 letters to his younger brother; 196 letters from Chekhov have survived.

GEORGY MITROFANOVICH CHEKHOV (1870–1943) Chekhov's cousin on his father's side, who became an agent of the Black Sea–Azov Shipping Agency in Taganrog upon leaving school. Chekhov was very fond of Georgy, as can be ascertained from the affectionate letters he sent him periodically throughout the course of his life, in which he expresses himself in simple language, dwelling for the most part on personal matters.

IVAN PAVLOVICH CHEKHOV (1861–1922) Chekhov's younger brother. Ivan Chekhov – Vanya – worked as a schoolteacher from 1879 onwards, first in Voskresensk and later in Moscow. Chekhov was close to the reliable and kind Ivan, whom he wrote to sporadically throughout the course of his life, often about their shared passion for fishing.

MIKHAIL MIKHAILOVICH CHEKHOV (1851–1909) Chekhov's cousin on his father's side. Mikhail Mikhailovich left Taganrog in his early teens to be apprenticed to the Moscow merchant Ivan Gavrilov, who later employed Chekhov's father. Misha became one of Chekhov's first correspondents. The high regard in which he held him in the letters he sent him from Taganrog was not maintained once he moved to Moscow himself, although the cousins' relations remained cordial.

MIKHAIL PAVLOVICH CHEKHOV (1865–1936) Chekhov's youngest brother. Mikhail Pavlovich – Misha – graduated from the law faculty of Moscow University in 1889 and worked initially as a tax inspector in provincial towns outside Moscow. In 1894 he moved to Uglich, and from 1902 worked in Suvorin's book-selling business. Besides contributing stories to various second-tier journals, Misha Chekhov published a book on agriculture and after his brother's death became his first biographer, writing the introductions to the six-volume collection of letters edited by his sister, and numerous memoirs. Of all his siblings, Chekhov was least close to Misha.

MITROFAN EGOROVICH CHEKHOV (1836–94) Chekhov's uncle, younger brother of his father. Mitrofan Chekhov was a trader in Taganrog, as his father had been (albeit more successful), and a pillar of the local community, serving as a churchwarden, engaging in various charitable activities and maintaining links with Russian monasteries on Mount Athos. The few letters Chekhov wrote to his uncle are respectful and formal.

NIKOLAY PAVLOVICH CHEKHOV (1858–89) Chekhov's older brother. Nikolay – Kolya – went to art school in Moscow after leaving school in Taganrog in 1875 together with Alexander, but he dropped out before graduating, in keeping with his increasingly wayward lifestyle. He started contributing illustrations to the comic journals for which his brother later wrote in 1881, but did not live to fulfil his considerable promise, surrendering first to alcoholism then tuberculosis, the disease which led to his untimely death in 1889. Chekhov was very close to Nikolay, particularly in the early 1880s, and the tight-lipped silence he maintained following his death belies the intensity with which he grieved him.

PAVEL EGOROVICH CHEKHOV (1825–98) Chekhov's father. Although he was born as a serf on the estate of Count Chertkov in Voronezh province, his own father bought his family's freedom in 1841. Pavel Egorovich became an apprentice in Taganrog in 1844 and married Evgenia Morozova ten years later; the first of their seven children (Alexander) was born in 1855 (the youngest, Evgenia, died in infancy). After opening his first grocer's shop in 1857, as a merchant of the third guild, Chekhov's father – 'Papasha' – became a stalwart member of the community in Taganrog, like his younger brother Mitrofan. Similarly devout, he conducted several church choirs in which his eldest sons were forced to sing and was a member of Taganrog's trade delegation for a while. Although his business was initially profitable, Pavel Egorovich later went bankrupt and fled to Moscow in 1876. From 1877 to 1890 he worked as a clerk at the warehouse of the merchant Ivan Gavrilov, living mostly on-site, but spent his last years at Melikhovo, the country estate bought by his son. A far more dutiful son than his elder brothers, Chekhov was always respectful to his father to his face but could never forgive him for administering corporal punishment during their childhood. Their relationship was never close (Chekhov found his father pompous and overbearing) and their correspondence neither lengthy nor voluminous. Pavel Egorovich mellowed a great deal in his later years, however (there is unmistakable affection in Chekhov's last letter to his father), and his unexpected death came as a great shock to the family.

EVGENIA YAKOVLEVNA CHEKHOVA, neé Morozova (1835–1919) Chekhov's mother. Like his father, Chekhov's mother – 'Mamasha' – had lowly origins but her family's freedom had been purchased earlier; her father was a merchant based in Ivanovo province. Following his death in 1847, she moved to Taganrog with her mother and sister and became a dutiful wife to Pavel Chekhov when they married in 1854. Once Chekhov moved to Moscow, he lived with his mother for the rest of his life, taking her to Yalta after the death of her husband and the sale of Melikhovo. They were extremely close, as is evident from the touching letters Chekhov sent her in his last years. Evgenia Yakovlevna had received little

education (her medieval-looking handwriting was as unsophisti-
cated as her literary style), and so her son's letters to her were
usually short and to the point.

MARIA PAVLOVNA CHEKHOVA (1863–1957) Chekhov's younger
sister. After receiving the nearest equivalent of a university education (which women were still barred from receiving at that time),
Maria – Masha – worked as a geography and history teacher at a
girls' Gymnasium in Moscow and also studied painting. At Melikhovo she assisted her brother with his medical practice and the
building of schools and increasingly took responsibility for domestic
matters. Chekhov came to rely even more on Masha when he
became ill. She had already forgone the opportunity of getting
married in order to devote her life to him, and after he died founded
a museum in his house in Yalta (which became her permanent home
until her own death), published the first edition of his letters and
wrote numerous memoirs.

SERGEY DIAGHILEV (1872–1929) Art historian, critic and impresario, founding editor of the lavishly illustrated, modernist journal
The World of Art in 1898, and creator of the Ballets Russes. Chekhov
became acquainted with Diaghilev at the end of his life, but declined
his invitation to edit the St Petersburg-based *World of Art*, whose
aesthetic credo he only partly sympathized with.

MIKHAIL DYUKOVSKY (1860–1902) Teacher and then inspector
of a Moscow school, family friend. Chekhov wrote Dyukovsky
seventeen letters between 1883 and 1893.

EVGRAF EGOROV (dates unknown) Retired artillery officer and
zemstvo leader in Nizhny Novgorod province who became acquainted
with the Chekhov brothers in the 1880s when his battalion was sta-
tioned at Voskresensk. This was where Ivan Chekhov worked as a
teacher, and where the Chekhov family spent their summer holidays.

PAVEL FILEVSKY (1858–after 1906) Fellow pupil at the Taganrog
Gymnasium, which he left in 1877, two years before Chekhov.
After graduating from Moscow University in 1881, Filevsky went
back to Taganrog to teach history at the Gymnasium and later
wrote a number of books about the town's history. Chekhov wrote
only one letter to Filevsky as far as can be ascertained.

KONSTANTIN FOTI (dates unknown) Mayor of Taganrog, whom Chekhov wrote to in connection with donating books to the town library.

MIKHAIL GALKIN-VRASKOY (1834–?) Head of the prison administration of the Ministry of the Interior. Chekhov wrote to Galkin-Vraskoy in 1890 before setting out for Sakhalin, hoping for his assistance (none was forthcoming).

VIKTOR GOLTSEV (1850–1906) Journalist and critic who initially trained as a lawyer. Goltsev became editor of the Moscow-based journal *Russian Thought* in 1885. Chekhov became friendly with Goltsev after he started contributing to the journal in 1892; they were particularly close in the last years of his life. There are 101 extant letters from Chekhov to Goltsev, who was one of only a handful of friends addressed as *ty* rather than *vy*, the Russian equivalents of the French *tu* and *vous*.

DMITRY GRIGOROVICH (1822–99) Writer and friend of Dostoyevsky best known for a series of short stories published in the 1840s, and an early champion of Chekhov's prose. It was Grigorovich who, impressed with the stories he had begun to read in *The Petersburg Newspaper*, wrote Chekhov a famous letter in 1886 urging him to take his writing more seriously; it was a turning point in Chekhov's literary career.

PAVEL IORDANOV (1858–1920) Doctor, member of the Taganrog municipal authority and head of the town library. Chekhov began sending regular parcels of books to the Taganrog library in 1896 and thereafter began a correspondence with Iordanov about the library's needs and about the town museum which he suggested should be founded. Chekhov also corresponded with Iordanov about the erection of a statue to Taganrog's founder, Peter the Great, to mark the town's bicentenary in 1898.

NIKOLAY KHLOPOV (1852–1909) Writer and dramatist. There are two extant letters from Chekhov to Khlopov.

ALEXANDRA KHOTYAINTSEVA (1865–1942) Painter, friend of Chekhov. She was initially a friend of Chekhov's sister, who had studied painting with her, and was one of his many admirers.

ALEXEY KISELYOV (died 1910) Landowner and later land captain, friend of the Chekhov family. Chekhov got to know the Kiselyov family through his brother Ivan when he was working as a teacher in Voskresensk, outside Moscow. He rented a summer dacha for three years in the late 1880s on Kiselyov's nearby estate at Babkino and later exchanged occasional letters with him.

MARIA KISELYOVA (1859–1921) Wife of Alexey Kiselyov, children's writer, friend of Chekhov. Their correspondence of about sixty letters, often about literary technique, extended from 1885 to 1900.

OLGA KNIPPER (1870–1959) Actress at the Moscow Art Theatre, Chekhov's wife. Their correspondence began in 1899, soon after their friendship was established. More than eight hundred letters and telegrams had been exchanged between them by the time of Chekhov's death. They married on 25 May 1901, but continued to live mostly apart, with Chekhov remaining in Yalta while Olga pursued her theatrical career.

VERA KOMISSARZHEVSKAYA (1864–1910) Actress at the Imperial Alexandrinsky Theatre from 1896 to 1902, who founded her own company in 1904. She was the first Nina in *The Seagull*, in 1896, and began an intermittent correspondence with Chekhov the following year, sending him seventeen letters and seven telegrams, ten of which he replied to. Chekhov greatly admired Komissarzhevskaya as an actress, and there was clearly a degree of attraction between them, although their personalities were almost diametrically opposed.

NIKODIM KONDAKOV (1844–1925) Archaeologist, Byzantine art historian and academician who became acquainted with Chekhov in Yalta, where he also lived permanently from the end of the 1890s. Chekhov wrote Kondakov nine letters, and received twenty from him between 1899 and 1904.

ANATOLY KONI (1844–1927) Lawyer, writer, public figure. Chekhov made his acquaintance after returning from the island of Sakhalin.

YAKOV KORNEYEV (1845–1911) Doctor and surgeon, owner of the house on Sadovaya-Kudrinskaya which Chekhov rented for his family from 1886 to 1890, and which now houses the Moscow Chekhov House-Museum. Korneyev wrote Chekhov thirteen letters between 1886 and 1895; six letters from Chekhov have survived.

VLADIMIR KOROLENKO (1853–1921) Populist writer from the Ukraine known for his short stories and sketches, the best of which are set in Siberia. He was exiled to Yakutia for four years in 1881 because of his political activities, later settling in Nizhny Novgorod, and then St Petersburg. Chekhov met Korolenko in 1887; they both became honorary Academicians in 1900 and resigned simultaneously two years later when Gorky's election was blocked. They exchanged about thirty letters between 1888 and 1903.

VUKOL LAVROV (1852–1912) Publisher and editor of the liberal Moscow-based journal *Russian Thought* from 1880. After making his acquaintance in 1889, Chekhov broke off relations after the publication in *Russian Thought* of what he regarded as a slur on his character in its issue of March 1890. Fences were mended in the middle of 1892, after which Chekhov published several of his stories in *Russian Thought*, beginning with 'Ward No. 6', in November of that year. Chekhov wrote a total of about forty letters to Lavrov.

NIKOLAY LEIKIN (1841–1906) Prolific comic writer and journalist, editor of the Petersburg-based weekly magazine *Fragments* from 1882 to 1905. Chekhov got to know Leikin at the end of 1882 and soon after started contributing to *Fragments* and corresponding with its editor. This was Chekhov's first 'literary' correspondence, and it was intense at first, but then became increasingly fraught as Chekhov spread his wings as a writer. Chekhov wrote 168 letters to Leikin between 1882 and 1900, most of which were written before 1888, when he finally stopped writing for *Fragments*. Chekhov's relations with Leikin became much friendlier after this time.

IVAN LEONTIEV-SHCHEGLOV (1856–1911) Retired soldier, comic writer and dramatist, friend of Chekhov. Before becoming a writer, Leontiev (Shcheglov was his pen-name) fought in the Russo-Turkish War (1877–8) as an artillery captain. Chekhov met Leontiev in 1887 in St Petersburg and they began a correspondence which lasted until the end of his life, exchanging about 175 letters.

ELENA LINTVARYOVA (1859–1922) Doctor, friend of Chekhov. Elena was the second daughter of Alexandra Lintvaryova, a landowner on whose Ukrainian estate Chekhov rented a summer dacha for his family in 1888 and 1889. Chekhov became friendly with the whole family; there are seven extant letters from Chekhov to Elena Lintvaryova, and five from her to him.

DAVID MANUCHAROV (1867–1942) Railway technician who appealed to Chekhov in 1896 when his younger brother was exiled to Sakhalin after being arrested for underground political activities.

ADOLF MARX (1838–1904) German-born publisher and bookseller best known for his successful marketing of a weekly magazine called *The Meadow*, which from 1891 included the collected works of Russian and foreign writers as free supplements. Chekhov sold Marx the rights to the publication of his collected works in 1899, and they exchanged 120 letters between 1896 and 1904.

MIKHAIL MENSHIKOV (1859–1918) Retired sailor and journalist on the newspapers *The Week* and *New Times*. Chekhov became acquainted with Menshikov in 1892, and maintained friendly relations until his last years. They exchanged about 100 letters.

VLADIMIR MIKHNEVICH (1841–99) Journalist on the St Petersburg-based *News and Stock Exchange Paper*, to whom Chekhov wrote one letter in 1891.

LIDIA MIZINOVA (1870–1937) Schoolteacher, amateur actress and painter, friend of Chekhov. The attractive Lidia Mizinova – known affectionately as Lika, and sometimes as 'Jamais' – was initially a friend of Chekhov's sister, who taught at the same school, but she later became a friend of the whole family. Chekhov met her before he left for Siberia and developed a close relationship with her in the early 1890s, which did not, much to her chagrin, lead to marriage. She wrote Chekhov ninety-eight letters between 1891 and 1900; there are sixty-seven extant letters from him.

MARFA MOROZOVA (1840–1923) Chekhov's aunt, the wife of his mother's brother Ivan. There are three letters to her from Chekhov which have survived.

VLADIMIR NEMIROVICH-DANCHENKO (1858–1943) Writer, playwright, stage director, co-founder of the Moscow Art Theatre, friend of Chekhov. While they met in the mid 1880s, when both were contributors to the comic journal *The Alarm Clock*, their friendship and correspondence did not begin until 1888, but lasted until Chekhov's death. Nemirovich-Danchenko was one of the few people Chekhov addressed in his letters as *ty*, the first of which he wrote in 1895.

NIKOLAY OBOLONSKY (1857–after 1911) Doctor and friend of the Chekhov family. Dr Obolonsky treated Chekhov's brother Nikolay in 1889 and remained in touch with Chekhov by letter until the last years of his life.

IVAN ORLOV (1851–1917) Doctor, head of Solnechnogorsk *zemstvo* hospital. Chekhov became acquainted with Dr Orlov while he was living in Melikhovo. They exchanged fifteen letters in 1898 and 1899.

ALEXEY PESHKOV (pen-name MAXIM GORKY) (1868–1936) Autodidact writer from Nizhny Novgorod, political activist, friend of Chekhov. They became acquainted by letter when Gorky wrote Chekhov a fan letter in the autumn of 1898, and in person the following spring. They exchanged some eighty letters during the course of their friendship, which lasted until Chekhov's death.

STEPAN PETROV (1864–?) Archimandrite, then Bishop Sergy, acquaintance of the Chekhov family. Petrov was a neighbour of the Chekhovs when they lived at Sadovaya-Kudrinskaya in the late 1880s. After graduating from Moscow University, he took holy orders.

ALEXANDER PLESHCHEYEV (1858–1944) Journalist and theatre critic, eldest son of Chekhov's friend Alexey Pleshcheyev. In 1904 he became editor of a weekly Petersburg Theatre Diary.

ALEXEY PLESHCHEYEV (1825–1893) Writer, critic, editor, friend of Chekhov. Pleshcheyev had published his first book of poetry in 1846, before being arrested along with Dostoyevsky in 1848 as part of the Petrashevsky circle and exiled to Siberia. He became literary editor of *The Northern Herald* when it was founded in 1885 and met Chekhov when the latter made a visit to St Petersburg in December 1887. Pleshcheyev played an important role in Chekhov's literary career by publishing his story 'The Steppe', which was his debut in a literary journal. He became an important correspondent and friend to Chekhov in the last five years of his life. The sixty letters Chekhov wrote to him contain some of the most important pronouncements he made about his personal beliefs and literary stance.

YAKOV POLONSKY (1819–1898) Prolific writer best known for his lyric poetry. Chekhov met Polonsky during his visit to Petersburg in December 1887 and wrote three letters to him in 1888, in one of them asking his permission to dedicate his story 'Fortune' (1887) to him. Polonsky had nominated Chekhov for the Pushkin Prize in literature even before meeting him.

IGNATY POTAPENKO (1856–1929) Writer, dramatist and journalist, friend of Chekhov. Potapenko met Chekhov in Odessa in 1889. He became a frequent guest at Melikhovo, where he often gave impromptu recitals (he had graduated from the Conservatoire as a singer), often with Lidia Mizinova, with whom he became romantically involved in 1894, before going back to his wife. In 1896, Potapenko helped with the staging of *The Seagull*, in which Chekhov partially reflected the doomed love affair with Lidia Mizinova.

GRIGORY ROSSOLIMO (1860–1928) Doctor, Professor of Neuropathology at Moscow University, friend of Chekhov, and former classmate in medical school. Chekhov wrote his penultimate letter to Rossolimo from Badenweiler, which he was desperate to leave, and asked his friend to inform him about shipping routes and timetables.

ELENA SHAVROVA-YUST (1874–1937) Writer, actress, friend of Chekhov. Elena Shavrova became a published author at the age of fifteen when Chekhov recommended her first story to *New Times* in 1889; she had approached him to ask his opinion when both were staying in Yalta. Chekhov continued to proffer advice by correspondence when she was later married and living in St Petersburg. Shavrova was one of the many female admirers with whom Chekhov enjoyed a flirtatious friendship – he sent her sixty-nine letters during the eleven years of their correspondence (against her 130).

FYODOR (FRANZ) SHEKHTEL (1859–1926) Leading Russian modernist architect, friend of Chekhov. Shekhtel first became friends with Chekhov's brother Nikolay while they were students together and fellow contributors to comic journals. Chekhov dedicated his 1882 story 'Two Scandals' to Shekhtel, who later designed the annexe in the garden at Melikhovo and the Moscow Art Theatre building in 1902. Chekhov corresponded sporadically with Shekhtel in the 1880s and 1890s. In 1914 Shekhtel designed a new library for Taganrog, which was named after Chekhov.

ALEXANDER SMAGIN (?–after 1930) Ukrainian landowner, related to the Lintvaryovs, friend of Chekhov. They became acquainted in 1888 when Chekhov spent his first summer in the Ukraine and was thinking of buying a property there. Smagin proposed to Chekhov's sister in 1892, but was dissuaded from pressing his suit – Chekhov had a vested interest in Maria's remaining unmarried, and was successful in discouraging all her suitors.

VASILY SOBOLEVSKY (1846–1913) Lawyer, journalist, newspaper editor, friend of Chekhov. They met in Moscow in the 1890s, when Sobolevsky became one of the co-editors of *The Russian Gazette*, and remained on good terms until the end of Chekhov's life. Sobolevsky arranged for Chekhov to receive *The Russian Gazette* in Badenweiler and received one of the writer's last letters.

LEONID SREDIN (1860–1909) Doctor resident in Yalta, friend of Chekhov. They became acquainted in 1894, and in 1895 Chekhov wrote to thank Dr Sredin for sending him a photograph he had taken of the naval training ship *Berezan*, which had docked in Yalta. In a previous life this ship had been the *Petersburg*, whose passenger Chekhov had been during his fifty-day journey home from Sakhalin. Four and a half years later he could still remember the tiniest details, even down to the eyes of the ship's chef, a retired policeman.

LEOPOLD (LEV) SULERZHITSKY (1872–1916) Theatre director, artist, gardener and Tolstoyan. Chekhov met Sulerzhitsky in 1900 in Moscow and wrote to him a few times from Yalta. Sulerzhitsky became a director of the Moscow Art Theatre in 1905, after Chekhov's death a year earlier.

ALEXEY SUVORIN (1834–1912) Writer, publisher, newspaper owner, friend of Chekhov. Suvorin became a published writer of liberal persuasion in the 1860s but had built up a powerful publishing empire by the time he met Chekhov in December 1885, at the centre of which was the prominent right-wing newspaper *New Times*. Their correspondence began in February 1886, when Chekhov started publishing stories in *New Times*, and lasted for seventeen years, during which time Suvorin became his closest friend. They travelled twice to Western Europe together. Chekhov's 337 letters to Suvorin contain some of his most intimate confessions as well as some of his most penetrating discussions of contemporary theatre, literature and politics.

ANNA SUVORINA (1858–1936) Second wife of Alexey Suvorin. They met in 1887 during Chekhov's visit to St Petersburg and started corresponding two years later, although the earliest surviving letter from Chekhov dates from 1896.

MODEST TCHAIKOVSKY (1850–1916) Dramatist, librettist, biographer. Chekhov met Modest Tchaikovsky along with his brother Pyotr in 1888.

PYOTR TCHAIKOVSKY (1840–1893) Composer, acquaintance of Chekhov. Admirers of each other's work, they met in December 1888 in St Petersburg, and Tchaikovsky paid Chekhov a visit in Moscow the following October, after receiving a letter in which Chekhov asked for his permission to dedicate his short story collection *Gloomy People* to him. They exchanged six letters.

Prince ALEXANDER URUSOV (1843–1900) Lawyer and editor of the illustrated weekly magazine *The Russian Huntsman*. They became acquainted following Chekhov's return from Sakhalin at the end of 1890, and exchanged thirty letters over the following decade.

RIMMA VASHCHUK (1879–1958) Eighteen-year-old Moscow schoolgirl who sent Chekhov two of her stories and asked him if she had any talent ('I so love your works, and to judge from them it seems to me that you are so kind that you won't reproach me').

OLGA VASILIEVA (1882–?) Amateur writer, heiress, friend of Chekhov. Vasilieva met Chekhov during his winter in Nice in 1897–8, and asked his permission to translate his stories into English. She was one of his youngest admirers, and sent him ninety-seven letters in the last six years of his life; he sent forty-two replies.

ALEXANDER VESELOVSKY (1838–1906) Professor of Literature at St Petersburg University and President of the Literary Section of the Russian Academy of Sciences from 1899.

VLADIMIR YAKOVENKO (1857–1923) Doctor and psychiatrist, acquaintance of Chekhov. They got to know each other when Chekhov was living in Melikhovo. Dr Yakovenko set up and headed a psychiatric hospital in the area.

Nineteenth-century Russia

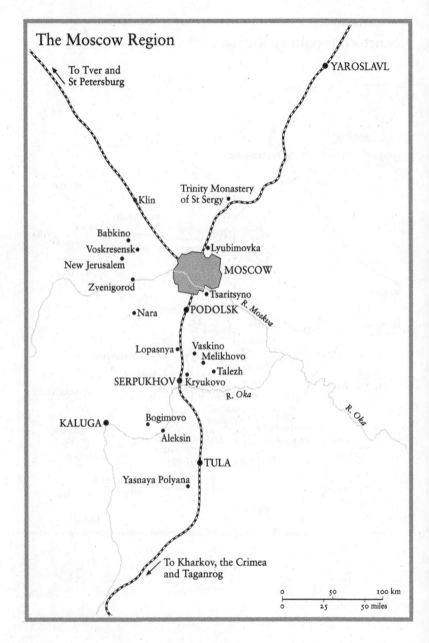

The Moscow Region

To Tver and
St Petersburg

YAROSLAVL

Klin

Trinity Monastery
of St Sergy

Babkino

Voskresensk

Lyubimovka

New Jerusalem

MOSCOW

Zvenigorod

Tsaritsyno

Nara

PODOLSK

R. Moskva

Lopasnya

Vaskino
Melikhovo

Talezh

SERPUKHOV Kryukovo

R. Oka

R. Oka

KALUGA

Bogimovo

Aleksin

TULA

Yasnaya Polyana

To Kharkov, the Crimea
and Taganrog

0   50   100 km
0   25   50 miles

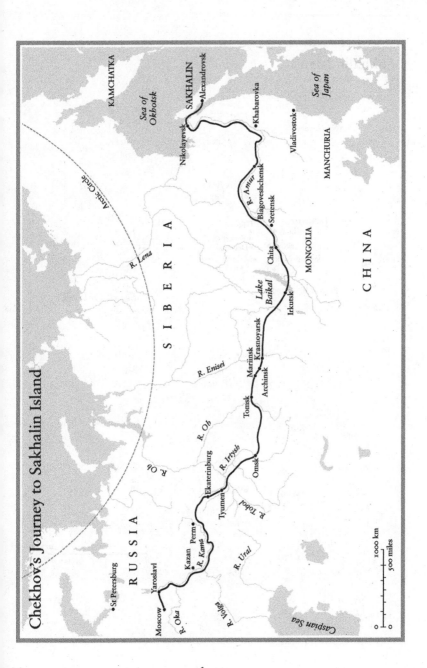

Chekhov's Journey to Sakhalin Island

KAMCHATKA

Sea of Okhotsk

SAKHALIN
• Alexandrovsk

Nikolayevsk

Sea of Japan

• Khabarovka

Vladivostok •

MANCHURIA

R. Amur

• Blagoveshchensk
• Sretensk

R. Lena

Chita

MONGOLIA

Lake Baikal

• Irkutsk

CHINA

Krasnoyarsk
• Mariinsk
• Archinsk

R. Enisei

Tomsk

Omsk

R. Ob

R. Irtysh

R. Tobol

Ekaterinburg

Tyumen

R. Ob

R. Ural

Perm
R. Kama

Kazan

SIBERIA

RUSSIA

St Petersburg •

Yaroslavl

Moscow
R. Oka

R. Volga

Caspian Sea

Arctic Circle

1000 km
500 miles

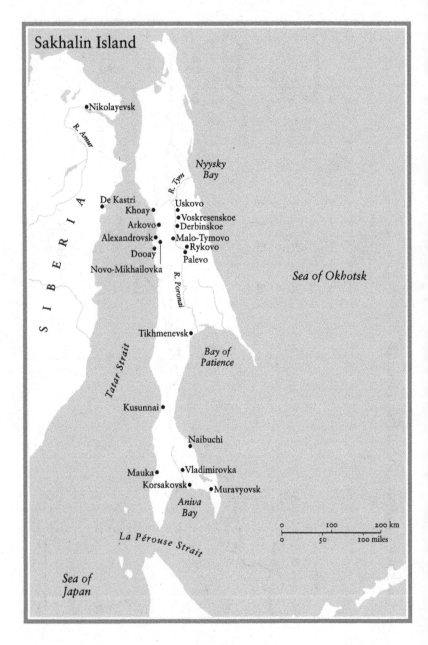

Sakhalin Island

Nikolayevsk

R. Amur

S I B E R I A

Nyysky Bay

R. Tym

De Kastri
Khoay
Uskovo
Arkovo
Voskresenskoe
Derbinskoe
Alexandrovsk
Malo-Tymovo
Rykovo
Dooay
Palevo
Novo-Mikhailovka

R. Poronai

Sea of Okhotsk

Tikhmenevsk

Bay of Patience

Tatar Strait

Kusunnai

Naibuchi

Mauka
Vladimirovka
Korsakovsk
Muravyovsk

Aniva Bay

La Pérouse Strait

Sea of Japan

0   100   200 km
0   50   100 miles

lxvi

A Life in Letters

1. To Mikhail M. (Mikhailovich) Chekhov, 7 December 1876, Taganrog

Dearest Cousin Mikhail Mikhailovich,

A few days ago I had the honour and pleasure of receiving your letter. In it you extend to me the hand of a brother, and I clasp it with feelings of pride and dignity as the hand of an elder brother. It was you who took the initiative in offering a sign of brotherly friendship, and it was an impertinence on my part to allow you to do so; in such a matter it should be for the younger to approach the elder, and therefore I ask your forgiveness. But the fact remains that a friendship of this kind formed part of my thoughts and my intentions from the very beginning.

I wanted to find, I dreamt of finding, a suitable opportunity to get to know you more closely, and then at last I received your letter. You occupy pride of place in my father's, my mother's and my brothers' letters. Mama sees in you much more than simply a nephew, she places you on a level with Uncle Mitrofan Egorovich, whom I know very well and of whom I shall never speak with less than admiration for his goodness of heart and his excellent, pure and jovial character. There is nothing I need to tell you about my brothers, I am sure you have already learnt for yourself everything there is to know. So you are greatly cherished by our family, and I feel that I know you from their letters. This was enough for me not to wait to seek out more favourable circumstances to make friends with a person such as yourself; I considered, and still consider, that I have a duty to honour someone who has earned the heartfelt respect of my family. You may thus imagine how welcome your letter was to me.

Of myself I have little to say, save that I am alive and well. I expect you will have heard plenty about me from my mother, and especially from Sasha and Kolya.[1] Please pass on my regards to your sister Elizaveta Mikhailovna and your brother Grigory Mikhailovich, and make sure they know that in the south of the country they have a cousin who enjoys receiving letters from various relatives. It would be a fine thing to have letters from them, if possible. I hope you won't mind my not standing on ceremony and asking you to write to me at least once a month? And please write informally, as a brother, so that there are no tensions between us. I need hardly say you won't find me staying aloof from you, and since one good turn deserves another I shall respond in kind. Since I have dragged in one proverb, here is another: there's no point in rushing to stick your head in the noose ahead of your elders and betters. So it is for you to take the first step. I am the number two, just as Kolya is to Sasha.

Please accept my deep bow and very best wishes for your happiness, meanwhile I have the honour to remain

Your respectful younger cousin and humble servant

A. Chekhov

My regards to Sasha and Kolya. Please tell Sasha that I have read *The Cosmos*.[2] I am sorry to tell him that it did not achieve the effect he desired: after I had read it I was still the same person. Tell Kolya his pictures are still at the Kursk railway station in Moscow, and he should go and say hello to them there. What a nuisance this war is,[3] keeping his pictures back like that!

1. Chekhov's elder brothers Alexander (Sasha) and Nikolay (Kolya). Nikolay was a painter.
2. *Der Kosmos: Entwurf einer physischen Weltbeschreibung* – unfinished five-volume magnum opus of German explorer Alexander von Humboldt (1769–1859), published in Russian translation 1848–63.
3. Russo-Turkish War, 1877–8.

2. *To Mikhail M. Chekhov, 1 January 1877, Taganrog*

Midnight precisely, 1877. Night

Dearest Cousin Misha,

I've just fired off two shots: one into the fence from my rifle, and one to Sasha from my pen. I fired off a toast to him: 'May your mathematical and scientific glory resound throughout this world like this shot' (but not in *that* world: there your sins will be on one side of the scales and your good deeds as counterweights on the other). Now, how can I fire at you without the gun misfiring? Insert two cartridges, and fire! Good shot sir! Well, the gun didn't blow up, however it just about broke the pen. After the bang-bang, the following words wing their way amid the smoke to Moscow: 'With this shot may all your misfortunes vanish like smoke, to be replaced by peace and money!' I drink your health with a jug of cold water instead of champagne, while mumbling this toast and penning this most idiotic of letters. If you are a believer in the New Year and its special characteristics, I send you my congratulations. Needless to say, as soon as midnight sounded I perpetrated an error, which means that I shall continue to make mistakes for the whole of the year: I mean that I dated this letter 1876 instead of 1877. I plan to be in Moscow for Easter; do you think that will be yet another mistake? Now my head is aching and my nose is wrinkling: the room stinks of gunpowder which hangs over the bed like a fog; the smell is appalling. The cause of this, you see, is that not only has my pupil[1] just let off a rocket flare in the room, but under cover of this has also contrived to let off one of his own uniquely pungent Cossack brand of rye-fuelled, authoritative detonations from that part of his anatomy not generally dignified with the name of artillery. The flare worked successfully, so my pupil is now looking inquiringly at me to see what I'm going to say about it. 'Get yourself to bed, you've smoked us out diabolically! Be off with you to your sty! Go to sleep!' And so, seeing that his flare failed to produce the

---

1. Chekhov stayed on in the family house after his parents fled to Moscow and paid for his room and board by tutoring the nephew of the new owner, Gavriil Selivanov.

desired effect, he starts telling me about the 'half-savage tribes of the aul', such being the way he describes his village and its Khokhol² inhabitants. It's so hot inside the room I can't sleep. I shall finish this letter and then go out, the devil knows why, maybe there'll be some excitement there. Give my greetings and best wishes to Grisha and Liza.³ All our Moscow lot will be asleep just now, I mean while I'm writing this letter. Well, so be it.

I can see that M. Chekhov will be saying to himself: 'What a stupid letter my cousin's written! What's wrong with him?' To which I will reply:

'The New Year has begun with a letter to you, so it follows that my first letter of 1877 is addressed to Misha. My head is full of such rubbish I can't make head nor tail of it myself. I wound up the year 1876 with a letter to Sasha, and now I'm beginning 1877 with a letter to you. Bravissimo, that's done then . . .' Now I'm going out to shoot some more, only not in the garden. Write to me, brother dear, if you have time; don't be lazy. If you don't have time I won't be offended, I have the sweetest nature in the world even though Mamasha (God grant her heart's desire) always said that I was born with an ingrained bad character. But I, God's humble and long-suffering servant, send her a jar of quince jelly. Vanya⁴ declines to send you his respects because according to him I am a scoundrel and a cheat and am liable to mangle the respects on purpose.

Me

i.e. A. Chekhov

Half-past midnight, 1 January 1877
Night (it may be tomorrow daytime, I'm not sure)
I sent you a postcard earlier. Did you get it? I have just read through this letter. It is very silly, not to mention the style reminding me of Lomonosov.⁵ But it can't be helped.

2. Affectionate but slightly disparaging term for a Ukrainian, somewhat similar to the way Scots are referred to as 'Jocks'.
3. Misha Chekhov's younger brother and sister, Grigory and Elizaveta.
4. Chekhov's younger brother, Ivan.
5. Mikhail Lomonosov (1711–65), a multi-talented Russian scientist and writer of humble peasant origin; the founder of Moscow University.

3. To Mikhail M. Chekhov, 10 April 1877, Moscow

Dear Cousin Misha,

As I've not had the pleasure of seeing you again, I'm taking up my pen. First, let me express my true fraternal gratitude for all that you have done for me during my stay in Moscow. Secondly, I am truly happy that we part now as intimate friends and brothers: it allows me to hope and trust that the eight hundred miles separating two cousins who keep up their correspondence will, now they have properly got to know one another, be no more than a trifling obstacle to maintaining our relationship. Now for a request to you, which, since it is a small one, I hope you will not find too difficult to fulfil: if I write to my mother care of you, please give her the letters in private, when you are alone together and not in the company of other people. There are some things in life that may only be said to one other completely trusted person; for this reason I sometimes have to write to Mamasha about matters other people should not know about, people to whom my secrets (and I do have secrets of a particular nature, which may or may not interest you, I don't know, but if you wish I shall be happy to tell them to you) are of no interest or, perhaps more properly, are of no concern. My second and last request is a rather more important one. Please be kind enough to continue offering comfort and support to my mother, who is physically and mentally in a very poor state.[1] She sees in you not just a nephew, but something much more. My mother's character is highly susceptible to the strong and positive influence represented by any kind of moral support from a third party. Well, you may think that is a pretty silly request. But it is one I believe you will understand, especially as I am speaking of 'moral', that is to say spiritual, support. Nothing in this malicious world is more dear to us than our mother, and therefore you will exceedingly oblige your humble servant by taking care of his mother, no more than half alive

---

1. Chekhov's mother's health suffered partly because Pavel Chekhov, her husband, remained unemployed for almost a year and a half before finding work in Moscow with Ivan Gavrilov, the merchant who also employed Chekhov's cousin Mikhail (Misha).

as she is. I am sure that we shall continue our correspondence as one would expect. By the way, I urge you to have no regrets at having opened your heart to me: I feel gratitude that you should place such trust in me. You may be sure, dear brother, that I value it most highly. Farewell; I send you my best wishes. My respects to Liza and Grisha, and to all your friends.

   Your cousin
   A. Chekhov

4. To Mikhail M. Chekhov, 9 June 1877, Taganrog

My very dearest Cousin Mikhail Mikhailovich,

   Not only you but all my Moscow relations are on my conscience. After two months' silence, I can at last wipe the sweat from my brow and write to you. You know cousin, I have to confess that May is the time when the pace is at its hottest for me, whereas for you it is Passion Week and Lent. And when the pace is as hot as it has been, one doesn't even have time to drink tea, let alone put pen to paper. I almost went out of my mind during these exams; it has been a period of anxiety and agitation during which I forgot all worldly pleasures and connections. First, let me congratulate you on the war, and secondly on the forthcoming marriage,[1] on your excellent brother-in-law, and on the betrothal of a sister at whose wedding, despite my advanced age, I would not only dance a *trepak*[2] with alacrity but would also down with you a modest glass of elixir, or as that celebrated Muscovite, 'our friend Isaak',[3] would put it, contraband liquor. Do please congratulate your sister for me on the forthcoming festivities, and please acquaint me with your future brother-in-law. From the bottom of my heart I wish them well and trust that they will become possessed of a not insubstantial pile of cash. I should regard it as a personal kindness if

1. Mikhail Chekhov's sister, Ekaterina, was shortly to marry Pavel Petrov, who later worked for the Muir and Mirrielees department store in Moscow.
2. A Russian folk dance.
3. A reference to the life of a monk from the Kiev Caves Monastery.

you would also go on the spree on my behalf. I expect you know that I finished up my exams all right, by which I mean that I passed into the seventh grade. Give my respects to Grisha and Liza. By the way, if you go to Kaluga, please give my compliments to your mother my aunt, and all your other sisters, who to my enormous chagrin do not know me any more than I know them. Please tell them: 'I am charged with presenting to you the compliments of your unknown acquaintance, your mysterious close relative.' Then continue: 'The closeness of this relative to you is unaffected by the fact that he resides twelve hundred miles from Kaluga, that blessed place of Shamil's refuge.'[4] It makes me very happy that you are giving your sister in marriage; I don't exactly know why, but it makes me happy. Farewell, cousin, we shall not see one another for seven years. It appears, or as Isaak would say, 'circumstances of a particular nature have contrived', that I shall not have occasion to travel through Mother Russia to Mother Moscow to see my own mother. Write to me more often, if you have time. Please send the photographs you promised. Our poor Taganrog is as poor as a pilgrim; the crops in the fields live better than you and me, they bloom better than the girls in Moscow, glowing brighter than gold sovereigns and growing faster than 25 per cent interest on your capital. As crops go, they are splendid. We're expecting a brilliant harvest. God grant the Russians victory over the Turk with his pipe, and a massive growth in business to accompany the harvest, then once again Papa and I will be able to make a reasonable living as merchants. But I think we will have to be patient for some time yet. I'll be a rich man, as sure as two and two make four (and I'll grow tall enough to touch the ceiling), and when I am I'll feed you on bread and honey and ply you with the finest wine for the brotherly way in which you respond to the respect and affection that now exists between us. You are a splendid fellow in many ways, let me tell you, not in flattery, but as a brother. May you live for a hundred years and then some!

Give my compliments to your comrades, they are also splendid

4. A reference to Shamil, the Muslim leader who tried to unite the Caucasian tribes against Russian annexation, and was captured by the Russians in 1859.

fellows, a world away from our pathetic Taganrog crowd of snobbish shop assistants who turn up their noses at you if you live down near the port and not in Bakhmut.[5] I felt very drawn to your friends, one can see at once that they are fine examples of the Russian people to whom both of us have the honour to belong, you and your humble servant, your cousin and friend

A. Chekhov

Please write to me more often! I'll keep pace with you, as much as you manage.

5. To Mikhail M. Chekhov, 29 July 1877, Taganrog

Dear Cousin Misha,

First, let me congratulate you on your safe return to Moscow from Kaluga, and secondly on the happy event of the marriage. I wish our mutual sister every happiness, and to her husband health, prosperity and all manner of earthly bliss. God grant this may not be the last wedding in your house, nor the last but one, nor even the antepenultimate, and that all such marriages will go off even more brilliantly than this one, which has brought great joy to our wise generation of Chokhovs.[1] Thanks to Ekaterina Mikhailovna for having set in train this process . . . and even though on this occasion I was not able to be present, I hope to celebrate future weddings in the house of Misha Chokhov and his nearest and dearest. I heard from my own family how magnificently you organized the wedding! I wish in my heart that more sisters could have brothers like you. You do more for your sisters, including your female cousins, than all of us put together would do for any of ours. All glory and honour to you! My only disappointment was not to have been there, and thus not being able to drink with you as we did in Moscow. I adore all kinds of revelry,

5. A town in southern Russia near Taganrog.
1. Mikhail Chekhov's family often called themselves Chokhov rather than Chekhov.

especially Russian revelry where the drinking of wine goes hand in hand with dancing . . . in a word, our brother Isaak is a very different animal from Akaky. I am in perfect health as I write, and trust that my letter will find you likewise in good health and a happy frame of mind. I received your invitation card on 16 July and thank you a thousand times for your kindness. But why don't you write to me? Do write, my friend! I wait for an envelope in your handwriting every day. Write and tell me how you are getting on, how your family is, how Elizaveta Mikhailovna is, whom I have not yet succeeded in getting to know properly. My best respects to Grisha. If you see my Papa, please tell him that I received his kind letter and am most grateful for it. My father and mother are the only people in the whole world for whom I will never grudge anything whatever. If ever I amount to something it will be their doing; they are wonderful people whose love for their children places them beyond all praise and outweighs all the disadvantages that stem from the hard life they have led. It ensures for them the sure and pleasing path in which they believe and trust with a devotion matched by few. If you consider your cousins in relation to the position of your uncle and aunt, you cannot but agree with me. Please tell my mother that I sent two packets containing money, and am surprised that they have not arrived. Give my greetings to our student and ask him to forgive me for not writing to him. I intend to write to him on the subject of polygamy, of which I am a defender. Sasha is a good person in his way; I don't know why he thinks of me as a nihilist. Please tell Kolya that there were two Jewish girls in Gavrilov's shop, Rosa Mikhailovna and Vera Mikhailovna Epshtein, who send their regards to him. Why don't you think up some boulevard somewhere where we can rendezvous?

Please send me the photographs you promised. If I get my picture taken I'll send mine to you first. Kindest regards to your colleagues at work, especially to Apollon Ivanovich, who has got to know me well and who even promised to write to me. And please give my very best respects to Elizaveta and Alexandra Mikhailovna. Write to me; I am proud to receive your letters and I cherish them. I have replied to the invitation from Kaluga. Pass on my regards to the Petrovs, and wish the best of good fortune to your devoted cousin, who in turn sends you his best wishes,

A. Chekhov

How did you find Vanya?

6. To Mikhail M. Chekhov, 4 November 1877, Taganrog

Dear Cousin Misha,

I take pleasure in congratulating you on your name day and wishing you every happiness and good fortune on this earth: first, good health, second, a ton of money, and third, success and happiness for your entire family, which represents for you – as my family does to me – the dearest thing that exists. I am conscience-stricken and ask your pardon, but all this time I have been too worried about lack of time to write to you. I received the photograph, and thank you for it. You and your sister Liza are very alike, and Grisha too. For this I am in your debt. I am in good health, and such being the case, am alive; I have only one thing wrong with me and unfortunately it causes as much suffering as toothache: I have no money. I have had no letters from Moscow for a long time, either from my parents or from you. It's most upsetting. How are you? Please write and tell me. Thank you for the greetings you sent me in your letter to Uncle Mitrofan Egorovich. There is nothing new under the sun in Taganrog, nothing whatsoever! Dreadfully boring! Not long ago I went to the theatre here and could not help comparing it with your Moscow theatres. Quite a difference! There is a huge difference generally speaking between Moscow and Taganrog. Moscow is a wonderful place; as soon as I graduate from the Gymnasium I shall fly to it on wings.

Write me a letter if you have time, it would give me so much pleasure. Is it true that Apollon Ivanovich has been taken for the army? If so, it's a rotten turn of events, really rotten. Aunt Fedosia Yakovlevna is very grateful to you for taking so much trouble over Alyosha. Please write and tell me how you are and how your family is, you would oblige me greatly by so doing. What impression did my brother Vanya make on you? Please pass on my regards to Grisha, Elizaveta Mikhailovna and Alexander Mikhailovich, and tell them I care deeply for their wellbeing. Give my respects as appropriate to your friends. Dear cousin, don't deprive me of the pleasure of your letters, and forgive me for my long silence.

Your brother

A. Chekhov

7. To Mikhail (Pavlovich) Chekhov, after 5 April 1879, Taganrog

Dear brother Misha,

I received your letter while yawning at the gates in a perfect agony of extreme boredom, so you may imagine with what marvellous timing your monster epistle made its appearance. Your handwriting is excellent, and I couldn't find a single grammatical mistake anywhere in your letter. There is however one thing I am not happy about: why do you portray yourself in such an exaggerated way as my 'worthless and insignificant little brother'? Do you really have such a strong sense of your own worthlessness? Not all Mishas have to be the same, brother. Do you know where it's right to confess your insignificance? To God perhaps, to intelligence, beauty and nature, but never to other people. Before other people you must be conscious of your worth. After all, you're no cheat but an honest person, are you not? Well then, have some respect for yourself as an honest fellow, and realize that an honest fellow is by no means worthless. Don't confuse 'humility' with 'recognizing your unworthiness'. Georgy is growing up.[1] He's a nice boy, and I often play *babki*[2] with him. He got the parcels you sent him. I am glad that you are reading; the habit of reading books is one you will appreciate more and more as time goes on. Did Madame Beecher Stowe[3] bring tears to your eyes? I used to read her

1. Chekhov's cousin Georgy, son of Pavel Egorovich's younger brother Mitrofan.
2. Translates as 'Knucklebones', a children's game.
3. Harriet Beecher Stowe (1811–96), the American author of the bestselling novel *Uncle Tom's Cabin* (1852).

some time ago, but then about six months ago I read through her book in a spirit of research. After that I experienced the disagreeable sensation, familiar to mortals, of having overindulged in raisins and currants. The hawfinch I promised you has flown off, his present whereabouts is unknown to me. I'll think of something else to bring you. I recommend the following books for you to read: *Don Quixote* (the full version, in seven or eight parts) – it's a great work. The author, Cervantes, can be placed almost on a par with Shakespeare. I suggest that my brothers read Turgenev's *Don Quixote and Hamlet* if they haven't already read it. I don't think that you, brother, would understand it. If you want to try an amusing travel book, have a look at something like Goncharov's[4] *The Frigate Pallada*. I send special greetings to Masha through you. Don't be upset that I am not coming right away. However bored one claims to be, time does fly. When I do come I shall bring a lodger with me who will pay 20 roubles a month and whom we shall be looking after personally. I am just off to haggle with his mother. Pray for me!! However effective your prayers, he'll still pay 20 roubles. After all even 20 roubles is not much, bearing in mind how expensive Moscow is and my mother's character – to feed her lodgers like gods. Our teachers take 350 roubles a head, and feed the poor little boys like dogs, with scraps from their roast meat.

A. Chekhov

8. To Pavel Filevsky, 27 October 1880, Moscow

Dear Pavel Petrovich,

I am being bold enough to trouble you once again with a request. Forgive the imposition, but I should be glad if you would write and let me know whether your stipend has come through yet, because I have not received mine for this year. What can this mean? I am in the most horrible difficulties, but your reply would at least tell me whether

---

4. Ivan Goncharov (1812–91), a prose writer whose best-known novel was *Oblomov* (1859).

I am alone in this or whether my friends are also, like me, still waiting for their grants. I have applied to the office, but as yet have had no reply. Have you heard anything yourself? I should be really grateful if you could let me know. Zembulatov[1] sends his regards to you. I wish you good health and happiness, and don't forget that I remain

Your humble servant

A. Chekhov

My address is: A. P. Chekhov, c/o Vnukova, Grachovka, Moscow
Best wishes to all my friends from school.

9. To Alexander Chekhov, 8 November 1882, Moscow

Dear Customs Officer and brother Alexander,

First of all let me inform you that all is well. Secondly, you are due 19 roubles 45 copecks from the *Moscow Sheet*. From the aforementioned sum I shall give Fedya 10 roubles, as previously agreed. The remainder I shall send to the Taganrog Customs for you to collect. Should I get my shoes out of pawn, or should I wait? I've completely run out of money. We receive, read, glory in and hugely enjoy your filthy letters. Fornicate not, that ye be not fornicated against. But you do fornicate, oh you do! Punch me in the stomach if you like; we medics forbid actual congress but not massage. Nikolka has gone to Voskresensk with Maria, it's Mishka's name day, Father is sleeping, Mother is praying, Auntie's thinking about herbs, Anna is washing dishes and is about to bring in the piss-pot, I am writing and wondering how many times tonight my whole body will be racked with pain for my presumption in daring to try to be a writer? I'm getting on with my medical studies ... There's an operation every day. Tell Anna Ivanovna that the old paperboy who sold *The Spectator*[1] has died in

1. Vasily Zembulatov, an old school friend from Taganrog who had also gone to Moscow University to train as a doctor.
1. A comic journal the Chekhov brothers contributed to.

hospital from cancer prostatae. We're just carrying on quietly as usual, reading, writing, hanging around in the evenings, drinking the odd glass of vodka, listening to music and singing, et caetera ... have some favours to ask you:

1 Catch a little smuggler and send him to me.

2 Ask Anna Ivanovna to accept my expression of the most sincere and benevolent wishes for her welfare, a thousand prostrate greetings and my desire to be her lucky little Sashkins.

3 Ask (eandem[2]) to be so kind as to describe the spiritual séance she witnessed, somewhere in Tula province apparently. Could she please give me a brief but detailed description: where? How? Who was there? Whose spirit was summoned? Did it speak? What time of day or night was it, and how long did it last? Please ask her to write it all down carefully and send it to me. This is vitally important. I shall be extremely grateful and will repay the favour.

4 Thou shalt not kill.

5 Write out a poem for me:

... when I was small

... I became

... a general ... remember?

This is also most important. Write it out for me, and remind me who wrote it ...

6 Write to me more often, and give more details. I rank your letters (when, that is, they contain anything besides Tula verses and descriptions of that fair town) as outstanding specimens of writing, and carefully preserve them. Write away.

7 Except. A predicate refers to the subject of a sentence, and if it does not refer to the subject then it is not a predicate ... And therefore please get from Uncle the photograph of us in a group (me, you, Ivan and Nikolay). Do you remember this photograph being taken at Strakhov's? Please send said picture. Essential.

I do miss you, even though you are a drunk.

Tell Anna Ivanovna her Gavrilka is a lying son of a bitch. I'm absolutely fed up with him.

2. her, i.e. Anna Ivanovna.

What is Anosha on about with that *Spectator* number he took exception to? Tell him we don't much care for any of the Loboda family numbers either, starting with Ivan Ivanych and ending with Anosha himself.

I am doing a bit of writing, but not much. You can read my 'Late Flowers'[3] in *Talk of the World*; get it from Uncle.

My stuff is going to be published in Piter[4] again.

Debag Shurka and pick Gershka up by the tail. Farewell, au revoir.

Why don't you come for the holidays . . . I still haven't sorted out my documents. If you're not in arrears yourself, could you fire off a letter to the Dean? Deans have nothing to do anyhow.

Is Uncle getting the newspapers regularly?

Rp. Alexandri penem
Annam Ivanovnam
Temporis nocturni q<uantum> s<ufficiat>
ut. fl. a congregatio No. 12. DS[5]

Caution! Do not shake the bottle.

Secretary Zakharin[6]

Excuse me, but doesn't something have to be written in the blank space?

What will come of all this? Well, suppose nothing comes of it . . . but what on earth will come of it?

I'd love to come to Taganrog to see you, and to Surazh to see Leonid. My advice to you is: don't pig yourself! You don't want to go getting fat!

3. An early story by Chekhov.
4. Piter – common Russian nickname for St Petersburg, which reflects how the city's name was originally spelt.
5. Prescription Alexander: apply Anna Ivanovna to the penis at night time as much as required to produce moisture before congress for twelve days. Caution!
6. A reference to a professor of medicine at Moscow University.

10. *To Nikolay Leikin, 12 January 1883, Moscow*

Dear Sir, Nikolay Alexandrovich,

In reply to your kind letter I am sending you a few things. I have received my fee, and am also getting copies of the magazine (on Tuesdays), and am indebted to you for both. Thank you also for your flattering invitation to continue our collaboration. I am especially pleased to be contributing to *Fragments*. I am not alone in being very attracted by the whole tenor of your journal, its appearance and the intelligence with which it is produced.

I am above all a great believer in short pieces, and were I myself to be the publisher of a humorous magazine I would be inclined to blue-pencil anything that smacked of prolixity. Among the Moscow editorial offices I seem to be the only one standing up for brevity (which doesn't, however, prevent me from occasionally trying to get away with more lengthy pieces . . . you can't always go against the tide!). All the same, I must admit that being held to a strict word count does cause me a certain amount of grief, and I often find it difficult to keep to imposed limits. For example . . . you don't accept articles of more than 100 lines, and I can understand why. I get my subject, sit down and start to write. From the very first phrase the injunction not to exceed 100 lines cramps my style. I abbreviate, sift, cut as much as I can, sometimes (as I cannot prevent my writer's instinct telling me) to the detriment of the subject and, most importantly, to the form. Once I've done all my cutting and compressing, I start to count . . . I get up to 100, 120, 140 lines (I've never written more than that for *Fragments*), lose heart, and . . . don't submit. Doubts creep in as soon as I spill over on to the fourth sheet of small-format writing paper . . . and so I don't send my story in. What usually happens is that I have to rehash the ending and send off something I didn't really want to . . . As an example, I'm sending you a piece entitled 'The Only Remedy'. I squeezed it right down and am sending it to you in the most digested form I can, but even so am still worried that it will be a bit too long for you. But I'm sure that if I had been able to write it at twice the length it would have been twice as good, and there would have been twice as much spice and substance in it . . . I do have some shorter things, but I do not have confidence in them. I might have sent them to you on another occasion, but I can't come to a decision . . .

All this is leading up to a plea: allow me a bit more space, up to 120 lines . . . I am sure I will not often take advantage of this extra licence, but the mere fact of knowing that I can do if need be would relieve me of anxiety.

In the meantime, please accept my respectful assurances of remaining your obedient servant,

Ant. Chekhov

PS Over the New Year I had prepared a package for you with material weighing almost an ounce and a half. But then the editor of *The Spectator* came along and took it off me; he is a friend so I could not stop him. Our editors deliver philippics against Muscovites who also write for Petersburg papers. But Petersburg takes less than the censors gobble up: they cut 400 to 800 lines from every edition of the poor *Alarm Clock*.[1] No one knows what to do about it.

11. To Alexander Chekhov, around 20 February 1883, Moscow

Esteemed brother, Alexander Pavlovich!

First, allow me to congratulate you and your other half on the happy outcome and increase in your kind, and the city of Taganrog on its latest citizeness.[1] May the newborn child live long (. . . cross yourself!), be filled to excess (cross yourself!) with physical and moral beauty, expressivity, understanding, and may she in the fullness of time snatch herself a valiant husband (cross yourself, you fool!), having previously ensnared and driven to despair all the Gymnasium pupils in Taganrog!!!

Having delivered myself of my congratulations, I shall now come

1. A popular weekly comic journal to which Chekhov contributed.
1. This refers to the birth of Alexander's daughter Maria.

straight to the point. Nikolka has just given me your letter to read. I shall put to one side the question of whether or not it was right for me to read it, because of lack of time. If the letter had just been about Nikolay, I would have confined myself to my congratulations, but your letter raises several extremely interesting questions all at once. It is these questions I want to discuss. Along the way, I shall respond to your previous scrawls. Sadly, I don't have the time to write as much as I should. For the sake of good order and discipline I must resort to a systematic response: your letter shall be examined from A to Z, point by point. I am a critic, and it is a work of literary interest. I have the right to do this because I have read it. Look at things as a writer and all will turn out well. Incidentally, exercising our critical faculties does us no harm as writers. But it is right to offer a word of caution: what I have to say concerns only the questions outlined above; I shall try to ensure that as far as possible my commentary avoids anything of a personal nature.

1) That Nikolka is wrong is not even worth disputing. Not only does he not reply to your letters, he doesn't even answer business ones; I have never met anyone ruder than him in this respect. For a year now he has been meaning to write to Lentovsky,[2] who wants to be in touch with him; a letter from a perfectly decent man, who wrote to him specifically requesting a reply, has been lying around on his bookcase unanswered for half a year, and it was only written so there would be an answer. It would be hard to find a more indolent person than our brother. And the worst of it is – he is incorrigible . . . Your letter will have moved him, but even so I doubt that he will find time to answer it. But this is beside the point. Let us begin with the style of your letter. I remember how you used to laugh at Uncle's pronounce-ments . . . You might as well laugh at yourself. Your pronouncements rival his for unctuousness. They have all the traits: 'clasp to your arms' . . . 'spiritual wounds' . . . The only thing missing is your bursting into tears . . . To believe Uncle's letters, he must have spent huge amounts of time in floods of tears. (Provincial life! . . .) Your letter is

2. Mikhail Lentovsky (1843–1906), an actor and impresario who hired the Hermitage gardens in Moscow in 1876 and put on variety shows.

one long tear-filled moan from beginning to end . . . All your letters are like that, as indeed is everything you write . . . One would think that, like Uncle, you consist of nothing but tear glands. This is not a joke, I'm not exercising my wit at your expense . . . I wouldn't have mentioned this weepiness, your breast heaving with joy or grief, these spiritual wounds, etc., if they had not been so inappropriate and . . . obnoxious. Nikolka (as you very well know) just fritters his time away; a good, strong Russian talent is going to waste in him, and all for nothing . . . In a year or two the voice of our artist brother will be stilled for ever. He's got himself mixed up with a crowd of boozers, worthless people like Yaron and other similar dregs . . . Have you seen the work he's turning out now? What on earth does he think he's doing? Everything that's cheap and vulgar . . . while all the time he has the makings of a fine picture standing in the hallway. He was approached by *Russian Theatre* to do illustrations for Dostoyevsky . . . He promised to do them, then broke his word, but those illustrations would have made his reputation and earned him his living . . . What can I say? You saw him six months ago, I hope you have not forgotten . . . And now, instead of giving him support, offering a good-natured and talented person some words of encouragement to strengthen his resolve, and being of inestimable help to him, you write him these pathetic, miserable lines . . . All they will do is make him wretched for half an hour, beat him round the head, diminish him . . . By tomorrow he'll have forgotten all about your letter. You are a wonderful stylist, you've read a great deal and written a great deal, you have as good an understanding of things as the next man, — and it would have cost you nothing to send a kind word to your brother. The very last thing he needed was to be scolded by you! If instead of weeping all over the place you had talked to him seriously about his painting, he would have settled down to paint and probably would have written back to you by now. You know how easy it is to influence him . . . 'I've forgotten you . . . this is the last letter I'll write to you' — what rubbish that is, that's not the point at all . . . the last thing you should be ramming home . . . You, a strong, educated, mature person, should be emphasizing everything that is vital, everything that is eternal, and affecting not the superficial emotions but the deepest human feelings

... You can do this ... You are clever, sensible, an artist. If I were God I would forgive you all your sins, of omission and of commission, in deed and in word, for that letter of yours with the description of the end-of-navigation thanksgiving service on the pier (complete with Captain Hatteras's ice-floes)[3] ... (By the way, after reading that letter, Nikolka was seized with an overwhelming desire to go and paint piers.) Even in your literary work you always lay stress on trivialities ... But you weren't born to be a subjective scribbler ... It's a tendency you've acquired, not an innate one ... It's the easiest thing in the world to give up this kind of acquired subjectivity ... All you have to do is be more honest: throw yourself overboard wherever you can, don't make yourself the hero of your own novel, get away from yourself at least for half an hour. One of your stories is about a young married couple who go through a whole meal doing nothing but kiss each other, whining and wittering on about nothing ... Not a single syllable of sense do they utter, just sweet nothings! You didn't write this for anyone else to read ... You wrote it because *you* enjoy this sort of aimless babbling. But if you were to describe the meal, the kind of food, how they ate it, what the cook was like, if you were to show the vulgarity of your hero who is so pleased with his idle happiness, your heroine's vulgarity and absurd love for her overfed, benapkined stuffed goose of a husband ... Of course everyone likes to see happy, well-fed people, but for a true description it's not enough just to tell us what *they* said and how often they kissed each other ... You need something else: a bit of detachment from the purely personal effect which newly married happiness always has on anyone who has not become completely embittered ... Subjectivity is a terrible thing. It's bad enough that it completely exposes feeble writers. I would lay a bet that priests' daughters and female clerks everywhere are in love with you from reading your works, and if you were a German you would never have to buy your own beer in any beer hall with a German barmaid. If it weren't for this squelchy, sloppy subjectivity

---

3. A reference to a novel by Jules Verne (1828–1905), *Voyages et aventures du capitaine Hatteras* (*Journeys and Adventures of Captain Hatteras*), published in two volumes in 1866.

of yours you would have the makings of a really worthwhile artist. You have such a marvellous sense of humour, your wit is so barbed, the accuracy with which you poke fun at people is so telling, your style has such fluency, you've endured so much, had such a wealth of experience ... Ach! All that material going to waste. If you could only have shoved a bit of it into your letters you could have sparked Nikolay's imagination ... You could forge steel, not manifestos, from your material. You could become such an indispensable person! Please try, write to Nikolka, write again, talk sense to him, good, honest sense – you are a hundred times cleverer than he is, – just write to him and you'll see what comes of it ... He will answer your letter, lazy though he is ... But don't moan at him and don't depress him: he's depressed enough as it is ...

'You don't have to be very sensitive,' you go on, 'to understand that when I went away I cut myself off from my family and condemned myself to oblivion ...' From this we are supposed to understand that you have been forgotten. You so obviously don't believe a word of it that it's not even worth talking about. There's no point in lying, my friend. Knowing our mother's tendency to complain, and also Nikolay's habit of affectionately remembering and kissing the whole world when he is drunk, that is something you simply can't say; you could only have written such a thing as a direct expression of your own tear ducts. 'I expected, and of course am still waiting ...' This is a dig at us, isn't it? ... Yes, sometimes it really is appropriate to turn the knife, but this is neither the way nor the language in which to do it. You've lifted it from your 'Little Sister'[4] story, but there are more apposite things of yours you could have quoted from.

2) 'Father wrote to me saying that I had failed to justify myself' etc. This is something you've said 100 times. I don't understand what you want from Father. He doesn't like the smoking of tobacco and illicit cohabitation – do you want him to be a different person from the one he is? You might move our mother and our aunt somewhere along those lines, but not Father. He's made from the same flinty stone

4. This story was never published.

as the schismatics,[5] no less, and is totally unbudgeable. That is probably his strength. However sweetly you write to him, he will always sigh and write back to you in exactly the same way, and the worst of it is, he will suffer ... How can you not know this? It's very strange ... Forgive me, brother, but I think there's another tune being played here, and it is not a very pleasant one. You're not so much trying to swim against the tide as trying to ingratiate yourself with it ... Why do you care what some schismatic thinks of your cohabitation? Why suck up to him, what is it you're after? Let him look on it however he pleases ... It's his own, schismatic, affair. You know you're right, well then there's where you make your stand whatever people may write to you and whatever suffering it may cause them ... The whole meaning of life resides in protest, my friend, so long as it's not mealy-mouthed.

Everyone has the right to live with whomever he likes and in whatever way he chooses – that is the privilege of any grown-up person, but apparently you don't believe in this right, or at least you feel the need to set the law on the Pimenovnas and Stamatiches[6] of this world. What do you yourself feel about your cohabitation? It's your home, your hearth, your grief and joy, your poetry, but you fuss over this poetry as if it were a watermelon you'd stolen, you look at everyone with suspicion (what does he think about it?), rub everyone's nose in it, moan and groan ... If I were one of your family, I'd be rather offended. Do you care what I, or Nikolay, or Father think? What business is it of yours? They won't understand you, any more than you will understand 'the father of six children', just as you have never understood Father's feelings ... Close as they are to you, they won't understand you, and there's no need for them to do so. Live your life, that's all you have to do. It's impossible to feel for the whole world at once, but you want us to feel for you. As soon as you see on our faces a hint that we don't care, you start complaining. Oh Lord,

5. A reference to the mid seventeenth-century schism when reforms of the ritual in the Russian Orthodox Church were opposed by Old Believers, conservative members of the Church.
6. A cook and a Greek broker, both previously regular customers at Pavel Chekhov's shop in Taganrog.

how manifold are Thy works! If I were in your position and had a family, not only would I not pay any attention to anyone else's opinions, I wouldn't want to try to understand them. This is my 'I', my department, and no little sisters have any right (by virtue of the natural order of things) to poke their well-intentioned, sensitive noses into it, in search of understanding! I wouldn't write to tell people about my joy at becoming a father . . . They won't understand, they will simply laugh at your declarations – and will be right to do so. You've made Anna Ivanovna sing to your tune as well. When we met in Moscow she was already in floods of tears, asking 'At thirty years of age isn't it . . . too late?' As if we had been asking her . . . Whatever we think is our business, and you don't have to explain yourself to us. I'd rather have my head banged against the wall than allow my wife to humiliate herself before my brothers, however high and mighty those brothers might be! So, anyway . . . that's a good subject for a story. But I've no time to write it.

3) 'I have no right to make demands on my sister . . . she has always had . . . the worst possible impression of me. She is incapable of seeing into my soul . . .' (Seeing into my soul . . . Doesn't that remind you of [Saltykov-Shchedrin's][7] village policeman who can read people's hearts?) You're right of course . . . Our sister loves you, but she has no conception of the person you are . . . The façade you say she puts on is purely the result of her being *afraid* to think about you. This is only natural! Just try to think, when did you ever have a proper, human conversation with her? When she was growing up, when she was studying seriously, did you ever say or write a single serious word to her? It's the same story as with Nikolay. You never say anything, so it's no wonder that she doesn't know you. Strangers have done more for her than you, her closest kin . . . She could have absorbed a lot from you, but you are too miserly. (You won't surprise her with love, because love without good deeds is dead.) Just now she is in the middle of fighting a battle, and what a desperate battle it is! Incredible! Everything she was expecting to be her life's work has crashed in ruins

7. Mikhail Saltykov-Shchedrin (1826–89), the greatest nineteenth-century Russian satirist.

about her ears . . . She now has all the qualities of one of Turgenev's heroines . . . I'm not exaggerating. This is the most fertile soil you can imagine! But you choose to make a fuss and be offended at her not writing to you! What should she write to you about? She did sit down once, thought and thought about what to say, and ended up writing about Fedotova[8] . . . There were other things she wanted to say, but she felt that anyone reading her words would probably sneer at them like [your university friends] Tretyakov and Co. I confess that I'm more irritable with the family than I should be. I'm generally an irritable sort of person. I'm often rude and unfair, but why do you think it is our sister tells me things she would not tell any of you? The answer is probably that I have not seen her purely as a 'dearly beloved sister', just as I didn't turn my back on Mishka, who is someone one absolutely *needs* to talk to . . . After all, she is a person, and very much a person. You just treat her facetiously, borrowing money from her to buy a table and a clock on credit . . . Great pedagogy! Her parents aren't going to look after her on this earth. It's not their job . . .

'I'll say nothing about Anton. You're on your own . . .'

From a purely gentlemanly perspective, I ought to pass this by without comment. But at the start of this letter I said that I would not descend to the personal . . . I will stick to that, but I do just want to add one 'question . . .' (Terrible how many questions there are!) There exists in this wide world a dread disease, with which no writer, not one, can claim to be unacquainted! . . . (There are many writers, but only a few of us. Our camp is not nearly numerous enough. The disease is rife in this camp. The people in it cannot understand one another.) I've written too much here! Must cross it out . . . It's a form of arrogance, people belonging together in the same camp and not wanting to understand one another. An evil affliction! We are family, we breathe the same air, we think alike, we have the spiritual affinity of kinsfolk, but at the same time . . . we can be mean-spirited enough to write 'I'll say nothing!' What overweening arrogance! There are so few of *us* that it is our absolute duty to support one another . . . well, yes, *vous comprenez*! However vile our behaviour may be to one another

8. Glikeria Fedotova, an actress at the Imperial Maly Theatre in Moscow.

(it is in fact hardly so at all!), we must honour the smallest sign that we 'belong to the salt of the earth'. We, that includes me, you, the Tretyakovs, our own Mishka, stand above the crowd, we're the elite ... We know our collective duty: it is to think, to have a head on our shoulders ... Whoever is not of us is against us. And here we go denying one another! We grumble, whine, sulk, gossip, spit in each other's faces! Look at the number of people Tretyakov and Co. have humiliated! Now that they've drunk *Bruderschaft*[9] with 'Vasya' [Malyshev][10] they feel they are entitled to write off the rest of humanity as narrow-minded provincials! I am so stupid I can hardly blow my own nose, there is so much I have not read, but the God I pray to is the same God as you do – and that ought to be enough for you to value me as worth my weight in gold! Stepanov is a fool, but he has been to university and knows a thousand times more than Semyon Gavrilovich or Vasya, yet there they were making him bang his head against the side of the piano after the can-can! Disgusting! A wonderful understanding of people and a wonderful way to make use of them! A fine thing it would be if I stuck a dunce's cap on Zembulatov because he hadn't heard of Darwin! Even though he was brought up in the serf-owning tradition, he nevertheless opposes it – and for that alone I love him! If I had to reject A, B, C ... D, one person after another, I would finish up in total isolation!

We newspapermen suffer from a disease – the disease of envy. Instead of rejoicing at your success, people envy it and like to put ... a sting in the tail! Rub in some salt! But all of them pray to the same God, they all do the same work, every last one of them ... Such small-mindedness! Such lack of breeding ... And how it poisons life!

There's work to be done, so I must stop. I'll write again some time. What I have written here has been out of friendship, on my word of honour; no one has forgotten you, no one holds anything against you ... so there is no reason not to write to you as a friend.

9. Translates as 'brotherhood' and implies switching from the formal *vy* to the more intimate *ty*.
10. Vasily Malyshev, a school inspector, was the uncle of Leonid Tretyakov, with whom Chekhov was at university.

My respects to Anna Ivanovna and to a certain Ma.[11]

Are you receiving *Fragments*? Let me know. Leikin himself sent you the confirmation.

Upon which, I have the honour to send you my deep respects.

A. Chekhov

Would you like a few nice little subjects?

I've written stacks! Twenty roubles' worth! More, even . . .

12. *To Nikolay Leikin, 21 and 24 August 1883, Moscow*

Dear Nikolay Alexandrovich,

What I am sending you herewith is not of my best. The writing is feeble, the story unpolished and painfully trivial. I have better subjects, I could have written more and earned more as well, but this time the fates are against me! I am currently writing in the most awful conditions, with a great weight of non-literary activities hammering mercilessly at my conscience, a visiting relation's baby screaming in the next room, while in another room my father is reading aloud to my mother from [Leskov's] 'The Sealed Angel' . . . Someone has got the music box going, so I have to listen to [Offenbach's] *La Belle Hélène* . . . I'd like to slope off to the dacha, but it's one o'clock in the morning . . . It would be hard to imagine a worse situation for someone who wants to be a writer. My bed is occupied by the visiting relation [Alexander Chekhov]; he keeps buttonholing me and starting to talk about medical subjects. 'My daughter probably has colic; that's why she's crying all the time.' I am unfortunate enough to be a doctor, so everybody seems to think they have to talk to me about medicine. And when they get tired of discussing medicine, they start on literature . . .

The situation is quite impossible. I'm cursing myself for not having gone to the dacha, where I would probably have had a decent sleep

11. Chekhov's niece, Maria.

and written you a story, and the main thing is, medicine and literature would have been left in peace.

I shall take myself off to Voskresensk in September, if the weather is good enough. I was delighted with your last story.

The baby is screaming her head off!! I promise myself faithfully never to have children of my own ... The French don't have many children, probably because they are scholarly people and write stories for *L'Amusant*. I've heard they are now being urged to have more children – that would be a good subject for *L'Amusant* and *Fragments*, perhaps a cartoon captioned 'The State of Affairs in France'. In comes a policeman demanding that the couple get on and make babies.

Farewell. All I can think of is how and where to get my head down for a decent sleep.

I have the honour to be your respectful

A. Chekhov

13. To Alexander Chekhov, between 15 and 28 October 1883, Moscow

Disgraceful brother o'mine, Alexander Pavlovich,

First of all, don't be a raggedypants, forgive me for being so slow in answering your letters. This is more due to lack of time than laziness; I've had not a free minute, not even to lay out the cards for a game of patience. My final exams are coming up (despite your desire, you toad, that I would fail to get through to the fifth year), and if I pass them I shall be able to call myself by the same title as the esteemed Kachilovsky.[1] Just as the tears of the mouse affect the cat, just so is the idleness of my former years catching up on me now. Woe is me! I am having to learn almost everything again from scratch. Then, not only have I got the exams looming over me, there are also cadavers to work on, clinical studies with the inevitable history of diseases, hospital rounds ... the more I work, the more I feel I'm not up to it.

1. A popular Taganrog doctor.

My mind has lost its ability to cram; I'm getting old, there's the writing . . . people complaining they can smell when I've had a drink, and so on and so on. I am really worried I might fail one of the exams. I need a holiday, but . . . summer is still a long way off! The thought that the whole winter still lies before me sends shivers down my spine. However, mustn't ramble . . .

We have some news. I'll start a new page.

My dear friend Fyodor Fedoseyevich Popudoglo died on 14 October. It's an irreplaceable loss for me. He was not a particularly gifted writer, although his picture has appeared in *The Alarm Clock*. His life was spent in and around writing, and he had a wonderful nose for literature; to a raw beginner like yours truly such people are like gold. I used to go on the sly to see him in Kudrino,[2] like a thief in the night, and he would pour out his soul to me. He liked me, and I knew him through and through. He died of meningitis, despite being under the care of such a distinguished physician as myself. There were twenty doctors treating him, but I was the only one to diagnose the true nature of his illness while he was alive. May he rest eternally in the Kingdom of Heaven! He died of drink and the indulgence of friends, whose *nomina sunt odiosa*[3] down the ages. Foolishness, negligence and an irresponsible attitude towards life – such were the causes of his death at the age of thirty-seven.

Now for the second piece of news. Leikin came to see me. He is a splendid person, but not a particularly generous one. He stayed in Moscow for five days and spent the whole time urging me to persuade you not to sing your swansong, as you told him you were going to do. He thinks you're angry with him. He likes your stories very much, and the only reason they don't get published is that you don't really understand *Fragments* and what the magazine is about.

This is what Leikin said:

'He's caught the atmosphere of the customs house perfectly, it's all very crisply observed and there is plenty of material there, but no! he will insist on dragging in some old double-dutch which gives the

2. The area or street in Moscow Chekhov moved to in 1886.
3. 'Names are odious'.

impression that he's not quite certain about something . . . If only he would write just plain 'Customs House' with good Russian names, that would get past the censors with no trouble at all.'

And where you are not going in for double-dutch, you stick in a deadly dose of lyricism. What you must do is continue writing, you will eventually find your true path. You will find your early reverses easily outweighed by the pleasure of earning a little extra cash. And who cares about the reverses anyhow? You'll see your stuff in print in *Fragments*.

Leikin brought along with him my favourite writer: the famous N. S. Leskov.[4] He came over to our place; he came with me to the Salon and to the Sobolev Lane[5] dens of vice . . . He gave me a signed copy of his works. One night I was out with him. He turned to me, half-drunk, and asked: 'Do you know who I am?' 'Yes, I do.' 'No, you don't. I'm a mystic.' 'I know that too.' Then he goggled at me with his rheumy old eyes and prophesied: 'You will die before your brother.' 'Very possibly.' 'Thee I anoint with oil, even as Samuel anointed David . . . You must write.' The man is a mixture of an elegant Frenchman and an unfrocked priest. But he's considerable. I'll call on him when I'm in Piter. We parted friends.

As far as fish and Santorini wine are concerned, you will have to apply to Father, who is as we know an expert in legal matters. As for me, I have to admit that I have completely run out of money and have no time to earn any. The fact that I'm not stirring myself to find a job for you is pure selfishness: I want to spend the summer with you in the South. Don't look for a dacha, as it might not be right. We'll look for one together.

The gluttony with which you talk about your red tomatoes and your blue aubergines makes it hard to recognize the lyricist in you. You shouldn't eat rubbish like that, my brother! Those things are abominations, and unclean. Aubergines may be acceptable when they are crisp against the teeth, but when they are marinated (hideously,

4. Nikolay Leskov (1831–95), a prose writer whose short stories include 'Sealed Angel' (1873) and 'Lady Macbeth of Mtsensk District' (1865).
5. A notorious red-light district in Moscow.

no doubt) they have a horrible, vinegary, damp smell. Eat meat, my brother! You'll be all skin and bones down there in that vile Taganrog if you stuff yourself full of the rubbish they sell in the market. You have a tendency to overeat anyway, and when you're drunk you're liable to eat things that aren't ripe. Your lady knows as much about housekeeping as I do about harvesting eiderdown, so that's a good reason to be extremely careful about your food and eat only what is good for you. Meat and bread. At the very least don't feed Mosevna[6] on whatever you happen to find lying about while she's growing up. Avoid her aunt's habit of spicing everything up with herbs, not to mention Father's spiced-up sauces, your 'time for a little snack' and Mama's tasty morsels. Your daughter needs educating in the aesthetics of the palate, if nothing else. Speaking of aesthetics, forgive me, my dear fellow, but there's more to being a parent than just what you say to your children. You need to teach by example. When you leave the clean linen all mixed up together with the dirty linen, the table covered in scraps of left-over food, filthy rags everywhere, your spouse going round with her tits hanging out and a bit of ribbon round her neck as filthy as Kontorskaya Street[7] – this kind of thing can ruin a little girl from her earliest years. Appearances are what little girls notice most of all, and you have allowed all appearances to sink to the lowest level. I must tell you in all honesty that I hardly recognized you when you were staying with us two months ago. Was that really you, you whose room used to be so spotlessly clean? You need to give that Katka[8] a good telling-off, brother! And speaking of another sort of cleanliness . . . you shouldn't use foul language. You're corrupting Katka, and soiling Mosevna's eardrums with your bad language. If I were in Anna Ivanovna's shoes, I'd give you a good thump every minute of the day. Give my regards to Anna and to my niece. All of us think the world of her. Your stuff hasn't come out in *The Alarm Clock* yet; as soon as it does I'll let you know.

    Chekhov

6. Alexander's baby daughter Maria.

7. Kontorskaya was the last Chekhov family home in Taganrog. Pavel Chekhov had a house built on the land there but had to abandon it when he went bankrupt in 1876.

8. A maid working for Alexander's family.

14. To Mikhail Chekhov, 15 April 1884, Moscow

Misha, my angel!

Please do me a favour and buy me a walking-stick, one you consider in good taste, costing at least a rouble but not more than two. I deserve your congratulations on emerging from a terrible trial. These examinations have completely worn me out.

Your

A. Chekhov

[*added in Ivan Chekhov's hand*] It would be very kind if you would buy me one too. I. C.

Forgive me for troubling you with such trifles.

15. To Nikolay Leikin, 25 June 1884, Voskresensk

Letter No. 1

Dear Nikolay Alexandrovich,

Practice makes perfect, evidently. To begin with, the story has not really come off. 'The Civil Service Exam' is a good subject in itself, drawn from life and something I do know about, but to do it justice I would need to work on it for rather more than an hour and be allowed more space than seventy or eighty lines . . . I wrote and wrote and then kept crossing out what I had written, worrying about space. I cut out the District Examiners' questions altogether, and the Post Office Inspector's answers, but they were actually the core of the examination. As well as that, the story suffered all sorts of vicissitudes, beginning on my writing desk and ending up in the pocket of a passing pilgrim. What happened was this: when I took the article to the local post office, I was disconcerted to discover that there is no collection on Sundays, so the earliest my letter could get to you in Piter would be Wednesday. This was a catastrophe. I had two choices: I could either rest on my laurels, or I could make a dash for the railway station (over twelve miles away) and hope to catch the mail train. I did neither. I have decided to entrust my correspondence to anyone I can find to take it to the station. I couldn't find a coachman, so I was obliged to make respectful salutations to a stout pilgrim . . . If she can manage to get to the station in time for the mail train and can deposit it in the right place, my troubles will be over, but if God wills that she should not be able to perform this service for literature, then you will get my story only when you open this letter.

Now, about the drawings. I have to confess right away that I am hopeless at devising witty captions for drawings. I can never for the life of me think of anything clever. Whatever captions I've sent you previously have been the fruit, not of a couple of minutes, but of all the ages I have lived through. I have exhausted my stocks, the good and the terrible alike, and now there is nothing left at all. Nevertheless, I have come up with a plan of action for the future: I'll just send you whatever comes into my head, whether it is any use or not – caption writers, like the dead, have no shame. In return, you are not to make me feel bad for sending you material which is of not the slightest use . . .

I probably could in fact devise captions, but – how? In company perhaps . . . reclining on a sofa in some nice drinking establishment, gossiping inconsequentially with friends, and lo! an idea might well pop into my head . . . I'm sure in such circumstances I could develop other people's notions as well, if they have any . . .

I am living in New Jerusalem[1] now . . . with aplomb, because I have in my pocket a licence to write prescriptions. Nature round here is magnificent. Open space, and no dachniks at all. Mushrooms, fishing, the ƶemstvo[2] clinic. The monastery is poetic. Standing listening to Vespers in the half-darkness of the galleries and arches, I think up subjects for a series of 'sweet sounds'. I have a lot of subjects, but am definitely not in the right state to write them . . . Please tell me, where could I find a publisher for 'large-scale' stories like those you saw in

1. Name given to the monastery founded in the seventeenth century and surrounding area.
2. The ƶemstvo was a form of local government introduced as part of Alexander II's reforms in the 1860s.

Tales of Melpomene?[3] Do you think *Talk of the World* would be interested? Anyhow, I'm too lazy . . . Please excuse me . . . I'm writing this letter lying down . . . How? I've got a book propped up on my stomach and I'm writing on it. I'm too lazy to sit up . . . Every Sunday in the monastery they have an Easter service with all its elaborate rituals . . . Leskov is bound to know all the specialities of our monastery. In the evening I walk about surrounded by the most colourful examples of men's, women's and children's fashions. I go to the post office to get my newspapers and letters from Andrey Egorych, and while there I rummage around in everyone's mail and read the addresses with all the zeal of the snooper with nothing to do. I got the idea for the 'Civil Service Exam' story from Andrey Egorych. An old man by the name of Grandpa Prokudin who's lived here for years calls for me in the mornings, he's mad on fishing, so I put on my big boots and go off with him somewhere like Ramenskoye or Rubtsovskoye to make an attempt on the life of a perch or a chub or a tench. Grandpa will happily sit there for a whole day; five or six hours are enough for me. I'm cramming food down myself and consuming a moderate amount of drink. My family is down here with me, boiling, baking and roasting the food my writing has paid for. It's not a bad life – the only problem is that I am idle and not earning much to speak of. If you are coming to Moscow, why don't you make the trip to New Jerusalem? It's so near . . . a twelve-mile cab ride from Kryukovo station, it takes about two hours and costs two roubles. My brother Nikolay will come with you. You could drag Palmin[4] along with you. You'll hear the Easter service . . . what about it? If you write and let me know, I could come and pick you up from Moscow . . .

I'm trembling with anxiety. I need to write a piece for *Fragments* this week, but haven't a single thing to write about. From now on I'll send you my stuff on Saturdays . . . You'll get it on Mondays.

I've been visiting a local Justice of the Peace here, Golokhvastov, who is a well-known contributor to *Rus*. I've also been seeing

3. The title of Chekhov's first collection of stories which he published himself in Moscow in 1884.
4. Fyodor Palmin (1841–91), a poet and translator who contributed to such journals as *The Alarm Clock*, *Fragments*.

Markevich, who is paid 5,000 a year from Katkov for his *Turning Points* and *Abysses*.

I've finished my studies . . . I think I wrote to you about this. Or maybe I didn't . . . I was offered a position as *zemstvo* doctor in Zvenigorod, but turned it down. (*A propos*, if you do come down, you could visit St Savva's Monastery[5] in Zvenigorod.) That's about it, I think; nothing else to tell you about. I send you my greetings and entrust myself to your holy prayers.

Ever your devoted and respectful servant,
District Physician and Doctor A. Chekhov

Oh, yes! I had my book printed on credit, with settlement due four months after publication. I have no idea what's happening about it in Moscow at the moment.

Now I should like to go and catch some fish . . . but alas! I have a commission from *The Alarm Clock* and obviously can't spare the time . . .

Please see my next letter. This one, due to circumstances beyond the editor's control, has got stale and run out of steam.

16. To Nikolay Leikin, 27 June 1884

Letter No. 2

I received your letter yesterday evening, dear Nikolay Alexandrovich, and read it with pleasure. It's no small pleasure getting letters at the dacha. Yesterday Andrey Egorych had no less than six for me, together with the newspapers and a copy of *Fragments*, so I enjoyed myself reading right up to midnight. I read every word, even the advertisements, and even the jokes by your new humorist E-ni[1] . . . I spent yesterday reading your letter and today I am replying to it . . . I

5. The Savvin-Storozhevsky Monastery, named after St Savva (see letter 17).
1. E-ni stands for 'Ezhini', a pen-name used by Nikolay Ezhov (1862–1941), a writer and journalist. After Chekhov's death he wrote a very disparaging memoir about him, in which he dismissed Chekhov as a mediocrity.

have just returned from carrying out a postmortem in a place six miles from Voskresensk. I went out there in a crazy troika with an ancient Court Investigator, a kindly, white-haired old soul, so decrepit he was barely breathing, who has spent the last twenty-five years dreaming of becoming a judge. I carried out the autopsy with the local district physician in a field beneath the leaves of a young oak tree on the village road . . . The deceased 'wasn't from round here', and the peasants on whose land the body was found begged us with tears in their eyes for Christ's dear sake not to carry out the procedure in their village . . . 'The women and children will be too frightened to sleep . . .' The Investigator glanced apprehensively at the gathering clouds and at first prevaricated, but when he realized that he would be able to make a pencil draft of his report, and that we were willing to start slicing up the body in the open air, he yielded to the peasants' request. A terrified village, witnesses, the local policeman with his badge, a poor widow keening 200 paces from where we were going to do the postmortem, and two peasants guarding the dead body . . . Beside the silent guards were the embers of a small bonfire . . . The body has to be protected day and night until the authorities come, but since they are peasants nobody will pay them for their pains . . . The body was dressed in a red shirt and new trousers, covered by a sheet, and on top of the sheet was a towel with an icon. We asked the policeman if he could get us some water; there was a pond nearby with plenty of water in it, but nobody would give us a bucket for fear that we would make it unclean. One peasant from this village, which is called Manekhino, devised a cunning plan: they would steal a bucket from neighbouring Trukhino, because no one minded about a bucket belonging to somebody else . . . When and where and how they were going to steal it was not clear, but they were terribly pleased with their stratagem and there were smiles all round . . . The actual postmortem revealed twenty broken ribs, a swollen lung and a strong smell of alcohol from the stomach. The death was violent, a result of strangulation. The drunk man's chest had been crushed by something heavy, probably a well-built peasant's knee. There were a number of abrasions on the body caused by attempts at resuscitation. Apparently the Manekhino peasants, when they found the body, rocked and pummelled it so enthusiastically for two hours that any future defence lawyer the murderer may have will have every right to call expert witnesses to state whether the ribs might not have been broken as a result of these attentions ... Somehow, however, I don't think in fact these questions will ever be asked. There will be no counsel for the defence, nor indeed any accused ... the poor old Court Investigator is so far gone that a sick bedbug would have no trouble evading his dim gaze, let alone a murderer ... I expect you are bored reading this, but I am overcome with a desire to write ... I'll add just one more revealing detail, and then shut up. The murdered man was a factory worker walking from the inn at Tukhlov with a barrel of vodka. Witness Polikarpov, the first person to discover the body beside the road, stated that when he saw the body there was a barrel of vodka beside it. Passing the body once again an hour or so later, he saw no barrel. Ergo the Tukhlov innkeeper, who doesn't have a licence to sell liquor off the premises, must have removed the barrel from the dead man in order to conceal the evidence. But that's quite enough of that. You protest about the way wetnurses are inspected ... well, what about prostitutes? Medical men (learned ones, naturally) who worry about 'the damage to moral susceptibilities' sustained by those who are thus inspected, have been debating this for a long time and have reached agreement that, at the end of the day, 'they have the goods and we have the money ... if it's all right for the medical police to inspect apples or gammon without being oversensitive about offending the person of the merchant, why should it not be all right to examine the goods offered by a wetnurse or a whore? If you're worried about giving offence, don't buy what is on offer.' If, because you are squeamish about offending her, you don't palpate a wetnurse you contemplate engaging, you run the risk of her presenting you with something a lot worse than rotten oranges, trichinosis-ridden ham or sausages that have gone off.

You have 600 dahlia shrubs – I can't understand what you see in this cold and uninspiring flower. It has an aristocratic, baronial exterior, but there's nothing inside it ... it makes you want to hack at its boring, arrogant head with your cane. However, *de gustibus non disputantur*. I resisted putting an advertisement in *Fragments* about my book not, as you insinuate, because I didn't think it would do any good, but simply because I didn't want to embarrass you: you don't have much space and would have thought it indelicate to charge me as much as you charge others ... If you can put in an advertisement, I'll be grateful. And if you can include a phrase to the effect that people from out of town can get the book through the publishers of *Fragments*, I'll be doubly so. I don't imagine there'll be many purchasers, so this announcement should not cause you much trouble. And if, contrary to all expectations, someone wanting to buy the book through you does turn up, all you would have to do is send me a quick letter with the fortunate individual's address, and that would settle the matter. But I accept that I know next to nothing about the publishing business ... so I leave it to you to do whatever is best ... Respectful thanks for your instructions. All that you write shall be carried out to the letter. I've gone on far too long! I go to the *zemstvo* hospital every other day to treat the patients there. I really should go every day, but I'm lazy. The *zemstvo* doctor is an old friend.

Votre

A. Chekhonte

17. To Nikolay Leikin, 14 July 1884, Zvenigorod

Dear Nikolay Alexandrovich,

At the present moment I am in the town of Zvenigorod where the fates have decreed that I should serve as *zemstvo* doctor, the incumbent having asked me to replace him for a couple of weeks. I spend half the day seeing patients (thirty to forty a day) and the rest of the time I relax or bore myself horribly sitting by the window looking out at the grey skies which for three days now have been relentlessly tipping down a most disagreeable rain ... In front of my window there is a hill with pine trees; to the right is the police chief's house, and further round in the same direction a scruffy little town which once was an important city ... On the left I see a ruined rampart wall, then a wood with the hallowed St Savva Monastery peeping out of it. The back porch, more accurately the back door, looks out towards the river over the stinking privy and some grunting pigs. It's Saturday. I'm rushing to send off some urgent work so as not to miss the post. I'll scribble out my story tonight and send it tomorrow. Please send letters to Voskresensk; they will be forwarded to me directly. I was in Moscow and heard that L. I. Palmin had married his old woman. He didn't say a word to me about it when I saw him. Don't mention to him that I passed on to you this prosaic news about a poetic person ... in any case, it may well already be old news to you! Farewell,

    Your

    A. Chekhov

18. To Nikolay Leikin, 10 December 1884, Moscow

Dear Nikolay Alexandrovich,

For three days now for no reason at all I have been bleeding from the throat. It has stopped me working, and also from coming to Piter ... it just came out of the blue, thank you kindly! It's three days since I've been able to bring up decent white phlegm, and there's no knowing when the medicines my colleagues keep cramming into me will start to work. Apart from that I'm fine ... I imagine the cause is a burst blood vessel ...

Mme Politkovskaya came to see me today ... it was awful! She was complaining about you: 'surely he could serialize my stories if he thinks they are too long!'

Why does Rykov appear in your leading article as having fair hair? He doesn't have anything of the sort ...

I've done my reports on the Rykov trial for *The Petersburg Newspaper*[1] ... now the thing will be to get some cash for them. If you are in the editorial office, could you please ask them to hurry up with my

---

1. Chekhov's first publications in *The Petersburg Newspaper* were a series of court reports on a famous embezzlement trial in Moscow: he later passed through the banker Ivan Rykov's place of exile when he was travelling through Siberia in 1890.

fee? An unemployed sick man would always rather have the cash sooner than later . . . I haven't seen Palmin, or Nikolay. My kinsmen stand afar off.[2] Thank you, I should be glad if the pharmacy would send the medicine as cheaply as possible; I expect it will give some relief.

I hope your subscriptions have started coming in well . . . I wish you twenty thousand subscribers . . .

I have patients of my own, just for fun . . . I ought to go and visit them, but at the moment I'm not able to . . . I don't know what to do about them . . . I could pass them on to another doctor, but it would be a pity to do that – after all, they do provide some income!

Farewell . . .

Your

A. Chekhov

Please preserve the mask of Ulysses . . . it seems that Palmin has been shooting off his mouth in the *Russia* office . . . Please write and tell him that I was not the author,[3] and I turned down the offer last year . . . We have this kind of provincial behaviour down here as well!

I'm drinking an infusion of ergot, which does no good at all . . .

I'll let you know about next week in good time.

19. To Mitrofan Chekhov, 31 January 1885, Moscow

Dear Uncle Mitrofan Egorovich,

First of all, I must thank you most sincerely for the kind thoughts and the love with which all your letters to my father are infused. Your good opinion matters greatly to us all, and to me in particular it is a source of pride and joy: the favour of good people brings honour and elevates our own opinion of ourselves! I won't apologize to you for

2. Quotation from Psalm 38, verse 11.
3. Chekhov had recently lampooned the publisher and journalists of the journal *Russia* in an article in *Fragments* under the pseudonym 'Ulysses'.

my long and persistent silence . . . I know you are too kind and sincere a man to look on this as bad manners or as signifying any change in our relations, and will look for another explanation. I know I won't find writing a letter to you satisfactory . . . No one who has spent hours and evenings in your company will be satisfied with less than a proper conversation; a letter, however long, could cover only a thousandth part of what I want to say . . . One reason I have not written is that I have been hoping that we will soon meet. I'm still hoping we will. Last summer I could not come to see you because I was standing in for a *zemstvo* doctor friend of mine who went on leave, but this year I plan to go on my travels and also to see you. In December I fell ill with blood-spitting, and decided to apply for some money from the literary fund to go abroad for a cure. I am a little better now, but still feel I need to make this trip. Wherever I go, whether abroad or to Crimea or to the Caucasus, I shall be sure not to bypass Taganrog.

I am delighted at your election to the Taganrog Town Council. The more the town can call on people of integrity and impartiality like yourself, the better place it will be . . . I regret that I have no opportunity to serve in my native town alongside you . . . I am sure that if I did work there, I would be less stressed, happier and enjoy better health, but the way my life seems to be mapped out, I shall have to stay permanently in Moscow. That is where my home and my career are now established. My working life is split into two: I would go to seed as a doctor in Taganrog and forget all that I have learnt; working as a doctor in Moscow, I have no time to go to the club and play cards. Only in the capital can I have a meaningful life as a writer.

My medical career is progressing, little by little. I've been treating a lot of people. I have to spend more than a rouble on cab fares every day. I have many acquaintances and therefore have a lot of patients. Half of them I treat free of charge, the other half pay me three to five roubles a time. (No doctor gets less than three roubles a visit in Moscow. The cost of labour is generally higher here than in Taganrog.) Needless to say, I have not yet managed to build up any capital, and see little prospect of doing so in the near future, but I live well enough and lack for nothing. As long as I stay alive and healthy, the family's situation is *assured*. I've bought new furniture, I've acquired a decent piano, keep two servants, arrange musical evenings at which people play and sing . . . I have no debts and see no need for them . . . Until recently I was getting meat and groceries on account, but I've stopped that now and pay for everything in cash . . . What the future will bring I can't say, but for the present I can't complain.

Mamasha is alive and well, and as ever the sound of grumbling can be heard coming from her room. But even she, perennial grumbler that she is, has come round to admitting that we live better in Moscow than we ever did in Taganrog. Nobody complains about her overspending the housekeeping, there is no illness in the house . . . We may not be living in luxury, but we're not going short of anything.

Ivan is out at the theatre at the moment. He's working in Moscow and is very happy about it; he is one of the best and most reliable members of our family. He is now firmly established on his own feet, and his future is solidly assured. He is honest and conscientious. Nikolay is thinking of getting married, Misha finishes his course this year . . . and so on and so forth. That's about all the news for this letter. I am concerned that you have not been receiving the newspaper; you should have been and will do so from now on. Please send the enclosed card to this address: Editorial Office, *News of the Day*, Strastnoi Boulevard, Moscow. It is likely to be a little while before I visit their offices, so the card will arrive before I do. Even if I am there earlier than expected, I'll get absorbed in conversation and forget about you getting the paper.

I kiss my aunt's hand and send my cousins my greetings. Regards to all my friends. Forgive me and don't forget your most obedient and eternally grateful

A. Chekhov

My address is: Dr A. P. Chekhov, Golovin Lane, Sretenka Street.

20. *To Mikhail Chekhov, 10 May 1885, Babkino*

Misha-Terentisha!

At last I've taken off my heavy boots, my hands no longer stink of fish and I can write to you. It's six o'clock in the morning, and everyone is asleep ... The silence is extraordinary ... Only the birds are chirping, as well as some creature scratching behind the wallpaper. I'm writing these lines sitting by the large, square window in my room, and as I write I glance from time to time through the window. Before my eyes unfolds an extraordinarily warm, caressing landscape: a little river, distant woods, the village of Safontyevo, a corner of the Kiselyovs' house ... in the interests of clarity I'll write things down point by point:

a) We had an awful journey here, to put it mildly. When we arrived at the station we hired what I can only describe as two apologies for humanity, an Andrey and a Panokhtey (?), at three roubles per ugly mug. (A troika costs six roubles at the post-station.) The human apologies drove us at a maddeningly slow pace, so that by the time we had got as far as the white church we were dying of hunger. We got something to eat at Eremeyev. From Eremeyev to the town took us four hours, because the road was so terrible. For more than half of the way I stumbled along on foot. We crossed the river at Nikulino, near Chikino. I was going on ahead (it was already dark by then), almost took a bath and drowned. Mama and Maria had to go across by boat; you can just imagine the shrieking and train-like screeching and other expressions of feminine alarm! When we got to the Kiselyovs' woods, the coachmen managed to sheer off one of the brake rods ... we had to wait and wait ... And so it went on; to cut a long story short it was one o'clock in the morning before we got to Babkino ... Sic!!

b) The doors of the dacha were unlocked ... We went in without disturbing our hosts, lit the lamp and what met our eyes far exceeded all expectations. The rooms are huge and have more furniture than we need ... Everything is marvellously comfortable and cosy. Ashtrays and matchbox stands, cigarette boxes, two washbasins, and ... goodness only knows what else our kind hosts have provided. A dacha like this near Moscow would cost at least 500. You'll see when you come. I settled myself in, unpacked my suitcases and sat down to take stock, drank some vodka and a glass of wine . . . and you know, it was so lovely to look out of the window at the darkened trees and the river . . . I heard the song of the nightingale and could hardly believe my ears . . . it was hard to forget that I wasn't still in Moscow. I slept wonderfully; the next morning Begichev came by hollering as loud as he could, but I didn't hear a thing and slept right on like a drunk cobbler.

c) I was setting a fish trap in the morning when I heard a shout of 'Crocodile!'. Looking up, whom should I see on the other bank but Levitan . . . He had ridden over . . . After coffee I went hunting with him and a hunter (a typical character) called Ivan Gavrilov. We wandered about for three and a half hours, covered about twelve miles and killed a hare. The hounds aren't up to much though . . .

d) Now, about the fishing. There isn't a lot to catch, some ruff and some gudgeon. I did get one chub, but such a tiddler that he wasn't really ready for the pan, and should have still been at school really.

e) You can catch some fish with a *zherlitsa*[1] trap. We got a huge burbot using Vanya's. But it's not worth using one at the moment, because there's no bait. Yesterday evening it was too windy to fish. Would you please bring some medium-size hooks for the traps with you? I haven't any left.

f) And oh, those traps! As it turned out they were quite easy to bring, and they weren't crushed in the luggage as we tied them on to the back of the cart . . . I have one in the river now, and it has already taken a roach and the biggest perch you ever saw in your life. It is so enormous that Kiselyov will come and dine with us today. We first put the other trap in the pond, but it did not catch anything there. Now we either have it beyond the pond in the feeder stream or in a reach of the river; yesterday there was a perch in it and just this morning Babakin[2] and I fished *twenty-nine* carp out of it. How about that? Today we shall have fish soup, fried fish and then jellied fish . . . So it would be a good idea to bring two or three more traps with you.

---

1. A particular kind of tackle used to catch pike.
2. Ivan Babakin was a young village boy who did errands for the Chekhov family.

You can get them in the fresh fish shops by the Moskvoretsky Bridge. I paid 30 copecks for mine, but they shouldn't cost more than 20 to 25. You can take them home in a cab, naturally.

g) Maria Vladimirovna is well. She presented Mama with a pot of jam and has generally been amazingly kind. She supplies me with jokes from (old) French magazines . . . We split the proceeds fifty-fifty. Kiselyov spends whole days with us. He drank three large glasses at supper yesterday. Begichev ate as well, but drank nothing . . . He had to content himself with longing glances at the vodka carafe.

h) I'm not drinking anything, but somehow or other the wine is all gone. The wine is so good that Nikolay and Ivan must each bring a bottle (in a suitcase, as I did). Wine is a godsend here. What could be more agreeable than sitting on the terrace after supper with a glass of wine! Tell them. This wine is particularly good . . . I bought it on Myasnitskaya Street, on the right-hand side going from the post office towards the city, in the Georgian wine shop. Giliai[3] knows which one, it's a white wine called 'Akhmet', or 'Makhmet' . . .

i) Levitan is living in Maximovka. He has recovered almost completely. All the fish he catches he inflates into crocodiles, and he has made friends with Begichev, who calls him Leviathan. 'It's so dull without Leviathan' sighs B, whenever the crocodile is absent.

k) The road is all right now and the river crossing so good that even Tyshko came yesterday. Tell Lilia to come for a week. There is masses of room, and the provender is outstanding. Invite her and tell her how to get here, explaining how much to pay the drivers and so on. It won't cost her much to get back, either. A week, minimum . . .

l) What's happening with Nikolay?

m) Please bring Olga's passport with you, some garlic sausage for Kiselyov (three or four sausages), bay leaves, pepper, large-format writing paper.

n) Please copy out June, July and August from the encyclopaedic dictionary – it's easier than bringing it with you. I got up at half past three this morning. I'm now drinking tea and shall go back to bed and sleep until coffee, then after coffee I'm going off with Kiselyov to have

3. Vladimir Giliarovsky (1853–1935), a well-known writer and journalist in Moscow.

a look at my traps. I wrote a lot yesterday and will send it off today.
The work's going well.

Your

A. Chekhov

I'm going hunting on Sunday. Vladislavlev is coming in a few days
and will bring a seine net with him. Then we shall really catch some
fish! Greetings to all.

21. To Mikhail M. Chekhov, 25 September 1885, Moscow

Dear Misha,

I am now back in Moscow. If there are still some boys you'd like
me to look at for treatment, then I am at Ivan Egorovich [Gavrilov]'s
service.[1] I see patients in the morning until lunchtime, i.e. from ten
o'clock until two o'clock. If you've changed your mind, just let me
know. If I move house or alter the hours of my practice, I'll let you
know in good time.

How are things with you, and how are you keeping? It would give
us great pleasure if you would remember our existence and come to
spend an evening with us. Best regards to you, and I clasp your hand.

Your

A. Chekhov

22. To Maria Kiselyova, 1 October 1885, Moscow

I am exercising the right of the strong to steal a piece of my sister's
territory, in order that, like Sofochka,[1] I may reveal to you the secrets
of my heart . . . and I hope that you will understand me better than

1. Chekhov had offered free medical treatment to boys working in Gavrilov's warehouse.
1. The writer Boleslav Markevich's personal secretary.

you do Sofochka. This is all because my poor heart is still full of nothing but memories of fishing rods, ruff, fish traps, that long green thing for worms ... camphor oil, Anfisa, the road over the marsh to the Daraganovsky woods, lemonade, going for bathes ... My mind is still so full of our summer that the first question I ask myself when I wake up in the morning is: are there any fish in the traps? It's hellishly boring in Moscow, in any case ... I went to the races and won four roubles. I am snowed under with work ... Respectful greetings to Alexey Sergeyevich, in the manner of a Collegiate Registrar greeting a Privy Councillor, or Father Sergy greeting Prince Golitsyn. Salutations and honourable regards to Seryozha and Vasilisa, who appear every night in my dreams. Meanwhile with all good wishes for your health and fine weather, I remain your devoted

A. Chekhov

23. To Alexander Chekhov, 4 January 1886, Moscow

Dear quarantine-enforcing exciseman Sasha!

A Happy New Year to you and your vale,* with all good wishes for great happiness and additions to your family ... May God grant you the best of good fortune. I expect you are angry that I have not written to you ... Well, I'm angry as well, and for the same reason ... You wretch! Raggedypants! Congenital pen-pusher! Why haven't you written? Have you lost all joy and strength in letter writing? Do you no longer regard me as a brother? Have you not therefore become a total swine? Write, I tell you, a thousand times write! It doesn't matter what, just write ... Everything is fine here, except for the fact that Father has been buying more lamps. He is obsessed by lamps. By the way, if I can find it on my desk, there is a rare titbit I'd like to send you, but I should be glad if you would return it to me when you have read it.

I've been to Piter, and while staying with Leikin endured, as the

* Mishka, being a poet, thought vale meant ...

Scriptures say, 'all manner of torments' . . . He did me proud with the meals he fed me but, wretch that he is, almost suffocated me with his lies . . . I got to know the editorial staff of *The Petersburg Newspaper*, and they welcomed me like the Shah of Persia. You will probably get some work on that paper, but not before the summer. Leikin is not to be relied upon. He's trying all kinds of ways to stab me in the back at *The Petersburg Newspaper*, and he'll do the same with you. Khudekov, the editor of *The Petersburg Newspaper*, will be coming to see me [later] in January and I'll have a talk with him then.

But for the love of Allah! Do me a favour, boot out your depressed civil servants! Surely you've picked up by now that this subject is long out of date and has become a big yawn? And where in Asia have you been rooting around to unearth the torments the poor little pen-pushers in your stories suffer? For verily I say unto thee: they are actively unpleasant to read! 'Spick and Span' is an excellently conceived story, but oh! those wretched officials! If only you had had some benevolent bourgeois instead of your bureaucrat, if you hadn't gone on about his pompous rank-pulling fixation with red tape, your 'Spick and Span' could have been as delicious as those lobsters Yerakita was so fond of guzzling. Also, don't let anyone get their hands on your stories to abridge or rewrite them . . . it's horrible when you can see Leikin's hand in every line . . . It may be hard to resist the pressure to prune, but you have an easy remedy to hand: do it yourself, pare it down to its limits, do your own rewriting. The more you prune, the more often your work will get into print . . . But the most important thing is: keep at it unstintingly, don't drop your guard for an instant, rewrite five times, prune constantly, don't forget that the whole of Petersburg is keeping tabs on what the Chekhov brothers are producing. I have never seen anything like the reception I got from the Petersburgers. Suvorin, Grigorovich, Burenin . . . they all showered me with invitations and sang my praises . . . and I began to have a bad conscience that I had been such a careless and slovenly writer. Believe me, if I had known I was going to be read in that way, I would never just have turned out things to order . . . Remember: people are reading you. And another thing: don't put the names of people you actually know into your stories. It's bad form: first, it's overfamiliar, and second, your friends lose respect for the printed word . . . One person I've got to know is Bilibin. He is a very decent fellow who is *completely* reliable in case of need. In two or three years' time he will be a very influential person in Petersburg press circles. He's going to end up editor of the *News* or *New Times* or something like that. So he is a person we need to have on our side . . .

Again, for the love of Allah! Since when have you been such a frigid tightarse! Who are you trying to impress with such pusillanimity? Things that other people might find genuinely risky merely make university men laugh, and laugh pretty condescendingly at that. But you seem to be in a rush to join the ranks of the faint-hearted! Why are you so frightened of being sent envelopes stamped with editorial trade-names? What do you think people can do to you if they find out you are a writer? Let them find out, you can spit on them! After all, you won't be beaten or hanged or sacked . . . By the way, when Leikin met your departmental director at a Credit Association meeting, he really went for him over the persecution you suffer for writing . . . The director was really embarrassed and started swearing . . . Bilibin writes but is also an impeccable employee of the Post and Telegraph Department. Levinsky publishes a comic magazine and has sixteen official posts. There are plenty of people in the Officer Corps, which has the strictest of regulations, who don't conceal the fact that they write. There may sometimes be a need for discretion, but you shouldn't be hiding away yourself – no, no! No, Sasha, it's time to pack up your depressed civil servants along with your persecution mania journalists, and bury them in the archives . . . Nowadays it is more true to life if you show Their Excellencies' lives being made hell by Collegiate Registrars and journalists poisoning the existence of other people . . . and so on. Excuse the moralizing, I'm only writing to you like this because it upsets me and makes me angry . . . You're a good writer, you could earn twice as much as you do and yet you're living off wild honey and locusts . . . all because of the crossed wires you have in your noddle . . .

I'm still not married, and I have no children. Life is not easy. There'll probably be some money in the summer. Oh, if only!

Please write! I think of you often, and rejoice when I remember you are alive . . . So don't be a fathead, and don't forget your

A. Chekhov

Nikolay is sitting on his backside. Ivan, as before, is being a real Ivan. Our sister is whirling round in a daze: admirers, symphony concerts, a big apartment . . .

24. To Viktor Bilibin, 1 February 1886, Moscow

Most amiable of humourists and barristers' assistants, most selfless of secretaries,* dear Viktor Viktorovich! Five times have I started a letter to you, and five times have I been torn away from my task. At last I have nailed myself to the chair and am writing. [several words in the original have been crossed out by an unknown hand] which gave offence both to you and to me, and which with your permission I declare closed, even though it has not even started yet in Moscow. I wrote to Leikin about it, and he gave me an explanation . . . I have just returned from visiting the well-known poet Palmin. When I read him the part of your letter that concerns him, he declared: 'I respect that man. He is very talented!' Whereupon His Inspiration raised aloft the longest of his fingers and graciously added (with an air of profundity needless to say): 'But Fragments will ruin him!! May I offer you a liqueur?'

We talked for a long time about many things. Palmin is a typical poet, if you admit the existence of such a type . . . He is a poetic person, constantly enthusing, and stuffed to the gills with subjects and ideas . . . You don't get tired talking to him. True, you have to drink rather a lot, but at the same time you can be sure that in the course of three or four hours' talk you won't hear one false word, one vulgar phrase, and it's worth giving up a bit of sobriety for that . . .

By the way, he and I tried to think up a title for my book. We racked our brains for ages but could not come up with anything other than *Cats and Carps* or *Flowers and Dogs*.[1] A title like *Buy this Book or Get a Sock in the Jaw!*, or possibly *May I Help You, Sir?* would be all right by me, but the poet considered them banal and hackneyed ... You couldn't think of a good title could you? As for me, I think all those portmanteau-word titles are (grammatically speaking) fit only for the pub ... I prefer Leikin's suggestion, which is: *A. Chekhonte. Stories and Sketches*, pure and simple ... although a title like that only really works if you're a celebrity, not a ∞ like me ... *Motley Stories*, now that wouldn't be too bad ... there are two possibilities for you ... Choose one of them and pass it on to Leikin. I rely on your taste, although I appreciate that this is as much an imposition as relying on you yourself ... But you won't mind ... When God wills that your house should catch fire, I'll lend you my hose.

Many thanks for your trouble over the clipping and for sending me the original. I don't wish to be in your debt, financially speaking, so am sending you a 35 copeck stamp you once sent me along with my fee, which I have never been able to get rid of. Now it will be your problem.

Next, the matter of my fiancée and Hymen ... With your permission I shall defer both these matters until [I write] next time, by which time I shall have recovered from the access of inspiration brought on by my conversation with Palmin. I am afraid of saying too much, too much nonsense that is. Ever since I was at school, when I speak of women I like, I've always had a tendency to spin out my words until they reach the *ne plus ultra*, the Pillars of Hercules ... Please thank your fiancée for remembering me and tell her that my own wedding will probably – alas and alack! The censor forbids me to say more ... My *she* is Jewish.[2] If she, as a wealthy young Jewess, has enough spirit to convert to the Russian Orthodox religion with all the consequences that entails, all will be well; if not, no matter. In any case, we have already quarrelled ... We'll make it up tomorrow, no doubt, but we'll be having another row within a week. She gets so annoyed by the obstacles her religion throws up that she breaks the pencils and the photographs on my desk; this is quite in character ... She has a

---

1. Nikolay Leikin published a collection of stories called *Carps and Pikes* in 1883.
2. Dunia Efros, a school friend of Chekhov's sister Maria.

dreadful temper ... There is not the slightest doubt that we shall divorce a year or two after we are married ... Anyhow, *finis*.

Your glee that the censors did not pass my 'Attack on Husbands' does you honour; I clasp your hand. However, it would have been much more pleasant to get 65 roubles than 55 ... Together with some friends I have instituted a 'Society for the Awarding of Horns' whose aim is to take revenge on the censors and everyone who relished my misfortune. The constitution has already been submitted for approval. I have been elected President by a majority of 14 to 3.

In the first number of *Ears of Corn* there is an article entitled 'Humorous Magazines'. What is this all about? By the way, when I was talking to you and your fiancée about young authors, I mentioned the name of Korolenko. Do you remember? If you're interested in getting to know him, get hold of *The Northern Herald*, where in issue 4 or 5 you can read his article 'Tramps'. I recommend it.

Please give my greetings to Roman Romanych. My emissary, the celebrated Moscow artist Shekhtel, went to see him the other day and will I'm sure have told him much more than the longest letter could have.

I need to write, but I just don't have any ideas ... What am I going to write about?

In any case, it's time to go to bed. I send you my regards and clasp your hand. I go out into the countryside every day on my medical rounds. What ravines, what views!

Your

A. Chekhov

Why haven't you mentioned the dacha? You complain about your health, but you aren't thinking about the summer ... You really must be a very dry, tough and immobile crocodile if you think of sitting out the whole summer in town. Surely it's worth giving up your job, and anything else that comes to mind, for the sake of two or three months of peace and quiet ...

I confirm receipt in full of the sum of 55 roubles 72 copecks, as signed and given under my hand

Doctor in private practice A. Chekhov

* A thought: editorial secretaries presumably don't envy editorial secretaries.

25. To Alexey Suvorin, 21 February 1886, Moscow[1]

Dear Sir, Alexey Sergeyevich,

I received your letter. Thank you for your flattering remarks about my work, and for publishing my story so quickly. You may judge for yourself how refreshing and even inspiring it has been for my writing to receive the generous attention of such an experienced and gifted person as you . . .

I share your views about discarding the story's ending, and am grateful to you for this helpful suggestion. I have been writing for six years, but you are the first person who has gone to the trouble of making suggestions and explaining the reasons for them.

My pen-name of A. Chekhonte probably does seem strange and contrived. But since I first dreamed it up 'at the dawn of my misty youth' I've grown used to it and don't notice its oddity . . .

I write comparatively little, not more than two or three little stories a week. I shall certainly be able to find time to write for *New Times*, but all the same it is a joyous relief that you are not imposing tight deadlines on my contributions. Deadlines always lead to haste and the feeling of having a millstone around one's neck, and I find both inhibiting. Deadlines are a particular problem for me since I am a doctor and have a medical practice . . . I can never guarantee that tomorrow I shall not be called away for a whole day . . . So I am always in danger of not finishing in time and being late with my copy . . .

The fee you propose is quite acceptable for the time being. If you could also arrange to send me copies of the paper, which I do not manage to see very often, I should be most grateful.

I am taking the opportunity of sending you another story, which is twice the length of the last one and, I fear, twice as bad.

I have the honour to remain

A. Chekhov

1. This was Chekhov's first letter to Suvorin.

26. To Dmitry Grigorovich, 28 March 1886, Moscow

Your letter, my dear, beloved bearer of good news, struck me like a bolt of lightning. I almost burst into tears I was so overcome with emotion, and now I feel that it has left a deep imprint in my soul. May God comfort your old age with the same tender blessings you showed towards my youth. I can find neither words nor deeds to thank you. You will already know of the reverence ordinary people have for the elect such as yourself, and you may therefore imagine what your letter has meant to my self-esteem. It means more than any diploma, and for a writer on the threshold of his career it is like a payment for the future and the present. I walk about as if intoxicated. It is quite beyond my powers to judge whether or not I truly merit this high accolade . . . I can only repeat that it has absolutely stunned me.

If it truly is the case that I have a talent that demands respect, then I confess before the purity of your heart that hitherto I have not respected it. It is true that I sensed this talent, but I have got used to treating it as worthless. All organisms are vulnerable to a whole series of external influences that may produce unjustified self-doubt, excessive hypochondria and suspicion . . . and I now realize that I have myself been exposed to quite a number of such influences. People close to me have always disparaged my writing and have never ceased to give me well-meaning advice not to abandon a proper profession for scribbling. I have hundreds of acquaintances in Moscow, including a few dozen writers, but I cannot remember any of them reading my work or thinking of me as an artist. Moscow has a so-called 'literary circle' where gifted people and mediocrities of all breeds and ages gather in a room in a restaurant once a week to exercise their tongues. If I were to read out just one phrase of your letter at one of these gatherings, they would laugh at me to my face. The five years I have spent lounging around newspaper offices have inured me to this general view of my literary nonentity; I soon became ready to accept this condescending view of my work – and my writing took a back seat! This is the first reason . . . The second is that I am a doctor and up to my ears in my medical practice. Never can there have been anyone with more occasion than I to lose sleep over the old saying about chasing two hares.

My excuse for writing all this to you is simply to offer you some justification, however inadequate, for my heinous sin. Until now I have approached my writing in a most frivolous, irresponsible and meaningless way. I cannot recall a *single* story on which I spent more than a day; indeed I wrote 'The Huntsman', which you liked, in a bathing hut! I've been writing my stories like reporters churn out pieces about fires: mechanically, half-asleep, caring as little for the reader as for myself ... Although while writing them I have tried, God knows why, not to waste images and descriptions that seemed valuable to me, but to save them and hide them carefully away.

My first impulse towards self-criticism resulted from a very generous and, so far as I can judge, sincere letter I received from Suvorin. After that I consciously tried to produce work of passable quality, but I still lacked any faith in my ability to write anything of real literary worth.

And then, out of a clear blue sky, came your letter. Forgive the analogy, but it was a jolt like getting a city magistrate's order 'to leave the city within twenty-four hours!' – that is to say, I felt immediately that I must absolutely extricate myself in the shortest possible time from the position in which I had mired myself ...

I agree with everything you say. When I actually saw 'The Witch' in print, I could clearly see for myself the cynical touches you pointed out. If I had taken three or four days, instead of just one, to write the story, they would have been eliminated.

I do intend to stop writing against short deadlines, but it will take some time to achieve this. It is just not possible for me to drag myself out of the rut into which I have fallen – not that I have anything against starving, something I have certainly done in the past, but I am not entirely my own master ... I write in my spare time, two or three hours during the day and part of the night; in other words only in time I can spare from more important work. In the summer, when I have more free time and can cut down on my living expenses, I shall settle down to some serious writing.

I cannot put my own name on the book because it is already too late: the cover has been designed and the book printed. You are not the first to say this; many people in Petersburg advised me not to spoil the book with a pen-name, but I did not listen, probably out of vanity. I am not at all satisfied with the book; it's nothing but a Russian salad, a formless mass of nonsensical student squibs cut to pieces by the censor and the sub-editors of the comic papers. I am sure that many people will be disappointed when they read it. If I had realized that it would in fact be read and studied by people such as yourself, I would never have allowed it to be published.

All my hopes are on the future. I am still only twenty-six. It may be that one day I shall manage to achieve something, although time is rushing by quickly.

Please forgive the length of this letter, and do not condemn a man who, for the first time in his life, has dared to indulge himself in the sweet pleasure of writing to Grigorovich.

If you can, please send me your photograph. The kindness you have shown me has so inspired me that I feel I should like to write not one page but a whole ream in reply. God grant you health and happiness, and may you be truly assured of the deep respect felt towards you by a grateful

A. Chekhov

27. To Nikolay Chekhov, March 1886, Moscow

Little Zabelin,[1]

It's been reported to me that you have taken umbrage at being teased by me and Shekhtel . . . Only the noble soul is capable of taking offence, but even so, if it is all right to laugh at Ivanenko[2] or me, or Mishka, or Nelly, why should it not be to laugh at you? That's not

1. This was a family joke shared with the Kiselyov family, from whom the Chekhovs rented a dacha in the 1880s: Zabelin was a local landowner and an alcoholic. Apart from Chekhov's brother Nikolay, another mutual friend (sometimes referred to as 'Big Zabelin') also had a drink problem.
2. Alexander Ivanenko (1862–1926), a musician and accident-prone close family friend of the Chekhovs.

fair . . . However, if you're serious and honestly feel offended, then I hasten to tender my apologies.

People only laugh at things that are funny, or things that they don't understand . . . take your choice. The second is more flattering, but alas! to me personally you are an open book. There are no mysteries in someone with whom one has shared the delights of Tatar hats,[3] Voutsinas,[4] Latin, and finally, life in Moscow. Besides, your life is not so psychologically complex that one needs a seminary education to understand it. I'll do you the honour of saying it straight. You feel angry and insulted . . . but the problem does not lie in the teasing or in Dolgov's amiable chattering . . . It lies in the fact that, as a decent human being, you feel yourself to be in a false position, and everyone who imagines himself at fault always looks elsewhere for justification: the alcoholic pleads his unhappiness, Putyata blames the censor, the bolter who runs from Yakimanka[5] in pursuit of lechery claims that his room was too cold, that his friends were laughing at him, and so on . . . Were I now to abandon my family to its fate, I'm sure I would seek to invent some excuse for this in our mother's character, or the fact that I am coughing up blood, or something of the sort. This is quite normal and excusable; it's human nature. And it is also true that you do genuinely feel yourself to be in a false position; I know this, otherwise I would not have described you as a decent person. If you were to lose that innate decency, it would be a different matter: then you would be more accepting of yourself as you are and not feel that you were living a lie . . .

It is also the case that you are not a mystery to me, and that you are sometimes excruciatingly funny. After all, you are a mortal man of flesh and blood, and it is only when we are impenetrably stupid that

3. A reference to a story the Chekhov family nanny used to tell about the Tatar Khan Saur, whose hat was buried in the southern steppe by Cossacks, who then built a large mound over it. This is how Russian peasants living on the steppe explained the mysterious *kurgans* around them, which were in fact Scythian burial mounds.
4. The name of the incompetent teacher from Cephalonia at the Greek parish school in Taganrog, where Chekhov and his brother Nikolay were both pupils for one year.
5. The Chekhov family apartment was situated on Yakimanka Street, named after the churches of St Joachim and Anna located on it. The Bolter is Nikolay himself.

we mortals are enigmas, and we are funny for forty-eight weeks of the year ... Don't you agree?

You have often complained to me that 'people don't understand you!!' Even Goethe and Newton drew back from making that complaint ... The only one who did make it was Christ, and then only in respect of his teaching, not of his inner self ... You are very well understood ... If you don't understand yourself, it's nobody's fault but your own ...

I assure you as your brother and someone close to you that I understand you and sympathize with you from the bottom of my heart ... I know all your good qualities as well as I know the back of my hand, I value them and have the greatest respect for them. I can enumerate them for you if you would like proof that I do understand you. I believe you are kind to the point of soft-heartedness, magnanimous, devoid of egotism, you would share your last copeck, you are sincere; a stranger to envy or hatred, you are open-hearted, you are compassionate towards men and animals, you are not spiteful and you don't bear grudges, you have a trusting nature ... You have been endowed from on high with that which the bulk of humanity lacks: talent. This talent places you above millions of people, for only one person in two million on this earth is an artist ... This talent would set you apart even if you were a toad or a tarantula, for everything is forgiven to talent.

You have only one fault. But in that fault lies the falseness of your position, your discontent and even the catarrh in your bowels. It is your complete lack of manners. Please forgive me, but *veritas magis amicitiae* ... The fact of the matter is that there are certain rules in life ... You will always feel uncomfortable among intelligent people, out of place and inadequate, unless you are equipped with the manners to cope ... Your talent has opened the door for you into this milieu, you should be perfectly at home in it, but at the same time something pulls you away from it and you find yourself having to perform a kind of balancing act between these cultivated circles on the one hand and the people you live among on the other. That telltale lower-class flesh of yours is all too apparent, the result of growing up with the rod, next to the wine cellar, and subsisting on handouts. It is hard to rise above that, terribly hard!

Civilized people must, I believe, satisfy the following criteria:

1) They respect human beings as individuals and are therefore always tolerant, gentle, courteous and amenable ... They do not create scenes over a hammer or a mislaid eraser; they do not make you feel they are conferring some great benefit on you when they live with you, and they don't make a scandal when they leave, saying 'it's impossible to live with you!' They put up with noise and cold, overdone meat, jokes, and the presence of strangers in the house ...

2) They have compassion for other people besides beggars and cats. Their hearts suffer the pain of what is hidden to the naked eye. So for example, if Pyotr realizes that his father and mother are turning grey from worry and depression and are lying awake at nights because they see him so seldom (and when they do, he's the worse for drink), he hastens to see them and cuts out the vodka. Civilized people lie awake worrying about how to help the Polevayevs, to pay for their brothers to go through University, to see their mother decently clothed ...

3) They respect other people's property, and therefore pay their debts.

4) They are not devious, and they fear lies as they fear fire. They don't tell lies even in the most trivial matters. To lie to someone is to insult them, and the liar is diminished in the eyes of the person he lies to. Civilized people don't put on airs; they behave in the street as they would do at home, they don't show off to impress their juniors ... They are discreet and don't broadcast unsolicited confidences ... They mostly keep silence, from respect for others' ears.

5) They don't run themselves down in order to provoke the sympathy of others. They don't play on other people's heartstrings to be sighed over and cosseted. They don't say: 'No one understands me!' or 'I've wasted my talents on trivial doodlings! I'm a whore!!' because all that sort of thing is just cheap striving for effects, it's vulgar, old hat and false ...

6) They are not vain. They don't waste time with the fake jewellery of hobnobbing with celebrities, being permitted to shake the hand of a drunken Plevako,[6] the exaggerated bonhomie of the first person they meet at the Salon, being the life and soul of the bar ... They regard

6. Fyodor Plevako, a well-known lawyer and judicial orator.

phrases like 'I am a representative of the Press!!' – the sort of thing one only hears from people like Rozdevich and Levenberg[7] – as absurd. If they have done a brass farthing's work they don't pass it off as if it were 100 roubles' by swanking about with their portfolios, and they don't boast of being able to gain admission to places other people aren't allowed in . . . True talent always sits in the shade, mingles with the crowd, avoids the limelight . . . As Krylov said, the empty barrel makes more noise than the full one . . .

7) If they do possess talent, they value it. They will sacrifice peace of mind, women, wine, and the bustle and vanity of the world for it . . . They take pride in it. So they don't go boozing with school teachers or with people who happen to have come to stay with Skvortsov; they know they have a responsibility to exert a civilizing influence on them rather than aimlessly hanging out with them. And they are fastidious in their habits . . .

8) They work at developing their aesthetic sensibility. They do not allow themselves to sleep in their clothes, stare at the bedbugs in the cracks in the walls, breathe foul air, walk on a floor covered in spit, cook their food on a paraffin stove. As far as possible they try to control and elevate their sex drive . . . Sleeping with a whore, breathing right in her mouth, endlessly listening to her pissing, putting up with her stupidity and never moving a step away from her – where's the sense in that? Civilized people don't simply obey their baser instincts. They demand more from a woman than bed, horse sweat and the sound of pissing; and more in the way of intelligence than an ability to swell up with a phantom pregnancy; artists above all need freshness, refinement, humanity, the capacity to be a mother, not just a hole . . . They don't continually swill vodka, they're aware they're not pigs so they don't root about sniffing in cupboards. They drink when they want to, as free men . . . For they require *mens sana in corpore sano*.

And so on. That's what civilized people are like . . . Reading *Pickwick* and learning a speech from *Faust* by heart is not enough if your aim is to become a truly civilized person and not to sink below

---

7. Rodzevich and Levenberg were minor Moscow journalists.

the level of your surroundings. Taking a cab over to Yakimanka and then decamping a week later is not enough . . .

What you must do is work unceasingly, day and night, read constantly, study, exercise willpower . . . Every hour is precious . . .

Shuttling backwards and forwards to Yakimanka won't help. You must roll up your sleeves and make a clean break, once and for all . . . Come back to us, smash the vodka bottle and settle down to read . . . even if it's just Turgenev whom you've never read . . .

You've got to get over your fucking vanity, you're not a child any more . . . you'll soon be thirty! Time to grow up!

I'm expecting you . . . We all are . . .

Your

A. Chekhov

28. To Mitrofan Chekhov, 11 April 1886, Moscow

I am writing to you, my dear Uncle, on Good Friday, on the eve of Easter Saturday. However, you will not receive this letter until after the 13th, and therefore I am quite entitled to kiss you three times from afar and to receive your reply 'He is risen indeed' and, if you will allow, a 10-copeck piece. So: Christ is risen! Please share this greeting with my aunt, and my male and female cousins, to whom I likewise offer my Easter greetings and my kisses. I wish you all happiness, peace and plenty and to you personally, my dear friend, everything you could desire from a person in whom you inspire such deep respect and devotion.

I ask your pardon for not having written to you for so long. You write a lot yourself,[1] and therefore will understand that a man who writes without ceasing from morning until night simply has no time! Whenever he has a spare moment he tries to devote it to reading or something other than writing. Yes, to speak frankly, I cannot under-

1. Chekhov's Uncle Mitrofan corresponded with monks at one of the Russian monasteries on Mount Athos.

stand those who only write to those they love from a sense of duty, and feel no need to wait for moments of true inclination, free from fears of insincerity or of the letter being too long.

Now, let us have a talk. We can begin with your departure. When you, Aunt [Lyudmila], Sasha and Father Anania got into the carriage and disappeared, our house felt empty. It was a long time before this feeling of loss passed; you are too dear a guest for parting with you to be easy. Remember that for us you are the *one and only*; we have never had, nor shall we ever have, a kinsman as close as you. It is not just because you are our blood-related uncle, but because none of us can remember a time when you were not our friend ... You always treated our failings with indulgence, always showed us integrity and true friendship, and on young people that has a tremendous effect! You may not have been aware of it, but you became our mentor, giving us the example we needed of spiritual cheer and courage, of tolerance, sympathy and gentle loving-kindness ... I press your hand and thank you from the bottom of my heart. Should God grant in ten or fifteen years' time that I set down an account of my life, I shall express my thanks before the entire reading public. But for the present I must content myself with clasping your hand.

At the moment the bells are ringing for matins. Everyone at home is asleep. Mama so tired herself out with the ham and Easter cakes that the heaviest cannon fire would not have awakened her.

Sasha left with you, but we still have her in our thoughts and still hope to see her again here soon. We all liked her very much, but I am not sure that she is getting the best treatment for her condition. If she should start to feel unwell again, do make sure she follows my advice. It wouldn't hurt for Georgy or Volodya to take her to the doctor and let him examine her. There is a Dr Eremeyev, Psalti's son-in-law, who lives near the Stone Steps.[2] If you take her to him you won't be going far wrong. In case, I am enclosing my card, which may serve as an introduction for Sasha. You can explain to Eremeyev the treatment I have been recommending.

2. The flight of steps built in the 1820s by Greek merchants in Taganrog in imitation of the steps leading to the Acropolis in Athens.

After you left us, just before Christmas, a Petersburg newspaper editor came to Moscow and took me back to Petersburg with him. He took me first class on the express, which must have cost him a pretty penny. When I got there I was so fêted that for about two months afterwards my head was still spinning from all the adulation. I had a magnificent apartment to stay in, a pair of horses, fabulous food, free tickets to all the theatres. Never in my life have I lived in such style as I did in Piter. As well as showering praise on me and offering me unstinted hospitality, I was presented with 300 roubles and sent home again first class . . . I seem to be much better known in Petersburg than I am in Moscow.

I am making steady progress with my medicine. It's very convenient for the family: even Fedosia Yakovlevna is my patient, and not long ago I treated Ivan. It's a handy thing to have a doctor in the house!

My sideline occupation, my writing, is also progressing in its own way. I now work for the biggest of the Petersburg papers – *New Times* – and get 12 copecks a line for my copy. Yesterday I received 232 roubles from that paper for three small stories which appeared in three issues. Wonders will never cease! I can hardly believe my eyes. And *The Petersburg Newspaper*, which is a smaller paper, gives me 100 roubles a month for four stories.

But all that is unimportant compared with what I am about to tell you. Russia has a major writer, Dmitry Grigorovich, whose portrait you will find in your book of *Contemporary Personalities*. Quite recently, without being acquainted with him and completely out of the blue, I received a long letter from him. Grigorovich is a figure of such enormous popularity and respect that you can imagine how pleased and surprised I was! Here are some passages from his letter: '. . . you have a *real* talent, a talent which sets you far above the writers of the younger generation . . . I am already over sixty-five; yet I have preserved such love for literature, I follow its successes with such fervour, I always feel such joy when I encounter something lively and gifted, that as you see, I cannot restrain myself from holding out both hands to you . . . When you come to Petersburg, I hope to see you and embrace you in person as I now do from a distance.'

It is a long and very generous letter, and I do not have time to reproduce it in full; when we see one another I can read it to you. When you consider that the letters of such people are regarded as museum treasures, can you wonder that I too should treasure them? I replied in the following manner: 'May God comfort your old age, my kind and much loved bearer of good news, with the same tender blessings you showed towards my youth!'

The old man was touched by my response, and sent me another long letter with his photograph. The second letter is wonderful.

The week after Easter I have been asked to return to Petersburg. I am all the rage there now. In May we are going to stay at our dacha at the Kiselyovs', where I invite you to join us, and later in the summer I shall come to visit you. *Probably* we shall see one another during the summer and have our fill of talk . . . I have to be in the south on business over the summer.

Mama is very happy that Ivan has got a job in a state school in Moscow, where he will be his own boss. He has a government apartment with five rooms. Servants, firewood and lighting are also all paid for by the state . . . Papa is also delighted that Ivan has bought himself a peaked cap with a cockade, and has ordered a professorial morning frock-coat with bright buttons.

Nikolay is working very hard now, but has trouble with his eyes.

I went shopping for some new clothes today, and now look quite the dandy.

Shekhtel came to see me today; he is my patient and pays me five roubles a consultation. He will join us when we end the fast. What a pity you can't also be with us for Easter! We'll have plenty to break the fast with. We would sing together, as we will on our return from the midnight service.

The bells have just rung at the Cathedral of Christ the Saviour.

I look forward to getting a letter from you (The Klimenko House, Yakimanka Street). If I have a free minute in Piter I'll write to you from there, but for now farewell and please do not forget your loving and respectful

A. Chekhov

Since our letters, dear Uncle, resemble intimate conversations between friends, may I ask you not to show mine to anyone outside your own family?

How is your ear?

Misha's negotiations with Ferapontov have not come to anything.[3]

Give my regards to Irinushka, if she has not forgotten me.

With reference to newspaper articles about the brotherhood, you slightly misunderstood what I was saying. I will explain more when we meet, but for now I will merely say that the best time to publish material about the brotherhood in the press would be immediately after the anniversary, in August ... And to make it more likely that the papers would carry this material, it would do no harm for the brotherhood to adopt a useful custom, that of annually sending the newspapers a report of the year's activities. They should be glad to print it, because nobody objects to praise for a good thing. I can send you the addresses the reports should be sent to.

29. To Nikolay Leikin, 13 April 1886, Moscow

He is risen indeed, my very dear Nikolay Alexandrovich!

Instead of the promised Saturday I am writing on Sunday evening, by which time the stomach has been crammed full of everything you can think of and the eyes are still glazed over from the succession of visitors.

The day passed most enjoyably. Yesterday evening I went to the Kremlin to listen to the bells, and wandered round the churches. Returning home about two o'clock, I had a drink and joined in some singing with two opera basses whom I found in the Kremlin and dragged home with me to celebrate the breaking of the fast. One of

3. Mitrofan Chekhov was the founder and treasurer of a Taganrog charitable society linked to a Russian monastery on Mount Athos. The plan had been for the Moscow publisher Ferapontov to issue the society's proceedings.

the basses gave a superb imitation of an archdeacon. I heard Great Vespers in the Cathedral of Christ the Saviour, and so on.

I received your book.

Giliai pulled a fast one on me. All he's got is a rash . . . I didn't find it a particularly amusing joke. I rushed over to see him the next day, wasting valuable time and money on a cab from Yakimanka to Meshchanskaya! You are critical of me for not going the moment I received his letter, but in fact there was no need for haste. His letter said: 'Three days ago I suffered a misfortune' – but three days is quite long enough for him to have got medical attention of some sort and to rule out any problems like broken bones or anything of that nature. I was sure he would be already well bandaged up, and that I was only being summoned because the old chatterbox didn't trust the first doctor he called.

Palmin is now one of my patients. The poet is mute. He is completely hoarse and has such an impossibly husky voice you can't help bursting out laughing. He got your book and photograph while he was here with me.

You ask what I do with all my money . . . I don't go out boozing, and I don't spend money on clothes, I have no debts,* but all the same from the 82 + 232 roubles I had from you and from Suvorin before the holiday only 40 are left, from which I have to part with 20 tomorrow . . . The devil alone knows where it all goes! I haven't yet had anything from Builov.

The weather is glorious.

I'm going to go and lie down now and read Lermontov.

Your

A. Chekhov

I'm sending you a story, 'An Enigmatic Nature', which you may hand over to the typesetters.

---

* I don't even have any kept women: love and *Fragments*. I get gratis.

30. To Franz Shekhtel, 8 June 1886, Babkino

Dearest but oh-so-sluggish Franz Osipovich,

I have received your letter. My response may be simply put: you are your own worst enemy . . . In the first place, you shouldn't take such a cavalier attitude towards exercise, and secondly, you should be ashamed to sit in stuffy old Moscow when you have the chance to come to Babkino . . . Staying in town during the summer is a sin worse than pederasty and sheep-buggering. It is wonderful here: the birds are singing, Levitan is doing his imitation of a Chechen, you can smell the grass, Nikolay is drinking . . . There is so much good air and expressivity in nature I have no power to describe it . . . Every twig cries out and begs to be painted by the Jew Levitan, who has a savings account in Babkino.

Nikolay has shaved his head and taken up with a turkeycock. His greatest pleasure in life is whistling to the turkey or imitating it. I write and write and write . . . and pass my time in idleness. Begichev came yesterday and opened a hairdressing salon.

Please don't come just for one week, but for two or three. You won't regret it, especially if you don't mind living like a pig, that is being content to do nothing but vegetate. Abandon your architecture! You are badly needed here. The thing is, we (that is Kiselyov, Begichev and ourselves) are planning to set up a properly constituted court, organized according to strict principles of jurisprudence, complete with prosecuting and defence counsels, in order to try the merchant Levitan. He stands accused of a) dodging military service, b) setting up a clandestine distillery (Nikolay must be drinking at his place because there is nowhere else to drink), c) maintaining a secret savings account, d) immorality and similar crimes. You will be required to address the court as public prosecutor. Your room has been beautifully decorated with sketches, and your bed has long awaited you.

Write and tell me when we should expect you. You'll get a triumphant reception.

We've got our own pharmacy here. There is plenty of room for exercise. The bathing is sensational. The fishing is terrible.

I clasp your hand.

A. Chekhov

[*added in Nikolay Chekhov's hand*] François, do come! I've truly come back to life here. To add to the physical pleasures there are spiritual ones; in the latter the turkey plays a not insignificant role. This is on account of his impressive military bearing, the equal of any general's, before which I prostrate myself in reverence. You must come, there are a lot of interesting things here.

31. To Nikolay Leikin, 30 July 1886, Babkino

Thank you for your letter, my dear, kind Nikolay Alexandrovich. And thank you for letting me off more lightly than I was expecting . . .

The day before yesterday I sent you a story after an interlude of three weeks. I am hoping the interlude has now come to an end, because only a few traces remain of the misfortunes which descended on my head. The gist of them is as follows:

1) I had atrocious toothache . . . The pain lasted three days and three nights . . . In the end I had to take myself off one night to Moscow, where I had two teeth taken out in one session. It was a very difficult extraction, it took a long time, it hurt like the devil, and I ended up with a dreadful headache which lasted two more days.

2) When I got back from Moscow, I realized to my horror that I was unable to sit or walk, because I had developed haemorrhoids. My bottom, adjacent to the piles, has been having a real field day and is still doing so. I tried to write lying down, but this was not very successful, especially as my general state was pretty horrible. Then five days ago I went to Zvenigorod to act as locum for a friend who is the *zemstvo* doctor there, where I was up to my neck in work and became ill myself. So there you are . . . Now, why didn't I let you know that I would not be sending you any stories? The reason is that every hour that went by I was hoping and hoping that I would be able to sit down and write . . . And Voskresensk still has no telegraph office . . .

I'm still ill. I'm in a foul mood, because I have no money (the whole of July I did no work anywhere), and my domestic circumstances are not particularly joyful . . . The weather is awful.

I received only one letter from you, in which you wrote about Timofey and my book. I did not get the one you sent asking how to get to Babkino; if I had received it you would long ago have got my directions as to how to find me. In any event, what you do is: take the Petersburg line to Kryukovo station, then get a coachman to take you to Voskresensk (New Jerusalem) or straight to me in Babkino. You can find out my address from any of the shops in Kryukovo, from the post office, the priest or the local policeman or the magistrate. The whole family would be very pleased to see you and I should be so happy to repay a little of the hospitality you have shown me.

Now about my book. I didn't see a single copy in any of the bookshops when I was in Moscow. Vasiliev has no copies ('I had some earlier, but not now'), nor were there any at the Nikolayevsky station[1] although previously there had been, and so on. If you think the book is going to come out in the autumn, then I'll wait to put an advertisement in *The Russian Gazette*.

The thick journals[2] have been paying some attention to my book. *Virgin Soil* hated it, describing my stories as the ravings of a lunatic. *Russian Thought* praised it, while the *The Northern Herald* devoted two pages to the wretched fate in store for me, even though they liked the book . . .

I received an invitation from *Russian Thought* yesterday. I'll write something for them in the autumn. There is no point in your asking me when I plan to be in Moscow: I don't know myself. Send your power of attorney to my country address here; if you had sent it earlier, I would have carried out your commission long ago.

My sister is going to Moscow at the beginning of August to look for an apartment. I'll be moving back there in September.

We're having dreadful weather at the moment. The rain lashed down all summer and shows no sign of ever stopping. The river has

1. The main railway station for trains to St Petersburg.
2. The popular term for the highbrow literary journals published monthly.

overflowed its banks just like the spring floods, so that today we could catch fish with a bit of thread. The crops are rotting and the harvest is spoiled – like the summer has been.

Brother Agafopod[3] is in Moscow, Nikolay is here with me.

How is Praskovia Nikiforovna's health? Is all that bother with the Senate over Fedya finished and done with yet? My respects to both of them, and my best wishes . . .

Is there any other news? I feel like falling into bed now . . . Farewell, and good health to you.

Our deepest respects to Apel Apelich.[4] All honour and glory to his sexual activities! If he's incapable of doing anything else, at least let him copulate!

Your

A. Chekhov

32. To Maria Kiselyova, 29 September 1886, Moscow

I received your 'Galoshes' from Alexey Sergeyevich yesterday, dear Maria Vladimirovna. The moment I got it I settled down to read it, smirking balefully, screwing up my eyes and rubbing my hands together in maliciously gleeful anticipation . . .

I'll give you my full response to 'Galoshes' in due course. In the meantime I can say, in general and roughly speaking, that from a literary point of view it is stylishly written, lively and succinct. I think my response will be favourable.

Your pen-name of Pince-nez is well chosen.

It goes without saying that I shall be very happy to be your official literary agent, broker and cicerone. Such an appointment is most flattering to my vanity, and no more difficult to perform than carrying your bucket on your way home from fishing. Should you wish to be advised of the conditions under which I shall accomplish the work, kindly take note:

3. Nickname for Alexander Chekhov.
4. Leikin's dog.

1) Write as much as you possibly can! Write, write, write . . ., until your fingers break under the strain. (Calligraphy is the most important thing in life!) Write more, aiming not so much at the intellectual nourishment of the masses as at the sad fact that, owing to your unfamiliarity with the 'small press', initially at least a good half of your stuff will be sent back to you accompanied by a rejection slip. On the subject of rejection, I promise not to deceive, dissemble or evade the issue. Don't let it upset you; even if half what you send is returned, it's still worth more than whatever the Bohemian produces for *The Children's Holiday*.[1] And as for the effect on self-esteem . . . I don't know about you, but I got used to it long ago . . .

2) Write about different subjects, funny, sad, good, bad. Let's have a stream of stories, trifles, jokes, witticisms, puns, and so on and so forth.

3) Translations from foreign languages are quite permissible, so long as you don't break the Eighth Commandment . . . (You'll be sent to hell for 'Galoshes' after 22 January!) Avoid popular subjects. However obtuse our editor friends may be, you can't accuse them of not knowing the Paris literary scene, especially of the Maupassant kind.

4) Write it all out in one go, having full confidence in your pen. I say this in all sincerity: compared to you eight out of ten people who now write for the 'small press' are amateurs and no-hopers.

5) In the 'small press' brevity is considered the prime virtue. The best guide is the size of writing paper you use – like that on which I am now writing to you. The moment you get to eight or ten pages – stop! Anyhow, writing paper is so much easier to post . . . Those are my conditions.

Now that you have absorbed the exhortations of a wise genius such as myself, please accept my assurances of the most sincere devotion. And Alexey Sergeyevich, Vasilisa and Sergey can also sign on the dotted line for them too if they would like.

I haven't seen the widow Khludova yet. I have been going to the

1. Chekhov's brother Misha contributed to a journal called *The Children's Holiday* under the pseudonym of the Bohemian.

theatre. Not a single pretty woman . . . Just snoutiful, harridaceous mordemondaines. It's all getting rather frightening . . .

Farewell, and give my greetings to everyone.

Respectfully your

A. Chekhov

Life itself is gradually turning into a complete mordemonium. Everything is grey, you never see any happy people . . .

Nikolay is here with me. He is seriously ill, utterly exhausted from haemorrhaging in the stomach. Yesterday his condition really alarmed me, but he is so much better today that I am already allowing him a spoonful of milk every half an hour. He's lying there looking pale, stone-cold sober and meek as a lamb . . .

Life is tough for all of us. In my serious moments, I am struck by the thought that people are being illogical when they are repelled by death. So far as my understanding goes, life consists exclusively of horrors, squabbles and banalities, sometimes all at once and sometimes one after the other . . . I see I have become addicted to the *New Times* style of belletristic writing. My apologies.

Ma[ria]-Pa[vlovna] is well. We're broke.

33. *To Maria Kiselyova, 13 December 1886, Moscow*

First of all, dear Maria Vladimirovna, allow me to present you with a story now in print about how famous writers make use of their familiarity with 'garlic'. The story brought me in 115 roubles. After that, how can one not be drawn to the Jewish race?

I take grave offence at your reproaches over Yashenka, Mme Sakharova and the others. Can you possibly be unaware that I have long forsworn the vanities of the world, all earthly pleasures, and now devote myself unceasingly to medicine and literature? A more well-intentioned and respectable individual than me would be hard to find the wide world over. I think even Archimandrite Venyamin is a bigger sinner. Even the memory of Ekaterina Vasiliyevna no longer stirs my imagination.

'A Bad Place' was a slip of the pen. 'A Bad Joke' it remains.

I hope that at the Day of Judgement I shall be forgiven for Anna Pavlovna.[1] As God is my witness, I plead not guilty!

If you will permit me, I propose to steal two descriptions of the weather from your two latest letters to my sister, for my own stories. They are excellent. Your writing style is truly masculine; in every line (except when you are talking about children) you show that you are really a man. Naturally, this should be most gratifying to your self-esteem, since generally speaking men are 1,000 times more elevated and better than women.

I had a holiday in Piter, or rather I spent day after day roaming round the city, paying calls and acknowledging compliments that my soul rejects. Alas and alack! In Piter I am becoming as fashionable as Nana.[2] While the name of Korolenko, who is a serious writer, is practically unknown to editors, the whole of Piter seems to be reading my drivel. Even Senator Golubev is reading it . . . It's very flattering, but it outrages all my literary instincts . . . I can't be happy with a public that lionizes literary lapdogs because they can't recognize an elephant when they're standing in front of one, and I am absolutely certain that once I start writing seriously I won't be recognized by so much as a dog.

Nadezhda Vladimirovna, with whom I had dinner, has lost weight, and so has Vladimir Petrovich.[3] Evidently Piter is a city not conducive to plumpness.

Ma-Pa is thrilled with her trip. So she should be! The officers in her carriage made a huge fuss of her, and she was as well looked after in Piter as Queen Pomare.[4] She was entertained everywhere she went . . .

Her room has no ventilation, as usual!

Your brother has been to see us twice. He was complaining that

1. Maria Kiselyova's father felt Chekhov had based his character Anna Pavlovna in his story 'The Husband', whom he describes as pale and long-nosed, on her.
2. The heroine of Emile Zola's (1840–1902) novel *Nana* (1880), a Parisian courtesan.
3. Mariakiselyova's father, Vladimir Petrovich Begichev (1828–91), was from 1864 to 1881 Inspector of Repertoires, and from 1881 to 1882 Administrator of the Moscow Imperial Theatres. Discussion of Alexey Kondriatiev, director of the Maly Theatre, relates to attempts to get Begichev's play *The Firebird* into production.
4. Aimata Pomare (1822–77), queen of Tahiti until 1852.

he can never find Kondratiev at home. If Kondratiev doesn't do anything, we could bring Shekhtel into play. He is a great friend of Lentovsky.

My greetings to Alexey Sergeyevich, Istra, the Daraganovsky woods, Sergey and Vasilisa.

What is the Counterfeit Coin[5] getting up to these days?

Finally, wishing all your family all earthly bliss, I remain your respectful and devoted

A. Chekhov

34. To Maria Kiselyova, 14 January 1887, Moscow

Your 'Larka' is very charming, dear Maria Vladimirovna. The story has the odd rough spot, but its succinct and masculine style make up for any defects. As I don't feel, however, that I should be the sole person to sit in judgement on your labours, I propose sending it to Suvorin, who really understands what's what in this field. I'll let you know in due course what he says . . . And now, with your permission, I have a bone to pick with you over your criticism of my work. Even the fact that you praised 'On the Road' has failed to assuage my authorial ire, and I now leap to the defence of 'Mire'. Get ready now, hold tight to the back of your chair, I don't want you dissolving in a swoon. So, here goes . . .

Criticism, even of the most abusive and illegitimate kind, is usually met with respectful silence – as is demanded of literary etiquette. It's simply not done to answer back, and those who break this rule run the risk of being justly condemned for overweening vainglory. But since your criticism harks back to our evening talks on the back porch of the Babkino annexe or out on the terrace of the main house, with Ma-Pa, the Counterfeit Coin and Levitan, and since it is also more concerned with general topics than the purely literary aspects of my

5. This was the nickname the Chekhov family gave to the Kiselyovs' dog.

story, I feel I may be forgiven for any crime against etiquette in allowing myself to continue our discussion.

In the first place, I have no more liking than you do for the kind of literature we are talking about. As a writer and as an ordinary man I prefer to steer well clear of it, but if you want my honest and unvarnished opinion, I must tell you that the question as to whether or not such writing has a right to exist remains an open one even though Olga Andreyevna may think she has settled it once and for all. No critic in the world today – and this includes you and me – can muster convincing arguments to justify banning such literature. I do not know who is right: Homer, Shakespeare, Lope de Vega, and those old masters who, not fearing to dig around in the 'dung heap', were far more morally robust than we are; or the writers of our own day who on the page are primness itself but whose hearts are as cold and cynical as their lives? I do not know whose taste is worse: the Greeks, who saw no shame in hymning love as it truly is in its natural state, or the readers of Gaboriau, Marlitt and Pierre Bobo?[1] This question, like those concerning non-resistance to evil, free will and so forth, is one to which only the future holds the key. All we can do is pose the question; if we try to answer it, we go beyond the limits of our competence. You argue that Turgenev and Tolstoy eschewed the dung heap – but this throws no light at all on the problem. Their fastidiousness proves nothing; after all, the generation of writers that came before them considered it degrading even to depict peasants or officials below the rank of Titular Councillor, let alone 'men and women of the criminal class'. In any case, no one period, however fertile, gives us the right to pronounce on the superiority of one tendency over another. Nor does what you say about the corrupting influence of this particular tendency address the problem. Everything in this world is relative and approximate. Some people will be corrupted even by literature written for children, the kind of people who gleefully ferret out the spicy passages in the Psalms and the Proverbs of Solomon. Equally there are those whose hearts become purer the more they soil their hands with the messy business of living. Journalists,

1. 'Bobo', the minor novelist and playwright Pyotr Boborykin (1836–1922).

lawyers and doctors, people to whom all the hidden places of human wickedness are an open secret, are not noticeably more immoral than other people. Most realist writers are more moral than the average archimandrite. When all's said and done, real life wins over literature every time for cynicism; the man who has already drunk a whole barrel-full will hardly get any drunker for having one more glass.

2) It is perfectly true that the world is 'awash with men and women of the criminal class'. Human nature is flawed, so it would be surprising if the only people we come across in this world were to be the righteous. Those who think the task of literature is to extract a 'pearl' from a gang of villains deny its very essence. The justification for calling literature an art form is that it depicts life as it really is. Its purpose is the honest and unconditional truth. To limit its functions to nothing but the extraction of 'pearls' would threaten its very existence as much as insisting that when Levitan paints a tree he should ignore its inconveniently grubby bark or its yellowing leaves. I agree that a 'pearl' is a lovely thing, but the writer is surely not a confectioner or a beautician or an entertainer. The writer is a man bound by contract to his duty and to his conscience. In for a penny, in for a pound: however degrading he may find it, he has no choice but to overcome his squeamishness and soil his imagination with the filth of life . . . The writer is no different from your average newspaper reporter. How would you regard a reporter who, from misplaced delicacy or a willingness to pander to his readers, never wrote about anyone but honest burghers, idealistic ladies or virtuous railwaymen?

To the chemist, there is no such thing on this earth as an impure substance. The writer must be as objective as a chemist. He must turn his back on the subjective preferences of the world and recognize that dung heaps have a useful role to play in the countryside, that ignoble passions are every bit as much a part of life as noble ones.

3) Writers are children of their age and therefore must, like everyone else, conform to the external dictates of society. Accordingly they do not have licence to overstep the bounds of decency. But that is the only thing we have the right to demand of the realist writer, and since you do not criticize either the form of 'Mire' or the manner in which

it was realized, I assume you think I must not have overstepped the mark in this respect.

4) I confess that my conscience is not something I often pay much attention to when I write. I attribute this to force of habit, and to the inconsequential nature of what I write. Hence I am not talking about myself when I express one view of literature or another.

5) You say: 'If I were the editor, I would send this piece back to you for your own good.' Why stop there? Why not point the finger at editors who print this kind of story? Why not condemn the Press Affairs Directorate for allowing pernicious newspapers to be published?

The fate of literature (great and small) would be a sorry one indeed if it were left to the mercy of individual opinions. That is the first point. The second is that nowhere would we be able to find a police force competent in the field of literature. I accept that the writing profession will always be vulnerable to all kinds of rogues sneaking into its ranks, and therefore it will never be possible entirely to eliminate restraints and truncheons. But no matter how hard you cogitate you will never be able to invent a better policing system for literature than criticism and the individual conscience of the writer himself. People have been trying since the creation of the world, but no one has yet come up with anything better . . .

Are you seriously suggesting that I should turn down 115 roubles and be humiliated by an editor? Some people, including your own father, are delighted by the story. Others write angrily to Suvorin, heaping all sorts of abuse on the paper and on me, and so on and so forth. Who is right? Where is the one true arbiter to be found?

6) You go on to say: 'You should leave writing like this to sad, mean-spirited hacks like Okreyts, Pince-nez and Aloe.' May Allah forgive you if you really believe this! Sneering at little people just because they are little does no honour to the human heart. The lower ranks are just as important in literature as they are in the army: if your head tells you this, how much more so should your heart . . .

Oof! I've chewed on this bone so long I'll have worn you out completely . . . If I had realized my critique would go on as long as this, I would never have started it in the first place. I humbly ask your pardon!

We are coming to see you. We meant to leave on the 5th, but . . . were delayed first by a medical congress, then by St Tatyana's Day,[2] and finally there will be a party on the 17th to celebrate 'his' name day!![3] This last will be a magnificent ball complete with Jewesses, turkeys and Yashenkas.[4] We will fix a day to come to Babkino after the 17th.

So you read my story 'On the Road' . . . How do you like my daring? I write about 'clever things' and am not afraid. The story raised a real furore in Petersburg. Not long before, my subject was non-resistance to evil and that also shocked the public. I got good reviews in all the editions of the papers that came out over the New Year, and in the December issue of *Russian Wealth*, the magazine that publishes Lev Tolstoy, there is a thirty-two page article by Obolensky entitled 'Chekhov and Korolenko'. The fellow raves about me, and demonstrates that I am a greater artist than Korolenko . . . I expect he's wrong, but all the same I am beginning to feel that I do have one merit: I am the only one scribbling his rubbish in newspapers and not publishing in the thick journals who has caught the attention of the lop-eared critics: this has never happened before . . . I got roasted in *The Observer*, but they were roundly taken to task for doing so! By the end of 1886 I felt like a bone that had been tossed to the dogs . . .

Vladimir Petrovich's play will be published by *Theatre Library*, and so will get good distribution to all the major cities.

I've written a play [*Swan-song*] myself, on four scraps of paper. It lasts fifteen or twenty minutes, the smallest drama the world has ever seen. The famous actor Davydov,[5] currently a member of

2. St Tatyana's Day, on 12 January, marked the date of the foundation of Moscow University in 1755 and the commencement of the winter vacation. It was celebrated annually by students, faculty and alumni with much revelry, a tradition revived in 2004.

3. 17 January was Chekhov's birthday.

4. Maria and Nadezhda Yanova, patients who became friends of Chekhov, and enjoyed a flirtatious relationship with him.

5. Vladimir Davydov (1849–1925), an actor at the Korsh Theatre who had previously worked at the Imperial Alexandrinsky Theatre in St Petersburg, to which he later returned. He was the first actor to play the eponymous role in *Ivanov*.

Korsh's[6] company, will star in it. It will be published in *The Season*, so should get a pretty decent circulation. All in all, it's much better to write small things than big things, they're less pretentious and the public likes them. What more can one ask? The play took me an hour and five minutes to write. I started another but haven't finished it, as I don't have time.

I shall write to Alexey Sergeyevich when he returns from Volokolamsk . . . My best respects to everyone. I may, I trust, count on your forgiveness for having written you such a long letter? My hand simply ran away with itself.

A Happy New Year to Sasha and Sergey. Is Seryozha getting copies of *Around the World*?

Your devoted and respectful

A. Chekhov

35. To Alexander Chekhov, 17 January 1887, Moscow

Your Chaste Excellency!

To thank you adequately for transferring the money would entail mastering the style of Uncle Mitrofan Egorovich. Thank you! Without your intervention the money would have taken a week longer to come than it did. I forgive you for giving me this trouble, and I shall be glad if you would accept a commission of one hundredth of one per cent . . .

My congratulations to both my nephew and his parents, the former for his own angel's name day and the latter for the offspring whose name day it is. I wish them the best, the very best of everything!!!

I am waiting for Leikin to arrive, and my heart is sinking. I know he will again wear me out. Relations between me and this Quasimodo have really soured. He offered me a pay rise, which he had made conditional on my sending in copy on time, but I turned it down and

6. Fyodor Korsh (1852–1923), the owner of one of the first private theatres in Moscow, founded in 1882 and named after him.

now he's sending me alternately tearful and pompous letters, accusing me of causing a drop in the number of his subscribers, of betrayal, duplicity and so on. He claims, falsely, that he is constantly getting letters from subscribers asking why Chekhonte is no longer writing? He's annoyed with you for not writing . . . I'm going to demand 12 copecks a line.

In fact, I should be glad to stop working for *Fragments* altogether, because I am repelled by writing trivial pieces. I want to write on a bigger scale or nothing. We spent St Tatyana's Day splendidly. I'm having an *evening* this evening. Come along.

Are you seeing anything of Suvorin? Are you writing at all? What are you writing? I imagine you've proposed to the Suvorinites that they should use what you write? Generally you need to put yourself about more, spare no effort. Golike is a delightful German. I have no intention of writing to him. Bilibin is also a good fellow, but with someone he doesn't know he behaves like an inert, grey mass that you have to push round: limp, pale and boring. But once you get used to him he is a very worthwhile person.

Your aunt received the three roubles.

Since by the end of January I shall have again run out of money, and since I should like if possible to avoid both the moans of the family and the necessity of borrowing, both of which have a depressing effect on my health, I shall trouble you once more with a transfer. Please help me out, and I will send you a prescription.

My situation is ridiculous! I had 220 roubles plus another 20 roubles from *The Alarm Clock*, but there are only 30 roubles left and they will all be gone by 22 January. Tell me please, dear heart, when shall I be able to live like a human being, that is, work without being in such straits that I have to ruin my reputation by producing rubbish?

Have you seen la Suvorina? Her sister's husband came to see me over the holidays. Somewhat reluctantly I had to return the visit and meet her mother and sister.

What sort of work are you doing for *New Times*? Does it have any creative side to it?

You must write to me. In view of your straitened circumstances and in order not to swell the ranks of the proletariat, you must stop having children. In this you will be following the wishes of Malthus and of Pavel Chekhov.

Be well, and give my greetings to all. Give Kokosha and Totosha[1] my blessings; they must be kept in good condition to work 'cos their mummy and daddy have to eat . . . Petersburg loves money.

Asking your blessing, we remain your loving brother and sister

Antony and Meditsina Chekhov

In addition to my lawful wedded wife of medicine, I have a mistress – literature – but I speak not of her, since those who live outside the law[2] will surely perish unlawfully.

36. To Mitrofan Chekhov, 18 January 1887, Moscow

Dear Uncle Mitrofan Egorovich,

Yesterday I had the pleasure of receiving a wonderful present: a letter from you and one from Georgy. Both are so lovely and so affectionate that I am not putting off my reply but writing at once.

First of all may I send you my best wishes for a happy New Year, and express to you my grateful thanks for your kind remembrances of your sincere admirer, and your generous indulgence towards his incorrigible silence. I am infinitely at fault before you and your family. My only excuse is the extent to which the sheer mass of writing work and business correspondence has worn me out. Several times I was on the point of writing to you, but never actually managed to do so. On your name day I went with my sister to Petersburg, where I spent a whole week and in the whirl of social obligations I did not have a single free minute; over the holidays I was so overwhelmed with work that at Mother's name-day celebrations I almost collapsed from exhaustion.

1. Alexander's sons Nikolay and Anton.
2. An ironic reference to Pavel Chekhov's moralizing diatribes.

I have to tell you that I am now the most fashionable author in Petersburg. This is plain from the newspapers and magazines, which at the end of 1886 were all featuring me and trumpeting my name in all directions and praising me more than I deserve. The result of this growth in my literary reputation has been a flood of commissions and invitations, followed inevitably by hugely increased work and attendant fatigue. My work makes demands on the nerves, it's unsettling and gives rise to a lot of tension ... Being in the public eye carries responsibilities, and that makes it doubly burdensome ... Every newspaper review has its effect on me and on my family ... For instance, in the December issue of the magazine *Russian Wealth*, the critic Obolensky wrote an article headed 'Chekhov and Korolenko', in which he devoted fifteen to twenty pages to praising me to the skies and demonstrating how superior I am to another young author, Korolenko, whose name is heard all over both of our capital cities. This article caused a commotion in our household. *New Times* and *The Petersburg Newspaper* – two of the biggest Petersburg newspapers – also prattle on about Chekhov ... My stories are read out at evening parties, everywhere I go people point me out, I have so many acquaintances I cannot cope with them all, and so on, and so forth ... There's never a day's rest, and I feel as if I'm permanently on tenterhooks. So I count it a real blessing that you do not scold me for my silence ... God grant we see each other soon and can make up in conversation what has to be omitted from our all too rare correspondence.

The Pushkin edition promised by *The Ray* does not cost six roubles – this is a trick on the part of the publisher. If you have not yet signed up for *The Ray*, write to me and I will send you the complete Pushkin (as a present to Georgy in thanks for his letter). My good friend Suvorin, the publisher of *New Times*, is issuing a Pushkin edition on 29 January on special offer, at the fabulous price of two roubles including postage. Such things can only be done by people of stature and wisdom such as Suvorin, who grudges nothing in the cause of literature. He owns five bookshops, a newspaper, a magazine, a huge publishing firm, an establishment worth millions – all achieved by the most honourable and attractive attitude to work. He is a native of Voronezh, where he was formerly a teacher in a district school.

Whenever we meet we talk about Olkhovatka, Boguchar and so on.[1] I see him twice a year, when I go to Petersburg. He pays me *100 roubles* for a single story – as you can see from the enclosed statement from the editorial office, according to which I received 111 roubles for a Christmas story.

Georgy asked me for some copies of newspapers with my work in them. I would have been happy to fulfil his request, but alas! I have practically stopped working for any of the humorous papers, and anyhow they are not worth reading. I don't like them. My best work is in *New Times*. I could send it to you free, but the truth is I feel awkward asking favours of Suvorin. He gave me so many presents in December that I now hesitate to ask even the merest trifle . . . Georgy must be patient for a little while. If you have not yet sent your subscription to *The Ray*, I shall *immediately* send you the Pushkin. You have my word on it. It may be some consolation to Georgy. Along with it I'll send you my book, which is a compilation of some of my lighter pieces; I collected them together, not so much to be read as to have some record of my early literary activities. Papa will send you the books, so if they do not arrive please get in touch with him and ask him about them.

I shall put a blue pencil mark in the contents page against the pieces in my book I am pleased with. The rest should be seen only as examples of the sort of potboiler one is obliged to turn out when one is desperate for money.

Volodya is correct. It is better to write 'Vladimir' with a Russian 'i' than a Latin one; the latter is a completely redundant letter. If it were up to me I would dispense altogether with the 'yat', the 'fita' – what a stupid letter! –, the 'izhitsa' and the 'i'. The only result of these letters is to get in the way of school work and confuse busy people who don't have time for grammatical arcana; they are nothing but useless adornments to our syntax.[2] It is true that you cannot own 'the world' [using the Latin 'i'], but then you cannot own 'peace' [using the Russian 'i'] either, although it is possible to call a person 'the master

1. Chekhov's father and uncle were born in Olkhovatka, a district of Voronezh province.
2. These letters disappeared when Russian orthography was reformed in 1918.

of the world'.[3] Tell Volodya that peoples and history are right to honour their elect, freely and without fearing that in so doing they are blaspheming against the greatness of God or raising man to divine status. They may do so for reasons of gratitude, or reverence, or admiration for the noble qualities displayed by the greatest of their fellows, qualities that mark people out from their peers and bring them nearer to God. When we honour a man, it is not the man himself whom we honour but the noble qualities in him, specifically the innate divine spark which he has succeeded in developing to a high degree. For instance we may bestow the title of 'great' on our outstanding Tsars, even though corporeally they may be no more distinguished than Ivan Ivanovich Loboda.[4] The Pope is styled 'His Holiness', the Patriarch's title includes the word 'Universal' although he has no connection with any planet other than Earth; Prince Vladimir was dubbed 'Master of the World' although in reality he was ruler of no more than a scrap of land, princes are called 'Your Most Radiant Highness' and 'Your Enlightened Majesty' when you get a thousand times more light from a Swedish match than you would from them, and so on. We do not lie when we use such titles, nor are we guilty of hypocrisy and exaggeration, we are simply expressing our feelings of admiration, just as a mother does not lie when she addresses her child as 'my treasure'. A sense of beauty speaks in and through us, and beauty cannot tolerate the commonplace and the vulgar; it is beauty that makes us resort to the kind of similes that Volodya's mind may reject but his heart will understand. For example, we compare black eyes with the night, blue eyes with the azure sky, curly hair with waves, and so on; even the holy scriptures do not disdain comparisons such as 'thy belly wider than the heavens', or 'the radiant sun of truth', or 'the rock of faith', etc. Man's feeling for beauty knows no boundaries or constraints. This is the justification for a Russian prince calling himself 'Master of the World'; but this title may also be applied to my friend Volodya because titles are given not for meritorious service, but to honour and remember outstanding people who once lived

3. The Russian word *mir* means both 'peace' and 'world'.
4. Chekhov's own maternal uncle, Vanya.

among us . . . If your scholar finds my arguments unconvincing, here is one more that should carry the day: it is no sin against love to exalt people even to the level of God, on the contrary, it is an expression of it. What we must never do is humiliate people. Better to address someone as 'my angel' than 'you fool', even if men are more like fools than they are angels.

That is all I have to say, after which please allow me to express to you my most sincere devotion. Please convey my greetings to my aunt and to my sister and brother cousins, to Irinushka and to all my friends.

Your

A. Chekhov

My address is: The Korneyev House, Sadovaya-Kudrinskaya, Moscow.

I'm writing to Georgy at the same time.

I entertained a large number of guests yesterday, among them A. A. Dolzhenko,[5] who plays the violin and the zither; he has turned out to be a marvellous person. He comes to see us twice a week and has become very attached to us. He is exceedingly witty, honest and decent. The poor fellow is utterly at sea over 'yat', 'fita' and 'i' . . . He can't write to save his life, and this gives him a good deal of grief. But in other ways he is as gifted as the late Ivan Yakovlevich [Loboda].

37. To Chekhov Family, 10 March 1887, St Petersburg

My dear Readers,

Fyodor Timofeyich[1] on his nightly forays round the roofs has a much easier time than I had travelling to Piter. To start with, the train went so slowly there were fifty-six hours in every twenty-four; secondly, I forgot to take a pillow with me. Thirdly, the carriage was full to bursting, and fourthly, the cigarettes I smoked were so terrible that not only my throat but my galoshes were rasping: do find out

5. Chekhov's cousin Alexey, son of his maternal aunt Fedosya (Fenichka).
1. Fyodor Timofeyich was the Chekhov family cat.

what kind of tobacco Vasilisa buys. It's quite extraordinary: the water in the carafe smells like a latrine, the cigarettes are disgusting . . .

You will not be surprised to learn that I was in a highly overwrought state while I was on the train. I dreamt of coffins and torch-bearers and was haunted by images of typhus, doctors and such like . . . Generally it was a dreadful night, comforted only by the dear and lovely Anna, with whom I occupied myself the whole way.*

Kavaliergardskaya Street is as far from Nevsky, where I was staying, as Zhitnaya Street is from Kudrino. Alexander's apartment is spacious enough, but not very elegant or attractive.

Alexander is in fact perfectly well. All that had happened was that he imagined he was ill, became depressed and frightened, and that's why he sent that telegram.

Anna Ivanovna actually does have typhoid fever, but not very severely. I consulted with the other doctor. We agreed to treat her according to my regimen. He invited me to his house. I'll go.

The typhoid fever that is raging throughout Petersburg at the moment is a particularly virulent form. The commissionaire at Leikin's offices, a tall, thin old man whom you may remember, Masha, died of it yesterday.

I'll send money tomorrow. It's eleven o'clock on Monday evening, and I'm in my room. As soon as I finish this letter I shall go and see Alexander.

I'm not sure when I shall be back. It's lovely spring weather.

I lunched at Leikin's. Anna Arkadievna[2] has been ill with typhoid fever, and has lost a lot of weight. The illegitimate children are healthy and cheerful. The elder one seemed very nice and affectionate today.

I'm scared.

Greetings to all: the backless dog,[3] Fyodor Timofeyich, Korneyev and all.

Your

A. Chekhov

2. Anna Solovyova, an employee at *Fragments*, later married Viktor Bilibin.
3. The elderly family whippet, Korbo, suffered from scabs which gave a bald patch along his back.

When you write, address your letters to me at *Fragments*.

I'll take Alexander the rissoles that were left over from the journey – this is for Mamasha-Tarakasha's information. Mamasha, I ate only half the bread so there are one and a half French loaves left (profit of 7½ copecks). Alexander does have some money.

I'm bored . . .

* Karenina, I mean.

38. To Maria Chekhova, 3 April 1887, Oryol

I'm in Oryol, and it's 4.50 in the morning.

The coffee I'm drinking tastes like smoked fish. The fields are clear of snow, and I'm enjoying the journey. I have no envelopes, so won't be sending you a travel diary. Take Vanya's advice on everything: he has a positive attitude and a strong character.

Regards to all

A. Chekhov

39. To Maria Chekhova, 4 April 1887, Slavyansk

Saturday, 7 a.m.

Mist and low cloud. Not a thing to be seen. The birds, crocodiles, zebras and other insects have all hidden. I slept wonderfully. I've had good company the whole way. Christ is risen! – after all you won't get this letter until two or three days after Easter. I'll write to you at length from Taganrog. I can see Khokhols and bulls. The intellectuals scurrying about the railway carriages remind me of the Kamburovs.[1] Mangy lot, they are.

Votre à tous

A. Chekhov

1. The two Kamburov brothers were distant relatives of the Chekhovs.

40. To Nikolay Leikin, 7 April 1887, Taganrog

Christ is risen, my dear Nikolay Alexandrovich! I got your letter yesterday, brought to me by a postman with a red coat and a good-natured expression on his mug. Having handed me the letter he put down his bag on the bench near the washing-up basin and sat down for a cup of tea in the kitchen, not in the least bit worried about the other letters. It's completely Asiatic here! Everything is so Asiatic I can hardly believe my eyes. The 60,000 inhabitants of this town do absolutely nothing except eat, drink and procreate; they have no other interests whatsoever ... Wherever you go you see Easter cakes, painted eggs, Santorini wine, babies at the breast, but no newspapers, no books ... The situation of the town is magnificent in every respect, the climate is wonderful, there are fruits of the earth in abundance, but the residents are totally inert ... They are all musical, imaginative, witty, highly-strung, sensitive people, but it all goes completely to waste ... There are no patriots, no one on the make, no poets. There's not even a decent baker.

On Saturday I am going to Novocherkassk, where I shall be best man at the wedding of a rich Cossack girl. I'll get drunk on the Don wine, then come back to Taganrog, and on the 14th I'm heading off to the Donets. But please continue to write to me in Taganrog.

I have a small favour which I should be grateful if you could do for me quickly: would you please find out from your black-bearded masseur what is considered the best *practical* massage technique? It would be a kindness to write the answer on a postcard and send it to Dr Ivan Vasilievich Eremeyev, Taganrog. You would oblige me very much in this, because in May my colleague and I have an exceedingly fat man to massage. Please don't forget to do this for me.

The women they have here!

Yesterday I went to look at the sea. Marvellous! My only problem is a bout of bowel inflammation brought on by the change in water and diet, and I keep getting the runs. And the WCs are out in the yard, at the back of beyond ... Nasty accidents have been known to happen on the way.

I have written a story for the *Paper* and will take it to the station to send it together with this letter.

Please write to me. Best wishes to Praskovia Nikiforovna and Fedya. Farewell.

Your

A. Chekhov

41. To Chekhov Family, 7 April 1887, Taganrog

Gracious Readers and Devout Listeners!

With trepidation I herewith continue my account, observing strict chronological order.

2 April   The journey from Moscow to Serpukhov was very tedious. My travelling companions proved to be solid citizens who incessantly discussed the price of flour. I arrived in Serpukhov at seven o'clock. The Oka is a nice, clean little river. Steamers go down it to Kashira and Kaluga; I wouldn't mind going some time.

I got to Tula, fairest of cities, at eleven o'clock. On the train I met an officer, Volzhinsky, who gave me his card and said I should call on him in Sevastopol. He had come from Moscow, where his brother, a doctor who was visiting a medical convention there, had contracted typhus and died, leaving a widow. In Tula there was *schnapps-trinken*, mild intoxication and *schlafen*. I slept curled up in a ball, like Fyodor Timofeyich, with the toes of my boots up near my face. At Oryol I woke up and wrote a postcard to send to Moscow. The weather was fine; there was not much snow there.

At twelve o'clock, Kursk. An hour's wait, a glass of vodka, a wash in the lavatory and some cabbage soup. We changed trains. The carriage was packed. As soon as we left Kursk I made new acquaintances: a cheerful landowner from Kharkov, a bit like Yasha Korneyev, a lady who had gone to Petersburg for an operation, a police inspector from Tim, a Khokhol officer, a general in the uniform of a provost-marshal. We discussed social problems. The general was a clear-thinking liberal with a gift for expressing himself succinctly; the police inspector was the type of gaunt old hussar-like sinner pining for his strawberry beds; he put on airs like a governor, keeping his mouth open for what seemed like ages before uttering a word, and when he did utter one he gave a long-drawn-out growl like a dog: eh-eh-eh-eh. The lady injected herself with morphine and sent the men out for ice at each station . . .

Cabbage soup at Belgrad. We arrived at Kharkov at nine o'clock. Touching farewells to the inspector, the general and others. Now the carriage was almost empty. Volzhinsky and I each took one of the long bench seats and soon went off to sleep without recourse to Mama's bottle. I awoke at 3 a.m.; my officer was getting his things together to leave. Lozovaya station. We parted, vowing to visit each other(?!). I fell asleep again as we travelled on, waking up at Slavyansk, where I sent you another postcard. More companions: a landowner who reminded me of Ilovaisky, and a railway ticket-collector. We discussed the railways. The ticket-collector told us how the Lozovaya–Sevastopol railway line had stolen 300 carriages from the Azov railway and painted them in their livery.

Khartsysk. 12 noon. Fabulous weather. You could smell the steppe and hear the birds singing. I saw some old friends – the kites flying over the steppe . . .

Little kurgans,[1] water towers, new buildings – all familiar and memorable. A bowl of exceptionally delicious rich cabbage soup from the buffet, followed by a stroll along the platform. Young women. A young woman (or a lady, who knows?) in a white blouse was sitting at the end window of the second floor, languorous and beautiful. I looked at her, she looked at me . . . I put on my pince-nez, she put on hers . . . Oh miraculous vision! My heart leapt and I continued on my way. Diabolically, disgracefully wonderful weather. Khokhols, oxen, kites, little white houses, small southern rivers, the Donets branch lines with a single telegraph wire, the daughters of landowners and tenants, ginger-coloured dogs, greenery – it all flashed by as if in a dream . . . It was very hot. The inspector began to be a bore. I still had half the rissoles and the pies left, but they were beginning to smell

1. Scythian burial mounds.

a bit off . . . I put them underneath the seat opposite with the remains of the vodka.

Five o'clock, and we could see the sea. Here is the Rostov line curving gracefully round, then the gaol, the almshouses, the loutish young men, the goods wagons . . . Belov's hotel, the clumsy architecture of St Michael's Church . . . I am in Taganrog. Egorushka meets me, a strapping lad dressed to the nines with a hat, rouble-and-a-half gloves, a cane, the works. I didn't recognize him, but he knew who I was. He hires a cab and off we go. It's like Herculaneum or Pompeii: no people, just sleepy-looking louts and vacuous-looking idlers instead of mummified remains. The houses are all dilapidated, the stucco falling off and not repaired, the roofs unpainted, the shutters closed . . . Beyond Politseiskaya Street the road degenerates into mud, which gets so sticky and uneven when it dries that you can't drive any faster than walking pace, and then only with great care. Finally, we arrive . . .

'It's, it's . . . Antoshechka . . . he's arrived!'

'De-e-e-arest boy!'

Beside the house is a shop looking like a soap box. The porch is in the terminal stages of decay, its only remaining impressive attribute its immaculate cleanliness. Uncle is just as he was, except his hair is noticeably greyer than before. He is just as affectionate, gentle and sincere. Lyudmila Pavlovna is 'so pleased' to see me, she forgets to put in the good tea and generally feels the need to apologize and make things up, quite unnecessarily. She keeps casting suspicious glances at me to check that I am not being critical, but overall is very warm and hospitable. Egorushka is a nice young lad and for Taganrog pretty decently turned out. He's a bit of a dandy and likes admiring himself in the mirror. He bought himself a 25-rouble lady's gold watch and goes out with girls. His circle of acquaintances includes Mamaki, Goroshka and Bakitka and similar young females who, like others of their ilk, have been put on this earth solely to occupy the large amount of vacant space in the heads of the youths. Vladimirchik, who resembles that scrawny, stooping Mishchenko who used to room with us, is a gentle soul. He says little and seems to have a nice nature. He is preparing to be a pillar of the church; his plans include entering a seminary and becoming a Metropolitan. So Uncle will have his

Metropolitan as well as his supply of halva. Sasha has not changed a bit, and Lyolya is indistinguishable from Sasha. What is immediately noticeable is the exceptional affection the children have for their parents and for one another. Irina has become very stout. The rooms are just as they were, with dreadful portraits and Coats & Clark[2] prints stuck up everywhere. There are enormous pretensions to refinement and luxury, but taste is in as short supply as femininity on a muddy boot. It's cramped, hot, there are not enough tables, and it's all very uncomfortable. Irina, Volodya and Lyolya all sleep in one room; Uncle, Lyudmila Pavlovna and Sasha in the other. Egor sleeps on top of a trunk in the front room. They don't generally have supper, quite sensibly, because if they did, the heat from the kitchen and the stoves, which they keep going however warm the weather, would long ago have blown the house into the air. The privy is in the back of beyond over by the fence; it is sometimes used by thieves as a place of concealment so that relieving oneself at night can be a greater hazard to life than taking poison. The only tables they have seem to be either card tables or little round ones for purely ornamental purposes. No spittoons, nowhere to wash your hands properly . . . the napkins are grey with dirt, Irinushka has grown flabby and coarse . . . all in all, it's so bad one could shoot oneself! I don't care at all for Taganrog manners, I can't bear them and would go to the other end of the earth to avoid them.

Selivanov's house is empty and falling down. It was depressing to look at, and I wouldn't want to have it for all the money in the world. I am amazed that we could ever have lived in it. Selivanov, by the way, is living on his estate, having banished his Sasha . . .

I have a cup of tea and then go out with Egor for an evening stroll along the High Street. The streets are clean and better paved than in Moscow. It smells of Europe. Aristocrats keep to the left, democrats to the right. More girls than you could shake a stick at: tow-haired ones, dark-skinned ones, Greeks, Russians, Poles . . . The fashion is for olive-green dresses and blouses. Everyone in Novostroyenka seems

2. A Scottish textile company which gave away free colour lithographs as prizes with the threads it sold. Chekhov's uncle liked to frame them and hang them in his house.

to have gone in for this olive colour, not just the aristocrats (i.e. the mangy Greeks). Big bustles are not worn; only the Greek women wear them large, the others don't dare.

Later in the evening I go back home. Uncle robes himself in his churchwarden's outfit; I help him put on his large medal, which he is wearing for the first time. Laughter. We set off for St Michael's Church. It's dark. No cabs to be had. Dock workers and local tearaways, many of them carrying little lanterns, flit in silhouette along the streets, reeling from church to church. Uncle Mitrofan's church is very effectively illuminated from the ground right up to the tip of the cross. The Loboda house with its brightly lit windows stands out from the surrounding darkness.

We enter the church. It's grey, mean and drab. The only illumination comes from the candles in the windows, but Uncle's face is lit with such a beatific smile that it makes up for any lack of electric light. Like the church at Voskresensk, this one is not especially beautifully decorated. We sell candles. Egor as a liberal and a dandy does not sell any, but stands to one side and looks on with an air of detachment. Vladimirchik, on the other hand, is clearly in his element . . .

The procession with the Cross. Two idiots lead the way waving Bengal lights[3] which puff smoke and sparks over the congregation. The congregation likes this very much. The founders, benefactors and worshippers of the church stand in the vestibule with Uncle at their head and wait, icons in their hands, for the Procession to return . . . Vladimirchik sits on top of a wardrobe sprinkling incense into the brazier. There is so much smoke it is hard to breathe. But now here are the priests and the holders of the banners, and a solemn hush descends. All eyes are turned to Father Vasily . . .

Suddenly the voice of Vladimirchik rings out from above the wardrobe: 'Papochka, should I put in some more incense?'

Matins begins. I go with Egor over to the cathedral. There are no cabs, so we have no option but to walk. In the cathedral everything is done properly, with solemn ceremony. The choir is splendid, the voices sumptuous, although the vocal discipline is poor. Pokrovsky has

3. Flares.

aged and gone grey; his voice has lost focus and power. Grigorevich is like a corpse.

I meet Ivan Ivanovich Loboda in the cathedral, having spotted the red, fleshy back of his head from afar off. We spend the rest of the service chatting.

We come back from the cathedral on foot, my legs numb and aching, and break our fast in Irinushka's room: wonderful Easter cake, disgusting sausage, grey, dingy napkins, stuffy air and the smell of the children's blankets. Uncle broke his fast in Father Vasily's house. Having eaten my fill and drunk some wine, I lay down and fell asleep to more sounds of 'it's . . . it's . . . it's . . .'

In the morning, an invasion of priests and choristers. I go to visit the Agalis, which pleased Polina Ivanovna. Lipochka wouldn't come out to see me because her jealous husband wouldn't let her. Nikolay Agali is a strapping booby who spends his time entering for exams he has no hope of passing and dreaming of getting into Zürich University. He is very stupid. From the Agalis I went on to Mme Savyeleva, who lives on Kontorskaya Street in one tumbledown wing of a dilapidated house. She has two minuscule rooms with two spinsterish couches and a cradle. Yakov Andreyiches,[4] homely and ingenuous, peep out from underneath the beds. Evgenia Yasonovna lives apart from her husband, with two children. She has become terribly ugly and dried up; her face shows how unhappy she is. Her Mitya is working somewhere in the Caucasus, living a bachelor life in some Cossack village there. He's a swine.

I try Eremeyev next, but he's not at home so I leave a note and go on to Mme Zembulatova. As I picked my way to her house through the New Bazaar, I could not help noticing how dirty, empty, lazy, uncivilized and boring Taganrog is. There is no such thing as a literate sign to be seen; one even said 'Rushia [instead of 'Russia'] Inn'. The streets are deserted; dockers with smug, ugly mugs, sharp young men in their long overcoats and caps, Novostroyenka types in their olive-green dresses, the beaux, the girls, the peeling stucco, the all-pervading inertia, the willingness to put up with the cheapest rubbish

4. The Chekhov family name for chamberpots.

and to avoid all thoughts of the future – all this staring you in the face is so repulsive that Moscow, with its dirt and typhus, seems by comparison very attractive . . .

Zembulatova provided Santorini and small talk. After seeing her I went back to Uncle's house. Lunch was soup and fried chicken ('You've got to have a bird for a holiday meal, child! Why not spoil yourself once in a while?'). While we were at table, in burst one of the Kamburovs, an individual with a pronounced five o'clock shadow and a white waistcoat, who had evidently already made considerable inroads on the Santorini on his unsteady progress from one visit to the next. He works in a bank, and his Anglofart of a brother lives in Warsaw, also working in a bank. 'I say!' he blurts out, 'why not come over to my place? I always read your pieces on a Saturday. My father's such a character! You should come and meet him. Oh, I suppose you've forgotten I'm married now. I've a daughter, you know! . . . How you've changed!' etc., etc.

After lunch (soup with hard rice and chicken) I went over to see Khodakovsky. Pan Khodakovsky lives pretty well, although in somewhat less luxurious style than he did when we knew him before. His fair-haired Manya, a plump, well-cooked piece of Polish meat, has a good profile but looks disagreeable *en face*. She has bags under her eyes and overactive sebaceous glands. She looks as if she could be a real goer; I found out later indeed, that last season she all but ran off with an actor, after going so far as to sell her rings, earrings and such. This is between ourselves, of course . . . Generally I get the impression that it is the height of Taganrog fashion to run off with an actor. Quite a lot of men wake up to discover their wives and daughters have gone missing.

From Pan Khodakovsky I went to the Lobodas. The whole family has aged quite terribly. Anosha is as bald as the moon, Dashenka has put on a lot of weight, Varenka is older, thinner and desiccated; when she laughs her nose goes down to meet her face and her chin wrinkles up to her nose. Marfa Ivanovna also looks much older and has gone grey. She was very pleased to see me and agreed to come to Moscow with me.

At the Lobodas I met the immortal Tsarenko, jolly, talkative and liberal. Pyotr Zakharych is very much alive; he was delighted to see me and wanted to hear about all our family ... He talks in a hoarse, extraordinarily gruff voice, you can't listen to him without wanting to laugh; he was married, but divorced his wife. On my way home from the Lobodas I met Mme Savelyeva with her daughter. The daughter is the image of her father; she laughs all the time and already speaks beautifully. When she thanked me for helping her put on one of her galoshes that had fallen from her foot, she looked at me languorously and said: 'Come and stay the night with us!'

When I got home I found Father Ioann Yakimovsky there, a plump, overfed priest who expressed polite interest in my medical work and, to Uncle's enormous satisfaction, was so condescending as to remark: 'What a joy for parents to have such excellent children.'

There was also a reverend deacon, who wanted to talk to me and informed me that their choir at St Michael's (a collection of starving jackals drilled by an alcoholic choirmaster) was considered the best in the town. I assented, knowing perfectly well that neither Father Ioann nor the reverend deacon has the slightest understanding of singing. A sexton seated a respectful distance away kept casting longing glances at the jam and the wine which the priest and the deacon were consuming with relish.

By eight o'clock Uncle Mitrofan, his entire household, Irina, the dogs, the rats that live in the store cupboard, the rabbits – were all fast asleep in the land of Nod. I had no choice but to go to bed and sleep myself. I slept on the sofa in the sitting room, which has not, I noticed, grown at all and is just as short as it always was. To stretch out on it meant either sticking my feet indecently up in the air or putting them down on the floor. I thought of Procrustes and his bed. I covered myself up with the hard, suffocating pink quilted blanket, which became unbearable during the night as the stoves Irina had stoked up made their presence felt. Only in my fantasies and dreams could Yakov Andreyich offer any relief, as only two people in Taganrog can afford such a luxury: the mayor and Alferaki. Everyone else either has to piss the bed or embark on a voyage of discovery to goodness knows where.

6 April   I wake up at 5 a.m. Overcast sky. A nasty, chill wind is blowing that reminds me of Moscow. I'm bored. I wait for the cathedral bells and go to the late service. It is lovely inside the cathedral, everything done right, and it's not boring. The choir sings well, not too vulgar, and the congregation consists entirely of young ladies in olive-green dresses and chocolate blouses. Many of them are very pretty, so much so that I regret that I am not Mishka with his addiction to pretty girls. Most of the girls round here are attractive, with splendid figures and not averse to a little flirtation. There are simply no beaux here, if you don't count the Greek businessmen and the somewhat dubious Kamburov brothers, so officers and visiting gentlemen have the field to themselves.

After the cathedral I went to see Eremeyev. He has set himself up very well indeed, Moscow-style. Now that I have seen his enormous apartment I am inclined to disagree with Alexander when he says it's not possible to live decently in Taganrog. His house was full of visitors, including all the local grandees, tawdry and limited people for the most part, although if you could be bothered you might be able to pick out a few worthwhile ones. I met one officer, Dzheparidze, who is a local celebrity for having fought a duel. I saw some of the doctors, among them Familiant, Rombro and Iordanov. Eremeyev came home himself at three o'clock, drunk as a lord. He was thrilled to find me there and swore eternal friendship; I didn't even know him particularly well but he insists that he has no more than two real friends in the world: Korobov and me. We sat down to lunch and cracked open a bottle. An excellent dinner: soup without hard rice, and chicken. Despite the cold wind we went to the Quarantine[5] after lunch. The Quarantine is awash with comfortable but inexpensive dachas; we could rent one for next year, but I felt there were just too many of them, it could get very noisy and crowded. There are some cottages on land belonging to the Kompaneisky mill, but I don't like this area much. Many people were advising me to drive five miles out of Taganrog to Miyus, where there are more dachas for sale at bargain prices. You can buy a very nice dacha there, with a little garden and a beach, for 500 to 1,000 roubles. Cheaper than mushrooms.

5. A large piece of land on the coast just outside Taganrog earlier used as a quarantine.

42. *To Maria Chekhova, 20 April 1887, Zverevo*

I've left the Zverevo–Voronezh line and am now on the Donets line. In Zverevo I had to wait from nine in the evening until five in the morning. Great fun!!!

Bare steppe: kurgans, kites, larks, blue horizon . . .

On Thursday I shall be in Novocherkassk, and on Sunday I shall rejoin the Donets line. It's a shame I'm on my own. Everything is very interesting.

The only person in Moscow I've had a letter from is Ivan; no one else in the Kudrino household has seen fit to write, for some reason.

A. Chekhonte

Greetings to all.

43. *To Chekhov Family, 30 April 1887, Ragozina Valley*

30 April   A warm evening. Because of the clouds there's not much to see. The air is heavy and smells of grass.

I am staying in Ragozina Valley at Kravtsov's. A little house with a thatched roof and some outbuildings made of flat stone. Three rooms with earthen floors, crooked ceilings and windows that open from the bottom up . . . The walls are festooned with rifles, pistols, sabres and whips. The chests of drawers and the windowsills are piled high with cartridges, tools for repairing rifles, tins of powder and little bags of shot. The furniture is all wonky and chipped. I have to sleep on a decrepit couch with hardly any upholstery left on it; it is very hard. For six miles around there is no such thing as a latrine or an ashtray or similar aids to comfortable living. If you need to renew acquaintance with Mlle Merde, you have to go down into the ravine (whatever the weather) and choose your bush. Before sitting down, however, you are well advised to satisfy yourself that the ground beneath said bush is free of vipers and suchlike creatures.

The local population consists of old Kravtsov, his wife, the Cornet

Pyotr who has wide red stripes down his trouser legs, Alyokha, Khakhko (i.e. Alexander), Zoika, Ninka, Nikita the shepherd and Akulina the cook. There are innumerable dogs, every last one of them foul-tempered, mad and unwilling at any hour of the day or night to let me pass. I need an escort to go anywhere, otherwise there would be one less writer in Russia. The dogs have names like Mukhtar, Wolfie, Whiteleg, Gapka and so on. The worst is Mukhtar, an old hound with what looks like bits of old rope hanging down from his snout instead of a coat. He hates me, and every time I step outside the house he hurls himself at me with a snarl.

Now, I'll tell you about the food. In the morning we have tea, eggs, ham and pork dripping. At midday there is a soup made from goose, which consists of a liquid resembling the slurry you would find in the water some fat market women have been bathing in, then roasted goose with marinated sloes or turkey, roast chicken, kasha with milk and sour milk. They don't seem to go in for either vodka or pepper. At five o'clock they make a kasha in the woods from millet and pork dripping. In the evening there is tea, ham, and whatever is left over from lunch. I forgot to say that after lunch we have coffee made from roasted dung, to judge from the taste and the smell.

Among the pleasures are shooting bustards, camp fires, trips to Ivanovka, target practice, teasing the dogs, concocting the gunpowder mixture for Bengal lights, talking politics, building stone towers, and so on.

The principal activity here is rationalized agronomy instigated by the young Cornet, who has invested five roubles and 40 copecks in buying books on agriculture from Leikin. The main emphasis is on that branch of agriculture concerned with wholesale slaughter; this continues all day and all night without interruption. They kill sparrows, swallows, bumblebees, ants, magpies and ravens, so they don't eat the bees; they kill the bees so they don't spoil the blossom on the fruit trees, and they cut down the trees so they don't exhaust the soil. A cycle is thus created, albeit a somewhat original one, based on the latest findings of science.

Everyone retires at nine o'clock in the evening. Sleep tends to be disturbed by the howling of the Whitelegs and the Mukhtars out in the yard, while Setter replies with a furious volley of barking from underneath my bed. I am woken by the sound of rifle fire: my hosts shooting through the window at some creature threatening the domestic economy. If I need to leave the house at night I have to rouse the Cornet in order not to be torn to pieces by the dogs, so the Cornet's sleep is wholly dependent on the amount of tea and milk I have drunk the previous evening.

The weather is lovely. The grasses are tall and flowering. I've been observing the bees and the people, among whom I feel like Mikhluko-Maklay.[1] There was a very beautiful thunderstorm yesterday evening.

The most magnificent aspect of the surroundings here are the mountains. They look like this:

Not far away are some mines. I'm leaving early tomorrow morning to go over to Ivanovka (fifteen miles) on a one-horse cart to pick up my mail.

I am suffering from haemorrhoids and my left leg hurts. I've had a letter from Misha, but nothing from Alexander.

We eat turkey eggs. The turkeys lay them in the woods on last year's leaves. They don't use a knife to slaughter chickens, geese, pigs and so on here. They shoot them.*

Farewell.

A. Chekhov

Regards to all.

* The shooting is non-stop.

1. Nikolay Mikhluko-Maklay (1846–88), traveller, scholar and public figure.

44. To Chekhov Family, 11 May 1887, Taganrog

With trepidation,[1] I continue. On leaving the Kravtsovs' I went to
the Holy Mountains. I had to leave the Azov line and rejoin the Donets
line in order to go from Krestnaya station to Kramatorovka. The
Donets railway line looks something like the following tangle, in
which the central circle represents Debaltsevo station and the other,
smaller circles are a collection of Bakhmuts, Izyums, Lisichansks,
Lugansks and God knows what other horrors:

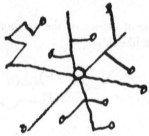

All the branch lines look exactly like one another, like the Kamburov
family, so that one is as liable to get into the wrong train at Debaltsevo
as to mistake [Levitan's dog] Vesta in the dark for the [Kiselyovs']
Counterfeit Coin. I, however, was so resourceful and on the ball as to
avoid muddling up my trains, and arrived successfully at Kramatorovka at seven o'clock in the evening. Stuffy, a smell of coal, a Jewish
lady with sour-looking Jew children, and an hour and a half to wait.
From Kramatorovka I took the Azov line to Slavyansk. A dark evening.
The cab drivers refused to take me to the Holy Mountains at night, and
suggested that I spend the night in Slavyansk, which I was most happy
to do seeing that I was exhausted and limping with pain like forty thous-
and Leikins. The town is three miles from the station and the cart ride
there cost 30 copecks. The town is rather like Gogol's Mirgorod:[2] it

1. An untranslatable play on the Russian words *s trepetom*, which, when run together,
mean 'like a little bustard'.
2. The name given to the cycle of stories about Ukrainian life written in 1835 by Nikolay
Gogol (1809–52), following on from *Evenings on a Farm Near Dikanka* (1831–2).

has a barber's shop and a watchmaker's, so one may assume that in a thousand years' time it will have a telephone. The walls and fences are covered with posters advertising a menagerie; weeds and excrement lie all along the bottom. Pigs, cows and other domestic animals wander along dusty streets that have grass growing in them. The houses have a friendly and welcoming air, like benevolent grannies, the pavement is soft and the streets wide, the air full of the scent of lilac and acacia. You hear the distant sound of nightingales singing, frogs croaking, dogs barking, someone playing a mouth organ, a woman squealing . . . I stayed at the Kulikov Hotel, where I got a room for 75 copecks. After sleeping on boards and in troughs it was a delight to see a bed with a mattress, a washbasin and – oh! blessings of kind fate – a Yakov Andreyich. (As a seasoned world traveller I have reached the indisputable conclusion that Yakov Andreyich is a much more useful and pleasant companion than Yakov Alexeyich [Korneyev], Yakov Sergeyich Orlovsky or even Yashenka M.!) Leafy branches push their way in through the wide-open window, and a warm breeze blows . . . Stretching luxuriously and screwing up my eyes like a cat, I demanded food and for 30 copecks was served an enormous portion of roast beef, bigger than the biggest chignon, which could equally well have been called roast beef or a cutlet or even a meat pie, that under normal circumstances I would have left to one side except and which I was as ravenously hungry as Levitan and his dog out hunting.

It was a wonderful morning. On account of the national holiday (6 May),[3] the cathedral bells were ringing. Mass was just coming to an end and people were streaming out: policemen, magistrates, army officers and other ranks of the blessed. I bought two copecks' worth of sunflower seeds and for six roubles hired a sprung carriage to take me to the Holy Mountains and (two days later) back again. We left town along lanes literally drowning in a profusion of cherry, apricot and apple blossom. The birds sang without pause for breath. Passing Khokhols, presumably taking me for Turgenev, doffed their caps, my driver Grigory Polenichka kept jumping down from his box to fiddle with the harness or lash out at the small boys running after the carriage

3. 6 May was the birthday of Nicholas II, the heir to the throne.

... The line of pilgrims stretched all along the road. Everywhere white hills and mountains, a bluish-white horizon, tall rye, the occasional oak forest – the only things missing were crocodiles and rattlesnakes.

I arrived at the Holy Mountains at twelve o'clock. It is an exceptionally unusual and beautiful place: a monastery on the banks of the Donets river at the foot of a towering white cliff with gardens, oak trees and ancient pines apparently suspended one above the other all the way up it ... The trees seem to be clamped on to the cliff, as though there is some kind of force pushing them up and up. The pines literally hang in mid-air, so that it's hard to believe they won't come crashing down on your head. The cuckoos and nightingales never let up day or night ...

The monks, who are extremely kind and pleasant people, gave me an extremely unpleasant room with a mattress as flat as a pancake. I spent two nights in the monastery and brought away with me a mass of impressions. Because of its being St Nicholas's Day, there were about fifteen thousand pilgrims thronging round me, eight-ninths of them old women. I never knew there were so many old women in the world; if I had known, I would long ago have shot myself ... I shall write something for *New Times* and when I see you I'll also tell you about my encounters with the monks and the medical treatment I gave to some of them and the old women. The services never stop: the bells ring at midnight for Matins, at five o'clock for early mass, at nine o'clock for late mass, at three o'clock for the akathist[4] and at six for compline. Before every service you hear the lament of a handbell in the corridors, and a monk runs up and down pleading like a creditor trying to get at least five copecks in the rouble:

'Lord Jesus Christ, have mercy on us! Matins is beginning!'

I felt a bit awkward just staying in my room, so got up and went out ... I found a lovely spot on the banks of the river and sat out the services there. I bought an icon for Aunt F[edosia] Y[akovlevna].

The monastery provided food for all the fifteen thousand: cabbage

4. From the Greek *akathistos* (literally, 'not sitting'), an ancient liturgical hymn of devotion in the Orthodox Church, consisting of twenty-four stanzas, alternately long (the *ikos*) and short (the *kontakion*).

soup, dried gudgeon and gruel. It was all delicious, as was the rye bread.

The bells were magnificent. The choir was bad. I joined the icon procession, which takes place in boats.

I won't write any more now about the Holy Mountains, because I could not possibly set it all down, I'd only make a hash of it if I tried.

On the return journey I had a six-hour wait at the station, which was miserable. In one of the trains I was in I caught sight of Sozya Khodakovskaya; she paints herself all the colours of the rainbow and looks like an old shop window.

I spent all night in the third-class coach of a disgusting, clapped-out goods train that dragged itself painfully along, so was one exhausted son of a bitch when I arrived.

Now I am back in Taganrog, to more exclamations of 'It's . . . it's . . . it's . . . !', the short couch again, the Coats prints on the walls, the stinking water in the washbasin . . . I've been out to Little Oaks[5] and the Quarantine and have been walking in the gardens. Lots of orchestras playing and millions of girls. Yesterday I was sitting talking to one girl, one of the local nobility, in the Alferakis' garden. Pointing to an old woman she said: 'Just look at that shitty old thing! She even walks like a piece of shit.'

Some of the girls are quite pretty, but I decided to remain faithful to the Yashenkas. I've been studying local life. I've been to the post office, to the bathing spots, to Kasperovka . . . I've made a discovery. Taganrog has a Myasnitskaya Street.

There is a sign on the main street which says: 'Sintastic fruit drinks on sale here'. The stupid arsehole must have misheard 'synthetic' and written down 'sintastic' instead!

If I send you a wire to the dacha saying 'Tuesday local Alexey', it means that I'm arriving on Tuesday by the local train and please can you send Alexey to meet me. Of course it may not in fact be Tuesday, because I don't know which day or what time I shall get home and start work.

5. A literal translation of Dubki, a wooded area outside Taganrog whose oak trees were planted by Peter I, the city's founder, in the early eighteenth century.

I feel sick when I write. I have no money, and if I weren't such an expert at living off other people I really don't know what I would do. The scent of the acacias is all around. Lyudmila Pavlovna has grown very fat and looks like a Jewess. The mind that can plumb the depths of her mind has not yet been created. Listening to her, I am lost in wonder at the inscrutability of the fates that occasionally fashion such a rare pearl. She is a unique creation. Although I have not completely forgotten all the anatomy I ever learnt, when I contemplate her skull I begin to doubt the existence of such an organ as the brain.

Uncle is a delight, and just about the best person in the whole town.

A. Chekhov

I had a letter from Maria Vladimirovna.

45. To Nikolay Leikin, 14 May 1887, Taganrog

I received your letter today, my dear Nikolay Alexandrovich. It is so hot and stuffy that I hardly have strength to write, yet write I must because tomorrow, the 15th, I return to Moscow and by the evening of the 17th I shall already be in Voskresensk at the dacha. It follows that this letter must mark an interruption in our South–North correspondence, and I should like to conclude it by expressing my profound gratitude to you for the letters you have written to me, which gave me so much pleasure during my Kalmyk[1] life here.

When am I going to visit you on your estate? The answer is, when I gather enough strength to come to Piter, and this will happen as soon as I publish two or three stories for the Saturday supplement and accumulate 150–200 roubles or so. In any event I would certainly like to take up your kind invitation, and shall try to visit you no later than 10 June.

Please keep for me the noble scion of Apel and his whore Rogulka, so long as he's a male, not too ugly, and not the result of your mongrels

1. A Buddhist nomadic people who lived on the steppe.

having assisted Apel to shag Rogulka while she was on heat. I will come and collect him.

I am not long back from the Holy Mountains, where I found myself among about fifteen thousand pilgrims. I gained a mass of impressions and material and have no regrets at having spent a month and a half on the trip. The vile and horrible side of it all is that I am penniless; this poisons every pleasure. Tomorrow I shall be back on the road and shall arrive in Moscow without a copeck. I shall have to rush off and start borrowing money straight away, taking a little bit from everyone. You are no exception, and would infinitely oblige me by sending, as soon as you receive this letter, 40 roubles or so as a 'first consideration'; you can address it to me in Voskresensk and the moment I get there I will send you some stories while giving thanks to heaven above for granting me such a generous editor. I am as poor as a church mouse; while I was on my travels I wore out not just myself but my clothes, which are filthy and ragged, and I even managed to rip a hole in my crotch during a spot of how's your father.

Farewell, and give my regards to all your family.

Until we meet, soon I hope, your

A. Chekhov

Palmin never gives up, does he; he deserves to be exhibited at a medical convention as a rare example of a new disease: apartmentomania.

46. To Nikolay Leikin, 22 May 1887, Babkino

Hell's bells and a hundred devils, it's 3 degrees Réaumur!!!

Your anger, my dear Nikolay Alexandrovich, will have dissolved into invisible mist as soon as you return home to Ivanovskoye from Petersburg and find the letter I sent you the day I left Taganrog, which must have accompanied me on the mail train. What an astonishingly pitiless and hardhearted man you are! You scold me for wandering round the South and not writing for *Fragments* . . . Well, if I didn't write anything I was counting on your indulgence and on your understanding that a travelling man has no time for authorship. It's true I did write something for *The [Petersburg] Newspaper*, but that was under duress and most reluctantly, purely to spare my family the need to go out begging. What I wrote was disgusting, clumsy, an abomination to pen and paper. Had my family not been penniless, of course I wouldn't have written anything for that paper either. I did happily write a lot of letters, so this aspect of your complaint does not bear examination. Anyhow, may God forgive you! When the desire to travel seizes you or Bilibin I shall feel under obligation to change places with you, and settle the score for my almost two months of idleness.

Well, sir, we are having a pretty cold snap. The son of a bitch now writing to you is frozen to the marrow, and cannot wait for Palmin's phoebuses and zephyrs to quit their empyrean alehouse and come to warm up us poor dachniks. My dacha has no stoves; it has a kitchen, but no fireplace. Brrrr!! I am sitting in my autumn coat trying to produce a Saturday story, but my brains seem to be able to disgorge nothing but icicles.

I'm suffering from haemorrhoids. They are not purely the result of my sedentary life; their aetiology owes something also to excesses of Bacchus and Venus, heart trouble, ailments of the liver and the gut. My haemorrhoids are hereditary, that is to say my veins have inherited a tendency to swell. This means that I get ganglions not only *in recto* but on my shins, so that they look like ulcers. I think the problem with my legs comes partly from my not spending much time sitting down, but always walking about . . .

I hope you are in the best of health. I shall come at the beginning of June, when I earn the right to do so and when I have recovered from all my travelling. It may not cost much to go round Lake Ladoga, but getting to Piter isn't cheap. I hope you are no longer starving, and that you are not denying yourself a sociable glass of vodka from time to time.

I should very much like to see you so that I can tell you about my travels; I also want to see the Neva in her summer garb.

The doctors of the town of Taganrog send you their thanks for the newspaper cuttings about massage.

Greetings to Praskovia Nikiforovna and to Fedya, and likewise to yourself in the mirror.

Be well,

Your

A. Chekhov

47. To Yakov Korneyev, 9 September 1887, Moscow

Most long-suffering and merciful one! Thou who lovest the righteous and art merciful to sinners!

In place of rent for the apartment I am sending you a volume of my excrement. For the apartment – alas! – I shall pay what I owe in one hundred years' time (or before if I receive a remittance). Should you wish to dispute this, pray present your claim to an arbitrator.

Bankrupt A. Chekhov

48. To Georgy Chekhov, 17 October 1887, Moscow

Very many thanks, my dear cousin, for remembering me and not scolding me for my long silence. If you can imagine me in my study you will be able to understand why I do not write to you very often. I write the *whole* day long, so that it is even uncomfortable to hold a pen in my fingers. I have been meaning for some time now to reply to your last letter, but have been very busy recently. Here is some evidence to support this:

We have heard that A. P. Chekhov has written a comedy in four acts entitled *Ivanov*. The subject of the play is new. The first performance is planned to take place in Moscow.

Not only this, but I have had many urgent matters and business correspondence to attend to. The only relief I get is when I go to visit my patients. I don't go to the theatre, I don't visit friends, and have become such a stay-at-home that Mamasha and Aunt F[edosya] Y[akovlevna] have started calling me Grandpa. I'm longing for the summer so that I can start going out into the world again and have a holiday.

We have no news to report. We are getting on fine, everyone is well and we have plenty of everything we need. Your Uncle P[avel] E[gorovich] has aged a great deal, but is as cheerful and active as ever. He becomes mellower and kinder with each year that passes. He stays with Vanya in his state apartment; he has his own room there but spends the day and has his meals with us here.

My last book, which was published by Suvorin, is doing *splendidly*. I take great pride in doing better business than the Lobodas. I, dear cousin, have turned into a merchant! I sell newspaper articles, plays, books and medical consultations. I get at least a thousand roubles for a play; not long ago I sold the rights of fifteen or so shop-soiled old stories, which had all appeared in print before, for 150 roubles for a one-time publication. And so on. In short, business is booming.

Please continue writing to me at this address: The Korneyev House, Sadovaya-Kudrinskaya. What I should like to hear from you is:

1) What news is there?
2) How is the health of my uncle and aunt. How is Uncle's ear?
3) Where is Volodya?

Sanya and Pecheritsa should not imagine that I have forgotten about them. I have the clearest recollection of the way they tried to attack me in the summer. I am sending my photograph, which I would be grateful if you could give to them.

Would you please let me know Anisim Vasiliyevich's address?

Did I by mistake leave a book behind at your house: Bezhetsky's[1] *In the Land of Mantillas and Castanets*? If I did, would you please send it to me when you have a chance? I seem to have left books scattered all over the place.

Please tell your father that I should be very pleased to have a letter

---

1. The pseudonym of Alexey Maslov (1852–?), a writer, lieutenant-general and a teacher at the Engineers' Academy. A military correspondent for *New Times* during the Russo-Turkish War, he met Chekhov in 1886.

from him. I value his friendship very highly. Give my best greetings to everyone, I wish all of you health, success in your work and studies, and don't forget me.

I published a description of the Holy Mountains in *New Times*. One young man, the nephew of a bishop, told me that he had seen three bishops reading my description: one was reading aloud, the other two were listening. They liked it, so I presume it was appreciated in the Holy Mountains as well. Thanks to the Holy Mountains I earned myself 100 roubles. I also described the steppe, and this also went down very well, especially in Petersburg. Farewell. I look forward to your letter.

Your

A. Chekhov

Concerning Father Bandakov's[2] sermons I will make inquiries with Suvorin when I get to Petersburg, and then immediately pass on the information to your father.

Tell your mama I have not forgotten about the seeds. I will send them, but only on condition that Sanya manages the garden according to the highest rules of art. The seeds can be sown not only in the front garden but all along the fence.

49. To Alexander Chekhov, 20 November 1887, Moscow

Well, the first night of the play [*Ivanov*] is over . . . I'll tell you everything as it happened. First of all: Korsh promised me ten rehearsals, but actually allowed me four, of which only two could properly be described as rehearsals, since the other two were more like tournaments for the actors to hone their skills in verbal disputation and invective. The only two members of the cast who knew their lines

2. Father Vasily Bandakov (1807–90) was a priest based in Taganrog who achieved national renown for his pithy, down-to-earth sermons, which were collected together and published in numerous volumes. He was a good friend of the Chekhov family.

were Davydov and Glama; all the others trusted to the prompter and their own inner convictions.

Act One   I am backstage in a small box like a police cell. The family sits shivering with nerves in a box in the dress circle. Against my own expectations I am calm, not suffering from nerves. But the actors are very nervous, crossing themselves in apprehension. Curtain. Entry of the star, whose benefit evening this is. His lack of authority, complete ignorance of his part and the presentation to him on stage of a wreath all combine to render my play unrecognizable. Kiselyovsky, on whom I had placed great hopes, did not speak a single one of his lines correctly. Literally, *not one*. He made everything up. Despite this and the inadequacy of the direction, the first act was a great success. Lots of curtain calls.

Act Two   The stage is full of people. Guests. Nobody knows his lines, everything is mixed up, everyone speaks gibberish. Each word feels like a knife wound in my back. But – oh, my Muse! – this act is a success too. We all take a curtain call. Congratulations all round.

Act Three   The acting is all right. Huge success. I am called out three times, and while I am taking my bows Davydov grasps my hand and Glama, in true Manilovesque[1] style, presses my other hand to her heart. A triumph of talent and virtue.

Act Four, Scene One   It goes all right. Curtain calls. But then there is a long and tiring interval. The audience grumbles, unused to having to leave their seats and go to the buffet between scenes. The curtain rises. It's beautiful: through an arch is seen a table laid out with food for a wedding. Flourishes of music. On come the bridegroom's friends: they are supposed to be drunk, so they have to fool about in an obvious sort of way and act the goat, which they do in a fashion that appals me: circus tricks and taproom horseplay. Then on comes Kiselyovsky: his scene is heartstoppingly poetic, but my Kiselyovsky doesn't know his lines and is as drunk as a cobbler, so what was intended to be spare, poetic dialogue turns into something vile, leaden and incomprehensible to the audience. At the end of the play the hero dies because he cannot endure the insult he has been offered. The public, by now

1. Manilov, an excessively vapid and ingratiating character in Gogol's *Dead Souls* (1842).

thoroughly tired and disgruntled, did not understand this death, which the cast had insisted upon (I have an alternative version). The company and I take our curtain calls; booing could clearly be heard during some of them, although it was drowned out by the applause and the foot-stamping.

All in all, I feel exhausted and depressed. It was a horrible experience, even though the play was definitely a success (Kicheyev and Co. disagree). My theatrical friends say they have never seen such a fracas, such a mélange of applause and catcalls, and never have there been such fierce arguments as now rage over my play. There has never been an author who has taken a second act curtain call at Korsh's theatre.

The next performance of the play is on the 23rd. It will have my alternative ending and some other changes – I shall dispense with the bridegroom's friends.

More details when we meet,

Your

A. Chekhov

Please tell Burenin that now the play has opened I am back in the groove, and settling down to my Saturday contributions.

50. To Alexander Chekhov, 24 November 1887, Moscow

Well, dearest Gusev,[1] the fuss has died down and all the anxieties dispelled, so that once again I am sitting at my desk peacefully writing stories. You cannot imagine what has been going on. From an insignificant piece of shit, my little play (I've sent a copy to Maslov) has turned into God knows what. I've already written to you about how there was such a commotion in the audience at the first performance that the prompter – who has worked in the theatre for thirty-two years – had never seen anything like it in his life. They roared and shouted, clapped and hissed; there was nearly a punch-up in the bar,

1. One of Chekhov's many nicknames for his brother – and later the title of a story.

students in the gallery wanted to chuck someone out and two of them got themselves ejected by the police. The whole place was in an uproar. Our sister almost fainted. Dyukovsky got palpitations and ran out, and Kiselyov for some reason buried his head in his hands and called out an anguished 'What am I going to do now?'.

The cast was very tense. Naturally, nothing I wrote to you or to Maslov about their performance and their attitude to my work must go any further. There were reasons for what happened . . . Apparently the leading lady's daughter was seriously ill and at death's door, and how can anyone give a convincing performance in a situation like that? Kurepin[2] was quite right to praise the cast.

The day after the first night there was a review by Pyotr Kicheyev in *The Moscow Gazette* which described my play as an insolently cynical, immoral pile of rubbish. *The Moscow News* liked it.

The second performance went pretty well, although not without a few surprises. An understudy took over (with no rehearsal) from the actress with the sick daughter. We got curtain calls after Act Three (twice) and Act Four, but there was no more hissing.

That's about it. My *Ivanov* will have another performance on Wednesday. Everyone has calmed down now and returned to their accustomed ways. We have circled the date of 19 November in our diaries and will celebrate it every year with a drink, because it will be a long time before the family forgets this day.

I'm not going to write to you any more about the play. If you want to find out what it's about, ask Maslov to give you his copy and read it. Reading the play won't give you any indication as to why there was such a fuss; you won't find anything out of the ordinary in it . . . Nikolay, Shekhtel and Levitan – that is to say the artists – insist that on stage it is so original that it is a strange experience to watch, but you can't tell that from reading it.

NB If you come across anyone in *New Times* proposing to criticize the actors who took part in my play, please ask them not to. They were splendid in the second performance.

2. Alexander Kurepin (1847–91), a Moscow journalist who edited *The Alarm Clock*, 1882–3.

Well sir, in a few days I shall be going to Piter, and will try to make it there by 1 December. Whatever happens we shall celebrate your eldest chick's name day together ... You'd better warn him there won't be a cake.

Congratulations on your promotion. If you really are the secretary now, could you insert a notice to the effect that '*Ivanov* received its second performance at Korsh's Theatre on 23 November. The cast, especially Davydov, Kiselyovsky, Gradov-Sokolov and Kosheva, were invited to take numerous curtain calls. The author was called for at the conclusion of the third and fourth acts.' Something along those lines ... With a notice like that, the play will get another performance and I shall get an extra 50–100 roubles. But if it's a problem to do this, don't bother ...

What is amiss with Anna Pavlovna? Allah Kerim! Obviously the Petersburg climate doesn't agree with her.

I received the 40 roubles, thank you.

Are you fed up with me? I feel like I've been behaving like a psychopath all month.

Giliai is going to Piter today.

Be well, and forgive me my psychopathy. It's over; I'm back to normal now. Our little sis, whose own psychopathy throughout the month of November has approached near-hysteria levels, is also herself again.

I wrote to Maslov thanking him for his telegram.

Your

Schiller Shakespearovich Goethe

51. To Chekhov Family, 3 December 1887, St Petersburg

Gracious gents and ladies!

I am writing to you from the offices of *Fragments*, where I am awaiting Golike,[1] with whom I am due to have lunch. I'm staying

1. Roman Golike (1849–?), the owner of the printing firm which published *Fragments*.

with Alexander. The dirt, the stink, the crying, the lies – a week there is enough to drive a man out of his mind and make him as dirty as a cook's dishtowel.

Nevertheless, Piter is wonderful. I'm in seventh heaven. The streets, the cabs, the food, everything is excellent and there is no end to the intelligent and decent people here. I meet new people every day. Yesterday, for example, I spent from half past ten in the morning to three o'clock with Mikhailovsky (who criticized me in *The Northern Herald*), Gleb Uspensky[2] and Korolenko: we ate, drank and chatted together in the friendliest manner. I see Suvorin, Burenin and others like them every day. All of them vie with one another to ply me with invitations and praise me to the skies. They are all in raptures over my play, although they think I ought to have taken more care over it. The only copy I have goes from hand to hand, and I can't get hold of it in order to submit it to the censor.

Suvorin is peeved that I let Korsh have the play. He doesn't think that either Korsh's company or the Moscow public understood *Ivanov*. The Moscow reviews have caused much amusement here. Everyone is waiting for me to stage the play in Piter, and is confident of success, but after Moscow I have become so disenchanted with my play I can't make myself even think about it; I am seized by a mixture of inertia and revulsion. As soon as I call to mind the horrible mess those shits of Korsh's made of *Ivanov*, the way they mangled the words and wrecked the sense, I feel nauseated and start feeling sorry for the poor audiences who had to leave the theatre empty-handed. I feel sorry for myself and for Davydov.

Suvorin is very excited by my play. Isn't it amazing: no one who saw the Korsh production came away with any conception of Ivanov's character, I heard nothing but criticism and complaints, but here there is universal agreement that Ivanov is a perfectly well-drawn character and needs nothing added or taken away from him.

Anna Arkadievna has grown very pretty. I'll bring back a photo-

2. Gleb Uspensky (1843–1902), a dedicated populist writer and son of a government official from Tula, the author of essays and stories about rural life.

graph of her for Ivan. Wouldn't he like a wife? She would be very suitable.

Alexander is well established among his *New Times* colleagues, and gets on well with them. His children are well, but don't utter a word.

I dined with Leikin yesterday and spent the night at his house. I ate my fill, had a wonderful sleep and a break from the dirt!

The December issue of *The Herald of Europe* has a big article about me.

I've put on weight over the past three days. How I wish I could live here all the time! When I think that I have to go back to a Moscow teeming with Gavrilovs and Kicheyevs, I feel quite ill.

I've met quite a few ladies, some of whom have invited me to call on them. I'll go, although their words of praise all carry overtones of that 'psychopathy' Burenin wrote about.

I shall bring a whole load of books back with me.

I don't think Korsh will put on any more performances of my play now. Some idiot at *New Times*, who had overheard but not understood a conversation I was having with Suvorin, wrote such a rude piece in the paper about Korsh's company that I kicked up a great fuss. Suvorin called the idiot an 'unprincipled scoundrel' and Korsh, I imagine, fainted from shock. The fool had hoped to curry favour with me, but the upshot was a disaster. If Korsh does decide to drop it from the repertoire, so much the better. Why should I go on covering myself with shame? To hell with all of them!

I'm writing. Did Misha get the parcel? Golike has arrived; I must go to lunch.

Greetings to all. I'll send some money, not much but as often as I can.

When I go to visit Bilibin, his wife refuses to come out and meet me.

I wish everyone good health and a happy disposition. Anything you may have heard from Korneyev about a slap in the face for Petersburg University is complete rubbish. There are a lot of lies in the world.

A. Chekhov

52. *To Dmitry Grigorovich, 12 January 1888, Moscow*

St Tatyana's Day (Anniversary of the University)
I shall not attempt to tell you, dear Dmitry Vasiliyevich, how important and precious to me was your last wonderful letter. I confess that I was unable to restrain myself from making a copy and sending it to Korolenko, who is, by the way, a most admirable person. Your letter did not make me too ashamed, since it caught me at work on something for a thick journal. Here then is my response to the essential part of your letter: I have made a start on a substantial work. I have completed slightly more than thirty pages, and anticipate adding to them another sixty or so. The subject I have chosen for my thick journal debut, one that has not been written about for a very long time, is the steppe.[1] I depict the plain, the lilac horizon, the sheep farmers, the Jews, the priests, thunderstorms at night, the birds of the steppe, and so on. Each individual chapter contains a separate story, linked, like the five figures in a quadrille, by characters who have a close relationship to one another. My aim is to give the chapters a common feeling, a common smell; this is helped by the device of having one character thread his way through all of them. I feel that in much of it I have been successful; there are passages where you can really smell the hay, although overall some of it has come out rather strange and perhaps rather too original. I do have a tendency to go to extremes; this comes from my lack of experience at writing at length, and from my constant and ingrained fear of writing too much. As a result my pages turn out so laconic as to appear positively compressed; impressions pile up one against another in a great heap; unbroken chains of scenes, or flashes of illumination as you call them, jostle one after another so much that it becomes tiring to the reader. Thus the general effect is less a complete picture than a dry, detailed catalogue of discrete impressions, something like a synopsis. Instead of a unified artistic representation of the steppe, what I offer the reader is an 'encyclopaedia of the steppe'. Well, practice makes perfect. In any case I am not daunted. Even encyclopaedias have their

---

1. 'The Steppe' was published in March 1888 in *The Northern Herald*.

uses. This one may open people's eyes and show them what riches, what realms of beauty lie still untapped and how much room there still is for the Russian artist to breathe. If my little story serves to remind my colleagues about the steppe, which they have forgotten, if just one of my dry, roughly sketched themes gives a poet somewhere cause for thought, I will be happy. You, I know, will understand my steppe and will forgive my unintended transgressions. And they really are unintended for the simple reason that, as must now be apparent, I still *do not know how* to write at length.

In the summer I shall resume my unfinished novel. It embraces an entire district (from the point of view of both landowner and the *zemstvo*), and the daily lives of several families. 'The Steppe' as a theme is somewhat exclusive and specific; its pastoral monotony becomes wearing as soon as it stops being purely a background and becomes a subject in and of itself. My novel will deal with people, ordinary men and women, members of the intelligentsia; love, marriage, children – the setting has the comfort of familiarity, and therefore will not be tiring to read about.

The suicide of a seventeen-year-old boy is a grand subject and a tempting one, but the prospect of taking it on is certainly daunting! An event that has caused such universal anguish calls for a response of equally anguished power, but do any of our writers have the necessary inner depth? No. You believe that such a theme would bring results, but you are basing this judgement on yourself; your generation, after all, has not only talent but erudition, training, phosphorus and iron. Talented people of our generation, however, lack anything of the kind, and, to be honest, it is all to the good that they avoid serious issues. If you were to suggest your young man to them, I feel sure that X would, with the best of intentions, descend to libel, slander and blasphemy, Y would contrive to insert some trivial, feeble piece of political special pleading, and Z would explain away suicide in terms of psychosis. Your boy is an innocent, kind creature, seeking God, a loving, delicately sensitive soul that has suffered deep wounds. To capture such a character one has to be able to suffer oneself, but our modern bards can do nothing but whine and snivel. As for me, as well as all the above, I am lazy and supine.

V. N. Davydov came to see me a few days ago. He acted in my play *Ivanov*, and that was how we became friends. When he realized that I was on the point of writing to you, he became very animated, sat down at the table and wrote a letter to you himself, which I am enclosing.

Do you read Korolenko and Shcheglov? The latter is much talked about. I think he has talent and originality. Korolenko continues to be the darling of the public and the critics; his book is selling famously. Among poets, the one who is beginning to stand out from the crowd is Fofanov.[2] He is truly gifted, but the others are pretty worthless as artists. The prose writers are not bad, but the poets are really very feeble. The public is uneducated and ignorant, its outlook on the world so blinkered as to be almost non-existent. Koltsov the cattle-dealer may not have been particularly well-versed in grammar, but he had far more integrity, wisdom and real culture than all our young poets of today put together.[3]

My 'Steppe' is to be published in *The Northern Herald*. I will write to Pleshcheyev and ask him to make sure you are sent an offprint.

I am so glad that you are now experiencing less pain. This was the main problem with your health; the rest is less important. Your cough is not a serious matter; it had nothing to do with your malady. I am sure it was just the result of a cold and will disappear when the weather gets warmer. Today is the day on which we drink copious toasts to the health of those men who instructed me in the art of cutting up corpses and writing out prescriptions. I am sure your health also will be drunk, because we never let an anniversary pass without drinking a celebratory toast to Turgenev, to Tolstoy and to you. The writers drink to Chernyshevsky, Saltykov-Shchedrin and Gleb Uspensky, while the lay public (students, doctors, mathematicians and the like), to which as a disciple of Aesculapius I belong, still keeps to the old traditions and resists any substitution for the names of the heroes it grew up with. I am sure that so long as Russia still has forests, ravines

2. Konstantin Fofanov (1862–1911), a poet whom Chekhov met when they both contributed to *Fragments*.
3. Alexey Koltsov (1809–42), from an uneducated background, combined cattle-dealing with writing poetry.

and summer, so long as the song of the sandpiper and the lapwing is heard in the land, neither you nor Turgenev nor Tolstoy will be forgotten, any more than Gogol will be forgotten. Even if the very people on whom your characters are based become extinct and are forgotten, you yourself will remain whole and undamaged. That is your strength, and consequently our joy.

Forgive me for wearying you with such a long letter, but my hand ran on of its own accord, and I wanted to talk to you for longer.

I hope this letter reaches you in warmth, good spirits and good health. Come to Russia in the summer: Crimea is said to be as good as Nice.

Thank you again for your letter. I send you my best wishes and remain your most sincerely devoted

A. Chekhov

53. To Yakov Polonsky, 18 January 1888, Moscow

For several days, dear Yakov Petrovich, I have been pondering how best to reply to your letter, but nothing worthy or apposite has come to mind, and I have therefore come to the conclusion that I have yet to learn the proper way of responding to letters as good and generous as yours. It was an unexpected New Year's gift for me, and if you can think back to your own past when you were starting out on the road, then you will understand how much it has meant to me.

I feel ashamed at not having written to you first. The fact is that I have long wanted to, but was too diffident and cowardly to do so. I did not think that our conversation, close though it brought me to you, gave me the right to such an honour as correspondence with you yet. Forgive me for such pusillanimity and meanness of spirit.

I have received your book and your photograph. Your portrait already hangs above my desk, and the whole family has been reading your prose. What makes you say that your prose is encrusted in moss and hoarfrost? If the reason is that the public nowadays reads nothing except newspapers, it is very far from justifying such a cold, autumnal judgement. I had no misgivings at all when I embarked on reading your prose – or rather, I was firmly biased in favour. The fact is that long ago, when I was studying the history of literature, one truth was so perfectly clear to me that it amounted practically to a law: all the great Russian poets have been magnificent prose writers. Hammer and nails will never be able to drive this predisposition from my head, and it was most certainly present during those evenings when I was reading your prose. Perhaps I am wrong, but in my opinion Lermontov's 'Taman' and Pushkin's 'The Captain's Daughter', and the prose of other poets as well, prove the affinity between the richness of Russian verse and the refinement of the best prose.

To your desire to dedicate a poem to me I can reply only with a deep bow and a request to be allowed to dedicate to you in the future a story which I shall write with particular love. Your kindness has touched me and I shall never forget it. In addition to the warmth and inner delight any dedication from a writer brings, your 'At the Door' holds a special value for me: it deserves to be lauded in an entire article from the pen of a recognized authority, because it means that in the eyes of the public I shall now have two yards added to my stature.

Concerning working for newspapers and illustrated magazines, I completely agree with you.

Isn't it the same whether a nightingale sings in a big tree or a bush? The requirement that talented people should *only* publish in thick journals is small-minded, smacks of servility and is harmful like all prejudices. This prejudice is stupid and ridiculous. There was a point to it when the publications were headed by people with clearly defined physiognomies, such as Belinsky,[1] Herzen[2] and so on, who not only paid a fee, but drew people to them, taught and educated them, but now when we have some very dreary stiff-collared people with dogcollars running these publications, allegiance to thick journals won't stand up to criticism, and the difference between a thick journal and a cheap newspaper is only quantitative, that is to say, from the

1. Vissarion Belinsky (1811–48), a famous nineteenth-century literary critic.
2. Alexander Herzen (1812–70), a writer, journalist, author of an important memoir, *My Past and Thoughts* (1868), and a novel, *Who is to Blame?* (1847).

point of view of an artist, it is not worthy of respect or attention. There is one convenient aspect to writing for a thick journal, though: a long piece won't get chopped up and is printed whole. When I write a long story, I will send it to a thick journal, and the small ones I will publish wherever the wind and my will want to take them.

Incidentally, I am at the moment writing a long piece that will probably appear in *The Northern Herald*. It's a small novella in which I depict the steppe, the people of the steppe, the birds, the nights, and so on. I am enjoying the writing of it, but because I am so unused to writing at length, I sometimes worry about getting tired, not managing to say quite what I want to, and not being serious enough. There are many passages which will not be understood by either the critics or the public; both will find them trivial and unworthy of attention, but I rejoice in advance that precisely these pieces will mean something to, and be appreciated by, two or three literary gastronomes, and that is enough for me. In general, I am not happy with my story. It strikes me as unwieldy, boring and too narrowly focused. A subject like the steppe, its nature and its people, is bound to appear narrow and irrelevant to today's reading public.

I shall probably be coming to Petersburg at the beginning of March to bid farewell to some dear friends and set out for the Kuban. I plan to spend April and May in the Kuban and around the Black Sea, and the summer in Slavyansk or on the Volga. In the summertime I can never stay put in one place.

Allow me to thank you once again for your letter and for the dedication. I deserved neither. I wish you health and happiness, and please believe in the sincere admiration and love of your devoted

A. Chekhov

PS A few days ago I returned from the country. Even in winter the countryside is wonderful. If only you could see the blinding white of the fields and the woods with the sun shining on them! It is so bright it hurts the eyes. I found myself having to do a postmortem on a cow that had suddenly died. Even though I am a doctor, not a vet, I sometimes have to turn my hand to veterinary work if there is no specialist around.

54. To Alexey Pleshcheyev, 3 February 1888, Moscow

Greetings, dear Alexey Nikolayevich,

'The Steppe' is finished and is ready to send off. When I began it there was not so much as half a copeck's worth, now suddenly it's getting on for a rouble. I started off intending to write between thirty and forty pages and ended up with nearer to eighty. The effort and strain of writing at such unfamiliar length has quite tired me out; I found it very hard going, and feel I have written a whole lot of nonsense.

Please be indulgent!!

The actual subject of 'The Steppe' is not important. If the story has even a moderate success, I shall use it as the basis of a major novella and expand it with a sequel. You won't find any characters that require close attention or need filling out.

All the time I was writing it I felt as if I were surrounded by the smell of summer and the steppe. It would be marvellous to go there!

I appeal to you, my dear friend, not to stand on ceremony and to tell me, should this truly be the case, that my story is meretricious and commonplace. I desperately want to know the unvarnished truth.

If the editorial board considers it acceptable for *The Herald*, I am happy to oblige it and its readers. Please do your utmost to ensure that it appears complete in one issue, because – as you will agree when you read it – it cannot be cut. Please ask them to keep some offprints for me; I should like to send some to Grigorovich and to Ostrovsky[1] ... We have already talked about the advance payment. I will only add that the earlier I can have it the better, because I am as down and out as the flea in Veinberg's[2] comic sketch. If the publisher[3] asks you what the fee should be, tell her that I am in her hands and, sinner that

1. Pyotr Ostrovsky (1839–1906), literary critic and brother of the dramatist Alexander Ostrovsky (1823–86), whose works included *The Storm* (1860) and *The Forest* (1875).
2. Pavel Veinberg (1846–1904) performed in variety shows.
3. Antonina Sabashnikova, publisher of *The Northern Herald* from 1885 to 1888.

I am, have been dreaming in the depths of my heart of 200 per printer's sheet.

Please excuse my troubling you. Perhaps one day, if we both should live, fate will afford me the happy chance of doing you a service in return.

'The Steppe' is written in separate exercise books. Please cut the binding thread when you receive the package.

Farewell, and may good fortune be yours.

I am having a rest now. Tomorrow I shall hurry to Ostrovsky. Give my greetings to your family and to Shcheglov.

Your cordially devoted debutant

Antoine Chekhov

My 'Steppe' is more like a steppe encyclopaedia than a short story.

55. *To Alexey Pleshcheyev, 9 February 1888, Moscow*

I've just had 500 roubles delivered to me from Junker's[1] office, dear Alexey Nikolayevich! They must be from *The Northern Herald*, as there is nowhere else they could have come from. Merci!

Your last letter overjoyed and encouraged me beyond words. I would happily give up drinking wine and smoking for the rest of my life to receive such letters. The previous one, however, which I answered by telegram, somewhat disheartened me. I felt awkward and guilty that I had to trouble you by raising the question of the fee. I am very badly in need of money, yet I detest talking about it, especially with people as good as yourself. Anyhow, the devil take it! I am sorry that in the part of the letter where I said I was dreaming of getting 200 roubles, I did not express myself clearly. There has never been any question of my making demands or putting inflexible conditions, still less an ultimatum. My parenthetical hint about 200 roubles arose from my complete unfamiliarity with the fees paid by thick journals, and because 200 roubles did not seem to me too inflated a figure. I based it on the benchmark of *New Times*, by which I mean that when

1. A banking firm.

I was calculating a fee for 'The Steppe' I was aiming at earning no less and no more than I would have got from Suvorin, who pays me 15 copecks a line. But it never crossed my mind to issue an ultimatum. I always accept what I am offered: if *The Northern Herald* gives me 500 a printer's sheet, I'll take it, if 50, I'll take that too.

In return for the promise to publish 'The Steppe' in full and to send me regular copies of the journal, I promise you the most excellent Don wine when we go down the Volga in summer. It is sad that Korolenko does not drink, because not to be able to drink when travelling, when the moon is shining and the crocodiles are peeping at you from the water, is as inconvenient a deprivation as not being able to read. Wine and music have always acted on me like a natural corkscrew. Whenever I'm on the road and feel my heart or my mind blocked up, all I have to do is drink a glass of wine, the cork flies out and I take wing again.

Korolenko will, in fact, be with me tomorrow. He is a good soul. It is a great pity that his 'On the Way' was plucked bare by the censor's office; it ('On the Way' I mean, not the censor's office) is an artistic but notably outspoken piece of work. Why on earth did he submit it to a journal that is subject to the censor? And why did he call it a Christmas tale?

I am hastening now to buckle down and produce some smaller things, but find it hard to control my urge to write something big. Ah, if you only knew what a theme for a novel is sitting in my grey matter at the moment! What wonderful women! What funerals, what weddings! If only I had the money, I would take myself off to the Crimea, sit under the cypress trees and write my novel in a month or two. I have already completed three printer's sheets of it, can you imagine! Actually, what I am saying is not entirely true: if I did have any money I would be in such a spin that all thoughts of novels would fly upside down out of the window.

When I have finished the first part of the novel I shall, with your permission, send it to you to read through, but I shall not send it to *The Northern Herald* as it won't be suitable for a censor-subject journal. I am greedy, and enjoy peopling my work with a host of characters, so my novel will be a long one. Also, I get fond of the people I invent, and one likes to spend time with those to whom one is partial.

As for Egorushka,[2] I do intend to continue him, but not just now. Silly old Father Khristofor has already passed away. Mme Branitskaya is living in terrible conditions. Varlamov is still whirling around. You wrote that you liked the idea of Dymov . . . Life has a way of throwing up mischievous natures such as Dymov's, not to be dissenters or tramps nor to settle for a peaceful existence, but to be full-blown revolutionaries . . . But there will never be revolution in Russia, and Dymov will end up drinking himself to death or in gaol. He is a superfluous man.[3]

Once, in 1877, when I was travelling, I contracted peritonitis, and spent a night of agony in a coaching inn belonging to one Moisey Moiseyich. The Jew spent the whole night without a break giving me mustard poultices and compresses.

Have you ever seen the high road across the steppe? That's where we should go! The crosses are all still there, but the wide open spaces are already not as they were, and now the railway has been laid to bring us closer together; hardly anyone travels by road; little by little the grass will grow up and in ten years' time the road itself will have disappeared or have transformed itself from a giant into an ordinary thoroughfare.

It would be a good idea to take Shcheglov along with us. He has turned completely sour and views his literary future through smoked glass. He needs to breathe some fresh air and see some new faces.

Tomorrow I am going to enjoy myself at the wedding of a tailor who is a rather good writer of verse and who, in honour of my talent (*honoris causa*), mended my jacket.

I have bored you enough with my prattle, and therefore will close. Good health to you, and may all your creditors be heartily damned . . . An importunate tribe, worse than mosquitoes.

Cordially yours

A. Chekhov

Doesn't *The Northern Herald* usually send proofs to authors?

2. The main character of 'The Steppe', a nine-year-old boy.

3. A character in Russian fiction, a prime example of whom is Lermontov's Pechorin (*A Hero of Our Time*, 1837–40), who sees himself as disillusioned and at odds with society.

56. To Nikolay Khlopov, 13 February 1888, Moscow

Dear Nikolay Afanasievich,

I have read through your story; it is good and will probably be published, so I believe it is worth my passing on to you the following as soon as possible. But if you count on it as a serious step forward and are going to make your debut with it, I do not believe it will be successful. The reason lies not in the subject or its execution, but in some little things that can be corrected – a carelessness, typical of Moscow writers, in polishing phrases, and some details which are not very important in themselves but which offend the eye.

Let us begin with some intrusive phrases that weigh as heavy as cobblestones. For example, on page 2 there is a phrase: 'he twice came to see me for a duration of half an hour'. Or 'on Iona's lips there suddenly appeared a slow, somewhat embarrassed, smile'. Just as you cannot say 'the rain began to pour down in a lengthy manner', I think you will agree that it is inappropriate to talk about a slow smile 'suddenly appearing'. However, these are minor points ... This one is more significant: where did you derive your model for the churchwarden Sidorkin? Naturally such people as churchwardens and elders do exist, but no churchwarden or elder, not even a merchant of unchallenged power and influence, would have the right to move a sexton from one position to another ... Only a bishop can do that. It would be more plausible if Iona were to be simply transferred from the town to the country for drunkenness.

The passage in which Iona savours his five acres like a spider with a fly is excellent, but what made you spoil his pleasure by describing his unlikely and unconvincing efforts with the plough? Was this really necessary? You surely know that anyone who tries his hand at ploughing the first time in his life won't manage to get the plough going at all – that's the first thing. Secondly, surely it would have been more profitable for the sexton to rent out his land to grow corn? Number three, you can't teach an old dog new tricks ...

'I sit up on the crossbeam that connects the house with the store-room' – page 16. What is this crossbeam? The character of the clerk with his jacket and bits of straw in his hair is the kind of stereotyped cliché you find in the comic papers. Clerks are more intelligent and more unhappy than is commonly believed. And so on.

At the end of the story the sexton (I like this, it is very *à propos*) sings 'Bless, my soul, the Lord, and lift up your heart . . .' There is no such prayer. There is one, however, that goes 'Bless, my soul, the Lord, and with all my heart His holy name . . .'

My last observation: you have a habit of scattering punctuation marks, which should serve as guideposts to the reader, like buttons on the uniform of one of Gogol's municipal mayors. There are too many dots and not enough full stops.

In my opinion these minor details spoil the music of your writing. If it were not for them, your story would be exemplary. I trust you will not take my 'moralizing' amiss and will understand that I write as your trusted confidant and with a purpose: bearing in mind what I have said, don't you think it would be a good idea to make some revisions to the story? It should not take you more than a couple of hours to polish and rewrite it, and I believe it will not suffer for it.

I repeat: even without any revision 'Iona' is good and will be published, but if you are determined to make a serious debut with it, from my experience of the Petersburg critics, it will not succeed as it is.

I await your response and ask your pardon for my unasked-for interference.

I wish you good health,

Your

A. Chekhov

57. To Mikhail Chekhov, 14 March 1888, St Petersburg

I'm writing from the *New Times* offices. Leskov has just come into the room. If he doesn't interrupt, I'll be able to finish the letter.

I got here safely, but had a wretched journey thanks to Leikin, who never stopped talking. He prevented me from reading, eating and sleeping . . . The little shit kept boasting and pestering me with questions the whole time; I would just be nodding off when he would poke me and ask: 'Did you know my "Bride of Christ" has now appeared in Italian translation?'

I have been staying at the Moskva, but today I am moving to the *New Times* place, where Mme Suvorina has offered me two rooms with a grand piano and a couch in the alcove. I expect I shall find that staying with the Suvorins cramps my style somewhat.

I gave the biscuits to Alexander. His family is in good health, well-fed, well and cleanly dressed. He is not drinking at all, which was quite a surprise to me.

It's snowing, and very cold. Wherever I go the talk is of my 'Steppe'. I've been to see Pleshcheyev, Shcheglov and some other people, and this evening I am going to see Polonsky.

I've moved to my new lodgings. Grand piano, harmonium, luxuriously upholstered couch, Vasily the valet, bed, fireplace, marvellous writing desk – these are the good things. As for the less good things, they are legion. To begin with, I can't possibly come home tipsy and with female company . . .

Before lunch – a long conversation with Mme Suvorina on how much she loathes the human race, followed by how she bought a jacket today for 120 roubles.

After lunch we talk about migraine, and the children never take their eyes off me because they are waiting for me to say something incredibly clever. They think I am a genius because I wrote 'Kashtanka'.[1] One of the Suvorins' dogs is called 'Fyodor Timofeyich', another 'Auntie' and a third 'Ivan Ivanych'.[2]

Between lunch and tea I pace from corner to corner of Suvorin's study while we philosophize, his wife butting in with inopportune comments from time to time in a deep bass voice or pretending to bark like a dog.

Tea. A conversation about medicine over tea. When I am finally released I sit in my study out of earshot of any voices. Tomorrow I

1. Chekhov's story about a dog which ends up performing in a circus.
2. The Suvorins' dogs were named after other animal characters in 'Kashtanka'.

shall make my escape for the whole day: I shall go to see Pleshcheyev, to Sabashnikova's *Herald*, to Polonsky's, to Palkin,[3] and shall not return until late at night, with my feet worn down to the ankles. Incidentally, I have a W.C. all to myself and a separate street entrance – without these I should simply want to curl up and die. My valet Vasily is better dressed than I am and the possessor of a noble countenance. It feels peculiar to have him tiptoeing reverently about trying to anticipate my every wish.

All in all, being a writer has its problems.

I should like to go to sleep, but my hosts don't retire before three o'clock in the morning. Supper isn't served here, but I'm too lazy to go to Palkin.

I have the honour to send you my respects. Regards to everyone.

Votre à tous

A. Chekhov

I'm too lazy to write, and I'm not left in peace anyhow.

Night. I can hear the click of billiard balls: Gey[4] is playing with my Vasily. When I go to bed I find a glass of milk and some bread beside it; I find I'm hungry. When I lie down I read the *Dragonfly* tear-off calendar.

This is the sum of my great and brilliant achievements on arrival in Petersburg.

58. To Alexey Pleshcheyev, 25 April 1888, Moscow

Christ is risen, my dear future guest! Best wishes for the festival and may all good fortune befall you.

Yesterday I received a letter from my brother, who went at my request to inspect the dacha we have rented. He writes that the

3. Palkin was a popular restaurant on Nevsky Prospekt earlier patronized by Dostoyevsky, who lived nearby.
4. Bogdan Geyman, the journalist in charge of the foreign section in *New Times* from 1876.

countryside is wonderful, the river wider and deeper than the Moscow river, the garden old, even ancient, and neglected. There is a yard with a dirty pond in it that never dries out, two emancipated young ladies, and so on. There are no conveniences whatsoever. The luxury you feared finding there is, even in its most rudimentary form, non-existent. The front porch has collapsed and the whole estate is a far from picturesque ruin. According to the letter, the furniture is absolutely dreadful . . . Well then, such is the cosy nest into which I am trying to entice you! But however bad it is, I think it must be healthier and more spacious than the Petersburg tundra. You must *definitely* come.

You have been worrying that we will allocate you the best room . . . well, there are no best rooms in our dacha, all of them are worst rooms . . . All you'll get is a bed and a chair . . . Oh all right, I suppose we might be generous and allow you a table, but don't expect a card table, it will be something wobbly on three legs . . . On the other hand, we shall eat, drink and be merry with superb and shameless abandon.

Like *la belle Hélène*,[1] my little story can now cry 'I'm ready! I'm ready!' I've finished it and will send it off tomorrow. It's as dry as the Solvichegodsky District Statistical Review.

There are pike-perch and carp in the River Psyol – what a pity you are not a fisherman! Catching pike is a higher and sweeter pleasure than making love!

Don't forget to send a wire from Kursk.

You leave Moscow at three o'clock in the afternoon and will arrive in Kursk at 11.30 the next morning. You will get to Vorozhba at eight o'clock (you have to change there) and to Sumy at 11.30 at night, so that you will be at the dacha by midnight.

Best wishes to all your family for the holiday.

Good fortune attend you

Your

A. Chekhov

1. The heroine of Offenbach's (1819–80) *opéra bouffe*, *La belle Hélène* (1864).

59. *To Ivan Chekhov, 10 May 1888, Sumy*

I'm about to go into the town, so must be brief. I'll go through the points one by one:

1) Everyone is fit and well. Little by little the coughs and colds are disappearing.

2) The apartment is roomy and comfortable, but there are no conveniences; you have go behind a bush and into the ditch. When the weather is dry and warm, 'having to go in the fresh air' does have its charms, but what will it be like when it's raining and cold, or when you have the runs?

3) The river is broad, deep and beautiful. There are the following fish in it: perch, bream, ide, perch-pike, aspius-rapax (a kind of chub), chub, roach, sheat-fish, osmerus, pike-roach . . . The first fish I hooked was a pike, the next one a big perch. Round here they use a bit of crayfish neck to catch perch with. There are thousands and thousands of crayfish. The fish in the pond aren't biting though.

4) We have fishing rods and floats. Bring as many hooks as you possibly can, *of all sorts and sizes*, big, medium-sized and small. Bring some with flies for us, and some without that we can give to the Khokhols and Khokholesses. We need big hooks for the sheat-fish – like this, or even a little bit bigger. Bring some fishing line and strings. There are plenty of boats, and people are used to fishing from boats here. Nobody will steal our perch tackle.

5) Our hosts are very nice people but not particularly jolly, weighed down by their woes. One of the Lintvaryova daughters, a woman doctor, has become blind from a tumour on the brain; she is incurably ill. The family as a whole is a serious one. There's no small talk. They are cultivated people and know about everything.

6) Food is not as cheap as our mother thought it would be.

7) A bottle of Santorini in Sumy costs 35 copecks.

8) We get the *World Illustrated* here.

9) We went on a river trip to see a mill. And yesterday we went off somewhere or other in a cart to see a country house.

10) The Khokhols are tremendous fishermen. I've already got to know many of them and am learning their wisdom. Yesterday, the feast of St Nicholas, they went up and down the Psyol in boats and played their violins.

And what conversations we've had! I couldn't possibly write them down, you have to hear them.

Best regards to Papa, to my aunt and to Alexey. It's rather cold today, but yesterday I was going about in a silk shirt. Be well.

Your

A. Chekhov

Can you buy for me about three roubles' worth of little books, some sacred and some secular (The Blessed Filaret,[1] Grigorovich, Gogol, things like that), which I want to give to the worm-diggers. I can't remember who publishes them. From the sacred books, only choose the *Lives of the Saints*.

60. *To Alexey Suvorin, 30 May 1888, Sumy*

Dear Alexey Sergeyevich,

I am replying to the letter I received from you yesterday. It arrived in an envelope so torn, crumpled and dirty in appearance that my hosts and family guests assigned it a strong political coloration.

I am staying on the banks of the River Psyol in the annexe of an old manor house. I rented it on impulse, without ever having set eyes on it, but so far have no grounds for repenting of it. The river is broad and deep and full of islands, fish and crayfish, the banks are beautiful and everywhere is green ... But the main thing is that there is so much space I can't help feeling that I have acquired for my hundred roubles the privilege of living in a limitless expanse. Nature and life seem to have been organized according to the same pattern, one so ancient that publishers no longer seem to find it of any relevance, not

1. A monk who lived on Mount Athos.

to mention nightingales that sing day and night, the sound of dogs barking far away, old, overgrown gardens, completely neglected estates, very poetic and still home to the souls of beautiful women, not to mention old servants, former serfs with one foot in the grave, and young girls thirsting for the most clichéd kind of romance; not far from me there is even the cliché of a watermill (of sixteen wheels), with a miller and his daughter, who always sits at the window obviously waiting for something. Every single thing I see and hear seems familiar to me from ancient lore and fairy tales. The only hint of novelty is a mysterious bird – the 'water bittern', which sits somewhere far off among the reeds and day and night utters a cry somewhere between a knocking on an empty barrel and the lowing of a cow marooned in a byre. Every Khokhol has seen this bird, but each one describes it differently, so that in fact no one has seen it at all. There is something else new, something quite different, but it's artificial and therefore not really new.

Every day I go down to the mill by boat, and in the evenings I set off for the islands to go fishing with some fishing maniacs from the Kharitonenko factory.[1] I've had some interesting conversations with them. On Whitsun Eve the maniacs will spend the whole night long on the islands fishing, and I shall join them. Some of them are marvellous characters.

My landlords have proved to be extremely pleasant and hospitable people. As a family they repay study; there are six of them in all. The mother is a very kind, comfortably upholstered old lady who has had more than her share of suffering in life. She reads Schopenhauer and goes to church for the akathist, conscientiously reads each issue of *The Herald of Europe* and *The Northern Herald*, and knows the work of novelists I've never dreamt of. The fact that the painter Makovsky[2] once stayed in her annexe is extremely important to her, and now she has a young writer staying there. When she talks to Pleshcheyev a kind of shudder of piety sweeps through her body, and she rejoices in

1. Its owner – a sugar magnate – built a sumptuous mansion, opposite the Kremlin, which after the Revolution became the British Embassy.
2. Nikolay Makovsky (1842–86).

every moment that she has been 'granted the privilege' of seeing the great poet.

Her eldest daughter is a doctor and the pride of the whole family. The peasants call her, somewhat extravagantly, a saint, but there is undoubtedly something truly remarkable about her. She has a brain tumour which has left her totally blind, and suffering from epilepsy and constant headaches. She knows perfectly well what lies in store for her and speaks with extraordinarily dispassionate stoicism of her imminent death. I am no stranger to treating patients who will soon face death, and it has always given me an odd feeling to hear such people speaking and smiling and crying in my presence. But in this case, seeing a blind woman laughing and joking on the terrace and listening to my *In the Twilight* being read to her, what seems strange to me is not that a woman doctor is about to die, but that we ourselves have no sense of our own death and carry on writing *In the Twilight* as if we were never going to die.

The second daughter is also a doctor, a quiet, shy, endlessly good spinster, who loves everybody and is not at all good-looking. She suffers agonies over her sick patients, and worries over them to the point of psychosis. When we consult together, we don't always agree: I tend to be optimistic where she sees only approaching death, and I increase to twice the strength the doses she prescribes. When it is obvious that the patient is inevitably going to die, my lady doctor does not at all feel doctor-like. On one occasion she and I were examining patients together at the clinic, one of whom was a young Khokhol woman with a malignant growth on the glands in her neck and on the back of her head. The cancer had spread to so many places that any kind of treatment was unthinkable. And because the woman was presently feeling no pain but within six months would die an agonizing death, my doctor looked at her with an expression of profound guilt as though asking forgiveness for her own good health and for the inability of her doctoring to help the patient. She is diligent about the running of the household and understands its smallest details. She even understands horses; when, for example, a trace horse refuses to pull properly or shows signs of nervousness, she knows exactly how to deal with the situation and put the coachman right. She loves family life, and even though her own destiny has denied it to her seems to dream continually of it; when there are musical evenings in the big house with singing and playing, she paces rapidly and nervously up and down in the darkness along the path under the trees like a caged animal . . . It seems to me that she has never in her life done anyone the slightest harm, and that she has never had and never will have a moment's happiness.

The third daughter, a graduate of the Bestuzhev courses,[3] is a young woman built like a man, strong and bony as a bream, muscular, sunburnt and noisy. When she laughs you can hear her a mile off. She passionately loves the Ukraine and its people. She built, and paid for with her own money, a school on the estate at which she teaches Khokhol kids Krylov's fables in Ukrainian translation. She visits the tomb of Shevchenko as Turks go to Mecca. She wears her hair long, dresses in a corset and a bustle, does her share of the housekeeping, loves singing and laughing, and even though she has read Marx's *Kapital* is by no means averse to the clichés of love. However, I don't think she will get married as she is rather plain.

The elder son is a quiet, modest, clever, somewhat luckless but hardworking young man. He is unpretentious and appears content with what life has served up to him. He was expelled from university in his fourth year, but doesn't make it an occasion to boast. He doesn't talk much. He loves farming and the land, and lives in harmony with the Khokhols.

The second son is a young man obsessed with Tchaikovsky, whom he worships as a genius. He himself is a pianist, and dreams of living as a Tolstoyan.

So there you have a thumbnail sketch of the people among whom I am now living. As for the Khokhols, the women remind me of Zankovetskaya[4] and all the men of Panas Sadovsky.[5] There are lots of visitors.

3. Higher women's courses and at the time the nearest thing to a university education for women in St Petersburg. Women could not attend university.
4. The actress Maria Zankovetskaya (1860–1934).
5. The Ukrainian actor Mikola Sadovsky or Panas Saksagansky. Chekhov confuses the two names.

A. N. Pleshcheyev is staying with me. Everyone looks on him as a demigod; those whose buttermilk he deigns to accept consider themselves blessed and offer him bouquets of flowers. He is invited everywhere, and so on. One of the people staying with my landlady is a schoolgirl from Poltava named Vata, and she is particularly attentive to him. But he just 'listens and goes on eating', and carries on smoking his cigars, which give his female admirers headaches. He is ponderous in his movements and displays the lethargy of old age, but none of that stops the fair sex inviting him to go on boat trips or out to neighbouring estates, and singing him songs. He presents himself here as he does in Petersburg, that is to say as an icon to which people address their prayers because it is old and once hung next to genuinely miracle-working icons. Apart from him being a very good, warm and sincere man, I personally see him as a reliquary full of traditions, interesting memories and amiable commonplaces.

I've written a story and already sent it to *New Times*.

What you write about 'Lights' is absolutely fair. 'Nikolay and Masha' run right through it like a crimson thread, but what was I to do? My inexperience with long forms of writing makes me very nervous; while I am writing I am frightened by the thought that my story is too long, and I try to compress it as much as I can. The final scene between Kisochka and the engineer seemed to me an important detail but it was simply clogging up the story, so I cut it out and reluctantly had to replace it with 'Nikolay and Masha'.

You write that neither the discussion about pessimism nor Kisochka's story illuminates or resolves in any way the question of pessimism itself. It doesn't seem to me that it is the job of writers of fiction to decide questions like God, pessimism, etc. The writer's task is only to describe those who have said or thought something about God and pessimism, how, and in what circumstances. The artist should not be a judge of his characters or what they say, but an impartial witness. I overheard two Russians having a confused and hopelessly inconclusive conversation about pessimism, and my task was to convey this conversation in the same form as I heard it. The verdict will be given by the members of the jury, i.e. the readers. I have no responsibility other than to be talented, by which I mean that I must be capable of distinguishing between testimony which is important and testimony which is not, be skilled at illuminating my characters and speaking in their language. Shcheglov-Leontiev takes me to task for ending the story with the phrase: 'Nothing can be understood in this world.' He believes that the psychologically perceptive artist *must* understand – that is what his psychological gifts are for. But I don't agree. It's time for writers, especially writers of real artistic worth, to realize, just as Socrates realized in his time and Voltaire in his, that in fact nothing can be understood in this world. The crowd thinks it knows and understands everything; and the stupider it is, the broader the compass of its perceived horizons. But if writers whom the public trusts could only bring themselves to admit that they understand nothing of what they see, that would be a great advance in the realm of thought, a great step forward.

On the subject of your play, you really should not knock it. Any faults it has are not due to any lack of talent or perception, but to the nature of your own creative abilities. You are more inclined towards a strict kind of art, inculcated in you by your familiarity with and love for classical models. If you could imagine your *Tatyana*[6] written in verse, you would see her faults in quite a different light. If you had written it in verse form, no one would notice that the characters all speak in the same voice, and they would escape criticism for philosophizing and talking like an essayist rather than in normal human speech. In a classical verse form, all this would fade into the background like smoke into the air, and consequently *Tatyana*'s signal lack of vulgar language and trivial actions, which contemporary dramas and comedies exhibit to excess, would not be noticed. You would get the same effect if you gave your characters Latin names and dressed them in togas ... The shortcomings of your play cannot be overcome, because they are an organic part of it. Better console yourself with the thought that they are the product of your best qualities, and that if only you were able to donate these same shortcomings to playwrights

6. Chekhov's one-act play *Tatyana Repina* (1889) was a continuation of Suvorin's play of the same name of 1886 and based on the story of an actress who took poison on stage to punish her lover.

like, for example, Krylov[7] or Tikhonov,[8] their plays would be more interesting and more intelligent than they are.

Now about future plans. At the end of June or the beginning of July I shall go to Kiev, and from there down the Dniepr to Ekaterinoslav. Then I'll continue to Alexandrovsk and so to the Black Sea. I shall stay for a while in Feodosia. If you really do plan to go to Constantinople, could I perhaps accompany you? We could go and see Father Paisy, who will prove to us that Tolstoy's teaching comes straight from the devil. I shall spend all of June writing in order to have enough money for the trip. From the Crimea I shall go to Poti, from Poti to Tiflis, from Tiflis to the Don, and from the Don to the Psyol . . . In the Crimea I plan to start work on a lyrical play.

I think I've rambled on enough in this letter! I must bring it to a close. Give my regards to Anna Ivanovna, Nastya and Borya. Alexey Nikolayevich sends you his greetings. He is not very well today, having trouble with his breathing and his pulse stumbles, like the way Leikin walks. Farewell, be well and God grant you good fortune.

Your sincerely devoted

A. Chekhov

61. To Kazimir Barantsevich, 4 July 1888, Sumy

My dear Kuzma Protapych,

You forgot your galoshes and your trousers at my house! If you believe in omens, this means that you will visit me often in the future, which gladdens me exceedingly.

Everything is fine with us here. My family, the Lintvaryovs and the crayfish all send their regards to you, kind-hearted Barbos sends you his Jesuitical smile and dear Zhuk is winking his one eye at you.

---

7. Viktor Krylov (1838–1906), a playwright and the head of repertoire at St Petersburg's imperial theatres.

8. Vladimir Tikhonov (1857–1914), a journalist and playwright.

I wish you good health and happiness, and may the heavenly angels protect you and your little goslings.

Your

A. Chekhov

PS To which museum should I send your trousers?

62. *To Chekhov Family, 22–23 July 1888, Feodosia*

Dear Household,

I am writing to let you know that I shall leave Feodosia tomorrow. My laziness is responsible for driving me out of the Crimea. I have not written a single line nor earned a single copeck; if my vile, lotus-eating life continues for another week or two I shall be completely penniless and the Chekhov family will be forced to spend the whole winter at Luka. I had every intention of writing a play and two or three stories while I was in the Crimea, but it is clear that it is easier to fly up alive into the southern skies than it is to write so much as one line beneath them. I get up at eleven o'clock and go to bed at three o'clock the next morning, and spend the whole day eating, drinking and talking, talking without stopping. I have turned into a machine for talking. Suvorin is also doing nothing, and he and I have thought up new solutions to all the problems of the world. The days pass in an endlessly replete stream, the cup of life overflows . . . Lounging about on the beach, Chartreuse, punch, fireworks, bathing, good cheer at supper, trips, songs – all such pleasures make the days go by so quickly that you hardly notice them; time flies while the drowsy head nods off to the sound of the waves and refuses to get down to work . . . The days are warm, the nights airless and Asiatic . . . No! I've got to get away!

Yesterday I went to Shakh-mamai, to Aivazovsky's[1] estate, twenty

---

1. A. K. Aivazovsky (1817–1900) was a painter celebrated for his depiction of seascapes.

miles from Feodosia. It is a wonderful place, almost like something out of a fairy tale. It's the sort of estate one might imagine in Persia. Aivazovsky himself is an energetic old man of seventy-five and makes an impression of being somewhere between a benign Armenian and a fastidious archbishop. He is full of self-importance, with soft hands which he offers to you like a general. He is not very intelligent, but he is a complex character and worth studying, embodying as he does in one person a general, an archbishop, an artist, an Armenian, a simple grandfather and an Othello. His wife is a young and extremely beautiful woman, whom he keeps on the tightest of reins. He is intimate with sultans, shahs and emirs. He collaborated with Glinka on *Ruslan and Lyudmila*. He was a friend of Pushkin, but has never read him, in fact he has never read a book in his life. If you suggest to him that he might like to read something, he replies: 'Why should I read, when I have opinions of my own?' I spent a whole day there and had lunch. It was a long, slow lunch with endless toasts. During it, by the way, I made the acquaintance of Tarnovskaya, a lady doctor married to a famous professor. She is an obese lump of meat. Stripped naked and painted green she would be a frog straight out of the swamp. After talking to her, I mentally crossed her off my list of doctors . . .

I see many women; Suvorina is the best of them. She is as eccentric as her husband and doesn't think like a woman. A lot of what she says is nonsense, but when she wants to talk seriously she speaks with independence and intelligence. She is head over heels in love with Tolstoy and therefore cannot stand contemporary literature. To hear her talk on the subject you would think that I, Korolenko, Bezhetsky and others like us are her personal enemies. She has an amazing capacity for ceaseless chatter about nothing in particular, but it is the chatter of a talented and interesting person and so one can listen to it without tiring, like a canary. All in all she is an interesting, clever and good person. In the evenings she sits weeping on the sand beside the sea, and in the mornings she laughs and sings gipsy songs . . .

One of two things will happen next: either I shall come straight home, or I shall disappear off the face of the earth. In the first case expect me in a week, in the second, don't.

My regards to the Lintvaryov family: to Alexandra Vasiliyevna, to Zinaida Mikhailovna, to my good friend and comrade [Elena Mikhailovna], to Natalia Mikhailovna, to Pavel and Georgy Mikhailovich and all good Orthodox Christians. Regards also to Antonida Fyodorovna and her little ones.

Suvorina is sitting in my room as I write, simultaneously pleading, 'Please let me read your letter!' and cursing me. I'm off to the town now.

I'll send some money in the next day or two.

We *do* have money to buy a farm – 2,000 roubles. Suvorin has presented me with two boats and a wagon. The boats are apparently splendid ones; I shall try to get them sent to the Psyol. He bought them from the Petersburg Yacht Club. One of them is a sailing boat.

I kiss Mama's hand. I hope you are all well-fed, that you have enough tobacco, and so on. Don't worry about the money. Even more important, don't worry about there not being any.

Love to you all.

A. Chekhov

3 a.m. Saturday morning   I have just come in from the garden and had a late supper. I've said my farewells to the ladies of Feodosia, with no end of kisses, good wishes, good advice and outpourings of feelings. The steamer comes in an hour and a half. I'm going with Suvorin's son, and we are just going to follow our noses. The wind is getting up; I'm bound to be sick.

You will get another letter in two or three days.

Please keep the *New Times* issue of 20 July for me – in fact, please keep all the papers.

Tell Lidia Fyodorovna her comb is still in one piece and has proved its worth: every minute I comb sand from my head.

Address letters (if there are any) to me care of Suvorin in Feodosia. He will know where I am.

It's stifling!

It lies heavy on my conscience that I did not say goodbye to Elena Ivanovna and Lidia Fyodorovna when I left the house.

63. *To an Unidentified Recipient, 25 July 1888, Sukhumi*

I'm in Abkhazia! I spent the night in the New Athos Monastery, and I've been in Sukhumi since this morning. The landscape is enough to drive you out of your mind, it's so extraordinary. Everything is new, fabulous, crazy and poetic: eucalyptus trees, tea bushes, cypresses, cedars, palms, donkeys, swans, buffalo, blue-grey cranes, and the chief delight of all – mountains, mountains, mountains as far as the eye can see . . . At the moment I'm sitting on a balcony watching a procession of Abkhazians dressed like Capuchin monks at a masked ball go lazily by; across the road is an avenue of olive trees, cedars and cypresses, and beyond that the dark blue sea.

It's so unbearably hot, I'm cooking in my own sweat! The red lace on my shirt has completely lost its stuffing from the heat and is oozing red dye over everything. Shirt, forehead and armpits – you could wring them all out. Somehow I think a swim might be the only answer . . . It's getting on for evening . . . I'll soon be back on board. You wouldn't believe, my friend, how delicious the peaches are here! As big as a large apple, velvet and so juicy . . . When you eat one, the flesh squeezes out through the fingers . . . I left Feodosia on the *Yunona*, arrived here today on the *Dira*, and tomorrow will be on the *Babushka* . . . I've become a connoisseur of boats, but haven't yet been sick on any of them.

In New Athos I met Bishop Gennady, Bishop of Sukhumi, who travels through his diocese on horseback. A curious individual.

I bought my mother a little icon, which I'll bring back with me.

If I stayed in Abkhazia for just a month, I'm sure I would write fifty or so irresistible stories. There are a thousand subjects peeping out of every bush, every shadow and half-shadow on the mountainsides, the sea, the sky. It's a crime that I can't paint or draw.

Well, stay alive and well, and may the heavenly angels protect you. Regards to all.

Your

A. Chekhov

Don't think that I'm going to Persia.

64. *To Alexey Suvorin, 29 August 1888, Sumy*

On 20 September, dear Alexey Sergeyevich, my summer holiday comes to an end and I shall return to Moscow. My address will be the same as last year: The Korneyev House, Sadovaya-Kudrinskaya, Moscow. If you pass through Moscow on your way home, and have time, please come and visit me or at least let me know so that I can see you and accompany you to the station.

I have been thinking recently about your encyclopaedic dictionary. If you really do plan to publish it, let me know in good time: I'll write to you with my ideas, which you may find useful.

The day before yesterday I came back from Poltava province. I looked at a farmstead there, but could not reach agreement on the price and so took myself off again. I happened to be there at threshing time. The harvest was magnificent. Everyone who had sown wheat was making 25 to 30 roubles an acre, while the rye was so heavy that in the course of a single day while I was there a six-horsepower steam threshing machine threshed 10,000 pounds, and the workers were fainting with fatigue, the sheaves were so heavy! It was tiring work, but exhilarating, like a good dance. When I was a child, staying with my grandfather on Count Platov's estate,[1] I used to spend whole days from dawn to dusk under orders to sit beside the steam engine and write down the pounds of grain that were threshed: the whistling and hissing, the deep bass, spinning-top-like noise of the steam engine under full load, the creaking of the wheels, the lazy movements of the oxen, the cloud of dust, the blackened, sweating faces of fifty men – all this is etched in my memory as clearly as 'Our Father'. This time I spent hour after hour watching the threshing, and felt supremely content. When the steam engine is working it seems almost a living thing, it has a sly, playful expression; the people and the oxen by contrast are the ones who seem like machines. There aren't many privately owned locomotives in Mirgorod district, but anyone can hire

1. Count Matvey Platov (1751–1818), a hero of 1812, was the original owner of the estate in the Don region where Chekhov's grandfather was employed as a manager.

one. The engine is like a prostitute, it goes round all the district drawn by six oxen offering itself to anyone who wants it. It costs a little over 10 copecks a hundredweight, about 40 roubles a day. One day it clanks away in one place, the next day in another, and everywhere it goes its arrival is an event to be celebrated, like that of a visiting archbishop.

I liked the farmstead I looked at very much. It was a snug, poetic little place. Wonderful piece of land, a water meadow, a pond, an orchard with masses of fruit, a fish pond and an avenue of lime trees. It lies between two large villages, Khomuts and Bakumovka, neither of which has a doctor, so it would be an excellent place for a surgery. Everything is very cheap there. The place swarms with Jews, among the mangiest specimens you could hope to find anywhere. Jews are cowardly people, they're always wanting treatment for something or other. The Cossack owner and I fell out over 300 roubles. I can't and won't go higher than the price I offered him, since what he is asking is unreasonable. If he does eventually agree, I'll leave my power of attorney with a friend to conclude the deal, and it may well be that by October I shall be joining the august company of Shponkas and Korobochkas.[2] If the purchase does go through, I will take advantage of your offer and borrow 1,500 roubles, but only, I beg of you, on the strict condition that you treat my debt as a real one, that is you don't allow our relationship or the friendship between us to have any bearing whatsoever on the way it is to be discharged, you will make no discounts or concessions, otherwise this debt will place me in the kind of position you can imagine. In the past, when I have owed money, I have invariably found myself playing the hypocrite – a deeply unpleasant, psychopathic condition. I can't help being extremely suspicious and deceitful in money matters as a rule. I'll tell you honestly, just between ourselves, that when I started working for *New Times* I felt like I was in California (before *New Times* I never got more than seven to eight copecks a line), and I promised myself I would write as much and as often as possible in order to earn more money – there's

2. Characters created by Gogol in his story 'Ivan Fyodorovich Shponka and his Aunt' and his novel *Dead Souls*.

nothing wrong with that; but when I got to know you better, and when I felt at ease with you, my suspiciousness began to torment me, so that my work for the newspaper, which was linked to getting a fee, came to lose its real value, and so I started to talk and promise more than I actually delivered; I started to fear that our relationship would be clouded by a feeling that you were more important to me as a publisher than as a person, and so on and so forth. It's all stupid and degrading, and merely goes to show that I attach a great deal of importance to money, and there's nothing I can do to alter that. Only when our relationship cools will I agree to a fixed working arrangement and financial terms with the paper, but for now I shall remain someone you do not need. As a friend I'm ready to jump through hoops for the paper and for the encyclopaedic dictionary, I'll undertake any kind of task for the latter *pour plaisir*, I'll write the odd story for the Saturday supplement once a month, but I wouldn't take up a regular position in the paper even if you offered me a million roubles. This doesn't mean that my ties with you are closer or more deeply felt than are other people's; it just means that I am defective in having been born, and having studied and grown up and begun to write, in a milieu where money plays an obscenely important role. Forgive me for this unpalatable candour; I feel I must once and for all explain something you probably find incomprehensible.

In any case, I have written to my brother asking him to keep back the proceeds from my books and 25 per cent of my fees. In that way the debt should be repaid in eighteen months to two years.

Yesterday I had a letter containing some dreadful news: the late Alexander Ostrovsky's son died from diphtheria on the eve of his wedding; after the funeral his bride poisoned herself with carbolic acid; her brother has fallen from his horse and smashed himself up badly.

Goodbye for now, keep well. Did the pharmacist prescribe phenacetin? My respects to Anna Ivanovna, Alexey Alexeyevich, his family, the Vinogradovs and the children. If I do buy the farmstead, I shall start issuing invitations to visit my climatic station. I'll send Alexey Alexeyevich a map of the area.

God grant you good spirits and peace in your soul.
Warmest greetings
A. Chekhov

I shall stop writing large-scale pieces for a while and concentrate on smaller things. I'm bored with the former.

If Alexey Alexeyevich wants to write to me he should address the letter to me in Moscow.

65. To Alexey Suvorin, 11 September 1888, Moscow

I believe this letter will find you still in Feodosia, dear Alexey Sergeyevich.

I shall be happy to look at the proofs of the Moscow Aesculapian[1] section of your yearbook,[2] and will be pleased if this is useful to you. They haven't been sent to me yet, but I am sure they will be soon. I'll try to be meticulous and do the best I can, but I fear that in my hands it may turn out different from the Petersburg section, by which I mean it may be fatter or leaner. If you think there is justification for my fears, please cable the printers and ask them to send me the Petersburg proofs as well, so that I can compare them. It wouldn't do for Petersburg to appear like a fatted calf beside Moscow, or vice versa. Both capitals should be accorded equal rank, or Moscow slightly less at a pinch.

I propose to take the opportunity to include a directory of lunatic asylums in Russia. This is a new subject, of interest to doctors and zemstvo people. I won't include more than a brief listing. Next year, if you agree, I should like to take responsibility for the whole medical section of your yearbook, but for now I don't propose to do more than pour some new wine into the old bottles. That's all I can do for

1. Relating to medicine and the healing arts.
2. Suvorin published an annual almanac of general information for inhabitants of St Petersburg and Moscow.

the present, because so far I have neither a plan of how it should be done, nor the necessary material to hand.

You advise me not to chase after two hares at once, and you think I should give up all thoughts of a career in medicine. But I don't see why one shouldn't chase two hares at once, even literally: one can do this if one has enough hounds. Admittedly I don't have enough hounds (this time in the metaphorical sense), but being conscious of having two trades rather than just one does make me happier and more at ease with myself . . . Medicine is my lawful wedded wife, and literature my mistress. When I've had enough of one, I can go and spend the night with the other. You may well call this disorderly conduct, but at least it stops me getting bored, and in any event I am sure that neither of them is the loser from my infidelity. If it were not for medicine I would not be devoting my leisure moments and my private thoughts to literature; I haven't the discipline to do so.

I wrote a lot of nonsense in my last letter to you (I was feeling rather down), but let me assure you that when I touched on my relationship with you I was thinking only of myself, not of you. I have always taken at face value your readiness to offer me payments in advance, and your fundamentally generous attitude to me, and so on. One would have to have a very poor appreciation of you, not to mention be a 22-carat psychopath, to suspect that your proffered bread was actually a stone. What prompted me to go on about my misgivings was no more than my charming habit of being nervous about having a second story published in a newspaper too soon after the first one, lest people as scrupulous as I am should think I rush into print too often in pursuit of filthy lucre . . . I beg you to forgive me for starting up such an embarrassing and utterly pointless 'polemic'.

I had a letter from Alexey Alexeyevich today. Please pass on to him my advice, which is based on experience, that however pleasant and silver-tongued illustrators may be, you must always keep them firmly penned inside their boxes and never trust them an inch. You may tell him – and Borya too by the way – that I am acquainted with Mme Godefroy, the circus trick-rider. She is not beautiful at all. Aside from a classy riding technique and excellent muscles she has nothing to recommend her; everything else about her is rather ordinary and vulgar.

To judge from her face, however, she is probably quite a nice woman.

The young lady (from Sumy) who wanted me not to come and visit you was thinking of the 'tendentiousness' and 'the spirit of the age' she feared might infect me, rather than the kind of corruption you mentioned. She was afraid of my person falling victim to political influence. This lady is in fact a person of great integrity and a pure heart, but when I asked her how she knew Suvorin and whether she actually read *New Times*, she began to mumble, wagged her finger at me, and said: 'All I'm saying is I think you ought not to go.' Our young ladies and their politically motivated squires are undoubtedly pure souls, but nine-tenths of their spiritual purity is not worth a rotten egg. Their supine piety and purity all stems from their naive and nebulous liking or disliking for personalities and labels rather than for facts. It's easy to be pure when you can hate the Devil you don't know, while at the same time loving the God you lack the brains to doubt.

My respects to everyone,

Your

A. Chekhov

66. To Alexey Pleshcheyev, 4 October 1888, Moscow

Dear Alexey Nikolayevich,

I have made a fair copy of my story[1] for *The Northern Herald* and have sent it off to the editorial office. I'm exhausted. I'm now looking forward to getting my fee. All September I had no money, so I had to pawn a few odds and ends and generally battled like a fish against the ice. September is always a difficult time for me, but this year was particularly bleak, after I had spent the summer in idleness and borrowed against future income to pay living expenses. I owed Suvorin 400 roubles, and only managed to pay off 200 . . .

A while back I wrote to you from Korsh's Theatre. If he does put on *The Blockheads*, don't forget to draw up a contract, either through

1. 'The Name-day Party'.

me or through someone else. Korsh pays 2 per cent an act for original plays and 1 per cent for translations. It's not a lot of money, but it is still money and should not be thrown away ... Your *Blockheads* is not listed in the Dramatic Society's catalogue. By the way, Korsh is now paying the Society six roubles an act, not five. Svetlov is a fine actor and a very good sort.

Pavel Lintvaryov came to see me today; he is applying to enter the Petrovskaya Academy,[2] but it looks as though they are not going to accept the poor fellow. He is under surveillance.

Jean[3] Shcheglov is in Moscow at the moment. His *Dacha Husband* did not have much success in Moscow, but it looks as though it will do much better in St Petersburg and in the provinces. Pavlovsk doesn't mean anything to people here in Moscow, nor does a dacha husband, nor a dacha servant, nor service in a government department. It's a slight play and an amusing one, but at the same time annoying because of the moral pinned on to the dacha housewife's bustle. If dear Jean plans to continue in the style of *The Dacha Husband* he is not likely to be promoted above the rank of captain as a dramatist in my opinion. You can't simply go on endlessly chewing on the same old stereotyped characters, the same town, the same bustle. After all, Russia has plenty of interesting and entertaining subjects besides dacha husbands and bustles. In the second place, it's time we got rid of cheap moralizing. *The Caucasus Mountains* has no pretensions to morality, and that is why it has been so outstandingly successful. My advice to Jean is to write a big comedy, in five acts or so, and on no account to abandon fiction.

You will soon see Georges. He is going to Petersburg.

When I wrote to Anna Mikhailovna, I particularly asked her not to cut a single line of my story. This was not obstinacy or caprice, but anxiety that editorial changes might give my story the sort of overtones I've always dreaded. I kiss you warmly and remain your devoted and affectionate

A. Chekhov

2. The Petrovskaya Agricultural and Forestry Academy was founded in Moscow in 1865.
3. Jean was Chekhov's nickname for his friend Ivan Shcheglov.

67. To Alexey Pleshcheyev, 4 October 1888, Moscow

Scarcely had I posted a letter to you, dear Alexey Nikolayevich, than I got your news, which will be most unwelcome to Svetlov. I shall pass on your answer to him straight away, and strongly recommend *A Bad Man* instead.

Had I received your letter two hours earlier, I would have sent my story straight to you, instead of which it is now halfway to Baskov Lane.[1]

I should very much like to read what Merezhkovsky[2] has written. Farewell for the present. Please write to me when you have read my story. You will not like it, but I am not afraid either of you or Anna Mikhailovna. The people I am afraid of are those who continually sniff between the lines seeking out tendencies, and who try to put me down as a definite liberal or conservative. I am neither a liberal nor a conservative, I'm not a gradualist, nor a monk, nor am I indifferent. My sole desire is to be a free artist, nothing more, and I regret that God has denied me the strength to be one. I detest lies and violence in all their forms, and consistory secretaries are no less repugnant to me than Notovich[3] and Gradovsky.[4] Pharisaism, stupidity and tyranny do not only reign in merchants' houses and the gaol; I see them in science, in literature, among young people ... For this reason I feel an equal absence of attraction to policemen, butchers, scientists, writers and young people. I regard all trademarks and labels as badges of prejudice. My holy of holies is the human body, good health, intelligence, talent, inspiration, love and complete freedom – freedom from violence and lies, no matter what form these two last may take. That is the programme I would adhere to if I were a great artist.

1. The address in St Petersburg of the editorial offices of *The Northern Herald*.
2. Dmitry Merezhkovsky (1866–1941), a writer and religious thinker associated with the Symbolist movement, had written a lengthy review of Chekhov's prose.
3. Osip Notovich (1849–1914), a journalist and editor of the *News and Stock Exchange Paper*.
4. Grigory Gradovsky (1842–1915), a journalist on the *News and Stock Exchange Paper*.

But enough of this rambling. Be in good health.

Your

A. Chekhov

68. To Dmitry Grigorovich, 9 October 1888, Moscow

It is wonderful news, dear Dmitry Vasiliyevich, that you have at last recovered and have returned to Russia. People who have seen you tell me that you are in excellent health, as cheerful as before, that you have even given a reading of your new story, and that you now have a big beard. If your chest pains have really gone then they are not likely to reappear, but I expect the bronchitis will continue to give you trouble. It may have died down during the summer, but in the winter the slightest exposure to risk is liable to start it up again. Bronchitis is not dangerous in itself, but it interferes with your sleep and is debilitating and annoying. Cut down on your smoking, don't drink kvass[1] or beer, don't go into smoking rooms, wrap up warmly in damp weather, don't read aloud and try to moderate your normal fast walking pace. Minor precautions like this are somewhat restricting and can be just as irritating as the bronchitis itself, but what else can one do?

I am also happy to have received a letter from you. Your letters are short, like good poems. We do not meet very often, but I believe, and am almost convinced, that if it were not for you and Suvorin in St Petersburg, I would lose my balance and turn out frightful nonsense.

The prize was of course the greatest stroke of good fortune for me,[2] and it would be a gross untruth if I were to tell you I am not excited by it. I feel as if I have just successfully completed a course, not in a school or university but in an even higher establishment. All day yesterday and today I have been wandering about as if I were in love, doing no work, just thinking. Of course – and about this there can be

1. A non-alcoholic drink made from fermented black bread.
2. Chekhov had just been awarded the Pushkin Prize by the Imperial Academy of Sciences for his short story collection *In the Twilight*, published in 1887.

no doubt – I do not owe this prize to my own achievements. There are better and more necessary young writers than I, such as Korolenko, for instance, a very decent writer and a fine man, who would have received the prize if he had entered his book. Yakov Polonsky instigated the idea of my getting the prize, Suvorin supported it, and he sent in my book to the Academy. And then in the Academy you were my staunch backer. You must agree that without the three of you I would have had as much chance of seeing the prize as of seeing my own ears. I'm not being falsely modest or trying to persuade you that it was nothing but your collective partiality that won me a prize I don't deserve and so on – that's boring old hat; but I do want to say that I am conscious my good fortune is not due to myself alone. A thousand thanks; for the rest of my life I shall be grateful to you.

I have written nothing for the small press since the New Year. I publish my shorter stories in *New Times* and longer ones in *The Northern Herald*, which pays me 150 roubles a printer's sheet. I don't propose to abandon *New Times*, first because of my great attachment to Suvorin, and secondly because *New Times* is not the small press. My plans for the future are not settled. I want to write a novel, and I have a wonderful subject; there are times when I am gripped by a passionate desire to get down to it, but I evidently lack the necessary strength. I have begun work on it, but am afraid to go on. I made a firm decision not to rush matters, to write only when I really feel like it, to revise and polish my work; I plan to spend several years on the novel; I don't have enough energy to finish the thing all at once, in a single year, I am afraid of not staying the course, and in any case there is no particular need to hurry. I have a propensity for every year being dissatisfied with what I wrote the previous year; I always think that next year I shall be stronger than this year. That is why I am not rushing to stake everything on a decisive step at the moment. For if the novel were to turn out badly, I would have lost the game for ever!

All the ideas, women, men, scenes of nature I have collected for the novel are safely preserved and inviolate. I promise you they will not be squandered on meretricious work. The novel will take in several families and a whole district, complete with woods, rivers, ferry boats, railways. At the centre of this landscape are two principal figures, a man and a woman, with other individuals grouped around them like pawns. I do not yet aspire to a coherent political, religious and philosophical world view; my opinions change every month, and therefore I must confine myself to describing how my characters love, get married, have children, die, and how they speak.

Until the time comes for me to concentrate on the novel I shall carry on writing what I love, that is short stories of one to one and a half printer's sheets or less. Inflating trivial subjects so as to fill up large canvases is tedious work, although it can be profitable. It would be a great pity to introduce big subjects, and waste ideas and images that mean a lot to me, on potboilers produced to meet urgent deadlines. I shall bide my time until it is more propitious.

I have no right to forbid my brother to sign his work with his own name. He asked my opinion before doing so, and I told him I had no objection.

I had a wonderful time during the summer. Some of it I spent in the Kharkov and Poltava regions, then I went to the Crimea, Batum, Baku, and survived the Georgian Military Road. Many impressions. If I lived in the Caucasus I'm sure I would write fairy tales there. It's an astonishing country!

I shall not be in St Petersburg before November, but the moment I get there I shall present myself to you. In the meantime, let me thank you once again from the bottom of my heart, and wish you good health and all happiness.

Your sincerely devoted

A. Chekhov

69. To Alexey Pleshcheyev, 9 October 1888, Moscow

Forgive me, dear Alexey Nikolayevich, for writing to you on ordinary paper. There's not a single sheet of proper writing paper left, and I haven't the time or the inclination to wait until they bring me some from the shop.

Grateful thanks for reading through my story,[1] and for your last letter. I value your opinions. I have nobody to talk to in Moscow, and I rejoice that in Petersburg there are good people who don't find it too tedious to correspond with me. Yes, dear critic, you are right! The middle of my story is boring, grey and monotonous. I was being lazy and careless when I wrote it. Because I am so used to short stories that consist of little more than a beginning and an end, I lose interest as soon as I feel that I am writing a middle, and tend to make too much of a meal of it. I am glad that, rather than keeping your opinions to yourself, you came out with your suspicion that I might be worried people would take me for a liberal; that insight has really caused me to look deep into my heart. Now that I've thought about it, it seems to me that in fact I could more readily be accused of gluttony, drunkenness, irresponsibility, coldness – anything you like – than a desire to appear, or not appear, anything at all . . . Secretiveness has never been one of my failings. If I have strong feelings for you or Suvorin or Mikhailovsky I don't conceal it. If I feel drawn to my heroine, Olga Mikhailovna, a liberal woman who has had higher education, I don't hide it, and I think that is quite clear. Nor do I conceal my respect for the *zemstvo*, for which likewise I have a great deal of time, as I do for trial by jury. What is certainly more dubious in my story is the way I attempt to balance the pros and cons. But the balance I am trying to achieve is in fact not between conservatism and liberalism, which seem to me beside the point, but between the lies and the truth my characters exhibit. Pyotr Dmitrich tells lies and plays the fool in court, he is a hopeless case and an impossible person to live with, but I have no wish to conceal that he is an attractive and gentle person by nature. Olga Mikhailovna lies every time she opens her mouth, but again it would be wrong not to acknowledge that this causes her pain. It is quite wrong to produce the Ukrainophile as evidence. I did not have Pavel Lintvaryov in mind. Heaven's above! Pavel Mikhailovich is an intelligent and modest young man who thinks for himself and doesn't try to ram his opinions down the throats of all and sundry. The Lintvaryovs' Ukrainophilia is a love of warmth, way

1. 'The Name-day Party'.

of dress, language and one's native soil. My targets were the pompous idiots who take Gogol to task because he didn't write in Ukrainian, and who posture and try to appear superior by the simple device of pasting labels on their foreheads, when in truth they are nothing but useless, bloodless, boneheaded idlers with empty skulls and empty hearts. As for my characterization of the 'man of the sixties', I tried to err on the side of caution and brevity although he really deserves a sketch all to himself. He is one I let off lightly. He is typical of the feeble, ineffectual sort of ignorance that has usurped the true spirit of the sixties; he and those like him picked up five or six second-hand ideas when they were in the fifth form at school, got stuck on them, and will continue doggedly parroting them until the day they die. They are not so much frauds as fools, who believe their own claptrap and understand little or nothing of what they are mumbling about. They are stupid, deaf and heartless. You must have heard them droning on about life today, not that they have a clue what it is about, and harking back to the sixties, which are equally a closed book to them. They hate students, schoolgirls, women, writers and every aspect of modern life, and they believe that's all there is to being a man of the sixties. They are as dull as a hole in the ground and as dangerous as a gopher to all who pay heed to them. The sixties were a sacred time, and allowing stupid gophers to usurp them is to trivialize them. No, I shall not delete either the Ukrainophile or this silly goose who so irritated me. He was boring enough even when he was at school, and he's just as boring now. When I create or talk about characters like him, I do not think in terms of conservatism or liberalism, but of vacuousness and pretentiousness.

Now for some minor points. When my Military Medical Academy student is asked in which faculty he is studying, he answers simply: 'the medical faculty'. Only a student who is specifically interested in the distinction between the Academy and the University would trouble himself to spell it out in plain language to a member of the public. You're right that the conversation with the pregnant peasant woman smacks of Tolstoyanism. That is indeed how it strikes me now. But the conversation is not important; I only put it in so that the miscarriage would not strike the reader too much *ex abrupto*. Because I am a doctor and would not like to disgrace myself professionally, I feel a certain obligation to prepare the ground for events of a medical nature. And you are also right about the back of the head. I sensed this when I was writing it, but as I had invested in it quite a lot of observation, I lacked the courage to cut it out altogether; it seemed a pity to waste it.

You are also right to say that a person who has just been crying cannot tell a lie. But only partly. Lying is like alcoholism; liars lie even on their deathbeds. The other day an officer from a noble family, engaged to a young lady we know, tried unsuccessfully to shoot himself. The man's father, a general, has not been to visit his son in hospital, and will not do so until he knows the reaction of polite society to his son's attempted suicide ...

I have been awarded the Pushkin Prize! Oh, if only I could have had the 500 roubles in the summer, when I would have been able to enjoy them, instead of now in winter, when they will just go to waste!

Tomorrow I shall sit down and write a story for the Garshin anthology,[2] and will try to make it a good one. As soon as it begins to take some sort of recognizable shape, I shall let you know and keep my promise. I doubt if it will be ready before next Sunday. I am in a very anxious state at the moment, and not working well.

Please put down the Lintvaryovs for one copy of the anthology, and Lensky,[3] the actor, for another ... In any case I will send you a list of my subscribers. How much is the book going to cost?

I sent the response to Svetlov a long time ago.

I like Sumbatov's[4] Chains. Lensky is wonderful as Proporiev. Be well and happy. The prize has rather unsettled me; my thoughts are

2. An anthology of work put together in memory of the writer Vsevolod Garshin (1855–88), who had recently committed suicide. He had completed twenty short stories, including 'Red Flower' (1883), by the time of his death.

3. Alexander Lensky (1847–1908), an actor, director and theatrical teacher. From 1876 to 1882 he acted at the Maly Theatre in Moscow and from 1882 to 1884 at the Alexandrinsky in St Petersburg. He returned to the Maly in 1884, where he spent the remainder of his working life.

4. Alexander Sumbatov (1857–1927), an actor, playwright and theatrical figure. He adopted the pseudonym Yuzhin and was also referred to as Prince Sumbatov-Yuzhin (see letter 235, for example).

whizzing round my head more stupidly than ever. My family sends their respects, as do I to yours. It's cold.

Your

A. Chekhov

70. To Alexey Suvorin, 10 October 1888, Moscow

The news about the prize has had an overwhelming effect. It roared through my apartment and all round Moscow like a thunderclap from the immortal Zeus. These last few days I've been walking around as if I'm in love; my mother and father are indescribably thrilled and spout the most frightful rubbish, and my sister, guarding our reputation with the pedantic severity of a lady at court, has been making the rounds of friends and broadcasting the news. Jean Shcheglov talks darkly of literary Iagos and of the five hundred enemies the 500 roubles are certain to bring me. I happened to meet Lensky and his wife, and they made me promise to go and dine with them; then I met a lady talent-spotter who also invited me to dinner; then the inspector of the Meshchanskoye school[1] came to see me to congratulate me and to buy 'Kashtanka' for 200 roubles, hoping 'to make something on the deal' . . . I think even Anna Ivanovna, who ranks Shcheglov and me somewhere below Rasstrygin, might invite me to dinner now. All those Xs, Zs and Ns who write for *The Alarm Clock*, *The Dragonfly* and *The Rag* have bestirred themselves and can now look to the future with hope. I must say it again: second- and third-rate magazine writers should put up a statue to me, or at the very least present me with a silver cigarette case; I have paved their way to the thick journals and into the hearts and approval of respectable people. So far that is my only achievement: nothing that I have written and that has brought me this prize will survive in people's memory for even a decade.

I've been terribly lucky. I had a wonderful summer, spending hardly

1. A school founded in Moscow by the Society of Merchants for boys and girls of the *meshchanstvo* – 'lower-class town dwellers'.

any money and managing not to saddle myself with too many painful debts. The River Psyol, the sea, the Caucasus, the farm, the book trade (my *In the Twilight* brought in something every month) – all smiled on me. In September I managed to work off half the money I owe, and I wrote a story of two and a half printer's sheets which netted me more than 300 roubles. A second edition of *In the Twilight* has been published. And now, like a bolt from the blue, suddenly this prize!

In fact, things are going so well that I keep looking suspiciously at the heavens. I shall soon have to hide under the table and sit there quietly out of the way, keeping my voice down. Until I feel I am ready for a serious new venture, by which I mean embarking on a novel, I shall stay like that, writing short, unpretentious stories and little plays, neither scaling the heights nor falling from them but plodding on as steady and even as Burenin's pulse: ∿∿∿∿∿∿ . I shall follow the advice of the Khokhol who said: 'If I were the Tsar I'd pinch a hundred roubles and keep my mouth shut.' So long as I remain the little Tsar of my own ant-hill, I'll steal my hundred roubles and scurry off with them. I seem to have begun to write a load of nonsense, however.

People are talking about me now. Strike while the iron is hot. You'd better put three advertisements in a row for my books, and then again on the 19th when the prize is officially announced. I'm going to tuck the 500 roubles away to buy a farmstead with, and I'll do the same thing with the earnings from the books.

What am I to do about my brother?[2] He gives me nothing but grief, and what grief. Sober, he is an intelligent, modest, honest and gentle person, but drunk he is unbearable. He completely loses control after two or three glasses, and starts telling lies. When he wrote that letter he was in the grip of a passionate desire to concoct a harmless but effective fabrication. He has not yet got as far as hallucinating because in fact the amount he drinks is comparatively small. I can tell from his letters to me when he is sober and when he is drunk: the first kind are reasonable and sincere, the second a tissue of lies from start to finish.

2. Alexander.

There is no doubt that he has an addiction to drink. What is this addiction? It is a psychosis analogous to morphine addiction, onanism, nymphomania, etc. Alcohol addiction is generally inherited from the father or mother, grandmother or grandfather. But our family has no history of drunkenness: my grandfather and my father used to get pretty drunk when there were guests, but it didn't stop them going to work when they had to, or getting up in time for early mass. Wine improved their temper and made them witty and amusing; it gladdened their hearts and sharpened their wits. Neither my brother the teacher nor I ever drink alone, we don't know much about wine, we can drink as much as we want and still wake up with a clear head. One day last summer a professor from Kharkov and I decided to get drunk. We drank and drank but then had to give up as it was obviously having no effect: when we woke up the next morning it was as if we had not touched a drop. But Alexander and my artist brother go berserk after two or three glasses and sometimes have a real craving for drink . . . Whom they take after, God only knows. All I know is that when Alexander drinks there is a reason behind it, something will have made him unhappy or discouraged. I don't know where he is living. If it is not too much trouble, please send me his home address, and I'll write him a politic, censorious but affectionate letter. My letters do have an effect on him.

I'm glad my leading article was approved. I'm sending the story I mentioned to you, about the young man and prostitution,[3] to the Garshin anthology.

My spirit is uneasy. However, it's not serious. Regards and greetings to all your family. I've sent the list of doctors to the directory; I had to rewrite it. If you agree, next year I should like to take over the whole medical directory. I shall do a lot of hunting this summer. Be well and at peace.

Your

A. Chekhov

3. The story is 'An Attack of Nerves', sometimes known as 'The Nervous Breakdown'.

I had a letter from Maslov: 'Twice now you've advised me to marry. What do you mean by this advice, honoured sir?'

I'm sending you a story by a teacher called Ezhov. It's as immature and naive as its heroine Lyolya, and that makes it good. I've cut out all the boring bits. Even if you find the story no good, please don't chuck it out. My protégé would be very hurt.

71. To Alexey Pleshcheyev, 10 or 11 October 1888, Moscow

Can you really find no evidence of 'ideological tendencies' in my last story? Not long ago you were telling me that my stories lack any element of protest, that you find in them no sympathy and antipathy ... But surely, isn't this story[1] one long protest against falsehood from beginning to end? Isn't that an ideological tendency? No? Well, then, either I'm no good at getting my point across or else I can't bite any harder than a flea ...

I'm afraid of the censor. He's sure to remove the passage where I describe Pyotr Dmitrich's actions as a judge in court. After all, all judges are like that these days.

Oh, how I must bore you!

A. Chekhov

72. To Alexander Chekhov, 13 October 1888, Moscow

Drunkard!

Your going to the Academy was by no means a pointless exercise: I won the prize. Since you also played a part in obtaining this crown of laurels for me, I hereby send you part of my heart. Pray accept said part and eat it.

You seem to have no commercial instincts. There should have been

1. 'The Name-day Party'.

a prominent advertisement for my books in the issue in which the prize was announced. Do bear in mind that the prize is going to be officially announced on 19 October, so there should be advertisements for the books on the 19th and 20th as well.

Suvorin has informed me that you have been beaten up by some officer or other, who apparently also threatened to beat up Fyodorov and Suvorin. While relating this joyful family occasion to me, Suvorin dispassionately inquired, in tones reminiscent of Mitrofan Egorovich, 'what exactly is an addiction to drink? My father-in-law also drinks . . .' and so on in that vein. I explained to him a little about addiction, and told him you had not been hallucinating. I gave him another explanation for the 'officer'. I told him that when you are under the influence you are prone to hyperbole and ecstasy, you get in a fog and lose your bearings, forget who you are and what you do for a living, turn down the corners of your mouth, spout rubbish, shout out to the world that you are Chekhov – and the morning after you're as sick as a dog . . . In the evening and at night you spew lies and in the morning you vomit . . . I asked him either to give you the sack or else to put you under the jurisdiction of the Resident.[1]

A little while ago I wrote a leading article for Suvorin. He printed it and now wants another. I'm not going to write articles for the editorial page, but why don't you? That would straight away put you in a secure position.

NB When you've been drinking, don't try to hide it from the editorial staff and don't try to justify it. It's better just to be straightforward about it, like Suvorin's father-in-law, or Gey and the Resident. But most important of all, do try to buckle down seriously to work, because someone who does good work thereby buys himself immunity from reproach.

Anyhow, what the hell do you want to drink like that for? Drink by all means in company with decent people but don't drink alone or with any old riff-raff. Getting tight is a great release, a boost; so

1. Pseudonym for Alexander Dyakov, a *New Times* journalist known for his pronounced reactionary views.

drink for that. But turning good vodka into a dreary, sour-tasting, sick-making debauch – ugh!

All of us send our love. M. M. Chokhov is going to marry the daughter of a merchant and is getting ten grand as a dowry; I could only wish the same for you.

If it's not too much trouble, could you arrange to send me via carrier a package of five of each of my books? And if the printers could let me know the cost of publishing my [*Motley*] *Stories*, I could be tempted.

Please add to the parcel one copy of Bezhetsky's *On the Way*, and ask the author if he would decorate the book with his autograph.

You need to develop more directness and sincerity in your relationships with people, to say less and be more straightforward in your dealings with them. Growl when you're angry, laugh when you're amused, answer when you're asked something. Father always smiled at customers and visitors even when he was sick to death of Swiss cheese; he was always responding to Pokrovsky even when he hadn't asked him anything; and he used to write begging letters to Alferaki's wife and Shcherbina that he had no business writing . . . In this respect you are terribly like Father! For instance, if this officer really did beat you up, why was it necessary to tell the world about it? All right, so he beat you up, but what has that to do with the editorial staff? There's nothing they can do either to help you or to protect themselves against assault.

If we do reasonably well with the books, let's buy a Ukrainian farmstead. You should try to get some money together: for 600 roubles I could buy you a piece of land in a place beyond your wildest dreams. If I buy a farmstead, the land could be split into sections, each of which should not cost more than five to six hundred roubles. A modest building to live in would cost about the same, depending on how many rooms it has: you have to allow about 100 roubles per room.

Be well, and give my greetings to the cubs.

Your

A. Chekhov

73. To Alexey Suvorin, 14 October 1888, Moscow

Greetings once again, Alexey Sergeyevich! I presume Jean Shcheg-lov gave you either yesterday or today my letter with a story by my protégé Ezhov in it. But I'm now replying to your last letter. First, about my coughing blood. I first noticed it three years ago when I was attending the [Moscow] circuit court: it went on for about three days and caused quite a commotion in my soul and in my home. There was a lot of blood. It came from my right lung. Subsequently I've noticed some bleeding once or twice a year, and sometimes there has been a lot of blood, by which I mean what I cough up would be thick and red, but sometimes not that much ... The day before yesterday, or the day before that, I don't remember exactly, I noticed some blood in the evening, but today it has stopped. I get a cough every winter, autumn and spring, and on damp days in the summer. But the only time it worries me is when I see blood: there is something sinister about blood flowing from the mouth, like the glow of a fire. If there is no blood I don't worry about it, and I'm not threatening Russian literature with 'yet another loss'. The point is that consumption and other serious lung diseases only manifest themselves through a particular set of symptoms, and I don't have that particular combi-nation. In itself losing blood from the lungs is not serious; sometimes it can pour out for a whole day and frighten the life out of the patient and his family, but – and this is the case more often than not – it does not end up in the patient's death. So it may be useful to know, in case it should happen, that if anyone not known to be a consumptive should suddenly start bleeding from the mouth, there is no need for alarm. A woman can lose half her blood without ill effects, a man slightly less than half.

If the bleeding I experienced in that circuit courtroom had been a symptom of incipient consumption, I would long ago have departed this life – that is my logic.

As for my brother, I can only express my gratitude to you. I'm sure you will agree how bad it would have been for a hallucinating, lying drunk to be left entirely without moral support. You wrote to me, I wrote to him, and between us we have done what was needed. Had it not been for your letter, many things about my brother would have been incomprehensible to me, and that is the most distressing thing of all.

For several days now my schoolboy lodger, Ashanin's[1] grandson, has been in bed delirious, with a temperature of 40 degrees and an aching head. You can imagine how alarmed we all are, I in particular! His mother is such a charming woman; there are not many like her. I had been worrying over whether or not to send her a telegram; she would have been devastated by it, the boy is her only son, but on the other hand I felt I did not have the right not to let her know. Fortunately, the youngster has pulled through, and the dilemma has resolved itself. Incidentally, I had a visit from his school teacher, a downtrodden individual struggling helplessly against the flood of regulations with which he is bombarded, not a very clever man and hated by the children for his strictness (he has a habit of taking a boy by the shoulders and shaking him: just imagine the hands of someone you detest clutching at your shoulders). He was very awkward, did not once sit down and spent the whole time complaining about the school board, which he said had turned him and his colleagues – the teachers – into sergeant-majors. We competed with one another in expressing our liberal credentials, and chatted about the south – apparently we both come from there – sighing over it nostalgically ... When I said to him 'How freely one breathes in our southern schools!' he waved his hands hopelessly and departed.

These teachers have to visit the homes of their charges as part of their duties; though when they do they often find themselves in stupid situations, especially when they encounter a crowd of guests, which results in general embarrassment.

I will speak to Korsh about [Maslov's] *The Seducer of Seville*, and will suggest actors, but I don't think they will produce it! They would need special scenery and costumes in order to put it on, and Korsh is such an old skinflint. And he doesn't have the actors to play the roles.

---

1. The pseudonym of the writer Boleslav Markevich (1822–84).

I think you should recommend to Maslov that if he hasn't the time to write a comedy, he should turn out a vaudeville . . . After all, the only difference between a full-length play and a one-acter is one of scale. Why don't you write a vaudeville* on the quiet, under a pseudonym? I'll get you into the Dramatic Society.

Your

A. Chekhov

Here's a specimen of the kind of letter my brother the teacher receives:

Highly esteemed Ivan Pavlovich!

I have the honour to inform you that my son, Nikolay Rensky, did not attend school on the 12th inst. on our instructions. On the evening of 11th he was at a wedding in church, and was accidentally locked in by an oversight of the refectory servitor. After a lengthy search, we brought him home two hours later. Being concerned that the shock might have a deleterious effect on his nervous system, we kept him at home on the following day in order to calm him.

Your humble servant

Deacon Dmitry Nikiforovich Rensky

* drama or comedy

74. To Alexander Chekhov, 6 or 7 November 1888, Moscow

Korbo, canis clarissimus, mortuus est. Gaudeo te asinum, sed non canem esse, nam asini diutius vivunt.

[Korbo, a dog of honour and renown, has passed away. I rejoice that you are not a dog but an ass, since asses live longer.]

75. To Alexey Suvorin, 24 or 25 November 1888, Moscow

Women who screw (or shag, as they say in Moscow), on any old sofa, are not so much crazy as like nymphomaniac cats. The sofa is a most inconvenient piece of furniture. It is far more frequently indicted for its role in lechery than is actually the case. I have only once in my life had recourse to a sofa, and I had cause to curse it.

I have seen fallen women and sinned on many occasions, but I take leave to doubt Zola and the woman who said to you 'Right, let's do it.' Debauched people and writers like to present themselves as gourmets and connoisseurs of fornication; they are bold, resolute, resourceful, they have intercourse in thirty-three different positions on everything but a knife blade, but this is all talk; in reality all they do is screw cooks and visit one-rouble brothels. All writers lie. It's not as easy to make love to a woman in town as their writings claim. I have never encountered an apartment (at least not a respectable one, obviously) where it would be possible to upend a woman in a corset, skirt and bustle on to a chest, or a couch, or the floor, and do her without attracting the attention of the servants. All these descriptions of doing it standing up or sitting down, etc., are so much nonsense. The best place is in bed, and the remaining thirty-three possibilities, whether of the simple or the complex variety, are only suitable for separate hotel rooms or a barn. Having an affair with a woman from a respectable background can be a very long-drawn-out business. In the first place, it has to be at night, secondly you have to make your way to the Hermitage, thirdly when you get there they tell you they don't have a room free so you have to go in search of an alternative nest for your assignation, fourthly when you finally get to the room your lady loses heart, is overcome by an access of gentility and begins to tremble and exclaim 'Oh my God, what am I doing?! No! No!', a good hour is spent disrobing and talking, and fifthly on the way back your lady wears an expression on her face as though you had raped her, and constantly mutters 'No, I shall never be able to forgive myself!' All this is rather a far cry from 'Right, let's do it!' Of course, there do exist times when a man can sin as easily as letting off a gun

– bang bang, let's do it! – but they occur so rarely as not to be worth mentioning. Don't believe the stories you hear! Trust in the exploits of brave lovers as little as you do hunters' tales. Remember the saying: 'the one in pain will always moan'; the more chaste a man is, the more he loves talking about his amorous adventures and the thirty-three positions in which they took place. No one loves smut as much as old maids and widows who no longer have a lover. Writers should always beware of old wives' tales and romantic epics. If Zola himself had enjoyed sexual intercourse on tables, underneath tables, against fences, in dog kennels, in carriages, or had seen with his own eyes others doing so, then you could believe in his novels, but if what he wrote was based on gossip and the anecdotes of friends, then he was being slapdash and careless.

Ah, what a story I've started![1] I shall bring it with me and hope you will read it. The subject is love, and I have chosen to cast it in the form of a fictional satirical sketch. An honourable man goes off with the wife of another honourable man, and writes down his opinion about it: he lives with her – his opinion; they break up – another opinion. I touch *en passant* on the theatre, on the prejudices inherent in 'incompatible beliefs', on the Georgian Military Road, on family life, on the inability of the contemporary intellectual to deal with same, on Pechorin, on Onegin, on Mount Kazbek . . . Lord save us, what a Russian salad it is! The wings of my brain are flapping furiously, but I haven't a clue where they're trying to take me.

You say that writers are God's chosen people. I cannot argue with that. Shcheglov calls me the Potemkin[2] of literature, so obviously it's not for me to talk about the path of thorns, the disappointments, and so on. I cannot say whether I have suffered more than a cobbler, a mathematician or a railway guard. Neither do I know whether it's God speaking through my lips or some other lesser being. The only minor unpleasantness I feel entitled to declare is one I suspect you have also experienced. It is this. You and I both like ordinary people;

1. 'The Duel'.
2. Grigory Potemkin (1739–91), soldier and statesman, and a favourite of Catherine the Great.

but we are liked because people see us as being out of the ordinary. For example, I am always being invited by all and sundry to be wined and dined like the obligatory general at a wedding; my sister is indignant at being invited along just because she is the writer's sister. No one is prepared to like us as ordinary people. It follows that if one fine day our dear friends were to see us as ordinary mortals, they would no longer like us but start feeling sorry for us instead. And that is horrible. It's horrible, because what attracts them to us is precisely those qualities in ourselves we often do not like and do not respect. It's horrible to realize that I was on the right lines when I put that discussion about celebrity between the engineer and the professor into my story 'The First Class Passenger'.

I want to go and bury myself on a farmstead. To hell with them! At least you have your bolthole in Feodosia.

A propos Feodosia and the Tatars. The Tatars were swindled out of their land, yet no one spares a thought for their welfare. They need schools. You ought to write an article demanding that instead of pouring money into that Dorpat University of Sausages for useless German students, the Ministry should instead spend it on schools for Tatars, who can be of some use to Russia. I would write it myself, but I haven't the skill.

Leikin sent me a most amusing comedy he has written. He truly is one of a kind.

Be well and happy.

Your

A. Chekhov

Tell Maslov that the fate of his play is in the process of being decided, and the decision might go either way. They have put on one Spanish play and it was not very successful, so they are dubious about putting on another one.

76. To Alexander Chekhov, 2 January 1889, Moscow

O wisest of secretaries!

Good wishes to your resplendent self and your progeny on the New Year, and for your further happiness. May you win two hundred thousand and be appointed a full member of the Privy Council, and furthermore enjoy the best of health and daily bread in measure sufficient even for such a glutton as yourself.

On my recent visit to you, both during the time we spent together and when we parted, it was as though there was a misunderstanding between us. I shall come again soon; in order to dispel the misunderstanding I think I ought in all sincerity and conscience to tell you what brought it about. I was seriously angry with you and was still angry when I left, which I now regret. On my first visit to you, what wrenched us apart was your *appalling* treatment of Natalia Alexandrovna and your cook. Forgive me, but to treat women in such a manner, whoever they may be, is unworthy of a decent, caring human being. What heavenly or earthly power granted you the right to make them your slaves? Constant bad language of the most filthy kind, raising your voice to them, criticizing them, capricious demands at lunch and dinner, endless complaints about how your life is nothing but penal servitude and accursed drudgery – is not all that the mark of a coarse bully and despot? However worthless and sinful a woman may be, however close your relations with her, you have no right to sit drunk in her presence, without your trousers on, and the sort of language factory hands would blanch at in the presence of a woman spewing out of your mouth. You think decency and good manners are mere prejudices, but surely there are things you should spare, such as female weakness, the children – you should at least spare the poetry of life even if you have done with the prose. No decent husband or lover would allow himself to talk coarsely to a woman about pissing and wiping her bum, to make dirty jokes about the relations of the bedroom, to root about verbally in her sexual organs. This corrupts a woman and sets up barriers between her and the God in whom she believes. No man with any respect for women, no educated and caring man, would expose himself without his trousers to the maid, yelling 'Katka, get me the potty!' at the top of his voice . . . When men go to bed with their wives at night they show proper decorum in tone and manner, and in the morning they hasten to put on their tie and dress decently in a way that does not offend. You may think this pedantic, but it is rooted in something you will understand if you think back to the fundamental role played in a person's upbringing by their surroundings and the little details of life. There is as great a difference between a woman who sleeps between clean sheets and one who dosses down on a dirty old rag, guffawing whenever her lover lets out a fart, as there is between a drawing room and a pigsty.

Children are sacred and pure beings. Even bandits and crocodiles have children who may be counted in the ranks of the angels. We ourselves can crawl into any hole we like, but the atmosphere surrounding them should be fitting to their status. You shouldn't allow yourself to use foul language in front of them, or insult the servant, or snarl at Natalia Alexandrovna, 'Go to hell, leave me alone. I don't want you here!' Nor should you make them the plaything of your moods: alternately kissing them tenderly and stamping on them in a frenzy. It's better not to love at all than to love as a despot. Hatred is a much more honest emotion than love à la Nasreddin,[1] who was given sometimes to raising up his favourite Persians to be satraps, and sometimes to impaling them on stakes. You should never take a child's name in vain, but you habitually describe every copeck you give or think of giving to someone else as 'one taken from the children'. If you really mean that you are taking it from them, it follows that you must have started off by *giving* it in the first place, and it isn't very attractive to draw attention to one's good deeds and charitable gifts. It comes across like a reproach. Most people live for their families, but it doesn't occur to most of them to claim any special merit for that, and it's certainly rare to come across someone like you, who when lending someone a rouble has the nerve to say: 'I'm depriving my children by doing this.' It hardly shows respect for the sanctity of

1. Nasreddin (1831–96), who is mentioned in Chekhov's story 'On the Road' (1886), became Shah of Persia in 1848. A Russian translation of a travelogue written by him was published in St Petersburg in 1887.

children to keep repeating from your well-fed, warm-clad, daily tipsy state that *every* penny you earn goes on the children. Enough already!

I ask you to remember that your mother's youth was ruined by despotism and lies. Despotism and lies also destroyed our own childhood, so much so that we become sick and fearful when we remember it. Think back to the terror and disgust we used to feel whenever Father made a fuss at lunch about the soup having too much salt in it, or cursed Mother for being a fool. Now he cannot forgive himself for all those things . . .

Despotism is a crime thrice over. If the Day of Judgement is not a chimera, you will be more harshly judged by the Sanhedrin than Chokhov or Ivan Gavrilov. You know perfectly well that the gods blessed you with that which is lacking in ninety-nine out of 100 people: by nature you are infinitely generous and affectionate. For that very reason, 100 times more is expected of you. Furthermore you are a university man, and regard yourself as a journalist.

The problems of your situation, the bad character of the woman you have to live with, the idiocy of cooks, the backbreaking work you have to do, the accursedly wretched life you are leading – none of these things excuse your bullying. Better to be the victim than the executioner.

Natalia Alexandrovna, your cook and your children are weak and defenceless creatures. They have no rights over you; you can throw them out of the door at any moment and laugh at their weakness if you wish. But you should not make them feel that you have this power over them.

I have stated my case as best I can, and my conscience is clear. Be generous and consider our misunderstanding at an end. If you are honest and not devious, you will not regard this letter as stemming from any malicious objectives, such as a wish to insult you or bad feeling on my part. In all that passes between us I desire only sincerity. I don't need anything else. We have nothing to fall out about.

Please write and tell me that you are not angry either, and that the black cat which crossed our path has now vanished.

Your

A. Chekhov

77. To Alexey Suvorin, 7 January 1889, Moscow

I'm sending you a chit on which I'd like you to scribble your signature and send it back to me. You will thereupon become a member of the Society [of Russian Dramatic Writers and Opera Composers] from 7 January until a date precisely fifty years after your death. This pleasure will cost you a mere 15 roubles.

Today I've sent you two alternative passages for my *Ivanov*. If an actor of subtlety and energy were going to be playing the role of Ivanov, there would be many more additions and alterations I would want to make. But alas! Ivanov is to be played by Davydov. This means that everything has to be written in a shorter and greyer style, given that all refinements and nuances will coagulate into a boring, grey soup. Could Davydov ever be capable of encompassing both gentleness and ferocity? When he plays serious parts he seems to switch on a little machine in his throat that speaks his lines for him in a sort of dull, feeble monotone . . . I feel sorry for poor Savina, who has to play the apathetic Sasha. I like Savina very much as an actress, but if Davydov is simply going to mumble his way through, then however many trimmings I give to the character of Sasha, there's no way I can make it work. I feel really embarrassed that Savina is going to act such nonsense in my play. Had I known at the time that she was going to be Sasha and that Davydov was going to be Ivanov, I would have called the play *Sasha* and built the whole structure around her, tacking Ivanov on as a peripheral character. But how was I to know that?

Ivanov has two monologues that are critical to the play: one in Act III and one at the end of Act IV . . . The first must be spoken as poetry, the second as a wild rant. Davydov can't handle either of them. He does them both 'sensibly', i.e. in an interminably limp way.

Can you please let me know Fyodorov's[1] first name?

I should be very happy to read a paper to the Literary Society on

---

1. Fyodor Fyodorov-Yurkovsky (1842–1915), a director at the Alexandrinsky Theatre.

the source of my ideas for *Ivanov*. I could turn it into a public confession. I had been cherishing for some time my dream of encapsulating everything ever written about miserable people who do nothing but whine, and my *Ivanov* is an attempt to draw a line under this kind of writing. I'd been thinking that all Russian novelists and playwrights felt obliged to depict unhappy people, and that they all wrote instinctively, without concrete images or any real focus on the subject. As far as the theory is concerned I have more or less hit the target, but I am a long way from having realized it successfully in practice. I ought to have waited! I'm glad now that I did not listen to Grigorovich's advice two or three years ago to write a novel. Imagine how much good material I would have wasted if I had listened! His idea is that 'talent and freshness conquer everything'. It would be truer to say that talent and freshness can ruin everything. Other, no less vital, attributes are needed besides talent and material. The first necessity is maturity, and after that *a sense of personal freedom*; this is a feeling that has only very recently begun to grow in me. Before, it was completely lacking; I successfully substituted for it a frivolous, careless and wholly irresponsible attitude to my work.

What upper-class writers have always taken for granted, those from humbler origins must sacrifice their youth to acquire. Try writing a story about a young man, the son of a serf, a former shop boy and chorister, schoolboy and student, brought up to be respectful of his betters and to kiss the priest's hand, to submit to the ideas of others, to be grateful for every crust of bread, who is constantly thrashed, who goes out without galoshes to tutor other people's children, who gets into fights, torments animals, savours the taste of good dinners with rich relations, unnecessarily plays the hypocrite before God and his fellows purely from a realization of his own insignificance – and then go on to tell the story of how this young man drop by drop wrings the slave out of himself until, one fine morning, he awakes to feel that flowing in his veins is no longer the blood of a slave, but that of a complete human being . . .

There is in Moscow a poet named Palmin, one of the meanest of men. He banged his head a little while ago, and I treated him. He came to have the dressing changed today, and brought me a bottle of genuine ylang-ylang, costing three roubles and 50 copecks. I was very touched by this.

Well, be in good health, and forgive this long letter.

Your

A. Chekhov

78. To Alexey Suvorin, 5 March 1889, Moscow

Dear Alexey Sergeyevich,

I am enclosing my story 'The Princess'. Devil take her, I'm fed up with her: she lay about on my desk all the time asking me to finish her; well now I have, but she's not in perfect shape. If you don't plan to publish her in the immediate future, please send me a proof so that I can polish her up a bit.

I'm writing another story now. I'm absorbed in it and can hardly drag myself away from my desk. By the way, I've bought myself a new desk.

Thank you for promising to send the dictionaries. One good turn deserves another . . . In return for the dictionaries I shall send you a cheap and useless present which nevertheless only I can give you.[1] You'll have to wait and see what it is. May I remind you about your large photograph and Shapiro's[2] photographs of me? If Shapiro has sent them to you, please send them on . . .

Svobodin[3] has been to see me, and told me among other things that you apparently received a letter from some parent whose son shot himself after seeing my *Ivanov*. If this letter is not a myth, please send it to me and I will add it to those I already have about *Ivanov*. I didn't read *The Citizen* 1) because I don't subscribe to this paper, and 2) because I am sick of *Ivanov*; I can't read any more about him, and I get a queasy feeling whenever people launch into earnest, cogent conversations about him.

1. Chekhov's parody sequel to Suvorin's play *Tatyana Repina*. See p. 139, n.5.
2. A St Petersburg photographer with a studio on Nevsky Prospekt.
3. Chekhov had become friends with Pavel Svobodin when the latter played Shabelsky in *Ivanov* in St Petersburg in 1888.

Yesterday I went out of town to listen to the gipsies. They sing very well, these wild creatures. Their singing is like a train crashing down a high embankment: a whirlwind of shrieking and banging . . .

Pay no attention to Leikin. I'm not spitting blood, I'm not depressed and I'm not losing my mind. If you were to believe everything you hear about me in Petersburg just now, then I'd be gushing blood, I'd have totally lost my wits, married Sibiryakova[4] and got myself a dowry of twenty million.

I bought Dostoyevsky[5] in your shop and am now reading him. It is good, but very long and self-indulgent. Very pretentious.

Tell me, why on earth have we allowed the French to make a laughing-stock of Ostrovsky's *The Storm*?[6] Who ever thought that would be a good idea? The only reason the play was put on was to give the Frenchmen another chance to look down their noses and gossip knowingly about things they find intolerably boring and incomprehensible. All these translator gentlemen should be packed off to Siberia for their unpatriotic and irresponsible behaviour.

I am planning to write *The Wood Demon* either in May or in August. By dint of pacing up and down during lunch I've mapped out the first three acts quite satisfactorily, but I only have a sketchy idea of the fourth. Act III is so scandalous that when you see it you will say: 'The man who wrote this must be a devious and cruel character.'

My deepest respects to Anna Ivanovna and the children. I wish them the best of health.

Your

A. Chekhov

So Potemkin didn't win on 1 March![7]

4. The widow of a Siberian goldminer.
5. A reference to Dostoyevsky's collected works, published in St Petersburg in 1889.
6. Alexander Ostrovsky's play had recently been staged in Paris in French translation.
7. Chekhov had not won the lottery.

79. To Nikolay Obolonsky, 29 March 1889, Moscow

Dear Nikolay Nikolayevich,

Please be so kind as to go and see my sick brother Nikolay Pavlovich Chekhov. He lives near the Red Gates, in Ipatieva's apartment (No. 42) in the Bogomolov house, Kalanchevskaya Street. He is suffering from pn. cruposa. If you would like me to come with you, let me know when I can catch you at home, or come to my house tomorrow. I make so bold as to suggest the latter course of action because of your promise to come and visit me (if you remember our supper conversation at Korsh's). It would be excellent if you could let me know by telegram. I live in Y. A. Korneyev's house on Sadovaya-Kudrinskaya.

If you decide to go to see my brother on your own, please be aware that although he lives a thoroughly bohemian life he has not been drinking at all for two months now. He has always had a weak pulse. I made arrangements for him to have eight dry cupping-glasses put on him, and have prescribed warm compresses. Forgive me in God's name for presuming so unceremoniously on your time and trouble.

I send you my best wishes,

Respectfully yours

A. Chekhov

80. To Alexey Suvorin, 8 April 1889, Moscow

A Happy Easter to you, Anna Ivanovna, Nastyusha and Borya, and may you enjoy prosperity, fame, honour, peace and happiness all your lives.

The weather in Moscow is disgusting: mud, cold and rain. The artist obstinately persists in running a temperature of 39 degrees. I visit him twice a day. My mood is like the weather. I'm not doing any work, just reading or pacing up and down. However, I don't really mind having the time to read. It's more enjoyable than writing. I feel that if I could live another forty years and spend the whole time reading, reading, reading, and learning how to write with talent, that is to say succinctly, then in forty years' time I would be able to blast everyone from such a big cannon that the heavens would tremble. But for now I am just as Lilliputian as all the rest.

The family is tidying, spring-cleaning, baking, cooking, dusting, running up and down the stairs. The place is in an uproar. I'm off to see the artist. Keep well. Come away with me, let's go down the Volga or to Poltava.

Your

A. Chekhov

81. To Maria Chekhova, 26 April 1889, Sumy

Bring me a pair of felt shoes, which you can buy for a rouble. I am the same size as Ivan.

The weather is lovely, but it is no greener here than in Moscow. The air is marvellous, the Psyol majestically gentle.

The fish traps arrived in good shape.

Greetings to Papa, the Ivans, Auntie and her offspring, the Korneyevs, the Lenskys, Vermicelli, Macaronova and all the others.

We are looking forward to seeing you.

Nikolay is in good spirits.

Did Ivan send off the vaudeville?

Don't skimp on expenses for the journey.

The cherries and the lilac are not out yet. Artemenko was terribly pleased to see me when I arrived.

Your

Antonio

The bittern is booming. The nightingales and frogs keep you awake. Buy an A string for the mandolin.

[On the back: To Maria Pavlovna Chekhova, The Korneyev House, Sadovaya-Kudrinskaya, Moscow, for forwarding to Akaky Petrovich Nakakiev][1]

82. To Alexey Suvorin, early May 1889, Sumy

I can't believe my eyes. A short while ago it was snowing and cold, and now I am sitting by an open window and listening to non-stop shrieking from nightingales, hoopoes, orioles and other such creatures. The Psyol is majestically gentle, the colours of the sky and the distant horizon are warm. The apple and cherry trees are covered in blossom. Geese stroll about with their goslings. In a word, spring has arrived in all its finery.

Stiva has not sent the boats, so we have nothing in which to go on the water. Our hosts' boats are somewhere in the woods with the forester, so I content myself with walking along the banks, acutely envying the fishermen dashing about in their canoes. I rise early, go to bed early, eat lots, write and read. The painter [Nikolay] coughs and gets irritable. Things are not going well for him. As I have no new books I'm going over old ground rereading things I have read before. I'm reading Goncharov by the way, and am surprised: why did I ever think him a first-class writer? His *Oblomov* is really not good at all. Ilya Ilyich as a character is overdone; he is simply not strong enough to sustain a whole book. He is just a flabby layabout like hundreds of others, he's not a complex character, but a commonplace and trivial one; making a social type out of such a person is to elevate him way above his status. The question I ask myself is: without his laziness, what would Oblomov have been? And my answer is: nothing. If so, he should just carry on snoring. The other characters are paltry, they have a Leikinish smell about them, half-baked and carelessly done. In no way do they exemplify their time, and they tell

1. Nonsense name with scatological associations, reminiscent of the hero of Gogol's story 'The Overcoat', Akaky Akakievich.

us nothing new. Stolz I find completely unconvincing. The author informs us that he is a splendid fellow, but I don't buy it. He's a sly, smug rogue who thinks highly of himself. He's half contrived and three-quarters pompous. Olga is also contrived and has been dragged in by the tail. But the worst of it is, the whole novel is cold, cold, cold . . . I'm crossing Goncharov off my list of demigods.

By way of contrast, what immediacy and strength Gogol has, and what an artist he is! His story 'The Carriage' is worth 2,000 roubles alone. Sheer delight, nothing less. He is the greatest of all Russian writers. The first act of *The Government Inspector* is the best, the third act of *Marriage*[1] the weakest. I'm going to read him aloud to the family.

When are you going away? How I should love to go somewhere like Biarritz just now, where there will be music to listen to and plenty of women. If it weren't for the painter I really would come chasing after you. I'd find the money somewhere or other. I give you my word that next year, if I live and am healthy, I will definitely go to Europe. All I need to do is wheedle 3,000 roubles out of the theatre management, and finish my novel, of course.

There are no copies of *In the Twilight* or *Stories* on your bookstand at the Sumy railway station, and there haven't been any *for some time now*. And in Sumy I'm a popular author, because I'm living here. If Mikhail Alexeyevich would send them another fifty copies, they'd all sell.

The dogs howl appallingly at night, and stop me sleeping.

My *Wood Demon* is coming along nicely.

Warmest regards to Anna Ivanovna, Nastya and Borya. Last night I had a dream about Mlle Emilie.[2] Why, do you think? I can't imagine.

Be happy and remember me in your prayers.

Your

Akaky Tarantulov

1. Gogol's two plays, written in 1836 and 1842 respectively.
2. The Suvorins' French governess.

83. To Alexey Suvorin, 4 May 1889, Sumy

I'm writing to you, dear Alexey Sergeyevich, having just returned from catching crayfish. The weather is marvellous. Everything is in song, in bloom and ablaze with beauty. The garden is already quite green; even the oak trees are in leaf. The trunks of the apple, pear, cherry and plum trees are painted white to protect them from worms, and in combination with their white blossom they look strikingly like brides at a wedding: white dresses, white garlands and an air of innocence as though they feel ashamed to be looked at. Every day a myriad new creatures come into existence. Nightingales, bitterns, cuckoos and other denizens of the feathered kingdom never cease their racket for a moment day and night, to the accompaniment of the frogs. Every hour of the day and night has its own characteristic sound, so for instance at nine o'clock in the evening the cockchafers start up literally with a roar . . . The nights are moonlit and the days are bright with sunshine . . . The result of all this is that my mood is splendid, and if only it were not for the artist coughing all the time, and the mosquitoes, who seem to be immune even to Elpe's prescription,[1] I'd be a complete Potemkin.[2] Nature is an excellent tranquillizer. It calms one, that is makes one indifferent to one's fate. And in this world one must be indifferent to one's fate. You can only see things as they truly are and be capable of working if you don't care about what lies in store for you – of course I'm speaking of intelligent people with noble natures; those who are egotistical and vacuous are quite indifferent enough as it is.

You write that I have become lazy. It doesn't follow that I'm any lazier than I was before. I am working just as hard now as I was three to five years ago. It has long been my custom to work, and to look as though I'm working, from nine in the morning until lunch and then again from tea in the evening until I go to sleep. In this respect I'm just like any government clerk. If this amount of work fails to produce

1. A reference to the science correspondent for *New Times*.
2. Meaning 'I'd be in clover'.

two stories a month or an income of ten thousand a year, the fault lies not with my laziness, but with my mental and physical make-up: I don't love money enough for medicine, and I don't have enough passion, and therefore talent, for literature. My fire burns steady but low, it is not a matter of sparks suddenly erupting into flame, and that is why I don't write fifty or sixty pages in a single night, or get so absorbed in work that I deny myself my bed when sleep calls; and for the same reason I neither commit egregious idiocies nor achieve startling insights. I am afraid that in this I much resemble Goncharov, whom I don't like but whose talent stands ten heads above mine. I lack great passion; and as if that were not enough, during the past two years, for some reason I can't put my finger on, I have developed a pathological aversion to seeing my works in print. I've become indifferent to reviews, to conversations about literature, to gossip, to success and failure, to earning big fees – in a word I have become the fool of fools. It's as though my soul has gone into hibernation. The only explanation I can find for it is that my personal life has also gone into hibernation. It is not that I'm frustrated or worn out or depressed, I've simply become somehow less interesting. Someone should put a bomb under me.

You'll be surprised to learn that I have finished the first act of *The Wood Demon*. It has turned out not badly, if a bit long. I feel much stronger than I did when I wrote *Ivanov*. The play will be ready by the beginning of June, so stand by, theatre managers! It should net me 5,000 roubles. The play is most peculiar, and I am amazed that such odd things can flow from my pen. But I fear the censor may not pass it. I'm also writing a novel, which is more congenial and closer to my heart than *The Wood Demon*, where I have to dissemble and play the fool all the time. Yesterday evening I remembered that I had promised Varlamov[3] I would write a farce for him. So today I wrote it, and have already sent it off to him. See how I can churn it out when I have to! And you say I'm lazy!

I notice you're at last taking notice of King Solomon. Whenever I

---

3. Konstantin Varlamov (1848–1915), an actor at the Alexandrinsky from 1875, for whom Chekhov wrote a 'jest in one act' entitled *A Tragedian Despite Himself*.

have talked to you about him in the past, you've just nodded wisely and obviously paid no attention. I think Goethe took the idea of writing *Faust* from Ecclesiastes.

I liked the tone of your letter about Likhachov[4] very much. In my opinion it could be a model for a polemic on any subject.

I went to the theatre in Sumy and saw *Second Youth*. The costumes and scenery were so terrible that the play was more like *Below Stairs* than *Second Youth*. There was a drum beating backstage in the last act. They are planning to produce *Tatyana Repina* and *Ivanov*. I shall go and see them. I can just imagine what Adashev will be like!

Please send me my copy of *Tatyana Repina*, if it has been published.

My brother has written to me saying that he's been having a bad time with his play. I'm delighted to hear it. Let him suffer. When he came to see *Tatyana Repina* and my *Ivanov* he was extremely condescending, knocking back the cognac in the intervals and graciously dispensing criticism. Everyone seems to think they are entitled to critique a play, as if it were the easiest thing in the world to write one. What they don't realize is that, difficult though it is to write a good play, it is twice as difficult, appallingly so, to write a bad one. Wouldn't it be wonderful if the entire theatre audience could be boiled down into a single person, and this single person wrote a play that you and I could watch from Box One and boo off the stage!

Alexander's problem is that he is inexperienced and rewrites too much. I am afraid many of his effects don't come off, then he torments himself in fruitless struggles with them.

Please bring me back some banned books and newspapers from abroad. I would have acompanied you had it not been for the artist.

God is not mocked: he has taken both [D. A.] Tolstoy and Saltykov[5] into the next world, thereby reconciling what formerly appeared irreconcilable. Now both are rotting, and both can be equally indifferent. I have been told that many people rejoiced at Tolstoy's death; to me this seems a bestial reaction. I find it hard to believe in the future

4. Vladimir Likhachov (1849–1910), a poet, dramatist, translator and one of the organizers of the anthology in memory of Garshin.
5. Dmitry Tolstoy (1823–89), Minister of Internal Affairs, 1882–9; Mikhail Saltykov-Shchedrin (1826–89), satirical writer.

of those good Christian souls who, even as they vent their hatred of the police, welcome the death of another human being because they see in it a sign of the angel of deliverance. You can't imagine how revolting it is to see women rejoicing in death like this.

When will you return from abroad? Where will you go after that?

Shall I really sit here on the banks of the Psyol until autumn? Oh, that would be terrible! After all, spring won't last for much longer.

Lensky has suggested I go with him when he tours to Tiflis. I'd go if it wasn't for the artist, who is not in brilliant shape.

Please tell Anna Ivanovna that I wish her the most enjoyable journey from the bottom of my heart.

If you go to the roulette tables, put twenty-five roubles on for me, for luck.

Well, God grant you health and all good fortune.

Your

A. Chekhov

84. To Nikolay Obolonsky, 4 June 1889, Sumy

Greetings to you, dearest Doctor! Suffer me not to be punished for my silence, rather command me now to speak. The reasons I have not written to you for such a long time are the following excellent ones: first, I did not know whether you were in Moscow or in the Caucasus; secondly, I was myself planning to accompany my sister to the Caucasus; and thirdly, I have been waiting every day for Nikolay to write out his *curriculum vitae* for you, as promised. Yes, and the other thing is that it is terribly boring and difficult to write when you know that there is nothing good or happy to write about. Matters stand badly with the artist [Nikolay]. The days are warm and he is drinking a lot of milk, but his temperature is the same as before, and his body weight decreases with every day that passes. His cough gives him no peace. For the first month we were here in the country he spent half the time out in the fresh air, but now he stubbornly keeps to his room; he comes out for half an hour at a time, but reluctantly and lethargically;

he sleeps a lot and is delirious while sleeping; he prefers to doze sitting up than to lie down because from the second half of May onwards the latter position has brought on his coughing ... His appetite is reasonable. I'm giving him ipec, quinine, atrop. [atropine] and so forth.

I hope you won't mind if I don't go on. All it will do is depress you. How are you? What are you doing with yourself? Is the 'club of contented idiots' still in existence? Are there plenty of pretty girls in Kislovodsk? Is there a theatre down there? In general, are you having a good summer? Write and tell me. If there are no chickens one must make do with bouillon; if you can't go to the Caucasus, letters from there go some way towards slaking one's thirst. You promise to send me a whole poem. All right. I'll respond with a story.

I may in fact come to Kislovodsk, but if I do it will not be before August. You know the reason. But if I do come, I'll immediately write a three-act play for Korsh. I did make a start on a full-length play for money, and wrote two acts, but then had to give it up. It just won't come. But I really should finish it, because it's already promised for Svobodin and Lensky's benefit performance, and all the newspapers have already been gossiping about it.

Our 'guest season' has started. Suvorin was here for a week; Svobodin is here now; tomorrow the cellist[1] and somebody else are coming from Moscow. If it weren't for the coughing from the next room, life would on the whole be enjoyable. When I grow up and can have my own dacha, I shall build three wings specifically for guests of both sexes. I think I prefer noise to fees.

Going back to the artist: when I was bringing him down from Moscow, he was very sick halfway here. He is still vomiting. And one other, more significant, detail: he is showing symptoms of a laryngeal infection. This is particularly worrying because I am rather weak on diseases of the throat, and there does not seem to be a laryngoscope anywhere in the district. Is there an inhalation you can recommend? One of the local physicians insists that the best thing is creosote.

We're having a drought here. There is no rain, the crops are very

---

1. Marian Semashko, a cellist and family friend of the Chekhovs.

poor and the fruit has all been eaten by worms. There will be no harvest at all. The fish aren't biting either.

The artist talks about you every day, and every day asks me to get him some writing paper so that he can write to you. He's got himself a kitten to relieve the boredom and plays with it as if it were a child. He's priming the face of a wall clock; he wants to paint a woman's head on it.

My family sends its greetings and once again its deep gratitude to you. I'm going to go and see Nikolay now and make sure he writes to you. I'll send his letter separately.

I look forward to the poem, and in the meantime warmly press your hand, wish you an expanding practice and yet more romances with the houris of Kislovodsk, and remain your cordially devoted

A. Chekhov

My address is: Sumy

85. To Nikolay Obolonsky, 17 June 1889, Sumy

The artist has passed away. Details in a letter, or when we meet, but for now please forgive my writing in pencil.

I warmly clasp your hand,

Yours with all my heart

A. Chekhov

86. To Franz Shekhtel, 18 June 1889, Sumy

Nikolay died of consumption yesterday, 17 June. He lies now in his coffin with a most beautiful expression on his face. May the Kingdom of Heaven be his, and health and happiness to you, his friend . . .

Your

A. Chekhov

87. To Mikhail Dyukovsky, 24 June 1889, Sumy

Dearest Mikhail Mikhailovich, I am replying to your letter. Nikolay was already suffering from consumption when he left Moscow. The outcome was never in doubt, although we did not know it would be so soon. With every day that passed his health grew worse, and for the last few weeks Nikolay was not living, but suffering: he had to sleep sitting up, the coughing never stopped, he felt he was suffocating, and so on and so forth. If in the past he had sins on his conscience, they will have been expiated a hundredfold by such suffering. At first it made him angry, his rage was painful to behold, but the month before he died he became as meek as a lamb, affectionate and extraordinarily calm. He dreamt of recovering and starting to paint again. He spoke often of you and of his relationship with you. Memories were just about his only remaining pleasure. A week before he died he took communion. He died fully conscious. He did not feel death was imminent, or at least he never talked about it.

Lying in his coffin he had a most beautiful expression on his face. We took a photograph of him, but I do not know whether any photograph can succeed in conveying this expression.

The funeral was splendid. According to southern custom, he was borne by hand into the church and out of it again to the grave-yard, in an open coffin with banners, without torch-bearers and without a hearse. The girls carried the coffin lid and we carried the coffin itself. The bells were rung in the church while we carried him. He was buried in the village churchyard, a very peaceful and welcoming place, where birds sing constantly and the creeping velvet grass smells sweetly. As soon as the funeral was over we placed a cross on the grave, which can be seen from far off across the fields. Tomorrow is the ninth day[1] and we shall hold a requiem for him.

1. In the Orthodox Church, a special service for the departed, a *panikhida*, is performed on the day of a person's death, and on the third, ninth and fortieth day following it.

All the family thank you for your letter; Mama wept when she read it. It is all very sad, my dear friend.

I am so glad that you are getting married. Congratulations and may I wish you all that is customary on your marriage.

I have not written at length to you, because the subject is not one that can be covered in two pages or so. I shall tell you more of the details when we meet, but for now I wish you health and happiness.

All my family send you their best regards.

Your

A. Chekhov

88. To Alexey Pleshcheyev, 3 August 1889, Yalta

My very dear Alexey Nikolayevich, can you imagine, I am neither abroad nor in the Caucasus, but have already been holed up for two weeks on my own in a one and a half rouble room in that city of Tatars and hairdressers, Yalta. I was supposed to be going abroad, but fetched up unexpectedly in Odessa and stayed there for ten days; having eaten up half of my fortune on ice cream (it was very hot), I travelled on to Yalta. There was no point in coming here, and there is no point in staying here either. I swim in the mornings and expire from the heat in the afternoons. In the evenings I drink wine and at night I sleep. The sea is magnificent, the vegetation unimpressive, everyone is either Jewish or ill. Every day I make up my mind to leave, but somehow I keep not doing so. But I need to leave. My conscience is pricking me horribly. It's shameful to be living so sybaritically when things are awry at home. When I left the atmosphere was depressed and fearful.

The present letter has two objectives: 1) to greet you and remind you of my sinful existence, and 2) to ask you to let Anna Mikhailovna know that she will have a story[1] from me no later than 1 September. This is a definite promise, as I have almost finished it. Despite the heat

1. 'A Dreary Story', which appeared in *The Northern Herald* in November 1889.

and the temptations that abound in Yalta, I am writing. I have already written 200 roubles' worth, i.e. about one complete printer's sheet.

I started a play before I left home, but gave up on it. I've had enough of actors. To hell with them!

I am a lucky man today. While I was out swimming, I narrowly avoided being killed by a lout with a long, heavy pole. My head was about one centimetre away from the pole, and this is all that saved me. Such a miraculous escape from death has channelled my thoughts into reflections appropriate to the circumstance.

There are many young ladies in Yalta, but not one of them is pretty. There are a good many writers as well, but none with any talent. Plenty of wine, but not a drop of it drinkable. The only good things are the sea and the ponies. When you ride on them they rock you as if in a cradle. Living is cheap; a person on his own can live here on 100 roubles a month.

Greetings from Petrov, long-term resident, printer, Don Juan and lover of poetry. He is sitting opposite me as I write and is about to treat me to dinner. He is deaf and therefore speaks terribly loudly. The place is full of cranks.

Should you feel inclined to present me with a letter, please address it to Sumy, whither I shall return no later than 10 August.

As a result of the heat and my wretched, melancholy mood, the story is turning out rather boring. But at least the subject is new, so perhaps people will find it interesting to read.

I was told by one of the local poets that Elena Alexandrovna [Lintvaryovna] is planning to come here. Tell her not to come before the grapes ripen, that is not before 15–20 August.

Give my regards to all your family. I embrace you and remain, as always, your sincerely devoted Antoine Potemkin (a sobriquet bestowed on me by Jean Shcheglov).

By the way: what is Jean doing? Is he still violating Melpomene? If you see him, please pass on my regards.

89. To Elena Lintvaryova, 6 September 1889, Moscow

Greetings, most honoured and kindest of doctors!

We eventually arrived in Moscow, in good shape and without any unforeseen adventures. We started on the food at Vorozhba and finished it just before we got to Moscow. There was a terrible smell coming from the chickens. Masha spent the whole journey pretending to be unacquainted with Semashko and me, because travelling in the same carriage was Professor Storozhenko, her former lecturer and examiner. To punish this display of pettiness I launched into a raucous account of my time as a cook in the service of Countess Keller and how amiable my employers were. Each time I took a swig of my drink, I saluted my mother and expressed the hope that she would find a good position in Moscow. Semashko impersonated a valet.

It is cold in Moscow, the rooms have not been cleaned and the furniture is shabby. I have left my soul behind in Luka. I would like to tell you a thousand warm words. Were it the custom to offer prayers to blessed women and maidens in advance of the heavenly angels translating their souls to paradise, I would long ago have penned an akathist to you and your sisters, and would declaim it every day on bended knee, but as this practice is not customary I must content myself by lighting in my heart the eternal flame in your honour, and asking you to trust in the sincerity and constancy of my feelings. I need hardly tell you that pride of place in these feelings is occupied by my gratitude.

Please give my best regards to all your family, omitting no one, not Grigory Alexandrovich, nor Domnushka, nor Ulyasha. I hope that Egor Mikhailovich has ceased his swinish behaviour, I mean messing about with his piglet. Tell Alexandra Vasiliyevna that she acted quite improperly in not charging me anything for the small annexe. She accepted something from Dekonor and is doing so from Artemenko, and I hope I am in no way inferior to them.

I already had visitors yesterday, the day I arrived. My family joins me in sending you cordial greetings, as does Semashko.

When I told Ivan how Valentina Nikolayevna had packed my bags, he thought for a minute, scratched behind his ear and sighed deeply. The bags were packed with such artistry that I was reluctant to unpack them.

Is Natalia Mikhailovna cold-blooded?

Well, may God preserve you all.

Your sincerely devoted

A. Chekhov

I enclose my erysipelas.[1]

90. To Pyotr Tchaikovsky, 12 October 1889, Moscow

Dear Pyotr Ilyich,

This month I am preparing for publication a new collection of my stories:[1] these stories are as dull and tedious as autumn, monotonous in tone, their artistic elements inextricably entangled with the medical, but none of this prevents me from having the temerity to approach you with a humble request for your permission to dedicate this little book to you. I hope very much that you will feel able to respond positively, because in the first place the dedication would afford me great pleasure, and in the second it would go some small way towards satisfying those profound feelings of admiration with which I think of you every day. I conceived the notion of dedicating the book to you as long ago as the day when we were lunching together at Modest Ilyich's and I learnt that you had read my stories.

If, in addition to granting me your permission, you would kindly send me your photograph, I shall have received more than I deserve, and you shall have my undying gratitude. Forgive me for troubling you in this way, and allow me to send you my best wishes.

Your sincerely devoted

A. Chekhov

1. A severe skin rash, also called St Anthony's Fire, caused by a streptococcal infection.

1. *Gloomy People*, published in St Petersburg in 1890.

91. To Pyotr Tchaikovsky, 14 October 1889, Moscow

Dear Pyotr Ilyich,

I am very, very touched, and infinitely grateful to you. I am sending you a photograph and some books, and would send you the sun as well if it belonged to me.

You forgot your cigarette case at my house. I'm sending it to you. You will find that three cigarettes are missing: they were smoked by the cellist, the flautist and the teacher.

I thank you again, and ask your permission to remain your sincerely devoted

A. Chekhov

92. To Alexey Suvorin, 17 October 1889, Moscow

I wrote to you yesterday about the medical section of the yearbook. Ostrovsky, about whom I have also written to you before, has lugged over a whole stack of his sister's stories today.

Goreva is getting a comprehensive mauling and roasting, and this is of course most unjust, as only people who do harm should be mauled and roasted in public, and even then never indiscriminately. But Goreva is truly awful. I went to her theatre once, and nearly died of boredom. Her actors are dingy, and her pretentiousness oppressive.[1]

You have no reason to congratulate yourself on having got into my play. It's premature for that little bird to sing.[2] Your turn is yet to come. I will at some point, should I live long enough, depict our nights of talking in Feodosia, and our fishing expedition when you walked up and down the decking at the Lintvaryovs' watermill – but that is all; for the time being there's nothing else I need from you.

1. The actress Ekaterina Goreva founded a theatre company in 1889 in Moscow which lasted for two years.
2. Suvorin had heard that two of the characters in *The Wood Demon* were based on him and his wife.

You are not in the play, and it is not possible for you to be, no matter how Grigorovich, with his characteristic perceptiveness, may see to the contrary. The play deals with a boring, self-satisfied, wooden man who without understanding the first thing about it has been lecturing on art for twenty-five years; a man who spreads gloom and despondency to all around him, suppressing all laughter, music and so on and so on, while himself remaining perfectly content. Please do not trust all those gentlemen who begin by trying to find the worst in everything, judging everything by their own standards and attributing to others their own vulpine and badgerly traits. Oh, how delighted Grigorovich is! And how pleased they would all be if I were to slip a little arsenic into your tea, or if I turned out to be a Third Department[3] spy. You will, of course, say that none of this matters. But it does matter. If my play were to be on the stage now, the public would be saying in its incorrigibly lazy and superficial way: 'So that's what Suvorin is really like! That's the sort of person his wife is! Hmm . . . well, I never did! We didn't know they were like that.'

It is pathetically trivial, I agree, but the world is destroyed by such trivialities. A few days ago at the theatre I was talking to a writer from St Petersburg, and when he heard that at various times during the summer Pleshcheyev, Barantsevich, you, Svobodin and some others had been staying with me, he sighed and said: 'That won't do your reputation any good, you know. You're making a big mistake if you think you can rely on any of them.'

What he meant was that I had invited these people in order to get write-ups for myself, and had asked Svobodin because I might be able to palm off my play on him. The taste in my mouth after this conversation was as if I had just drunk a glass of ink full of flies instead of vodka. Things like this are insignificant pinpricks, but without them human life would be entirely blissful, instead of half of it being revolting, as it is now.

If someone offers you coffee, don't go looking for beer in it. If I present you with the ideas of the Professor, trust me and don't look for Chekhov's ideas in them, thank you kindly. There is only one

3. The tsarist secret police.

notion in the entire story to which I subscribe, and that is the one the Professor's son-in-law, the scoundrel Gnekker, has got into his head: 'The old boy's gone crackers!' Everything else is invented and purely the fruit of my imagination ... I don't understand where you find polemics. Surely you don't value any opinions whatever by concentrating on their specific centres of gravity to the exclusion of everything else, without taking into consideration how they are expressed, where they come from, and so on? On that basis even Bourget's *Disciple*[4] would constitute a polemical book. For me as a writer, none of these opinions has any value whatsoever in itself. The question is not what the opinions actually consist of: they are not fixed nor are they new. The whole point lies in the nature of the opinions, their dependence on external influences, and so on. They should be scrutinized like objects, or like symptoms, with total objectivity and with no attempt either to prove or disprove them. If I describe an attack of St Vitus's Dance, you wouldn't study it from the perspective of a choreographer, would you? It's just the same with opinions. It was absolutely not my purpose to dazzle you with my views on theatre, literature and so on; all I meant to do was use my skill and experience in order to describe the vicious circle into which a good and intelligent man has blundered – a man who, despite his willingness to take life as God gives it and behave like a good Christian, grumbles resentfully like a peevish slave and tears strips off people at precisely those times when he is struggling with himself to say something nice about them. He has every intention of standing up for his students, but all that comes out of his mouth is hypocrisy and Resident-style abuse ... Anyhow, it's a long story.

Your sons are certainly very promising. They have increased the price of the Hundred Chapters calendar[5] while reducing its size. They promised me a small barrel of wine for my stories but diddled me out of it; then to mollify me they stuck in my portrait facing one of the Shah of Persia. *A propos* the Shah: I recently read a poem called

---

4. *Le Disciple* (*The Disciple*), a novel by the French writer Paul Bourget (1852–1935).
5. Illustrated calendar published by Alexey and Mikhail Suvorin which reprinted some of Chekhov's early stories.

'A Political Concert', which went something like this: 'And the habitually eccentric Persian Shah went to Paris to compare his cock with the Eiffel Tower.' Come to Moscow. We'll go to the theatre together.

Your
Chekhov

93. *To Maria Chekhova, 14 January 1890, St Petersburg*

Unforeseen circumstances will keep me here for a few more days yet. I'm alive and well. No news at all. Actually, I saw Tolstoy's *The Power of Darkness*[1] the other day, and I have been to Repin's[2] studio. Anything else to report? Nothing else. It's mostly very dull.

I went to a wretched exhibition today with Suvorin, who is standing beside the desk as I write these lines and saying: 'Tell them you went to a wretched exhibition today with the notorious wretch Suvorin.'

Alexander and the children are well.

Regards to everyone I know. I've nothing else to write about.

Your
A. Chekhov

Georges Lintvaryov is hanging about in Petersburg.

I'm waiting for a letter from Misha about *The Artist*[3] magazine and about *The Wood Demon*.

1. A play written by Tolstoy in 1887.
2. Ilya Repin (1844–1930), Russia's most celebrated realist painter.
3. Theatrical, musical and artistic journal published in Moscow from September to April between 1889 and 1895. Chekhov did not want his play *The Wood Demon*, which had just been performed in Moscow, to be published in *The Artist*, and had written to his brother Misha from St Petersburg asking him to get the script back.

94. To Mikhail Galkin-Vraskoy, 20 January 1890, St Petersburg

To His Excellency Mikhail Nikolayevich Galkin-Vraskoy
Your Excellency, Mikhail Nikolayevich,

In view of my intention during the coming year to visit eastern Siberia for scientific and literary purposes, and to visit both the central and southern parts of the island of Sakhalin during the course of my journey, I humbly request all possible assistance that Your Excellency may be able to afford me to further my stated objectives.

Assuring you of the greatest respect and sincere devotion, I have the honour to remain, Sir, Your Excellency's most humble servant

Anton Chekhov

95. To Alexey Pleshcheyev, 15 February 1890, Moscow

I am replying to your letter, dear Alexey Nikolayevich, the moment I received it. Was it really your name day? Yes it was, and I forgot! Please forgive me, my dear friend, and accept my belated congratulations.

Did you really not like *The Kreutzer Sonata*?[1] I don't say that it is a work of immortal genius – I'm not able to judge that – but I do consider that, compared to most of what is being written today both here and abroad, it would be hard to find anything to compare with the importance of its theme and the beauty of its execution. Aside from its artistic merits, which are in places stupendous, we must above all be grateful to the story for its power to excite our minds to their limits. Reading it, you can scarcely forbear to exclaim: 'That's so true!' or alternatively 'That's stupid!' There is no doubt that it has some irritating defects. As well as those you have listed, there is one for which it is hard to forgive the author, and that is his arrogance in

1. A controversial story by Tolstoy, advocating celibacy, written in 1889.

discussing matters about which he understands nothing and is prevented by obstinacy from even wanting to understand anything. Thus his opinions on syphilis, foundling hospitals, women's distaste for sexual intercourse and so on, are not only contentious but show what an ignorant man he is in some respects, a man who has never in his long life taken the trouble to read one or two books written by specialists on the subject. But at the same time the story's virtues render these faults so insignificant that they waft away practically unnoticed, like feathers on the wind, and if we do notice them they serve merely to remind us of the fate of all human endeavour without exception, which is to be incomplete and never entirely free of blemishes.

So my Petersburg friends and acquaintances are angry with me? On what grounds? For not boring them with my presence, which has for long been a trial to myself? Please set their minds at rest, and tell them that, while it is true I ate a great many lunches and suppers in Petersburg, I failed to conquer *one single woman*. Tell them that every evening I fully expected to be leaving on the express, but each time was delayed by friends and by the *Maritime Almanac*, of which I had to read every published issue going back to 1852. During my month in Piter I achieved more than my young friends would in a whole year. Anyhow, let them be angry if they wish!

All the other gossip is complete nonsense, like the rumour that Shcheglov and I set off for Moscow by carriage because our friends fell for a spoof telegram young Suvorin had sent them; the idea that the Ministry sent 35,000 couriers galloping after me in order to offer me the governor-generalship of the island of Sakhalin is also absolute rubbish. My brother Misha had written to the Lintvaryovs telling them I was busy with preparations for my journey to Sakhalin, and they obviously did not understand what he was saying. If you see Galkin-Vraskoy, please tell him not to worry about getting his reports reviewed: I shall devote a lot of space to them in my book and will immortalize his name. As a matter of fact the reports are not very good: they have a wealth of good material in them but the bureaucrats who wrote them didn't know how to make use of it.

I spend all day, every day sitting, reading, and copying out excerpts. There is nothing either in my head or on paper except Sakhalin. Derangement of the mind. *Mania Sachalinosa*.

I recently dined with Ermolova.[2] A wild flower amidst a bouquet of carnations absorbs added fragrance from its elegant companions. Similarly, two days after dining with a star, I still feel her radiance around my head.

I have been reading Modest Tchaikovsky's *Symphony*. I enjoyed it. It makes a very strong impression when you read it. I think the play should be successful.

Farewell, my dear friend, please come to see us. Greetings to your family. My sister and mother send you their best wishes.

Your

A. Chekhov

96. To Alexey Suvorin, around 20 February 1890, Moscow

Thank you for taking so much trouble. I need to look at Kruzenstern's atlas[1] either now or on my return from Sakhalin, but preferably now. You say the map in it is not a good one, but that's just why I need it. I already have a good one which I bought from Ilyin[2] for 65 copecks.

I've been spending day after day reading and writing, reading and writing . . . The more I read, the more convinced I become that two months is not enough to achieve even a quarter of what I have set out to do, and I cannot spend more than two months on Sakhalin because

2. Maria Ermolova (1853–1928), a celebrated Russian actress.
1. A supplement consisting of more than 100 maps and designs, published with Kruzenstern's three-volume *Journey Round the World in 1803, 1804, 1805 and 1806* (St Petersburg, 1809–12).
2. Alexey Ilyin, general-lieutenant, cartographer, proprietor of a cartographic firm and map shop in St Petersburg and Moscow.

those wretched steamers won't wait![3] The work I am engaged on now is varied but very tedious ... I must turn myself into a geologist and then a meteorologist and then an ethnographer, and since I'm not experienced at any of this I get bored. I shall go on doing my research about Sakhalin until March, until I run out of money, and then I'll settle down to write some stories.

I don't recall why it was that I wrote to Pleshcheyev about hanging myself. I expect I was drunk at the time. I was writing, naturally, in jocular vein, something like: 'for this I should have been simultaneously hanged and promoted to general.' I most definitely deserved the latter, because the amount I drank while I was in Piter should have made the whole of Russia take pride in me! I also remember that I wrote to Pleshcheyev saying that during my time in Piter I got as much done in a month as my young friends, the ones who were for some reason annoyed with me, would do in a whole year; I wasn't exaggerating, for each one of my young friends is twelve times as idle as I am. While staying with you I read and saw and heard a great deal, and pestered many more people besides Galkin, and all this without taking into account all the wine-drinking and pacing up and down.

Mme Lenskaya[4] has smeared lard on her face. Mamyshev[5] came to see me, complaining that they had sent his collar with the thirty-year guarantee to Zvenigorod instead of to Volokolamsk, where he lives. I told him the man to blame was you.

If your library contains a copy of Vysheslavsky's *Sketches in Pen and Pencil*, please send it to me. I would be very grateful.

Ostrovsky also came to see me and asked what had happened about his sister's book. I told him that you and Neupokoev[6] were unhappy with the drawings and the format of the book. He said that if the drawings were not acceptable they could be discarded and new ones commissioned, and that the format, like other such matters, was entirely up to the printer. Do I have your permission to write and tell

3. Navigation closed in the winter months because of the ice.
4. Lidia Lenskaya, the wife of the actor Alexander Lensky.
5. Vasily Mamyshev, a judge in Tver province and later a legal investigator in Zvenigorod, who married Suvorin's sister.
6. Arkady Neupokoev (1848–1906) ran Suvorin's printing press.

him that his book will be printed in the summer? Ugh, how vilely his cigars stink! I recoil in horror from the cursed things every time he comes. He told me that his brother the Minister has diabetes.

The Kreutzer Sonata is a success in Moscow.

Why aren't you sending me any stories [by young writers]? Today or tomorrow I shall send you a story by Lazarev (Gruzinsky).[7] Your agreement to increase the fee to my protégé Ezhov and send him copies of the paper brings tears to my eyes and causes my voice to tremble in gratitude as I stretch out my arms heavenwards, and call down blessings of every imaginable bliss on you and your family for ever and ever amen.

My work in Sakhalin will make me look such a learned son of a bitch that you will simply have to throw up your hands. I have already lifted a great deal of information and insights from other people's books, that naturally I shall present as my own. In our pragmatic era there is no other way. Tell Alexey Alexeyevich that he should go to the banks of the Murgab River. I read that the Queen of Romania has written a play about the daily life of the common (?) people and that she is to put it on in a Bucharest theatre. This is one author whom one will not be permitted to boo. But I would love to go and do so.

Lensky has been saying that 'apparently they want to put on' Maslov's play. I've heard no more about it though.

Keep well. May God grant you his blessings.

Respectfully yours

Heinrich Blokk & Co.

How are your esteemed horses? It would be good to go for an outing somewhere.

7. Alexander Lazarev (pseudonym Gruzinsky) (1861–1927), a minor writer.

97. To Alexander Chekhov, 25 February 1890, Moscow

Infusorio!

I need as much and as detailed information as I can get about what the newspapers have published about Sakhalin, because my interest in the articles goes beyond the purely factual information in them. The facts and figures are clearly important in themselves but, Gusev, I also need to know the historical context in which they have been set out. The articles were written either by people who had never been to Sakhalin and had no conception of what it was really like, or by interested parties who had invested capital in Sakhalin business and wanted to protect their innocence. The rashness of the first and the deviousness of the second alike obscure the truth and impede progress, and, as such, can be even more revealing to the researcher than the factual information itself, which is for the most part random and inaccurate; the elements I am talking about brilliantly illuminate our society's attitude to the whole business, and to imprisonment in particular. You can only understand an author and his motives when you read his article in full.

In any case, leave the Public Library out of your rounds from now on. You have done enough there. Our sister will transcribe the remainder; I have commissioned her to start digging around in the Rumyantsev Library from the third week in Lent. For you, O fool, I shall find other work. Kneel and ask my forgiveness. You will find complete instructions in a letter to be received in the fourth or fifth week of Lent. On the subject of lice I can tell you only one thing: I am mortally afraid of dirt. Oblomov's Zakhar[1] and Alexander Chekhov agree in maintaining that there is no way lice and bedbugs can be avoided; this is a highly scientific view but, and you may find this hard to imagine, I actually know quite a few families to whom these creatures are unknown. There are many remedies for lice. Ask at any chemist for a decoction of sabadilla.

1. Oblomov's lazy servant in Goncharov's novel.

We are all well. Regards to Natalia Alexandrovna, to Kuka and to my godson.

Your benefactor

A. Chekhov

98. To Alexey Suvorin, 9 March 1890, Moscow
Forty Martyrs and Ten Thousand Larks[1]

We are both wrong about Sakhalin, but you probably more so than I. I am going there perfectly convinced that my trip will make no useful contribution either to literature or to science: I have neither knowledge nor time nor ambition to do so. I have no plans to emulate Humboldt, or even Kennan;[2] I simply want to produce a couple of hundred pages so that I can repay a little of what I owe to medicine, which, as you know, I treat like a pig. I may well find that I shall be unable to write anything at all, but even if such be the case, the trip loses none of its attractions for me: I shall discover and learn a great deal from all the reading, looking around and listening. Even before setting out, the books I have had to read have taught me a great deal that everyone should know under pain of forty lashes, but which I have hitherto been completely ignorant about. Besides, as I see it, the journey will occupy six months of unremitting physical and mental toil, and I need this because I'm a Khokhol[3] and have already started to get lazy. I must pull myself together. My trip may well prove to be

1. The Feast of the Forty Martyrs of Sebastia was celebrated in Russia by the baking of lark-shaped rolls to mark the coming of spring.
2. Alexander von Humboldt studied the geography of Siberia at the invitation of the Russian government in 1829. The American journalist George Kennan (1845–1924) travelled to Siberia in 1885–6 to study the conditions of political exiles there; the book he published about his travels, *Siberia and the Exile System* (London, 1890), was predictably banned in Russia, and Chekhov read the Russian translation that had just been published in London.
3. Chekhov indeed had Ukrainian blood, and also came from the south.

nothing but a pointless, stubborn whim, but just think about it for a moment and tell me what I have to lose by going. Time? Money? Comfort? My time is worth nothing, I never have any money anyhow, and as for privations I shall spend twenty-five to thirty days, no more, travelling by horse, and the rest of the time I shall be sitting on the deck of a steamer or in a room somewhere bombarding you with letters. Perhaps I won't get anything at all from the trip, but surely to goodness there will be two or three days which I shall remember for the rest of my life, whether delightful or painful. And so on, and so forth. There you have it, my good sir. You may not find any of this very convincing, but what you write is no more so. For instance, you say that nobody needs Sakhalin or finds it at all interesting. Can this really be so? Only a society that does not deport thousands of people to Sakhalin at a cost of millions could find it entirely devoid of usefulness or interest. Sakhalin is the only place, except for Australia in former times, and Cayenne, where one can study a place that has been colonized by convicts. All of Europe is interested in it, so how can it be that we are not? A mere twenty-five or thirty years ago our own Russian people performed amazing feats exploring Sakhalin, enough to make one glorify the human spirit, but none of this matters to us; we know nothing of these people, we just sit within our own four walls complaining that God did a bad job when he created mankind. Sakhalin is a place of unbearable suffering, on a scale of which no creature but man is capable, whether he be free or in chains. People who have worked there or in that region have faced terrifying problems and responsibilities which they continue to work towards resolving. I regret that I am not a sentimental person, otherwise I would say that we should make pilgrimages to places like Sakhalin as the Turks go to Mecca, and sailors and penal experts should study Sakhalin the way soldiers study Sevastopol. It is quite clear from the books I have been reading and am still reading, that we have let *millions* of people rot in gaol, and let them rot to no purpose, treating them with an indifference that is little short of barbaric. We have forced people to drag themselves in chains across tens of thousands of miles in freezing conditions, infected them with syphilis, debauched them, hugely increased the criminal population, and heaped the blame for the whole thing on red-nosed prison supervisors. All Europe now knows that the blame lies not with the supervisors, but with all of us, but we still regard it as none of our business, we're not interested. The much-vaunted sixties did *nothing whatsoever* for sick people or for prisoners, thus violating the principal commandment of Christian civilization. These days at least we try to do something for the sick, but for prisoners we do nothing at all; prison administration holds no interest whatsoever for our judiciary. No, I assure you, Sakhalin is necessary and interesting, and the only regret I have is that it is I going there rather than somebody more experienced in the field, and more able to generate interest in society at large. My personal reasons for going are trivial.

As for my letter about Pleshcheyev, what I wanted to say to you was that although my young friends were criticizing my inactivity, I can plead in my defence that I have still achieved more than they ever do, which is precisely nothing. At least I read through the *Maritime Almanac* and went to see Galkin, but they did nothing at all. That's all there is to say about it, I think.

We are having some splendid student unrest here. It all started in the Petrovskaya Academy, when the administration forbade the taking of girls into the students' hostels, suspecting them not just of prostitution but of politics. The disorders spread from the Academy to the university, where the earnest seekers after knowledge, reinforced by mounted Hectors and Achilles heavily armed with pikes, are now making the following demands:

1. Full autonomy for universities
2. Full academic freedom
3. Full and free access to university education regardless of faith, nationality, gender and social standing
4. The unrestricted right of Jews to enter the university and enjoy the same rights as other students
5. Freedom of assembly and recognition of student organizations
6. The establishment of university and student courts
7. The abolition of police inspection functions

8. A reduction in tuition fees.

I jotted this down from a leaflet I saw, with a few abbreviations. I think the spark that set off the fire came from a crowd composed of Jewish youths and members of that sex which is clamouring to be admitted into the University, even though they are five times worse prepared than the men, who are themselves not very well prepared and who with rare exceptions study vilely when they get there.

I've sent back to you: Krasheninnikov,[4] Khvostov and Davydov,[5] *Russian Archives* (1879, vol. III) and *Proceedings of the Archaeological Society* (1875, vols 1 and 2).

Would you kindly send me the next part of Khvostov and Davydov, if there is one? Also, it's vol. V of *Russian Archives* 1879 I need, not vol. III. I will send the other books tomorrow or the day after.

I am very sorry indeed for Gey, but there is really no need for him to torture himself as he does. There are excellent treatments for syphilis now, and no doubt that he can be cured.

Along with the books, please send me my vaudeville *The Wedding*.[6] I don't need anything else. Come and see Maslov's play.

Be well and happy. I am no more ready to believe that you are an old man than I believe in the fourth dimension. First, you are not old yet in any way that I can see; you think and work enough for ten men and the way your mind works is anything but senile; secondly, I am ready to swear that you are not suffering from any maladies except migraine, and thirdly, old age is only a bad thing for bad old men, a burden only to those who are themselves a burden to others, while you are a good person and not a burden to others. Fourthly, the distinction between youth and old age is at root a relative and pro-visional one. Consequently you will please allow me, out of respect

4. Stepan Krasheninnikov (1713–55), the author of a book about the Kamchatka peninsula in the Russian Far East, published in St Petersburg in 1885.
5. Nikolay Khvostov (1776–1809), a naval officer, and Gavriil Davydov (1784–1809), a naval officer and explorer, wrote a two-part book about their voyage to America, published in St Petersburg, 1810–12.
6. Chekhov's one-act play, written in 1889.

for you, to throw myself into a deep ravine and dash my head to smithereens.

Your

A. Chekhov

Some time ago I wrote to you about Ostrovsky. He has been to see me again; what should I tell him?

Do go to Feodosia! The weather is wonderful.

99. To Ivan Leontiev (Shcheglov), 16 March 1890, Moscow

Greetings, dear Jean, how long it is since we were in touch! The will of capricious fate has caused my poor muse to don dark glasses, abandon her lyre and busy herself with ethnography and geology . . . Forgotten are sweet sounds and glory . . . all, all forgotten. This is why I have not written to you for so long, my friend and former colleague (I say 'former' because I am no longer a literary man but a Sakhalinian).

How are you getting on, how are you feeling? What is the state of your nerves, your plays, your grandmother? Please write me even one line in your tragically awful handwriting and don't abandon me . . . I'm going away in April, so we are not likely to see one another again before January!

My itinerary is shaping up like this: Nizhny, Perm, Tyumen, Tomsk, Irkutsk, Sretensk, down the Amur to Nikolayevsk, two months on Sakhalin, Nagasaki, Shanghai, Hong Kong, Manila, Singapore, Madras, Colombo (Ceylon), Aden, Port Said, Constantinople, Odessa, Moscow, Piter, Tserkovnaya Street.

If I escape being eaten by bears and convicts on Sakhalin, if I am not killed by typhoons in Japan or by the heat in Aden, I shall return in December and rest on my laurels waiting for old age and doing precisely nothing. Wouldn't you like to come with me? We shall devour sturgeon on the Amur and swallow oysters at de Kastri, fat, enormous oysters such as are nowhere to be found in Europe; on

Sakhalin we shall buy bearskins to make fur coats for four roubles a skin, in Japan we'll get ourselves a dose of Japanese clap, and in India each of us will write an exotically flavoured story or vaudeville called 'Bully for the Tropics!' or 'The Involuntary Tourist' or 'A Captain *au Naturel*' or 'The Theatrical Albatross' or something. Let's go!

Do drop me a line, just *ein wenig*. Be well, and give my greetings to your most kind and hospitable wife; all my family send our warmest regards to you.

Your

A. Chekhov

100. *To Modest Tchaikovsky, 16 March 1890*

Permit me to cross out the thirteenth swallow,[1] dear Modest Ilyich, it's an unlucky number. A few days ago the editor of *The Artist* came to see me urging me to employ all my eloquence in persuading you to let your *Symphony* appear in his magazine at the start of next season. I asked him how much he would pay. He replied: 'Not much, since I don't have any money.' Nevertheless, should you feel inclined to accept, bear in mind that *The Artist* pays 150 to 250 roubles for an original play running in a State theatre – not per printer's sheet, but for the whole work, the swines! But since *Symphony* has already appeared in a lithographed edition by Rassokhin, they won't pay you as much as 250. Let me know whether you agree or not, but I advise you not to commit yourself finally because by autumn your plans may have changed; I would give them a non-committal answer. Tell them you will bear it in mind. That will be quite enough for them.

I am sitting at home the whole time reading about the price per ton in 1883 of Sakhalin and Shanghai coal; about amplitudes and the NE, NW, SE and other winds which will blow on me as I observe my

1. A reference to the swallows depicted on the notepaper on which he was writing.

personal brand of seasickness off the shore of Sakhalin. I read about the soil, the subsoil, about sandy clay and clayey sand. However, I have not yet completely lost my mind; yesterday I even managed to send off a story to *New Times*,[2] and soon I shall send *The Wood Demon* to *The Northern Herald* – this with great reluctance since I dislike seeing my plays in print.

Within the next ten days or two weeks the little book[3] I dedicated to Pyotr Ilyich will be published. Such is my admiration for him that I am ready to mount a guard of honour day and night by the steps of the house where he lives. If Russian artists are ranked in order of greatness, he must now occupy second place after Lev Tolstoy, who has long occupied the first place. (Repin I would place third, and myself ninety-eighth.) I have long harboured the impertinent dream of dedicating something of mine to him. It would be a poor scribbler's partial and trivial attempt to pay tribute to his colossal talent which, owing to my musical ineptitude, I am utterly unable to convey on the page. Sadly, the book I have had to use to realize this dream of mine is not one I consider the best. It consists of a series of exceptionally gloomy, psychopathological sketches and has a gloomy title, and so my dedication will probably strike not only Pyotr Ilyich himself but his admirers as inappropriate.

Are you really a Chekhist?[4] I humbly thank you. But no, you are not a Chekhist, merely an exceptionally tolerant person. I send you my best wishes for good health and happiness.

Yours truly,

Chekhov

Moscow, Kudrino

2. 'Thieves'.
3. *Gloomy People*.
4. Modest had signed his last letter to Chekhov thus.

101. To Vukol Lavrov, 10 April 1890, Moscow

Vukol Mikhailovich!

On page 147 in the book review section of the March issue of *Russian Thought*, I came across the following phrase: 'As recently as yesterday, even the high priests of unprincipled writing such as Messrs Yasinsky and Chekhov, whose names . . .' etc., etc. I appreciate that it is not usual to respond to criticism, but in this case it may not be criticism but pure libel. Even libel I might have been prepared to overlook, but since in a few days' time I shall be leaving Russia, perhaps never to return, I could not leave this calumny unanswered.

I have never been an unprincipled writer, nor – what amounts to the same thing – a scoundrel.

It is true that my entire literary career has consisted of an unbroken series of mistakes, sometimes grievous ones, but the cause of this lies in the limitations of my talent and has nothing whatsoever to do with whether I am a good or a bad person. I have never blackmailed anyone, nor have I ever libelled or denounced anyone. I have eschewed flattery, lies and insults. In short, while I should be happy to throw out as worthless many of my stories and leading articles, there is not a single line of which I am now ashamed. I must assume that by 'unprincipled' you refer to the sad fact that I, an educated man whose work is often seen in print, have done nothing for those I love; my activities have, for example, left no trace on the *zemstvo*, the new law courts, the freedom of the press, freedom in general, and so on. If such is indeed the case, then I can only say that *Russian Thought* should regard me as an ally rather than attack me, since in these respects it has done no more than I have. And that is the fault of neither of us.

Even when judged objectively as a writer, I do not deserve to be accused publicly of lacking principles. Up till now I have led a sheltered life within four walls; you and I meet one another no more than once every two years or so, and I have never in my life encountered Mr Machtet[1] – from this you may judge how seldom I leave my house; I

---

1. Grigory Machtet (1852–1901), a minor writer.

studiously avoid literary soirées, parties, meetings and so on, I have never visited any editorial office without being invited to do so, and have always tried to act in such a way that my friends regard me more as a doctor than a writer; in short, I have always conducted myself with discretion in writing circles, – the present letter is my first immodest action in ten years of writing. I am on excellent terms with my colleagues; I have never presumed to sit in judgement either on them or on the magazines and newspapers for which they write because I do not consider myself competent to do so, moreover I believe that in the present subservient position of the press, any word uttered against a journal or a writer should be regarded not merely as an unkind and insensitive attack, but as actually criminal. Hitherto, the only magazines and newspapers to which I decline to contribute have been those whose manifestly inferior quality is obvious to all, but when I am obliged to choose between one publication or another, I have habitually favoured those who most needed my services for material or other reasons. This is why I have always worked for *The Northern Herald* rather than for your paper or for *The Herald of Europe*, and it is also why I have earned no more than half what I could have, had I taken a different view of my obligations.

Your accusation is libellous. There is no point in asking you to retract it, since it has already appeared in print and cannot now be simply chopped out with an axe. Neither can I excuse it as a careless or irresponsible lapse, because I am quite aware that your editorial office consists of unimpeachably decent and civilized people who, I trust, do not simply write and read articles but take responsibility for every word they write. The only recourse I have is to point out your error, and ask you to believe in the genuinely heavy heart with which I am writing you this letter. It goes without saying that professional collaboration and even social acquaintance are impossible after your accusation.

A. Chekhov

102. To Alexey Suvorin, 15 April 1890, Moscow

So, my dear friend, I'll be leaving on Wednesday, or Thursday at the latest. Goodbye until December. Stay happy. I received the money, many thanks, although fifteen hundred is rather a lot and I've nowhere to stow it. I would have been able to buy some things in Japan in any case, as I had scraped up enough for that.

I'm feeling rather as if I were preparing to go to war, although I don't anticipate any dangers except toothache, which I invariably get when I travel. The only document I am taking with me is my passport, nothing else, so I may well have some awkward encounters with the powers that be, but such things are only ephemeral problems. If there is anything I'm not allowed to see, I shall simply write in my book that they would not let me see it, and *basta!* think no more about it. If I should drown or anything like that, please note that everything I have and may have in the future belongs to my sister; she will settle all my debts.

I shall definitely wire you, but I'll be writing to you more often. The address for telegrams is: Chekhov, c/o *Siberian Herald* offices, Tomsk. I should definitely get any letters written before 25 July; if they're written after that and sent to Sakhalin I won't get them. In addition to letters and cables, kind sir, please parcel up and send me all kinds of printed rubbish, starting with brochures and ending with newspaper cuttings. They will be therapy for my Sakhalin blues; but please only send me things I can throw away after reading them. My address for letters and parcels will be: Alexandrovsk Station on Sakhalin Island, or Korsakovsk Station [on the mainland]. Use both addresses. In return for these services I will make additional payment outside the normal terms of agreement in the form of an ivory carving of a naked Japanese lady, or something analogous to the venerable duck that sits on your bookcase in front of the table. When I'm in India I shall write you an exotic story.

I won't write anything for *New Times* while I'm travelling except pieces for the Saturday supplement. My letters to you will be private; if any of my travel notes strike you as being worth publishing, by all means pass them on to the editorial staff. In any case, I'll see what it's like when I'm there. It wouldn't be a bad idea to write some articles of forty to seventy-five lines.

I'm taking my mother with me as far as the Trinity Monastery, where I shall leave her, and my sister is also coming with me as far as Kostroma. I lied to them that I shall be back in September.

I'll look round the University in Tomsk. As they only have one faculty there, and it's a medical one, I hope not to appear too much of an ignoramus.

I've bought myself a half-length fur coat, a waterproof leather officer's coat, some heavy boots and a large knife with which to cut sausage and to hunt tigers. I'm armed from head to foot.

So, goodbye then. I'll write to you from the Volga and from the Kama. My warmest regards to Anna Ivanovna, Nastyusha and Boris.

Your

A. Chekhov

103. To Chekhov Family, 23 April 1890, on the Volga
Early morning, on board the steamer Alexander Nevsky

Dear Tungus[1] friends! Was it raining when Ivan returned from the monastery? There was such a downpour in Yaroslavl that I had to wrap myself up in my leather coat. First impressions of the Volga were poisoned by the rain, by streaming cabin windows and by Gurlyand's[2] wet nose – he came to the station to meet me. Yaroslavl in the rain is not unlike Zvenigorod, and its churches remind one of the Perervinsky Monastery; lots of illiterate notices, dirt everywhere, jackdaws with great big heads stalking along the road.

Once aboard, the first thing I did was give full rein to my special talent, that is to say I went to sleep, and awoke to the sun shining.

1. An indigenous Siberian tribe.
2. Ivan Gurlyand, a student at the law school in Yaroslavl who later worked at the Ministry of the Interior.

The Volga is not bad: water meadows, sun-drenched monasteries, white churches; an incredible sense of space; lovely places to sit and fish wherever you look. Classy young ladies wander along the bank nibbling green grass; you hear an occasional shepherd's pipe. White seagulls just like young Drishka[3] fly above the water.

The steamer itself is not up to much. The best thing about it is the W C, which is perched high up with four steps leading to it, so it could easily be mistaken by an inexperienced person like Ivanenko for a royal throne. The worst thing on the steamer is the food. Here is the menu, complete with idiosyncratic orthography: grin cabbidge soup, sossidge with collyflower, fry sturgeon, baked kat pudding ('kat', it turned out, is 'kasha'). Bearing in mind that my money has been earned by blood and the sweat of my brow, I could wish that the situation were the other way round, i.e. the lunch was better than the lavatory – especially since my insides have so completely seized up with all the Santorini wine Korneyev poured down me that it looks as though I shall get to Tomsk before needing the lavatory at all.

I have a travelling companion: Kundasova.[4] I have no idea where she is going, nor why, and when I ask her about this she launches into mysterious speculations about someone she was supposed to meet in a ravine near Kineshma, after which she dissolves in hysterical laughter, stamps her feet and elbows her way in any old where, not giving a fart. We have left Kineshma, and its ravines, behind, but she is still on board, which is of course very nice for me. Incidentally, I saw her eat yesterday for the first time in my life. She does so much as other people do, but mechanically, as if she were chomping her way through some oats.

Kostroma is a nice town. I saw Plyos, home of the torpid Levitan; and I saw Kineshma, where I strolled along the boulevards and observed the local beaux. I went into a chemist's shop there to buy some Berthollet's salt for my tongue, which as a result of the wine I drank has acquired the consistency of Moroccan leather. The moment he caught sight of Olga Petrovna, the pharmacist expressed joy and

3. Nickname for Darya Musina-Pushkina, an actress friend.
4. Olga Kundasova, a family friend and one of Chekhov's many female admirers.

embarrassment in equal measure; evidently they were old friends and to judge from their conversation had visited the ravines of Kineshma together on several occasions in the past. See what beaux they have there! The pharmacist's name is Kopfer.

It's cold and a bit boring, but quite entertaining on the whole.

Every few minutes the ship's whistle sounds, making a noise midway between an ass's bray and an Aeolian harp. In five or six hours from now I shall be in Nizhny Novgorod. The sun is just coming up. I slept the whole night through like a true artist. I have succeeded in holding on to all of my money – by dint of continually clutching it to my stomach.

There are beautiful tugs on the river; each one tows four or five barges. It's rather like watching an elegant young intellectual straining to run ahead but all the time being hampered by clumsy women dragging importunately at his coat-tails – a wife, a mother-in-law, a sister-in-law, a grandmother.

I bow to the ground to Papasha and Mamasha; to the waist to all others. I hope that Semashko, Lidia Stakhievna [Mizinova] and Ivanenko are behaving themselves. It would be interesting to know who is now going to go out boozing with Lidia Stakh until five in the morning? It's a good thing Ivanenko has no money!

The trunk Misha bought me, thank you kindly, is falling apart. My health is perfect. My neck doesn't hurt at all. Yesterday I didn't have a drop to drink.

Please get the book of Fofanov's poems from Drishka. Give Kundasova the French atlas and Darwin's *Voyage*[5] which are on the shelves. Ivan should do this.

The sun has now gone behind a cloud, the sky is overcast and altogether the wide Volga has a gloomy appearance. Levitan shouldn't live on the Volga, it casts a pall over the soul. Although it wouldn't be such a bad idea to have a little estate on the river bank.

I send my best wishes to you all, hearty greetings and a thousand bows.

---

5. The Russian translation of Darwin's account of his voyage on the *Beagle* was published in St Petersburg in 1865.

Misha, please explain to Lidia Stakh how to send books as printed matter, and give her the receipt for the Gogol. You remember that one volume of Gogol was returned to Suvorin as a model for the bookbinders, so there should be three more volumes.

If the steward would only wake up, I would order a cup of coffee. As it is I shall have to drink water, from which I get no pleasure. My regards to Maryushka and to Olga.[6]

Well, keep well and happy. I shall write to you regularly.

Your homesick Volga Boatman, Homo Sachaliensis,

A. Chekhov

Regards to Granny.

104. To Nikolay Obolonsky, 29 April 1890, Ekaterinburg

Hooray!!

Sending a telegram to Vorozhba seemed to me, on mature reflection, a risky step. Vorozhba seemed in any event rather a vague concept: after all, the place you were getting married was twenty-five miles away, and how could I possibly rely on anyone actually delivering my telegram to you? It would not have occurred to you to inquire at the post office; celestial beings like you no longer have anything to do with lowly amphibia like us . . .

I thought it better to write you a touching letter.

And so, my very dear, kind and golden friend Nikolay Nikolayevich, I congratulate you and Sofia Vitaliyevna upon your marriage in the eyes of the law and wish both of you happiness, prosperity, peace, harmony, success in all your affairs and eighteen children of both sexes. I cry hooray! to you as I drink your health (in spirit, of course).

I am now sitting in Ekaterinburg, with my right foot in Europe and my left in Asia. The weather is, to put it mildly, execrable . . . Alas,

6. Maria Belenovskaya (Maryusha, Maryushka) had been the family's cook since 1884; Olga Gorokhovaya worked for the family as a maid.

how my life has changed! The whiteness of 18-rouble shirts has now been replaced by snow covering the roads; warmth has been replaced by bitter cold; instead of delightful people like yourself I see only people with the high cheekbones and bulbous foreheads of Asiatics who, one would think, have resulted from the coupling of Urals pig-iron with a beluga whale . . . Sigh with pity for me, as I sigh with envy for you.

Please assure Sofia Vitaliyevna of my sincere respects, and once again please accept my best wishes.

Be well and happy, and don't forget your

A. Chekhov

105. To Konstantin Foti, 3 May 1890, Tyumen

Dear Konstantin Georgevich,

My uncle Mitrofan Egorovich has written to tell me that in conversation with him you were pleased to express the wish that I send my books to the Taganrog Public Library. Such a mark of high esteem is more than I deserve; it greatly flatters my pride as an author, and I find it hard to express my gratitude to you. I am glad of any opportunity to serve my native town, to which I owe so much and towards which I continue to entertain the warmest feelings.

When I set out from Moscow on my travels I left instructions for three of my books to be sent to you. The fourth book – *Motley Stories* – is at the moment sold out and will be published in another edition when I return, that is to say not before the New Year. By the way, I also asked for a copy of Tolstoy's *The Power of Darkness*, signed by the author, to be sent to you; I hope the town library will accept this small gift from me, as in due course I hope it will accept all the books signed by their authors I presently have in my possession, which I am collecting and keeping expressly for the library of my home town.

Allow me to send you my best wishes and to trust in my sincere respect

A. Chekhov

106. *To Evgenia Chekhova, 4 May 1890, Ishim*

I'm alive, in good health and all is well. I've learnt how to brew coffee, but I find I need two spoonfuls a cup, not one. Regards to all the family and to the Lintvaryovs. There's no greenery anywhere, everything is frozen. My feet are terribly cold.

Be well, don't fret.

Your respectful son, A. Chekhov

There's literally not a hint of greenery anywhere yet.

107. *To Alexey Suvorin, 20 May 1890, Tomsk*

At long last greetings from Siberian Man, dear Alexey Sergeyevich! I have been missing both you and our correspondence terribly.

I shall nevertheless start from the beginning. They told me in Tyumen that there would be no steamer to Tomsk until 18 May. I had to take horses. For the first three days every joint and tendon in my body ached, but then I got used to it and had no more pain. But as a result of the lack of sleep, the constant fussing with the baggage, the bouncing up and down and the hunger, I suffered a haemorrhage that rather spoilt my mood, which was not in any case particularly sunny. The first few days were bearable, but then a cold wind started to blow, the heavens opened and the rivers overflowed into the fields and the roads, so that I kept having to swap my vehicle for a boat. The attached pages will tell you about my battles with the floods and the mud; I didn't mention in them that the heavy boots I had bought were too tight, so that I had to plough through mud and water in felt boots which rapidly turned into jelly. The road is so bad that in the last few days I've only managed to cover forty miles or so.

When I went away I promised once I got as far as Tomsk to let you have some notes on the journey, since the road from Tyumen to Tomsk is one that has been described and exploited a thousand times. But your telegram, sir, requested some Siberian impressions from me as soon as possible, and you were even so cruel as to chastise me for having a poor memory, i.e. apparently forgetting about you. It was absolutely impossible to get anything down on paper while travelling; I had with me a little diary and a pencil, and all I have to offer you is whatever I jotted down in it. I don't want to write at too great length, and I want to avoid a confusing jumble, so I have divided my impressions into separate chapters. I am sending you six chapters now. They were written *for you personally*. Everything I have written has been for you only, and therefore I have not worried much about my observations being too subjective or containing more of Chekhov's feelings and thoughts than of Siberia. If you find any of it interesting and worth publishing, you may submit it to the scrutiny of a benevolent public above my name and publish individual chapters in very small doses. You could give the notes an overall title of 'From Siberia', with individual parts 'From the Trans-Baikal', 'From the Amur', and so on.

You will get another instalment from Irkutsk, where I am going tomorrow. The journey there will take at least ten days, because it is a very bad road. I'll send you several chapters from there, even if you don't want to publish them. Read them, and if they start boring you, just send me a cable saying 'stop'!

I've been as hungry as a horse all the way. I filled my belly with bread in order to stop thinking of turbot, asparagus and suchlike. I even dreamt of buckwheat kasha. I dreamt of it for hours on end.

I bought some sausage for the journey in Tyumen, if you can call it a sausage! When you bit into it, the smell was just like going into a stable at the precise moment the coachmen are removing their foot bindings; when I started chewing it, my teeth felt as if they had caught hold of a dog's tail smeared with tar. Ugh! I made two attempts to eat it and then threw it away.

I received a telegram and a letter from you, in which you wrote that you want to publish an encyclopaedic dictionary. I don't know why, but the news about the dictionary gave me great pleasure. Do publish it, my friend! If you think I would have anything to contribute to it, I'll set aside November and December. I plan to be in Piter for those two months. I'll sit and work from morning till night.

I wrote out a fair copy of my travel notes in Tomsk, in the shabbiest hotel room imaginable, but diligently and trying hard to please you. He's probably a bit bored and hot in Feodosia, thought I, so it will be nice for him to read about somewhere cold. These notes replace the letter that I was writing to you in my head the whole time I was travelling. In return, please send me your critical articles, except the first two, which I have read. Could you also please arrange for me to be sent Peschel's *Ethnology*,[1] with the exception of the first two instalments, which I already have?

Mail comes to Sakhalin both by sea and overland across Siberia, so if anyone is going to write to me I shall be able to receive correspondence regularly. Don't lose my address: Alexandrovsk Station, Sakhalin Island.

Oh Lord, my expenses are mounting up! Thanks to the floods I had to pay all the coachmen almost twice and sometimes three times as much as usual, for they had to work hellishly hard, it was like penal servitude. My suitcase, a nice little trunk, has proved not to be very suitable for the journey: it takes up too much room, bashes me continually in the ribs as it rattles about, and, worst of all, is threatening to fall to pieces. 'Don't take trunks on a long journey' well-meaning people told me, but I only remembered this when I had got halfway. What to do? Well, I have decided to let my trunk take up residence in Tomsk, and have bought myself some piece of shit made of leather, but which has the advantage of flopping on the floor of a tarantass[2] and adopting any shape you like. It cost me 16 roubles. Anyway, to continue . . . It would be sheer torture to take post-chaises all the way to the Amur. I would simply be shaken to pieces with all my belongings. I was advised to buy my own carriage. So I bought one today for 130 roubles. If I don't succeed in selling it when I get to Sretensk, where

1. A Russian translation of the German geographer Oskar Peschel's *Abhandlung zur Erd- und Völkekunde* (Leipzig, 1877) was published in instalments by Suvorin beginning in 1890.

2. An old-fashioned four-wheeled carriage pulled by three horses, which could travel at a speed of about 8 mph. It had a folding hood but neither springs nor seats and travellers simply reclined on its floor, having first put down straw and blankets to cushion the ride.

the overland part of my journey ends, I shall be left without a penny and will howl. Today I dined with Kartamyshev, the editor of *The Siberian Herald*. He's a local Nozdryov,[3] a flamboyant sort of fellow . . . Drank six roubles' worth.

Stop press! I have just been informed that the Assistant Chief of Police wants to see me. What can I have done?!?

False alarm. The policeman turned out to be a lover of literature and even a bit of a writer; he came to pay his respects. He's gone home to collect a play he's written; apparently he intends to entertain me with it . . . He'll be back in a moment and again interrupt my writing to you . . .

Write and tell me about Feodosia, about Tolstoy, the sea, the goby, the people we both know.

Greetings, Anna Ivanovna! God bless you. I often think of you.

Regards to Nastyusha and Borya. If it would give them pleasure I shall be delighted to throw myself into the jaws of a tiger and summon them to my aid, but alas! I haven't got as far as tigers yet. The only furry animals I've seen so far in Siberia have been hundreds of hares and one mouse.

Stop press! The policeman has returned. He didn't read me his play, although he did bring it with him, but regaled me instead with a story he had written. It wasn't bad, a bit too local though. He showed me a gold ingot, and asked me if I had any vodka. I cannot recall any occasion on which a Siberian has not, on coming to see me, asked for vodka. This one told me he had got himself embroiled in a love affair with a married woman, and showed me his petition for divorce addressed to the highest authority. Thereupon he suggested a tour of Tomsk's houses of pleasure.

I've now returned from the houses of pleasure. Quite revolting. Two a.m.

What has Alexey Alexeyevich gone to Riga for? You wrote to me about this. How is his health? From now on I'll write to you punctually from every town and every station where I change horses, i.e. everywhere I have to spend the night. What a pleasure it is to have to stop

---

3. A character in Gogol's *Dead Souls*, portrayed as a drunken bully and a braggart.

for the night! Scarcely do I flop into bed but I'm asleep. Out here, when you keep going through the night without stopping, sleep becomes the most treasured prize there is; there is no greater pleasure on earth than sleep when you are tired. I now realize that in Moscow or indeed in Russia generally I have never really craved sleep. I just went to bed because it was time to do so. Not like now! Another thing I've noticed: you have no desire to drink when travelling. I haven't drunk a thing. I have smoked a lot though. I don't seem to be able to think properly; my thoughts just don't cohere. The time goes very quickly, so that you hardly notice it's moved on from ten o'clock in the morning to seven o'clock in the evening; the evening simply flows seamlessly into the morning. It's like being ill for a long time. My face is covered in fish scales because of all the wind and rain, so that when I look in the mirror I hardly recognize my former distinguished features.

I won't describe Tomsk. All Russian towns are the same. Tomsk is a dull and rather drunken sort of place; no beautiful women at all, and Asiatic lawlessness. The most notable thing about Tomsk is that governors come here to die.

I embrace you warmly. I kiss both Anna Ivanovna's hands and bow to the ground before her. It's raining. Goodbye, keep well and happy. You mustn't complain if my letters are short, slapdash or dry, because one is not always oneself while on the road and cannot write exactly as one would wish. This ink is appalling, and there always seem to be little bits of hair and other things sticking to the pen.

Your

A. Chekhov

Please describe your house in Feodosia. Do you like it?

108. To Chekhov Family, 20 May 1890, Tomsk

Dear Tungus friends! It's already Whitsuntide where you are, but here not even the willows have begun to come out and there is still snow on the banks of the Tom. I leave tomorrow for Irkutsk. I've had a rest. There was no particular point in hurrying on as the steamers across Lake Baikal don't start until 10 June, but now I'm on my way anyhow.

I am alive, in good health, and have not lost any of my money; the only problem is a slight soreness in my right eye, which is aching.

Everyone is telling me to return via America, since you apparently die of boredom sailing with the Voluntary Fleet:[1] too much official military stuff, and you hardly ever put in to port.

Kuzovlyov, the customs officer who was exiled here from Taganrog, died two months ago in extreme poverty.

Having nothing better to do, I set down some travel impressions and sent them to *New Times*; you'll be able to read them some time after 10 June. I didn't go into anything in much detail. I was writing off the cuff – not for glory but for money, and to pay off some of the advance I received.

Tomsk is a most boring town. To judge from the drunks I have met and the supposedly intelligent people who have come to my room to pay their respects, the local inhabitants are deadly boring. At all events I find their company so disagreeable that I have given instructions that I am not receiving anyone.

I've been to the bathhouse and had some laundry done – five copecks a handkerchief! I bought some chocolate from sheer boredom.

Thanks to Ivan for the books; I can relax now. Please send him my regards if he's not with you. I have written to Father, and would have written to Ivan except that I don't know for certain where he is living or where he has gone.

In two and a half days' time I shall be in Krasnoyarsk, and in seven and a half or eight days in Irkutsk. Irkutsk is a thousand miles from here.

I've just made some coffee and am about to drink it. It's morning, and the bells will soon start ringing for late mass.

1. Founded by voluntary public subscription in 1878 to be a buttress against the Turkish navy and protect Russia's Asian coastlines, the fleet was largely subsidized by the government. The original three steamers which participated in the Russo-Turkish War had been joined by eleven others by 1890, some of which were converted so that they could be used to transport convicts to Sakhalin and other penal institutions, as well as freight to Vladivostok.

The taiga[2] starts at Tomsk. So we'll see.

Best regards to all the Lintvaryovs and to our dear old Maryushka. I hope Mama won't worry and will pay no attention to bad dreams. Are the radishes ripe yet? There are none at all here.

Well, stay alive and healthy, and don't worry about money, there will be enough. Don't spoil the summer by skimping too much.

Your

A. Chekhov

My soul is crying out. Have mercy on me, my poor old trunk will be left behind in Tomsk and I'm buying myself a new one, soft and flat, which I can sit on, and which won't fall to bits from all the shaking around. So my poor old trunk has been condemned to end its days in exile in Siberia.

109. To Chekhov Family, 25 May 1890, Mariinsk

Spring has begun; the fields are turning green, the leaves are coming out, and there are cuckoos and even nightingales singing. It was wonderful early this morning, but at ten o'clock a cold wind started blowing, and it began to rain. It was very flat up to Tomsk, and after Tomsk it was forests, ravines and such like.

I sentenced my poor trunk to exile in Tomsk for its unwieldiness, and purchased instead (for 16 roubles!) a ridiculous object that now sprawls inelegantly on the floor of my carriage. You may now boast to everyone that we own a carriage. In Tomsk I bought a barouche with a collapsible hood etc. for 130 roubles, but needless to say it has no springs, as no one in Siberia acknowledges springs. There are no seats, but the floor is large enough and flat enough to let you stretch out full length. Travelling will be very comfortable now; I fear neither the wind nor the rain. The only thing I do fear is broken bones, because the road is truly terrible. I

2. Northern coniferous forest.

am endlessly getting on boats: twice this morning, and tonight we have to cover three miles by water. I am alive, and quite well.

Be well,

Your

Antoine

110. To Alexander Chekhov, 5 June 1890, Irkutsk

European brother!

It is of course not very pleasant to live in Siberia, but better to be an honourable man there than to live in St Petersburg having the reputation of a drunk and a blackguard. Present company excepted, naturally.

When I was preparing to leave Russia, O brother, I wrote to tell you that you would be receiving a great many instructions from me. I didn't manage to write to you before I left, I had no opportunity to write while I was travelling, and now that I think of it I realize that I don't after all have a long list of instructions, but just one, which I ask you to accomplish under pain of being disinherited. It is this: when our sister tells you she needs money, put on your trousers and go along to the *New Times* bookshop: there they will give you what is due to me from my books, and you can send it all to our sister. That's it.

Siberia is a big, cold country. There seems no end to the journey. There is little of novelty or interest to be seen, but I am experiencing and feeling a lot. I've battled with rivers in flood, with cold, unbelievable quagmires, hunger and lack of sleep . . . Experiences you couldn't buy in Moscow for a million roubles. You should come to Siberia! Get the courts to exile you here.

The best of the Siberian towns is Irkutsk. Tomsk is not worth a brass farthing, and none of the local districts is any better than that Krepkaya in which you were so careless as to be born.[1] The worst of

1. Alexander was born in the village where his grandparents lived, because his parents had been forced to abandon Taganrog when it came under bombardment during the Crimean War (1854–6).

it is that in these little provincial places there is never anything to eat, and when you're on the road this becomes a matter of capital importance! You arrive in a town hungry enough to eat a mountain of food, and bang go your hopes; no sausage, no cheese, no meat, not so much as a herring, nothing but the sort of tasteless eggs and milk you find in the villages.

Generally I'm happy with my journey and glad that I came. It's hard going, but on the other hand it's a wonderful holiday. I'm enjoying my vacation.

After Irkutsk I go on to Lake Baikal, which I shall cross by steamer. Then it's 660 miles to the Amur, and from there I take a boat to the Pacific. The first thing I shall do when I get there is have a swim and eat oysters.

I arrived here yesterday and immediately made my way to the baths, then went to bed and slept. Oh, how I slept! Only now do I understand the true meaning of the word.

I hope you are well. Deepest respects and best wishes to Natalia Alexandrovna, to the silent Kuka and to my namesake. My address is: Alexandrovsk Station on Sakhalin Island. Write and tell me how you are getting on, and any other news. Write as often as you can to the family, life's a bit dull for them.

Blessings be upon you with both hands.

Your Asiatic brother A. Chekhov

111. To Chekhov Family, 6 June 1890, Irkutsk

Greetings, dearest Mama, Ivan, Masha and Misha and everyone. I am with you in spirit . . .

In the last long letter I wrote to you I said that the mountains round Krasnoyarsk resembled the Don ridge, but this is not really the case: looking at them from the street, I could see that they surrounded the town like high walls, and they reminded me strongly of the Caucasus. And when I left town in the early evening and crossed over the Enisei, I saw that the mountains on the far bank were really like the mountains of the Caucasus, with the same kind of smoky, dreamy quality . . . The Enisei is a wide, fast-flowing, lithe river, more beautiful than the Volga. The ferry across is wonderful, very skilfully designed in the way it goes against the current; I'll tell you more about its construction when I'm home. So the mountains and the Enisei have been the first genuinely new and original things I have encountered in Siberia. The feelings I experienced when I saw the mountains and the Enisei paid me back a hundredfold for all the hoops I had to jump through to get here, and made me curse Levitan for being so foolish as not to come with me.

Between Krasnoyarsk and Irkutsk there is nothing but taiga. The forest is no denser than at Sokolniki, but no coachman can tell you where it ends. It seems endless; it goes on for hundreds of miles. Nobody knows who or what may be living in the taiga, but sometimes it happens in winter that people come down from the far north with their reindeer in search of bread. When you are going up a mountain and you look up and down, all you see are mountains in front of you, more mountains beyond them, and yet more mountains beyond them, and mountains on either side, all thickly covered in forest. It's actually quite frightening. That was the next new experience I had . . .

Beyond Krasnoyarsk the heat and the dust began. The heat is terrible, and I have banished my coat and hat. The dust gets into your mouth, up your nose, down your neck – ugh! To get to Irkutsk you must cross the Angara on a flat-bottomed ferry; and just then, as if on purpose, a strong wind gets up . . . I and the officers who are my travelling companions have spent the last ten days dreaming of a bath and a sleep in a proper bed, and we stand on the bank reluctantly getting used to the idea that we may have to spend the night in the village instead of in Irkutsk. The ferry simply cannot put in to shore . . . We wait an hour or two, and – oh heavens! – with a supreme effort the ferry gets to the bank and ties up alongside. Bravo, we can have our bath, supper, and sleep. How sweet it is to steam in the bath-house and then sleep!

Irkutsk is a splendid town, and very civilized. It has a theatre, a museum, municipal gardens with music playing in them, good hotels . . . No ugly fences with stupid posters and wasteland with notices saying it's forbidden to stay there. There is an inn called the 'Tagan-rog'. Sugar costs 24 copecks and pine nuts are six copecks a pound.

I was bitterly disappointed not to find a letter from you. If you had written anything before 6 May I would have received it in Irkutsk. I sent Suvorin a telegram but got no reply.

Now, about sources of filthy lucre. When you need some, write (or send a cable) to Alexander and ask him to go to the *New Times* bookshop and collect my royalties *for the books*. That's the first thing. The second is, read the enclosed letter carefully and post it in August. Keep the certificate of posting. I have written to Alexander.

Don't forget to look out for my winning ticket.

Did I write to Misha telling him that I shall probably come home via America? There's no need for him to rush off to Japan.

I am alive and well, and I haven't lost any of the money. I'm saving some of the coffee for Sakhalin. I'm drinking excellent tea, after which I feel pleasantly stimulated. I see a lot of Chinese. They are a good-natured people and far from stupid. At the Bank of Siberia I was given money straight away, received cordially, treated to cigarettes and invited out to the dacha. There is a wonderful patisserie, but everything is hellishly expensive. The pavements here are made of wood.

Last night the officers and I went and had a look round the town. We heard someone shouting for help about six times; it was probably somebody being strangled. We went to look, but didn't find anyone.

Hold a mass on 17 June, and on the 29th celebrate with as much style as you can.[1] I shall be with you in spirit, and you must drink my health. Greetings to Papa, to the Lintvaryovs, Jamais,[2] Semashechko, Ivanenko and Maryushka. Well, look after yourselves, and may God keep you. Try not to forget your relative who misses you, A. Chekhov

All my clothes are creased, dirty and torn. I look like a bandit!

1. 17 June 1890 was the first anniversary of Nikolay Chekhov's death; 29 June was Pavel Chekhov's name day.
2. 'Jamais' was the nickname of Lidia Mizinova.

I probably won't bring any furs back with me. I don't know where they sell them and I'm too idle to inquire.

The cabs here in Irkutsk have springs. It's better than Ekaterinburg and Tomsk. Totally European.

When travelling you need to take at least two large pillows, and definitely dark pillowcases.

What is Ivan doing? Where has he gone? Did he go south?

From Irkutsk I go on to Baikal. My travelling companions are gearing themselves up to be seasick.

My big boots have stretched now and become more comfortable to wear; my heels aren't sore any more.

I've ordered buckwheat kasha for tomorrow. I remembered about curd cheese while I was on the road, and have started eating it with milk whenever I get to a station.

Did you receive any of the postcards I sent from the little towns I passed through? Please keep them: they will help you tell how long the post takes. It's not very quick hereabouts.

112. To Chekhov Family, 13 June 1890, Listvenichnaya
By the shores of Lake Baikal

I'm having the most frustrating time. On 11 June, that is the day before yesterday, we left Irkutsk in the evening, in the hope of making the Baikal steamer which was departing at four o'clock in the morning. When we reached the first station, they told us that there were no horses, so we could not continue our journey and had to spend the night there. The following morning we set out again and reached the landing stage at Lake Baikal about noon. On inquiring, we were told there would not be another steamer before Friday 15 June. So all we could do was sit on the shore until Friday, look at the water, and wait. All things eventually come to an end, and usually I don't mind waiting, except that on the 20th the steamer sails from Sretensk to go down the Amur, and if we miss that one we will have to wait until the 30th for the next steamer. God have mercy, when shall I ever get to Sakhalin?

We came to Lake Baikal by way of the banks of the Angara, which flows out of Baikal until it gets to the Enisei. Have a look at the map. The banks are very picturesque. Mountain after mountain, and all completely covered with forest. The weather has been marvellous, calm, sunny and warm; as I was travelling I felt extraordinarily well, so well in fact I find it hard to describe. It was probably due to the rest I had had in Irkutsk and to the fact that the banks of the Angara are just like Switzerland.[1] Somehow new and original. We followed them until we came to the mouth of the river, then turned left, and there was the shore of Lake Baikal, which in Siberia they call a sea. Just like a mirror. You can't see the other shore, of course: it's more than fifty miles away. The shoreline is steep, high, rocky and tree-clad; to the right and to the left are promontories which you can see jutting out into the sea like those of Ayu-Dag or Tokhtabel near Feodosia. It's like the Crimea. The Listvenichnaya station is situated right by the water's edge and is astonishingly like Yalta; if the houses were white it would be completely like Yalta. Except that there are no buildings up on the hills: they are too sheer and it would be impossible to build on them.

We got ourselves billeted in a sort of little barn, not unlike one of the Kraskov dachas. The Baikal starts right outside the windows, a couple of feet below the foundations. We're paying a rouble a day. Mountains, woods, the mirror-smooth Baikal – all spoilt by the knowledge that we must stay here until Friday. What are we going to do with ourselves? Also, we don't yet know what we're going to eat. The local population eats nothing but wild garlic. There's no meat or fish; despite their promises, they haven't provided any milk for us. They fleeced us of 16 copecks for a small loaf of white bread. I bought some buckwheat and a small piece of smoked ham and asked them to cook it up into a sort of mush; it tasted awful, but there was nothing we could do. One must eat. We spent all evening going round the village looking for someone to sell us a chicken, but to no avail . . . There's plenty of vodka though! Russians are such pigs. If you ask

1. Chekhov had never been to Switzerland – he had actually never been abroad at this point.

them why they don't eat meat and fish, they will tell you that there are problems with supplies and transport and so on, but you'll find as much vodka as you want even in the most remote villages. You would think it ought to be much easier to get hold of fish and meat than vodka, which costs more and is harder to transport . . . No, the point is that it is a lot more enjoyable to sit and drink vodka than make an effort to catch fish in Lake Baikal or rear cattle.

At midnight a little steamer docked; we went to have a look at it and also to find out if there might be something to eat. We were told we could have lunch the following day, but that it was night-time now, the stove in the galley was not lit, and so on. We gave thanks for 'tomorrow' – at least there was some hope! But alas! Just then the captain came in and announced that the ship would be leaving at four in the morning for Kultuk. Great! We drank a bottle of sour beer (35 copecks) in the cafeteria, which was too small even to turn round in, and saw what looked like amber beads sitting on a plate: this was omul[2] caviar. We went back to our quarters to sleep. The very idea of sleep has become repellent to me. Each day you have to lay your coat out on the floor wool-side up, then put your rolled-up greatcoat and a pillow at the top, and you sleep on these lumpy hillocks in your trousers and waistcoat . . . Civilization, where art thou?

Today it's raining, and Baikal is shrouded in mist. 'Most diverting' as Semashko would say. It's boring. I really should settle down to some writing, but it's hard to work when the weather is bad. The prospect before me is rather thankless; it would be all right if I were on my own, but I have these officers and an army doctor with me, and they love talking and arguing. They don't understand much, but they talk about everything. One of the lieutenants is also a bit of a Khlestakov[3] show-off. You really need to be alone when you are travelling. It's much more interesting to sit in a coach or in your room with your own thoughts than it is to be with people. In addition to the army people a boy called Innokenty Alexeyevich is travelling with us; he's a pupil at the Irkutsk Technical School; he resembles that

2. A fish of the salmon family found in Lake Baikal.
3. Khlestakov – the main character in Gogol's play *The Government Inspector*.

Neapolitan who spoke with a lisp, but nicer and more intelligent. We are taking him as far as Chita.

You must congratulate me: I managed to sell my carriage in Irkutsk. I won't tell you how much I got for it, otherwise Mamasha will fall over in a dead faint and won't be able to sleep for five nights.

You should receive this letter around 20 to 25 July, but maybe later. I'll send one or two more letters to Sumy, and then start sending them to Moscow. But what address shall I use?[4] You'll have to think of something. It is essential that you wire me your Moscow address. Where should you cable me? I'll let you know the address.

I am so glad, Masha, that you were in the Crimea. I sent a telegram to you in Yalta care of Sinani, the Karaim who sits in Asmolov's [book] shop.[5] Did you get it? It included a reply to Gorodetsky,[6] who had favoured me with an inordinately long telegram. I don't think Gorodetsky will get anywhere. In the first place, he cannot write decently and is basically not very talented, like all baptized Jews, and in the second place Vyshnegradsky's journey to Asia is not interesting enough to justify commissioning a journalist (i.e., paying travel expenses, *per diems*, etc.).

Look after your dear selves and don't worry about me. Where is Ivan? Regards to him. Also to Ivanenko, Semashko and Jamais. Grateful obeisances to the Lintvaryovs for their telegram.

The fog has lifted. I can see clouds on the mountains. Ah, devil take it! You'd think you really were in the Caucasus . . .

Au revoir,

Your Homo Sachaliensis

A. Chekhov

---

4. Rather than pay rent through the summer while they were at the dacha, the impecunious Chekhovs gave up the house on Sadovaya-Kudrinskaya they had lived in since the autumn of 1886 and put their furniture into storage.

5. Chekhov later became good friends with Isaak Sinani, a Karaim Jew, who later opened his own bookshop on the seafront in Yalta.

6. A Yalta journalist and bookseller whom Chekhov met in 1889.

113. To Chekhov Family, 20 June 1890, Shilka, on board the steamer Ermak

Greetings, dear household members! At last I can take off my filthy, heavy boots, my worn-out trousers, my blue shirt shiny with dust and sweat, I can wash and dress myself again like a normal human being. No more sitting in a tarantass; I am ensconced in a first-class cabin on board the Amur steamer *Ermak*. This change in my fortunes took place about ten days ago, and in the following way. I wrote to you from Listvenichnaya to tell you about missing the Baikal steamer, which meant I would have to cross the lake not on Tuesday but on Friday, and therefore not get to the Amur steamer until 30 June. But fate can play unexpected tricks. On Thursday morning I was walking along the shore of Lake Baikal and spied smoke coming from the funnel of one of the two little steamers there. Upon my asking where she was bound for, I was told she was going 'over the sea' to Klyuyevo, having been engaged by some merchant or other to take his wagon train across to the other side of the lake. Well, we also needed to go 'over the sea', and the place we needed to get to was Boyarskaya. How far was Boyarskaya from Klyuyevo? Sixteen miles, they said. I rushed off to find my travelling companions and suggested to them that we take a chance on going to Klyuyevo instead. I say 'chance', because we risked not finding any horses when we arrived at Klyuyevo, which consists of nothing but a landing-stage and a few huts, and then we would have to sit around there and miss the Friday steamer. This would have been a worse fate than the death of Igor,[1] since that would mean having to wait until the following Tuesday. My companions nevertheless agreed to risk it, so we collected our belongings and gaily stepped on board, heading straight for the cafeteria: anything for some soup! My kingdom for a plate of soup! The cafeteria was absolutely disgusting, and built like the smallest W C you can imagine. But the

1. Mentioned in the story of Princess Olga and the Drevlyans in the Russian Primary Chronicle, a work compiled by monks in Kiev detailing the history of the eastern Slavs until the early twelfth century.

cook, a former serf from Voronezh called Grigory Ivanych, proved to be a master of his craft and fed us magnificently. The weather was calm and sunny, the turquoise waters of Lake Baikal clearer than the Black Sea. People say that in the deepest places you can see down almost as far as a mile, and indeed I myself saw rocks and mountains drowning in the turquoise water that sent shivers down my spine. The trip across Baikal was wondrous, utterly unforgettable. The only bad thing was that we were in third class, the deck being fully taken up by the merchant's wagon horses, and they were stamping about during the whole voyage like raving lunatics. These horses added a certain flavour to my voyage: I felt as if I was on some sort of pirate ship. At Klyuyevo the watchman agreed to take our luggage to the station; he set off in his cart and we followed behind on foot beside the lake through the most magnificent and picturesque scenery. It's beastly of Levitan not to have come with me! The track led through the forest: woods to the right up the mountainside, woods to the left dropping down to the lake. What ravines, what crags! The colours round Baikal are warm and gentle. The weather was very warm, by the way. After a five-mile walk we came to Myskansk station, where a passing official from Kyakhta gave us excellent tea[2] and where we managed to get horses so that we could travel on to Boyarskaya. All this meant that we left on Thursday instead of Friday, and, better still, we got away a whole twenty-four hours ahead of the mail, which usually grabs all the horses from the station. We pressed on neck and crop, nourished by the faint hope that we might reach Sretensk by the 20th. I'll wait until I see you to tell you about my journey along the banks of the Selenga and then across Trans-Baikal, except to say that the Selenga is utterly beautiful, and in Trans-Baikal I found everything I have ever wanted: the Caucasus, the Psyol valley, the area round Zvenigorod, and the Don. In the afternoon you can be galloping through the Caucasus, by nightfall you are in the Don steppe, and next morning you wake from a doze and find yourself in Poltava – and it's like that for all six hundred miles. Verkhneudinsk is a nice little town, Chita

2. Kyakhta, just north of the border with Outer Mongolia, was the centre of the Russian–Chinese tea trade.

not so nice, a bit like Sumy. Needless to say, there was no time even to think of eating or sleeping; we rattled on, changing horses at stations and worrying about whether or not there would be any horses at the next one, or whether we would have to wait there for five or six hours. We covered 130 miles a day, and that's the most you can do in summer. We were completely dazed. During the day the heat was terrible too, and then it got very cold at night, so that I had to put on my leather jacket over my cotton one; one night I even had my coat on. Well, on we went and on we went, and this morning we arrived at Sretensk, exactly one hour before the steamer sailed, having tipped the coachmen at the two last stations a rouble apiece.

And so has ended my mounted journey across the wide land. It has taken me two months (I left on 21 April), and if you don't count the time spent travelling by rail and ship, the three days I was in Ekaterinburg and the week at Tomsk, a day in Krasnoyarsk and a week in Irkutsk, two days at Baikal and the days spent waiting for floods to subside so that boats could sail, you get an idea of the rapidity of my progress. I have had as good a journey as any traveller could wish for. I have not had a day's illness, and of the mass of belongings I brought with me have lost only a penknife, the strap from my trunk and a little tub of carbolic ointment. I still have all my money. Not many can travel like that for thousands of miles.

I got so used to travelling by road that now I feel somehow ill at ease, scarcely able to believe that I am no longer in a tarantass and am not hearing the jingling of the harness bells. It is a strange feeling to be able to stretch out my legs fully when I lie down to sleep, and for my face not to be in the dust. But the strangest thing of all is that the bottle of cognac Kuvshinnikov presented me with did not get broken and has not lost a drop. I promised him that I would uncork it on the shores of the Pacific.

We are travelling down the Shilka, which joins the Argunya at Pokrovskaya station and thence flows into the Amur. It is no wider than the Psyol, perhaps not even as wide. The banks are rocky, all cliffs and forests, and full of game. We tack from side to side in order to avoid running aground or bumping the stern against the banks – the steamers and barges are always bashing alongside one another. It's very stuffy. We have just stopped at Ust-Kara, where we disembarked five or six convicts; there are mines and a hard-labour prison there.

Yesterday I was in Nerchinsk, not exactly a brilliant little place, but one could live there, I suppose.

And how are you living, ladies and gentlemen? I am completely in the dark about how things are with you. Perhaps you could club together and find a 10-copeck piece to send me a wire.

The boat is going to tie up at Gorbitsa for the night, where I shall post this letter. The nights can be misty hereabouts and it is not safe to navigate.

I am going first class, because my travelling companions are in second class and I am keen to get away from them. We were all on the road together (three in a tarantass), slept together, and have all got fed up with each other, especially I with them.

Give my regards and greetings to all my friends. I kiss Mamasha's hand. As Masha is in the Crimea I am addressing this letter to Mamasha. Where is Ivan? Was Papasha in Luka for 29 June?[3]

My handwriting is dreadfully shaky because the boat shudders all the time. It's hard to write.

A little interlude. I went down to see my lieutenants and drink tea with them. They both slept well and are in a good mood . . . One of them, Lieutenant Schmidt (not a pleasant-sounding name to my ears), from an infantry regiment, is a tall, well-fed, loud-mouthed Courlander[4] and a real Khlestakov show-off. He sings bits from all the operas but with as much ear for music as a smoked herring. He is an unhappy, rather ill-bred fellow who has squandered his entire travel allowance, knows Mickiewicz[5] by heart, is candid to a fault and can talk the hind legs off a donkey. Like Ivanenko he loves to talk about his uncles and aunts. The other officer, Meller, is a quiet, modest cartographer and a highly intelligent fellow. If it weren't for Schmidt, one could happily go a million miles with him, but when Schmidt is around shoving his oar into every conversation, I get bored with him

3. Chekhov is writing knowing the letter will arrive after the 29th.
4. Courland, an historic region and former duchy in Latvia, situated between the Baltic Sea and the Western Dvina River.
5. Adam Mickiewicz (1798–1855), the Polish national poet.

too. Anyhow, what do you care about these lieutenants? They are not very interesting.

Look after your health. We seem to be approaching Gorbitsa.

Hearty greetings to the Lintvaryovs. I shall write separately to Papasha. I sent a postcard to Alyosha from Irkutsk. Farewell! I wonder when this letter will get to you? Probably it will be at least forty days from now.

I embrace and bless you all. I'm missing you.

Your

A. Chekhov

Tomorrow I am going to put together the form of the telegram which you can send to me in Sakhalin. I'll try to get into thirty words everything I need to know, and you must try to adhere strictly to it.

The gadflies are biting horribly.

114. To Alexey Suvorin, 21 June 1890, on board the Ermak

River Amur, near Pokrovskaya

This is to inform you that the steamship *Ermak* shakes as if it has a fever and so therefore there is not the slightest possibility of my writing anything. Thanks to such nonsense, all the hopes I had placed on the journey by steamship have foundered. Nothing is left to me except to eat and sleep.

I sent you a telegram yesterday from Gorbitsa. I send you my greetings.

Your

A. Chekhov

115. To Chekhov Family, 23–26 June 1890, en route from
Pokrovskaya to Blagoveshchensk

I've already written to tell you how we ran aground. At Ust-Strelka, where the Shilka flows into the Argunya (look at the map), the ship, which draws two and a half feet of water, struck a rock which holed her in a few places, and as the hold began to take in water we settled on the bottom. They set to pumping out the water and patching the holes; one of the sailors stripped naked and crawled into the hold up to his neck in water, and felt about for the holes with his heels. Each hole was then covered from the inside with heavy sailcloth smeared with caulk, after which they placed a board over it and inserted a bracing strut on top of the board which reached up to the roof of the hold – and that was the hole repaired. They went on pumping from five o'clock in the evening until nightfall, but the water level did not go down; they had to stop work until the following morning. The next morning they discovered some more holes, so they carried on pumping and patching. The sailors pumped while we, the passengers, strolled about the decks, gossiped, ate and drank and slept; the captain and the first mate were taking their cue from the passengers and were obviously not in any hurry. To our right was the Chinese shore, to our left the village of Pokrovskaya with its Amur Cossacks. You could either be in Russia or you could cross over to China – up to you, nothing to stop you either way. During the day the heat was unbearable, and I had to put on a silk shirt.

Lunch is served at twelve noon and supper at seven o'clock in the evening.

By a piece of bad luck, the steamer coming in the opposite direction, the *Herald*, with a mass of people on board, could not get through either and both ships have ended up stuck fast. There was a military band on board the *Herald*, and the result was an excellent party; all day yesterday we had music on deck which entertained the captain and the sailors and no doubt delayed the repairs to the ship. The female passengers – particularly the college girls – were having a ball:

music, officers, sailors … ah! Yesterday evening we went into the village, where we listened to more of the same music, which the Cossacks had paid for. Today the repairs are continuing. The captain is promising that we shall be off again after dinner, but his promises are made so languidly, his eyes wandering somewhere off to the side, that he's obviously lying. We're not in any rush. When I asked one of the passengers when we were likely to be on our way at last, he asked: 'Aren't you enjoying being here?' And he's right, of course. Why shouldn't we stay here, so long as it's not boring?

The captain, the mate and the agent are as pleasant as can be. The Chinese down in third class are good-natured, amusing people. Yesterday one of them was sitting on the deck singing something very sad in a treble voice, and while doing so his profile was more amusing than any cartoon drawing. Everyone was watching him and laughing, but he paid not the slightest attention. Then he stopped singing treble and switched to tenor – good God, what a voice! It was like a sheep bleating or a calf mooing. The Chinese remind me of gentle, tame animals. Their pigtails are long and black, like Natalia Mikhailovna's. Mention of tame animals reminds me: there is a tame fox cub living in the bathroom, which sits and watches you while you wash. If it hasn't seen anybody for a time, it starts to whimper.

We have some very strange conversations! The only topics of conversation round here are gold, the gold fields, the Voluntary Fleet, and Japan. Every peasant in Pokrovskaya, even the priest, is out prospecting for gold. So are the exiles, who can get rich here as quickly as they can get poor. There are some nouveaux riches who won't drink anything but champagne, and who will only go to the tavern if someone puts down a red carpet for them stretching right from their hut to the door of the inn.

When autumn comes, would you please send my winter coat to the *New Times* bookshop in Odessa, first asking Suvorin's permission, which you must do for form's sake. I shan't need galoshes. Also send any letters for me and a note of your address. If you should have any spare money, you could also send 100 roubles to the same address marked for transfer to me, in case I should need them. You will need to mark them to be transferred to me, otherwise I shall have to hang about getting them from the post office. If you don't have any spare, it doesn't matter. When you get to Moscow, suggest to Father that he take some potassium bromide, because he gets dizzy spells in the autumn; if this happens you must apply a leech behind his ear. Anything else? Yes, ask Ivan to buy from Ilyin (the shop in Petrovsky Lane) a map of the Trans-Baikal area printed on cloth, and send it in a printed-matter wrapper to this address: Innokenty Alexeyevich Nikitin, pupil at the Technical School. Please keep all newspapers and letters for me.

The Amur is an extraordinarily interesting and unusual region. It seethes with life in a way that you can have no conception of in Europe. It (life here, that is) reminds me of stories I've heard about life in America. The banks of the river are so wild, so unusual and so luxuriant one wants to stay here for ever. As I write these lines it is now 25 June. The steamer vibrates so much it's hard to write. We are on our way once more. I've already travelled over six hundred miles down the Amur, and have seen a million magnificent landscapes; my head is spinning with excitement and delight. I saw one cliff that would cause Kundasova to expire in ecstasy, were she to take it into her head to oxidize herself at the foot of it, and if Sofia Petrovna Kuvsh[inni-kova] and I were to arrange a picnic at the top of it, we could say to one another: 'You can die now, Denis, you will never write anything better.'[1] The landscape is amazing. And it's so hot! It's warm even at night. The mornings are misty, but still warm.

I stare at the banks through binoculars and see masses of ducks, geese, divers, herons and all manner of long-billed creatures. It would be a glorious place to rent a dacha!

Yesterday we passed a little place called Reinovo, where a man in the gold business asked me to visit his sick wife. When I left his house, he pressed a wad of banknotes into my hand. I felt guilty and tried to refuse the money, handing it back and saying that I was a rich man myself; the discussion went on for some time with each

1. Potemkin allegedly uttered these words to the playwright Denis Fonvizin (1745–92) after the first performance of his play *The Adolescent*.

of us attempting to persuade the other, but in the end I still found I had 15 roubles left in my hand. Yesterday a gold dealer with a face just like Petya Polevayev's came to lunch in my cabin; he drank champagne throughout the meal instead of water and treated us to it as well.

The villages here are like those on the Don; the buildings are a little different, but not much. The locals don't observe Lent, and they eat meat even during Passion Week; the young women smoke cigarettes and the old ones pipes – that is the custom here. It's odd to see peasant women smoking cigarettes. What liberalism! Ah, what liberalism!

The air on board gets red hot from all the talking. Out here nobody worries about saying what he thinks. There's no one to arrest you and nowhere to exile people to, so you can be as liberal as you please. The people grow ever more independent, self-sufficient and understanding. If a conflict should arise in Ust-Kara, where there are convicts working (among them many political prisoners who aren't subject to a hard-labour regime), it would spread unrest right through the whole Amur region. There's no culture of denouncing people here. A political prisoner on the run can take a steamer all the way to the ocean without fearing that the captain will turn him in. In part this can be explained by a complete indifference to what goes on in Russia. Everybody would say: 'What has that to do with me?'

I forgot to write and tell you that the coachmen in Trans-Baikal are not Russian but Buryat.[2] They are a funny lot. Their horses are viperish; they loathe being put into harness and are crazier than horses pulling fire-engines. To harness the trace horse you first have to hobble its legs; the moment the hobble is removed, the troika takes off like a bullet, enough to take your breath away. If the horse isn't hobbled it will kick over the traces and gouge chunks out of the shafts with its hooves, tear the harness to shreds and generally give an impression of a young devil caught by his horns.

2. Mongolian people whose lands were located north of the Russian–Mongolian border, near Lake Baikal.

26 June

We are getting near Blagoveshchensk now. Be well and happy, and don't get too used to my not being with you. But perhaps you already have? A deep bow and an affectionate kiss to you all.

Antoine

My health is excellent.

116. *To Alexey Suvorin, 27 June 1890, Blagoveshchensk*

Greetings, dearest friend! The Amur is a very fine river indeed; I have got from it more than I could have expected, and for some time I have been wanting to share my delight with you, but for seven days the wretched boat has been juddering so much that it has prevented me from writing. Not only that, but it is quite beyond my powers to describe the beauties of the banks of the Amur; I can but throw up my hands and confess my inadequacy. Well, how to describe them? Imagine the Suram Pass in the Caucasus moulded into the form of a river bank, and that gives you some idea of the Amur. Crags, cliffs, forests, thousands of ducks, herons and all kinds of fowl with viciously long bills, and wilderness all around. To our left the Russian shore, to our right the Chinese. If I want I can look into Russia, or into China, just as I like. China is as wild and deserted as Russia: you sometimes see villages and guard huts, but not very often. My brains have addled and turned to powder, and no wonder, Your Excellency! I've sailed more than six hundred miles down the Amur, and before that there was Baikal and Trans-Baikal . . . I have truly seen such riches and experienced such rapture that death holds no more terrors for me. The people living along the Amur are most unusual, and they lead interesting lives, not at all like ours. All they talk about is gold. Gold, gold – nothing else. I feel foolish and disinclined to write, so I'm writing very briefly and like a pig; I sent you four printer's sheets today about the Enisei and the taiga, and I'll send you something later about Baikal, Trans-Baikal and the Amur. Don't throw anything away; I'll collect it all up and use it for notes to tell you in person what I seem to be unable to put on paper. I have changed ships and am now on the *Muravyov*; I'm told it is a much smoother vessel, so perhaps I shall be able to write while I'm on board.

I'm in love with the Amur and would be happy to stay here for a couple of years. It is beautiful, with vast open spaces and freedom, and it's warm. Switzerland and France have never known such freedom: the poorest exile breathes more freely on the Amur than the highest general in Russia. If you were to live here you would write a lot of splendid things that would give the public a great deal of pleasure, but I am not up to it.

Beyond Irkutsk one starts to encounter the Chinese, and by the time you get here they are more numerous than flies. They are a very good-natured people. If Nastya and Borya could get to know some Chinese, they would leave their donkeys in peace and transfer their affections to the Chinese. They are nice animals and quite tame.

The Japanese start at Blagoveshchensk, or rather Japanese women, diminutive brunettes with big, weird hair-dos. They have beautiful figures and are, as I saw for myself, rather short in the haunch. They dress beautifully. The 'ts' sound predominates in their language. When, to satisfy your curiosity, you have intercourse with a Japanese woman, you begin to understand Skalkovsky,[1] who is said to have had his photograph taken with a Japanese whore. The Japanese girl's room was very neat and tidy, sentimental in an Asiatic kind of way, and filled with little knick-knacks – no washbasins or objects made out of rubber or portraits of generals. There was a wide bed with a single small pillow. The pillow is for you; the Japanese girl puts a wooden support under her head in order not to spoil her coiffure – it looks something like this.[2] The back of her head rests on the concave part. A Japanese girl has her own concept of modesty. She keeps the light on, and if you ask her what is the Japanese word for such and such a thing she answers directly, and because she doesn't know much Russian points with her fingers or even picks it up, also she doesn't

1. Konstantin Skalkovsky (1843–1905), a mining engineer and minor writer.
2. Chekhov's original drawing is in the manuscript only and therefore not available for reproduction in this volume.

show off or affect airs and graces as Russian women do. She laughs all the time and utters a constant stream of 'ts' sounds. She has an incredible mastery of her art, so that rather than just using her body you feel as though you are taking part in an exhibition of high-level riding skill. When you climax, the Japanese girl picks a piece of cotton cloth from out of her sleeve with her teeth, catches hold of your 'old man' (remember Maria Krestovskaya?) and somewhat unexpectedly wipes you down, while the cloth tickles your tummy. And all this is done with artful coquetry, accompanied by laughing and the singsong sound of the 'ts' . . .

When I invited a Chinaman into the cafeteria to stand him a glass of vodka, he held the glass out to me, to the barman and to the waiters before drinking it, and said 'velly nice, eat!'. That is Chinese formality. He did not drink it down in one go, as we do, but in sips, nibbling something after each sip. He then thanked me by giving me some Chinese coins. Astonishingly polite people! They don't spend much money on clothes, but they dress very beautifully, and they are discriminating in what they eat, which they do with a sense of ceremony.

There is no doubt that the Chinese are going to take the Amur[3] from us. Or rather, they will not take it themselves; others will take it and give it to them, the English, for example, who control China and are building strongholds everywhere. The people who live along the Amur are a very sardonic lot; they find it highly amusing that Russia is so exercised about Bulgaria, which isn't worth a brass farthing, and pays no attention whatever to the Amur. It is an improvident and foolish attitude to take. However, the politics must wait until we meet.

You sent me a telegram saying that I should make my return journey via America. I was indeed thinking of doing just that, but people are warning me against it because of the cost. There are other places besides New York where you can transfer money to me; you can do so in Vladivostok, through the Bank of Siberia in Irkutsk — they welcomed me warmly when I was there. I still have some funds

3. The Amur runs along the Russo-Chinese border and its ownership was a constant bone of contention.

left, although I am spending them like water. I lost more than 160 roubles on the sale of my carriage, and my travelling companions, the lieutenants, have taken more than 100 roubles off me. But, in fact, I don't think I shall need any money transferred. If the need arises I'll let you know in good time.

I am feeling extremely well. Judge for yourself – after all, I've been living out in the open day and night for more than two months now. And all that physical exercise!

I'm rushing to get this letter finished, as the *Ermak* is due to sail back in an hour's time taking the mail with it. It will be some time in August before you receive this letter.

I kiss Anna Ivanovna's hand and pray to heaven for her good health and happiness. Has Ivan Pavlovich Kazansky been to see you, the young student with the neatly pressed trousers who makes you feel depressed?

Along the way I've done a bit of doctoring. In Reinovo, a little place on the Amur inhabited exclusively by gold dealers, one of them asked me to see his pregnant wife. As I was leaving his house he pressed a wad of banknotes into my hand; I felt guilty and tried to give them back, assuring him that I was a very wealthy man and didn't need the money. It ended by my giving the packet back to him, but somehow there were still 15 roubles left in my hand. Yesterday I treated a small boy and refused the six roubles his mother thrust into my hand. I'm sorry now I didn't take them.

Be well and happy. Forgive me for writing so disgracefully and with so little detail. Have you written to me in Sakhalin?

I have been swimming in the Amur. Bathing in the Amur, talking and dining with gold smugglers – is that not an interesting life?

I must run to the *Ermak*. Farewell!

Thank you for the news about my family.

Your

A. Chekhov

117. To Chekhov Family, 29 June 1890, near Khabarovka, on board the Muravyov

There are meteors flying all round my cabin – fireflies, just like electric sparks. Wild goats were swimming across the Amur this afternoon. The flies here are enormous. I am sharing my cabin with a Chinaman, Son-Liu-li, who chatters incessantly about how in China they cut your head off for the merest trifle. He was smoking opium yesterday, which made him rave all night and stopped me getting any sleep. On the 27th I spent some time walking round the Chinese town of Aigun. Little by little I am entering into a fantastic world. The steamer shakes so much I can hardly write. Yesterday evening I sent Papasha a congratulatory telegram. Did it arrive all right?

The Chinaman has now launched into a song inscribed on his fan. I hope you are all well.

Your

Antoine

Regards to the Lintvaryovs.

118. To Maria Chekhova, 17 July 1890, Sakhalin

Received telegram. Well. Flat is fine. People are nice. Good conditions. Will return in autumn. Will bring many interesting things. Greetings to Trosha, the respected comrade,[1] Ivanenko, Jamais, everyone. Miss you. It's hot.

---

1. 'Trosha, the respected comrade': nicknames for Elena and Natalya Lintvaryova.

119. *To Maria Chekhova, 14 August 1890, Sakhalin*

Felicitations. Am well.[1]

120. *To Alexey Suvorin, 11 September 1890, Tatar Strait, on board the* Baikal

Greetings! I'm sailing south through the Tatar Strait which separates North from South Sakhalin. I have no idea when this letter will reach you. I am in good health, although from all sides I see the green eyes of cholera staring at me, waiting to ensnare me. Cholera is everywhere – in Vladivostok, Japan, Shanghai, Chifu, Suez, even on the moon it seems – quarantine and fear are everywhere. They are expecting that cholera will strike in Sakhalin, so ships are being held in quarantine; in short, things are in a bad way. Some Europeans have died in Vladivostok, among them the wife of a general.

I stayed on North Sakhalin for exactly two months, and the local administration welcomed me there with exceptional cordiality, even though Galkin had written not a word about me. Neither Galkin, nor Baroness Muskrat[1] nor the other geniuses I was stupid enough to turn to for help, lifted a finger to help me: I had to do everything entirely on my own account.

Kononovich, the general in charge of Sakhalin, is an intelligent and decent person. We got on well together right away, and everything turned out fine. I shall bring some papers back with me which will show you that the context in which I was working was as good as it could be. I saw *everything*, so the question now is not *what* I saw, but *how* I saw it.

I don't know exactly what will come from this, but I have achieved

1. 15 August was Maria Chekhova's name day.
1. Baroness Varvara Ikskul (a Baltic German name – Uexküll) von Gildenbandt (1854–1929).

a good deal, enough for three dissertations. I rose every morning at five o'clock, went to bed late, and laboured all day under great pressure at the thought of how much I had still to accomplish. But now that my own experience of hard labour is over, it's hard to avoid the suspicion that in seeing all the trees I missed the wood.

By the way, I patiently carried out a census of the entire population of Sakhalin. I went to all the settlements, visited every hut and talked with everyone. I used a card system to take notes, and now have records of about ten thousand convicts and settlers. In other words, there are no convicts or settlers on Sakhalin with whom I did not meet and talk. I was especially glad to be able to make records of the children, and hope that this information will prove to be of value for the future.

I dined with Landsberg[2] and sat in the kitchen of the former Baroness Heimbruck[3] . . . I visited all the celebrities. I was present at a flogging, after which I had nightmares for three or four nights about the executioner and the dreadful flogging-bench. I talked to convicts who were chained to their wheelbarrows. One day I was drinking tea in a mine, when Borodavkin, the former St Petersburg merchant who is serving a sentence here for arson, took a teaspoon out of his pocket and presented it to me. All in all it was a huge strain on my nerves and I vowed never again to come to Sakhalin.

I would like to write to you more fully, but a lady in the cabin is screaming with laughter and jabbering without ceasing, and I don't have the strength to write any more. She has been guffawing and chattering without a moment's peace since yesterday evening.

This letter will come to you via America, but I don't think I shall go that way. Everyone agrees that the route through America costs more and is more boring.

Tomorrow I shall catch a distant glimpse of the island of Matsmai, off Japan. It is now getting on for midnight, darkness is on the face of the waters and the wind is blowing. It's a mystery to me how the ship

2. Karl Landsberg, a guards officer exiled to Sakhalin.
3. Baroness Olga Gembruk (Heimbruck), a convicted criminal who was exiled to Sakhalin.

can keep going and stay on its bearings in such pitch-black conditions, not to mention in such wild and uncharted waters as the Tatar Strait.

When I remember that I am over six thousand miles away from the world I know, I feel overwhelmed with lethargy, as though it will be a hundred years before I return home.

My most profound respects and heartiest greetings to Anna Ivanovna and all your family. May God grant you happiness and all your desires.

Your

A. Chekhov

I'm depressed.

121. To Evgenia Chekhova, 6 October 1890, South Sakhalin Island

Greetings, dear Mama! I'm writing this letter to you on what is almost the eve of my departure from here back to Russia. We wait every day for the Voluntary Fleet steamship, hoping that it will be here at the latest by 10 October. I'm sending this letter to Japan, from where it will come on to you via Shanghai, or possibly America. At present I am billeted at the Korsakovsk station, where there is no post or telegraph office, and where ships only put in once a fortnight at most. One boat did come in yesterday, bringing me a pile of letters and telegrams from the north. From them I learnt that Masha enjoyed being in the Crimea; I thought she would prefer the Caucasus. I learnt that Ivan has hopelessly failed to master the art of cooking the schoolmasterly kasha, mixing up the grains with the oats. Where is he at the moment? In Vladimir? I learnt that Mikhailo, thanks be to God, had nowhere to live all summer and so stayed at home, that you went to the Holy Mountains, and that Luka was boring and rainy. It's strange! Where you were it was rainy and cold, while from the moment I arrived in Sakhalin until today it has been warm and bright; sometimes there's a light frost in the mornings and one of the mountains has snow on the top, but the earth is still green, the leaves have not fallen and nature all around is smiling, just like May at the dacha. That's Sakhalin for you! I also found out from letters that the summer at Babkino was marvellous, that Suvorin is pleased with his house, that Nemirovich-Danchenko is not happy, that Ezhov's wife has died, poor fellow, and finally that Ivanenko and Jamais are writing to each other and that Kundasova has gone off somewhere, nobody knows where. I shall personally put Ivanenko to death, and I suppose that Kundasova is, as before, wandering the streets waving her arms about and calling everybody scum, and therefore I am not rushing to grieve for her.

At midnight yesterday I heard a ship's siren. Everyone jumped out of bed: hooray, our ship must have come in! We all got dressed, took lanterns and went down to the jetty, where indeed we saw in the distance the lights of a ship. Everyone thought it must be the *Petersburg*, the ship on which I will be sailing to Russia. I was thrilled. We climbed on board a dinghy and rowed out; we rowed, and rowed, and at last the dark bulk of the ship loomed out of the mist before us. One of us croaked out: 'Ahoy there! What ship are you?' The answer came back: *Baikal*! Oof, curses, what a disappointment! I'm homesick, and fed up with Sakhalin. After all, for three months I've seen no one besides convicts or people who have no topic of conversation other than hard labour, floggings and prisoners. A wretched existence. I am longing to get to Japan, and then on to India.

I am very well, if you don't count a twitch in my eye which seems to be bothering me often just now, and which always seems to give me a bad headache. My eye was twitching yesterday and today, so I am writing this letter to the accompaniment of an aching head and a heaviness throughout my body. My haemorrhoids also remind me of their existence.

The Japanese Consul Kuze-San lives at Korsakovsk with his two secretaries, whom I have got to know well. They live in the European style. The local administrative establishment made an official visit today with all due pomp and circumstance, to present them with medals they had been awarded; I went along with my headache, and had to drink champagne.

While staying here in the south I went three times from the Korsakovsk station to visit Naibuchi, a place lashed by real ocean waves. Look at the map and you will find poor, benighted Naibuchi on the eastern shore of the southern island. These waves destroyed a boat with six American whalers on board; their ship was wrecked off the coast of Sakhalin and they are now living at the station, stolidly tramping the streets. They are also waiting for the *Petersburg* and will sail with me.

I sent you a letter at the beginning of September via San Francisco? Did you get it?

Greetings to Papasha, to my brothers, to Masha, to my Aunt and to Alyokha, to Maryushka, Ivanenko and all my friends. I'm not bringing any furs; there weren't any on Sakhalin. I wish you good health, and may heaven preserve you all.

Your

Anton

I'll be bringing presents for everyone. The cholera has abated in Vladivostok and Japan.

122. To Mikhail Chekhov, 16 October 1890, Vladivostok

Will be in Moscow on 10 December. Going via Singapore.

123. To Maria Chekhova, 6 December 1890, Vorozhba

Will see each other tomorrow. All come and meet me. Large amount of luggage. Get supper ready. Antoine.

124. To Alexey Suvorin, 9 December 1890, Moscow

Greetings, most dear friend!

Hooray! Well, here I am at last, sitting at my desk offering up prayers to my dilapidated penates and writing to you. I have such a wonderful feeling, as if I had never left home. I'm well and happy to the very marrow of my bones. Here is a very brief report for you. I spent not two months on Sakhalin, as reported in your paper, but three months and two days. I worked very intensively and carried out a full and detailed census of the entire population of Sakhalin. I witnessed *everything* except capital punishment. When I see you I shall show you a whole trunk full of memorabilia of life in a convict labour camp, all of it invaluable raw material. I learnt a lot, but have brought back with me many unpleasant memories. While I was actually living on Sakhalin, the only feeling I was aware of was a bilious discomfort in my gut as if I had eaten rancid butter, but now I am able to contemplate it in retrospect, Sakhalin appears to me like a complete hell. For two months I worked without respite or thought for myself, and by the third month I could no longer stand the bitter taste I have mentioned, nor the wretched tedium, nor the thought that cholera was threatening to spread from Vladivostok to Sakhalin, meaning that I might be facing the prospect of having to spend the winter in a prison camp. But, heaven be praised, the cholera stopped in its tracks and on 13 October a steamer carried me away from Sakhalin. So then I was in Vladivostok. Of the entire Far Eastern region and our eastern seaboard, with its fleets, its special problems and its Pacific aspirations, I have only this to say: unbelievable poverty! Poverty, boorishness and barbarism enough to drive one to despair. Only one in a hundred is an honest man; the other ninety-nine are thieves who bring disgrace to the name of the Russian people . . .

We gave Japan a miss as cholera was raging there, so I did not buy you anything Japanese; the 500 roubles you gave me to buy presents I spent on things I needed myself, a crime for which you have every right to condemn me to exile in Siberia. The first foreign port we put in to on the voyage was Hong Kong. The bay is wonderful; I have never, even in pictures, seen so much marine activity; the roads are splendid, horse-drawn trams, a funicular railway up the mountain, there are museums, botanical gardens; everywhere you see evidence of how well the English look after those who work for them. There is even a sailors' club. I rode in a rickshaw, that is to say a chaise pulled by a man, bought all manner of trinkets from the Chinese, and got very indignant when I heard my Russian travelling companions complaining about the English exploiting the natives. Yes, I thought, perhaps the English do exploit the Chinese, the Sepoys and the Hindus, but on the other hand they give them roads, running water, museums, Christianity. You also exploit people, but what do you give them in return?

As soon as we left Hong Kong, the ship began to roll heavily. Because it was not laden it pitched as much as 38 degrees, and we were afraid of capsizing. I discovered that I do not suffer from seasickness, which was a pleasant surprise. Two people died as we were on our way to Singapore, and their bodies were thrown overboard. When you see a dead man wrapped in sailcloth somersaulting into the water, it is a shocking realization that the bottom lies several miles below, and you cannot help thinking that you too might die and be tossed into the sea. The horned cattle fell sick, and, by command of Dr Shcherbak and your humble servant, the herd had to be slaughtered and thrown overboard as well.

I don't remember much about Singapore, because while driving round the island I became sad for some reason and almost burst into tears. After that came Ceylon, which was paradise. I travelled more than seventy miles by train, and enjoyed my fill of palm groves and bronze-skinned women. When I have children of my own, I shall be able to boast to them: 'Well, you little sons of bitches, once upon a time I had intercourse with a black-eyed Hindu girl, and where do you think that was? In a coconut grove, by the light of the moon!' From Ceylon we sailed on for another thirteen days and nights without stopping and nearly went out of our minds with boredom. I didn't mind the heat however. The Red Sea is a depressing place, but I found I was moved by the sight of Mount Sinai.

God's world is good. Only one thing in it is vile: ourselves. How little justice and humility there is in us, how shabby our idea of patriotism! A drunken, debauched wreck of a man may love his wife and children, but what good is his love? The newspapers all tell us how much we love our great Motherland, but what is our way of expressing this love? In place of knowledge there is limitless impudence and arrogance, in place of work there is idleness and bestiality; there is no justice and the idea of honour goes no further than 'pride in one's uniform' – a uniform which is most usually to be found decorating the docks in our courts. What we must do is work, and let everything else go to the devil. Above all we must be just, and everything else will follow.

I desperately want to talk with you. My soul is a seething cauldron. There is no one else I want, because you are the only person I can talk to. To hell with Pleshcheyev. And the actors, too.

I received your telegrams, but in so impossibly garbled a state as to be unintelligible.

I travelled from Vladivostok to Moscow with the naval officer son of Baroness Ikskul (the selfsame Muskrat). His mama has been staying at the Slavyansky Bazaar,[1] and I'm now on my way to see her, as for some reason she has asked me to call. She is a fine woman; at least her son adores her and he is a decent, upright young man.

I am very happy that I managed to get by without Galkin-Vraskoy! He did not write a single line about me, so I arrived on Sakhalin as a completely unknown quantity.

When shall I see you and Anna Ivanovna? How is she? Please write and tell me everything in detail, as it looks unlikely that I shall be able to get to you before the holidays. My greetings to Nastya and Borya; when I do come to you I shall hurl myself at them brandishing a knife and issuing blood-curdling shrieks to prove that I have been in a prison camp. I shall set fire to Anna Ivanovna's room and preach sedition to the unfortunate public prosecutor, Kostya.

I warmly embrace you and your household, with the exception of The Resident and Burenin, both of whom I send merely my regards and who ought long ago to have been sent to Sakhalin.

1. A well-known hotel in central Moscow.

I had many opportunities to talk to Shcherbak about Maslov, whom I like very much.

May the heavens preserve you.

Your

A. Chekhov

125. To Ivan Leontiev, 10 December 1890, Moscow

Greetings, dear Jean! The fates have decreed that once again the wandering star has returned to your constellation. I am back in Moscow, and writing to you again. Once more, greetings.

I don't propose to give you a description of my journey and my time on Sakhalin, because even the briefest account would make this letter so long it would never end. I will say no more than that I am extremely pleased, well-fed and so full of enchantment that I want nothing more from life and would have nothing to complain of were I now to be struck down by paralysis or carried off by dysentery. I am a man who can say: 'I have lived! It is enough.' I have been in Hell, represented by Sakhalin, and in heaven, that is to say on the island of Ceylon. Oh! the butterflies, the creepy-crawlies, the flies, the cockroaches!

The journey itself, especially crossing Siberia, was like a long-drawn-out, debilitating illness: it was very arduous having to travel, travel and keep on travelling, but then, when it was all over, how light and airy were the memories of everything I had been through!

I spent three months and three days on Sakhalin. I'll tell you when we meet what my work there achieved, but now let us talk of events nearer home. Is it true that Pleshcheyev has inherited two million? How is your health, what are you writing at the moment and what are your literary plans? You've said farewell to your grandmother's house and to life in Petersburg . . . Congratulations on entering a new era . . . God grant you every happiness and success in your new abode.

My health was good the whole time, except that I caught a cold in the Archipelago, where there were storms and a very cold north-easterly wind; now I spend the whole time coughing and blowing my nose, and in the evenings I run a temperature. I must deal with it.

My family is beaming with happiness.

Ah, my angel, if you only knew what sweet animals I've brought back from India with me! Two mongooses, about the size of a young cat, most cheerful and lively beasts. Their qualities are: courage, curiosity and affection for human beings. They will take on a rattle-snake and always win, they are not afraid of anyone or anything; as for their curiosity, if there are any parcels or bundles in the room they will not leave a single one untied; whenever they meet a new person the first thing they do is wriggle into his pockets to have a look and see what's there. If you leave them alone in a room they start to cry. You really will have to come down from Petersburg to see them.

I'm off to see my aunt. Keep well.

I shall probably not be in Petersburg before the New Year. Please give your wife my sincere greetings.

Your

A. Chekhov

All my family send their regards.

126. To Georgy Chekhov, 29 December 1890, Moscow

My dear cousin, grateful thanks to you and your family for thinking of me. I had a letter from your papa when I was in Odessa, and from you when I arrived in Moscow. I haven't replied to either of them before now, because I am terribly distracted by people all the time. I have an endless stream of different visitors coming to see me, and not one of them ever stops talking. I have become like your father, who has only to take up his pen or his book for some garrulous monk or high-up person to come into the shop and start exercising his tongue.

Well, sir, I am alive and well, and when I finally arrived home I found everyone alive and well there. I expected my trip would have plunged us into debt, but God spared us even that. Everything worked out so well it was as if I had never been away. It is amazing to think that throughout a journey lasting eight months, with its inevitable privations, I was never ill for a day, and the only thing I lost was my little knife.

To tell you all about my travels would be as hard as counting the leaves on a tree. It would take several evenings to do it. I went right across Siberia and covered three thousand miles by horse, lived three months and three days on Sakhalin, and then came back on a ship of the Voluntary Fleet. I was in Hong Kong, Singapore, on the island of Ceylon, I saw Mount Sinai, I was in Port Said, I saw the islands of the Greek Archipelago, from where we get olives, Santorini wine and long-nosed Greeks, who incidentally everywhere in the world except Taganrog are considered terrible scoundrels and ignoramuses; I saw Constantinople. I got tossed about in boats, battered by every kind of monsoon and north-easterly wind, but I was never seasick, and had as good an appetite when we were rolling and pitching about as when it was flat calm.

Misha has told me many good things about you. I am sincerely happy for you, and also for Volodya. Is he taller than you now? If so, that's bad. When he becomes an archbishop, the little deacons will be too short to put his mitre on for him. When I see Pyotr Tchaikovsky I will ask him about you. What did he do when he was with you in Taganrog?[1] Did he come to your house? He is now the second most famous person in Moscow and Petersburg. Lev Tolstoy is No. 1, and I am No. 877.

I've been sent a small cask of Santorini wine from Corfu as a present. No offence, but what disgusting wine! I've quite got out of the habit of drinking it.

Please write me a fuller letter, regardless of expense and paper. Spread yourself over three pages.

I'll be in Taganrog in the spring or summer.

My deepest respects and a thousand warmest wishes to Uncle, Aunt,

---

1. Tchaikovsky's brother Ippolit ran a shipping business in Taganrog which employed Chekhov's cousin.

the seminarist, both the girls and Irinushka. Stay well, happy and wise, and most important of all, kind.

We all send our regards.

Your

A. Chekhov

127. To Maria Chekhova, 14 January 1891, St Petersburg

I'm as exhausted as a ballerina after five acts and eight scenes. Dinners, letters I can't be bothered to answer, conversations, all kinds of nonsense. I'm supposed to go out to lunch on Vasilievsky Island now, but I don't feel like it and I've got work to do. I shall stay another three days and then see: if the merry dance continues I'll either come home or go to stay with Ivan in Sudogda.

I seem to be shrouded in a thick, vague fog of ill feeling which I just can't understand at all. People invite me to lunch and hymn me with vulgar dithyrambs of praise, but at the same time have their knives out for me. Why? The devil alone knows. I think I would be giving the greatest pleasure to nine-tenths of my friends and devotees if I decided to shoot myself. And how tawdry are their expressions of their tawdry little feelings! Burenin tears me to pieces in his articles, although it's not done to criticize a colleague on the same newspaper; Maslov (Bezhetsky) declines to accept the Suvorins' invitations; Shcheglov gleefully relays all the gossip about me, and so on. It's all so terribly stupid and boring. They're not real people, they're more like some species of mildew.

I've run across Drishka; she's staying in the same house as I am. I'll see her tomorrow.

My *Children*[1] has come out in a second edition, and I got 100 roubles for it.

I'm quite well, but going to bed rather late.

I spoke to Suvorin about you: you will not be going to work for

1. Suvorin had brought out a collection of Chekhov's stories about children in 1889.

him. I'm against it. He is very attached to you, and in love with Kundasova.

Regards to Lidia Egorovna Mizyukova.[2] I await her programme. Tell her to eat no food made from flour, and to stay away from Levitan. She will not find a better suitor than me, neither in the Duma nor in Heaven.

Shcheglov has just arrived.

Grigorovich came to see me yesterday; he kissed me repeatedly, told a lot of lies and wanted me to tell him about Japanese women.

Irakly has also arrived.[3] I need to speak to him, but the telephone is not working.

Regards to all.

Your

A. Chekhov

128. To Vladimir Mikhnevich, 17 January 1891, St Petersburg

Dear Vladimir Osipovich,

Rumour has it that my lambskin hat with streaks of grey is at your house. Would you be kind enough to give it to the bearer of this note? Your own hat accompanies this note; it has been in the offices of *New Times* for three days or so. The blame lies at your door, since you left Svobodin's earlier than I did.

Respectfully yours,

A. Chekhov

2. A reference to Lidia Mizinova.
3. Father Irakly was a Buryat priest with whom Chekhov became friendly on Sakhalin. They returned to Russia together and Father Irakly stayed with the Chekhovs when he first arrived in Moscow.

129. To Anatoly Koni, 26 January 1891, St Petersburg

Dear Anatoly Fyodorovich,

I have not rushed to answer your letter since I shall be staying in Petersburg until at least Saturday.

I am sorry that I did not visit Mme Naryshkina,[1] but judged it would be better to wait to do so until after my book has come out, by which time I shall be better able to deal with all the material I have collected. My brief Sakhalin past now appears to me so enormous that whenever I try to talk about it I scarcely know where to begin, and it always seems to come out all wrong.

I shall try to describe in some detail the situation of children and young people on Sakhalin. It is quite extraordinary. I saw starving children, girls as young as thirteen acting as kept women, girls of fifteen pregnant. Girls start a life of prostitution as young as twelve, sometimes before the onset of menstruation. Church and school exist only on paper; the upbringing of children depends entirely on the environment they happen to live in and the surroundings of a penal colony. I made a note of a conversation I had with one ten-year-old boy while I was carrying out a census of the settlement of Verkhny Armudan, where the settlers are destitute to a man and are reputed to be fanatical card players. I went into one hut: none of the grown-ups was at home; a young boy was sitting on the bench, a fair-haired, round-shouldered lad with no shoes, lost in thought. We started talking:

I   What is your father's patronymic?

He   Don't know.

I   What do you mean, you don't know? You're living with your father and you don't know his name? For shame!

He   He's not my real father.

I   What do you mean – not your real father?

He   He lives with my ma.

1. The president of a ladies' charitable organization which helped exiled families on Sakhalin.

I Is your mother married or a widow?

He Widow. She came because of her husband.

I What do you mean, because of her husband?

He She killed him.

I Do you remember your father?

He No, I don't. I'm illegimate. Ma had me when she was on the Kara.

Travelling with me on the Amur steamer to Sakhalin was a convict in leg irons who had murdered his wife. His daughter, a motherless little girl aged six, was with him. I watched him when he came down from the upper deck to the WC, followed by his daughter and a guard. While the convict sat on the WC, the little girl and the soldier with his rifle waited outside the door. When the convict climbed back up again, the girl clambered up behind, hanging on to his fetters. At night the little girl slept hugger-mugger with the convicts and the soldiers.

I remember a funeral I was at on Sakhalin. They were burying the wife of a settler who had gone away to Nikolayevsk. Around the freshly dug grave stood four pallbearer convicts – ex officio, the finance officer and I (who had been wandering around the cemetery like Hamlet and Horatio), the dead woman's Circassian lodger who had nothing better to do, and a woman convict who had turned up out of pity: she had brought along with her two of the dead woman's children, one still not weaned and the other, Alyoshka, a four-year-old boy in a woman's jacket and blue trousers with brightly coloured patches at the knees. It was cold and damp, the bottom of the grave was full of water, and the convicts were laughing . . . You could see the sea. Alyoshka peered with interest into the grave; he wanted to wipe his frozen little nose but the long sleeves of the jacket kept getting in the way. While the earth was being shovelled into the grave, I asked him:

'Alyoshka, where's your mother?'

He waved his hand like a landowner who's just lost at cards, laughed and said: 'They've buried her!'

The convicts laughed; the Circassian came up to us and asked what he should do with the children – it wasn't his job to feed them.

I encountered no infectious diseases on Sakhalin, and found very little congenital syphilis. But I did see children who were blind, dirty and covered in sores, all diseases that bear witness to neglect.

Of course I'm not in a position to resolve the issues of the children. I don't know what should be done about them. But it does appear to me that you won't get anywhere by relying on charity and a few crumbs from the table of penal and other appropriations; I believe it is very harmful to have to depend mainly on charity, which in Russia is at best a haphazard affair, and on surpluses that never in fact occur. I think it would be far better if this problem were to be addressed by funding from the state.

My address in Moscow is: The Viergang House, Malaya Dmitrovka.

Allow me to thank you for your friendly reception of me and for your promise to visit. I remain your sincerely respectful and devoted

A. Chekhov.

130. *To Alexey Suvorin, 31 January 1891, Moscow*

The amazing astronomer[1] came to visit, and I said to her: 'Suvorin and I mentioned you about three times, and he sends you his regards.' She said: 'Go to hell.' She is mourning the death of Kovalevskaya.[2]

When I got home I found gloom and despondency. My clever and dearly beloved mongoose has fallen ill and is lying motionless under a blanket. The little wretch won't eat or drink. Our climate has laid its cold hand over him and is trying to kill him. Why?

I've received a very sad letter. When we lived in Taganrog we were friendly with a well-to-do Polish family. To this day I have nostalgic memories of the cakes and preserves I consumed in this family's house when I was a schoolboy; there was music and young ladies and liqueurs, and we used to catch goldfinch in the big, wild garden. The father was an officer in the Taganrog customs service,

1. The 'astronomer' was a nickname given to Olga Kundasova, who had earlier worked at the Moscow Observatory.
2. The mathematician Sofia Kovalevskaya (1850–91).

and then he was arrested and put on trial. The family, which included two daughters and a son, was destroyed by the investigation and the trial. When the elder daughter married a Greek crook, the family adopted a little orphan girl. They brought her up, and then she developed tuberculosis of the knee and had to have her leg amputated. Their son, Hercules, a medical student in his fourth year, a splendid young man and the hope of his family, then died of consumption . . . This was followed by dreadful poverty . . . The father wandered round the graveyard desperate for a drink, but without the constitution for it: vodka simply gave him terrible headaches, and his thoughts remained as sober and black as ever. They have now written to me to say that the younger daughter has consumption, a lovely, plump young lass . . . This letter is from the father and he is asking me for a loan of *ten* roubles . . . Ach!

I was very reluctant indeed to leave you, but am glad that I did not stay an extra day, as leaving demonstrates that I still have some willpower. Here I am already writing to you. By the time you come to Moscow I shall already have finished the story, and I'll come back to Petersburg with you.

Tell Borya, Mitya and Andryusha that I *vitupero* [reprimand] them. In the pocket of my fur coat I found scraps of paper on which was written: 'Shame on Anton Pavlich, shame on him!' *O pessimi discipuli! Utinam vos lupus devoret!* [O most vile students! May you be devoured by wolves!]

My family has only just received the letter I posted to them from Sakhalin on 31 August. How is this possible?

I couldn't sleep last night, and reread *Motley Stories* for the second edition. I have chucked overboard more than twenty of the stories.

Pray accept this assurance of my sincere respect and devotion. I certify my reverence for your esteemed family.

Your

A. Chekhov

My regards to the censor Matveyev. I suggested to Anna Ivanovna that he and Ivan Pavlovich Kazansky be invited to Feodosia for the whole summer. They are such good company!

131. *To Ivan Chekhov, after 7 February 1891, Moscow*

I asked the famous teacher D. I. Tikhomirov[1] to request the Literacy Committee to put together a library [of textbooks] and send it to Sakhalin. You will see his reply on the reverse of this. A huge quantity of books has now been sent. Suvorin's bill for the textbooks amounts to 666 roubles. I had lunch yesterday with Morozova, the millionairess, and had been intending to ask her to pay this bill, but somehow my tongue clave to the roof of my mouth; I'll wait for a better occasion.

We are all well. I have been writing frantically since I returned home. For the moment it is all going swimmingly, but who knows what will come later? Generally, life is quite dull. Are you receiving the newspaper?

Keep well and free from harm, and try to avoid falling down drunk at night on the shards from broken bottles, of which I feel sure Dubasov has a plentiful supply.

I firmly clasp your hand,

Your

A. Chekhov

The mongoose has been ill and nearly died, but he's well again now and back to making mischief.

132. *To Alexey Suvorin, 5 March 1891, Moscow*

Let's go!!! I'm ready to go wherever and whenever you want. My soul is leaping with joy. It would be silly for me not to go, because when shall I have another chance? But I must inform you, my dear friend, of the following circumstances:

1) I have nowhere near finished my work. If I put it off until May, then my Sakhalin work cannot start before July, and that is dangerous,

1. Dmitry I. Tikhomirov (1844–1915), an important figure in popular education.

because the impressions I am carrying with me are already beginning to evaporate and I risk forgetting much of it.

2) I have no money at all. If I leave my work unfinished and take 1,000 roubles for the trip and for living expenses afterwards, I shall get into such a mess that the devil himself would not be able to pull me out by the ears. At the moment I am still all right, because I am being very careful and living more modestly than a churchwoman making communion loaves, but if I go off with you everything will go to the devil, the bills will mount up and I'll find myself with debts I can't pay. The mere thought of a 2,000-rouble debt makes my heart sink.

There are other factors, but they are all minor compared to the work and the money. So will you please turn over my thoughts in your mind, put yourself in my skin for a moment and try to decide if it wouldn't perhaps be better for me to stay behind? You will object that my reservations are piffling ones. But abandon your point of view and try to see it from mine.

I'll wait for your answer as soon as you can give it to me.

My story is coming along, but I haven't got very far yet.

I've been in the country with the Kiselyovs. The rooks have arrived already.

Your

A. Chekhov

133. To Maria Chekhova, 17 March 1891, St Petersburg

Twelve o'clock midnight

I have just been to see the Italian actress Duse[1] as Shakespeare's Cleopatra. I don't know Italian, but she was so wonderful it was as though I understood every word. A superb actress. I have never seen anything like her. Watching Duse, I was overcome by the melancholy reflection that we have to develop our own temperament and taste via

1. Eleonora Duse (1858–1924), the celebrated Italian actress.

such wooden players as Ermolova and her colleagues, whom we consider great because we have never seen better. Duse made me understand why theatre in Russia is so dreary.

I sent you a promissory note for 300 roubles today. Did you receive it?

After seeing Duse, how nice to read the address I am enclosing herewith. My God, how can our taste and our sense of justice have sunk so low! And it was written by students, God help their souls! Whether it's Solovtsov or Salvini, it's all the same, both of them arouse 'an ardent response in the hearts of the youth of today'. I wouldn't give half a copeck for those hearts.[2]

I'm leaving at half past one tomorrow afternoon for Warsaw. Keep well, all of you. I send you my best regards, all of you, even the mongoose, who doesn't deserve them.

I'll write.

With all my heart

A. Chekhov

134. To Chekhov Family, 20 March 1891, Vienna

My dear Chekh friends!

I am writing to you from Vienna, where I arrived at four o'clock yesterday afternoon. The journey was fine, I travelled from Warsaw to Vienna in luxury worthy of Nana; my carriage in the Société Internationale des Wagons-Lits train had beds, mirrors, enormous windows, carpets and so on.

Oh, my dear Tungus friends, if only you could know how magnificent Vienna is! There is no comparison with any other city I've ever seen in my life. The streets are wide and immaculately paved, there are masses of boulevards and squares, all the houses have six or seven

---

2. Chekhov had sent his sister a cutting from a newspaper in which some Kharkov students paid tribute to the actor and later actor-manager Nikolay Solovtsov (1858–1902), and was amazed they made no distinction between him and the Italian actor Tomaso Salvini.

storeys, and as for the shops – well, they are not shops so much as an utterly stupefying dream come true! The ties alone in the windows run into billions! And what amazing things they have in bronze, china, leather! The churches are enormous, but their size caresses rather than oppresses the eye because they seem to have been spun from lace. St Stephen's Cathedral and the Votiv-Kirche are particularly beautiful, more like cakes than buildings. The parliament building, the Town Hall, the University, all are magnificent; yesterday I understood for the first time that architecture is truly an art form. And in Vienna this art form is not scattered about randomly as it is with us, but extends in terraces for miles on end. There are many monuments. Each little street has its bookshop, and sometimes you see Russian books in their windows, but alas! not books by Albov[1] or Barantsevich or Chekhov, but books by all kinds of anonymous authors who write and publish abroad. I spotted Renan's book, also *Secrets of the Winter Palace*, and other things. It is a strange feeling to be able to read and say whatever one likes.[2]

Pay heed, ye heathens, to the cab-drivers they have here, damn their eyes! None of your droshkies, these are all handsome new carriages with usually a pair of horses, splendid ones at that. Upon their boxes sit real dandies in jackets and top hats, reading their newspapers and distinguished by the most obliging civilities.

The food is excellent. There is no vodka, but instead there is beer and pretty decent wine. One disadvantage is that they make you pay for bread. When you get your bill, they ask you '*wieviel Brötchen?*' – how many rolls have you scoffed? Then they present you with a bill for each one.

The women are beautiful and elegant, like just about everything else here.

I find I have not completely forgotten my German. I understand what people say to me, and they can understand me.

---

1. Mikhail Albov (1851–1911), a writer who became one of the editors of *The Northern Herald* in 1891.
2. Joseph Ernest Renan's (1864–1910) *Philosophical Studies* and Paul Grimm's novel *Secrets of the Winter Palace* were banned in Russia.

It was snowing as we crossed the border. There's no snow here in Vienna, but it is very cold.

I miss home, I miss all of you and suffer pangs of guilt at having once more abandoned you. But never mind; once I am home again you won't see me stirring from the house again for a year. My love to everyone, without exception. Papa, will you do something for me? Please get for me, at Sytin[3] or wherever you can find it, that popular print of St Varlaam, the one where he is riding on a sleigh with the bishop standing on a balcony in the distance, and the saint's life printed underneath.[4] Please buy it for me and leave it on my desk.

It looks as though we are not going to Spain, but we shall go to Bukhara.

Semashko, did you write to Ivanenko? Did you talk to Lika about the position at the Duma?

I send you all my best wishes. Think of me, abject sinner that I am. My respects to all, I embrace you, bless you, and remain

Your loving

A. Chekhov

Everyone we meet can see that we are Russians. They don't look me in the eye but gaze at my hat with the grizzled grey streaks in it. They probably think I'm a wealthy Russian count.

Did I write and tell you about Alexander's children? They are well, and make a very good impression.

My greetings to the handsome Levitan.

3. Ivan Sytin (1857–1934), a publisher and bookseller.
4. The account of St Varlaam tells how he believed devoutly that snow and ice would save the summer harvest and promised he would visit the Bishop of Novgorod by sleigh. On the appointed day, snow fell up to his waist.

135. *To Ivan Chekhov, 24 March 1891, Venice*

I am now in Venice, where I arrived the day before yesterday from Vienna. I must say that for sheer enchantment, brilliance and *joie de vivre* I have never in all my life seen a more wonderful city than Venice. Where you expect to find streets and lanes there are canals, instead of cabs there are gondolas, the architecture is staggeringly beautiful and every little corner has its historical or artistic interest. You drift along in a gondola seeing the palaces of the Doges, Desdemona's house, the homes of famous painters, churches ... And inside these churches sculpture and paintings such as one sees only in dreams. In a word, enchantment.

I sit in a gondola from morning till night and glide through the streets or stroll around the famous piazza of St Mark. It's a square, as smooth and clean as a parquet floor. Here is St Mark's Cathedral – something which defies description – and over there is the Doges' Palace, and other buildings which affect me like beautiful part-singing by a choir, that intense pleasure which comes from incredible beauty.

And the evenings! Dear God! You could expire from the un-familiarity of it all. There you are in your gondola, it's warm, quiet and you can see the stars above ... There are no horses in Venice, so it is as quiet as in the fields. Gondolas dart about all around ... Here comes one floating by, decorated with lanterns. In it are sitting a double bass, violins, a guitar, a mandolin and a valve cornet, two or three ladies, some gentlemen, you hear singing and music, operatic arias. And their voices! A little further on, and here's another boat with singers, and yet another, so that at midnight the air is still filled with tenors, violins, all manner of sounds that tug at your heartstrings.

Merezhkovsky, whom I met here, has been driven clean out of his mind with ecstasy. It's quite easy for a poor, humble Russian to lose his wits in this world of beauty, riches and freedom. You simply want to stay here for ever, and when you stand in a church and listen to the organ being played it makes you want to convert to Catholicism.

The tombs of Canova and Titian are magnificent. Great artists are buried in churches here, like kings. People don't despise art here as they do in our country; even the most explicitly naked depictions, statues and paintings are given sanctuary in the churches.

There's one painting in the Doges' Palace with more than ten thousand human figures in it.

Today is Sunday, and there will be musicians playing in St Mark's Square.

Anyway, stay well. I wish you every blessing. If you should come to Venice, it will be the most wonderful thing ever to happen in your life. You should see the glass that is made here! By comparison, our bottles are so hideous it quite turns the stomach to think of them.

Your

A. Chekhov

136. To Maria Kiselyova, 25 March 1891, Venice

I'm in Venice. Send me to a lunatic asylum. The gondolas, St Mark's Square, the water, the stars, the evening serenades, the mandolins, the Falerno wine – in a word, I'm gone! Think kindly of me.

The shade of the beautiful Desdemona sends her smile to the head of the *zemstvo*. I send my regards to all.

Antonio

The Jesuits send you their regards.

137. To Chekhov Family, 26 March 1891, Venice

It's raining as hard as you can imagine, and *Venezia bella* has ceased to be particularly *bella*. There's a feeling of melancholy wafting from the water, and it makes one long to flee to somewhere where the sun is shining.

The rain made me think of my leather raincoat. I have an idea the rats have been nibbling at it. If this is so, could you please quickly put it in for repair – there's a shop dealing in waterproofs on Petrovka called Piechlauer or Wiechlauer or something.

How is Signor Mongoose? Every day I dread learning of his demise.

I now realize that when I was telling you yesterday how cheap Venice is, I was exaggerating somewhat. It's the fault of Mme Merezhkovskaya; she was telling me how many francs a week she and her husband were paying, when what she actually meant was how much a day. Even so, things are pretty cheap here. A franc is worth about the same as a rouble at home.

We're off to Florence.

May the Holy Madonna bless you.

Your

A. Chekhov

I have seen Titian's *Madonna*.[1] It is lovely. But it is a pity to have wonderful paintings jumbled up with worthless pictures which ought to have been thrown out but instead have been preserved out of the spirit of conservatism which prevails among people. It's absolutely incomprehensible how many of these pictures have survived.

The house where Desdemona lived is available to rent.

138. To Chekhov Family, 29 March 1891, Florence

I'm in Florence. I've worn myself out dashing from one museum to another and from one church to another. I saw the *Venus dei Medici* and thought that were she to be dressed in the sort of clothes people wear nowadays she would look most unattractive, especially around the waist. I'm well. The sky is overcast and Italy without sun is like a face behind a mask. Be well.

Your

Antonio

The Dante statue[1] is beautiful.

1. At the Frari.

1. A statue erected in 1865 in the Piazza Santa Croce to mark the 600th anniversary of Dante's birth.

139. *To Maria Kiselyova, 1 April 1891, Rome*

The Pope of Rome has bade me congratulate you on your saint's day and to wish you as much money as he has rooms. He has eleven thousand of them, after all! After wandering round the Vatican I was overcome with fatigue, and when I got home my legs felt as if they were made of cotton wool.

I take my lunch at the table d'hôte with the other guests. Can you imagine, there are two little Dutch girls sitting opposite me: one of them reminds me of Pushkin's Tatyana, and the other of her sister Olga.[1] All through the meal I watch them both and see in my mind's eye a little spick and span white house with a little round tower, excellent butter, superb Dutch cheese, Dutch herrings, a fine-looking pastor, a thoroughly reliable teacher . . . and it makes me want to marry a nice little Dutch girl so that I can have my picture painted side by side with her on a tray beside our spick and span little house.

I've seen everything I was supposed to and dragged myself everywhere I was told. If someone gave me something to smell, I smelled it. Now I am drained of all feeling except exhaustion and a longing for cabbage soup with buckwheat kasha. Venice put me under her spell and turned my head, but the moment I left, Baedeker[2] and bad weather took over.

Farewell, Maria Vladimirovna, may the Lord God preserve you. The Pope and I send our deepest respects to His Excellency, to Vasilisa and to Elizaveta Alexandrovna.

Ties are amazingly cheap here; they're so cheap I may have to start eating them. Two for a franc.

I'm going to Naples tomorrow. Wish me luck in meeting a beautiful Russian lady, preferably a widow or divorcée. All the guidebooks say that a love affair is an indispensable condition for touring Italy. Well,

1. Tatyana and Olga are characters in Alexander Pushkin's (1799–1837) verse novel *Eugene Onegin* (1833).
2. Karl Baedeker (1801–59), the pioneering German publisher of travel guides.

what the devil, I'm ready for anything that comes along. Why not an affair?

Don't forget this miserable sinner, your sincerely devoted and respectful

A. Chekhov

Best regards to the starlings.

140. To Chekhov Family, 1 April 1891, Rome

On arrival in Rome I went to the post office and did not find a single letter. Each of the Suvorins had several letters. I decided I would pay you back in kind, that is not write to you at all, but never mind! It's not that I am so fanatical about getting letters, but there's nothing worse than being on your travels and not having any news. What have you decided about the dacha? Is the mongoose still alive? Etc., etc., etc.

I've visited St Peter's, the Capitol, the Colosseum, the Forum; I've even been to a *café chantant*, but it has not been as enjoyable as I expected. The weather hasn't helped; it's been raining. It's too hot for an autumn overcoat, and too cold for a summer one.

Travel is very cheap here. All it costs is 400 roubles to come to Italy, and even then there would be money left over for souvenirs. If I had been on my own, or with Ivan, say, then I would have come back with the impression that it is much cheaper to go to Italy than to the Caucasus. But, alas, I'm not on my own, I'm with the Suvorins ... We stayed in the best hotel in Venice, like doges, and here in Rome we're living like cardinals, because our hotel is the former palace of Cardinal Conti, now the Hotel Minerva: two huge drawing rooms, chandeliers, carpets, fireplaces and all kinds of useless clutter, costing us 40 francs a day.

My back is aching and the soles of my feet are burning from all the walking we've done. I'm appalled to think how far we must have walked!

I can't quite understand why Levitan didn't take to Italy, it's an enchanting country. If I were an artist with no ties and plenty of money I would spend the winters here. After all, it's not simply that the natural surroundings and the warmth of Italy are beautiful in themselves, Italy is the only country where art reigns over all, and simply to be aware of this is very stimulating.

I am well. I hope you are too. Regards to all.

Your

A. Chekhov

141. To Mitrofan Chekhov, 1 April 1891, Rome

I'm writing to you, my dear Uncle, from the Vatican, where the Pope lives. There are altogether eleven thousand rooms in the Vatican, but I got tired after only visiting thirty or forty of them. The famous Cathedral of St Peter is right next to the Vatican.

So greetings to you from the Vatican and St Peter's! Best regards to all, and my best wishes.

Your

A. Chekhov

142. To Chekhov Family, 7 April 1891, Naples

I went to Pompeii yesterday to have a look round. As you know, this is a Roman city that was completely buried in AD 79 by lava and ash from Vesuvius. I walked through the streets of the city and saw houses, temples, theatres, squares . . . I was amazed by the Romans' ability to combine simplicity with function and beauty.

After looking at Pompeii I had lunch in a restaurant and then decided to set out for Vesuvius, a decision fuelled by the excellent red wine I had drunk. I had to go on horseback to the foot of Vesuvius, and today in consequence several parts of my mortal frame feel as if I had survived a visit to the Third Department where I had been soundly beaten. Dragging oneself up Vesuvius is sheer torture: ash, mounds of lava, molten rock that has congealed in waves, hummocks full of all manner of things better left undescribed. One step forward, half a step back, the soles of your feet are sore, your chest aches ... On you plod, but the summit is as far away as ever. Give up and turn back? No, I would be too ashamed, and besides I would expose myself to ridicule. I started the ascent at two thirty, and got to the top at six. The crater is several score metres across; I stood on its lip and looked down as if into a cup. The ground all round about is covered in a deposit of sulphur that gives off clouds of vapour. Evil-smelling white smoke belches forth from the crater itself, molten rock and sparks fly everywhere, and Satan lies snoring beneath the smoke. There is a huge cacophony of sounds: waves breaking against the shore, the heavens thundering, rails clattering, boards crashing down. It is terrifying, and yet one is gripped by a desire to leap straight down into the monster's mouth. I now believe in Hell. The lava is so hot a copper coin will melt in it.

Going down is as awful as climbing up. You sink up to your knees in ash. I'm terribly tired now. I rode home through little villages and past villas: the air smelled wonderful and the moon was bright. I breathed in the air, looked at the moon and thought about *her*, Lika Lenskaya that is.

None of us, my dear aristocrats, will have any money this summer, and the thought of this quite puts me off my food. If I had come solo, this trip would have cost me 300 roubles, but as it is I owe 1,000. All hopes must rest on those stupid amateurs who are going to produce my *Bear*.[1]

Signori, did you manage to find a dacha? Your behaviour to me is disgraceful, you don't write to me at all and I have no idea at all what is going on at home.

My profoundest regards to all. Be well and happy, and don't completely forget your

Antoine

1. Chekhov's popular one-act farce (1888).

143. To Chekhov Family, 15 April 1891, Nice
Monday of Holy Week, 1891

I received a postcard from Papasha yesterday which had been sent on to me from Rome; I learnt from it that you have already rented a dacha. Well, thank the Lord for that. I'm very happy both for you and for myself. Don't rush the move; do it little by little, with God's help. Take out subscriptions to *The Russian Gazette* and *News of the Day*, and give the new address to *New Times* and *Fragments*. I'll write myself to *The Historical Herald* and *The Northern Herald*.

We are staying in Nice, at the seaside. The sun is shining, it's warm and green and the air smells nice, but it's windy. The famous Monaco is an hour's drive away, and there you find a little place called Monte Carlo, where roulette is played. Think of the halls in the Assembly Hall of the Nobility, beautiful and high-ceilinged, but wider. The Monte Carlo halls have big roulette tables, and I'll explain the game to you when I return. I went there on my third day here, and lost. Gambling is horribly seductive. After we'd lost our money, I sat down with Suvorin's son and we thought long and hard about working out an infallible system of winning. We went back yesterday with 500 francs each; my first stake won two gold sovereigns, then I won again and then again; the pockets of my waistcoat were weighed down with gold; I was even holding in my hands French coins from 1808, as well as Belgian, Italian, Greek and Austrian money . . . I've never seen so much gold and silver. I started to play at five o'clock, and by ten o'clock hadn't a franc left; all I had was the comforting thought that at least I had my return ticket to Nice. So there you are, ladies and gents! Of course you will say: 'What a dreadful thing to do; here we are starving, while he plays roulette.' You are quite right, and have my full permission to slit my throat. But I'm very pleased with myself: at least I shall now be able to tell my grandchildren that I have played roulette and have some experience of the feelings the game stimulates.

Next to the casino roulette is another roulette game – the restaurant. They fleece you mercilessly, but the food is magnificent. Everything that is set before you is a complete creation before which you can but bow the knee in reverence; you wouldn't actually dare to eat it. Each morsel is decorated with artichokes, truffles, nightingales' tongues, everything you can think of ... And God in heaven above, how despicable and vile this life is, with its artichokes, its palm trees, its scent of wild oranges! I adore luxury and wealth, but this roulette-style luxury reminds me of nothing so much as a luxurious water-closet. The very air has a whiff of something that offends your sense of decency and vulgarizes nature itself, the sound of the sea, the moon.

Yesterday was Sunday and I went to the local Russian church. Particularities: they have palm leaves here instead of pussy willow and ladies sing in the choir instead of boys, which makes the singing sound a bit operatic; they put foreign money on the collection plate, the churchwardens and ushers speak French, and so on. They sang Bortnyansky's Seventh 'Cherubim' Cantata marvellously, and a simple 'Our Father'.

Of all the places I have visited up to now, Venice has made the strongest impression and the best. Rome was more or less like Kharkov, Naples was dirty. I wasn't overimpressed by the sea, because I had had enough of it in November and December. Damn it, I seem to have been doing nothing but travel for a whole year. Hardly was I back from Sakhalin when I went off to Petersburg, and then back there again and on to Italy ...

If I don't return in time for Easter, remember me in your prayers when you break your fast and accept my felicitations from afar. You must know how terribly I shall miss not being with you on Easter night.

Are you keeping all the newspapers for me?

Regards to all: Alexey and Auntie, Semashko, the handsome Levitan, Likisha of the golden curls, the old lady, everyone in fact. Keep well, and may heaven bless you. I have the honour to present my report and to remain your homesick

Antonio

Regards to Olga Petrovna.

144. To Chekhov Family, 17 April 1891, Nice

Well, it's beginning to look as though I shall not manage to get back to Moscow in time for the holiday. We are setting off for Russia tomorrow, but on the way will take in Milan and the Italian Lakes (Como, Lago Maggiore), then on to Berlin, so it will be the week after Easter before I am back in Moscow.

The weather is still bad.

If our dacha is near the river, I implore you, *signori*, to buy at least two fish traps.

I trust you have already obtained the mongoose's harness? Was the little horror at the Natural Scientists' meeting?

I'm doing a little bit of writing, although it is very hard to do any on the road.

Christ is risen! I kiss you all three times for Easter and beg your forgiveness for not getting home in time for the holiday. I'm not much looking forward to a sad and lonely Easter eve.

Farewell for now, keep well. Ask Ivan not to leave. Best regards to the Kuvshinnikovs.[1]

Your

A. Chekhov

I have grown terribly tired of a life consisting of breakfast and dinner and sleeping. One spends a powerful amount of time doing that when travelling. It's much better in Siberia in this respect, where travellers don't have time for breakfast or dinner or sleep. You don't eat there, and as a result feel as though you are on wings.

1. Sofia Kuvshinnikova (1847–1907), an amateur artist, and Dmitry Kuvshinnikov, a doctor, had been Moscow friends of Chekhov's since 1888. Sofia Petrovna's affair with Chekhov's friend Levitan was later made the satirical subject of his story 'The Grasshopper' (1892).

145. To Chekhov Family, 21 April 1891, Paris

Today is Easter. So, Christ is risen! This is the first time I have ever been away from home for Easter.

I arrived in Paris on Friday morning and went straight away to the Exhibition.[1] The Eiffel Tower is indeed very, very tall. I only saw the other Exhibition buildings from the outside, because the cavalry were inside them in case of disorder. They were expecting riots on Friday. Crowds of people were out on the streets, shouting and whistling and generally getting very excited and being chased off by the police. All you need to see off a big crowd here is ten policemen. They charge in a group and the crowd scatters like a bunch of lunatics. I had the honour of being charged myself: a gendarme grabbed hold of my shoulder and started to push me in front of him.

There is a tremendous amount of traffic. Every street swarms and seethes with life. More like the Terek in full spate than a street. Noise and uproar everywhere. The pavements have tables all over them, and sitting at the tables are Frenchmen, who evidently feel as much at ease on the street as they do at home. Wonderful people. But you can't really describe Paris; I'll wait until I get home to tell you about it.

I went to Easter service at the Embassy church.

A retired diplomat by the name of Tatishchev has attached himself to us. The Paris correspondent Ivan Yakovlev-Pavlovsky,[2] who used to live with us in the Moiseyev house,[3] with the Fronshteins, has

1. The 1889 Exposition Universelle was held to mark the centenary of the French Revolution. Spread out over 960,000 square metres along the Champ de Mars, the Trocadéro, the Invalides Esplanade and the Quai d'Orsay, it was dominated by the Eiffel Tower, which was originally supposed to have been taken down afterwards.
2. Ivan Pavlovsky (pseudonym Yakovlev) (1852–1924) was the Paris correspondent for *New Times*. Before emigrating, he had been arrested in Russia for political activities and deported to Siberia. He was supported in Paris by Turgenev before the latter's death in 1883.
3. The building in Taganrog where Pavel Chekhov had his grocery shop.

become a sort of local aide-de-camp to us and goes everywhere with us. Pleshcheyev and his son and daughters are here too. As you can see, there are a lot of us. A whole colony of Russians.

Tomorrow or the day after we shall leave for Russia, which means that I'll be in Moscow by Friday or Saturday. I shall be coming through Smolensk, so if you feel inclined to meet me, come to the Smolensk station.

If I can't get away on Tuesday or even Wednesday, I shall still be in Moscow no later than Monday, so please ask Ivan not to leave until I arrive.

I'm worried you may have run out of money.

Misha, to save your immortal soul would you please get my pince-nez mended? They can put in the same lenses as yours. I am really suffering without spectacles; I went to the exhibition of paintings at the Salon and couldn't see half the pictures because I am so short-sighted. Russian painters, by the way, are much more serious than the French. Levitan is a king compared to the landscape painters I saw yesterday.

This is the last letter I'll be writing to you. *Au revoir.* I left with an empty trunk and am returning with a full one. Each of you will receive according to his or her merits.

The best of health to you all.

Your

A. Chekhov

146. To Alexander Urusov, 3 May 1891, Moscow

Dear Alexander Ivanovich,

It was only yesterday that I received your letter inviting me for a cup of tea 'with consequences' on my return from Sodom and Gomorrah. Since the last time we saw one another I have been in Italy, Paris, Nice, Berlin, Vienna . . . In Paris I saw naked women.

In any case, here is my address for the summer: Aleksin Station, Syzrano–Vyazemsky railway line.

Keep well, till we meet again.
I am off to Aleksin today to listen to the nightingales.
Your
A. Chekhov

147. To Alexey Suvorin, 10 May 1891, Aleksin

I received your letter, *merci*. The person who uses the number 1 as a pen-name is Dedlov-Kign,[1] a writer and interesting traveller, whom I know of but have not read. Yes, you are right, I am in need of balm for my soul. What would give me great pleasure, I might even say joy, would be to read something serious, not just about myself but in general. I pine for some serious reading, and none of the Russian criticism I've read recently nourishes me, it only irritates. I would dearly love to read something new about Pushkin or Tolstoy – that really would be balm to my idle mind . . .

I also miss Venice and Florence, and would be prepared to climb Vesuvius again; Bologna, however, has faded from my memory and become somewhat tarnished, and as for Nice and Paris, when I think about them, 'I read the lines of my life with revulsion' . . .[2]

In the latest issue of *The Herald of Foreign Literature* there is a story by Ouida[3] translated from the English by none other than our very own Mikhail, the tax inspector. Why don't I know any languages? I think I'd be very good at translating fiction; when I read other people's translations I always mentally change the language and the word order and end up with something light and ethereal, like lace.

On Mondays, Tuesdays and Wednesdays I work at my Sakhalin book, and the other days, except Sundays, at my novel. On Sundays I write little stories. I'm enjoying working, but alas! my family is large, and when I'm writing it's rather like being a crayfish in a cage

1. Vladimir Kign (pseudonym Dedlov) (1856–1908) was also a critic.
2. Paraphrase of a line from Pushkin's poem 'Remembrance' (1828).
3. 'Rainy June' (1885), a story by Ouida, the pseudonym of Marie Louise de la Ramée (1839–1908), the author of forty-five novels.

with other crayfish: a little crowded. The weather is wonderful every day, the dacha's situation[4] is dry and healthy, there is forest all around . . . Lots of fish and crayfish in the Oka. I can see trains and steamers. All in all, if it weren't so cramped, I'd be very, very happy.

When will you be in Moscow? Please write. You won't like the French exhibition much, so be prepared for that. You will like the Oka though, when at 5 a.m. we board a rotten old tub at Serpukhov and sail off to Kaluga.

I have no intention of getting married. My desire now is to become a bald little old man and sit behind a big desk in a nice study.

Keep well and peaceful. Respectful bows to all your family. Please write to me.

Your

A. Chekhov

I'm writing a vaudeville. This is the cast: Anna Ivanovna, Aivazovsky, General Bogdanovich, Ivan Ivanovich Kazansky and Makarov the censor.

148. To Lidia Mizinova, 17 May 1891, Aleksin

Golden mother-of-pearl and filigree-threaded Lika! It is three days now since the mongoose ran away and now he will never come back to us. The mongoose is no more. That's the first thing.

Secondly, we are leaving this dacha and taking up residence in the upper floor of Bylim-Kolosovsky's[1] house, the same who poured out milk for you but forgot to offer you berries. We will tell you in good time the day we are moving. Come and smell the flowers, catch fish, go for walks and howl.

Ah, fair Lika! All the time you were howling and watering my right

4. This dacha was a four-roomed wooden house, at the edge of a birch wood, found by Misha in Aleksin, a small town on the River Oka, one hundred or so miles south of Moscow.

1. Evgeny Bylim-Kolosovsky, the Chekhovs' new landlord, nicknamed Gege.

shoulder with your tears (I managed to get the stain out with benzine), and while you were munching your way through slice after slice of our bread and beef, we were greedily feasting our eyes on your face and the back of your head. Ah Lika, Lika, diabolically beautiful Lika! When you go out promenading with somebody or sit in the Society [of Art and Literature] and when what we were talking about comes to pass, do not despair but come to us, and we will hurl ourselves on you with might and main and fold you in our embrace.

When you are with Trofim in the Alhambra, I desire you to put out his eyes accidentally with a fork.

Your well-known friend
Guniyadi-Yanos[2]

The female guard presents her compliments. Masha asks you to write and tell us about the apartment. The address here is not Aleksin Station, but just the town of Aleksin.

149. To Maria Chekhova, 5 July 1891, Bogimovo

Masha! Hurry home, because your absence has caused our intensive domestic economy to fall into utter disarray. There is nothing to eat, the flies have taken over, there is an appalling miasma emanating from the WC, the mongoose has smashed a jar of preserves, and so on and so forth.

All the dachniks are sighing and bemoaning your departure. There is news. Gege continues to get no sympathy from anyone, and rushes pointlessly about the yard. His cross-eyed Usirisa still smiles to your face, just as she did when you were here all the while putting needles into the sour cream behind your back. Spider Man busies himself from morning till night with his spiders.[1] He has already itemized five spider legs, now there are only three to go. When he has finished with the

2. The name of a mineral water with laxative properties.
1. Another holidaymaker on the estate was the zoologist Vladimir Vagner.

spiders, he will start work on the fleas, which he is going to catch on his aunt. The Kiselyovs spend every evening at the club, and however heavily I hint, cannot be persuaded to leave.[2]

Arguments at table are, as ever, few and far between – only every lunch and every supper. The weather is hot, there are no mushrooms. Suvorin has not come yet. Elena has returned, and is already running up and down the staircases. I repeat, there is no news of any kind.

My compliments to Baroness Ikskul and all the Lintvaryovs, the Sakharovs and Markovs. Buy a cake of soap and present it to Lilia: let her wash her phiz with it.

Don't forget to remind Sushkin that I left a bottle of liqueur with him by mistake.

Come back soon, we're missing you terribly. We have just caught a frog and given it to the mongoose. He ate it.

All the best. The socialists keep themselves to themselves; presumably plotting separatism. They will long be remembered in Ukraine. Stay well, and bring the baroness down with you. You must convince her that we are hellishly bored here without her.

Your

Antonio

150. *To Lidia Mizinova, late July 1891, Bogimovo*

Dear Lika,

If you have decided to dissolve your touching *ménage à trois* for a few days, I shall persuade my brother to delay his departure for Moscow. He was planning to leave on 5 August. Come on the 1st or the 2nd. We are longing for your arrival.

Oh, if you only knew how my stomach hurts!

Your loving

M. Chekhova[1]

2. These Kiselyovs, relatives of the zoologist Vladimir Vagner, were not related to the Kiselyovs who owned the estate at Babkino.

1. This letter was actually written by Chekhov himself.

151. To Lidia Mizinova, June–July 1891, Bogimovo

Dear Lida,

Why all these reproaches? I am sending you my ugly mug. We shall see each other tomorrow. Don't forget your little Petka.[1] I kiss you one thousand times!!!

I've bought Chekhov's stories. What a delight they are! You should buy them too.

Regards to Masha Chekhova.

What a sweetie-pie you are!

152. To Lidia Mizinova, June–July 1891, Bogimovo

Dear Lidia Stakhievna,

I love you passionately, like a tiger, and I offer you my hand.

Marshal of Mongrility Golovin-Rtishchev

PS You must convey your response in mime. You are cross-eyed.

153. To Pyotr Tchaikovsky, 18 October 1891, Moscow

Dear Pyotr Ilyich,

I have a friend, a cellist and former student of the Moscow Conservatoire, called Marian Semashko, a first-rate person. Knowing that I was acquainted with you, he has asked me on several occasions to use my good offices with you: is there perhaps somewhere, either in the capitals or in the provinces, Kharkov for instance, or abroad, where he might find a suitable position, and if so, would you be kind enough

---

1. On the photograph of himself that Chekhov sent Lidia Mizinova was the inscription 'To Lidia from Petya'.

to speak for him? I know from experience how tedious such requests are, and I hesitated long before troubling you, but today I determined to do so and beg you from the kindness of your heart to forgive me. It grieves and distresses me that such an excellent professional as Semashko should be forced to drift around without serious work, not to mention that his appeals to me are so piteous that I have no power to resist. Nikolay Kashkin[1] knows him well.

I am alive and in good health, writing a great deal but publishing little. *New Times* will shortly publish my long novella *The Duel*, but you will not read it in the paper. I shall send you the book, which is due to appear at the beginning of December. *Sakhalin* is not yet finished.

Once again, forgive me for troubling you.

Your sincerely respectful and infinitely devoted

A. Chekhov

154. To Alexey Suvorin, 18 November 1891, Moscow

I am looking forward to your story, and you must send it to me as you promised. I love your stories, because they have something no one else's work has. Something that is very touching.

I read your letter about influenza and Solovyov.[1] I found it had an unexpectedly cruel flavour. Expressions like 'I hate' do not become you, and for you to beat your breast in public and cry 'I am guilty, guilty, guilty' is so arrogant it made me feel quite ill. When the Pope assumed the title of 'Most Holy' the head of the Eastern Church called himself in pique the Slave of the Slaves of God. Likewise you make a public acknowledgement of your sinfulness in order to spite Solovyov for having the cheek to call himself Orthodox. Do you really think

1. Nikolay Kashkin (1839–1920), a professor at the Moscow Conservatoire where Tchaikovsky himself taught until 1878.
1. Chekhov is referring to one of the regular 'Little Letters' Suvorin published in *New Times*, which concerned the ideas of the religious thinker Vladimir Solovyov (1853–1900).

that words like Orthodox, Judaic, Catholic have anything at all to do with purely personal qualities or merits? In my view anyone who has the word inscribed in his passport has no choice but to style himself Orthodox. Whether or not you are a believer, whether you are a prince or an exile doing hard labour, you are still basically Orthodox. So Solovyov was not making any particular claims when he replied that he was not a Jew or a Chaldean, but Orthodox . . .

I continue to grow dull, stupid, increasingly indifferent, and weak; I'm coughing too, and I am already beginning to think that my health will never recover its former strength. However, it's all in God's hands. The idea of having to undergo treatment and fuss over my physical condition produces in me something akin to revulsion. I'm not going to be treated. I'll take the waters, and take quinine, but I can't bring myself to be examined.

The reply to *The Russian Gazette* has been sent. They will be very grateful. In all matters of money and obliging people you are such a gentleman I could never hope to match you, because I don't know how.

Be well. Please write, otherwise I shall be horribly bored.

Your

A. Chekhov

(continued)

No sooner had I written this letter to you than I received yours. You say that by going to the back of beyond I'm abandoning you. In fact my intention in moving to a farmstead in the Ukraine is in order to be nearer Petersburg. You see, sir, if I don't have to keep up an apartment in Moscow, I can spend all November, December and January in Petersburg. This is what would make it possible. It would also make it possible for me to spend all summer doing nothing. I'll look for an estate for you, but you're wrong not to like the Khokhols. The people who live in Poltava province aren't children and they aren't actors; they're real people, well fed and happy to boot.

Do you know what I find helps my cough? When I'm working, I spray some turpentine on the edge of the desk and breathe in the fumes. And when I go to bed I spray some round the bedside table and other nearby objects. The spray evaporates more quickly than the liquid itself. Turpentine has rather a pleasant smell. I also drink Obersalzbrunnen, I don't eat any hot dishes, I don't talk much, and I scold myself for smoking too much. I repeat, you should wrap up as warmly as you can, even inside the house. Keep away from draughts in the theatre. Look after yourself like a hothouse plant, otherwise the cough will take a long time to get rid of. If you want to try the turpentine, buy the French kind. Take quinine once a day, and watch you don't get constipated. Influenza has entirely removed from me any desire to drink spirits. They taste foul. I don't have my normal two glasses at night, and so take a long time to get to sleep. I wish I could take ether.

I'm looking forward to the story. Why don't we each write a play in the summer? I mean it! How much time can we afford to waste?

Your

A. Chekhov

155. To Evgraf Egorov, 11 December 1891, Moscow

Dear Evgraf Petrovich,[1]

Here is the story of my abortive attempt to come and see you. I was coming not as a journalist, but on behalf, or perhaps I should say with the agreement, of a small group which wants to do something for the people who are starving. The fact is that the public has lost confidence in the administration, and is therefore reluctant to make donations. Thousands of fantastic rumours and stories about waste, bare-faced robbery, etc., are in circulation. People are wary of the Diocesan Department, and have completely lost patience with the Red Cross. The owner of unforgettable Babkino, himself a land captain,[2] tore a strip off me in no uncertain terms: 'The Moscow Red Cross is

1. Evgraf Egorov was a retired artillery officer Chekhov had got to know while spending his summers near New Jerusalem at the Babkino estate in the mid 1880s.
2. Land captains were established in 1889 to control and discipline the peasantry. The posts were usually filled by the landowning nobility.

a den of thieves!' When the general attitude is such, the administration can hardly expect much in the way of serious support from the public. Yet at the same time the public does want to help, because its conscience is far from easy. Several groups were formed among the Moscow intelligentsia and plutocracy in September; they put their heads together and talked and fussed and sought advice from knowledgeable people in the field, and the whole object of their discussions was to find ways of circumventing the administration and setting up independent mechanisms to get aid directly to the people who needed it. They decided to send their own agents into the famine-afflicted regions, to familiarize themselves with the situation on the ground, organize soup kitchens, and so on. Some influential high-up people in these circles went to Durnovo[3] and requested permission to do this, but Durnovo refused, saying that the organization of relief was the sole responsibility of the Diocesan Department and the Red Cross. The upshot was that the private initiative was completely nipped in the bud. Everyone felt as though they'd had cold water thrown over them, and got thoroughly discouraged. Some were angry, others simply washed their hands of it. You need the courage and authority of a Tolstoy to go against the stream, defy the prohibitions and the general climate of opinion, and do what your duty calls you to do.

Now, sir, about my own position. I was a great supporter of the private initiatives, since everyone has a right to do good in whatever way he sees fit; but the whole debate about the administration, the Red Cross, etc., seemed unreal and irrelevant to me. I felt that, given cool heads and kind hearts, there would be ways of getting round all the ticklish problems that people were worried about, and that there was no necessity to drag the Minister into it. When I went to Sakhalin I did so without so much as a single letter of recommendation, and I still succeeded in achieving everything I needed to; why then would I not be able to go to famine areas? And then I remembered administrators like yourself and Kiselyov, and all the land captains and tax inspectors I know, people of impeccable conduct and morality who deservedly enjoy the widest trust. So I decided to try to bring together,

3. Ivan Durnovo (1830–1903) was Minister of the Interior from 1889 to 1895.

if only in a small area, the twin engines of the administration and the
private initiative. That was why I immediately wanted to come to see
you and get your advice. The public trusts me, as it would you, and I
feel I could count on success. You may recall that I sent you a letter.
Then Suvorin arrived in Moscow. I complained to him that I did not
know your address; he sent a cable to Baranov,[4] and Baranov was
kind enough to send your address to me. Suvorin then came down
with influenza. Usually, whenever he comes to Moscow we are insepar-
able for days on end together, talking about literature, of which he
has an unrivalled knowledge. This is how it was on this occasion, and
it ended with my also getting influenza, upon which I took to my bed
suffering from paroxysms of coughing. Korolenko was also in Moscow
and found me in this stricken state. For a month I lay ill with lung
complications, and during that time I stayed at home doing absolutely
nothing. I'm on the mend now but still coughing, and I can't seem to
put back any of the weight I lost. That is the whole sorry story. Had
it not been for the flu, you and I together could perhaps have winkled
out two or three thousand or even more from the public, depending
on circumstances.

I understand your irritation with the press. Knowing the real
situation, you get as annoyed by hacks pontificating as laymen pontificating about diphtheria annoy me as a doctor. But what can we do?
What? Russia is not England, and it isn't France. Our newspapers are
not wealthy organizations, and they don't have many people at their
disposal. It costs a lot of money to send an Engelhardt[5] to the Volga,
or a professor from the Petrovskaya Academy, and a newspaper can't
afford to spare an experienced and talented colleague from his desk
where he is needed. *The* [London] *Times* would be able to organize at
its own expense a census of famine-stricken provinces, would dispatch
someone like Kennan to every district and pay him a subsistence
allowance of 40 roubles a day, and then we would have some reliable
information. But what can *The Russian Gazette* or *New Times* do? To
them, an income of 100,000 seems like the wealth of Croesus. As for

4. Nikolay Baranov (1837–1901), governor of Nizhny Novgorod from 1885 to 1897.
5. Nikolay Engelhardt was a popular investigative reporter for *New Times*.

the journalists themselves, they are all city-dwellers and all they know
about the country is what they've picked up from Gleb Uspensky.
They are really in a completely false position: they turn up in a district,
sniff around, scribble something and then they're off again. The hack
has no material resources, no freedom of action and no authority. For
200 roubles a month he dashes hither and thither hoping to God not
to get bawled out on account of the inevitable inadvertent misrepresen-
tations. He feels guilty. However, it's not he who is guilty but Russian
backwardness. Western correspondents have good maps to refer to,
encyclopaedias, statistical research documents; in the West, a journalist
can write his article sitting at home. But what about ours? Our
correspondents have to scavenge for their information in casual conversations and from rumours. For heaven's sake, there are only *three*
districts in the whole country that have been investigated up to now:
Cherepov, Tambov and one other. That's in the whole of Russia! All
right, the newspapers lie, the journalists are just colts still wet behind the
ears, but what is to be done? *We cannot not write.* If the press were to
keep silent, we would be in an even worse position, you must surely
agree with that.

Your letter and your scheme to buy cattle from the peasants have
jolted me from my inaction. I am ready with all my heart and with all
my powers to work with you and to do whatever you would like me
to. I have thought about this for a long time, and this is my conclusion.
We cannot rely on the rich. It's too late for that. Every wealthy man
has stumped up as many thousands as he was ordained to give. Now
we should concentrate all our efforts on the man in the street, who
will contribute a rouble or half a rouble. All the people who were
exercising their tongues in September on the subject of the private
initiative will by now have found a safe haven working in one or other
of the commissions or committees. So the little man is all we have left.
We should announce a subscription. If you write a letter to the editor,
I will have it published in *The Russian Gazette* and *New Times*. To
achieve the combination of elements I referred to above, we could
both sign the letter. If you feel that your official position makes this
awkward, we could make it a report from a third party, to the effect
that such and such a project has been organized in ward 5 of the

Nizhny Novgorod district. We can say that the project is operating very successfully, thank God, and contributions are requested to be sent to Land Captain E. P. Egorov at address so-and-so, or to A. P. Chekhov, or to the editor of such and such newspaper. The vital thing is that the letter must ring absolutely true. If you write giving all the details I will add something of my own, and it's in the bag. We must ask for contributions, not loans. Nobody will be interested in lending money, it's too much of a fuss. It's hard enough to give; getting it back is even harder.

I only know one rich person in Moscow – Varvara Morozova, a well-known philanthropist. I took your letter to her yesterday. At the moment she is completely taken up with the Literacy Committee, which is organizing soup kitchens for schoolchildren. Literacy and horses are incommensurable entities, so Mme Morozova could only promise me the support of her committee if your plans include establishing soup kitchens for schoolchildren, and if you can send her detailed information. I felt *uncomfortable* about asking her for money just at the moment, since everyone perpetually ransacks her and harries her like a cornered fox. So all I could do was beg her not to forget us whenever she is in touch with any of her commissions or committees, and that she promised to do. Your letter and project have also been passed on to Sobolevsky, the editor of *The Russian Gazette*, just in case. I'm collaring everyone and telling them the project is already organized.

Any roubles and half-roubles I get I shall send on to you immediately. And please make whatever use of me you can think of; I want you to be in no doubt that it would be the greatest joy for me to do anything at all, however small, since up to now I have done nothing whatsoever to help the starving or those who are supporting them.

We all send our greetings to you, except Nikolay, who died of consumption in 1889, and Fedosia Yakovlena (if you remember, she came to visit Ivan at the school), who died in October, also from consumption. Ivan is now teaching in Moscow, and Misha is a tax inspector.

Keep well,

Your

A. Chekhov

156. To Alexander Smagin, 11 December 1891, Moscow

Once again, greetings to you, Excellency.

Thank you for your telegram. We are waiting urgently for a reply, because the 20th is not far off now. The moment I receive a telegram from Masha I shall get busy with the power of attorney and transfer the money to you.[1]

Well now, honoured sir, on to another subject. I am staying put in Moscow, but in the meantime my business in Nizhny Novgorod is going full swing! Together with a friend, a thoroughly excellent person, a land captain in the most remote part of Nizhny Novgorod province, where there are no landowners, no doctors, not even any educated girls (who can be found in great number even in Hell these days), we have started off a little enterprise that we think will net us around a hundred thousand. As well as all kinds of other famine-relief projects, the main thing we are trying to achieve is to save next year's harvest. Since the peasants now have to sell their horses for next to nothing and practically give them away, there is a real danger that the fields will not get ploughed for the spring sowing, and the famine saga will be repeated all over again. So our plan is to buy the horses, feed them and return them to their owners in the spring. The scheme is well and truly up and running, and in January I shall go down there and observe the fruits of our endeavour. This is the reason for my letter. If during one of your riotous feasts you or anyone you know should happen to be in a position to collect some roubles or 50 copecks to aid the starving, or if some Korobochka[2] should leave a rouble in her will to the same cause, or if you yourself should win 100 roubles at cards, pray remember all of us sinners in your holy prayers and share a smidgeon of the bounty with us! Not necessarily immediately, but whenever is convenient, so long as it is no later than the spring. By then the horses will no longer belong to us. All contributors will

1. Before Chekhov purchased his estate at Melikhovo, he was negotiating to buy a rural property in the Ukraine.
2. A dim-witted widow in Gogol's *Dead Souls*.

receive a detailed report about every copeck spent, in verse if desired, penned to my commission by Giliarovsky. In January we shall announce it in the press. Any loot can be sent to me, or direct to the front line: Land Captain Evgraf Petrovich Egorov, Bogoyavlennoye Station, Nizhny Novgorod province.

What made you think our feelings towards Sumbatov had cooled? On the contrary, we are as much in thrall to his talents as we ever were.

Can it really be true that I am coming to live in Sorochintsy or near there? I can't believe it, but it would be wonderful if I did. I'd fish for gudgeon all summer and autumn, and in the winter make a bolt to Petersburg and Moscow . . .

Please write.

Yours with affection

A. Chekhov

157. To the Management of the Moscow Zoo, 14 January 1892, Moscow

Last year I brought back with me from the island of Ceylon a male mongoose (defined in Brehm as mungo).[1] The animal is in good health and condition. As I am about to leave Moscow for some considerable time and cannot take him with me, I humbly request the Management to accept the animal from me, and to send for him today or tomorrow. The best method of transporting him would be in a small basket with a lid and a blanket. He is quite tame. I have been feeding him on meat, fish and eggs.[2] I have the honour to be respectfully yours,

A. Chekhov

1. Alfred Edmund Brehm (1829–84), a German zoologist, was best known for the encyclopaedia *Illustriertes Tierleben. Eine allgemeine Kunde des Tierreichs* (1864–5). In volume 1 of the Russian translation the mongoose was attributed to the monkey family.

2. A representative of the zoo's management wrote to Chekhov on 15 January advising of the creature's safe arrival.

158. To Alexey Suvorin, 22 January 1892, Moscow

Well, sir, I'm back from Nizhny Novgorod province. As I hope we shall soon be seeing one another, and as I plan to write something about the famine tomorrow or the day after, I shall write only briefly now: the press is definitely *not* overstating the famine. Things are very bad. The government is not doing too badly, it's helping wherever it can, but the *zemstvo* is either incompetent or hypocritical; there is practically nothing coming in from private charity. I saw 900 kilos of rusks come from Petersburg for twenty thousand people. As the Gospel says, these donors were expecting five loaves of bread to feed the five thousand.

I had quite a journey. There was a raging blizzard and one evening I lost my way and barely made it alive. It was a horrible feeling. I went to visit Baranov. I had lunch and dinner with him, and travelled back to the station in the governor's carriage.

Generally speaking, the administration is not putting obstacles in the way of private initiatives, at least not in Nizhny province, just the opposite in fact. People can do what they like.

I found the proofs of 'Kashtanka' when I got home. Dear God, what terrible drawings! My dear friend, I would rather give the artist 50 roubles from my own pocket to take these illustrations away. What on earth does he think he is doing? Three-legged stools, a goose laying an egg, a bulldog instead of a dachshund, oh dear ...

If only there were as much talk and action about the famine in Moscow and Petersburg as there is in Nizhny, there would be no famine.

And how wonderful the people are who live down there! Healthy, vigorous peasants, each one more handsome than his neighbour – each one could be a model for the merchant Kalashnikov.[1] And they are intelligent.

I've just heard that the Moscow magnate Shelaputin has malignant anthrax.

1. The hero of 'The Song About the Merchant Kalashnikov' by Mikhail Lermontov (1814–41).

Well, I am looking forward to seeing you so that we can go to Bobrov together. Please write and tell me when you will be in Moscow.

Your

A. Chekhov

Ask Alexey Alexseyevich to send me the article about oil by Batsevich, the mining engineer, as soon as he can. I forgot to read it when I was in Petersburg.

A. Chekhov

159. To Evgraf Egorov, 6 February 1892, Voronezh

My dear and most kind Evgraf Petrovich, I am now writing to you from Voronezh province. As in Nizhny, the Governor invited me to dinner and I had both to talk and to listen to a great deal about the famine. The horse business has been set up in the following way: Governor Kurovsky buys the horses wherever he can get hold of them, as you do, and he has already bought about four hundred of them. Each horse obtained from the Don region costs about 50–60 roubles, not counting the cost of feed. Kurovsky does not keep the horses, but farms them out to peasants as soon as possible after the purchase. He brings peasants who have no horse in from the famine districts, and says to them: 'Here's a horse for you. Use it to transport grain.' The peasant takes his new horse and can thus earn money to keep himself and the horse. In the spring they say to him: 'This is the amount you have earned, and this is the amount the horse cost. Therefore, this is what you have left (or alternatively this is what you still owe).' In effect, the peasant gets the horse as a loan, and the loan is progressively worked off bit by bit.

Voronezh is a hive of activity. Famine relief is organized here on a much sounder basis than in Nizhny province. They're not just distributing grain, but even such things as portable ovens and coal. Workshops and many soup kitchens have been set up. There was a performance at the theatre yesterday in aid of famine victims, and it was completely sold out. Kurovsky is a civilized and sincere person; he works as hard as Baranov does. He is a civilian, and for a governor that is actually a great advantage: he has much more freedom of action. Anyhow, we'll talk about all this when we meet.

I saw Sofia Alexandrovna Davydova and gave her your address. She is a businesslike, kind and modest woman, who I believe can achieve much.

My letter about Nizhny Novgorod and Voronezh provinces will be published in *The Russian Gazette*.

Regards to all your family, I hope you keep well. Please write. I shall be in Moscow about the 10th–12th.

Your

A. Chekhov

160. To Alexey Suvorin, 3 March 1892, Moscow

Lensky sent me a ticket yesterday for a student performance. His students were doing [Ostrovsky's] *The Abyss* in the Maly Theatre. It's an astounding play. In a million years I could never have written the last act. It is a whole play in itself, and when I have my own theatre something I shall do is present this act on its own. Two of the students were very good. When I praised one of them, Lensky wrinkled his face; obviously this particular student is not one of his favourites.

I make discoveries every day. It is terrible having to deal with liars! The man who is selling the property, an artist, tells one lie after another, stupidly, even when there is no need to – and as a result there are daily disappointments. Every moment you wait for a new instance of deceit, and it becomes very wearing. We are all accustomed to writing and saying that it is just merchants who give short measure and cheat you, but what about the gentry! Just to look at them can turn your stomach. They're not people, they're plain ordinary kulaks,[1]

1. A derogatory term for a rich, tight-fisted peasant. The Russian word *kulak* means 'fist'.

worse even than kulaks, since the peasant kulak works for what he takes, while the only thing my artist does is take, then he stuffs himself and swears at the servants. Can you imagine, since last summer the horses have not seen a single oat or a handful of hay, and they're given nothing but straw to chomp on, although they work hard enough for ten. The cow gives no milk because she doesn't get enough to eat. The man's wife and his mistress live under the same roof; the children are filthy and ragged. The place stinks of cats. There are bedbugs and giant cockroaches. The artist affects devotion to me body and soul, while all the time teaching the peasants to cheat me. Since the boundaries of my land and woods are hard to establish by eye, he has been encouraging the peasants to show me a large wood which actually belongs to the church. But they didn't do what he said. It's all so stupidly degrading and vulgar. What especially disgusts me is that this starving, dirty swine thinks I'm just like he is, scrabbling after every copeck and up for every kind of crooked deal. The peasants are downtrodden, frightened and surly.

I'm sending you a note about country estates. I'll make some inquiries when I get there.

They tell me in your shop that *Kashtanka* is selling very well. If this is the case, then it would be good to bring out a second edition as soon as possible.[2]

You want to build a theatre, while I passionately desire to go to Venice and write . . . a play. I'm so relieved not to have an apartment in Moscow any longer! This is a happy circumstance I have never in my life been able to enjoy until now.

How is Alexey Alexeyevich's health? I don't understand why it was he needed to have showers.

Every good wish!

Your

A. Chekhov

---

2. The story 'Kashtanka' was published separately as a small book. A second edition was permitted by the censor on 12 April 1892.

161. To Alexey Kiselyov, 7 March 1892, Melikhovo

Lopasnya Station, Moscow–Kursk. This is our new address. Now for some details. Did we ever buy ourselves a barrel-load of trouble with this pig in a poke! I'll say we did – a huge, unwieldy estate which, if it were in Germany, would undoubtedly be the property of a duke. It has 576 acres divided into two sections. Strip farmed. There are more than 270 acres of woodland that in twenty years' time will be forest, but for the present looks more like shrubland. I'm told it will be good for producing shafts [for carts or sleighs], but at the moment it looks unlikely ever to produce anything more than birch rods. I'm supplying this information for the benefit of Mesdames et Messieurs teachers and land captains.

We have an orchard. A park. Big trees, long avenues of limes. There are barns and granaries, quite new and handsome. There is a hen house built on the latest scientific principles. A well with an iron pump. The whole estate is barricaded off from the world by a wooden palisade-like fence. The courtyard, garden, park and barns are also fenced off from one another. The house has both good and bad points. It is more spacious than a Moscow apartment, it's light and warm, the roof is iron, and the situation is good. It has a verandah that leads on to the garden, Italian windows and so on, but the bad points are that it is too low and too old, it looks extremely stupid and naive from the outside, while inside it is completely overrun by bedbugs and cockroaches which you can only get rid of by setting fire to them; nothing else has any effect.

There are some seed beds. In the garden, fifteen paces away from the house, there is a pond 35 feet long by 12 feet wide, with carp and tench in it, so you could fish out of the window if you wanted to. Beyond the yard is another pond, which I haven't yet seen. In another part of the estate is a river, probably not up to much. Two miles away, though, the river is wide and good for fishing. We have 38 acres sown with rye, and our intention is to sow oats and clover. We have already bought clover at 10 roubles for 36 pounds, but we can't afford oats at the moment.

The estate cost 13,000 roubles, and the deed of purchase cost another 750 roubles, making a total of 14,000. I paid the vendor, an artist, 4,000 in cash and took out a mortgage for 5,000 at 5 per cent over ten years. That leaves 4,000, which the artist will get from the Land Bank in the spring, when I mortgage the whole estate to a single bank. You can see what a good deal this is! In two or three years I'll be able to scrape together 5,000, which will allow me to clear the initial mortgage, and at that point I shall only owe the bank 4,000. But getting through the next two or three years will be no joke! The problem is not the interest, which isn't much, less than five hundred a year, but the whole business of having to think about due dates and all the unpleasantness connected with owing money. Furthermore, Your Excellency, so long as I live and carry on earning four or five thousand a year, a debt of this size hardly matters, it's actually an advantage even, since 470 roubles is a lot easier to pay than the 1,000 a Moscow apartment costs to rent. This is all fine and good, but supposing I were to leave you sinners and go on to another world, i.e. kick the bucket? Then Ma-Pa and my venerable parents will find a debt-ridden dukedom a burden so insupportable that they will cry aloud with lamentations to heaven above.

This enterprise has completely cleaned me out; I haven't a penny left.

Oh, if only you could come and visit us! It would be absolutely wonderful! First, it would be a great pleasure and very interesting to see you. Secondly, your wise advice would save us from a thousand stupidities. The truth is, we haven't a clue what we are doing. Like Rasplyuev,[1] all I know about agriculture is that the earth is black — and that about sums it up. Please write. What is the best way to sow clover? As rye, or as a spring crop?

Greetings and my best wishes to Maria Vladimirovna and Elizaveta Alexandrovna. I saw our dear Idiot[2] in Moscow before he left, and

1. A character in *Krechinsky's Wedding*, a play by Alexander Sukhovo-Kobylin (1817–1913), who exclaims that black earth is black.
2. Kiselyov's son Sergey.

heard from him that Vasilisa Pantalevna is in Moscow, therefore I am not sending my compliments to either of them in Babkino.

Your

A. Chekhov

During the day it's plus 2 degrees, but at night it goes down to minus 13.

162. To Alexander Chekhov, 21 March 1892, Melikhovo

Fireman Sasha! We have been receiving your journal and are gratified to read the profiles of distinguished fire chiefs and the lists of the medals they have been awarded. We live in the hope that you too, Sasha, will be awarded the Order of the Lion and the Sun.

We are living on our very own estate. Like Cincinnatus,[1] I spend my life in toil and eat my bread by the sweat of my brow. Mamasha fasted today and was taken to church by our very own horse, and such was the impetuous pace of the steed that Papasha fell out of the sleigh!

Papa is philosophizing as usual, and has been asking questions like: why does the snow lie here? Or: why are there trees over there, but none here? He spends all his time perusing the newspapers, upon which he informs Mamasha that there has been a society founded in Petersburg to oppose the classification of milk.[2] Like everyone from Taganrog, he is not capable of any work except lighting candles in church. He is very strict with the peasants.

We received a grandiloquent letter of congratulation from Uncle in which he assured us that 'Irinushka shed tears'.

Well, sir, regarding my financial affairs: they are in an extremely bad state, the estate expenses exceeding the income by a factor of ten. I can still hear Tournefort[3] saying: 'She needs to give birth, but we have no

1. A fifth-century BC Roman politician who also farmed.
2. A confusion with 'falsification'.
3. The French teacher at the Taganrog Gymnasium.

candle.' That's precisely my position: we need to sow, but have no seeds. The geese and the horses need fodder, but they can't eat the walls of the house. Yes, Sashechka, the love of money is not confined to Moscow.

There is a pond in the garden twenty paces away from the house, and it is quite deep, about 14 feet. How pleasant it will be to fill it with snow and look forward to the time when fish will be splashing around in its depths! And what about the ditches that need digging? . . . Digging ditches is just as agreeable an occupation as editing *The Fireman*,[4] don't you think? And what about getting up at five in the morning secure in the knowledge that you don't have to go anywhere, and no one will be coming to see you? And listening to the roosters, starlings, larks and tomtits all singing away? And getting piles of newspapers and magazines from another world?

But, Sasha, when the time comes for my estate to be auctioned off I shall buy a house with a garden in Nezhin and live there until I'm old and decrepit. 'All is not yet lost!' will be my cry when a stranger settles on my estate.

It will be a very poor show and a disgrace if you do not come and visit us in the summer and spend at least one day living the life of Cincinnatus. A lovely little estate right next to mine was sold not long ago for 3,000, with a house, outbuildings, a pond and 125 acres of land . . . It would have suited you down to the ground. Masses of raspberries and strawberries!

As Misha and I were shovelling snow into the pond today we remembered how you used to tease Beschinsky: '*Náum, Náum, ferkáche*' and so on.[5] How clever you were, Sasha!

My barns present an extremely naive appearance.

Keep well. Regards to Natalia Alexandrovna and your *pueri*. How is Mikhail's head? Is it still scabby? If it is, ask Natalia to send me details and I'll advise (gratis).

Your

Cincinnatus

4. 'The Bulletin of Firefighting in Russia' was a monthly illustrated journal published between 1892 and 1896 by the wealthy Count Alexander Sheremetiev. Its first three issues were edited by Alexander Chekhov.

5. This was a Taganrog taunt addressed to Naum Beschinsky, the Chekhovs' neighbour. *Ferkáche* may be a corruption of the German word *verkatert* – 'hung over'.

The second issue of *The Fireman* is better put together than the first.

Your relations are highly gratified by your present association with a count and the fact that your paper includes portraits of princes. Please, my dear, present my compliments to Their Highnesses and ask them if they would kindly spare a rouble as a gesture.

How much do you think the count would pay for a story about a conflagration? Would he give me a hundred roubles?

163. To Alexey Suvorin, 6 April 1892, Melikhovo

I know Amfiteatrov.[1] He is talented. Apparently he wrote his article in collaboration with his friend Passek, who graduated as a lawyer and lectures somewhere on law, and that is why half his piece deals with lawyers and lecturers in jurisprudence. Rakshanin[2] – well, their name is legion, there are hordes of people like him.

It's Easter. We have a church, but no clergy. The whole parish clubbed together and managed to scrape up 11 roubles to hire a monk from the Davydovo Monastery; he began taking services here on Friday. The church is dilapidated and cold, the windows have bars on them, the shroud of Christ is a wooden board about a yard long with a faded picture on it. We (that is my family and my guests, young people) sang at the Easter service. It was very good and harmonious, especially the mass. The peasants were delighted and said they had never had a service so splendidly conducted. All day yesterday the sun shone, so it was warm. I went out into the fields in the morning; the snow has already gone, and for half an hour I was in a glorious mood: it was absolutely wonderful. Green shoots are already pushing through from the winter crop, and the grass is coming up in the woods.

You won't like Melikhovo, at least not initially. Everything is in miniature: there's a small avenue of lime trees, a pond the size of an

1. Alexander Amfiteatrov (1862–1938), a regular columnist on *New Times*.
2. Nikolay Rakshanin (1858–1903), a writer, dramatist and theatre critic.

aquarium, a small garden and park, and little trees, but when you have been round it a couple of times and really take it in, then the impression of smallness disappears. It is actually very extensive, despite the nearness of the trees. There are woodlands all round. And masses of starlings. The starling can justly say of himself: 'I will sing praises unto my God, while I have any being.'[3] He sings the whole day long, without stopping.

I shall go to Moscow on Thursday or Friday of this week to get money, for I am sore impoverished. If I go the week after Easter I will let you know, so that we can meet there.

My brother's 'ambulatory typhoid' is giving me a lot of worry. Besides the disorderly way of life this illness tends to bring in its train, it is ruining his health and he is ageing not by the day but by the hour. And the children are still very young. I hear he is parting company with Sheremetiev, who was, so Alexander said, paying him a decent wage. I have some sympathy with Sheremetiev, who was doubtless being bombarded by letters from Alexander, written under the influence of his disease. It's very sad.

I do hope we shall meet in Moscow.

God grant you all good fortune, and may you keep well.

Your

A. Chekhov

I have information from a very reliable source that the telephone conversation Alexander is alleged to have had with Sheremetiev is a pure invention made up by someone or other.

3. Psalm 146, verse 2.

164. To Alexey Suvorin, 8 April 1892, Melikhovo

I shall be in Moscow on Wednesday and Thursday of St Thomas's Week.[1] That is definite. When you set off for Moscow, send me a wire via Ivan to: Miusskoe School, Tver Gate, Moscow. I would come earlier, but the story is not yet finished.[2] I've had guests, guests, guests continually since Friday of Holy Week until today . . . and I haven't written a single line.

I really wouldn't know what to do with the giant photograph you say Shapiro wants to present me with. It would be a monstrously unwieldy gift. You say I was younger then. Yes, just imagine! Strange as it may seem, I turned thirty some time ago and already feel nearer to forty. I've not only aged physically but spiritually as well. I've become stupidly indifferent to everything, and for some reason this indifference dates back to the time of my trip abroad. When I get up in the morning, and when I go to bed, I feel as though my interest in life has dried up. It's either that illness the newspapers call overexhaustion, which one keeps reading about, or else it's the elusive emotional process designated in novels as a spiritual crisis; if it's the latter, then so much the better.

I've had a bad headache yesterday and today; it started with flashes in front of my eyes – a condition I have inherited from my mama.

The artist Levitan is staying with me, and yesterday evening we went out shooting woodcock. He shot at one and winged it. It fell into a puddle. I picked it up and saw its long beak, big black eyes and superb plumage. It looked at us in surprise. What were we to do with it? Levitan grimaced, shut his eyes and pleaded, his voice shaking: 'Hit it on the head with your rifle butt, my friend . . .' 'I can't,' I told him. He kept on nervously shrugging his shoulders, shaking his head and begging me to do it. The woodcock went on looking at us in surprise. In the end I had to do what Levitan wanted, and kill it. There was one beautiful loving creature less in the world, and two fools went home and sat down to dinner.

1. The week after Easter in the Orthodox calendar.
2. 'Ward No. 6'.

Jean Shcheglov, with whom you spent a dull evening, is fiercely opposed to heresies of all kinds, including the notion of intelligence in women. But beside, say, Kundasova, he seems like a novice in a nunnery. By the way, if you should see Kundasova, give her my regards and tell her we do hope to welcome her here. She is a very interesting person when she gets into the open air, much more intelligent than she is in the town.

Giliarovsky came to see me. My God, the things he got up to! He rode all my nags to the point of exhaustion, climbed trees, frightened the dogs and split logs to show how strong he is. He never stopped talking, either.

Be well and happy. *Au revoir* in Moscow!

Your

A. Chekhov

165. To Alexey Suvorin, 25 June 1892, Melikhovo

Did you finally get away from Petersburg? Or did you decide to delay your departure until Sunday? I've had no letters from you, nor any word, nor the story you promised to send. Where is it? Where are you? I am writing, at a guess, to Franzensbad; perhaps you are there? If so, hello at last. I've already written to you abroad, asking whether you plan to spend the autumn in Feodosia. If so, can I come with you? I should be happy to stay with you until as late as January.

Cholera has already reached Saratov. From there it will creep into Nizhny and Moscow, and along the Oka to Serpukhov and eventually Melikhovo. A most unwelcome guest. By rights, after the famine, it should have raged through the Volga region, but it is not going to do that. I look to the future without pain or fear.[1] Cholera asiatica travels fast, but like Podkolyosin[2] it is a feeble and irresolute creature. Either it will degenerate or it will be subdued by medication. Even in cesspits

1. Paraphrase of the line from Pushkin's poem 'Stanzas'.
2. The main character in Gogol's play *Marriage* (1841), who runs away to avoid being betrothed.

such as Baku, where a hundred thousand poor and hungry people live like Chinese coolies, the sufferers are counted in tens and even single figures rather than in hundreds. It's the same in Tiflis, despite the Maidan.[3] And it was the same story in Vladivostok in 1890: there was more talk about it than there were people actually stricken by the disease. But it will be tough for the doctors all the same. If cholera does appear in Serpukhov district then, sinner that I am, I shall be making a great noise, writing prescriptions, rushing about and sleeping badly. I've been reading up about it and feel well armed for the fray.

Russian people are not very perceptive about delicate feelings. My neighbour, a wealthy manufacturer, came to see me today with his small son who needed some treatment for a throat infection. As he was leaving he offered me three roubles. I said: 'What's that for? Come, come!' He thanked me and put the money back in his pocket.

Please write and tell me what is going on abroad. What are you doing with yourself, where are you going next, are you not bored yet?

I had a letter from Chertkov.[4] He's looking for something substantial 'for well-educated readers' and asked me straight out what my fee and conditions would be, warning me at the same time that whatever he could pay would entirely depend on sales. What do you think I should tell him?

The astronomer did not come; she has vanished somewhere or other. I'm worried she may be ill and prostrate somewhere, too proud to tell anyone where she is. She is absolutely crazy. If I knew where she was I would write and tell her to come here.

I do not believe a wife is necessarily innocent just because she shares a bed with her husband. Therefore if a certain party refused to see a doctor, there must have been other factors. In any case, how does Pleshcheyev know she refused? Pleshcheyev always finds something to be disappointed in. One would have to be as dumb as a sheep to take his affection seriously and believe in his friendship. Merezhkovsky genuinely loved him and imagined that he was loved in return. The

3. The name for the market square in Tiflis (Tbilisi).
4. Vladimir Chertkov (1854–1936), a disciple of Tolstoy, was an editor of The Intermediary, the publishing house they set up to produce cheap editions of morally edifying literature for the masses.

last time he went abroad he did so not for any desire of his own or his wife's, but to please the suffering Pleshcheyev, who had been writing him tearful letters and begging him to come. And now Pleshcheyev is disappointed ... What does he mean by it? It's just the sybaritic grumbling of an old man, that's all.

Svobodin came to visit me recently. He is very thin and haggard, and has gone grey; when he sleeps he looks like a corpse.[5] Extraordinary gentleness, a calm tone of voice, and a pathological aversion to the theatre. Seeing him brought me to the conclusion that a man preparing to die cannot love the theatre.

There's no news. Keep well and in good spirits. Please write to me. If it's too boring to write, bring yourself here instead. Greetings to Anna Ivanovna and the children.

Your

A. Chekhov

166. To Evgraf Egorov, 15 July 1892, Melikhovo

My dear Evgraf Petrovich, I fear I have nothing favourable to write to you, since I do not know a single doctor who is not fully occupied at the moment, and my acquaintances do not run to any medical students. Even if I were to come across someone medically qualified, I doubt whether I would be very successful at persuading him, because I don't think any doctor would be willing to come to your district for a monthly salary of 250 roubles.

We are also having to move heaven and earth here; there are so few doctors in Serpukhov district that when cholera does strike us we shall be practically defenceless. Even I, God's humble servant, have been roped in to be a medical sanitary inspector. I go round the villages giving lectures. The day after tomorrow the sanitary committee is going to meet and tackle the problem of where to get doctors and medical students. I doubt whether we shall come up with any answers.

5. Svobodin was suffering from tuberculosis and would die of the disease in October 1892.

So you are not going to be able to have a rest after the famine. It is a most upsetting and chastening business.

I am just off to the monastery to ask them if they would be prepared to erect a shelter in which we can quarantine patients. Keep well and may heaven protect you. My respects to your family.

Your

A. Chekhov

167. To Alexey Suvorin, 1 August 1892, Melikhovo

My letters pursue you, but you are elusive. I have written to you many times, including to St Moritz, but judging by your letters you have not received anything from me. First, there is cholera in and around Moscow, and it is bound to come to our area in the near future. Secondly, I have been appointed a cholera doctor, and my patch includes twenty-five villages, four factories and a monastery. I spend my time organizing, getting quarantine shelters built and so on, and I feel very lonely because I find everything to do with cholera very alienating. The work involves constant travelling, endless discussions and pettifogging details, and it tires me out. There is no time to write. Literature has long been abandoned, and I am poverty-stricken and wretched because I considered it appropriate to my situation and my independence to turn down the salary local doctors are paid. I'm tired of it all, but if you take a bird's-eye view of cholera it has many interesting aspects. It's a shame you are out of Russia at the moment; much fine material for your regular column is going to waste. This cholera epidemic has more good than bad about it, so it is radically different from what we saw with the famine last winter. This time everyone is working furiously hard. What is being achieved at the trade fair at Nizhny[1] is a miracle, enough to make even

1. The fair at Nizhny Novgorod, the commercial centre of Russia, was the largest in the country: 'While Moscow is the heart of Russia and Petersburg is its head, Nizhny Novgorod is its purse.' Chekhov was referring in his letter to a report in *The Russian Gazette* about the opening of stalls selling disinfectants at a fixed price; they were given away to the poor. The number of medical orderlies specializing in disinfection had also just been increased from twenty-five to one hundred.

Tolstoy have some respect for medicine and for the involvement of the educated classes generally. It looks as though the cholera has been successfully lassooed. Not only has the number of infections fallen, but the proportion of people dying from it is lower as well. In the whole Moscow region there are no more than fifty cases a week, whereas down on the Don cholera is claiming a thousand victims a day. That is a formidable difference. We district physicians are pretty well prepared: we have a solid programme for action, so there is every reason to suppose that in our own areas we shall also be successful in reducing the incidence of cholera deaths. We have no assistants, we have to be both doctor and nurse at one and the same time. The peasants are coarse, dirty and suspicious; but the idea that our efforts will actually make at least a small difference stops one noticing any of this. Of all the Serpukhov doctors I am the most pathetic; my horses and carriage are wrecks, I don't know the roads, I can't see anything once evening falls, I've no money, I get exhausted very quickly, above all I can never forget that I need to be writing, and what I really want to do is wash my hands of the cholera and sit down and write. And I want to talk to you too. I feel utterly alone.

Our attempts at agriculture have been crowned with complete success. We had a decent harvest, and by the time we've sold our grain Melikhovo will have provided us with more than a thousand roubles. The vegetables are spectacular: we have mountains of cucumbers and incredible cabbage. If it were not for this accursed cholera, I could say I have never spent a better summer than this one.

The astronomer paid us a visit. She is living at the hospital with the lady doctor, and poking her nose into cholera matters in a typically female way. She exaggerates everything and sees intrigues everywhere. Strange creature. She has got used to you and likes you, although, as Chertkov would say, she hardly belongs in the ranks of those whom the censor finds acceptable. Shcheglov is wrong; I don't like that sort of literature.[2]

Nothing has been heard of any cholera uprisings, although there

2. A reference to a novella by Shcheglov which lampooned the activities of The Intermediary publishing house.

have been rumours of some arrests, some proclamations, and so on, and I hear that the writer Astyryov[3] has been sentenced to fifteen years' hard labour. If our socialists have any intention of exploiting the cholera for their own ends, they will earn my contempt. Foul means to worthy ends make the ends themselves foul. It's all right for them to give doctors and medical assistants a hard time, but why deceive the people? Why pander to their continuing ignorance and behave as if their crude prejudices were holy writ? I can't believe that the mere promise of a bright future can atone for this disgusting lie. If I were a politician, I would never traduce the present for the sake of the future, even if an ounce of falsehood were to guarantee me a hundredweight of bliss.

Are we going to see one another this autumn? Shall we be together in Feodosia? After your foreign travels and my experiences with the cholera we would have so many interesting things to tell one another. Let's spend October in the Crimea. I promise you it won't be boring. We'll write, talk, eat . . . Feodosia is quite free of cholera now.

Please write to me as often as possible, bearing in mind the extremity of my situation. I'm finding it hard to be very cheerful at the moment, but your letters prise me away from my cholera preoccupations and take me for a little while into another world.

Keep well. Give my greetings to my old school friend Alexey Petrovich.

Your

A. Chekhov

I intend to treat cholera by the Cantani[4] method: large enemas with a solution of tannin at a temperature of 40 degrees, and a subcutaneous

3. Nikolay Astyryov (1857–94), an ethnographer, statistician, writer and public figure associated with the underground terrorist 'People's Will' organization in St Petersburg. He was arrested on 30 March 1892 for writing and distributing an appeal to peasants about the 1891 famine in Samara province, and died in prison before he was sent into exile. Chekhov became acquainted with him at the end of the 1880s.

4. Arnoldo Cantani (1837–93), an Italian doctor who developed methods of treating cholera.

infusion of a solution of household salt. The former are a highly effective remedy: they provide heat and they reduce diarrhoea. The infusion sometimes works wonders, but sometimes causes heart failure.

168. To Alexey Suvorin, 25 November 1892, Melikhovo

You are not difficult to understand, and you have no need to castigate yourself for an inability to express yourself clearly. What I offered you, a man addicted to strong drink, was nothing but sweet lemonade. You gave the lemonade its due, but observed quite correctly that there was no alcohol in it. Nothing being written today contains any alcohol, that necessary ingredient, as you point out very clearly, for inebriation and enslavement. Why should this be so? Let us put 'Ward No. 6'[1] and me personally to one side and talk in general terms, for that is more interesting. Let us, if it won't bore you too much, talk about first causes and consider the times we live in as a whole. Tell me honestly, who among my contemporaries, that is between thirty and forty-five years of age, has given the world a single drop of alcohol? Are not Korolenko, Nadson[2] and all the playwrights of today pure lemonade? Have you ever been knocked overboard by the paintings of Repin or Shishkin?[3] It's all charming stuff, talented and admirable, but you can never forget for a moment that what you really want is a decent smoke. For science and technology our age may be one of greatness, but for people like us it's a stodgy, sour, dull sort of time, and we ourselves are sour and dull, capable of producing no

1. Chekhov's short story was published in November 1892 in *Russian Thought*.
2. Semyon Nadson (1862–87), a 'civic' poet. The critic D. S. Mirsky memorably condemned Nadson's poetry as being 'devoid of all life and strength. It marks the low-water mark of Russian poetical technique; and his great popularity the low-water mark of Russian poetical taste', *A History of Russian Literature From its Beginnings to 1900*, New York, 1958, p. 360.
3. Ivan Shishkin (1832–98), a landscape artist famous for his countless paintings of trees and woods.

more than gutta-percha boys, and the only person who can't see this is Stasov,[4] whom nature has endowed with the rare ability to get high on any old slops. This state of affairs is not, as Burenin thinks, due to stupidity, lack of talent or arrogance, but to a disease more damaging to the artist than syphilis or sexual impotence. We definitely lack that '*je ne sais quoi*', and so when the skirts of our muse are lifted up nothing is to be seen there but an empty space. You must remember that all those writers we call great, or even just good, who have the power of intoxicating us, share one very important characteristic: they move in a specific direction and draw you along with them, so that you sense not just with your mind but with your whole being that they have a goal, like the ghost of Hamlet's father, which had a distinct purpose in coming and quickening his imagination. Some of these writers, according to their quality, have immediate aims: the abolition of serfdom, the liberation of one's country, politics, beauty – or simply, as in the case of Denis Davydov,[5] vodka. Others have more distant aims: God, life beyond the grave, the happiness of mankind, etc. The best of these writers are realists and depict life as it is, but because every line they write is like sap, saturated with a consciousness of their goal, you derive from them a sense not just of life as it is but of life as it should be, and it is this that captivates you. But we – what do we do? We describe life as it is, but once we have done that – whoa there! We dig in our heels and won't budge another inch, however hard you whip us! We have neither immediate nor distant goals, our souls are empty. We have no politics, we don't believe in revolution, we have no God, we're not afraid of ghosts, and personally I don't even fear blindness or death. A man who desires nothing, hopes for nothing and fears nothing cannot be an artist. I don't know whether or not this is an illness; it's not important what name you give it, but

4. Vladimir Stasov (1824–1906) had a long career as a librarian in the St Petersburg public library but also worked as a critic and a tireless apologist for Russian music and art.
5. Denis Davydov (1784–1839), a soldier and poet. In Mirsky's thumbnail description of his 'hussar' poetry, Davydov 'sings the praise of a reckless valo[u]r, on the field of battle as well as before the bottle', *A History of Russian Literature From its Beginnings to 1900*, p. 82.

the fact is that we are facing a critical situation. I cannot say what will become of us in ten or twenty years' time; it may be that things will have turned out quite differently by then, but for the time being it would be unwise to expect anything significant from us, irrespective of whether we have any talent or not. We write mechanically, subscribing to long-established conventions which lay down that some people should become civil servants, some businessmen, and some writers ... You and Grigorovich consider me an intelligent person. Yes, I am intelligent, at least to the extent that I do not hide my sickness from myself, do not lie to myself, and do not conceal my hollowness by stuffing it full of scraps scavenged from other men, like the ideas of the sixties and so on. I'm not planning to throw myself down the stairs as Garshin did, but I refuse to delude myself with hopes of a better future. I am not to blame for my sickness, and it is not up to me to cure it, for we must assume that this sickness has its own good purposes which are hidden from us, and that it has been sent to us for a reason ... 'She had a reason, a good reason, to stay with the hussar!'[6]

Well, sir, now about intelligence. Grigorovich thinks that intellect can prevail over talent. Byron was a pretty clever man, as clever as a hundred devils, but what has survived is his talent. If you tell me that X talks rubbish because his intellect has overwhelmed his talent, or the other way round, then I will tell you this is because X has neither intelligence nor talent.

Amfiteatrov's articles are far better than his stories, which read like translations from Swedish.

Ezhov writes that he has collected, or rather selected, some of his stories, and he wants to ask you to publish them in book form. He has influenza, and so has his daughter. All the stuffing has been knocked out of him.

I am coming to Petersburg, and if you don't throw me out would like to stay with you for almost a month. I may take off to Finland for a while. When will I come? Don't know. All depends on how soon I

6. Slight misquotation of an epigram by Lermontov.

can write a story about eighty pages long in order not to have to borrow money in the spring.

May the heavens keep you.

What about a trip to Sweden and Denmark?

Your

A. Chekhov

169. To Alexander Chekhov, 6 February 1893, Melikhovo

Thank you, Sashechka, for going to all that trouble. When I become an Actual State Counsellor,[1] in recognition of your efforts I shall suffer you to approach me without showing due regard for my rank, i.e. without the obligation to address me as Your Excellency. I can wait another month, because my passport runs out on 21 February, but no more than that. Tell Ragozin[2] that if he doesn't send me a passport by 1 March, I shall write to Vukov in Taganrog.

Not all is completely well with us. I'll itemize the matters point by point:

1) Father is ill. He has severe pain in his spine and numbness in his fingers. Neither condition is permanent but comes and goes, like angina pectoris. Both symptoms are clearly manifestations of old age. He ought to have treatment, but the lord and master continues to insist on eating all the wrong things and refuses to cut down on anything: pancakes for lunch, hot gruel for supper and all kinds of rubbishy

1. A very high civil service rank in the Table of Ranks, the equivalent of a major-general in the army. Out of fourteen ranks only three were higher.
2. Lev Ragozin was the director of the Medical Department of the Ministry of the Interior. Now that Chekhov was no longer a resident of Moscow, he no longer had the right to live either there or in St Petersburg since he was officially a *meshchanin* – a lower-class townsperson or petty bourgeois. To reside in St Petersburg he had to have noble status, which his brother helped to procure by liaising with Ragozin's Medical Department. After being appointed to an honorary civil service post which bestowed residence privileges, Chekhov promptly retired so that he could then have the right also to live in Moscow.

snacks. He says of himself: 'I'm a martyr to paralysis', but won't take any advice.

2) Masha is ill. She has been in bed with a high temperature for a week, and we thought it must be typhoid. She is getting better now.

3) I am ill with influenza. I can't do anything and am irritable.

4) The pure-bred calf's ears have got frostbite.

5) The geese have chewed off the cockerel's comb.

6) Guests come all the time and stay the night.

7) The *zemstvo* management committee wants a medical report from me.

8) The house is subsiding in places and some of the doors won't shut.

9) The icy weather continues.

10) The sparrows are already copulating.

Actually, you may ignore the last point if you wish. Actually, sit down at your desk, and, while picking your nose, give serious consideration to the question of immorality among sparrows. But if you don't want to, don't.

The photographs arrived as ordered. But since every chest and windowsill in the house is already stacked high with photographs, your gift failed to produce much of an impression. Of all occupations in this world, the two I consider most useless are woodwork and photography.

Please inform Nikolay and Anton of the following. Grandma and Auntie Masha have promised that if they do their lessons well, learn to say their prayers and recite poems by heart, and if they are not rude to Misha or to one another, they will be sent presents in Lent. But if Natalia Alexandrovna writes to tell us they are not behaving themselves in a manner befitting children of a provincial state secretary, all they will receive is the hole without the doughnut. Anton is pigeon-chested and he must do some gymnastics. You can't live with a chest like that.

My head aches and the influenza is making me feel rather miserable. There is a distinctly hospital-like atmosphere in the house.

My respects to Natalia Alexandrovna together with my best wishes for prosperity, peace and health. Regards to the children and Gagara[3] as well.

Be well.

Your

A. Chekhov

170. To Nikolay Leikin, 16 April 1893, Melikhovo

My dear Nikolay Alexandrovich,

The dachshunds[1] finally arrived yesterday. They had got cold and hungry and tired on the way from the station, and were fantastically happy to be here. They raced round all the rooms jumping up affectionately on to everyone and barking at the servants. As soon as they had been fed, they felt completely at home. During the night they dug up all the soil from the window boxes, complete with the seeds that had been sown in them, and distributed the galoshes from the front porch through all the rooms in the house. In the morning, when I was taking them for a walk in the garden, they caused panic in the breasts of our yard dogs, who had never in all their lives seen such monstrous creatures. The bitch is prettier than the dog. There is something not quite right, not only with his face, but also with his hind legs and rump. But both of them have such kind and grateful eyes. What have you been feeding them on, and how often? How do I train them not to answer calls of nature inside the house, and so on? Everybody has fallen for the dachshunds; they are now the main topic of conversation. My most grateful thanks for them. The bitch had a collar with an inscribed tag on it; I am returning it to you complete, along with some pennies for the cost of sending them. At least I can defray the costs of all the trouble you went to.

We are having perfectly disgraceful weather. For example, at six o'clock this morning it was frosty, the sky was clear and the sun was

3. How Alexander's family referred to his mother-in-law.
1. Maria christened the dogs Brom (Bromide) and Khina (Quinine) and Chekhov attached patronymics: Brom Isayevich and Khina Markovna.

shining, and everything seemed to promise a fine day to come. But now, two hours later, the sky is overcast with clouds, there is a wind blowing from the north and it feels as though it might snow. There is already a lot of snow on the ground; the only way of getting about is on wheels, and even then at some peril. We've done no ploughing and haven't yet put out the cattle from their winter quarters. It looks as though it will be May before the beasts will be able to start grazing. We face disaster. The price of straw should be 30 to 33 copecks a pood,[2] but we are selling ours to our own people for 20 copecks and to outsiders for 22 copecks, and even though this includes a small premium as a nod to charity, 20 to 22 copecks seems a shamelessly low price to me. My mother and I struggle to get more, but can't seem to do anything.

You ask when I am likely to be in Petersburg? How can you be serious – who is going to Petersburg at the moment? If I do come, it won't be before winter.

Now for a little misunderstanding, which you are the only person in a position to resolve. Can you intercede on my behalf with Viktor Bilibin? He is offended with me because in one of my letters I am supposed to have asked you how many children he now has. He knows I am quite familiar with his domestic situation, so he probably regarded my inquiry as ironic and consequently offensive. One of two things must have happened: either I failed to express myself clearly enough to you, thus causing you to misunderstand what I was saying, or Viktor misunderstood what you said to him. Do be kind enough to show him the passage in my letter where I was asking about his children, or persuade him that he cannot have understood you aright. I should be very grateful.

It's cold! So depressing when the weather is bad.

I read that you have been elected a councillor, congratulations.

My best respects to Praskovia Nikiforovna and Fedya.

With very best wishes, most of all for good health,

Your

A. Chekhov

2. A pood was the equivalent of 36 pounds or 16.38 kilograms.

171. To Lidia Mizinova, 13 August 1893, Melikhovo

Dearest Lika,

The reason I haven't been writing to you is because there is nothing to write about. Life is so devoid of incident that all one feels is the flies biting, nothing else whatever. Come here, my dearest blonde creature, and we'll talk and argue and then make up. It is very boring without you, and I'm ready to pay five roubles for the chance to talk to you even for five minutes. We have no cholera here, although there is dysentery and whooping-cough, as well as rotten rainy weather, damp and coughing. Please come and sing to us, adorable Lika. The evenings are drawing out now, and there is nobody nearby with any inclination to dispel my boredom.

I shall be going to Petersburg as soon as I am allowed to, that is when the cholera epidemic is over. I shall probably base myself there in October. I keep dreaming of building something in that part of the world and moving there. But it is a vulgar dream: to avoid vulgarity one needs poetry, and I do not have enough poetry.

Money! Money! If I had money I would go to South Africa, about which I am currently reading some very interesting letters. One must have a goal in life, and that is exactly what travel provides.

Our cucumbers have ripened. Brom has fallen in love with Mlle Mirrielees.[1] We live quietly. We don't drink vodka and have given up smoking, but for some reason I am still overtaken by a tremendous desire to sleep after supper, and the room still smells of cigars. Gladkov has lost some weight; the prince[2] has put some on. Varenikov claims his clover is doing well. The great bungler Ivanenko continues to bungle and tread on the roses, the mushrooms, the dogs' tails and everything else. Will he get a job at Ivan's school? Do you know anything about this prospect? I am very sorry for the poor fellow, and if I thought it were an acceptable thing to do and would not be open

---

1. Two mongrel yard dogs who lived at Melikhovo were called Muir and Mirrielees by the Chekhovs, after a famous Moscow department store.
2. This was the Chekhovs' neighbour, Prince Sergey Shakhovskoi.

to misinterpretation, I would happily give him a piece of land and build him a house to live in. After all, he's not getting any younger!

I'm not getting any younger either. I feel that life is laughing up its sleeve at me, and that is what impels me to describe myself as old. Once my youth has finally evaporated and I feel a desire to start living as a proper human being but cannot manage to do so, at that point I shall be justified in saying: I'm an old man. Anyhow, all this is nonsense. Forgive me, Lika, but honestly there's nothing else to write about. I shouldn't be writing anyhow, I should be sitting near you and we should be talking.

Time to go and have supper.

The apples have ripened. I sleep seventeen hours a day. Lika, if you have fallen in love with someone and already forgotten me, please at least don't laugh at me. Masha and Misha have gone to Babkino to the Kiselyovs and don't seem to be enjoying it much. That's the news. Nothing more to write about. Potapenko and Sergeyenko came to visit. We all liked Potapenko; he sings very well.

Keep well, my dear Lika, and don't forget me. Even if you are dallying with some Tisha or other, find time to scribble a line to me.

Your

A. Chekhov

172. To Alexey Suvorin, 11 November 1893, Melikhovo

If the last letter you got from me was dated 24 August, you obviously never received those I sent you while you were abroad. Or perhaps you did receive them but forgot about them? Anyway, it doesn't matter.

Regarding the co-inheritor of Pleshcheyev's fortune,[1] I remember a conversation I had with a lawyer who was an assistant to Plevako. This man told me that there was one other woman with a claim to the

1. Pleshcheyev had died that year leaving a huge fortune which he himself had inherited very late in life.

inheritance, but that she had been bought off. At the time, for some reason, I had the impression that the lawyers had actively sought out this rival heiress so that they could frighten Pleshcheyev and screw more money out of him.

I am alive and well. My cough has got worse than it was, but I don't believe I am anywhere near being a consumptive. I've cut my smoking down to one cigar a day. I didn't stir from this place all summer; I treated patients and visited the sick, and waited for the cholera to strike . . . I saw a thousand patients and expended a huge amount of time, but of cholera there was no sign. I didn't write anything at all, but amused myself in the time I could spare from medicine by reading my unwieldy material for *Sakhalin* and putting it into some sort of order. The day before yesterday I came back from Moscow, where I spent two weeks in a sort of trance. Because my life there consisted of an uninterrupted succession of banquets and new acquaintances, I earned myself a new nickname: Avelan.[2] I have never felt myself to be such a free spirit. First, I had no apartment round my neck, so there was nothing to stop me staying wherever I liked, secondly, I still have no passport, and then . . . it was girls, girls, girls . . . All summer long I had been worrying myself sick about lack of money, but now that I'm spending less I am much more relaxed. I'm starting to experience a sense of release from financial cares, by which I mean that as I seem not to need more than two thousand a year, I can either write or not, as I please.

Pascal is very well done, but there is something unpleasant about Pascal himself.[3] When I get diarrhoea at night, I can put a cat on my stomach to act as a compress and keep me warm. Clotilde is like King David's Abishag – a cat to keep the monarch warm. Her lot in life is no more than to warm up an old man – what an enviable reason for

2. Fyodor Avelan (1838–1910), a Russian vice-admiral fêted in France following the signing of the Franco-Russian alliance. Alexander III had gone aboard a ship of the French Navy during an official visit to Kronstadt in August 1891 and had stood bareheaded while the 'Marseillaise' was played. In the autumn of 1893, a Russian naval squadron, led by Avelan, had paid a return visit to Toulon. The Russian newspapers were full of reports about how well he had been received.
3. A reference to Zola's novel *Le Docteur Pascal* (*Doctor Pascal*), 1893.

being on this earth! I have great sympathy for Abishag, who may not have written any psalms but was probably purer and more acceptable in the sight of God than the man who stole Uriah's wife away from him. Clotilde is a person, an individual in her own right, a young woman who must surely be in need of a young man, and – here you will excuse me – no one but a Frenchman, in the name of God knows what, would think of turning her into a hot-water bottle for a grey-haired old Cupid with stringy fowl's legs. I find it offensive to read of Pascal taking his pleasure with Clotilde rather than someone younger and stronger; old King David, pumping himself to exhaustion in a young girl's arms, is like a melon already touched by the early morning frosts of autumn but deluding itself that it can still ripen; to every fruit its proper season. And what nonsense it is anyway – is sexual potency really such an infallible index of life and health? Is only the stud a real man? Intellectuals become impotent at forty, while the ninety-year-old savage still manages to keep it up with ninety wives. Serf owners used to hang on to their virility and go on impregnating their Agashkas and Grushkas right up to the last gasp of extreme old age, when they would be carried off by a stroke. I'm not trying to read you a moral lecture, and I suppose my own old age will not be entirely free of attempts to 'draw my bow', as Apuleius has it in *The Golden Ass*. It's only human for Pascal to sleep with a young girl, nothing particularly wrong with that and it's his own affair; what I object to is Zola's applauding Clotilde for sleeping with Pascal, and giving this perversion the name of love.

The astronomer has become a pauper. She has grown old and is very thin, with dark circles under her eyes, strained nerves . . . The poor thing has lost faith in herself and that is the worst thing that can happen. Blessed is he who has no faith and never did have. People have tried to help her, but they always end up dashed against the rocks of her terrible *amour propre*.

Recently I have been overcome by irresponsibility, accompanied by an unprecedented attraction to people; literature has become my Abishag, and I am now so bound to her that I have begun feeling contempt for medicine. But the literature I mean is not the stories or novels you expect, or have given up expecting, from me, but the kind of thing I can read for hours on end stretched out on the sofa. I lack the necessary passion to write myself.

I'm not thinking of writing any plays. No inclination to do so. I have seen a lot of Potapenko. The Odessa Potapenko is as far removed from the Moscow Potapenko as the crow is from the eagle. The difference is astonishing. I like him better and better the more I see of him.

Sakhalin is being sent to the Central Office of Prisons in page proof rather than as galleys, although galley proofs were stipulated when I got permission to go to Sakhalin. I had a horribly bureaucratic letter from Central Office: 'Subsequent to receipt of your letter dated, etc., etc.' Not just 'with reference to', but 'subsequent to receipt of', and needless to say quoting an official number. How stuffy can you get?

I hear that you are writing a new play. I am so glad.

Well, goodbye for now. We'll discuss the stories when we meet. You will be in Moscow some time in November or December, won't you?

I send you my best wishes. When you come, I'll also put up at the Slavyansky Bazaar. Yasinsky is in Moscow at the moment.

Hooraaaaay!

Your

A. Chekhov

173. To Alexey Suvorin, 27 March 1894, Yalta

Greetings!! I've been in Yalta, deadly dull Yalta, for almost a month now, staying at the Hotel Rossiya. I'm in room 39, and next door in room 38 is your favourite actress Abarinova.[1] The weather is springlike, warm and sunny, the sea is all the sea should be, but the people are as dull, dreary and lifeless as you can possibly imagine. It was a stupid mistake for me to devote the whole of March to the

1. Antonina Abarinova (1844–1901), an actress at the Alexandrinsky Theatre.

Crimea; I should have gone to Kiev and lost myself in contemplation of the holy places and the Khokhol spring.

My cough hasn't quite gone, but I still intend to come back north to my penates on 5 April. I've been here quite long enough, and in any case I've run out of money. I only brought 350 roubles with me, and by the time you've dealt with travelling expenses both ways there are only 250 roubles left, and it's pretty hard to overindulge on that sort of money. If I'd had 1,000 roubles, say, or 1,500, I'd have gone to Paris, and that would have been a good thing for me for several reasons.

Generally speaking I'm well, but I have a few specific ailments, such as the cough, heart palpitations and haemorrhoids. A little while ago I suffered palpitations continuously for six days, and it was a truly horrible feeling. Since I gave up smoking for good I have lost my gloomy and anxious state of mind. Possibly because I no longer smoke, Tolstoyan morality has ceased to influence me; in the depths of my soul I feel rather hostile to it. This is, of course, unfair. There is peasant blood flowing in my veins, and peasant virtues just don't strike me as amazing revelations. Ever since I was a child I have been a firm believer in progress, and this could hardly have been otherwise when you take into consideration the enormous difference between the time when I was thrashed and the time when I stopped being thrashed. I have always loved clever people, quickness of temper, courtesy and wit, and I have always been as indifferent to the fact that some people pick at their corns or have foot bindings that stink to high heaven as I am that some young ladies have a habit of walking about in the morning with curling papers in their hair. But there was a time when I was strongly affected by Tolstoy's philosophy; it possessed me for six or seven years and I was affected not so much by his fundamental ideas – with which I was already familiar – than by the way in which he expressed them, his very reasonableness, and no doubt a species of hypnotism peculiar to him. But now something inside me protests against it: reason and justice tell me there is more love for mankind in electricity and steam than there is in chastity and abstaining from meat. It is true that war is evil and courts of law are evil, but that does not mean I have to go about in bast shoes[2] and sleep on top of the stove beside the labourer and his wife, and so on and so forth. But all this is really beside the point; it's not a matter of being for or against, what it amounts to is that whichever way I look at it Tolstoy has simply passed on, he is no longer in my heart, and when he departed he said, Behold, your house is left unto you desolate.[3] I've been granted, so to say, an exemption from billeting. These debates bore me, and when I read windbags like Max Nordau[4] I'm revolted. A man who is ill with a fever may not have much of an appetite, but he does want to eat something, and this vague fancy he will usually express as 'something a bit tart'. Well, that's what I want, something a bit tart. And it is not accidental, for this is exactly the feeling I sense in the air all around. It is as though we have all been infatuated, but now we have recovered from our infatuation and are seeking new objects for our passions. Russian people may well once again become interested in the natural sciences, and materialism will become fashionable again. Science is now achieving miraculous successes and may perhaps, like Mamai,[5] overwhelm the public with its sheer scale and grandeur. But it's all in the lap of the gods. Once you start philosophizing, your head spins.

A German from Stuttgart sent me 50 roubles for a translation of one of my stories.[6] How do you like that?

I support the copyright convention, but this has not stopped some swine of a journalist writing an article in which he claims that in discussion with him I expressed my opposition to the convention. Some of the things he says I said I couldn't even pronounce.

---

2. Peasant shoes or sandals usually made from the inner bark of the lime tree.
3. Luke 13, verse 35.
4. The real name of Simon Südfeld (1849–1923), whose notorious book called *Entartung* (*Degeneration*, 1892) condemned all manifestations of modernism as immoral and pernicious.
5. The fourteenth-century ruler of the Golden Horde, the westernmost province of the vast Mongol kingdom whose headquarters in Sarai, on the Lower Volga, Russian princes had to visit annually to pay tribute during the 240-year occupation. In 1380, Russian forces won an important battle against Mamai's army at Kulikovo, paving the way for their eventual liberation.
6. 'My Wife' (1892).

Write to me in Lopasnya. If you feel like sending me a telegram you can still catch me in Yalta, as I'm not leaving here until 5 April.

Keep well and at peace. How is your head? Are you getting as many headaches as before, or not? I've had fewer since I stopped smoking.

My deepest respects to Anna Ivanovna and the children.

Your

A. Chekhov

174. To Georgy Chekhov, 9 September 1894, en route from Feodosia to Yalta, on board the steamship Grand Duke Konstantin

Dear Georges,

I received your sad telegram today. I shall not attempt to console you, because I am grieving myself. I loved my late uncle with all my heart and respected him greatly.[1]

It was cold throughout my stay in Feodosia. The wind blew from the north-east, and if I had come to Taganrog by sea I would have had to stay in my cabin the whole time to keep warm. I hate the cold.

Please give my warmest greetings to my aunt, and to your sisters and to Volodya. I send them my deepest sympathy.

I will write again. At the moment I am on my way to Yalta, and from Yalta I shall go wherever God wills, probably abroad for two or three weeks. I embrace you warmly.

Your

A. Chekhov

Please write to me with all the details of the funeral. My temporary address is c/o New Times Bookshop, Odessa.

1. Chekhov's uncle Mitrofan died on 8 September 1894.

175. To Maria Chekhova, 13 or 14 September 1894, Odessa

I've been in Yalta. Now I'm in Odessa. Because I probably won't be home before October, I thought it would be a good idea to tell you the following:

1) As explained in the enclosed note you will receive money on 1 October.

2) Dig up the gladioli and have the tulips covered with leaves. I should be very glad if you could plant some more tulips. You can buy peonies and suchlike on Trubnaya Square.

3) There are now some vocational courses in Taganrog, where young girls between the ages of fifteen and twenty can learn the art of sewing in the latest fashions (*modes et robes*). Sasha, our late uncle's daughter, who is now seventeen or eighteen and a very nice, gentle girl, attended these courses and according to the mayor of Taganrog was considered their best student. She is in fact a superb seamstress. She has very good taste. Some time ago I was speaking to the mayor, and he was complaining that he finds it very difficult to get good teachers for the courses and has to import them from Petersburg, and so on. I said to him: 'If I were to send my cousin, whom you have been praising, to Moscow and put her to study with the best fashion designer, would you subsequently take her on as a teacher?' He replied that he would be delighted to do so. A teacher should earn 50 roubles a month – and that money would be very welcome for Uncle's family, which now faces poverty. So please give some thought to this: could we not do something for the girl? We could keep her for one winter in Moscow, and I would give her 15 to 20 roubles a month for her rent; she could stay with you, and it wouldn't be too much of a nuisance to you because she is, as I say, a splendid girl. The main thing is to try to help. Think about this before I come, and we can have a talk about it then.

4) On 14 September, the Feast of the Exaltation of the Cross, we should have given the constable a rouble. If we haven't done so, give it to him now.

5) When you send the horses to meet me, don't forget to send a warm hat with them.

6) It's cold in the south. It was pretty nasty in Feodosia, and you couldn't go out without an overcoat in Yalta. Apparently it was cold all summer.

A deep bow to everyone. Be well and don't mope.

Your

A. Chekhov

176. To Maria Chekhova, 29 September 1894, Milan

Dearest Masha, I'm in Italy, in Milan. I went to Lemberg (Lvov) where I saw an exhibition of Polish paintings, which I found feeble and insubstantial, shameful though Sienkiewicz[1] and Vukol Lavrov may find this admission. I've been in Vienna, where I ate some delicious bread and bought myself a new inkstand and a jockey cap with ear flaps. I went to Abbazia on the shores of the Adriatic, where I observed high-quality rain and boredom, and then Fiume in Trieste, whence enormous ships set sail for every corner of the world. Then I went to Venice, where without breathing a word against her, I acquired a nettle rash which I have still not managed to get rid of. In Venice I bought myself a glass painted in heavenly colours, three silk ties and a pin. I am now in Milan; I have been to see the cathedral and the Galleria Vittorio Emmanuele, so now there is nothing left but to go to Genoa, which has many ships and a splendid cemetery.[2] (By the way, in Milan I went to see a crematorium, this is a cemetery where the dead are burned in a furnace; I rather regretted that they do not burn some of the living, for instance heretics who eat meat on Wednesdays.)

I'll probably go on from Genoa to Nice, and from Nice straight home. It looks as though I shall be back by October, around the 12th to 15th of the month. In any event I will wire you the date of my arrival. I can just imagine what the mud is like at the moment!

1. Henryk Sienkiewicz (1846–1916), the most important and prolific Polish writer of the second half of the nineteenth century.
2. The Cimitero di Staglieno is situated on a hillside planted with cedars and cypresses outside the city, and is full of life-size marble sculptures and ornate tombs.

If you see Goltsev, tell him that I am writing a novel about Moscow life for *Russian Thought*. I am kept awake at night thinking about the laurels with which Boborykin has been crowned, so I am writing an imitation of his *The Crossing*. But tell Goltsev and Lavrov not to expect anything before December, because it's a long novel, somewhere between ninety-six and 128 pages.

I expect you are running short of money, if not completely out of it. Be patient for a week or so: I shall have a full statement of account from the *New Times* bookshop when I get to Nice, and then I can ask them to send us some money. We also owe the bank 180 roubles.

What is Potapenko doing these days? Where is he? Give him my regards.

The beer abroad is fabulous. If Russia had beer like this, I could become a serious drinker. Also, the actors are wonderful; their artistry exceeds the wildest dreams of us Russians.

I've been to the operetta and went to a performance of Dostoyevsky's *Crime and Punishment* in an Italian translation, and when I thought of our greatest and most experienced actors, I concluded that their acting doesn't even contain lemonade, let alone fire. Here actors and actresses put real human beings on the stage; beside them ours are mere pigs.

Yesterday I went to the circus, and I've also seen an exhibition.

Regards to Papa and Mama, and everyone. I'll be home in October.

I have a cough and a terrible itch from the rash, but otherwise I'm well.

I hear a lot of people here studying singing. Milan is full of foreign ladies learning to sing à la Lika and Varya, in pursuit of fame and fortune. Poor things, they have to exercise their vocal chords from morning till night.

I'm off to Genoa later today.

Keep well.

Your

A. Chekhov

If you can get together a large group to go abroad, you can do it very cheaply.

177. To Alexey Suvorin, 27 November 1894

I was recently in Serpukhov, where someone from Odessa insisted to me that Ivan Kazarinov, who treated us that time to the singing of the girls from the orphanage, died in the autumn.

I was doing jury service in Serpukhov, on a panel consisting of landowners, manufacturers and local merchants. The fates decreed that I should be called for every single case, so that by the end everyone burst out laughing when it happened yet again. Each time I was appointed jury chairman. I have drawn the following conclusions: 1) jurors are definitely not your average man in the street, they are people mature enough to be able to represent what one might call a social conscience; 2) in our milieu good people possess tremendous authority, irrespective of whether they are gentry or peasants, educated or not. Overall I was left with a very good impression.

I have been appointed a trustee of a village school in a place called Talezh. The teacher there earns 23 roubles a month, has a wife and four children, and hair that has already turned grey although he is only thirty years old. He is so ground down by poverty that whatever subject you talk to him about, he cannot stop himself bringing the conversation round to salaries. In his opinion, the only suitable subject for poets and prose writers is salary increases; when the new Tsar reshuffles his ministers there will probably be an increase in teachers' salaries, etc.

My brother Alexander visited us, stayed five days or so and left on 21 November. He is a sick and suffering man; when he has had a drink he is very difficult to be with, but it's not much easier when he is sober, as then he is ashamed of everything he did and said when he was drunk.

So, I owe you 1,004 roubles, that's all signed and settled. I agree the figure, and should like to make the following proposal: in order for me to clear my debts and start with a clean slate from 1 January, would it be possible for your shop to take 5,000 copies of *Motley Stories* for cash with a 40 per cent discount? If they agree to this, they could make over to you personally the balance of 1,004 on 1 January, and that would clear my debt. The reason I'd like to settle the last remaining amount I owe you quickly is that I have it in mind to ask you for more.

If you are thinking of publishing my collected stories in a series of volumes, then there is no urgency to carry out this idea right now; it can wait for a year or two so long as we agree that we should not go ahead as planned with reprinting *In the Twilight* and *Gloomy People*.

There's no snow, so there are no roads either. This is such a problem for country people, you can't even begin to imagine.

Best respects to Anna Ivanovna, Nastya and Borya. Please write and tell me all the news. Have you found, or do you have any prospect of finding, anything to publish? Can it really be the case that the existing warning guidelines will remain unchanged?[1]

Your

A. Chekhov

178. To Ivan Chekhov, 17 February 1895, Moscow

Mikhail Alexeyevich[1] and I invite you to join us at the Central Baths this evening, and afterwards to supper. Please come at 8.15 p.m.

I arrived today and must leave tomorrow. Regards to Sonya and Volodya.

Your

A. Chekhov

We shall have supper at the Grand Moscow Hotel.

1. Chekhov is asking about the censorship policy, following the accession of Nicholas II on 20 October 1894.

1. Mikhail Alexeyevich, Suvorin's son from his first marriage. He was exactly the same age as Chekhov, and ran the *New Times* bookshops his father had set up in Russian railway stations.

179. To Georgy Chekhov, 21 March 1895, Melikhovo

Dearest Georges,

While I was talking to Modest Tchaikovsky at the Mariinsky Theatre's Masked Ball during Shrovetide, I caught sight of a clean-shaven retired sailor in the distance and decided this must be your Tchaikovsky. I meant to have a word with him about you, but the room was very crowded and I lost sight of him before I had a chance to introduce myself.

I'm sitting at home in Melikhovo. I haven't gone anywhere, because all the money I could have spent on travel has gone on the building of a new stable block. I don't have a great desire to get up and go in any case, and I especially don't want to go to the Crimea, which I got fed up with some time ago. If I want a holiday I'll come to Taganrog and paint the town red with you. Nothing is healthier than the air of one's native place. If only I were a rich man and did not have to rely on what I can earn, I would immediately buy a little place in Taganrog by the sea where I could warm my bones in my old age. This last is already well within sight.

Don't be upset, don't torment yourself and don't put yourself needlessly in the way of temptation. Only time will determine whether you get to Petersburg.

Tell His Grace Vladimir that if he wishes to study medicine once he has finished his time at the seminary, I am at his service. Three hundred roubles would be enough for him to complete a course of studies in Tomsk, pay for attendance at lectures and come home to Taganrog for the holidays. I will be glad to advance this sum, a third, i.e. a hundred roubles, at a time, and he can return the money to me when he finishes the course. It would be an interest-free loan, and I can let it run for five years. The medical profession has the advantage that he would be able to live permanently in Taganrog. And I think that it can be quite an enjoyable profession, speaking as a doctor myself and not as a dog.

At present prices it costs hardly anything at all to get to Tomsk.

My deep respects to your mother and sisters. Keep well and happy, and don't forget me in your prayers. I would be grateful if you would find out and let me know Gutmakher's[1] first name and patronymic; he sent me his book. The Jew is not without talent, but he is a very proud man and can be malicious. As malicious as a pilgrim who has had his toes trodden on in the crowd.

We had 12 degrees of frost last night.

Your

A. Chekhov

My compliments to the Tarabrins.

180. To Alexey Suvorin, 23 March 1895, Melikhovo

I told you Potapenko was a very lively sort of person, but you didn't believe me. Every Khokhol has treasure buried in the depths of his soul. I think that when our generation grows old Potapenko will be the happiest of us all, and the one most full of the joys of life.

All right, I will marry if you want. But here are my conditions: everything must be as it was before, that is, she must live in Moscow while I live in the country, and I will come and visit her. I should never be able to stand the sort of happiness that carries on from one day to the next and from one morning to the next. When someone talks to me day in day out about the same thing in the same voice, I turn nasty. I turn nasty when Sergeyenko is around, for example, because he is very like a woman ('intelligent and responsive'), and because I can't get it out of my head that maybe my wife would be like him. I promise to be a splendid husband, but let me have a wife who, like the moon, will not appear in my sky every day. NB Having a wife won't make me write any better.

Are you going to Italy? Excellent, but if you are taking Mikhail Alexeyevich with you for the benefit of his health, running up and down

1. Alexander Gutmakher (1864–1921), a writer from Taganrog who wrote a book called *Taganrog Motifs*.

stairs twenty-five times an hour chasing after the *facchino*[1] and so on will do little to make him feel better. What he needs is to stay quietly by the sea and go bathing; if that does no good then he could try hypnotism. Give my greetings to Italy. I love Italy, despite your telling Grigorovich that I lay down in St Mark's Square and said: 'How good it would be if we could be lying on the grass somewhere near Moscow just now!' Lombardy made such an impression on me that I think I can remember every tree, and I can see Venice if I close my eyes.

Mamin-Sibiryak[2] is a very nice fellow and an excellent writer. His latest novel *Bread* (in *Russian Thought*) has been much praised; Leskov in particular was very enthusiastic about it. Some of his things are truly excellent, and the descriptions of peasants in his most successful stories are no way inferior to those in 'Master and Man'.[3] I am so glad that you have come to know him a little.

I've now been at Melikhovo for three years. My calves have turned into cows, my trees are now two feet high or more ... My heirs will be able to do good business from the timber, and will call me an ass, for heirs are never satisfied.

Don't go abroad too soon; it's cold there. Wait until May. I may go as well; perhaps we'll meet somewhere ...

Please write to me again. Is there nothing new in the realm of pointless but pleasant daydreams? Why has Wilhelm recalled General W.?[4] We're not going to go to war with Germany, are we? Oh no, then I'll have to enlist and perform amputations, and write reports for *The Historical Herald*.*

Ever your

A. Chekhov

*Do you think I could get an advance from Shubinsky for the reports?

1. Italian for hotel porter.
2. Dmitry Mamin-Sibiryak (1852–1912), a prose writer and the son of a priest from Perm; known for his novels of life in the Urals and Siberian mining towns.
3. This story by Tolstoy, about a landowner and his peasant who get stuck in a snowstorm, had just been published in *The Northern Herald*.
4. It was reported in *New Times* that General Werder, head of the large German colony in St Petersburg, had been recalled to Germany by Kaiser Wilhelm.

181. *To Maria Chekhova, 23 July 1895, Moscow*

Sunday

1) Suvorin and I are coming tomorrow, Monday.

2) Can you send the big tarantass to meet the express, please.

3) We won't have lunch, but please leave some soup for supper.

4) Tania[1] must stay and wait for our arrival, otherwise there'll be trouble.

5) Suvorin wants to talk to her about the theatre; evidently that is his main reason for coming to Melikhovo.

6) We'll bring some sweets and a few other things as well.

7) If we can't get tickets for the express, we'll either come on a relief train or the mail train. Ask Roman to wait for us.

8) With a better fable I might please, but fear to irritate the geese.[2]

A. Chekhov

PS Regards to the delectable widow Alexandra Lvovna.[3]

182. *To Alexander Chekhov, 11 August 1895, Melikhovo*

Duplicitous and free-thinking Sasha!

I'm approaching you in the hope that you will be able to fulfil this my undermentioned request. The day before yesterday, I was at Yasnaya Polyana when a man with a knapsack on his back came to see Lev Tolstoy begging for alms. This man has a cornea problem in both eyes and can see very little, so has to feel his way around. He's not fit for work. Tolstoy asked me to write and find out if there isn't a home the blind old wanderer could be packed off to? Since you are a specialist in blind matters, please don't refuse my request to write to the said

1. The writer Tania Shchepkina-Kupernik, who was staying at Melikhovo.
2. Chekhov is quoting inaccurately from a well-known Krylov fable.
3. Alexandra Selivanova-Krauze, a close friend of Chekhov from Taganrog days who was saying at Melikhovo.

wanderer telling him where he can apply and what to say in his application. His particulars are: former soldier Sergey Nikiforov Kireyev, fifty-nine years of age, lost the sight of both eyes ten years ago, residing at the Kireyev house in Kashira. You can write to him at Kashira.

I told Tolstoy about you; he was most displeased and denounced you for your dissolute life.

Quinine has had a pup, Saltpetre. No other news.

Profound respects to your spouse, and mental chastisement to your offspring, with my heartfelt wishes for them not to be cleverer than their parents. As for you, I desire that you should mend your ways and be a comfort to Papa.

Your benefactor,

A. Chekhov

183. To Alexey Suvorin, 21 October 1895, Melikhovo

Thank you for your letter, for your warm words and for your invitation. I will come, but probably not before the end of November as I have the devil of a lot on my plate at the moment. First of all, next spring I am building a new school in a nearby village where I serve as trustee; I have to have plans and estimates drawn up in good time and this entails a great deal of running about all over the place. Secondly, can you imagine, I'm writing a play, and this also will take me at least until the end of November to finish. I'm enjoying writing it, although I am doing dreadful violence to stage conventions. It is a comedy with three parts for women, six for men, four acts, a landscape (view of a lake); many conversations about literature, hardly any action and 185 pounds of love.

I read about Ozerova's disaster and felt very sorry for her. Nothing is more painful than failure. I can just imagine the poor little Jewess weeping and turning to ice when she saw the review in *The Petersburg Newspaper* describing her performance as plainly inept.[1] I read about

1. The actress Lyudmila Ozerova had just appeared in a production of Schiller's *Kabale und Liebe* (*Intrigue and Love*) at the Imperial Mikhailovsky Theatre in St Petersburg.

your theatre's success with *The Power of Darkness*, and of course it was right to have Domashova, rather than the 'little one' to whom (as you yourself say) you are so attached, play Anyutka. The Little One should play Matryona. When I visited Tolstoy back in August he told me, as he was drying his hands, that he had no intention of rewriting his play in any way.[2] Remembering this conversation now, I feel sure he knew then that the play would be passed for the stage *in toto*. I spent a day and a half with him, and it was altogether a wonderful time. I felt as relaxed there as in my own home, and it was just as easy talking with Lev Nikolayevich. I'll tell you the details when we meet.

My story 'Murder' will appear in *Russian Thought* in November, and another story, 'Ariadna', in December.

I'm appalled by something that has happened, and it's this. There is an outstandingly good journal published in Moscow called *The Surgical Chronicle*, which has a good reputation even abroad. The editors are two well-known surgeon/scientists, Sklifosovsky and Dyakonov. The number of subscribers has been increasing year by year, but even so it has always made an annual loss. Up until now, and this will continue until next January, Sklifosovsky has covered the loss from his own funds, but now he has been transferred to Petersburg. The consequence of this is that he has lost his Moscow practice and no longer has any spare cash. Neither he nor anyone else has any idea how the current year's deficit is to be covered, assuming there is one, but on the basis of previous years there will be, of the order of 1,000 to 1,500 roubles. When I heard the journal was faced with imminent collapse I became extremely upset at the idiocy of such a trifling sum mortally endangering an indispensable publication which should in any case be turning a profit in three or four years' time! The stupidity of the situation struck me with such force that I rashly said I would find a publisher, thinking this would not be at all difficult to do. So began my intensive quest, going the rounds begging and humiliating myself, having dinner with God knows whom, but all to no avail. The

2. In addition to his publishing activities, Suvorin, a playwright himself, had taken over a theatre in St Petersburg, where Tolstoy's play *The Power of Darkness* had just been staged.

sole remaining hope is Soldatenkov,[3] but he is abroad and won't be back until December, and it must all be settled by November. What a pity your printing works is not in Moscow! It would have spared me making a fool of myself in my unsuccessful attempts to be an honest broker. When we meet I'll paint you a full picture of the travails I have endured. If it weren't for the school building, which is going to cost me about 1,500 roubles, I would underwrite the publication of the journal myself, because I'm upset by such manifest stupidity and find it very hard to accept it. I plan to go to Moscow on 22 October with a proposition to put to the editors, that as a last resort they should apply for an annual subsidy of 1,500 to 2,000 roubles. If they agree, I'll rush up to Petersburg and start lobbying. How do I set about this? Will you give me some lessons? In the interests of saving the journal I'm prepared to see anyone at all, and will stand around in anyone's lobby for as long as it takes. If I succeed I shall heave a big sigh of relief and pleasure, because the rescue of a first-class surgery periodical is worth as much as twenty thousand successful operations. In any case, please advise me what I should do.

After Sunday you can write to me in Moscow, Grand Hotel, room 5.

How is Potapenko's play doing? How is Potapenko himself? I've had a despairing letter from Jean Shcheglov. The astronomer is destitute. Apart from that, everything is all right. I shall go and see operettas in Moscow; during the day I'll mess around with my play, and in the evening go to the operetta.

Deepest respects to you. Do please write, I implore you.

Your

A. Chekhov

3. Kozma Soldatenkov (1818–1901), industrialist, publisher and patron of the arts.

184. To Alexey Suvorin, 21 November 1895, Melikhovo

Well, sir, my play [*The Seagull*] is finished. I began it *forte* and finished it *pianissimo* – against every rule of dramatic art. It's turned out more like a novella. I am more dissatisfied than satisfied, and reading through my newly born play convinces me more than ever that I am not a playwright. Each act – there are four of them – is very short. Thus far it is only a framework, a sketch of a play really, and it will undergo a million changes before next season, but all the same I've ordered two copies to be typed on a Remington (the machine will make two copies at once) and will send one of them to you. But you must not show it to anybody.

I have not received your play *A True Word*; this may be because you sent it as printed matter and therefore it is now lying uncollected at Serpukhov.

Some woman, I have no idea who, under the mistaken impression that I was the author of the article about the floods,[1] sent me a letter addressed to the *New Times* office enclosing five roubles, asking me to pass the money on to the victims. Your people forwarded the whole thing to me at Lopasnya, and now I don't know what to do with the money. Would you please send the letter to Alexander and put five roubles in with it. I could have forwarded the letter to him myself, but I suspect he may be short of money at the moment, and I have no way of sending the cash by mail from here because there is no post office. I will return the five roubles to you when we meet, assuming I don't manage to give them away before then, to fire victims or to some organization that cares for orphans or the homeless. In the latter case I'll bring you a receipt.

Your letter describes the actresses in a most artistic way; as I read it all I could do was croak out: Yes! Yes! I'm glad I'm not in your shoes. The revival of *Ivanov*[2] will bring in 280 roubles for the first

---

1. The article about the floods in St Petersburg that year was in fact written by Chekhov's brother Alexander.
2. Suvorin was thinking of reviving Chekhov's play *Ivanov* at his theatre.

performance, 116 for the second, and, as I'm sure you won't be putting on a third, that will be that. That's what I think, anyhow. In your place on Sundays and holidays I would put on decadent plays and crowd-pleasers like *Parasha the Girl from Siberia* or *The White General*.[3] The public would also go for *Hamlet* and *Othello*, as long as you concentrate mostly on the scenery. I think you would also have success with the public (as long as ticket prices are low) if you were to put on *The Power of Darkness* and *Marriage*. They would only net 116 roubles, but that would still be better than bringing back gentlemen such as Ivanov from exile. You will say: it's easy to give advice from a distance. And you would be right.

Keep well and happy. I find a glass of beer a very effective remedy for insomnia. I'll be coming soon, but probably not before the beginning of December.

Your

A. Chekhov

Your article about Gorbunov[4] is tremendously good. You have no equal today for hitting the nail on the head.

185. To Marfa Morozova, 16 January 1896, Melikhovo

My dear Aunt,

I am sending you my photograph, only please do not show it to my new bride otherwise she will judge me incapable of any sinful action whatsoever, and this will cause her to shed tears of disappointment.

We are all alive and well and send you cordial greetings. I returned from Petersburg yesterday but shall be going back there in a week's time.

3. *Parasha the Girl from Siberia*, a play written by Polevoy; *The White General*, a play by Elizaveta Zalesova.
4. Ivan Gorbunov (pseudonym Gorbunov-Posadov) (1864–1910), one of the directors of The Intermediary publishing house.

I'll come and see you in March, but for now I kiss your hand and remain your loving

A. Chekhov

Regards to you all.

We now have our own post office. Letters to me should be addressed to: Lopasnya, Moscow Province.

186. To David Manucharov, 5 March 1896, Melikhovo

Dear David Lvovich,

None of the people I knew are still on Sakhalin Island, but I will try to do whatever I can for your brother at the earliest opportunity.[1] When I go to Petersburg I may be able to see someone who has some power, influence or connections on Sakhalin, and if I do I shall mention your brother. I'll write myself, if necessary, and will let you know in good time what transpires.

Reassure your brother; tell him even on Sakhalin there are good people who will not turn away from giving him help and advice.

I send you my best wishes, and am at your service,

Your

A. Chekhov

187. To Georgy Chekhov, 11 March 1896, Melikhovo

Dearest Georges,

Masha is sending the girls some flower and vegetable seeds. The Taganrog climate is warm enough for them to be sown and planted straight into the ground without the need to cultivate them beforehand

1. David Manucharov had appealed to Chekhov to help his brother, a former Petersburg University student and political prisoner, who was being exiled to Sakhalin after ten years' solitary confinement.

in a hothouse, so you don't have to follow the instructions on the packets.

I received the 22 roubles.

Work has already begun on building the Talezh school, and it should be finished by the end of May. I doubt whether I shall manage to tear myself away from home before then. As soon as I do though, I shall make straight for Taganrog.

Deepest respects and greetings to Aunt and the girls, and my respects also to Irinushka. I had a letter from Volodya in which he promised to enter the University. Maybe he will keep his promise; let's hope so.

Yours,

A. Chekhov

You're such a hypochondriac! Every time you eat something you start clutching at your stomach. And there was I planning to bring you some beer and some good Moscow sausage!

I'll send Tarabrin[1] a photograph a bit later on, when I get them from Piter.

188. To the Director of the Imperial Theatres, 15 March 1896, Melikhovo

To: The Director of the Imperial Theatres
From: Anton Pavlovich Chekhov

Application

I herewith present two copies of a play in four acts written by myself entitled *The Seagull*, and have the honour humbly to request that the same be submitted to the Theatrical-Literary Commission for inspection with a view to permission being granted for the play's presentation in the Imperial Theatres.

Anton Chekhov

1. Georgy Tarabrin, a doctor who worked in the hospital at Taganrog.

189. To David Manucharov, 21 March 1896, Melikhovo

Dear David Lvovich,

I'll try to answer your questions.

1) I was given permission to visit the prisons and settlements by the then governor-general of the Amur region, Baron Korf, on condition that I avoided contact with political prisoners, and I had to give my word of honour that I would abide by this. Therefore I seldom spoke to any political prisoners, and then only in the presence of official witnesses, of whom several had been assigned to spy on me. I therefore know little about the life of political prisoners on Sakhalin. They wear their own clothes and are not locked up; they work as clerks and in supervisory capacities, in kitchens for example, or as observers in meteorological stations. One I knew was a churchwarden, another a supernumerary assistant to a prison warder, another was in charge of the police department library, and so on. No political prisoner received any corporal punishment in my presence. There were rumours of depression among many of them, and instances of suicide – but again, only rumours.

2) If you have technical skills you should be able to obtain a position as a senior supervisor on Sakhalin working in the local workshops; they were desperately short of experienced managers when I was on the island. Senior supervisors earn 50 to 60 roubles a month or even more. To get an appointment you should apply to the Commanding Officer of the island or, if you are in Petersburg, visit the Central Prisons Bureau. I believe that if you were to approach the Head of the Bureau and explain to him that for family reasons you want to live and work on Sakhalin, he would give your request every consideration.

I send you my best wishes and remain at your service,

A. Chekhov

190. To Maria Chekhova, 11 April 1896, Melikhovo

Everything is just as it was, i.e. frost at night and a gradual thaw during the day. Today, Thursday, there is a cold wind. The pond is full. The pond in the field is also almost full; the water flows straight into it from the field so that there is almost no need for a ditch. The starlings are very busy. Please bring for Mother: two packets of fine needles Nos 7 and 8, two pounds of granulated sugar, two pounds of *baranka* rolls for Lent, two pounds of roasted nuts. Everything is fine in the greenhouse. Roman will go on horseback to the station. Get Father a quire of thirty-six-line ruled paper from Muir's – he needs it for his journal. I don't think the road will be passable just yet; in any case I'll send someone over to the station again on Tuesday, and write and tell you about our spring weather and the condition of the roads round here.

Your

A. Chekhov

191. To Pavel Iordanov, 10 June 1896, Melikhovo

Dear Pavel Fyodorovich,

I am sending you two cases of books for the town library, also a set of the Granat-Garbel Encyclopaedia,[1] with the exception of volumes IV and V, which I will send as soon as I receive them.

The books will be delivered to you carriage paid.

Allow me to convey to you my best wishes and to remain your sincerely respectful

A. Chekhov

1. Granat and Co., formerly Garbel and Co., published a desk encyclopaedia in Moscow in 1894.

192. To Ignaty Potapenko, 11 August 1896, Melikhovo

My dear Ignatius,

The play [*The Seagull*] is on its way to you. The censor has blue-pencilled the passages of which he disapproves on account of the indifference shown by the brother and the son to the actress's love affair with the writer. On page 4 I have cut out the phrase 'lives openly with this writer', and on page 5 'is only able to fall in love with young men'. If the alterations are accepted, stick the separate slips of paper I have prepared firmly down over the offending places and blessings will be upon you for ever and ever amen, and you will live to see the sons of your sons! If the alterations are not accepted, you can spit on the whole play; I do not intend to fuss any more over it, and I advise you to do the same.

On page 5, where Sorin says 'Tell me by the way, what's he like, her writer?' you can delete 'her' and just put 'this' instead. In the same speech, instead of 'You can't understand him. He never speaks', he can say 'You know, I don't really care for him.' Or anything else that comes into your head; a passage from the Talmud if you like.*

It is quite obvious from his tone that the son objects to his mother's amorous relationship. On page 37, the passage that has provoked such disapproval, he says to his mother: 'Why, why has this man come between us?' On the same page we can cut Arkadina's words: 'I know you cannot be happy about our intimacy, but . . .'; that's the lot. Have a look at the passages underlined in the blue copy.

When are you coming to Melikhovo?

To sum up, delete whatever you need to, so long as Litvinov gives some provisional indication that it will be enough to pass.

Thank you for the Mignon chocolate. I've eaten it.

On the 16th or 17th I'm going south and shall be in Feodosia where I shall pay court to your wife. Write to me in any case. After the 20th my address will be: c/o Suvorin, Feodosia.

Don't forget, there is still the committee to get through!!

---

* Perhaps the words: 'At her age too! Oh, how disgraceful!'

If you can track down an apartment for me, I'll spend all winter in Petersburg. All I need is one room and a WC.

Why don't we go off somewhere together? We've plenty of time. How about Batum or Borzhom? It would be nice to drink the odd glass of wine.

I warmly embrace you.

Ever in your debt,

A. Chekhov

Both copies need to have correction slips pasted into page 4. On pages 5 and 37 the appropriate lines will have to be crossed out. Anyhow, you know what to do. Forgive me for being so presumptuous and tedious.

I have underlined in green the passages I think may have to be deleted, i.e. those passages I believe the censor will find most offensive.

193. To Maria Chekhova, 20 September 1896, Melikhovo

Dear Masha,

If you can, please buy one hundred tulips (identical) at Immer's, otherwise we shall have no spring flowers.

Everything is fine at home. Vasily Zembulatov[1] is here at the moment.

Your

A. Chekhov

---

1. Vasily Zembulatov was an old school friend from Taganrog who had also gone to Moscow University to train as a doctor.

194. To Mikhail Chekhov, 18 October 1896, St Petersburg

The play flopped and was a complete disaster.[1] The atmosphere in the theatre was strained, a mixture of incomprehension and ignominy. The cast's performance was dreadful and stupid.

The moral is: don't write plays.

Never mind. I'm alive and well and in good heart.

Your big daddy

A. Chekhov

195. To Anna Suvorina, 19 October 1896, Melikhovo

Dearest Anna Ivanovna,

Are you angry that I left without saying goodbye? After the performance my friends were worried about me; someone came to Potapenko's apartment looking for me after one o'clock in the morning, there were also people looking for me at the Nikolayevsky station, then the following day they started coming round at nine o'clock in the morning, and at any moment I expected Davydov to turn up proffering advice and sympathy. It would have been touching, but absolutely unbearable. In any case I had already decided to leave the day after the first performance, whether or not it was a success. The din of triumph disorientates me, and I did the same thing after *Ivanov* – left town the following day. In short I was seized by an ungovernable urge to flee, but feared that if I came down to say goodbye to you, I would have been unable to resist the charming warmth of your pressure to stay.

I warmly kiss your hand, and hope to be forgiven. Remember your motto![1]

1. The first performance of *The Seagull*, at the Imperial Alexandrinsky Theatre, had indeed been a resounding failure, although subsequent performances were very successful.

1. The motto printed on her notepaper was *Comprendre – pardonner!*

My deepest respects to all. I shall return in November.
Yours devotedly
A. Chekhov

196. To Alexey Suvorin, 22 October 1896, Melikhovo

In your last letter (of 18 October) you thrice call me an old woman and a coward. What is the meaning of this libel? After the performance I dined fittingly at Romanov's, then went to bed where I slept soundly, and then the next day went home without uttering so much as a squeak of protest. Had I been a coward I would have run round to all the editors and the actors pleading anxiously for indulgence, I would have nervously made all kinds of unnecessary changes to the text, and would have stayed in Petersburg for the next two or three weeks attending performances of my *Seagull*, fretting, breaking out in a cold sweat, complaining . . . You yourself said, when you were with me the night after the performance, that the best thing for me would be to go away; and the following day I received a letter from you saying goodbye. Where in all this is the cowardice? I acted with the cold reasonableness of a man whose proposal has been rejected, and for whom the only thing remaining is to go away. Yes, my pride was hurt, but that hardly makes the heavens fall in; I had been expecting a failure and was prepared for it, as I told you in perfect sincerity beforehand.

When I got home I took a dose of castor oil and washed myself in cold water – and now I feel good enough to write another play. My exhaustion and irritation have passed and I no longer dread Davydov and Jean arriving to discuss the play. I agree with your suggestions – and thank you a thousand times for them. But please do not regret not having attended the rehearsals. There was actually only one, and nothing could be understood from it in any case; the play itself was completely invisible through the dreadful acting.

I received a telegram from Potapenko: colossal success. I had a letter from someone I don't know called Veselitskaya (Mikulich), in which she expresses her sympathy in tones that suggest a death in the family – most inappropriate. However, none of this matters.

My sister is delighted with you and with Anna Ivanovna, and I cannot tell you how glad I am of this, because I love your family as my own. She rushed home from Petersburg, presumably thinking I was about to hang myself.

The weather here is warm and damp, and many people are ill. Yesterday I treated a rich peasant whose bowels had completely seized up with faeces, and we had to administer the most colossal enemas. He survived. Please forgive me, I took away with me – intentionally – from your house *The Herald of Europe*, and – unintentionally – 'T. Filippov's Collected Articles'. I'll return the former, and the latter when I've read it.

Send me a parcel with the item Stakhovich took away and I'll return it straight away. One more request: please remind Alexey Alexeyevich that he promised me *All Russia*.[1]

I wish you all blessings, earthly and heavenly, and thank you with all my heart.

Your

A. Chekhov

197. To Elena Shavrova-Yust, 1 November 1896, Melikhovo

If, noble lady, you write purely as 'a member of the audience' at the first performance, then allow me – oh, do allow me! to cast the faintest shadow of doubt over your sincerity. Your haste to apply healing balm to the author's wounds has led you to assume that in circumstances such as these, this is an act nobler and more necessary than speaking the truth. You are kind, my dear Mask, very kind, and it does great honour to your generous heart. I did not myself see the whole of the performance, but what I did see was dull, insipid, depressing and wooden. I had no responsibility for casting the

1. A directory published in St Petersburg by Suvorin from 1895.

production, no new scenery was provided for it, there were only two rehearsals, the actors did not know their lines, and the resulting atmosphere on stage was one of panic and defeat; even Komissarzhev-skaya[1] failed to shine, although in one of the rehearsals her acting had been so wondrous that people in the stalls started crying and hung their heads . . .

In any case, I am grateful to you and very, very touched. My plays are to be published in a collected edition; as soon as they see the light of day I shall send you a copy, but you must let me know of any change of address. I don't know if *The Seagull* will be produced in Moscow; I have not seen or heard anything from anyone there. I expect it will be produced there eventually.

Well, how are you getting on? Why don't you have a go at writing a play? It is a sensation not unlike stepping into an unheated bath at a Narzan spa. Do try it. Incidentally, you seem to have become lazy and stopped writing altogether. This is not good.

I shall be at home until 15 or 20 November. Please write me a line or two, to stop me getting tired of life. I feel as though there is nothing to life, and never has been.

I send you my very best wishes, and once again all my thanks.

Your

A. Chekhov

198. To Anatoly Koni, 11 November 1896, Melikhovo

Dear Anatoly Fyodorovich,

You cannot imagine how delighted I was to receive your letter. I was only present in the auditorium for the first two acts of my play; after that I sat backstage acutely conscious all the time of the failure *The Seagull* was proving to be. Later that evening after the perform-ance, and the following day, everyone assured me that all my characters

1. Vera Komissarzhevskaya (1864–1910), who went on to enjoy a distinguished career, and later founded her own theatre, played the part of Nina in *The Seagull*.

were idiots, from the dramatic point of view my play was clumsy, crass, unintelligible, even senseless, and so on and on in that vein. You can imagine my state of mind, faced with disaster on a scale I had never dreamed of. I felt ashamed and annoyed with myself, and left Petersburg consumed by self-doubt. My thought was that if I had really written and produced a play so obviously crammed with hideous defects, I must have lost whatever sensitivity I ever possessed, and therefore the engine of my creativity must have suffered terminal collapse. By the time I arrived home I was getting letters from Petersburg telling me that the second and third performances had been successful. Several of the letters, some signed and some anonymous, praised the play and took the critics to task, but although they made pleasurable reading they failed to dispel my feelings of shame and disappointment, and I began to harbour a suspicion that if people were feeling the need to console me from the kindness of their hearts, then I must indeed be in a bad way. But your letter had a positive effect. I have known and greatly respected you for a long time, and I trust you more than all the critics put together. You knew this would be the case when you wrote your letter, and that is why it is so fine and so convincing. My mind is now at rest and I am able to reflect on the play and the performance without turning away in revulsion.

Komissarzhevskaya is a miraculous actress; at one of the rehearsals many of the people watching her were reduced to tears and declared that she is the greatest actress in Russia today. But during the perform-ance even she succumbed to the generally antipathetic feelings towards my *Seagull*; she seemed to lose all confidence and you could hardly hear what she said. She has been treated very coolly, quite unjustifiably so, by the press, and I feel very sorry for her.

May I thank you once again from the bottom of my heart for your letter. Please believe me when I say that I value more than I can say the feelings which prompted you to write to me, and I shall never, never, whatever happens, forget the concern you characterize at the end of your letter as 'unnecessary'.

Your sincerely respectful and devoted
A. Chekhov

199. To Lidia Miʒinova, 12–13 November 1896, Melikhovo

Dear Lidia Stakhievna,

I shall arrive on the express at eight o'clock on Saturday. Following is the detailed protocol of my arrival:

1) After the train has pulled in to the platform, having first satisfied myself that nobody has come to meet me at the station, I shall take a cab costing 20 copecks and go to the Grand Moscow Hotel.

2) Having deposited my luggage there and taken a room, I shall take a cab for 10 copecks and go to Theodore's, where I shall have my hair cut for 15 copecks.

3) My haircut having rendered me more youthful and handsome, I shall return to my room in the hotel.

4) At 10 p.m. I shall go to the restaurant in order to consume a half-portion of ham omelette. Should Lidia Stakhievna be with me at the time I will allot her a mouthful of my portion, and in the event of insistent demands will entertain her to a bottle of Three Mountains beer, the cost for same to be added to my bill.

5) Following supper I shall descend once more to my room and lie down to sleep, happy at last to be alone.

6) Awakening the following morning and having washed and dressed myself, I shall go to Sukharevka with a view to purchasing books.

7) I shall depart from Moscow on Tuesday morning, having restrained myself from any uncalled for actions or emotions and having permitted no person to take liberties, no matter how insistent the demands.

Goodbye, dear Lidia Stakhievna!

Respectfully

A. Chekhov

*200. To Vladimir Nemirovich-Danchenko, 20 November 1896,
Melikhovo*

My dear Vladimir Ivanovich,

As you can see, I am not responding immediately to letters either.
Masha is staying in the same place as last year, in the Kirchhoff house
on Sadovaya-Sukharevskaya.

Yes, the first performance of my *Seagull* in Petersburg was a
resounding flop. The theatre was rank with hostility, the very air was
awash with hatred and I shot out of Petersburg like a bomb, in
accordance with the laws of physics. You and Sumbatov are to blame,
since it was you who incited me to write the play.

I understand your growing antipathy to Petersburg; all the same
there are many good things about the place: for instance, Nevsky on
a sunny day, or Komissarzhevskaya, whom I consider a very great
actress.

I am in pretty good health and pretty good spirits as well. I fear my
spirits will soon begin to flag again though: Lavrov and Goltsev are
insisting on publishing *The Seagull* in *Russian Thought* – so now the
literary critics will be able to tear into me as well. This is a horrible
prospect, like landing in a big puddle in autumn.

Once again I'm imposing on you with a request. The Taganrog
Library is opening a reference section. Please could you let me have
for it the programme and regulations of your Philharmonic Society,
the governing regulations of the Literary Fund, and anything else you
have to hand that in your opinion has a general reference content. Do
forgive me for this exciting commission.

My respects to Ekaterina Nikolayevna, and keep well.

Your

A. Chekhov

Write and tell me something.

201. To Mikhail Chekhov, 27 November 1896, Melikhovo

On 26 November at six o'clock in the evening a fire broke out at home. It started in the passage round Mother's stove. From lunchtime until evening there had been a terrible smell of smoke and we all complained of the fumes, then by evening we could see tongues of flame in the gap between the stove and the wall. At first it was difficult to see what had actually caught fire, whether it was inside the stove or in the wall. The prince happened to be visiting us at the time, and he started chopping at the wall with an axe. But the wall would not give way, we couldn't manage to introduce any water into the gap and the flames kept climbing higher and higher, meaning there must have been a draught somewhere. Meanwhile, it was obvious that it wasn't just soot burning, but wood. We ring the bell. Smoke. Everybody crowds round. The dogs are howling. The peasants drag the fire engine into the yard. Commotion in the passage. Commotion in the attic. The fire hose splutters. The prince hacks away with his axe. A woman comes with an icon. Vorontsov discusses the situation. Result: one wrecked stove, one wrecked wall (the one opposite the WC), wallpaper torn to shreds on the wall between Mother's room and the stove, one wrecked door, floors covered in dirt, everywhere stinking of soot — and nowhere for Mother to sleep. And on top of all this, a brand new pretext for a certain person to fuss and scream and shout.[1]

I declare the cost of the damage as 200 roubles.

Lika is here. Best respects.

Your big daddy,

A. Chekhov

The stove had been extremely stupidly constructed.

1. Pavel Egorovich, Chekhov's father.

202. *To Maria Chekhova, 22 January 1897, Melikhovo*

No significant change has been detected in the health of E. Y. Chekhova. She claims to be better, and says she no longer feels bad in the mornings.[1] Early this morning (it was still dark) she was disturbed by doors banging as everyone left to go to the mill, and early yesterday there was a lot of bustling about to make sure the aubergines didn't freeze solid in the larder.

If you have time, could you please buy and bring back with you for Mother a quarter or half a pound of best-quality unpressed caviar, unsalted and with the eggs nicely separated. You can get it in the new fish shop or at Andreyev's. Keep well!

Your

A. Chekhov

We already have some groceries on order at Andreyev's.

If you don't have enough money to pay for the caviar, ask Andreyev to put it on our account and add it to the amount we owe.

203. *To Vladimir Yakovenko, 30 January 1897, Melikhovo*

Dear Vladimir Ivanovich,[1]

Having read your letter in *The Doctor*, I wrote off to Moscow requesting that you be sent a copy of my book *The Island of Sakhalin*.[2] In it you will find some reflections on corporal punishment and, incidentally, a reference to Yadrintsev,[3] whom I commend to you. If you were to write to Senator Anatoly Fyodorovich Koni, I think he

1. Chekhov's mother had fallen ill with flu and was troubled with varicose veins.
1. Vladimir Yakovenko was a local doctor who had set up a psychiatric hospital near Melikhovo.
2. Published serially in *Russian Thought* in 1893, and in full as a book in 1895.
3. N. Yadrintsev wrote an article on the situation of exiles on Sakhalin in *The Messenger of Europe*, 1875.

would be prepared to share with you the literary sources on which he drew for his biography of the celebrated philanthropist and prison doctor, Dr Haas. I also recommend that you read Kistyakovsky's[4] research into capital punishment, which includes an account of all the tortures ever inflicted by executioners on their victims.

I should mention, by the way, that lawyers and prison warders understand the term corporal punishment (in its narrow, physical sense) to embrace not only birchings, whippings and beatings with the fist, but also the use of fetters, the 'cooler', 'no lunch' as practised in schools, 'bread and water' regimes, forced kneeling for long periods or repeatedly bowing to the ground, and being chained up.

The census[5] has quite worn me out. I've never had so little time to do anything.

I send you my best wishes and warmly press your hand.

Your

A. Chekhov

My profoundest respects to Nadezhda Fyodorovna and Doctors Genike and Vasiliev.

You will find in court proceedings of torture cases statements by doctors that give a clear account of the effect of corporal punishment on the health of the body.

Koni's address is: Anatoly Fyodorovich Koni, 100 Nevsky Prospekt, St Petersburg.

204. To Alexey Suvorin, 8 February 1897, Moscow

The census is finished. The whole business has totally lost its attraction for me, since I had to wear my fingers to the bone counting and writing and supervising fifteen enumerators. The enumerators

4. Kistyakovsky's *Research Into Capital Punishment* went into a second edition in its first year of publication in 1896.
5. The first and only national census was carried out in the Russian Empire in January and February 1897.

356

worked very well, and so pedantically I had to laugh. By contrast, the land captains, who were responsible for the census in the rural districts, behaved disgracefully. They did nothing, understood little of what they were supposed to be doing, and signed themselves off sick whenever things got particularly difficult. The best of them was a drunken Khlestakov-type loudmouth – at least he was a character if only a farcical one – but all the others were such colourless individuals it was a real trial to have anything to do with them.

I am in Moscow, staying at the Grand Moscow Hotel, but not for long – ten days or so, and then home. I'll be busy all through Lent and during April with joiners and caulkers and those sorts of people, as I'm building another school. The peasants came to me with a deputation asking for one, and I just did not have the strength of mind to refuse. The *zemstvo* is contributing a thousand and the peasants have collected a total of three hundred, but the total cost of the school won't come out a copeck less than three thousand. So once again I shall have spent all summer long worrying about money, scratching it together here and there, wherever I can. Country life is altogether very demanding. *A propos* these imminent expenses, may I ask whether you have sent the agreement to the theatre management?

Who do you think has been paying me calls? None other than Ozerova, the famous Hannele.[1] She arrives, puts her feet up on the sofa and looks away, then when it is time to go she puts on her jacket and worn-out galoshes as awkwardly as a young girl ashamed of her poverty. She is like a little queen in exile.

The astronomer, however, has considerably cheered up. She has been running about Moscow giving lessons and engaging in debates with Klyuchevsky.[2] Her health is a little better, and she is evidently beginning to get back into her stride. I have in my keeping a sum of 250 roubles which we collected for her, but that was a year and a half ago and she has not touched it yet.

1. Lyudmila Ozerova played the part of Hannele in Hauptmann's 1893 play *Hanneles Himmelfahrt* (*Hannele's Journey to Heaven*), which was staged at Suvorin's theatre in St Petersburg in 1895.
2. Vasily Klyuchevsky (1845–1911), a famous historian and professor at Moscow University.

The authorities have searched the apartment of Chertkov, the well-known follower of Tolstoy, and have taken away everything the Tolstoyans had collected about the Dukhobors and other sects.[3] As a result, all the evidence against Mr Pobedonostsev[4] and his angelic cohorts has suddenly disappeared as if by magic. Goremykin went to see Chertkov's mother and told her: 'Your son may choose between going to the Baltic provinces, where Prince Khilkov is already living in exile, or abroad.' Chertkov chose London, and is leaving on 13 February. Tolstoy has gone to Petersburg to see him off, and had to have his warm overcoat brought up to him yesterday. A lot of people are going to see Chertkov off, even Sytin, and I am sorry that I cannot do the same. Not that I have particularly warm feelings towards the man, but what has been done to him has deeply, deeply offended me.

Might you be able to come to Moscow for a while on your way to Paris? That would be good.

Your

A. Chekhov

205. To Alexey Suvorin, 1 March 1897, Melikhovo

I stayed in Moscow for twenty days and spent all my advances, but now I'm back at home, leading a chaste and sober existence. If you will be in Moscow during the third week of Lent, I'll come as well. At the moment I am busy with building works (not on my own account but for the *zemstvo*), but I'll be able to get away; you just need to send me a wire to Lopasnya a day or two beforehand. I expect you will see

3. Religious sects like the Dukhobors ('Spirit Wrestlers') were banned by the authorities from practising their faith. As a pacifist, Tolstoy took up the cause of the Dukhobors when they began to suffer persecution over their refusal to serve in the imperial army (and later donated the profits from the publication of his last novel, *Resurrection* (1899), in order to enable them to emigrate to Canada), and Chertkov was sent into exile for his active involvement in the affair.

4. Konstantin Pobedonostsev, Procurator of the Holy Synod from 1880 to 1905, was a powerful and highly reactionary figure in the Russian government.

at the theatrical convention the plans for the huge People's Theatre we are hoping to organize. *We* are representatives of the Moscow intelligentsia (the intelligentsia is looking to find the capital, and the capital is not averse to collaborating). What we will end up with is a handsome, well-planned building which contains a theatre, auditoria, a library, reading room, cafés and so on all under one roof. The plans are ready, the constitution is now in the process of being drawn up, the only outstanding detail is a trifling half a million roubles. It will be a joint stock company, but not a charitable organization. We anticipate that the government will authorize us to issue 100-rouble shares. I'm so enamoured of the project that I already have complete faith in it, and I wonder that you also don't think of building a theatre. First of all there's a need for it, secondly it's enjoyable and will fill two years of your life. If the theatre is a good building, not badly planned like the Panayev one [in St Petersburg], it can't fail to be profitable.

Recently I arranged a performance in Serpukhov in aid of the school. The actors were amateurs from Moscow; they were excellent and didn't ham it up at all, better than many professionals. The audience came dressed in Paris fashions and real diamonds, but all we managed to raise was 101 roubles.

There is no news, or rather there is, but it is either dismal or uninteresting. People are talking a lot about the plague and the war,[1] and about the merger between the Synod and the Ministry of Education. The artist Levitan (the landscape painter) seems to be near death. He has a dilated aorta.

I'm not having much luck at the moment. I wrote a story about peasant life,[2] but I'm being told that it won't pass the censor and I must cut it in half. That means another loss.

If it's good spring weather when we are in Moscow, let's go to the Sparrow Hills and to the convent.[3] We can then go together from Moscow to Petersburg, where I have a particular matter I must deal with.

1. Between Turkey and Greece.
2. 'Peasants'.
3. The Novodevichy Convent, located in the south-west of Moscow, near the Sparrow Hills, is where Chekhov and his father are buried.

I wrote to you but you did not reply, so I commissioned my brother to come and see you and find out what is going on. I also asked him to investigate the whereabouts of the agreement the theatre office sent me, which it now wants back.

Is it true that Davydov has resigned from the Alexandrinsky Theatre? Capricious old hippopotamus.

Well, here's to our meeting soon. In the meantime, please write me a line or two. Best respects to Anna Ivanovna, Nastya and Borya.

Your

A. Chekhov

206. To Elena Shavrova-Yust, 2 March 1897, Melikhovo

Dear Colleague,

The conspirator will in all probability arrive in Moscow on train No. 14 at noon on 4 March. If you have not already left Moscow, send me a telegram with just one word: 'home'. Just write: Chekhov, Lopasnya. Home.

If, further, you accept my invitation to lunch with me at the Slavyansky Bazaar at one o'clock, then substitute for 'home' the word 'accept'. The telegraph boy may think I have offered you my hand and my heart, but what do we care what the world thinks!!

I'm coming just for one day, a flying visit, and don't plan to stay anywhere; I'll spend the night in the restaurant. However, in the third week of Lent I am coming to Moscow for a longer stay, four days or so, and then I shall be able to pay you a visit.

With my best wishes,

The Conspirator

207. To Franz Shekhtel, 7 March 1897, Melikhovo

Dearest Franz Osipovich,

On Monday last I was in Moscow and went to see Levitan. He told me that Pavel Tretyakov[1] had already reached agreement with the painter Braz[2] to paint my portrait, and I am now the one who is holding things up. I must write to Braz and let him know when I shall be in Petersburg (in the fifth week of Lent or the second half of May), but I don't know Braz's address or how to find it out. Do you know where he lives, or could you find out from someone, also what his first name and patronymic are, and so forth? Once I have the answers to these questions I can write to Piter straight away.

I examined Levitan by auscultation, and things are not good. His heart doesn't so much beat as pound. Instead of a steady tck-tck you hear something like pff-tck. In medical terminology this is known as 'audible arhythmia'.

How did you get on with Sventsitsky? He is a good Aesculapian.

I shall be coming in the third week of Lent to see one or two people at the convention, then I'll drop in to see you. In the meantime I press your hand warmly and wish you all earthly and heavenly blessings.

Your

A. Chekhov

1. Pavel Tretyakov (1832–98), founder of the first public collection of Russian art, in 1892.
2. Iosif Braz (1872–1936), a painter who had studied with Repin at the Academy of Arts in St Petersburg. He painted Chekhov at Melikhovo in 1897 and in Nice in 1898, but Chekhov liked neither painting.

208. To Georgy Chekhov, 18 March 1897, Melikhovo

Dearest Georges,

I received two letters from you sent from Anapa, but didn't reply to either of them, the reasons being, first, I had no time: I've had all kinds of work to do and a lot of business to deal with, because from early youth my head has always been at war with my heart; and secondly there was nothing to write to you about. Life continues uneventfully, giving us nothing to brag about.

We have snow here; the rooks have arrived but there are no starlings as yet; the weather is dank, the road is in a terrible state, in a word it's all horrible. In Taganrog, however, I expect spring is already in full flower! I envy you, and shall continue to envy you until the middle of April, when we shall probably have some good weather here.

I am going to Petersburg in the sixth week of Lent to have my portrait painted for the Tretyakov Gallery. I'll be back for Passion Week and shall then stay at home until the end of May. I am engaged on building work this year: a school in the village of Novoselki, midway between Melikhovo and the station.

There is no news at all. Quinine has whelped, bringing into the world a copper-coloured pup, to whom in recognition of the firmness of his character we gave the name Major. But the other day Major breathed his last. You may remember we had a big yard dog called Sharik, and he has also perished as a result of having his throat gnawed by Zalivai, a hound we had been given. That's all the news we have.

Now I should like to ask you to do me a favour. A little while ago the Taganrog Gymnasium celebrated the hundredth anniversary of its foundation and the director published an historical account which I read about in *World Illustrated*. Could you kindly get hold of this memoir somehow or other, and send it to me printed-matter rate? Best of all would be if you could see the director personally and ask him to let you have a copy of his great work; you might at the same time find out from him whether Venyamin Evtushevsky[1] has been

1. Venyamin Evtushevsky (?1885–after 1949), the son of Andrey Evtushevsky, the brother of Chekhov's aunt Lyudmila (widow of Mitrofan Chekhov).

excused from paying fees to the school. You should know *in the strictest confidence* that I offered to pay Venyamin's fees for the first semester of the year on condition that the school's own charitable society paid the second semester. I made this proposal to the governing council of the school via M. N. Psalti, and if they have accepted it then I am prepared to continue the arrangement in subsequent years. Please tell the director this, but say nothing about it to Andrey Pavlovich or to your mother. I didn't tell them the truth, merely told them I had been to see the director.

What about Volodya? How is he getting on? Write and tell me all details. I warmly press your hand and send my best respects to my aunt and cousins. Keep well and forgive your cousin for his tardiness.

Your

A. Chekhov

209. *To Lidia Avilova, 24 March 1897, Moscow*

Here is my criminal record: on Friday evening I began to spit some blood. The following morning, Saturday, I went to Moscow, and at 6 p.m. went with Suvorin to the Hermitage to have dinner. Hardly had we sat down to table when a vigorous flow of blood started streaming from my throat. Suvorin took me to the Slavyansky Bazaar and summoned doctors. I lay in bed there for twenty-four hours but now I'm back home, that is to say in my room in the Grand Moscow Hotel.

Your

A. Chekhov

210. *To Maria Chekhova, 25 or 26 March 1897, Moscow*

Please don't say anything to mother and father.
A. Chekhov

211. *To Elena Shavrova-Yust, 26 March 1897, Moscow*

Alas and alack! I had already arrived in Moscow, on my way north, when a scandal suddenly occurred in my lungs and blood started to come from my throat – so here I am, confined to bed in the clinic, and reduced to writing on paper that has recently, as you see, had a carafe standing on it.

I shall eventually be let out of here but not, apparently, before Easter . . . Please write to me, otherwise I shall expire from boredom: Professor Ostroumov's Clinic, Devichie Polye,[1] Moscow.

Alas, alas! Please send me something to eat, some nice roast turkey for instance, because they give me nothing but cold bouillon.

Greetings to you, I press your hand.

Your colleague

A. Chekhov

212. *To Rimma Vashchuk, 27 March 1897, Moscow*

My dear madam,

I read your story 'In the Hospital' in the clinic where I am presently confined. I am replying to you lying in bed. From the point I have marked in red pencil on, the story is very good. The opening, however, is banal and superfluous. You certainly should continue writing, provided of course in the first place that the activity gives you pleasure, and in the second that you are still young enough to learn the proper and literate use of punctuation marks.

Regarding your 'Fairy Tale', it strikes me as less a fairy tale than a random collection of words like 'gnomes', 'fairy', 'dew', 'knights', all of which are fake diamonds – at least they are so on our Russian soil, which has never been trodden on by knights or gnomes, and where

1. Coincidentally close to the Novodevichy Convent to which he had planned an excursion with Suvorin earlier in the month.

you will be hard put to find anybody capable of imagining a fairy dining on dew and sunbeams. You should forget all that stuff: your task is to be a sincere artist writing only about what exists or what you think ought to exist, painting pictures of life as it is.

Going back to your first story: it is not a good idea to write too much about yourself. When you write about yourself you fall into the trap of exaggerating, and therefore run the risk of ending up with nothing for your pains because either you will fail to convince your readers, or your outpourings will leave them cold.

With my best wishes,

A. Chekhov

213. *To Rimma Vashchuk, 28 March 1897, Moscow*

Instead of being angry, I suggest you read my letter a little more carefully. I believe I clearly told you your story was *very good*, except for the beginning, which gave the impression of having been unnecessarily tacked on. It is not my job to give or withhold permission for you to write. I referred to your youthfulness because at thirty or forty years of age it is too late to start; and I mentioned the necessity of learning the correct and literate use of punctuation marks because in a work of art they often play the part of notes in a musical score, and this is something you cannot learn from a textbook, but only from instinct and experience. Getting pleasure from writing does not mean it is a game you play for amusement. Getting pleasure from something means that you love doing it.

Forgive me, it is not easy to write; I am still lying in bed.

Please read my letter once again and stop being angry. I wrote to you in absolute sincerity, and I am now writing to you again because I sincerely wish you success.

A. Chekhov

214. To Alexey Suvorin, 1 April 1897, Moscow

The doctors have diagnosed active pulmonary tuberculosis at the apex of my lungs and ordered me to change my way of life. The first I understand, but the second I don't, because it is almost impossible. They say I must definitely live in the country, but don't they realize that full-time country living entails constant problems with peasants, animals and the elements in all their aspects, and that you're as likely to escape getting burnt in hell as you are to protect yourself from cares and troubles in the country. But as far as possible I will try to mend my ways, and I have already told Masha to announce that I am giving up my local medical practice. This will be at once a relief and a severe deprivation to me. I shall give up all my district responsibilities, buy myself a dressing gown, warm myself in the sun and eat a lot. I have been told to eat six times a day, and got into trouble when the doctors found out how little I have been eating. I am forbidden to talk much, go swimming, and so on and so forth.

Apart from the lungs, all my organs have been found to be in good working order; I saw no need to inform the doctors that I sometimes have trouble with impotence of an evening.

Until now I have always imagined I drank as much as I could without harming myself, but the check-up has shown that I have been drinking less than my entitlement. What a pity!

The author of 'Ward No. 6' has now been moved from Ward No. 16 into Ward No. 14. This is a spacious room with two windows, lighting that could have been designed by Potapenko, and three tables. The bleeding is much less now. After Tolstoy came to see me the other evening (we talked for a long time) I had another large haemorrhage at four in the morning.

Melikhovo is a healthy place to be; it stands right on a watershed and is high up, and therefore free from fever or diphtheria. After general consultation it was decided that I should not move anywhere else, but should stay at Melikhovo. We just need to arrange it so that it is a bit more comfortable to live in. When I get fed up with being there I can go to the neighbouring estate, which I have rented for the times when my brothers come to stay.

I have visitors all the time, bringing flowers, sweets and comestibles. Bliss, in a word.

I read in *The Petersburg Newspaper* about the performance in the Pavlova Hall. Tell Nastya that had I been present I would most certainly have presented her with a bouquet of flowers. My deepest respects and my greetings to Anna Ivanovna.

I can now write sitting up, not lying down, but as soon as I have finished writing I return to my sickbed.

Your
A. Chekhov
Please write, I beg you.

215. *To Alexander Chekhov, 2 April 1897, Moscow*

Here's the story. Almost every spring since 1884 I have coughed up a bit of blood. But this year, following your rebuke to me for accepting the blessing of the Most Holy Synod, I was so upset by your unbelief that in the presence of Mr Suvorin I suffered a severe haemorrhage and was taken to the clinic. Here I was diagnosed with pulmonary apical tuberculosis and accordingly awarded the right to describe myself, should I so desire, as an invalid. My temperature is normal, I do not suffer from night sweats nor any particular symptoms of weakness, but I dream of archimandrites and the future looks generally extremely uncertain. Although the disease has not yet progressed very far at all, I nevertheless ought not to delay making a will in order to prevent you making off with my estate. I am to be discharged from here on Wednesday of Passion Week and will go straight to Melikhovo. After that, we shall see. I have been told to eat a lot. Therefore it's not Papa and Mama who need to be fed, but me. Nobody knows anything about my illness at home, so rein in your customary malice and don't blab about it in your letters.

My story,[1] in which I (partially) recount the fire at Melikhovo when you were there in 1895,[2] will appear in the April issue of *Russian Thought*.

My deepest respects and greetings to your wife and children, from the bottom of my heart, naturally.

Keep well.

Your benefactor

A. Chekhov

216. To Alexey Suvorin, 7 April 1897, Moscow

If I were to trust the way I feel, I am in perfect health, but I seem to have swelled up from all the time I spent lying about doing nothing. I shall be discharged from the clinic at noon on Thursday, then I shall go home and carry on living there as I did before. You write that laziness is my ideal state. That is not entirely accurate; I despise laziness as I despise weakness and flabby emotional responses. I was not talking about laziness but about idleness, moreover I said that idleness was not an ideal, merely that it was one of the indispensable conditions for personal happiness.

If the tests of Koch's new drug yield successful results, I shall certainly go to Berlin. Eating more is doing me no good at all. They have now been force-feeding me for two weeks, but to very little effect; I'm not putting on any weight.

I ought to get married. A sharp-tongued wife might be able to cut

1. 'Peasants'.

2. A reference to a fire at Melikhovo in April 1895. Epifan Volkov, a peasant from the village of Melikhovo, burnt his mother's house down when drunk and was arrested the next day. Aware of the desperate predicament of Volkov's mother, Chekhov corresponded with and met the local investigator, arguing that Volkov had been merely irresponsible and should be released, as he was needed at home. Alexander Chekhov also became involved as he was staying in Melikhovo at the time. Chekhov was able to bail out Volkov and the case was formally closed a year later.

in half the number of my visitors. Yesterday I had a constant stream; it never stopped. They came in two by two, all of them telling me not to speak, but asking me questions at the same time . . .

In any event, please address letters to me at Lopasnya after next Thursday. What is happening to the edition of my collected plays? It seems to have got stuck somewhere. Thank you for your letter, and God grant you good health.

Your

A. Chekhov

217. To Mikhail Menshikov, 16 April 1897, Melikhovo

Dear Mikhail Osipovich,

My lungs have been misbehaving a bit. On 20 March I was on my way to Petersburg but started to cough up blood and had to stay in a clinic in Moscow for two weeks' treatment. The doctors have diagnosed pulmonary apical tuberculosis and forbidden me to do virtually everything I find interesting.

Please give my warmest greetings and grateful thanks to Lidia Ivanovna and to Yasha. I much appreciate their friendship and concern for me.

I have a headache today. It is rather spoiling the day, but the weather is wonderful and the garden is full of sounds. Inside there are guests, laughter and the piano being played, and outside there are starlings.

The censor has snipped out a sizeable chunk of 'Peasants'.

I am most grateful to you. I press your hand and wish you all happiness. My sister sends you her regards.

Your

A. Chekhov

Every cloud has a silver lining. I had a visit in the clinic from Lev Nikolayevich [Tolstoy], and we had an exceptionally interesting conversation – exceptionally interesting for me at any rate, because I listened more than I spoke. We discussed immortality. He accepts the idea of immortality in the Kantian sense, proposing that all of us (human beings and animals) will continue to live on in some primal state (reason, love), the essence and purpose of which is a mystery hidden from us. However, this primal state or force appears to me to be a shapeless mass of jelly, into which my 'I', my individuality, my consciousness, would be absorbed. I don't feel any need for immortality in this form. I don't understand it, but Lev Nikolayevich finds it astonishing that I don't understand it.

Why has your book[1] not come out yet? Jean Shcheglov visited me in the clinic. He is much better, in fact he has recovered completely. He is moving to Petersburg.

218. *To Maria Chekhova, 6 June 1897, Melikhovo*

It is hot, quiet, dry, dusty. Everything is fine. Isayich and Markovna are inflamed with passion. A little dog, just like a vixen, has taken to coming over from Vorontsov's. Ivanenko went away but is coming back today; he and I caught fifty-seven carp the day before yesterday. Seryogin came on Tuesday; he is going straight on to Novorossiisk. The strawberries have ripened. The roses are blooming most luxuriously. I'm sending you, printed-paper rate, an article about the production at the Rzhevskaya school. Old Anna is watering the vegetables; Potapenko is ploughing. There's no news. Nothing more to add.

Regards and best wishes to all,

Ivan Ivanovich Loboda[1]

1. Menshikov had withdrawn his collection of articles, *Thoughts About Happiness*, in 1896 over censorship fears. It was finally published in 1898.
1. A joke – Ivan Loboda was Chekhov's maternal cousin.

219. To Nikolay Leikin, 4 July 1897, Melikhovo

Dear Nikolay Alexandrovich,

I shall be in Petersburg around 15 July, and shall try to bring the puppies back here with me when I return. I'll be happy and very grateful to have them, whatever colour they are, white or coloured.[1] I had been thinking it might not be a bad idea to go on from Petersburg to the exhibition in Stockholm but in fact I don't think I will; I'd like to see Stockholm and the Swedes, but somehow the exhibition itself doesn't much appeal. One exhibition is very like another, and they are all tiring.

I am overrun with guests at the moment. I haven't room for them all, nor bed linen, nor much inclination to talk to them and play the genial host. I have been eating heartily in order to put on weight, and have now recovered my health so successfully that I can no longer claim the privileges of an invalid, such as abandoning my guests when I feel like it, and I'm now allowed to talk as much as I like.

I am going away soon, so at the moment am doing nothing except wandering round the garden and eating cherries. I pick twenty at a time and stuff them all into my mouth at once. They taste better like that.

Suvorin is in Petersburg. He writes that the Literary-Artistic Circle has taken a lease on the Maly Theatre for five years. His son Alexey is ill with typhoid fever. There is no news in Moscow; but there are persistent and widespread rumours that I am planning to publish a newspaper. The new mayor is getting a lot of praise. Sytin, the famous publisher, has been awarded the Order of St Stanislav[2] and has bought a large estate.

The weather just now is marvellous. Haymaking is over, and we're about to get down to harvesting the rye, which is already ripe. The drought did a lot of damage, and although we now get rain every day

1. These were two laika puppies, Siberian hunting dogs, which were christened Nansen (after the Norwegian explorer) and Laika (laika, from the verb 'to bark').
2. An imperial decoration which was also awarded to Chekhov.

it only serves to freshen up the plants, it's too late to save what has already dried up and withered.

Well, until our next meeting, which I hope will be soon, I wish you health and happiness, and send my profound respects to Praskovya Nikiforovna and Fedya.

Your

A. Chekhov

---

220. To Nikolay Leikin, 27 July 1897, Schlüsselberg
Sunday, on board the Rybka

Dear Nikolay Alexandrovich,

I must have dropped my pince-nez on the jetty; they are round, with a cord. If they are found, please keep them for me; they cost about 10 roubles as the glass in them is foreign.

Your

A. Chekhov

---

221. To Pavel Iordanov, 29 August 1897, Melikhovo

Dear Pavel Fyodorovich,

I have sent you a few more books by express post – I expect by the time you receive this letter they will already have arrived in Taganrog.

On 1 September I am going abroad, first to Biarritz, where I shall stay until October, then on to somewhere where it will be warmer at that time of year. Should you wish to drop me a line, here is my address while I am abroad: M. Antoine Tchekhov, Biarritz, France.

I read in *The Taganrog Herald* that I am in Kislovodsk. This is not true; I haven't been to Kislovodsk this year.

Allow me to send you my best wishes and to clasp your hand.

Your

A. Chekhov

222. *To Alexandra Khotyaintseva, 17 September 1897, Biarritz*

Dear artist, you ask me whether it is warm here. It was cold and damp for the first few days after my arrival, but now it's like being in an oven. It is especially hot after lunch, which consists of six rather rich dishes washed down by a whole bottle of white wine. The most interesting thing here is the sea: even when the conditions are completely calm you can hear the roar of the breakers. I sit on the Grande Plage from morning till evening voraciously reading the newspapers, while before my eyes passes a motley crowd of government ministers, rich Jews, Adelaides,[1] Spaniards, poodles; the women's dresses, the gaily coloured parasols, the brilliant sunshine, the expanse of water, the cliffs, the harps, the singing – put all this together and it's a hundred thousand miles from Melikhovo.

When are you coming to Paris? It's nice there at this time of year.

There was a cowfight in Bayonne a few days ago, Spanish picadors tussling with the cows. These furious and remarkably agile little animals were chasing the picadors round the ring just like dogs. The crowd went mad.[2]

Konstantin Makovsky is here, painting portraits of women.

Keep well. Give my respects to your mother and brother, and remember me in your prayers. Thank you for your letter.

Your

A. Chekhov

1. A name Chekhov gave to smartly dressed ladies with lorgnettes.
2. Chekhov clearly went to the circus in Bayonne, on a Sunday when cows were also let into the arena along with the bulls more usually fought.

223. To Evgenia Chekhova, 4 October 1897, Nice

Dear Mama,

As Masha is probably not at home, I'm sending this business letter to you.

If Karl Wagner from Riga sends the poplars, don't plant them now, as it's too late in the season. Just put them in the garden and cover the roots with soil, and we'll plant them in the spring. If they don't arrive now it means they will be sending them in the spring. The post office receipt for the 10 roubles I sent to Karl Wagner is in the basket in my study with all the other receipts, which should be carefully kept.

I am alive and well and lack for nothing; I eat and sleep a lot. It's warm here, and when I go out of doors I don't need an overcoat. I'm staying in a Russian pension, by which I mean a hotel run by a Russian lady. I have a big room with a fireplace and a carpet which covers the whole floor, and I also have my own bathroom where I can wash. We have a Russian cook, Evgenia; her cooking is like a French chef's (she has been living in Nice for thirty years) but every so often we have borscht or fried mushrooms. We have plenty of coffee, starting at seven o'clock in the morning. There are orange and Seville orange trees in the garden, as well as palm trees and oleanders as tall as our linden trees. The oleanders are all in bloom. The dogs wear muzzles, and there are all kinds of breeds. A day or two ago I saw a long-haired dachshund, an elongated beast a bit like a hairy caterpillar. The cooks here all wear hats; domestic carriages are pulled by donkeys, which are quite small, about the size of our Kazachok.[1] It's very cheap to have laundry done here, and they do it very well.

Deepest respects to Papasha, Maryushka and everyone. Please don't worry about me; everything is fine at the moment and I am very much enjoying myself. I have more money than Deyev.[2]

1. One of the ponies of Melikhovo.
2. A Moscow banker.

Keep well, live in peace and joy and let nothing you dismay.
Your prayerful
Father Antony

When you see Father Nikolay Filippovich, please pass on my respects.
Give Maria Timofeyevna the stamps from the envelope.

224. To Lidia Avilova, 6 October 1897, Nice

Your letter was forwarded from Lopasnya to Biarritz, and from there it was sent on to me in Nice. My address here is: Pension Russe, Nice, France, and my name should be written like this: Antoine Tchekhoff. Do please write to me again, and if you have had anything published, send that too. Let me have your address, by the way. I'm sending this letter via Potapenko.

You complain that my characters are gloomy. Alas, this is not my fault! They come out like that without my necessarily wanting them to, and when I am writing I don't feel as though I am writing gloomily. In any case, I'm always in a good mood when I'm writing. It is a well-documented fact that pessimists and melancholics always write in a very upbeat way, whereas cheerful writers generally manage to depress their readers. My temperament is inclined to be cheerful; at least for the first thirty years of my life I have lived, as they say, content with my lot.

My health is reasonable in the mornings and very good indeed in the evenings. I'm doing nothing, not writing nor feeling much inclination to write. I've grown terribly lazy.

Keep well and happy. I press your hand.
Your
A. Chekhov
I shall probably live abroad all winter.

225. To Alexey Suvorin, 25 October 1897, Nice

Your letter was a terrible blow to me. I was so looking forward to seeing you, I wanted to spend time with you and talk to you, and the truth is I really do need you! I had prepared a whole basketful of topics for conversations and arranged marvellously warm weather – and then suddenly, this letter. I am terribly disappointed!

Nemirovich[-Danchenko] is staying on the floor below me at the Pension Russe, and he was also looking forward to seeing you.

You are preoccupied by your theatre, and I also have my worries. My *Surgery* journal still has one foot in the grave, and once more it is down to me to do whatever has to be done to rescue it, since I am the only doctor with any knowledge of, or connections to, the world of literature and publishing. Scientifically speaking the journal is outstanding, fully able to stand comparison with the best in Europe. Can you give me some advice: how on earth are we to secure a subsidy of three to four thousand roubles a year? If it means I have to go to the lengths of pretending to be the publisher myself, I'll happily do exactly that and stand barefoot and bareheaded outside Witte's front door for a week with a candle in my hand.[1] If you can just advise me how to proceed I will submit the application myself or get the editor to do so.

I've had another episode of coughing blood, lasting three or four days, but now I am fine, leaping about and feeling quite well. I've written two stories and sent them off.

If you reconsider and decide you do want to come to Nice after all, send me a telegram and I'll come to meet you. In any event, wherever you go please cable me the day you leave Paris, so that I know where to write to you and what sort of mood you are in. I very much hope you are not downcast.

Keep well. Deepest respects and greetings to Mikhail Alexeyevich and to Pavlovsky.

1. Count Sergey Witte was Minister of Finance from 1892 to 1903.

It has been sunny, warm and quiet all day. What a splendid country!
Your
A. Chekhov
I shall stay in Nice all winter.

226. To Anna Suvorina, 10 November 1897, Nice

Dearest Anna Ivanovna,

Thank you very much for your letter. I've read it and am immediately sitting down to answer. You ask about my health. I feel in fine
form and outwardly I seem to be in perfect health, but the problem is
that I keep coughing blood. There is not much blood, but it does
continue for some time, and the last haemorrhage, which is still going
on today, started three weeks ago. Because of this I have to submit to
various privations: I don't go out after three o'clock in the afternoon,
I don't drink any alcohol at all, I don't eat hot food, I don't walk fast,
I don't go further than the street, basically I'm not living, I'm a vegetable. This annoys and depresses me, and leads me to find everything
that my Russian dinner-table companions say vulgar and stupid, so
that I have to make a continual effort not to be rude to them.

But for God's sake don't mention my coughing blood to anyone;
what I have told you is strictly between ourselves. When I write home
I tell them I am perfectly well, and there is no point in writing anything
else because the truth is I do feel perfectly well in myself, and if they
knew at home that I was still losing blood there would be weeping
and wailing.

Now, concerning the little affair you wanted to know about. When
I was in Biarritz I had some French lessons from a nineteen-year-old
girl called Margot. As I was leaving Biarritz and saying goodbye to
her, she announced that she would definitely come to Nice. And
probably she is here, but I cannot seem to find her anywhere . . . and
I still can't speak French.

The weather here is heavenly; it's hot, calm and very gentle. The music competitions have begun. The streets are full of orchestras, noise, dancing and laughter. When I see all this I think to myself how silly I have been not to live abroad for long periods before. As long as I'm alive, I don't think I'd spend another winter in Moscow now for all the tea in China. As soon as October comes round, I'll be off and away from Russia. The landscape round here doesn't attract me much, I find it quite alien, but I adore the warmth, I love the culture . . . And you see the culture oozing out of every shop window, every raffia basket; every dog smells of civilization.

How is Nastya? How is Borya? Warmest greetings and deep respects to them. Please don't be too proud and grand to write to me as often as you can; I need letters. I kiss your hand 100 × 100 times and wish you all happiness. Thank you once again.

Yours with heart and soul,

A. Chekhov

My regards to Konstantin Semyonovich.

227. To Maria Chekhova, 12 November 1897, Nice

Dearest Masha,

I received the cheque for 400 roubles. *Mille remercîments.* I've replied to letters from Lika and Levitan, but from Olga Petrovna[1] I have heard not a word; please tell her this from me. Of course you must not pay Ladyzhensky[2] anything, but you should write to him; I think he is in Petersburg now. Find out what happened in the elections and write and tell me. Who is the chairman? There should be more money due to you from *Ivanov*.

Now, about my health. Everything is fine. *Je suis bien portant.* In French, 'healthy' is '*sain*', but this word is only used to apply to food, or water, or the climate. When speaking of yourself you say '*bien portant*' or '*se porter bien*', which literally means to carry yourself well,

1. Olga Kundasova.
2. Vladimir Ladyzhensky (1859–1932), a poet and active figure in the *zemstvo*.

to be in good health. When you greet someone, you say '*Je suis charmé de vous voir bien portant*', 'I am glad to see you are well'. After '*charmé*', or any word denoting an emotional state or an activity by any of the five senses or memory, the verb is usually followed by '*de*'. For instance: '*j'oublie de vous donner de l'argent*' – 'I've forgotten to give you some money'. '*Bien*' means 'good' or 'well', and can also be used in the sense of 'very'. '*Vous êtes bien bon*' – 'You are very kind'. '*Ça me semble bien cher*' – 'That seems very expensive to me'. '*Je vous remercie bien*' – 'Thank you very much'. At our age it is difficult, very difficult, to learn French, but it is possible to make some progress. Don't learn from Olga Petrovna, read something with the help of a dictionary, five or ten lines a day, and learn one expression a day. Here's an example of something you can learn today: '*la pièce*' – 'thing', 'piece'. If someone asks you how many books or coins or rooms you want, you answer: '*trois pièces*', '*sept pièces*', three or seven of whatever it is. Tomorrow, learn '*monter*' – 'ascend', 'climb'; or '*descendre*' – 'descend'. Use the Makarov dictionary. That way you will learn thirty words a month, in their common French usage. I speak very badly, but can already read fluently, and I can write letters in French. Keep well. Your description of the annexe was so enticing it made me want to come home immediately.[3]

Your

A. Chekhov

228. To Maria Chekhova, 3 December 1897, Nice

Ma chère et bien aimable Marie,

If you are brought or sent some worthless object, don't register surprise and ask why on earth anyone would want to send such junk

3. Maria had written to her brother to tell him about the new furnishings for the two-room cottage in the garden at Melikhovo, which they had built as guest accommodation for the summer months. Chekhov sometimes used it as his study (he wrote *The Seagull* there), and was pleased to hear from his sister that its interior now looked as smart as a chocolate box.

halfway round the world. The fact is that opportunities to send things come up without warning; you usually find out by sheer chance that someone is going back to Russia, and so you just send whatever you manage to grab from the desk, a magnifying glass, say, or a cheap pen ... A certain Miss Zenzinova is going to get in touch with you next week, a young lady who is the daughter of the tea merchant Zenzinov. She is going to bring you something, but please don't open it while she is there because if she sees that she has brought worthless objects such a distance, she will be offended. The Zenzinovs were staying at the Pension Russe and gave me tea in the evenings. Judging by their appearance and their tastes, as a family they are something like the Lintvaryovs. Be friendly to the girl, i.e. thank her for all the hospitality I received from her parents in Nice, say a couple of nice things to her, and her Papa will send you a quarter of a pound of tea for your trouble.

Put the magnifying glass on my desk.

Have a look in my room and see what volumes of Brockhaus's dictionary are missing, and write and tell me: I'll try and arrange to have them sent.

The wife of General Shanyavsky, the gold dealer, came to visit me. I shall return the compliment tomorrow. I'd rather have been visited by a sack of gold than by her.

Do take photographs of the laikas and send me the pictures – you do have a camera, don't you? Everybody is interested in them here and wants to know what sort of breed they are. There aren't any laikas here.

Larousse's new geographical atlas is going to cover the entire world. It will come out in fifty parts.

Best respects to everyone. Keep well. There is no news to speak of, all is well.

Your

A. Chekhov

229. *To Maria Chekhova, 1 January 1898, Nice*

Yesterday, on New Year's Eve, a Russian family from Cannes sent me flowers, and now my room is full of their scent. I didn't stay up to see the New Year in, but retired to bed at eleven o'clock. This morning the Consul sent me a bottle of vintage wine (1811). Happy New Year! The weather is beautiful again. I am, as usual, in the best of health, although not nearly as fat as the photograph makes me out to be. I took Alexandra Khotyaintseva to Monte Carlo yesterday to show her the roulette tables, but like all women she lacks that proper sense of curiosity which men find such a spur, so nothing makes much of an impression on her. She is wearing the same dress as she was when she was at Melikhovo. She is by far the most intelligent of all the Russians at the Pension Russe dinner table.

There is no other news. Everything is fine. Deepest respects to all.
A. Chekhov

230. *To Fyodor Batyushkov, 23 January 1898, Nice*

Dear Fyodor Dmitriyevich,

Here are the proofs, which I am returning to you. The typesetter left no margins, so I have had to paste in my corrections.[1]

Please send the offprints of the article you wrote about me to me here in Nice. I plan to stay here, probably until April, and expect to be very bored, so your article will perform a double service.

The talk here is of nothing but Zola and Dreyfus.[2] An overwhelming majority of the intelligentsia backs Zola and believes Dreyfus is innocent. Zola has grown tremendously in stature; his protest articles have brought in a breath of fresh air, and now every Frenchman can feel that there is, thank God, such a thing as justice in the world, and that if an innocent man is convicted there will be someone to stand

1. 'A Visit to Friends'.
2. See n. 1 to following letter, no. 231.

up for him. The French newspapers are exceptionally interesting, in comparison to the uselessness of the Russian ones. *New Times* is absolutely disgusting.

Please be sure to send some copies of my story to my sister: Maria Pavlovna Chekhova, Lopasnya, Moscow Province.

We are having wonderful weather here; it's just like summer. All through the winter I never once had to put on galoshes or an autumn overcoat, and only twice had to take an umbrella with me when I went out.

Allow me to send you my best wishes and to thank you for your kind attention to me, which I value most highly. I warmly press your hand and look forward to receiving your article. I remain,

Sincerely and respectfully yours,

A. Chekhov

231. To Alexey Suvorin, 6 February 1898, Nice

A few days ago I saw a prominent advertisement for *Cosmopolis* on the front page of *New Times*, announcing the publication of my story 'The Visit'. First of all, the title is 'A Visit to Friends' not 'The Visit'. Secondly, this kind of publicity really grates on me; its scale is in any case quite out of proportion to the story itself, which is the sort that can be produced at the rate of one a day.

You write that Zola has begun to disappoint you,[1] but I must tell

1. The attacks on Zola in *New Times*, some of them by Suvorin himself, began when the writer took up the cause of defending Dreyfus. After publishing his famous letter 'J'Accuse' in *L'Aurore* in January 1898, Zola fled to England for eleven months to avoid being gaoled for libel. Captain Alfred Dreyfus, a Jew, had become the victim of a miscarriage of justice when falsely accused of passing French Ministry of War documents to Colonel Schwartzkoppen, the German military attaché in Paris in 1894. He was sentenced to life imprisonment on the penal colony on Devil's Island, situated off the coast of French Guiana. A French Secret Service agent had discovered evidence implicating a Major Esterhazy in 1896, but a fiercely anti-Semitic press campaign contributed to the conviction against Dreyfus being upheld at a second trial. Dreyfus was finally pardoned in 1899, but his conviction was not quashed until 1906.

you that over here the general feeling is that he has been reborn as a new and improved Zola. Like turpentine, the trial has cleansed him of the stains which had previously sullied his reputation, so that he now appears before the French in all his true shining radiance, demonstrating a purity and moral grandeur that no one suspected he possessed. Consider the scandal from the very beginning. The court-martialling of Dreyfus, whether or not it was just, produced a thoroughly upsetting and depressing effect on everyone (including you yourself, I recall). Everyone saw that during this degrading spectacle Dreyfus conducted himself like an upstanding, disciplined officer, while others who were present, like the journalists for example, behaved appallingly, hurling insults like 'Shut up, you Judas!'. Everyone came away from the event deeply unhappy and with a troubled conscience. Unhappiest of all was Dreyfus's defence counsel, Démange, an honest man who from the very beginning of the investigation suspected that there was something fishy going on behind the scenes. We then had the spectacle of the experts constantly running around Paris parroting the mantra that Dreyfus was guilty, in order to prove to themselves that they had not made any mistakes ... One of these experts turns out to be insane, the author of a monstrously inept system of graphology, and the other two are complete cranks. However hard one tries one can't avoid dragging into the discussion the War Ministry's Bureau of Information, the military consistory whose real job is to catch spies and read other people's letters, and the reason we can't avoid dragging in the Bureau is the revelation that Sandherr, its chief, was suffering from a progressive form of paralysis, with Paty de Clam being exposed as a local version of Berlin's von Tausch; and then there is yet another mystery in Picquart's abrupt and scandalous resignation. Then, right on cue, a whole series of judicial errors came to light. Gradually it has come to be realized that Dreyfus was actually convicted on the strength of a secret document that had been disclosed neither to the accused nor his defence counsel, and right-thinking people have seen this as a fundamental violation of the law. Whoever wrote this letter, whether it was Kaiser Wilhelm or the sun itself, it should have been disclosed to Démange. Speculation was rife as to what the letter might contain. The most absurd theories are in circulation. Dreyfus was an officer –

so the army immediately goes on the defensive. Dreyfus was a Jew –
so the Jews go on the defensive . . . everyone began to mutter about
militarism, about the threat posed by the yids. People with dubious
reputations like Drumont stuck their heads above the parapet; little by
little an unholy brew began to ferment in the soil of anti-Semitism,
soil that reeks of the abattoir. Whenever we feel something is wrong
inside us we look for the cause outside ourselves, and usually it does
not take us long to find it: 'The French have been fouling their
own nest', or 'it's the Jews', or 'it's Wilhelm . . .'. Capital, demons,
Freemasons, the syndicate, the Jesuits – they're all phantoms, but oh!
how they relieve our feelings of unease! Of course, they are symptoms
of something very unhealthy. The moment the French start talking
about yids, or the syndicate, what they are really doing is expressing
their own sense of something's being amiss, their acknowledgement
of the worm within, their dependence on these phantoms to soothe
their agitated consciences. And then, what about Esterhazy, that
bullying braggart straight out of Turgenev, a chancer long mistrusted
and despised by his colleagues? What of the suspiciously close resem-
blance his own handwriting bears to that in the *bordereau*,[2] the Uhlan
letters, the threats he uttered but for some reason never carried out,
and finally his mysterious court martial, with its bizarre verdict that
the *bordereau* had indeed been written in his handwriting, but not by
him . . . ? As time went on one could feel the pressure of the foul gas
building up and the atmosphere getting more and more suffocating
and depressing. The scuffle in the Chamber of Deputies was a purely
nervous, hysterical reaction to this pressure; Zola's letter and his trial
are also symptoms of the same condition. What would you expect,
other than for the best people of the nation to take the lead in raising
the alarm? For this is precisely what has happened: the first to speak
up was Scheurer-Kestner, described (according to Kovalevsky) by
Frenchmen who know him as a 'dagger blade', so transparent and
above reproach is he. The second was Zola. And now he is on trial.[3]

All right, Zola is no Voltaire, none of us are Voltaires, but there

2. A document listing items in a classified dossier.
3. Zola's trial took place from 7 to 23 February 1898 in Paris.

are times in life when circumstances conspire to make the accusation that one is not Voltaire quite beside the point. Think of Korolenko defending the Multan pagans and saving them from forced labour.[4] Or Doctor Haas: no Voltaire, but a man who lived a wonderful life and died content that he had done what he had done.[5]

My knowledge of the case comes from reading the stenographic transcripts, which are very different from what one reads in the newspapers. It is quite clear to me what lies behind Zola's stance. The main thing is that he is acting honestly, by which I mean his judgements are based not on the chimeras of others but on what he has seen for himself. It is, of course, possible to be both sincere and wrong, but the errors of the sincere do less harm than the consequences of the deliberately insincere, the prejudiced or the politically calculating. Even if Dreyfus is guilty, Zola is still right, because the writer's task is not to accuse or pursue, but to defend even the guilty once they have been condemned and are undergoing punishment. The question will be asked: what about politics, or the interests of the state? But great writers and artists should have nothing to do with politics except insofar as they themselves need protection from it. We already have no shortage of accusers, prosecutors and gendarmes without adding writers, who are in any case much more suited to the role of Paul than of Saul. And whatever the outcome of his trial, at the end Zola will be blessed with great joy, his old age will be happy, and when he dies his conscience will be clear, or at the very least lightened. The French people have suffered, and are ready to seize on any word of consolation or justified criticism that comes to them from without. Hence the enthusiasm with which they greeted Bjørnstjerne's letter, and the

4. A group of Udmurts in the Vyatka region had been falsely accused of murdering a beggar to offer up as a sacrifice in 1892, but were later exonerated as the result of Korolenko's campaign in the press.

5. Fyodor Haas ('Gaaz' when Russianized) was chief medical officer for the Moscow prisons from 1830 to 1850, and achieved fame by improving conditions for convicts. Although opposed by the government, through his efforts female convicts no longer had to have their heads shaved, heavy shackles were replaced by lighter ones, and sick and feeble convicts were no longer put in irons. Haas also built at his own expense a hospital for convicts and a school for their children.

article by our own Zakrevsky (which appeared in *The News* here), and hence their disgust at the vilification daily heaped on Zola by the gutter press, which they despise. However nervous Zola may seem to be in court, he nevertheless stands as an exemplar of French common sense, and for this the French love him and are proud of him, even though they are frightened enough by the generals' simplistic talk of war and the need to maintain the honour of the army to applaud it.

What a long letter! It's spring here, and feels like it does at Easter in the Ukraine: warm, sunny, the sound of bells, memories of the past. Why don't you come! Duse, by the way, is coming to act here.

You write that you have not been getting my letters. How can this be? I'll send them registered post.

I wish you good health and all happiness. Best respects and greetings to Anna Ivanovna, Nastya and Borya.

I've written this letter on paper from the offices of *Le Petit Niçois*.

Your

A. Chekhov

232. To Alexander Chekhov, 23 February 1898, Nice

Brother!!

As though to demonstrate that it has no objection to your chasing after theatre girls, the government decreed that there should be a performance of my *Ivanov* on 13 February. Also, Kholev, after consulting with Domashova and wishing to give you pleasure, ordered your *Platon Andreyich* to be removed from the repertoire and replaced by my *Proposal*. As you see, everything is going swimmingly.[1]

And my health is also in good shape, so you, my heirs, can afford to be joyful. Having broken one of my teeth, the dentist made three attempts at extracting it, as a result of which I got a periostitic infection of the upper jaw. The pain was fierce, and, thanks to the subsequent

1. Alexander Chekhov believed one reason his play *Platon Andreyich* was removed from the repertoire at Suvorin's theatre in St Petersburg was that there was no role for the actress Domashova, whom he described to his brother as Suvorin's 'concubine'.

fever, I had to endure the sort of condition that I so artfully depicted in my story 'Typhoid' and which those members of the intelligentsia watching your *Platon Andreyich* experienced. A nightmarish sensation. They lanced it the day before yesterday, so today I can once again sit at my desk and write. You will not inherit just yet.

I shall come home in April around the 10th. Until then my address will remain unchanged.

I had news from Yaroslavl that Misha has had a daughter. The neophyte parent is in the seventh heaven.

The attitude of *New Times* to the Zola affair has been simply vile. The boss [Suvorin] and I have exchanged correspondence on this subject (in extremely measured tones, be it said), and silence now reigns on both sides. I don't wish to write to him, nor do I wish to receive letters from him in which he justifies the insensitivity of his newspaper's stance by claiming that he approves of the military – I don't wish to receive letters from him because I got bored with it all long ago. I also approve of the military, but if I owned a newspaper I would not allow cacti[2] to publish Zola's novel in the Supplement[3] *without payment*, while at the same time flinging mud at the selfsame Zola in the rest of the paper – and in the name of what, pray? In the name of something which is in fact quite foreign to every single one of the cacti, namely a noble impulse and purity of soul. And in any case, to attack Zola while he is on trial is simply not literature.

I received your portrait and have already presented it to a French lady with the inscription: '*Ce monsieur a un immense article, très agréable pour dames.*' She thinks I am referring to some article you have written on the women's question.

Write to me, don't be shy. My respects to Natalia Alexandrovna and the children.

L'homme des lettres
A. Chekhov

2. A reference to Alexander Amfiteatrov (see letter 163, n. 1) and Vasily Lyalin (1854–1909), both of whom were columnists on *New Times*.
3. From 18 October 1897 *New Times* published in serial form Zola's novel *Paris* in its illustrated supplements every Wednesday and Saturday. Zola was not paid a royalty for the serialization. Suvorin published the complete novel in 1898.

233. *To Alexey Suvorin, 13 March 1898, Nice*

It's wonderful weather here, sheer delight. It's warm, hot even, the sky is bright blue, the sea is sparkling, the fruit trees are covered in blossom. I stroll around in a straw hat without a coat. I've become as lazy as an Arab, I do precisely nothing, and the more I look at myself and other Russians the more convinced I become that a Russian person is incapable of working except when the weather is bad.

Potapenko is here. He's also staying at the Pension Russe. Prince Sumbatov-Yuzhin left yesterday. The three of us went together to Monte Carlo and amused ourselves greatly. Kovalevsky has returned from Paris.[1]

You are getting more and more involved with the theatre, while I seem to be moving further away from it. This is a pity, since at one time the theatre gave me a lot of good things (and I earn good money from it as well; this winter my plays have enjoyed greater success in the provinces than ever before; even *Uncle Vanya* has been put on). There used to be no greater pleasure for me than sitting in a theatre, but now whenever I do I feel as though someone in the balcony is about to shout 'Fire!'. And I don't like actors; I suppose writing for the theatre has spoiled me.

So Nastya is getting married. How is Borya? I have high hopes of him. I should so much like to see him, and Nastya too.

A few days ago I sent a complete run of the French classics, 319 volumes, to the Taganrog Library. It cost me a pretty penny. Now I'm worried that the censor will hold them up and might even confiscate half of them.

Please telephone your book-keeper and ask him to reckon up my account for 1897, and to send me any money I am due, because I am completely out. If none is due, no matter, I'll get round it somehow or, more likely, find a way of dodging my creditors.

---

1. While in Nice, Chekhov became very friendly with the lawyer Maxim Kovalevsky, who had been dismissed from his post as a professor at Moscow University in 1887, and had a house in nearby Beaulieu.

I am well enough, but no more so than I was before. I have not put on so much as an ounce of weight, and it looks as though I never shall. I shall return home after 10 April, via Paris.

Regards and greetings to Anna Ivanovna and all your family, and a thousand warm wishes to yourself.

Your

A. Chekhov

I saw Rochefort today.[2]

234. To Maria Chekhova, 16 March 1898, Nice

Braz arrived the day before yesterday. He still wears the same frock-coat, which makes him look like a grasshopper, he seems more mature, isn't foppishly dressed and is generally a bit less flamboyant. His friend is with him, a landowner from Borovichka. They are both staying at the Pension Russe. Braz's first idea was to paint me out of doors, but that did not work out; then there was too much sun indoors and that didn't work out either. We had to look for a studio, which we eventually found. I am going to sit for him in the mornings, in bright-coloured trousers and a white tie. Braz is always talking about Velasquez and perpetually complains about Repin, whom he suspects of intriguing against him as a potential rival.

We go to Monte Carlo every day. Potapenko won 110 francs yesterday, but he's some way off the million he is looking for.

There is no way I can get out of going to Paris; the city of Taganrog has asked me to go and see Antokolsky in Paris and negotiate with him about the statue of Peter the Great.[1] I'll buy some underwear and a trunk there, and then I'll take the express train. Do you have any commissions for me? I'll be glad to carry them out.

It was cold here for a couple of days, and there was snow on the

2. Victor Rochefort edited *Intransigeant*, a Paris newspaper, with an anti-Dreyfus bias.
1. Peter the Great, Tsar of Russia from 1682 to 1725, founded Taganrog in 1698, and it was decided that a statue would be put up to him to mark the town's bicentenary.

mountains, but now it's hot again. Even when it's cold the thermometer still shows 8 degrees above zero. There are people swimming in the sea. There is no news, everything is fine. I haven't coughed up any blood for a long time. Regards to all. If you haven't transplanted the Berlin poplars near the gooseberry bushes to the park next to the pond, that should be done, now that it's spring. The same applies to the larches, at least one of them, the middle one, and also the elder by the balcony with the blocked-up window.

Keep well.

Your

A. Chekhov

235. To Alexander Chekhov, 26 or 27 April 1898, Paris

Dear Poor Relation!

I am leaving Paris on Saturday 2 May on the fast train (the *Nord Express*), and arriving in Petersburg on Monday, probably some time after noon. Brush your shoes, put on your best clothes and come to meet me. Etiquette demands no less, and in any case I have a right to expect it since I am your rich relation. Don't tell anyone I am coming, the only people I'm telling are you and Potapenko.

I am going straight to Moscow the same day, first class.

Your benefactor

A. Chekhov

I shall be on my own, without Suvorin.

I've been wearing a top hat.

236. To Lidia Avilova, 24–26 July 1898, Melikhovo

We have so many guests at the moment that I haven't been able to get round to answering your last letter. I wish I could write at greater length, but my hand seizes up at the thought that someone may come in at any moment and interrupt me. And indeed, just as I was writing the word 'interrupt', in came a girl to announce the arrival of a patient. I must go.

The financial situation has already been satisfactorily resolved. I have clipped all my little stories from *Fragments*, and have sold the rights to Sytin for ten years. And then it turns out that I can draw a thousand roubles from *Russian Thought*, which incidentally has raised my fee: they used to pay 250 roubles but this has now increased to 300.

I have grown sick of writing, and do not know what to do. I would be glad spend my life as a doctor, and would be prepared to take a position somewhere or other, but I no longer have the financial flexibility to do so. When I write now, or think about having to write, I find it as revolting as having to eat cabbage soup from which a cockroach has just been removed – excuse the analogy. It is not so much the writing that disgusts me, as the literary 'entourage' from which you can never hide and which you inevitably carry about wherever you go, as the earth carries its atmosphere.

The weather is wonderful and I have no desire to go anywhere. I have to contribute a piece to the August issue of *Russian Thought*; it's already written, it just needs finishing off.[1] Keep well and happy. There's no room for my usual rat's tail, so you are getting a bob-tailed signature.

Your
A. Chekhov

237. To Alexey Suvorin, 24 August 1898, Melikhovo

Sytin offered not three but five thousand roubles for my comic stories. I was sorely tempted but in the end decided not to sell; my heart's not really in another book with a different title. I'm tired of bringing out a new book every year under a new title, and it's an

1. 'About Love'.

untidy way to proceed. Whatever Kolesov may say, sooner or later I will have to publish my stories in a series of volumes called simply: Volume I, Volume II, Volume III and so on – in other words, my collected works. That would be one way out of the difficulty, and it's what Tolstoy is advising me to do. The comic stories I have just collected would make up Volume I. And if you have no objection, I could settle down to edit the later volumes when autumn and winter are well and truly upon us and I have nothing else to do. My plan is strengthened by the thought that it would be much better for me to edit and publish my works than to leave it to my heirs. New volumes won't affect sales of the old ones which are still unsold, as they will eventually disappear by a process of attrition from the railway bookstalls – where, incidentally, there appears to be a stubborn resistance to stocking my books. The last time I travelled on the Nikolayevskaya line[1] I didn't see any of them on the shelves.

I'm building another new school, my third. My schools are considered models of their kind; I mention this so that you should not think I threw away your 200 roubles on rubbish. I'm not going to Tolstoy's on 28 August, first because the journey will be cold and damp, and secondly, what would be the point?[2] Tolstoy's life is one long jubilee, and there is no reason to single out any particular day. Thirdly, Menshikov came in to see me straight from Yasnaya Polyana, and said that Lev Nikolayevich was grumbling and grimacing at the very thought of wellwishers coming to congratulate him on 28 August; and fourthly, I don't want to go to Yasnaya Polyana because Sergeyenko will be there. I was at school with Sergeyenko; he was an amusing fellow then, a good sport and something of a wit, but now that he sees himself as a great writer and intimate of Tolstoy (whom by the way he completely wears out), he has turned into the world's most crashing bore. He frightens me, he's like a hearse stood up on end.

Menshikov said that Tolstoy and his family very much want me to go to Yasnaya Polyana, and will be offended if I don't. ('But not on the 28th, please,' added Menshikov.) But I can only repeat that the

1. The main railway line between St Petersburg and Moscow.
2. Tolstoy celebrated his seventieth birthday on 28 August 1898.

weather has got damp and very cold, and I have started coughing again. They tell me I am much better now, but at the same time everyone keeps trying to chase me away. I'll have to go south, I think; I'm rushing around at the moment trying to get everything done before I go, so I don't have time to think about Yasnaya Polyana, although really I should go for a couple of days. And I'd like to.

Here is my proposed itinerary: the Crimea and Sochi to start with, then, when it gets too cold to stay in Russia, I'll go abroad. The only place I feel any inclination to go to is Paris; warm climes don't attract me at all. I'm dreading this journey, because it feels as if I am going into exile.

I received a letter from Vladimir Nemirovich-Danchenko in Moscow. He's really getting on with things. There have already been almost 100 rehearsals, as well as lectures for the cast.[3]

If we do decide to go ahead with the publication of my stories in a series of volumes, we should meet and talk before I go away, and also, incidentally, dig some money out of your office.

Where is Alexey Kolomnin[4] at the moment? If he is in Petersburg, could you please ask him to send me the photographs he promised as soon as possible.

Be well and happy, and I wish you all the best.

Your

A. Chekhov

Send me a telegram about something. I love getting telegrams.

238. To Pavel Chekhov, 20 September 1898, Yalta

Dear Papa,

The trees will be coming from Riga. I have already asked for five apple trees to be given to Father Grigory, and the other five planted

---

3. A reference to the newly formed company of the Moscow Art Theatre, which had started rehearsing *The Seagull* in preparation for its production that autumn.
4. Alexey Kolomnin (1848–1900), the widower of Suvorin's deceased daughter, ran Suvorin's financial operation.

somewhere in the garden, near the cellar. Some Berlin poplars are also coming, and they should be planted to replace the ones that have died from lack of water. The larches should go in the appropriate place in the park. Remind Roman that the park must be ploughed before the frosts start. The ground underneath the apple trees in the orchard needs digging over as well before the frosts start, and the raspberries separated from the gooseberry bushes. The roses must be covered with leaves after the first frost. The dog roses and the wild roses don't need to be covered at all.

Tell Masha to send me, as well as the hat, a cheap luggage strap (Bon Marché), some shirt-front studs (five) and a long black tie (the kind that looks like a paper knife for cutting books and that is tied in a bow).

Roman should tell the postmaster not to send on the *thick* journals to me; the ordinary ones will be quite enough.

My address is the Bushev dacha, Yalta. It's summer weather here, quite warm. I have two rooms, nicely furnished, and there's a large garden. But it's nicer in Melikhovo.

When you write me letters, please enclose some seven-copeck stamps in them, and whenever you send a parcel could you also put in twenty-five pre-stamped three-copeck envelopes.

Tell Masha that she will shortly be receiving from Petersburg a payment from my theatre earnings. I'm donating it to the construction of the Melikhovo school.

What sort of weather are you having?

Deepest respects and greetings to Mamasha, Masha, Maryushka and everyone. Keep well and happy and do not forget your homesick wanderer.

Your

A. Chekhov

I hope that everything is well and peaceful with you up there, and that you are not having lunch later than half past eleven.

239. To Maria Chekhova, 13 October 1898, Yalta

Heavenly kingdom eternal rest to father sad deeply sorry write details health good do not worry take care of mother Anton

240. To Maria Chekhova, 14 October 1898, Yalta

Dearest Masha,

Sinani got your telegram yesterday, 13 October at 2 p.m. The telegram was not very clear: 'How has Anton Pavl. Chekhov taken the news of his father's death.' Sinani was embarrassed and thought he should keep the news from me. The whole of Yalta knew about Father's death, but no one informed me and it was only in the evening that Sinani showed me the telegram. I then went to the post office and it was there that I read Ivan's letter, which had just arrived, telling me about the operation. I am writing this on the evening of the 14th, but am still completely without news.

Whatever the circumstances, this sad news, utterly unexpected as it was, has deeply grieved and shaken me. I am sorry for Father and I am sorry for all of you; I am thinking all the time of the turmoil you had to go through in Moscow while I was living peacefully in Yalta, and the thought constantly oppresses me. How is Mother? Where is she? If she does not return to Melikhovo (and it will be hard for her there alone), where will you settle her? There are many questions to be decided. I deduce from your telegram to Sinani that you are worrying about my health. If you and Mother are really worried, why don't I come up for a short time to Moscow? Or perhaps Mother would like to come to me here in Yalta to have a rest? She can have a look at the place, and if she likes it we could settle here permanently. The weather is always warm, you never need an overcoat, and everyone says it is a very comfortable place to spend the winter. So we could winter here in Yalta and move back to Melikhovo in the summer or go to Küchük-Köy, which is not far from Yalta.

If Mamasha decides she would like to come, she should cable me and I will go to Sevastopol to meet her. I can take her straight from the station to Yalta by carriage.

The fast train is very comfortable. Mamasha would find a very warm welcome here and she would be well taken care of. If you could manage to take some leave and come as well, even for a week, that would be wonderful. Apart from anything else we could talk through plans for the future. I feel that life in Melikhovo will not be the same now Father has died, as though the course of life there ceased with his death.

Once again, I am perfectly well. Please write to me, don't leave me in the dark. I received the parcel.

I'll write again tomorrow. Keep well. Regards to Mamasha, Vanya and Sonya.

Your

Antoine

241. To Vladimir Nemirovich-Danchenko, 21 October 1898, Yalta

Dearest Vladimir Ivanovich,

I am in Yalta, and plan to stay here for some time yet. The trees and grass are as green as if it were summer, it is warm, calm and dry, and today, for instance, it is not so much warm as just plain hot. I like it very much, and may well find myself settling permanently in Yalta.

I was deeply touched by your telegram. My thanks to you and to Konstantin Sergeyevich [Stanislavsky] and to the artists for kindly remembering me. Generally speaking, please do not forget me and write to me, even if only once in a while. You are very busy now that you are a director, but I hope you will still find the time to write to an idle fellow occasionally. Tell me chapter and verse, how did the cast react to the success of the first performances, how is *The Seagull* doing, what cast changes have there been, and so on and so forth. Judging by the newspapers the first night was brilliant, and I am very, very happy about that, more so than you can imagine. Your success proves once again that audiences and actors alike need intelligent theatre. But why is nobody writing about Irina–Knipper? Is there a problem of some kind? I didn't like your Fyodor, but Irina was quite exceptional; these days, however, Fyodor is more talked about than Irina.[1]

I am already getting involved in public life here. I have been appointed to the governing body of the girls' Gymnasium, so when I make a grand descent of the school steps all the little girls in their white capes curtsy to me. The estate Sinani mentioned is lovely, a poetic and attractive place, but wild, more like Syria than the Crimea. It only costs two thousand, but I shan't buy it, because I don't have two thousand. If I sell Melikhovo I will buy it.

I'm looking forward to *Antigone*[2] – I say looking forward, because you promised to send it. I need it badly.

I'm also looking forward to seeing my sister, who has sent me a telegram saying she is coming to Yalta. Together we shall work out what to do next. Now my father has died, my mother is hardly likely to want to go on living in the country. We shall have to come up with some new ideas.

Regards and greetings to Ekaterina Nikolayevna, Roksanova, Knipper, and deepest respects to Vishnevsky. I remember them fondly. Please write. I warmly clasp your hand.

Your

A. Chekhov

1. Unlike the Petersburg première two years earlier, the Moscow Art Theatre production of *The Seagull* was a huge success from the first performance. Chekhov had attended rehearsals before leaving for Yalta, and had been particularly struck when attending rehearsals for another production, A. K. Tolstoy's *Tsar Fyodor*, by Olga Knipper, the young actress who played the part of Irina – but it would be another year before they became properly acquainted.
2. The Moscow Art Theatre was rehearsing Sophocles' tragedy in Dmitry Merezhkovsky's translation.

242. *To Mikhail Chekhov, 26 October 1898, Yalta*

Dearest Michel,

No sooner had I sent you my postcard than I received yours. I knew what you all had to go through during our father's funeral, and my heart was heavy indeed. It was only on the evening of the 13th that I found out from Sinani that Father had died; for some reason nobody had sent me a telegram, and if I had not happened to go into Sinani's shop I would not have known anything about it for a long time.

I am buying a piece of land in Yalta on which to build a house in order to have somewhere to live in the winter. The prospect of a permanently nomadic existence, staying in hotel rooms at the mercy of porters and irregular meals and so on and so forth, sends shivers down my spine. Mother could spend the winter here with me. There's no such thing as winter here; it's now the end of October and the roses and all the other flowers are still trying to outdo one another, the trees are green and it's warm. There is plenty of water. You don't need anything besides the house itself, no outbuildings; everything can come under one roof. Coal and wood stores, caretaker's quarters, etc., are all in the basement. Hens lay all year round, but you don't need a separate hen house to keep them in, just a little fence. There is a baker's shop and a market nearby. So Mother would be quite warm and comfortable. Another thing: all through the autumn you can pick chanterelles and saffron milk caps in the woods round about, and that would be something our mother would enjoy doing. I don't plan to do any of the building myself, an architect will take care of all that. The house will be finished by April. Considering it is in a town it is quite a big plot of land, with enough space for a garden, flowerbeds and a vegetable plot. The railway will come to Yalta next year.[1]

Küchük-Köy won't do for a permanent place to live: it is just a dacha, very nice but worth buying only because it is so nice and so cheap.

As for getting married, which you insist I do, well, what can I tell

---

1. There continues to be no rail connection with Yalta. In Chekhov's time, travellers went via Sevastopol, either by steamer or by carriage.

you? Marriage is interesting only if it is for love; marrying a girl just because she is nice is exactly like buying something you don't need in a bazaar simply because it is pretty. The most important ingredient in family life is love, sexual attraction, one flesh; everything else is flimsy and boring, however carefully we may have tried to calculate. So the point is not to look for a nice girl, but one you love. A trifling obstacle, I'm sure you'll agree.[2]

Nothing but sad events to report in Serpukhov district: Witte has had a stroke, Kovrein ditto,[3] Sidorov has died, Vasily Ivanovich (the book-keeper) has consumption.

Masha arrives tomorrow. We shall put our heads together and discuss everything properly; I'll let you know what we decide.

Prince Urusov, the lawyer, is here. He has interesting things to say. He also wants to buy land here. Soon there won't be so much as a scrap left in Yalta, everyone is in such a rush to buy. My being a writer helped me to buy my property. Because of it they sold the land to me cheaply and on credit.

Keep well and give my regards to Olga Germanovna and Zhenia. It's not difficult to protect yourself against typhoid fever: it isn't infectious; all you have to do is avoid drinking water unless it has been boiled.

My *Uncle Vanya* is being put on all over the provinces and is a success everywhere. You never know when things are going to turn out well or badly. I had absolutely no expectations from this play. Keep well, and write to me.

Your

A. Chekhov

It is very good that Father was buried in Novodevichy. I was going to telegraph you to suggest it, but then thought it would be too late; you divined my wishes.

1. Mikhail Chekhov had suggested his brother get married, at least in order to experience fatherhood, and was hoping he might choose among his female acquaintances either the teacher Natalia Lintvaryova or the artist Alexandra Khotyaintseva, with both of whom he got on well.
2. Ivan Witte and Ivan Kovrein were local *zemstvo* doctors.

Doctor Borodulin is here and sends you his regards. A clerk in the State Bank was asking after you, he also wanted me to send you his regards.

243. *To Elena Shavrova-Yust, 28 November 1898, Yalta*

Dear Colleague,

I have just been to see your sister and had tea with her. With bagels. There was an interesting doctor there as well. Life here is generally not too bad. The weather is very pleasant, warm and clear, and everything tastes delicious. Someone has just brought me a jar of honey.

All the same I am homesick for Moscow, very homesick; I want to be there now with the awful weather and the wonderful bustle that stops you noticing it. I want to be in Moscow to see all my good friends, like you for example; I want to go to the theatre, to restaurants . . . You'll agree to come to Serpukhov again and perform in aid of the school. You will, won't you? I'm having another school built (that makes it my third), and I'm putting my head into the noose for the two and a half thousand needed. We'd go and have supper at Serpukhov station after the performance, wouldn't we? . . . But alas! I shall not get to Moscow before April, in fact I won't even be going to Moscow but to the country, the back of beyond, to see to the building works.

How are things with you? Is your poisonous 'Asp' story finished yet? Send it to me, I'd like to read it. I have no books here, nothing to read, I'm turning to stone from boredom, so much so that I shall probably end up throwing myself off the mole into the sea or getting married. Your sister gave me Gnedich to read,[1] but it turned out I had already read these stories . . . Sinani has given me the Customs Tariff to read. I've nothing else to do, so I'm even reading that.

Forget that I'm a writer, write to me as a doctor, or better still as a

1. Pyotr Gnedich (1855–1925), a writer and playwright.

patient, and your conscience will lie easy. Do not suffer anguish thinking that your letters encroach on the great writer's precious time, because he is spending it lying all day on his bed staring at the ceiling or reading the Customs Tariff. I press your hand.

Your

Antoine

244. To Alexey Peshkov (Gorky), 3 December 1898, Yalta

Dear Alexey Maximovich,

Your last letter gave me much pleasure. Heartfelt thanks. *Uncle Vanya* was written a long time ago, a very long time ago; I have never seen it on the stage. In the past few years it has had a good many performances in the provinces, possibly because I published it in a complete edition of my plays. In general I am not now particularly warmly disposed towards my plays; I lost interest in the theatre some time ago and no longer have any desire to write for it.

You ask me for my opinion of your stories. What is my opinion? There is not the slightest doubt of your talent, it is a genuine, a major talent. It manifests itself, for example, with extraordinary strength in your story 'In the Steppe', so strongly that I even feel a touch of envy at not having written it myself. You are an artist and a highly intelligent man, you have extraordinary sensitivity and plasticity, by which I mean the way you describe things is such that one can see and touch them with one's hands. This is true art. There's my opinion for you, and I am very glad to be able to give it to you. I repeat, I am very glad, and if we could meet one another and talk for an hour or two you would realize how greatly I esteem you and what hopes I place on your gifts.

Shall I speak now of your shortcomings? That is more difficult. When it is a question of talent, analysing defects is like criticizing a great tree that grows in a garden; what matters is not the tree itself but the tastes of the person who is looking at the tree. Don't you agree?

I'll start by saying that in my opinion you show a lack of restraint.

You are like someone in a theatre audience expressing his delight in so exuberant a fashion that neither he nor anyone else can hear the play. This lack of restraint is most apparent in the descriptions of nature with which you intersperse your dialogues; reading them one wishes them shorter, more concise, two or three lines at the most. The frequent invocations of languor, murmurings, velvetiness and so on lend your descriptions a kind of rhetorical uniformity – this can become dispiriting and slightly wearing. There is also a lack of restraint in the way you depict women ('Malva', 'On the Rafts') and in the love scenes. It has nothing to do with the scale of your work or your broad brush strokes, it has everything to do with lack of restraint. And you are rather given to using words that strike one as out of place in the sort of stories you write. Words like 'accompaniment', 'disc', 'harmony'[1] are apt to jar. You make frequent references to waves. There is a feeling of tension, almost wariness, in the way you treat educated characters; this comes not from any lack of perception in your observation of educated people, because you do know them, but from an uncertainty about which direction you should approach them from.

How old are you? I don't know you or anything about you or where you come from, but I feel that while you are still young you should leave Nizhny and spend two or three years rubbing up against literature and literary people; not in order for the cockerel to learn how to crow still more loudly, but in order to dive head first, once and for all, into literature, and grow to love it; life in the provinces is also apt to age people quickly too. Korolenko, Potapenko, Mamin and Ertel are all outstanding people; you might find them a bit boring at first, but after a year or two, once you have got used to them, you will come to appreciate their true qualities, and their company will more than compensate for the disagreeable and inconvenient aspects of metropolitan life.

I am hastening to post this letter. Keep well and happy. I warmly clasp your hand. Thank you again for your letter.

Your

A. Chekhov

1. None of these words have Slavonic roots.

245. To Maria Chekhova, 8 December 1898, Yalta

Well my dear, I'll start with the news. It's good news, and quite a surprise. Don't jump to the conclusion that I want to get married and have proposed. I couldn't restrain myself, I've taken the plunge and gone and bought Küchük-Köy. I paid exactly two thousand for it and have already completed the deed of purchase, and when I go out there in a few days I'll already be the owner, taking a mattress and sheets with me. The house has four rooms, a Tatar-style annexe, a kitchen, a cow byre, a tobacco store, a spring with water straight from the cliff, a dray cart, a set of scales, a sideboard, a cupboard, two tables, a dozen bentwood chairs, a divan and a cast-iron stove. The land extends for three acres and takes in a vineyard, cliffs and a splendid view. The sea is marvellous, and there is sand. So as from today I am the proprietor of one of the most beautiful and interesting properties in the Crimea. We can keep a cow there, one horse, one donkey, some ducks and hens. Look back at the letter I wrote to you about Küchük-Köy last September. I paid cash for the property, so there is not a copeck of debt with it. The heavy millstone of debt I will have round my neck is entirely attributable to the dacha in town, it amounts to around ten thousand or a little under; the interest on this will be about 600–700 roubles a year, including capital repayments. The most attractive aspect of the new purchase is that the property doesn't need a penny spent on repairs, and the price was so low it was like something out of a fairy tale. But don't tell anyone about it just yet, apart from Vanya and Misha, and of course Mamasha, who will probably be very pleased with the property. She will find it exceptionally quiet, cosy and warm all the time, and also clean.

Work is progressing at Autka. I called on the highways chief today, and he told me they won't have to take so much as an inch of land from us when they widen the road, and they will put up a fence and supporting wall by the roadside at public expense. The local council has already approved the plans.

I sent a story to *The Week*;[1] the answer came today: they have sent me 500 roubles. It's hot again today.

So don't tell anyone about my new acquisition, because I am afraid it might get into the newspapers and be put about that I've bought an estate for a hundred thousand. There's no need for a caretaker at Küchük-Köy; I can simply lock it up and take the key with me; I shall need to buy a samovar and a set of crockery (plates and forks) for the new place; I can keep them here until someone goes out. There's no cellar, but you can keep milk in jugs immersed in cold spring water, in a little hole in the ground somewhere by the spring.

A very beautiful lady has just come to pay a call on my landlady. Well, keep well, and regards to all. If it upsets you that I have bought Küchük-Köy, don't worry too much about it, the money won't be lost; it can always be sold, and with a decent profit too, especially once the railway comes here.

The deed of purchase is being sent from Simferopol where it is being certified by a senior notary, and then I will send it on to you. Shapovalov is coming out with me to Küchük-Köy.

246. To Elena Shavrova-Yust, 26 December 1898, Yalta

Dear Colleague,

Both books – the lacerated blood of a troubled soul and the female nihilist – have arrived. The first gave me real pleasure, the second I had already read some time ago. I noticed that you wrapped *The Nihilist*[1] up in a sheet, then put it into a parcel which you sealed and covered all over with a thousand postage stamps – why such precautions? You could just have sent it by registered printed-matter rate.

We are still having lovely weather in Yalta.

They are writing from Moscow and banging all the drums about the big success *The Seagull* has had. But I'm generally not lucky

1. 'On Official Business'.
1. A novella by Sofya Kovalevskaya published in Geneva in 1892.

in the theatre, to such a catastrophic extent in fact, that inevitably one of the actresses fell ill after the first performance, and my *Seagull* has been taken off.

I am so unlucky in the theatre, so horribly unlucky, that were I ever to marry an actress I expect our child would be born an orang-utan or a porcupine.

Send me another book to read, and do write again.

Your

A. Chekhov

I forgot the most important thing: Happy New Year!!

247. To Alexey Peshkov, 3 January 1899, Yalta

Dear Alexey Maximovich,

I am replying straight away to two letters. First of all, let me send you my greetings for a happy New Year; I wish you much, much happiness, blessings old or new as you please.

It seems you did not fully understand me. When I wrote to you I was not referring to coarseness, but to the awkward way in which you sometimes employ obscure and foreign words, or at least words of non-Russian derivation. In other authors a word like 'fatalistic' would not grate, but your writing is so musical, so beautifully proportioned, that every tiny rough spot screams at you at the top of its voice. Naturally this is a matter of taste, and it may be that what I am expressing here is no more than the excessive irritability or conservatism of someone who long ago became set in his ways. I am reconciled to descriptions such as 'collegiate assessor' and 'captain of the second class', but I am very put off by words like 'flirtation' and 'champion' (when they appear in descriptions).

Are you self-taught? Your stories are the work of a complete artist and, in the true sense of the word, an educated man. Crudeness is the last thing to be found in your writing, you are clever, and you possess a refined and subtle sensitivity. 'In the Steppe' and 'On the Rafts' are your best things – did I tell you that before? They are outstanding pieces of writing, models of their kind, and they reveal an admirably schooled artist. I don't think I am wrong about this. Your only defect is your lack of restraint and grace. By grace I mean the practice of using the least possible number of movements to accomplish any given action. But what you do has a sense of excess.

Your nature descriptions are artistic; you are a true landscape painter. But your frequent use of personifications, when the sea breathes, the sky looks on, the steppe luxuriates, nature whispers, speaks or mourns, etc. – such anthropomorphisms tend to make your descriptions somewhat monochrome, sometimes cloying and sometimes obscure; the only way to achieve colour and expressivity in nature writing is by plain phrases such as 'the sun set', 'darkness fell', 'it started to rain', etc. – and you have this simplicity naturally, to a degree found in very few writers.

I did not care for the first issue of the revamped *Life*.[1] There was something not serious about it. Chirikov's story is naive and artificial, and Veresayev's is a crude imitation of something or other, perhaps Orlov, the husband in your story; it's a crude and naive sort of imitation too. No one is going to get far with stories like that. Although the general tone of your 'Kirilka' is well maintained, it is spoilt by the character of the land captain. Keep away from depicting land captains. Nothing is easier than to describe unsympathetic officialdom, and although there are readers who will lap it up, they are the most unpleasant and limited kind of reader. I find characters like land captains from our contemporary world as objectionable as [un-Russian] words like 'flirtation', although I may well be wrong for that very reason. But I have lived in the country myself, I know all the *zemstvo* bosses in my own and neighbouring districts, I've known them for a long time, and I find their personalities and their activities quite untypical and deeply uninteresting – and I'm right on this point, I think.

Now a word about living the life of a vagrant. It – vagrancy I mean – is a fine and seductive thing, but as the years go by one gets less agile and more rooted to one spot. Moreover the literary profession will of its very nature suck you in. Failures and disappointments make

1. A literary and political journal published in St Petersburg, 1897–1901.

time fly past quickly, so you don't notice real life, and I now think of my own past, when I was so free, as no longer mine but belonging to someone else.

The post has arrived and I must read the letters and newspapers. Be well and happy. Thank you for your letters and for making our correspondence fall so easily into a rhythm.

I warmly clasp your hand.

Your

A. Chekhov

248. To Vladimir Nemirovich-Danchenko, 29 January 1899, Yalta

Dearest Vladimir Ivanovich,

Sometime in the next few days, an army officer called Andrey Nikolayevich Leskov, the son of the writer, will come to the theatre and introduce himself to you. He wants to resign from the army, dreams of a stage career and now wishes to ask your advice. He is a very cultivated, highly strung young man with excellent manners, adaptable, he speaks well, and strikes me generally as having many fine qualities that far outweigh such shortcomings as his small stature and slightly nasal voice. Please spare him ten minutes, and lend a sympathetic ear.

This is what Yust writes: '*The Seagull* is going even better and more smoothly than at the second performance, although Stanislavsky overdoes his portrayal of Trigorin as a writer who has already grown feeble, both physically and morally, while the Seagull herself (*j'en conviens*) could be a touch more beautiful in the last act. But on the other hand Arkadina, Treplev, Masha, Sorin, the teacher (his linen suit is a triumph in itself), and the estate manager are all magnificent, real, living people . . .' See what sort of reviews I get.

There is a big change coming in my life: I've been negotiating with Marx, the negotiations now seem to have come to an end, and I feel as though I have finally, after a long delay, been granted a divorce by

CHEKHOV: A LIFE IN LETTERS

the Holy Synod. No more printers to deal with! No more formats or prices to think about, no new book titles to dream up![1]

Moscow is not replying to letters, even though I have written hundreds of them. I don't know what to do! Even the banks in Moscow don't reply, not to mention Nikolay Efros,[2] whose treatment of me is nothing short of disgraceful.

What a kindness it would be if the whole cast of *The Seagull* could arrange to have their photograph taken, in costume and make-up, and sent to me!

I'm bored here.

Well, keep well and happy. My best respects to Ekaterina Nikolayevna.

Your

A. Chekhov

249. To Maria Chekhova, 4 February 1899, Yalta

Dearest Masha,

When I was writing to you about the piano, what was in my mind was this: we should start thinking now, during the winter while you are in Moscow and I am in Yalta, about what we shall need in the Crimea, so that we don't have to do everything in a great rush once summer comes. The piano can stay at Ilovaiskaya's for the time being, and incidentally then people could play to me here. But you decide. It's not the most important thing.

The house will have a parquet floor upstairs, and the whole building has been slightly enlarged, so that Mamasha's room and the dining

1. Chekhov had just signed a contract with the German-born Petersburg publisher Adolf Marx, giving him the rights to produce a multi-volume edition of his collected works in return for 75,000 roubles – an astronomical sum at that time, but one which quickly proved to be highly disadvantageous to the author. Marx earned his money back in a year and then started to make a profit on Chekhov.

2. Nikolay Efros (1867–1923), a journalist, theatrical figure and editor of a Moscow journal called *The Family*; he had neglected to send Chekhov the issue of the journal which contained his story 'The Darling', and had not replied to his letters.

room will be about two and a half feet longer and wider, perhaps a little more than that. There will be a complete flat downstairs. Should your tower have a parquet floor?[1]

I have signed with Marx, and the deal is done, so Sergeyenko can talk about it as much as he likes and wherever he likes. Now everything has been settled it's no longer a secret. I shall receive 75,000, not all at once but in several instalments extending over almost two years, so that I can be quite confident of not running through the money in two years. This is how I have calculated it: 25,000 to clear all the debts, cover the building costs and so on; and 50,000 to go into the bank, which will produce 2,000 a year in interest.

In one of my recent letters I asked whether the Darskys[2] would agree to play Marina and the Pretender in Yalta on the second and third day after Easter as part of the Pushkin celebrations.[3] I've had no reply as yet. The suggestion arose because I heard that Olga Mikhailovna [Darskaya] was planning to come to the Crimea for a cure in the spring.

Has that young army officer Leskov been to see you? Or Menshikov, who is in Moscow at present?

I read in *The Courier* that Stanislavsky is playing Trigorin as a rather weak character. What sort of idiocy is this? After all, Trigorin is a person people are attracted to, they like him, in other words he's interesting, so deciding to play him as a weak, listless character is something only a pedestrian actor with no imagination would do.

Ye Gods, how drab society is here, and how uninteresting the people are! No, I could never think of permanently severing connections with Moscow! Keep well, and best respects to Mamasha.

Your

Antoine

1. Masha's room was all on its own on the top floor of the house, and so resembled a tower.
2. Mikhail Darsky (1865–1930) and his wife Olga Darskaya, née Shavrova (1875–after 1941), were both actors.
3. 1899 marked the centenary of Pushkin's birth, a date celebrated all over Russia. Chekhov was on the committee for events in Yalta, where a production of Pushkin's play *Boris Godunov* was planned.

People have written to tell me that Lev Tolstoy has been doing very good and very funny readings of my story 'The Darling', which was published in *The Family*.

What a marvellous place Küchük-Köy is! The house is un-locked, the owners are away, there's no caretaker. No overhead costs at all.

I'll send *Fashions*.

Korsh's girl borrowed 100 roubles from me here. Fyodor Korsh, her father, will send this money to you at Dmitrovka. It can go towards the March 200 roubles, for you and Mamasha's provisions.

250. To Ivan Orlov, 22 February 1899, Yalta

Greetings, my dear Ivan Ivanovich!

Our friend Krutovsky[1] came to see me and we talked about France and Panama, but I did not manage to introduce him to my Yalta friends because as soon as he had talked his fill of politics he went off to see the charming organ-grinders;[2] that was yesterday, and today he is in Gurzuf.

I have sold everything to Marx, my past and my future, so now I'm going to be a Marxist for the rest of my life. He will pay me 5,000 roubles for every twenty printed sheets of previously published prose; in five years I shall get 7,000 and so on, similar sums being added every five years so that when I am ninety-five I shall be worth tons and tons of money. For the total of everything I have already written I will get 75,000. I managed to beat him down over the income from my plays, which I and my heirs will continue to receive. Even so – alas – I am far from being a Vanderbilt. Twenty-five thousand has already gone bye-byes, and I don't get the balance right away but over two years, so I can't really go on the spree just yet.

1. Vsevolod Krutovsky, a horticulturalist friend of Orlov.
2. Chekhov's punning nickname for the family of his neighbour, the writer Sergey Elpatievsky.

There is no particular news. I'm writing very little. Next season my play [*Uncle Vanya*], which has not yet been performed in either capital,[3] will be produced at the Maly Theatre, so as you see that will bring in a bit. Work has hardly started yet on the house I am building at Autka, owing to the wet weather we had almost continually throughout January and February. I shall have to leave before the building work is finished. My mayonnaise (as Pastukhov, the publisher of *The Moscow Rag*, calls the *mayorat*) in Küchük-Köy is an enchanting place but almost impossible to get to. My dream is to build a cottage there, cheaply but in the European style, so that one can spend time there in the winter as well. It's only possible to stay in the present two-storey cottage during the summer.

My telegram about Devil's Island was not intended for publication: it was a strictly private telegram. It has provoked much indignant grumbling in Yalta. One longstanding resident here, Kondakov, a member of the Academy, said to me, referring to the telegram: 'I'm annoyed and offended.'

'What about?' I asked in astonishment.

'I'm annoyed and offended at not having written it myself.'

And, certainly, Yalta in winter is notorious for being a place not everyone can survive. Tedium, gossip, intrigues and shameless slanders. Altshuller is having a hard time settling in here; he is the subject of furious gossip among our esteemed friends.

Your letter quotes from the Scriptures. In reply to your complaints about the governor and the various setbacks you have encountered, let me offer another text: 'Put not your trust in princes, nor in the son of man . . .'[4] And let me also remind you of another expression relating to the sons of men, the same who are so gravely interfering in your life: 'the sons of our age'. It's not the governor who is to blame, but the entire intelligentsia, all of it, my dear sir, without exception. While the young people of our country are still students, they are honest and good people, they represent our hopes and the future of Russia, but

---

3. Moscow was still referred to as being one of the capitals of Russia, despite having been replaced by St Petersburg in 1712.
4. Psalm 146, verse 3.

the moment they become adults and set out on their own independent path, our hopes and the future of Russia vanish in a puff of smoke, leaving nothing behind on the filter but dacha-owning doctors, greedy functionaries and thieving engineers. Don't forget that Katkov, Pobedonostsev, Vishnegradsky are university men; far from being ignorant louts they're highly educated people, our professors and luminaries . . . I have no faith in our intelligentsia, which is hypocritical, false, hysterical, ill-educated and idle, and I have no faith in it even when it suffers and complains, because its oppressors spring from its own bowels. My faith is in individual people, and I see our salvation in individual personalities scattered all over Russia, whether educated people or peasants, that is where our strength lies although there are few enough of them. No prophet is accepted in his own country;[5] and the people I am referring to are not prominent; they do not dominate our society, but their work is nevertheless visible. In any case, science always moves forward, social awareness increases, moral questions begin to assume troubling characteristics, and so on and so forth – and all of this is happening independently of public prosecutors, engineers or governors, independently indeed of the intelligentsia en masse and in spite of everything.

How is I. G. Witte? Kovrein is here, and has found a nice place to live. Koltsov is feeling a little better. I press your hand. Keep well, happy and in good spirits. Please write!

Your

A. Chekhov

251. To Maria Chekhova, 10 March 1899, Yalta

I'm replying to your latest letter, dearest Masha. If the only houses for sale are wooden ones, and if it is healthier to live in a wooden house, then by all means go ahead and buy a wooden house, only on condition that it doesn't look like an inn, is as respectable looking as

5. Incorrect quotation of Luke 4, verse 24.

possible and isn't painted green. The only reason I mentioned stone when I wrote was because I was thinking of fire, which is a common hazard in Moscow. If you do buy a house, buy some furniture as well, although not too much. I need only two rooms – a study and a bedroom.

I shall come first to Moscow, and then, when it's a bit warmer and not so muddy, go on to Melikhovo. Then at the end of May I shall come back to Yalta to take care of the building work, and then go back again to Melikhovo. The contractor says the house will be finished long before August.

Write and tell me about the weather. When spring arrives and it starts getting warm in Moscow, I'll come without waiting for specific permission. So please write every three days telling me what the weather is like.

Don't send the telegrams I wrote to you about, as I have cancelled my participation in the Pushkin celebrations.

We've already done some planting on the plot where the house is being built; Mustafa the Turk, a reliable person, will look after it while I am away.

You are worried about the fact that I'm not going to receive all the money in the first instance, so it won't be available to increase our capital. But in the first place increasing the capital was not something I particularly had in mind, and secondly at the end of the year I shall be getting a further 30,000, which we will then be able to put to use. And winter is not so far off.

In Yalta the trees are already starting to blossom. Every day I go out driving in a carriage, I do it all the time. I had allowed myself 300 roubles for cabs, and so far I have not managed to spend so much as 20, but even so I can claim to have been for a lot of drives. I often go to Oreanda and Massandra. My most regular companion is a priest's daughter, as a result of which tongues are wagging and the priest is making inquiries about what sort of a person I am. I went to a party yesterday evening. My intestines are inflamed again and I have lost a bit of weight. Napoleon suffered from exactly the same intestinal catarrh, which during battles led him to hear reports from his aides and issue orders from a highly indecorous position.

1,388 roubles is certainly very little. My respects to Mamasha. I'm doing nothing and writing nothing except letters. Once I get to Melikhovo I'll do some writing.

Your

Antoine

Where shall I be staying in Moscow?

252. To Alexey Peshkov, 25 April 1899, Moscow

No word from you, my dearest Alexey Maximovich. Where have you disappeared to? What are you up to? Where are you planning to go?

I went to see Lev Tolstoy the day before yesterday.[1] He was full of praise for you, and said you were a 'splendid writer'. He likes your 'The Fair' and 'In the Steppe', but not 'Malva'. He said: 'One may invent anything one wishes, but one may not invent psychology, and that is precisely what one finds in Gorky: psychological inventions to describe things he has not himself felt.' So there you have it. I said we would go and visit him together when you are in Moscow.

When will you come to Moscow? On Thursday my *Seagull* will have a closed performance for my benefit, and if you are able to come I will give you a ticket. My address is: The Sheshkov House, Apartment 14 (entrance on Degtyarny Lane), Malaya Dmitrovka, Moscow. After 1 May I shall go to the country, where my address is Lopasnya, Moscow Province.

I am receiving mournful and vaguely conscience-stricken letters from Petersburg, and find it hard to know how to answer them, or indeed how to react in general.[2] Yes, life certainly has its complications when it is not a psychological invention.

Do send me a few lines. Tolstoy asked a great many questions about you; you have aroused his curiosity. He's obviously moved by you.

1. Tolstoy was staying nearby in Gaspra.
2. A reference to letters from Suvorin.

Keep well. I press your hand. My regards to your little Maxim.

Your

A. Chekhov

253. *To Mikhail Menshikov, 27 April 1899, Moscow*

Dear Mikhail Osipovich,

Here is my address: The Sheshkov House, Malaya Dmitrovka, Moscow. Or you can just put Dmitrovka, Moscow.

Lev Tolstoy came and visited me, but we did not manage to have a proper conversation as there were all sorts of other people here, among them two actors unshakeably convinced that nothing in the world could possibly be as important as the theatre. The following day I went to Tolstoy's and had lunch there. Tatyana Lvovna[1] had called on us before dinner, at a time when my sister happened not to be at home. Tatyana Lvovna said: 'Mikhail Osipovich has written suggesting I get to know your sister. He said we would have much to learn from one another.'

When I returned home after lunch, I passed this on to my sister. She was appalled, waved her arms about and cried: 'No, nothing would induce me to go there! Nothing in the world!'

My sister was so terrified by the idea that Tatyana Lvovna might have something to learn from her that to this day I have not succeeded in persuading her to call on her, and I'm feeling awkward about it. And as if on purpose, my sister has been out of sorts the whole time; she's been tired and depressed, and the mood at home has been generally dispiriting.

When I was sending a telegram from the telegraph office today and the telegraphist, a stout and rather breathless woman, saw my signature, she asked me: 'Are you Anton Pavlovich?' It turned out that I had treated her and her mother fifteen years ago. Joy unconfined! But

---

1. Tolstoy's daughter.

how old I am now! I've been a doctor for fifteen years already, and I'm still wanting to run after young ladies.

I expect still to be in Moscow between 1 and 3 May.

I'll send a story to *The Week* once I finally get to the country. I have plenty of subjects, but not the peace and quiet I need.

I warmly clasp your hand. Keep well and happy.

Your

A. Chekhov

Please write.

254. *To Olga Knipper, 16 June 1899, Melikhovo*[1]

What can this mean? Where are you? So stubborn is your refusal to give us any news of yourself that we are completely befogged and already beginning to think you must have forgotten us and got married down there in the Caucasus. If you really have got married, to whom? You haven't decided to give up the theatre, have you?

The writer is forgotten — oh how dreadful, how cruel, how treacherous!

Everyone sends you greetings. There is no news. There aren't even any flies. Nothing at all. Even the calves are not biting.

I had meant to come and see you off at the station, but fortunately was prevented by the rain.

I had my photograph taken twice when I was in Petersburg. I almost froze to death there. I shan't be going to Yalta before the beginning of June.

With your permission I warmly clasp your hand and send you my best wishes.

Your

A. Chekhov

Lopasnya, Moscow Province

1. This was Chekhov's first letter to the woman who would later become his wife.

255. *To Alexey Suvorin, 26 June 1899, Moscow*

I received two letters from you, neither of which had your country address. I wanted to write to you in Skuratovo, but wasn't sure of the address; I tried to find out, wrote to Konstantin Semyonovich, and then finally today I went into your shop – so now at last I am writing to you.

First of all, about the school plans. I have now overseen the building of three schools, and they are considered models of their kind. They are built of the best materials, the rooms are 12 feet high, they have Dutch stoves, the teacher has a fireplace and the teacher's apartment is a decent size – three to four rooms. The first two schools cost 3,000 apiece; the third is a bit smaller and cost just over 2,000. I'll get someone to take photographs and will send you the front elevation of all three, and I'll also send you the plans with all the dimensions marked on them. These, by the way, are not arbitrary, but are based on the requirements of the provincial *zemstvo*. But don't build this year; wait until next summer.

You are not mistaken, we are indeed selling our Melikhovo. After the death of my father we don't want to go on living there any more, its appeal seems have faded and become tarnished; and furthermore my own situation is uncertain: I don't know where I should live, who I am, what my profession is, and since I must spend the winters in the Crimea or abroad, it follows that I no longer need an estate, and I can't afford the luxury of owning one and not living on it. And from a literary point of view Melikhovo's usefulness was exhausted after 'Peasants', and held no further value for me.

Some prospective purchasers are coming to look at the place; I would be happy if someone were to buy it, but if nobody does then I'll close it up for the winter.

For the time being I am in Moscow. I go to the Aquarium,[1] watch the acrobats and talk to the fallen women. I was in Petersburg, but not for long. It was bitterly cold and I didn't even stay the night: I arrived on Friday and left on Friday. I did see Alexey Petrovich [Kolomnin].

1. Nightclub established in a Moscow garden by Charles Aumont.

My health is tolerable, almost good. If I were allowed to stay in Moscow for the winter I would probably start up some comercial (with one 'm') enterprise or other. For instance, I could open a bookstore exclusively for out-of-town customers, that is to say not a retail shop but a mail-order business, with one employee who would incidentally also have the job of cleaning my shoes. But alas, I am not permitted to stay in Moscow, they'll insist on packing me off to the sticks again.

I shall be going back to the country in two or three days' time, but don't send letters to Lopasnya, address them to me at the Sheshkov House, Malaya Dmitrovka, Moscow. There is always somebody staying here, so letters won't lie around unattended to.

Warm greetings and my best wishes to Anna Ivanovna, Nastya and Borya. I should love to come and see you, but I don't know when I shall be able to tear myself away to do so – perhaps in July, or later.

Keep well, peaceful, and cheerful.

Your

A. Chekhov

256. To Olga Knipper, 1 July 1899, Moscow

Yes, you are correct: the writer Chekhov has not forgotten the actress Knipper. Moreover, your proposal to travel from Batum to Yalta together strikes him as most enticing. I will come, but on the following conditions: one, immediately on receipt of this letter you are to send me, without a delay of so much as one minute, a telegram stating the approximate date on which you intend to leave Mtskhet, exactly as follows: 'To Chekhov, Sheshkov House, Malaya Dmitrovka, Moscow. Twentieth.' This shall signify that you will leave Mtskhet for Batum on 20 July. Two, I go straight to Batum and meet you there, without going to Tiflis. And three, you are to refrain from completely turning my head. Vishnevsky regards me as a very serious person, and I do not wish him to see that I am as weak as everyone else.

The instant I receive your telegram I shall write back to you – and all will be splendid, but in the meantime I send you a thousand cordial wishes and warmly press your hand. Thank you for your letter.

Your

A. Chekhov

We are selling Melikhovo. People tell me that now the summer has come my Crimean property at Küchük-Köy is sensational. You absolutely must come and spend some time there.

I was in Petersburg, and had my photograph taken twice. The pictures came out quite well. Prints are on sale priced at one rouble apiece, and I have already sent five to Vishnevsky, cash on delivery.

Better still for me would be if you were to cable me 'fifteenth', but in no circumstances may it be later than 'twentieth'.

257. To Maria Chekhova, 29 August 1899, Yalta

Dearest Masha,

Here is the latest state of affairs. The kitchen is already finished, and Maryushka's room as well. The parquet in your room is in the process of being laid; they were proposing to hang the wallpaper but I did not let them, telling them to wait for you to get here. My room and Mamasha's room will be completely ready by 1 September, which means the floors will be laid, the walls will be papered and the windows will have shutters. One room downstairs is being fixed up for Kurkin.[1] At the moment I am living in the annexe, and have made myself quite comfortable there. It's crammed full of stuff, however, and your cupboard has proved very useful for keeping my linen in.

Everything arrived in good shape. The table linen is all here and undamaged, and there are plenty of sheets. The cupboard arrived safely.

1. Ivan Kurkin, the *zemstvo* doctor Chekhov had got to know while living at Melikhovo (and possible inspiration for the character of Dr Astrov in *Uncle Vanya*), came to stay that autumn.

They won't touch the walls in the front hall either until you get here; the only rooms that will be wallpapered will be mine and Mamasha's. The workmen are racing to get the Waterproof[2] finished. The water in the well is fine.

We can get *News of the Day* and *The Russian Gazette* here, but not *The Courier*.

Do bear in mind that there will be a lot of people travelling on the train and on the steamer. When you get to Sevastopol, don't wait for the luggage to be brought out, but get hold of a cab straight away and then sit and wait in it. This is what all experienced travellers do to make sure of getting a cab. It will cost 75 copecks to get to the jetty with the luggage. One cab will be enough for you, as they are two-horse four-seaters. I will meet you at the jetty and Mustafa will look after the luggage.

I dined at the girls' Gymnasium yesterday. The atmosphere there is awash with gloom and despondency because the archpriest, the father of my friend, has denounced the chaplain who teaches religion in the school, as a result of which he has been sacked. All Yalta is in shock, and has reacted by ostracizing the archpriest and his daughter.

I'm writing this letter in the morning, after coffee. The spirit stove works very well. A bottle of milk costs 10 copecks, they sell it just round the corner.

The garden is not particularly extensive, but we'll find somewhere to keep hens.

I've left myself without money until December, so will have to borrow some.

Our land is good for growing clover. If you have time, please bring a pound [of seed] with you, and the same amount of timothy grass and lucerne [alfalfa].

I joined the 'Consumers' Society' yesterday, an organization with its own shop where you can buy groceries and drink; I bought fifty shares in it. Now all our goods can be delivered straight to the door. In the next few days I shall have a telephone installed.

Please tell Olga Leonardovna that her plant sends her his regards:

2. WC.

he arrived safely and is already sitting in the garden under the pear tree. I gave the chocolate hen to one of the girls at the school.

Upon which, I trust you are keeping well. Regards to Mamasha. I am in good health.

Your

Antoine

258. To Olga Knipper, 3 September 1899, Yalta

Dearest Actress, let me answer all your questions. I arrived safely. My travelling companions let me have the lower berth, and it then worked out that there were only two of us, me and a young Armenian. I drank tea several times a day, three glasses, with lemon each time, calmly and without rushing. I ate everything in the basket. But I found it rather undignified to have to fuss about in stations with my basket in search of hot water – a bit demeaning to the prestige of the Art Theatre. It was cold until we got as far as Kursk, but then it grew warmer and by the time we reached Sevastopol it was quite hot. In Yalta I was able to move into my own house, and I am now living there under the protection of the faithful Mustafa. I don't have lunch every day as it is quite a long way to go into town, and fiddling about with a kerosene stove also threatens to demean my prestige. In the evenings I eat cheese. I see quite a lot of Sinani, and I have already been twice to visit the Sredins; they studied your photograph with great emotion and ate all the sweets. Leonid Valentinovich is not feeling too bad. I don't drink the Narzan water.[1] What else have I to tell you? I seldom go to the [municipal] garden, but spend most of the time sitting at home thinking of you. When I passed Bakhchisarai I thought of you and remembered our travels together. My dear, remarkable actress and wonderful woman, if only you knew how much joy your letter brought me. I bow down low, low before you, so low that my forehead touches the bottom of my well, which has already been

1. Sparkling mineral water from Kislovodsk.

dug to a depth of 32 feet. I have got used to you and miss you, and cannot now bear the thought of not seeing you until the spring; I'm in a bad temper, in a word, and were Nadenka to find out what is happening to my heart, there would be quite a to-do.

The weather in Yalta is marvellous, except that for some unknown reason it has been raining for the past two days, making everything very muddy and obliging me to wear my galoshes. The walls are so damp there are centipedes crawling all over them, and frogs and young crocodiles leap about the garden. The green reptile in the flowerpot that you gave me, which I managed to convey here successfully, is now sitting in the garden warming itself in the sunshine.

A naval squadron has arrived in port. I've been watching it through binoculars.

There is an operetta in the theatre; performing fleas continue to serve the sacred cause of art. I have no money. Guests come often. Generally speaking it is boring, and it is an idle, pointless boredom.

Well, I warmly take your hand in mine and kiss it. Be well, cheerful, happy, work, leap about, enjoy yourself, sing and, if possible, do not forget the part-time writer and your devoted admirer

A. Chekhov

259. To Olga Knipper, 29 September 1899, Yalta

I received your admirably sensible letter with a kiss on the right temple, and your other letter with the photographs. Thank you, dearest actress, I am terribly grateful. Tonight is your first night,[1] and so in grateful recompense for your letter and for remembering me I send you my congratulations and a million good wishes for the opening of the season. I wanted to send a cable to the directors of the theatre with good wishes for everyone, but since nobody has written to me, because obviously I have been forgotten about and haven't even been sent the annual report (which was published recently according to the

1. The first night of the Moscow Art Theatre's second season.

newspapers), and since it's the same old Roksanova[2] playing the Seagull, I thought the best thing would be to pretend I had taken offence – hence my good wishes are for you alone.

It has been raining here, but the weather has cleared up now and it has turned cool. There was a fire in the town last night, and I got up and watched it from the verandah, feeling terribly lonely.

We are now living in the house and dining in the dining room; we even have a piano.

I have no money, not a penny, and all I can do is dodge my creditors. This state of affairs will continue until the middle of December, when Marx will send me a remittance.

I want to write something else sensible to you, but can't think of anything suitable. After all, I have no season just getting under way, there is nothing new or interesting in my life; everything is as it was. And I have nothing to look forward to except the weather getting worse, which is predicted to be just around the corner.

Ivanov and *Uncle Vanya* are on at the Alexandrinsky Theatre.

Keep well, my dear actress, magnificent woman, and may God keep you. I kiss both your hands and bow down to your feet. Do not forget your

A. Chekhov

260. *To Moscow Art Theatre, 1 October 1899, Yalta*

Eternally grateful send congratulations and good wishes bottom of my heart we will work conscientiously gladly tirelessly with one mind to ensure this splendid beginning serves as token of further achievements so that life of theatre will mark brilliant period in history of Russian art and all our lives trust in my sincerest friendship

Chekhov

2. Maria Roksanova (1874–1958), an actress at the Moscow Art Theatre (1898–1902) who played the role of Nina in *The Seagull*.

261. To Grigory Rossolimo, 11 October 1899, Yalta

Dear Grigory Ivanovich,

Today I sent Dr Raltsevich eight roubles and 50 copecks for the photograph, and five roubles for the annual subscription. I am sending a photograph of myself by registered post to your address, but it's not a very good one (it was taken when a bout of enteritis was playing havoc with me). My autobiography? I suffer from an affliction known as autobiographophobia. Being forced to read, let alone write, any details about myself is the purest torture. I have put down a few bare dates on a separate sheet of paper to send you, but that's the best I can do. If you wish, you may add that my letter of application to the Rector seeking admission to the University contained the statement that the faculty I desired to enter was the Faculty of Medicine.

You ask when we might see one another. This cannot be before the spring. I have been exiled to Yalta, a splendid exile perhaps, but still exile. Life passes tediously here. I am in reasonably good health, but only on some days. As well as everything else I suffer from haemorrhoids and rectal catarrh, and there are some days when the frequent calls of nature completely exhaust me. I'll have to have an operation.

I was very sorry not to be at the dinner and to miss the chance of seeing my colleagues. A Mutual Aid Society for alumni of our course would be a good development, but it would be a more practical and more achievable idea to set up a mutual aid fund similar to our literary fund. The fund would pay benefits to the family of any member who dies, and fresh subscriptions would only be sought after a member's death.

Might you consider coming to the Crimea in the summer or autumn? It's a good place for a holiday. The south coast has become a favoured destination for *zemstvo* doctors from Moscow province, by the way. They find the accommodation here comfortable and good value, and are always delighted with their stay by the time they leave.

If anything of interest happens, please write and tell me about it. I am truly bored here, and if I don't get any letters I may hang myself, learn to drink bad Crimean wine or take up with an ugly and stupid woman.

Keep well, I firmly press your hand and send my very warmest wishes to you and your family.

Your

A. Chekhov

[attached to letter to Grigory Rossolimo]

I, A. P. Chekhov, was born on 17 January 1860 in Taganrog. I was first educated at the Greek school attached to the Church of the Emperor Constantine, and later at the Taganrog Gymnasium. In 1879 I entered the Medical School of Moscow University. At the time I had only a vague knowledge of the University's different faculties, and I do not remember why I chose medicine, but I have had no subsequent regrets. I began publishing in weekly journals and newspapers during my first year, and by the beginning of the 1880s these literary activities had assumed a permanent, professional character. In 1888 I was awarded the Pushkin Prize. In 1890 I travelled to Sakhalin Island in order to write a book about our penal and hard-labour colony there. In addition to court reporting, reviews, articles of various kinds, news reports and everything written on a daily basis for newspapers that would now be difficult to trace and collect, I have in my twenty years of literary activity produced more than 4,800 pages of novellas and stories. I have also written plays.

I have no doubt that my involvement in medical science has had a strong influence on my literary activities; it significantly enlarged the scope of my observations and enriched me with knowledge whose true worth to a writer can be evaluated only by somebody who is himself a doctor; it has also provided me with a sense of direction, and I am sure that my closeness to medicine has also enabled me to avoid many mistakes. My knowledge of the natural sciences and the scientific method has always caused me to err on the side of caution, trying wherever possible to take scientific facts into consideration, and where this has not been possible preferring not to write at all. I should state incidentally that one of the conditions of creative art is that it cannot always accord completely with scientific facts; a death from poisoning cannot be portrayed on stage exactly as it occurs in reality. But even within the conventions there should always be a sense of correspondence with the facts, by which I mean that the reader or spectator should clearly be aware that it is a convention, and that the author genuinely knows what he is about.

I cannot be included among those writers who are hostile to science; neither would I wish to be counted among those who rely exclusively on their own wits to arrive at their conclusions.

As for practical experience as a doctor, when still a student I worked under the well-known *zemstvo* doctor Pavel Arkhangelsky at the Voskresensk Zemstvo Hospital (near the New Jerusalem Monastery), and later briefly as a doctor in the Zvenigorod Hospital. During the cholera epidemic of 1892–3 I was in charge of the Melikhovo section of Serpukhov district.

262. To Olga Knipper, 30 October 1899, Yalta

Dearest actress and best of friends, you ask if I'm excited. But in fact it was only when I received your letter on the 27th that I found out about the performance of *Uncle Vanya* that had taken place on the 26th. The telegrams started coming on the evening of the 27th, when I was already in bed. They read them to me over the telephone. They woke me up each time, and I had to dash over to the telephone in the dark, barefoot and freezing cold; then hardly would I get off to sleep again than there would be another ring, and then another. This is the first time in my life that my own fame has kept me from sleeping. Next day, when I went to bed, I put slippers and a dressing gown next to the bed, but by then there were no more telegrams.

The telegrams made no mention of anything except curtain calls and brilliant success, but I thought I could detect in them the slightest, subtlest hint of something which led me to suspect that the mood among you was not quite so universally sunny. This morning's news-papers confirmed my intuition. Yes, my actress, all you Art Theatre players are no longer satisfied by an ordinary, average success, you need a sensation, a twenty-one-gun salute, an explosion of dynamite. Ultimately you are spoiled, you have become so deafened by the talk of constant success, capacity or near-capacity box-office receipts, that you are already addicted to this drug, and in two or three years you will no longer be fit for anything. So there!

How are you, how are you feeling? I'm just the same, in the same old place; I've been doing some work and I've planted some trees.

But visitors arrived and stopped me writing. They sat for more than an hour and then they wanted tea, so we had to get the samovar going. Oh, what a bore!

Don't forget me, and don't let your friendship flicker out, so that we can go somewhere together again in the summer. Farewell, till we meet again! I suppose this will not be before April. If you were all to come to Yalta in the spring you could perform here and then have a holiday. That would be an amazingly artistic thing to do.

One of my visitors will take this letter and post it.

I firmly clasp your hand. Best respects to Anna Ivanovna and your military uncle.[1]

Your

A. Chekhov

Write to me, actress, in the name of all that's holy, otherwise I shall be bored. I feel as though I'm in prison and full of rage, terrible rage.

263. To Maria Chekhova, 8 November 1899, Yalta

Dearest Masha,

Everything is fine, there's no news. They've finally put the railings up on the fence; I was expecting them to look hideous but actually

1. Anna Ivanovna, Olga Knipper's mother. Her Uncle Sasha, Alexander Zaltsa, served in the army.

they are all right. The downstairs room is still not finished, the joiners are still messing about doing something or other. The balcony isn't finished either. There's been a tremendous amount of planting done in the garden; you won't recognize it. Stone pillars with two rows of barbed wire strung between them have been put up along the fence separating us from the neighbours and from the Tatar cemetery. We've been sent a barrel of pickled watermelons from Taganrog. That's all.

I got the pillow with lace trimmings. The lace has all been ripped off.

I have heard that Natalia Lintvaryova is coming to Yalta. Should I offer to put her up here?

I need a roller for sticking down envelopes and stamps, as my tongue is all cut to pieces. Please send one when you can.

I have just had a letter from Konshin.[1] He apologizes for being late with the payment, which he is supposed to have made by 4 November, and he says he and his wife like Melikhovo very much. So, keep well. Pass on my regards to Olga Leonardovna and Alexander Vishnevsky. It strikes me that Alexander V. ought to be the one to provide for Masha and her child. After all, he spent a lot more time in our house than Alexander the soldier did.[2]

What else is new?

Your

Antoine

264. *To Vladimir Nemirovich-Danchenko, 24 November 1899, Yalta*

My dear Vladimir Ivanovich,

Please don't be offended at my silence. There has been a general lapse in my correspondence. This is first because I have been doing

1. The timber merchant who purchased of Melikhovo.
2. Masha Tsyplakova, the Chekhovs' unmarried maid at Melikhovo and then Moscow, had just had a baby.

some literary work, secondly because I am reading proofs for Marx, and thirdly because I have been very busy with the number of ill people who come to Yalta, all of whom for some reason seem to turn to me. The proof-reading for Marx is pure penal servitude; I have only just finished the second volume, and if I had known before how hard it was going to be I would have demanded 175,000 from him, not 75,000. The sick people who come here, the majority of whom are destitute, appeal to me to find them somewhere to live, and this involves me in a great number of discussions and a lot of correspondence.

Of course, I am desperately bored here. I work during the day, and when evening comes I start to wonder where to go and what on earth to do with myself – and by the time the second act is beginning in your theatre I am already in bed. I get up while it is still dark, can you imagine; in the dark, with the wind howling and the rain lashing against the window.

You are much mistaken if you think that people 'write to me from all four corners'. None of my friends and acquaintances writes to me at all. All the time I have been here I have had no more than two letters from Vishnevsky, and one of those didn't count because he devoted it to an attack on some critics whose reviews I had not read. I also got a letter from Goslavsky,[1] but that didn't count either because it was about professional matters, matters about which I honestly hardly knew how to answer him.

I am not writing any plays. I've got a subject, 'Three Sisters', but I'm not going to settle down to it until I have finished the stories which have long been weighing on my conscience. It is now certain that you will have to go ahead next season without a play from me.

My Yalta dacha has turned out to be very comfortable; warm and cosy with a lovely view. The garden is going to be spectacular. I am planting it myself, with my own hands. I've put in more than a hundred roses alone, all of them the noblest and most elegant varieties, and fifty pyramidal acacias, lots of camellias, lilies, tuberoses, etc.

In the part of your letter where you talk about the theatre and how much you have become tired of the minutiae of theatrical life, I can

1. Evgeny Goslavsky (1861–1917), a writer and playwright.

dimly detect a tinkling sound like that of an antique bell. Oh, how I beg of you not to flag or lose your passion! The Art Theatre is creating the most glorious pages of the book that will in time come to be written of contemporary Russian theatre. This theatre is your proudest achievement, and although I have never once been inside it, it is the only theatre I love. If I lived in Moscow I would do my best to get a job on your staff, as a caretaker if I had to, merely to help in a small way and if possible to prevent you losing any of your passion for this most beloved of institutions.

The rain is coming down in sheets, it is quite dark inside. Be well, cheerful and happy.

I warmly press your hand. Give my deep respects to Ekaterina Nikolayevna and everyone in the theatre, with the deepest bow of all to Olga Leonardovna.

Your

A. Chekhov

265. To Maria Chekhova, 1 December 1899, Yalta

We are having appalling weather with snow, cold, mud and the sort of conversation one hears on the worst days in Moscow. Everyone says it is going to be horrible for the whole winter. All the visitors are fed up and angry. Bring with you things we can't get in Yalta: peas, lentils, more pince-nez cords, Belov sausage, anything else you can get hold of.

There is no news to report. The staircase has been varnished. Progress on the garden has been interrupted due to the disgusting weather, which is depressing. I will send Rayevskaya a photograph, but please write and let me know her first name and patronymic, and where she lives. Can you make arrangements for them to continue sending us *The Courier* and *News of the Day* after the New Year without waiting for us to renew our order? Ask Olga Leonardovna to come to us in Yalta for the whole summer; it's dull without her. Tell her I'll pay her wages.

Something has gone wrong with the telegraph office, no telegrams are getting through. I don't know how Tolstoy is.

Keep well. Everything is fine here.

Your

Antoine

266. To Olga Knipper, 2 January 1900, Yalta

Greetings, dearest actress! Are you angry that it is so long since I have written to you? I have in fact written to you often, but you have not been getting my letters because one of our mutual friends has been intercepting them at the post office.

I send you my congratulations and best wishes for your happiness in the New Year. I wish especially for your happiness, and I bow down to your feet. May you long be happy, rich, healthy and cheerful.

We are getting along fine here, eating, talking and laughing a lot, and often remembering you. When she returns to Moscow, Masha will give you an account of how we spent the holidays.

I shall not congratulate you on the success of *Lonely Lives*.[1] I still have visions of the company coming to Yalta, so that I shall see *Lonely Lives* on stage for myself and have the chance to offer you my hearty congratulations in the proper manner. I have written to Meyerhold in an effort to persuade him not to overdo his characterization of a tense person. After all, most people are tense and suffer, and for a minority of them this can cause acute distress, but you don't in the normal course of events come across people, at home or on the streets, who thrash about, roll around or clutch their heads, do you? Suffering should be portrayed as it is in real life, that is, not with the arms and legs but by a glance, a nuance, gracefully, not with gesticulations. The subtle emotional reactions that cultivated people feel naturally should be expressed physically in equally subtle ways. You will no doubt point to theatrical convention, but no convention can excuse insincerity.

1. Hauptmann's play *Einsame Menschen* (1891).

My sister says you were wonderful as Anna. Oh, if only the Art Theatre could come to Yalta!

Your company was highly praised in *New Times*. There has been a change of tack; evidently by Lent you will all be getting rave reviews. My new story ['In the Ravine'] – a very frightening one – will be in the February issue of *Life*. It has a crowd of characters and lots of scenery, a crescent moon and a bittern that booms Boo-oo! Boo-oo! somewhere far off in the distance like a cow locked in a barn. It's got everything.

Levitan is staying with us, and has painted a moonlit night at haymaking time on my fireplace. It has a meadow, corn stooks, a distant wood and the moon reigning over all.

Keep well, my dear, unique actress. I miss you very much.

Your

A. Chekhov

When will you send me your photograph?

How cruel you are!

267. To Olga Knipper, 22 January 1900, Yalta

Dearest Actress,

I received telegrams on 17 January from your mama and your brother, from your uncle Alexander Ivanovich (signed 'Uncle Sasha') and from N. N. Sokolovsky.[1] Please tell them how very grateful I am and pass on my sincere feelings of affection.

Why haven't you written? What has happened? Or are you entirely absorbed in the moiré silk lining of the lapels?[2] Well, I can't help that, you must do as you please.

I'm told you are definitely coming to Yalta in May. If this has already been decided, wouldn't it be a good idea to make arrangements

1. Nikolay Sokolovsky (1864–1920), a lawyer, writer and, from 1892, the co-publisher of *The Russian Gazette*.
2. A teasing reference to Olga's putative feelings for Vladimir Nemirovich-Danchenko, who was very attracted to her; Maria Chekhova had mentioned his silk lapels in a letter to her brother.

about the theatre in advance? The theatre here is leased out, and there is no way to get hold of it without coming to an agreement with the tenant, an actor called Novikov. I could open negotiations with him if I were commissioned to do so.

The 17 January, my name day and the day of my election to the Academy,[3] passed in a rather dull and gloomy way, because I was not feeling well. I am better now, but then my mother started feeling under the weather. These little misfortunes quite took away all the pleasure from my name day and the Academy nomination, and they also stopped me writing to you and answering your telegrams as quickly as I should have.

My mother is on the mend now.

I see quite a lot of the Sredins; they come over here and very, very occasionally I go over to them, but I do go. Dr Rozanov (one of those madmen we saw at Kokoz) will be in Moscow soon and will be seeing Masha; please make sure he gets into the theatre.

So, obviously you are not writing to me and don't plan to in the near future. The blame for everything lies with those moiré silk linings. I understand you too well!

I kiss your hand,

Your

A. Chekhov

268. To Mikhail Menshikov, 28 January 1900, Yalta

Dear Mikhail Osipovich,

I simply cannot work out what Tolstoy could be suffering from. Cherinov[1] told me nothing when he replied to me, and I can't deduce anything from what I read in the papers, nor from what you now write to me. If he had stomach or intestinal ulcers they would be manifesting themselves differently; there are none there, or possibly at some time

3. Chekhov had just been elected as an honorary member of the Imperial Academy of Sciences.

1. Mikhail Cherinov (1836–?1905), a professor of medicine at Moscow University.

he has passed some gallstones that damaged the wall of the intestine, causing lacerations that bled. Nor can it be cancer; cancer, if there were any, would show itself in his appetite, in his general condition and above all in his face. Most probably Lev Nikolayevich is in good health (apart from the gallstones) and will live for another twenty years. His illness alarmed me and kept me in a constant state of tension; I fear the death of Tolstoy. If he were to die, a large empty space would appear in my life. In the first place, there is no other person whom I love as I love him; I am not a religious person, but of all faiths I find his the closest to me and the most congenial. Secondly, when literature possesses a Tolstoy, it is easy and pleasant to be a writer; even when you know that you have achieved nothing yourself and are still achieving nothing, this is not as terrible as it might otherwise be, because Tolstoy achieves for everyone. What he does serves to justify all the hopes and aspirations invested in literature. Thirdly, Tolstoy stands proud, his authority is colossal, and so long as he lives, bad taste in literature, all vulgarity, insolence and snivelling, all crude, embittered vainglory, will stay banished into outer darkness. He is the one person whose moral authority is sufficient in itself to maintain so-called literary fashions and movements on an acceptable level. Were it not for him the world of literature would be a flock of sheep without a shepherd, a morass in which it would be hard for us to find our way.

To finish with Tolstoy, I want to say something about *Resurrection*, which I read straight through in one gulp, not in instalments or in fits and starts. It is a magnificent work of art. The least interesting aspect of it is the treatment of Nekhlyudov's relationship with Katyusha, the most interesting the princes, the generals, the aunts, the peasants, the prisoners and the prison guards. I found myself holding my breath when I read the scene with the spiritualist general, the commandant of the Peter and Paul Fortress, it was so good! And what about Mme Korchagina in her chair, and the peasant, Fedosya's husband! When this peasant describes his wife, he says of her that she 'can turn her hand to anything'. That exactly describes Tolstoy's pen: it can turn its hand to anything. The novel doesn't have an ending, or at least the way it finishes can't properly be called an ending. To write and write at such length and then make everything hinge on a text from the Gospels – well, that's just a little too theological for me. Having everything depend on a Gospel text is as arbitrary as dividing the prisoners into five categories. Why five and not ten? Why a text from the Gospels rather than one from the Koran? Before bringing in the Gospels to resolve everything, you first have to convince the reader of the absolute truth of what they say.

Am I boring you? When you come to the Crimea I'll interview you and then publish it in *News of the Day*. So much unctuous rubbish gets written about Tolstoy, the sort of thing you hear old women spouting about holy fools; I can't think why he bothers to talk to these Jews.

I have been unwell for the past couple of weeks, but I've struggled through. I'm now sitting with a Spanish fly blister under my left collarbone, and feeling better – not so much on account of the blister beetle itself as because of the red spot it leaves behind.

Of course I will send you my photograph. I was glad to have been made a member of the Academy, because I enjoy knowing that Sigma[2] will now be envious of me. But I shall be even happier to lose the title as a result of some misunderstanding or other – an eventuality that will undoubtedly come to pass, because the scholar Academicians live in dread that we are going to shock them. They were grinding their teeth when Tolstoy was elected – they regard him as a nihilist. At least that is what one lady, the wife of one of the current Privy Councillors, called him – a good enough reason in my view to give him my hearty congratulations.

I am not receiving *The Week*; do you know why this should be? The editors still have a manuscript by S. Voskresensky which I sent them, entitled 'The Foolishness of Ivan Ivanovich'. If it's not suitable, please send it back to me. Keep well, I firmly press your hand.

Greetings to Yasha and Lydia Ivanovna.

Your

A. Chekhov.

Do write!

---

2. Pseudonym of Sergey Syromyatnikov (1864–1934), a columnist for *New Times*, and from 1896 editor of the Petersburg newspaper *Rus*.

269. To Ivan Chekhov, 7 February 1900, Yalta

Dearest Ivan,

Did I write and tell you that I have bought a small piece of the seashore at Gurzuf? I am now the owner of a little bay with a marvellous view, rocks, bathing, fishing, and so on and so forth. Not far away, about three minutes' walk, are a jetty and a park. There is a little cottage but it's in rather a sorry state; it has three rooms and is built entirely of wood. I'm hoping that we, that is I, Mother, Masha and all our serf entourage, will spend the summer in Gurzuf. If you like, I will rent you a couple of rooms with a nearby Tatar, only you must write and let me know in advance. Go to Trubnaya Square and buy some fishing line and one of those pail-sized wicker cages shaped like a barrel for the fish, also some sinkers and all the rest of the tackle one needs for fishing. The new dacha has only one tree, a mulberry, but there is room to plant a hundred more, which I plan to do. Küchük-Köy will have to be sold. Everything is fine with us here; there is nothing new to report. Best regards to Sonya and Volodya. Keep well.

Your

Antoine

Why haven't you written?

270. To Olga Knipper, 14 February 1900, Yalta

Dearest Actress,

The photographs are very, very good, especially the soulful one where you have your elbows on the back of a chair and are wearing an expression of calm, demure melancholy but with a devilish little imp lurking in the background. And the other one has also come out very well, but it makes you look a little bit like a Jewess, a deeply musical student at the conservatoire who at the same time, just in case, is learning dentistry on the quiet and has a fiancé in Mogilev who resembles Manasevich.[1] Are you angry? Really, truly angry? It's my revenge for your not signing the photographs.

Of the seventy roses in the garden I planted in the autumn, only three have not taken. The lilies, irises, tulips, tuberoses and hyacinths are all pushing out of the ground. The willow is already coming into leaf, and the grass is already lush round the bench in the corner. There is blossom on the almond tree. I've put benches all round the garden, not fancy ones with cast-iron feet but wooden ones I'll paint green. I've built three bridges across the stream. I'm planting palm trees. Generally there's a lot that's new, so much that you won't recognize the house or the garden or the street. Just about the only thing that has not changed is the owner, who is the same lugubrious and sedulous worshipper of the talents resident in the vicinity of the Nikitsky Gates.[2] I've heard no music nor singing since autumn, and I haven't seen a single interesting looking woman; don't you think that would be enough to make anyone lugubrious?

I had decided not to write to you, but since you sent me the photographs I am releasing you from purdah and, as you see, am writing. I even agree to come to Sevastopol but, I repeat, you are not to let anybody know, especially Vishnevsky. I shall be incognito there and shall book into the hotel as Count Blackface.

I was joking when I said that your portrait made you look like a Jewess. Don't be angry, my precious one. Well, with that I kiss your hand and remain as ever your

A. Chekhov

What job is Ivan Tsinger[3] doing in your theatre at the moment?

1. Albert Manasevich, secretary to the Moscow Art Theatre Directorate.
2. Located at the top of Bolshaya Nikitskaya Street in central Moscow, near to where Olga Knipper lived.
3. The son of a professor of mathematics, Ivan Tsinger was a Tolstoyan and a stagehand at the Moscow Art Theatre.

271. To Olga Knipper, 19 February 1900, Yalta

Received sweets and wallet thank you dear Actress God grant you health and happiness you are kind and clever wonderful spring birds singing camellias flowering in my garden.

The Academician

272. To Alexey Suvorin, 10 March 1900, Yalta

Never has a winter dragged on so long for me as this one, the time simply crawls by without apparently moving at all, and now I see how stupid I was to leave Moscow. I have grown unused to the north and am not yet used to the south; just now the only thing I can think of to alleviate my situation is to go abroad. Spring in Yalta was immediately followed by winter: snow, rain, cold, mud – enough to make you spit.

The Moscow Art Theatre is coming to perform in Yalta the week after Easter, bringing all its scenery and props. Tickets for all four advertised performances were sold out in a day, despite greatly increased prices. The repertoire, by the way, includes Hauptmann's *Lonely Lives*, which I think is a marvellous play. I read it with huge enjoyment, even though I don't enjoy reading plays, but the Art Theatre's production is said to be amazing.

There is no news. Not quite true, there is one great event to report: Sergeyenko's *Socrates*[1] is being published in the Supplement to *The Meadow*.[2] I have been reading it, although it's been an effort. This is no Socrates but a peevish, dull-witted sort of fellow whose wisdom and claim on our attention seem to consist uniquely in his habit of

1. Pyotr Sergeyenko (1854–1930), an old school contemporary of Chekhov and a writer with the pseudonym Poor Yorick, whose play *Socrates* was published and performed in St Petersburg in 1900.
2. *The Meadow* was the very popular illustrated magazine published by Adolf Marx.

taking everything he hears at face value. The play lacks any whiff of talent, but it may well be successful because it contains words like 'amphora', and Karpov will say that it is spectacular.

News of the Academy. The President has been greatly offended both by Korsh's[3] book and by his polemics. Elections to Ordinary Membership were held on 5 February, and Professor Kondakov[4] was elected to the Pushkin Division. That makes three members, including Lamansky and Korsh. Kondakov wrote to me that 'the Division has decided for the time being not to hold elections for the remaining three places'; his view is that he is not personally likely to last until this 'time being' comes to an end. And there has been no official announcement of Kondakov's election; obviously it is being kept quiet so as not to alarm the literary fraternity.

There are so many consumptives here! Their poverty is terribly distressing. People who are gravely ill are barred from hotels and apartments, so you can just imagine what dreadful scenes one cannot avoid witnessing here. People are dying from emaciation, from the conditions they are forced to live in, from complete neglect – and all this in Tauris [the Crimea] of hallowed memory. It quite takes away any appetite for sun and sea.

Warm greetings to Anna Ivanovna, Nastya and Borya. Be well and happy.

Your

A. Chekhov

---

3. Fyodor Korsh (1843–1915), an academic (not to be confused with the theatre-owner) whose *The Water Nymph*, a book about the controversial ending of Pushkin's *Rusalka*, was published in 1897 in the journal *Russian Archive*.

4. Nikodim Kondakov (1844–1925), an academic, archaeologist and historian of Byzantine art. See p. 459 and note.

273. *To Maria Chekhova, 26 March 1900, Yalta*

Dearest Masha,

When you are preparing for your journey to Yalta, the most important thing to remember is that once the warm weather starts, one can't get any snacks in Yalta – no caviar, no olives, no ham, not even any halva for Mother. Bring about five pounds of such things. Also bring, or send with the other things, my top hat, some toilet soap and a wrap. There is no news, and there's no water in the pipes either. I've been completely overrun with visitors. Yesterday, 25 March, I had a constant stream of them all day; every doctor in Moscow and the provinces furnishes people with a letter asking me to find them a flat, help them get settled, as if I were some sort of agent! Mother is well. I hope you are too, come soon.

Your

Antoine

Get me some braces from Shanks', the English shop[1] – ordinary ones, not for cycling.

274. *To Pavel Iordanov, 27 April 1900, Yalta*

Dear Pavel Fyodorovich,

I am sending you some more books; please send for them to the Russian Steamship Trading Company. They were dispatched by passenger boat and should already be in Taganrog by now.

During Passion Week I had some bleeding from haemorrhoids, and have not yet managed to recover fully. In Holy Week Yalta had a visit from the Art Theatre, another thing from which I have not succeeded in recovering, since after surviving a long-drawn-out, quiet and boring winter I found myself up every night until three or four in

1. A shop in Moscow owned by James Stewart Shanks (1829–?).

the morning, and dining every day in multitudinous company – and this went on for more than two weeks. I am having a rest now.

What news from Taganrog? Did 'Helios'[1] get its planning permission? When is work supposed to start?

I send you my best wishes, and warmly press your hand. Keep well.

Your

A. Chekhov

275. To Evgenia Chekhova, 9 May 1900, Moscow

Dearest Mama,

I arrived in Moscow yesterday and saw Masha. She is leaving to come home on 13 or 14 May, along with the other Masha.[1] I will accompany her or come a little later. It's cold in Moscow, but I feel very well.

Don't pay Ostrovsky[2] for your teeth. I told him I, not you, would pay his bill. And please don't be embarrassed about it: you can't live without teeth, and anyhow Ostrovsky did the work very cheaply.

Be well. See you soon!

Your

A. Chekhov

Chin up and don't let anything worry you.

276. To Olga Vasilieva, 9 August 1900, Yalta

Dear Olga Rodionovna,

First let me send you my deep respects and my grateful thanks for the carpet, which I received some time ago, in the spring. I did not

1. A company commissioned to install plumbing, electricity and trams in Taganrog; the project did not go ahead.
1. The Chekhov family servant in Moscow.
2. Ilya Ostrovsky, a dentist in Yalta.

write to thank you before because I did not know where you were. I knew you could not be at home because the post office returned to me 'The Lady with the Little Dog', which I sent to you at Znamenskoye. (This story is now on its way to you again, in the same somewhat tattered state as I received it.)

Alas, I am really at a loss to know how to answer your question. I don't read English, so I don't see or know anything about the English magazines. My impression is that I am of such minimal interest to the English public that it will make no difference at all whether or not I am published in an English magazine. If you can wait a little I will make some inquiries, and if I discover anything useful I will immediately let you know.

Allow me once again to thank you most cordially, to press your hand and to send you my best wishes.

Your sincerely devoted

A. Chekhov

277. To Olga Knipper, 9 August 1900, Yalta

Hello, my Olya, my darling! I received your letter today, the first since you left.[1] I read it, read it again, and now I'm writing to you, my actress. After seeing you off I went to Kist's Hotel for the night;[2] the next day, because I was bored and had nothing else to do, I went to Balaclava. There I was forced to go into full-time hiding from ladies who recognized me and kept wanting to applaud me. I spent the night there and in the morning boarded the *Tavel* bound for Yalta. The voyage was hellishly rough. I'm now sitting in Yalta, bored, angry

1. Olga had come to stay with Chekhov in Yalta in the summer of 1900, and the new level of intimacy in their relationship is reflected in their switch, when writing to each other, from the polite *vy* form of address in Russian to *ty*, the equivalents of the French *vous* and *tu*.

2. This was the main hotel in Sevastopol, where the steamer from Yalta docked and where travellers would board the train for Moscow. There is to this day no railway station in Yalta itself.

and moping. Alexeyev[3] came to see me yesterday. We talked about the play,[4] and I gave him my word that I would have it finished no later than September. See what a clever old thing I am.

I still keep imagining that the door is about to open and you will come through it. But you won't, you're either rehearsing or you're in Merzlyakovsky Lane, far from Yalta and from me.

Farewell, may the powers of heaven keep you and the angels protect you. Farewell, my dear girl.

Your

Antonio

278. To Adolf Marx, 9 August 1900, Yalta

Dear Adolf Fyodorovich,

As long ago as last autumn, in November, I was sent Volume II [of the Collected Works] for final signature, fully paginated and, because I had by then read it several times, completely ready for the press. I duly signed, and waited for it to appear, but a few days ago I was surprised to receive from the printers several stories from this volume again, newly typeset . . .

I have another complaint. Late last year or early this year I received the proofs of several stories from Volume VIII or IX, but it is not clear to me why they had been typeset. I wrote to the printers asking them to keep to the order they had been given from the list you and I put together. I also wrote to you and to Yuly Osipovich. But a little later I again received the same stories. Now I have received them yet again, and I really do not know what to do . . . (These are the stories I refer to: 'The Darling', 'On Official Business', 'Man in a Case', 'Gooseberries', 'About Love', 'A Case History', 'A Visit to Friends', 'The New Dacha', 'The Pecheneg', 'On the Cart', 'Good People', 'In

3. Chekhov is referring to Konstantin Stanislavsky, whose real name was Alexeyev.
4. *Three Sisters.*

the Sea' and 'The Head Gardener's Story'.) Meanwhile time is passing, I am soon going abroad and shall be away for a long time . . .

I sent back the proofs of Volume III to you today. Allow me to send you my best wishes and to remain, respectfully yours,

A. Chekhov

279. To Olga Knipper, 14 August 1900, Yalta

My dearest one, I don't know when I am coming to Moscow; the reason I don't know is because, can you imagine, I am writing a play at the moment. Actually it's more of a dog's dinner than a play. It has so many characters – I may completely lose the plot and have to abandon it.

The yellow boots you ask about have not been cleaned since the day I saw you off. Nobody has cleaned me either. I go about covered in dust, fur and feathers.

Sonya and Volodya are still with us.[1] The weather is horrible, dry, and the wind never lets up . . . I'm not very happy, because I'm bored.

Keep well, my dear little German girl, don't be angry with me and don't be unfaithful to me. I kiss you warmly.

Your

Antoine

280. To Olga Knipper, 8 September 1900, Yalta

You write: 'Oh, everything is so, so confusing to me,' . . . It's good that you're confused, my dearest little actress, very good! It shows you're a philosopher, a woman of brains.

The weather's warmed up, hasn't it? Whatever the weather, I'm coming to Moscow on 20 September and will stay there until 1 October.

1. Ivan Chekhov's wife and son.

I shall sit in the hotel every day and write my play. Shall I write, or just make a fair copy? I don't know, my dear old girl. Something's a bit wrong with one of my heroines; I can't seem to do anything with her and it's really annoying me.

I got a letter from Marx today: he says my plays will be coming out in ten days' time.

I'm afraid you're going to be very disappointed in me. My hair is falling out frightfully, so much so that, who knows, in a week's time I may be a bald old gaffer. It must be something to do with the barber. As soon as I had my hair cut I started going bald.

Is Gorky writing a play or not? Wherever did *News of the Day* dredge up the news that *Three Sisters* is no good as a title? What nonsense! Maybe it isn't good, but I certainly don't plan to change it.

I miss you terribly – terribly, do you hear? All I eat is soup. It's cold in the evening, and I do nothing but stay at home. There are no pretty girls. The money is getting less and less, and my beard is going grey . . .

Dear heart, I kiss your hand – the right one and the left one. Be well and don't be downcast, stop thinking everything is so confusing to you.
Au revoir, my lovely Olya, my heart's crocodile!
Your
Antoine

281. To Evgenia Chekhova, 9 October 1900, Yalta

Dearest Mama,

I'm alive and well, and hope you are the same. There's nothing new in Yalta, the weather is as warm and summery as ever. There was a bit of rain, but nothing serious. The chrysanthemums are flowering gloriously, the crane and dogs say hello to you, Granny and Arseny[1] are flourishing.

1. Granny: Maryushka, the family cook, since retired; Arseny was the Russian gardener who replaced Mustafa when he left.

Give my regards to Vanya and his family, and to Masha. All best wishes to you.

Your

A. Chekhov

282. To Vera Komissarzhevskaya, 13 November 1900, Moscow

Dear Vera Fyodorovna,

I had hoped to answer your letter verbally and in person, because I did firmly intend to come to Petersburg. Various circumstances, however, prevented me from doing that, and so instead I am writing to you. The *Three Sisters* are ready, but their future, at least their immediate future, is lost in a mist of uncertainty. The play has turned out to be boring, sluggish and awkward; I say awkward, because for instance it has four female leads and an atmosphere of unparalleled gloom.

Your actors would find it not remotely to their taste if I sent it to the Alexandrinsky Theatre. Nevertheless I will send it to you, and you can read it and decide if it would be worth taking on tour in the summer. At present it is being read by the Art Theatre (it only exists in one copy), but after that I will take it back and make another fair copy. Then I shall have several copies typed up and shall hasten to send you one.

How wonderful it would be if I could just manage to tear myself away and come to Petersburg, if only for a day! Here it's like hard labour on the treadmill: I run around all day from morning till night making calls, and then at night sleep like the dead. My health was good when I came here, but now I have started coughing again, I'm in a foul mood, and people say my complexion is yellow. I'm very sad to hear that you are not well and not enjoying life. I saw Maria Ilyinishna;[1] probably she is already with you and you are on the mend,

1. Maria Ziloti, sister of the pianist and conductor Alexander Ziloti and cousin of Rachmaninov.

perhaps already completely better, which I wish and shall continue to wish with all my heart. So to repeat, they are now reading through my play at the Art Theatre, following which I shall make a new copy, have it typed and sent to you, I hope before December. The play is as complicated as a novel, and the mood, so I'm told, quite deadly.

I warmly kiss your hands – both of them – and send you my profound respects. May heavenly angels protect you.

Cordially yours

A. Chekhov

283. To Nikodim Kondakov, 6 December 1900, Moscow

Dear Nikodim Pavlovich,

Yes, I'm in Moscow! I came intending to stay three days, a week at the most, but got stuck here for almost two months. The weather here is marvellous, we've had no more than 3 degrees of frost, but today it's raining and muddy and the snow is the colour of coffee. Everyone is coughing and complaining, but I am flourishing, I've even put on weight. However, I'm leaving on Sunday the 10th; I already have my tickets and foreign passport. I'm going to Nice and then on to Africa. Just in case, my address will be 'Nice'.

I do not have a photograph of myself to hand, but if you need one you can write to the 'South' photographic studio in Yalta, and they will send you one. The proprietor is Sergey Vladimirovich Dziuba. If you like I can write to him.

Yesterday my sister brought me the parcel from the Taganrog refuges together with your letter. My most grateful thanks. If you will be in Moscow over the holiday season, you absolutely must go to the Art Theatre. Vladimir Nemirovich-Danchenko and Konstantin Alexeyev (Stanislavsky), the directors of the theatre, are very good people by the way, and would be happy to see you.

I have written a play and have already given it to the theatre. You see what a prolific writer I am. I'm not getting any letters from Yalta, and have no idea what is going on there. One disagreeable, or rather extremely disagreeable, event did occur: a student from Yalta, one Sinani,[1] has died here in Moscow. His father came for the funeral; I met him at the station and it was an agonizing experience to have to give him an account of his son's death.

And so, I shall soon be off. How long shall I be away? I do not know. I wish you all the very best, you and your family, to whom I send my deepest respects. I shall write to you from Nice. Keep well and happy.

With sincere respects, yours devotedly

A. Chekhov

284. To Olga Knipper, 14 December 1900, Nice

Hello my marvellous, angelic, Jewish soubrette! I have just arrived in Nice, had some dinner, and the first thing I'm doing is writing to you. Here is my address: Pension Russe, Rue Gounod, Nice, and for telegrams: Pension Russe, Nice. My head is spinning with the fatigue of the journey, so I shall not write much today, I'll write to-morrow, but for now just let me kiss you ten thousand times, my darling child. It's raining a bit, but incredibly warm. The roses are blooming, and all kinds of other flowers, you can hardly believe your eyes. The young people are in summer coats, there's not a hat to be seen. There is a monkey-puzzle tree growing right in front of my window, just like yours except that this one is the size of a big pine.

It was dull in Vienna; the shops were closed, and another thing: you told me to stay at the Hotel Bristol. It turns it was the best hotel in Vienna; they fleece you diabolically, they don't allow you to read newspapers in the restaurant, and everyone is dressed up to the nines, so outrageously fashionably that beside them I was ashamed and felt like some horny-handed Boer. I travelled from Vienna on the express,

1. Abram Sinani, son of the Yalta bookshop owner Isaak Sinani, committed suicide while studying in Moscow.

first class. We simply flew along, like a bird. I had a carriage all to myself.

Well, look after yourself, my dear heart. May God and His heavenly angels preserve you. Don't betray me, even in your thoughts. Write and tell me how the rehearsals are going. Generally, write as often as you can, I beg you.

Your

Antoine

I kiss you – understand that. I bow down to your feet.

285. *To Leonid Sredin, 26 December 1900, Nice*

Dear Leonid Valentinovich,

I send you my best wishes for the New Year; may it be filled with health, happiness and prosperity for you. This is now the second week that I have been staying in and around Nice, and – what can I say? It's a salutary experience, very salutary, to spend a whole winter in Yalta, because it seems like paradise here after Yalta. Yalta is Siberia! For the first couple of days I found myself actually laughing out loud at the novelty of being able to stroll about in a summer coat or sit in my room with the door open on to the balcony. The people on the streets are jolly and noisy and laugh a lot; not a policeman or haughty-visaged Marxist in sight ... But two days ago we had an unexpected frost and everything withered. Frosts are practically unknown here; no one could understand where this one had sprung from.

Do you happen to know where my mother and sister are at the present time? If they are in Yalta, please write and let me know if they are all right and how they are feeling. I have written to them, but not received any reply.

Give my greetings and respects to Sofia Petrovna, Nadezhda Ivanovna and the children. Write and tell me how Nadezhda Ivanovna is getting on in Yalta, and whether she misses the theatre. Tell me everything in detail, if you can. However lovely it is on the Riviera, one still misses letters from home. I hope my house hasn't fallen down?

I warmly clasp your hand and embrace you. Be well and happy.

Your

A. Chekhov

Give my regards to the Yartsevs.

286. To Olga Knipper, 28 December 1900, Nice

You can't imagine, dearest doggie, the terrible thing that has happened! Just now I was informed of a gentleman asking for me downstairs. I went down to see an elderly gent who introduced himself thus: Chertkov. In his hands was a bundle of letters, and it turned out that they were all addressed to me but he had received them because of the similarity of our names. One of your letters (there were three of them, the first three you sent) had been opened. What do you think of that? In future, obviously, you must put on the envelope: Monsieur Antoine Tchekhoff, 9 Rue Gounod (or Pension Russe), Nice. Be sure to put 'Antoine', otherwise I won't get your letters for ten or fifteen days after you've sent them.

Your strictures on the subject of Vienna, where you called me a 'lump of Slav blancmange', came a little late in the day; it's true that fifteen years ago I was a very inexperienced foreign traveller and missed seeing a lot of places I should have seen, but this time in Vienna I went everywhere it was possible to go. I did go to the theatre, but there were no tickets left. Later on, when I was leaving Vienna, I remembered that I had forgotten to look at the posters; agreed, that is very Russian behaviour. I bought myself a beautiful wallet at Klein's in Vienna; it was apparently only the second day his shop had been open. I also bought some luggage straps from him. You see, my dear heart, what a domesticated person I am.

You tell me off for not having written to my mother. My dear, I wrote many times to Mother and to Masha, but got no reply and it doesn't look as if I'll get one now. So I gave it up as a bad job. Not a line have I heard from them. You are right, I've always been a blancmange and that's what I shall go on being; I shall always feel I'm in the wrong although never knowing why.

Thank you for the word on Tolstoy. Shekhtel is here from Moscow. He won a load of money at roulette, and leaves tomorrow. Vladimir Nemirovich is here with his wife. Beside the other women here she seems so crass, like a Serpukhov merchant's wife. She buys all sorts of rubbish, at bargain prices. I'm sorry for him, having her around. He is, as always, a fine person, and the best of company.

It was cold, but now it's warm and we are in summer coats. I won 500 francs at roulette. Do I have your permission to play, darling?

There I was, rushing to finish the last act because I thought you all needed it. Now it seems you won't start rehearsing it before Nemirovich returns. If only I could have had another two or three days on this act, it might have turned out a bit juicier. [Gorky's] *The Three* is a good piece of work, but the writing is old-fashioned and therefore it is a tough read for people accustomed to literature. Even I found it hard going to get through it to the end.

Are you feeling better? I hope so! Even though when you're ill you're a good girl and write nice letters, don't even think of getting ill again.

There are a lot of ladies at the table I dine at, some of them from Moscow, but I keep my mouth tight shut. I just sit there silently with a haughty expression on my face, stubbornly chewing away or thinking of you. Every now and again the Muscovite ladies start up a conversation about the theatre, obviously hoping I will be drawn into it, but I stay silent and carry on eating. It is very nice to hear you being praised. And you get a lot of praise, just fancy that. People talk as though you were a good actress. Well, my dear child, keep well and happy. I am yours! Take me and eat me with olive oil and vinegar. I kiss you fervently.

Your

Antoine

287. To Olga Knipper, 11 January 1901, Nice

You cruel, savage woman, it's a hundred years since I had a letter from you. What can this mean? My letters are now delivered most punctiliously, and so if I'm not getting any, the blame can lie with none other than you, faithless one.

In a few days' time, assuming the sea subsides from its present turbulence, I shall set out for Africa. I'll still have the same address, i.e. 9 Rue Gounod, the people here will know where I am. I shan't spend long in Africa, a week or two.

The weather here is staying fine and summery, warm, wonderful; there are flowers, women, bicycles – but alas! for me at least it is just a print rather than an original painting.

Write to me, little ginger-haired doggie! Not to write me any letters is such a mean thing to do! You could at least tell me what is happening with *Three Sisters*. So far you haven't written to tell me anything whatsoever about the play, absolutely nothing except you say you've been to a rehearsal, or that there wasn't a rehearsal today. I shall definitely have to beat you, damn you!

Has Masha arrived in Moscow?

The days are passing, soon it will be spring, my glorious, wonderful actress, and we shall see each other. Write to me, my darling, I implore you.

Your

Antoine

288. To Konstantin Alexeyev (Stanislavsky), 15 January 1901, Nice

Dear Konstantin Sergeyevich,

Many thanks for your letter. You are, of course, a thousand times right, Tuzenbakh's corpse should not be seen on stage at all. I had the same thought when I was writing it, and mentioned it to you, if you recall. The fact that the end of the play is reminiscent of *Uncle Vanya* is not a big problem; after all *Uncle Vanya* is my play, not anyone else's, and people will accept echoes of yourself in your own work. Chebutykin's phrase 'Would it not please you to accept this date?' should be sung, not spoken: it comes from some operetta or other, but I couldn't for the life of me tell you which. You could ask the architect Franz Shekhtel, who lives in his own house, on the Garden Ring Road near St Ermolay's church.

Thank you very much for writing to me. Profound respects to Maria Petrovna[1] and all your artists; I send you all my best wishes. Keep well and happy.

Your

A. Chekhov

289. To Olga Knipper, 20 January 1901, Nice

Dearest little actress, tender exploitress of my heart, what made you send me that telegram? Surely it would have been better to wire me something about yourself than something so pointless. Anyhow, how is *Three Sisters?* To judge from letters I've been getting, you are all talking utter nonsense. The noise in Act III – what noise, pray? The only noise should be in the distance, far offstage, a muffled, vague sort of sound, while everyone on stage is tired out, nearly asleep . . . If you don't get Act III right the whole play will be ruined and I'll be booed off the stage in the declining years of my old age. Alexeyev's letters are full of praise for you and for Vishnevsky. Even though I can't see what you are doing, I praise you as well. Vershinin's 'tram-tram-tram' should be like a question, and yours should be, as it were, in reply, and it should strike you as such an original thing to say that you utter it with a slight smile . . . You should say 'tram-tram' and give a little laugh, not a loud one, just a hint. Your expression, meanwhile, should not be like the one you have in *Uncle Vanya*, but livelier and more youthful. Remember, your character is quick-

1. Maria Lilina (1866–1943), an actess at the Moscow Art Theatre and wife of Stanislavsky.

tempered, with a sense of humour. Anyhow, I'm counting on you, sweetheart, you are a good actress.

I said at the time that it would be difficult to carry Tuzenbakh's body across the stage of your theatre, but Alexeyev has been insisting that it won't work if the corpse isn't seen. I have written to him saying that the body should not be brought on, but I don't know if he has received my letter.

If the play is a failure, I shall go to Monte Carlo and lose every last copeck until I fall down in a stupor.

I'm already feeling the urge to leave Nice, I've had enough, but where to go? Africa is not a possibility at the moment as the sea is too rough, and I don't want to go back to Yalta. I shall have to be in Yalta by February in any case, and in April I'll be in Moscow with my doggie. After Moscow we can go off somewhere together.

There is nothing whatsoever new in my life. Keep well, my dear heart, astounding actress, don't forget me and love me just a little, at least a copeck's worth.

I kiss you and embrace you. I wish you all happiness. Four hundred roubles is little enough in all conscience; you are worth much more than that.

Keep well,

Your venerable

Antony

290. *To Maria Chekhova, 26 January 1901, Nice*

Dearest Masha,

I'm not going to Algiers, but to Italy. My address will be: Poste restante, Naples – that is, Naples, to be called for.

Keep well. I'll drift around Italy for a couple of weeks, and then go to the Crimea. There's no other news.

My respects to Efim Zinovievich and Evdokia Isaakovna.

Your

A. Chekhov

291. To Olga Knipper, 2 February 1901, Rome

My dearest girl, I'm now in Rome. Your letter, the first I've had from you in a whole week, arrived here today. I think the blame must lie with my play, I suppose it can't have been a success. I've not heard so much as a whisper about it, so obviously it must have been a failure.

Oh, what a wonderful country this Italy is! An amazing country! There's no corner, not a square inch of ground, that doesn't offer you something to stimulate the mind.

So, here I am in Rome. I'll go on from here to Naples, where I shall be for five days (meaning I shall get your letter there, assuming you've sent me one), then to Brindisi, and from Brindisi by sea to Yalta, via the island of Corfu, of course. You see, my sweetheart, what a seasoned traveller I am! In any case, going from place to place and seeing everything is much more agreeable than sitting at home and writing, even writing for the theatre. We, that is you and I, will go to Sweden and Norway together . . . shall we? It would give us something to remember in our old age.

I am now completely well, my dearest one. Don't worry about me, and keep well yourself.

I have just learnt that Mirolyubov[1] (Mirov), who publishes the *Everyman's Magazine*, is in Nervi, and I have written to him. If he is going to Corfu as well, I'll perhaps stay there as long as a week.

I have two travelling companions: Maxim Kovalevsky and Prof. Korotnev.

I warmly kiss you, my dear heart. Forgive me for not writing much. Even so, I do love my little dog very much. Have you ever been to Italy? I've an idea you have. If so, you'll understand my mood. This is my fourth visit to Italy, by the way.

I'm eating a tremendous amount. I got a letter from Nemirovich: he is full of praise for you.

Your

Antoine (the Venerable)

---

1. Viktor Mirolyubov (1860–1939), a writer, editor and former singer.

Masha has asked me to bring her back an umbrella and some shawls. What can I bring you? It's a pity I'm not going to Paris — Italian umbrellas aren't much good, apparently.

292. To Olga Knipper, 20 February 1901, Yalta

My divine, wonderful darling, I take you in my arms and kiss you passionately. I've been on the road for about two weeks without getting any letters, and thought you must have fallen out of love with me, but now suddenly a whole collection has turned up, from Moscow, from Piter and from abroad. I left Italy so soon because it was cold and snowing there, and I was missing your letters and fretting at not knowing what was happening. Only when I arrived here in Yalta did I find out anything much about *Three Sisters*; in Italy I could only get snippets, hardly anything at all. It seemed as though it had not been much of a success, because people who had read the newspapers weren't saying much about it, while Masha was praising it to the skies in her letters. Well, it's all one to me anyhow.

You ask when shall we see one another? In Holy Week. Where? In Moscow. Where shall we go? I don't know, we can decide when we see one another and talk about it, my marvellous clever darling, my glorious little Jewish girl.

It's nice and warm in Yalta, the weather is very good, the house is cosy, but in general I'm bored. Bunin is here,[1] and happily he comes to see me every day. Mirolyubov is also here, and until recently Nadezhda Ivanovna. Her hearing has deteriorated. Sredin seems to be in excellent health. Altshuller has put on weight.

Well, darling, they are calling me in to supper. I'll write again tomorrow, or maybe after supper. May God keep you. Write and tell me everything about Petersburg. Why doesn't Vishnevsky write to me?

I kiss you once again, my love.

Your holy father

Antony

1. The writer Ivan Bunin (1870–1953).

293. To Mikhail Chekhov, 22 February 1901, Yalta

Dear Michel,

I have returned from abroad and can now answer your letter. Moving to Petersburg to live will certainly be a good thing in itself and a lifeline for you, but as for working for Suvorin, I can't give you a definite opinion even after much thought. Needless to say, in your position I would much prefer to work in the printing press and keep away from the newspaper. *New Times* has a very bad reputation these days; the people who work there are fat and complacent (if you don't count Alexander, who doesn't see anything);[1] Suvorin himself is a liar, a terrible liar, particularly in his so-called moments of candour. By this I mean that he may well be sincere when he is saying something, but you cannot be sure that half an hour later he will not say the complete opposite. Whichever way you look at it it's an extremely difficult situation; may God help you, for any advice I am able to give you is hardly likely to be of much use. If you do go to work for Suvorin, keep in mind that he is an extremely easy person to fall out with, so make sure you have a civil service job up your sleeve, or train to become a barrister.

Suvorin has one good man working for him – Tychinkin, or at least he was a good man. His sons, I mean Suvorin's, are worthless in every sense of the word, and Anna Ivanovna has also become petty-minded. Nastya and Borya seem to be decent souls. So was Kolomnin, but he died recently.

Keep well and happy. Let me know what happens. Life in Petersburg will be good for Olga Germanovna[2] and the children, better than in Yaroslavl.

Write and tell me any details there are. Mother is well.

Your

A. Chekhov

1. Chekhov's brother Alexander was still on the staff of *New Times*.
2. Mikhail Chekhov's wife.

294. To Olga Knipper, 1 March 1901, Yalta

My dearest, don't pay any attention to the newspapers, don't read them at all, or you'll completely collapse on me.[1] Let this be a lesson to you to pay attention in future to your venerable holy father. Wasn't I saying, insisting to you, that no good would come of Petersburg? You should have listened to me. At all events, your theatre will never appear in Piter again – thank God.

As for me, I am going to give up the theatre altogether, I'm not going to write another play ever again. One can write for the theatre in Germany, Sweden, even in Spain, but not in Russia, where authors aren't respected, but just kicked in the teeth and not forgiven, either for their successes or their failures. You are encountering criticism for the first time in your life, and that is why you are so sensitive, but everything will be fine and you'll get used to it. However, I can just imagine how marvellous Sanin[2] must be feeling just now! I'm sure he's carrying all his reviews around with him in his pocket, his eyebrows pushed right up as high as they can go . . .

The weather is fabulous here, warm and sunny, the apricot and almond trees are covered in blossom . . . I shall be waiting for you in Passion Week, my poor, beleaguered actress, waiting and waiting, keep that in mind.

Between 20 and 28 February I sent you five letters and three telegrams; I asked you to wire me back – but not a word of a reply did I get. I had a telegram from Yavorskaya about *Uncle Vanya*.

Write and let me know until what date you will be in Piter. Write to me, my dear actress.

I am well, my word of honour.

I hug you

Your holy father

1. The Moscow Art Theatre had been receiving bad reviews while on tour in St Petersburg.
2. Alexander Sanin (1869–1956), an actor and director at the Moscow Art Theatre from 1898 to 1902.

295. To Nikodim Kondakov, 2 March 1901, Yalta

Dear Nikodim Pavlovich,

Grateful and heartfelt thanks for your book.[1] I read it with enormous interest and pleasure. You may like to know that my mother is a native of the Shuya district, and fifty years ago used to visit Palekh and Sergeyevo (which is two miles from Palekh) to visit her relations who were icon painters there. At that time they had a very good life indeed; the Sergeyevo relations had a two-storey house with a mezzanine, a very substantial dwelling. When I told my mother about your book she became very excited and started telling me all about Palekh and Sergeyevo and about this house, which was already quite old then. According to her memories, theirs was a good, prosperous life; they used to get commissions from big churches in Moscow and Petersburg.

Yes, there is no end to the greatness and variety of the power of the Russian people, but even their strengths cannot revive what has died. You talk of icon painting as a craft; like all crafts it gives rise to a cottage industry and little by little ends up producing the kind of work factory goods firms like Jacquot and Bonacoeur turn out. Even if you were to close these firms down, other manufacturers will spring up to take their place and produce paintings on boards, in the correct way perhaps, but that still won't bring Kholui and Palekh back to life. Icon painting thrived and was strong when it was an art rather than a craft, when it was led by truly gifted people; as soon as a school of 'painting' arose in Russia and artists began to be trained and to transform themselves into gentry, then the Vasnetsovs and the Ivanovs[2] began to appear, while back in Kholui and Palekh there remained only craftsmen, and so icon painting became a craft . . .

Incidentally, there are hardly any icons left in peasants' huts any more; all the ancient images there were once have perished in fires, to be replaced, if at all, by new ones painted on paper or tinfoil.

1. *The Current State of Popular Icon Painting*, St Petersburg, 1901.
2. Viktor Vasnetsov (1848–1926), Alexander Ivanov (1806–58), celebrated nineteenth-century painters.

I haven't seen *Henschel*, nor have I read it, and therefore have no idea what sort of play it is. But I do like Hauptmann and consider him a major playwright. In any case it would be hard to judge from just one act, especially if Roksanova was acting in it.

I have not been well recently. I had a coughing spell such as I haven't had for a long time.

Your book about icon painting is written with great warmth, in places with passion, and that is why it is so lively and interesting to read. It is certainly the case that icon painting in Palekh and Kholui is dying out, becoming extinct; I only wish that someone would appear who could write the history of Russian icon painting! It is a subject to which one could devote an entire lifetime.

However, my heart tells me that I'm already boring you. The general reaction to Tolstoy's excommunication[3] has been one of derision. It was stupid of the bishops to graft that piece of Church Slavonic text into the middle of their announcement. It was deeply insincere, or at least had a strong smell of insincerity about it. Keep well and in God's good care, and try not to forget your sincerely devoted and respectful

A. Chekhov

296. To Olga Knipper, 7 March 1901, Yalta

I've received an anonymous letter saying that you are carrying on with someone in Piter and are head over heels in love. Of course, I've suspected this for some time, you miserly little Jewess you. You've probably fallen out of love with me because of my extravagance in urging you on to ruin by sending a couple of telegrams . . . Well, so be it! Whatever the case I still love you as much as ever, and just cast your eyes at the paper on which I'm writing to you.

Skinflint, why didn't you write and tell me that you were staying

3. Tolstoy had just been excommunicated from the Russian Orthodox Church by the Holy Synod.

on in Petersburg for a fourth week and weren't going to Moscow? I was waiting and waiting and not writing because I thought you were going home.

I'm alive and seem to be well, even though I'm still coughing furiously. I'm working in the garden, where the trees are already coming out; the weather is marvellous, as marvellous as your letters that are now arriving from abroad. The latest letters are the ones sent on from Naples. Oh what a glorious, clever woman you are, my dear heart! I read each letter through a minimum of three times. So, I'm working in the garden but doing very little in my study; I have no inclination to do anything, I'm reading proofs and am glad of them to pass the time. I don't go in to Yalta very often, and have no desire to, but the Yaltese spend ages sitting with me out here, and every time they do my spirits sink and I promise myself I'll either go away or get married, so that I can have a wife to chase them off, the visitors that is. Then I can get a divorce in Ekaterinoslav province and marry again. Permit me to make you a proposal.

I brought you back some very good scent from abroad. Come and collect it in Passion Week. You must come, my dear, good, glorious creature; if you don't you will deeply offend me and poison my existence. I'm already looking forward to your coming, counting the days and hours. It doesn't matter that you have fallen in love with someone else and have already betrayed me, I still implore you to come, please just come. Do you hear, doggie? I love you, you should know that, and it is already hard for me to live without you. If the theatre starts getting ideas about keeping the company back for rehearsals over Easter, you must tell Nemirovich this would be a mean and swinish thing to do.

I just went downstairs to have some tea with bagels. I had a letter from Academician Kondakov in Petersburg. He went to see *Three Sisters* and is in indescribable raptures. You didn't tell me anything about the dinners that have been given in the company's honour, so please write and tell me about them now, for friendship's sake if nothing else. After all, I am your friend, your close friend, you doggie you.

I also got a long telegram from Solovtsov in Kiev today, about how the *Three Sisters* production there has been an enormous, incredible success, and so on. The next play I write is definitely going to be a funny one, very funny – at least in intention.

Well, old girl, be healthy, be cheerful, don't feel down, don't be sad. Yavorskaya has favoured me with a telegram about *Uncle Vanya*! Evidently she came to your theatre in the spirit of Sarah Bernhardt, no less, genuinely hoping that the fact of her presence would bring you all happiness. And you almost went and picked a fight with her!

I kiss you eighty times and hug you passionately. Don't forget, I'm waiting for you. Don't forget!

Your holy father

Antony

297. To Georgy Chekhov, 8 March 1901, Yalta

Dearest Georges,

Our almond and apricot trees blossomed long ago, it is gloriously warm and all would be fine and merry were it not for the cough which has been troubling me for ten days now. *Three Sisters* is indeed having a great success, but it needs to have three very good, young actresses, and the men must know how to wear uniforms. It is not a play written for the provinces.

There is no news, everything is just as before. Mother is well, she's fasting at the moment. The crane[1] walks all over the yard, behaving like a landlord. Write and tell me what is happening with the municipal library – are they getting more readers in?

Keep well. Give my respects to my aunt, your sisters, Volodya and Irinushka. I warmly clasp your hand.

Your

A. Chekhov

1. A crane that Chekhov kept as a pet in Yalta.

298. To Olga Knipper, 11 March 1901, Yalta

So you don't want to come to Yalta, my darling. Well, that's up to you, I won't try to insist. Only I am terribly reluctant to leave Yalta! I dread the trains, the hotels . . . However, none of this matters, I'll come to Moscow – *basta!*

You are happy and not depressed, and that makes you a wonderful, clever girl! You write that I am not fond of Petersburg. Who told you that? I love Petersburg; I have a great weakness for it. And I have so many memories bound up with that city! It's true I don't have much respect for the theatre in Petersburg, except for Savina[1] and – up to a point – Davydov; in fact, like your uncle Karl I entirely reject it and intensely dislike it. I had a letter today from Flerov,[2] who is not well: he's asking me to find him somewhere to stay in Yalta for the whole summer. I read about the assassination attempt on Pobedonostsev today . . .[3]

Your dear, glorious letters give me extraordinary pleasure. But why don't you like me signing myself 'holy father'? After all, I live here exactly like a monk, and I do have a monastic name. Please write to me, my dear good wonderful sweetheart, your letters affect me like the song of the nightingale; I love them very much. And I love your handwriting.

We shall soon be seeing one another, surely we shall, and that is so good! We'll meet, and then go somewhere together.

Well, good night, my darling. Be well and in good spirits, and don't forget

Your

Antoine

1. Maria Savina (1854–1915), a famous actress at the Alexandrinsky Theatre from 1874.
2. Sergey Flerov (1841–1901), a theatre critic who contributed to *The Moscow Gazette*. He wrote several articles on Chekhov between 1887 and 1900.
3. An attempt had been made on the life of the Procurator of the Holy Synod in St Petersburg on 8–9 March by N. Ligovsky.

299. *To Olga Knipper, 16 March 1901, Yalta*

Hello, my darling one! I will definitely come to Moscow, but am not sure about going to Sweden this year. I'm so tired of being a wanderer, also my health gives every sign of becoming that of an old man, so that apart from anything else, rather than a husband you'll be getting a grandad in me. I spend whole days rooting around in the garden, the weather is beautiful and warm, everything is blooming, the birds are singing, there are no visitors, life is nothing but a bowl of cherries. I've given up literature altogether, and when we get married I shall make you give up the theatre and we'll live together like plantation owners. Wouldn't you like that? Well, all right, you can carry on acting for five years, and then we'll see.

I happened on a copy of *Russian Veteran* today, a specialist army newspaper, and there out of the blue I saw a review of *Three Sisters*. The issue is No. 56, 11 March. It's all right, it is generally favourable and they didn't find any mistakes in military matters.

Write to me, my dear sweetheart, your letters bring me such joy. The reason you are unfaithful to me is that, as you say, you are a human being and a woman; well, all right then, go ahead and be unfaithful to me, just so long as you remain as wonderful and glorious as you are. I'm an old man, it's impossible for you not to betray me, I perfectly understand that, and if some time I betray you out of desperation, you'll forgive me, because you'll understand that there is grey in my beard and a devil behind my ribs. Isn't that so?

Are you seeing anything of Avilova? Did you make friends with Chumina? I expect you've taken up writing stories and novels on the quiet. If I find out you have, that will be the end, I'll divorce you.

I read of Pchelnikov's[1] appointment in the paper, and was surprised, especially at his having no qualms about accepting such an unlikely position. But they won't take *Doctor Stockmann* out of your repertoire, it's a conservative play after all.

1. Pavel Pchelnikov (1851–1919) ran the Moscow office of the Imperial Theatres from 1882 to 1898 and was Inspector of the Repertoire of Private Theatres from 1901.

Even though I have abandoned literature, from time to time I still write something from force of habit. I'm now writing a story entitled 'The Bishop'; it's a subject that has been knocking around in my head for about fifteen years.

I embrace you a hundred times, faithless one, and kiss you passionately. Write to me, write to me, my joy, otherwise when we marry I'll beat you.

Your venerable

Antoine

300. *To Olga Knipper, 19 April 1901, Yalta*

Dearest Actress, my dear heart,

Think about this: why don't we take a trip together down the Volga, at least as far as Astrakhan? What do you think? Give it some thought, I'll come soon and we'll go together to Yaroslavl or Nizhny or Rybinsk. We must spend this summer as comfortably as we can, which means as far away as possible from everyone we know.

It's raining here in Yalta. A horse has crushed one of Kashtanka the dog's paws, so I'm currently engaged in medical practice.

Mind you don't get too thin in Moscow, or else I shall come and drag you back to Yalta.

Well, stay healthy, light of my life.

I kiss you desperately.

Your

Antoine

301. *To Olga Knipper, 26 April 1901, Yalta*

Olka doggie! I'll come early in May. As soon as you get my telegram, go immediately to the Dresden Hotel and find out if Room 45 is available; in other words reserve as cheap a room as you can.

I'm seeing a lot of Nemirovich, he is very nice and doesn't put on airs. I haven't seen his wife yet. My main reason for coming to Moscow is to wander about and stuff my face. We can go to Petrovsko-Razumovskoye, and to Zvenigorod, we'll go everywhere as long as the weather is good. If you agree to come down the Volga with me we'll eat sterlet.[1]

Kuprin[2] seems to be in love, he's completely bewitched. His love is a huge, strapping woman, you know her, she's the one you've been urging me to marry.

If you give me your word that not a soul in Moscow shall know of our marriage until after it has taken place, then I'll marry you the very day I arrive. I don't know why, but I have a horror of weddings and congratulations and having to stand around with a glass of champagne in my hand and a vacant smile on my face. We can go straight from the church to Zvenigorod without going home at all. Or we could get married in Zvenigorod. Think about it, darling heart, think about it! Everyone says how clever you are, after all.

The weather in Yalta is pretty awful, with a biting wind. The roses are blooming, but not much; they'll flower extravagantly later on. The irises are magnificent.

Everything is fine with me, except for one minor detail – my health.

Gorky[3] hasn't been exiled, he's been arrested and confined to Nizhny. Posse[4] has also been arrested.

I embrace you, my Olka.

Your

Antoine

1. A fish of the sturgeon family.
2. The writer Alexander Kuprin (1870–1938).
3. Gorky had been arrested in Nizhny Novgorod on 16 April 1901 for revolutionary activities, and for possessing a mimeograph for the dissemination of subversive materials.
4. Vladimir Posse (1874–1940), a journalist who edited the journal *Life* from 1898.

302. To Evgenia Chekhova, 12 May 1901, Moscow

Dearest Mama,

I've arrived in Moscow and everyone is well. The weather is splendid, really warm. Tell Arseny to water the birch tree once a week, and the eucalyptus (it's next to the chrysanthemums and the camellias) once every two days. Don't let him prune anything. I'm staying at the Dresden Hotel on Tverskaya. Your friend Olga Vasilieva is here as well, so they tell me. Masha will come to Yalta very soon; I told her about the mushrooms. I've put your umbrella in for repair. My cough is better. Pass on my respects to Varvara Konstantinovna and the young ladies, to Maryushka and Arseny, and keep well and happy.

Your

A. Chekhov

303. To Adolf Marx, 24 May 1901, Moscow

Dear Adolf Fyodorovich,

I am returning the proofs to you with apologies for the delay of a few days. The fact is, your printers sent the proofs to me, not at the Hotel Dresden where I am staying, but to the address I was at last year, and then they were sent to my sister's apartment, but she is away . . . It was only by the merest chance that I received them.

Tomorrow I am going away to take a kumiss[1] cure, which I have been ordered to do by the doctors, and I shall probably be there for at least two months. I will send you my address tomorrow.

I send you my best wishes and remain your sincerely respectful and devoted

A. Chekhov

---

1. The drinking of kumiss, fermented mare's milk, was a popular health treatment in Russia.

304. To Evgenia Chekhova, 25 May 1901, Moscow

Dear Mama,

Give me your blessing, I'm getting married. Everything will stay as it was. I am now going off for a kumiss cure; the address is Aksyonovo, Samaro-Zlatoustovskoy. My health is better.

Anton

305. To Lidia Avilova, between 25 May and September 1901[1]

My deepest, deepest respects to you, and my thanks for your letter. You ask if I am happy? The first thing I have to tell you is that I am ill. And I know now that I am very ill. There you have it; take it how you will. I repeat, I am very grateful for your letter. Very.

You write of the sweet smell of the dew, to which I answer that the dew smells sweet and sparkles only on sweet-smelling and beautiful flowers.

I have always desired your happiness, and anything I could have done to bring it about I would have done with joy. But I could not.

And what is happiness? Who knows the answer to this? I for one, recalling my own life, am most vividly aware of being happy at precisely those moments when, as it seemed to me at the time, I was most unhappy. When I was young I was full of the joys of life – that is something different.

And so, once again my thanks, and all best wishes, etc.

Alyokhin

1. This letter was supposedly recalled from memory by Lidia Avilova, who claimed that she and Chekhov had a serious relationship, and that he referred to himself as 'Alyokhin', as in his story 'About Love', hence the signature in this letter. The tone of the letter and its language seem so un-Chekhovian that one wonders why it was included in the Academy of Sciences' definitive edition of Chekhov's collected works.

306. To Maria Chekhova, 30 May 1901, en route to Aksyonovo

Dearest Masha,

The plant in my study that looks like an onion needs watering once every three days. The birch tree needs three buckets-full once a week. The roses once a week, without fail. The camellias and the azalea will be all right just with the rain. The eucalyptus is in among the camellias and the chrysanthemums, and it should be watered as often as possible, every day.

We are sailing down the River Belaya to Ufa. It's very hot. Respects to Mama and everyone. I shall be back soon, sooner than you expect. Keep well. Olga sends her respects.

Your

Antoine

Tell Sinani to send my mail on to Aksyonovo.

307. To Maria Chekhova, 4 June 1901, Aksyonovo

Dearest Masha,

The letter you wrote advising me against getting married was sent on to me from Moscow and arrived here yesterday. I'm not sure whether I have made a mistake or not, but the main considerations impelling me to get married were, first, I am already over forty, second, Olga comes from a highly principled family, and third, if it should ever come to our having to part company, I can do so without a moment's hesitation just as if we were not married: she is an independent woman and well able to live on her own means. Then, it is most important to remember that this marriage will have absolutely no effect on my way of life, nor on those who have lived and are now living with me. Everything, I emphasize everything, will remain as it was before, and I shall continue to live alone in Yalta.

I am thrilled that you want to come here to Ufa province. If you have really decided to come, it would be wonderful. Come at the beginning of July; we'll stay here for a while and you can drink kumiss, and then we'll go down the Volga together as far as Novorossiisk and on to Yalta. The best way to come is via Moscow, Nizhny and Samara. It's further, but in the end it will save two or even three days. When I told Knippschütz you were coming, she was overjoyed.[1] Today she has gone into Ufa to do some shopping. It's rather dull here, but the kumiss tastes good; it's warm, and the food is not at all bad. One of these days we shall go fishing.

I'm sending you a cheque for 500 roubles. If you think this is too much cash to keep at home, deposit some of it in your name at the State Bank. Sinani will tell you how to do this. When you come, you will need to take a bit more than 100 roubles for travel tickets; I have money here to pay for the return journey.

The address for telegrams here is: Chekhov, Aksyonovo. If you decide to come to us, send just one word: coming.

Anna Chokhova is here staying with a seventeen-year-old girl, the daughter of the late Liza. She seems a very nice girl.

When you send your telegram to 'Chekhov, Aksyonovo', put a line at the bottom of the telegram and below it write 'Samaro-Zlatoustovskoy', like this:

Samaro-Zlatoustovskoy

Put this right at the bottom of the page.

The kumiss doesn't seem to upset my stomach. I seem to be tolerating it quite well.

A deep bow and my greetings to Mamasha. Please pass on my thanks to Varvara Konstantinovna for her telegram. Well, look after yourself and don't worry. Write more often, please.

Your

Antoine

---

1. Masha did not in fact make the journey and remained in Yalta that summer.

308. To Olga Vasilieva, 12 June 1901, Aksyonovo

Dear Olga Rodionovna,

I don't think you should sell for 125,000 roubles. There's no hurry after all. If something is valued on first sight at five roubles, it means you ought to be able to sell it for seven and a half. Wait a little, perhaps a year or even six months, and in the meantime some reliable person should go to Odessa and establish how much your house is really worth and whether it could be sold for a greater sum. Since you intend the proceeds to go towards paying for a hospital, the best person to go to Odessa would be a doctor, because he would have an interest and therefore be that much more reliable. I can recommend Dr Mikhail Alexandrovich Chlenov,[1] a medical practitioner and the most honest of men; if you write and let me know that you are happy for him to do this I will write to him, he will make the trip and then write to you.

Building a hospital is an excellent plan. But my advice to you is to secure the *zemstvo*'s approval first, that is to say, the hospital should be a *zemstvo* hospital. I believe you should expect to lay out ten to fifteen thousand roubles in the first instance; it is better to leave additional investment until later, when the project is already on its feet and working; things will be clearer to you then. Write to Dr Dmitry Nikolayevich Zhbankov in Smolensk (he is a *zemstvo* doctor) and ask him how to proceed and to whom to apply, emphasizing the pressing need for medical services. He will write back to you immediately and steer you in the right direction, but don't at this stage indicate how much you are minded to contribute, because this is something that will only become clear to you as time goes on.

Then please write and tell me how matters are progressing. The main thing is not to be in too much of a hurry.

My health has improved and I'm coughing much less. May you stay

1. Mikhail Chlenov (1871–1941), a dermatologist and professor of medicine at Moscow University.

in good health and under God's protection for many years. My best respects to the adorable Masha.[2]

Your

A. Chekhov

309. To Alexander Chekhov, 21 June 1901, Aksyonovo

Explain to me, O Lord, why you are not writing to me. Are you angry with me?

Well, I'm taking a kumiss cure at present, and my address (until 10 July) is: Aksyonovo, Ufa Province. After the 10th, the address will be as before, i.e. Yalta.

I owe you an apology: I failed to ask your permission and your blessing. You see, I've gone and got married, in a manner of speaking!

Keep well, and please write to me. Where is Misha? If he is in Petersburg, what is he doing? Tell him to write to me. Respects to the family.

Your kumissful brother

Antoine

NB This is certainly nothing like England!

310. To Maria Chekhova, 3 August 1901, Yalta

Dearest Masha,

I hereby bequeath to you for the remainder of your life my villa in Yalta, the money and the income from my stage works; and to my wife Olga Leonardovna my villa in Gurzuf and 5,000 roubles. You may sell the property should you so desire. To my brother Alexander I give 3,000, to Ivan 5,000 and to Mikhail 3,000, to Alexey Dolzhenko

2. Olga Vasilieva had adopted a little girl from an orphanage in Smolensk.

1,000 and to Elena Chekhova (Lyolya) 1,000 roubles if she does not marry. After your death and Mother's death the entire residue, with the exception of the income from the stage works, shall be put at the disposal of the Taganrog Municipality to be used in the support of public education, and the income from the stage works shall be given to my brother Ivan, and after his death to the Taganrog Municipality for the like support of public education.

I have promised to give 100 roubles to the peasants of Melikhovo village to pay for a road; I have also promised Gavriil Alexeyevich Kharchenko[1] of Moskalevka, Kharkov, that I will pay for his eldest daughter's Gymnasium fees until such time as he is relieved of the necessity to pay for her education. Help the poor. Take care of our mother. Live in peace.

Anton Chekhov

311. To Olga Knipper-Chekhova, 24 August 1901, Yalta

Dear heart, I got two postcards and one sealed letter from you, thank you! You are kind and good and I love you, I love you. I've had a headache all day today, a splitting one, and on top of that I've had one visitor after another from morning till night (just as I did yesterday). I can't do any work. Among the nicer guests, however, were Doroshevich and a doctor from Piter called Reformatsky.

The carpets are already down on my floor. It's very cosy. The stoves are going to be rebuilt. After the amount of watering you and I gave them, the roses have burst into flower.

I shall come to Moscow in September as soon as you write and tell me to. It's very dull without you. I've grown used to you, like a little boy; without you it feels cold and comfortless.

The school director and her sister-in-law Manefa came to see me. It's raining. Our new cook, a Polish woman called Masha, makes very

1. As a boy, Kharchenko had worked as an apprentice in Pavel Chekhov's shop in Taganrog.

nice meals. For the past three days we've been eating like human beings. My room has been tidied up, and Arseny cleaned my clothes today. Tatarinova[1] was here yesterday – did I write and tell you that?

You write 'my heart grows heavy when I think of the quiet sadness that seems to lie deep in your soul'. What nonsense, darling heart! There's no sadness and never has been; mostly I feel fairly content with life, and when you are with me I feel marvellous.

Write and tell me how you were received in the theatre, what plays are running at the moment and are planned for the future, and what you are going to be doing until 15 September. Write at length, don't be lazy. My letters to you are long, but my handwriting is small and so they come out looking short.

It's been rather cold, but it looks as though it will warm up now. It's calm and lovely; the roses are a riot of colour, in a word life is nothing but a bowl of cherries.

I hug you, my darling wife, I kiss you and bless you and beg you not to forget me, to write to me and to think of me often. When I come I'll kiss you without stopping for an hour, and then I'll go to the baths and the hairdresser, then have dinner and then go to sleep. All right? Sweetheart! What a dreadful portrait of you in *Holiday*! Oh my, oh my!

I kiss you on both palms.

Your

Antoine

312. To Olga Knipper-Chekhova, 3 September 1901, Yalta

Hello, dearest Olka! I didn't write to you yesterday, first because there were crowds of visitors, and second because I had no time; as soon as the visitors had left I sat down to work on a story.

Thank you, joy of my life; Mother was overjoyed by your letter.

---

1. Fanny Tatarinova (1863–1923), a resident of Yalta who published *The Yalta Sheet* before moving to Moscow, where she taught singing at the Moscow Art Theatre.

She read it through and then gave it to me to read out loud to her, upon which she had all kinds of nice things to say about you. There may be some truth in what you say about your jealous feelings, but you are such an intelligent person and have such a good heart that nothing you say about your so-called jealousy accords in any way with your character. You go on about how Masha will never accept you, and so on. What nonsense that is! You're exaggerating and not thinking straight, and I'm very worried that you might end up even quarrelling with Masha. This is what I want to say to you: be patient and say nothing for a year, just one year, and then you will see clearly how things truly stand. Whatever anyone says, however things may seem, just say nothing, not a word. Newly married couples always find that the best way to get on with life lies precisely in being willing for a time to let things be. Do listen to me, dear heart, be a good and clever girl!

I'll come whenever you write and tell me to, but definitely not a day later than 15 September. It shall be as you wish, but I'm not going to wait any longer than that. I'll stay in Moscow until December, unless you throw me out.

Please send me Nemirovich's play, my little German girl! I'll read it with great attention and bring it back with me in one piece.

I shan't bring many clothes with me; I can buy whatever I need in Moscow. I shall get warm underwear and an overcoat there but will bring my rug and galoshes with me (I'll travel in the old overcoat). In short, I'll do my best to come with as little luggage as possible.

I'm having the most enormous wardrobe built for myself and my wife. My wife is an extremely demanding woman, and I have to make life more comfortable for her. Yesterday I washed my hair in spirit.

I kiss and hug my dearest old girl. May God preserve you. A little while longer and we shall be seeing one another. Write to me, do please write, sweetheart! I shall never love anyone but you, not any other woman in the world.

Be well and cheerful!

Your husband

Anton

313. *To Evgenia Chekhova, 17 September 1901, Moscow*

Dearest Mama,

I've arrived in Moscow. My address is The Boitsov House, Spiridonovka. Masha is in good health and feels very well, and Olga the same. They both send their respects to you. It is cool in Moscow, but dry.

I will write to you often, so don't be downcast and just take things easy, as they come.

Keep well. Greetings to Maryushka, Arseny, Marfusha[1] and Maria.
Your

A. Chekhov

314. *To Alexey Peshkov, 24 September 1901, Moscow*

My very dear Alexey Maximovich,

I'm in Moscow and received your letter here. My address is: The Boitsov House, Spiridonovka. Before I left Yalta I went to see Lev Nikolayevich. He has become extremely partial to the Crimea; there is something there that gives him a childlike joy, but I did not think he was looking at all well. He has aged greatly, and that's the main thing wrong with him – old age, which has already overtaken him. I shall be back in Yalta in October, and if they give you permission to travel there, it will be wonderful. In the first place there are not many people in Yalta during the winter, no one to bore you or stop you working, and in the second place Lev Nikolayevich obviously misses having company and we would go to visit him.

Do finish your play, my dear friend. You feel it is not turning out as you would wish, but you shouldn't trust your feelings, they are deceptive. It is quite usual not to like a play while you are writing it, and not to like it afterwards, come to that; but let others be the judge

1. The Chekhov family cook in Yalta.

of that. Just don't give it to anybody to read, no one at all; send it straight to Nemirovich in Moscow, or send it to me so that I can pass it on to the Art Theatre. Later on, if you are not completely happy with something, you can always alter it in rehearsal, even right up to the eve of the first night.

Do you have the last section of *The Three*?

I'm forwarding to you a completely pointless letter.[1] I received an identical one.

Well, God be with you. Keep well and, if such a thing is possible for an inhabitant of Arzamas, happy. Give my respectful greetings to Ekaterina Pavlovna and the children.

Your

A. Chekhov

Please write.

315. To Olga Knipper-Chekhova, 29 October 1901, Yalta

My dearest, glorious, wise and wonderful wife, light of my life, greetings to you! I'm sitting at home in Yalta, and it feels so strange! The Sredins and the director of the girls' Gymnasium were here today, and already in my mind I've slipped back into the old boring and empty routine. Anyhow, the journey was very good, although after Sevastopol I didn't continue by road as there was a steamer going all the way to Yalta. It was fine and didn't take too long, although it was cold . . . it's not so much cold here as absolutely perishing; on the journey I was even cold in my overcoat.

Tatarinova is about to come and see me on business, and I'm anxious to get down to writing. Mother is well and says I could have stayed longer in Moscow. Sredin is also well, or at least looks well; he spent the whole time scolding his daughter-in-law.

My angel, my sweetheart, my darling doggie, please believe I love

1. Probably a reference to a letter from Mikhail Feofanov, a Russian translator who lived in Germany.

you deeply; don't forget me, and think about me all the time. Whatever the future may bring, even if you were suddenly to turn into an old woman, I would still love you for your soul and the sweetness of your disposition. Write to me, my dear little dog! Look after your health. If, God forbid, you should fall ill, drop everything and come to Yalta, I'll look after you here. Don't overtire yourself, my darling.

I've received a whole lot of photographs from Kharkov. A photographer came here in the summer and took pictures of me in all sorts of poses.

Dinner today was of the most elaborate nature – probably because of your letter. We had chicken cutlets and pancakes. The tongue we bought at Belov's got spoilt during the journey, or at least it seems to have; it's giving off rather an unpleasant smell.

May the good Lord bless you. Think of me, remember I'm your husband. I kiss you fervently, I hug you and kiss you again. The bed seems so lonely, fit only for a mingy, cantankerous old bachelor.

Write!!

Your

Antoine

Don't forget you're my wife; write to me every day.

Give my respects to Masha. I'm still eating the sweets your mother gave me. Give her my respects as well.

316. To Olga Knipper-Chekhova, 6 November 1901, Yalta

Well my dearest love, yesterday I went to see Tolstoy. I found him in bed. He's bruised himself and has had to lie down. His health is better than it was, but this is just because of the warm days we had at the end of October, and winter will be upon us all too soon! As far as I could tell he was glad to see me, and for some reason I was particularly glad to see him. His expression is kind and genial, but he looks like an old man, verging on the senile. He listens eagerly to what you have to say and is more than ready to talk. He still likes being in the Crimea.

Balmont came to see me today.[1] He is banned from Moscow now, otherwise he would have come to see you in December and you would have helped him get tickets for all the plays running in your theatre. He is a great fellow, and the main thing is, I've known him a long time and consider him a friend, as he does me.

How are you, my treasure and my delight? Sredin was here today and brought a photograph with him, the one we brought back from Aksyonovo but enlarged, so that we have both come out looking old, with our eyes all screwed up.

Sweetheart, use ordinary writing paper and envelopes when you write to me, because if you don't, by the time your letters reach me they show every sign of having been hurriedly opened. It's a lot of nonsense, but we are provincials down here my love, we're mistrustful people.

Are you really building a new theatre? When? Write and tell me these things, wife, otherwise it's so dreary; I feel as if I have been married for twenty years and this is the first time I have been apart from you. I will probably come in January; I'll wrap up warm and when I get to Moscow I'll stay indoors.

Keep well, my kind, gentle, glorious little German girl. I love you very much and cherish you.

I embrace you and cover you with kisses, keep well and cheerful. Thank you for your letters!

Your

Antonio

---

1. Konstantin Balmont (1867–1942), the Symbolist poet who in 1901 was exiled from all university towns in the Russian Empire for reading an anti-Tsarist poem at a public reading.

317. To Olga Knipper-Chekhova, 17 November 1901, Yalta

Dearest better half, the rumours you have heard about Tolstoy's illness and even death are quite baseless. There is and has been no significant change in his state of health, and nothing to suggest that his death is in any way imminent. It is true that he is weak and looks sickly, but he has no life-threatening symptoms except old age . . . so don't believe anything you hear. If, God forbid, anything should happen, I'll let you know by telegram. I'll refer to him as 'Grandpa', otherwise the telegram might not get to you.

Alexey Maximovich is here and in fine fettle. He is registered to stay in my house and is doing so. We had a visit from the local policeman today.[1]

I am writing and working, but, sweetheart, it's impossible to work in Yalta, utterly impossible. Life is so uninteresting, so cut off from the world, and above all so cold. I had a letter from Vishnevsky; you can tell him that I will write a play, but not before the spring.

The lamp is burning in my study as I write. So far it doesn't smell of paraffin, it works pretty well.

Alexey Maximovich is just the same, still the decent, intelligent and generous person he always was. Only one thing jars about him, or rather on him: his peasant blouse. I just can't get used to it, any more than I could to a chamberlain's uniform.

The weather is autumnal, not very pleasant at all.

Keep alive and in good health, light of my life. Thank you for your letters. Take care of yourself and don't get ill. Give my respects to your family.

I kiss you warmly and embrace you.

Your husband

Antonio

I'm in good health. Moscow had an incredibly good effect on me. I

1. Both Tolstoy and Gorky were under constant police surveillance for separate political reasons.

don't know who is responsible, you or Moscow, but I've hardly been coughing at all.

If you should see Kundasova, or anyone who will be seeing her soon, please let her know that Dr Vasiliev, the psychiatrist, is at present in Yalta, and is very seriously ill.

318. To Olga Knipper-Chekhova, 4 December 1901, Yalta

Hello my sweetheart, my better half! You are not pleased with my letters, I know that, and admire your taste. But how can I help it, my dearest, if I've been out of sorts all these last few days! You must forgive me and not be angry with your absurd old man.

Yesterday your letter really put me out of sorts, when you wrote that you would not be coming to Yalta for Christmas. I don't know what's the best thing for me to do. Some of the doctors say it's all right for me to go to Moscow, others say it is out of the question. But I simply can't stay here, I absolutely cannot!

What is this I hear about your taking a lease on the Aumont Theatre?[1] I understand you can't stay on in the old one; sooner or later you'll have a fire there, in any case it's not a central enough location. I'm always worried there might be a fire during the fourth act of *Three Sisters*, there is such a mad scrum of people on the stage.

Don't hold back, my doggie, write and tell me every little thing that finds its way into your head, no matter how irrelevant or trifling: you just can't imagine how essential your letters are to me, how calm and happy they make me feel. The thing is, I love you, that's what you must not forget.

I'm going to see Gorky in Oleiza today. I may see Tolstoy as well.

A wealthy Tatar came to see me yesterday, wanting to borrow money from me to be paid back with interest. When I told him that I

1. A theatre in Moscow in Kamergevsky Lane, where farces were staged. In 1902 it indeed became the new home of the Moscow Art Theatre, which had previously rented a theatre in Karetny Row.

don't lend money against interest and consider it a sin, he was astonished and didn't believe me. One of my close friends has borrowed 500 roubles 'just till Friday'. People are always borrowing from me 'just till Friday'.

I kiss and hug my lovely wife. Don't be upset, my darling, if for some reason you don't get a letter from me. It will be my fault, but I deserve compassion.

Your husband
Antonio

Aren't there any new plays? I had a letter from Fyodorov,[2] the author of *The Trees Blown Down*, in which he tells me he has sent a play to Nemirovich.

319. To Viktor Goltsev, 11 December 1901, Yalta

My dearest friend Viktor Alexandrovich,

I am lying in bed at the moment occupying myself with coughing blood. I'm eating nothing and doing nothing except reading the newspapers. Don't be angry with me, my friend. I'll get back to work as soon as I feel better.

Please don't mention my illness to anyone; I don't want it appearing in the papers. I've written to my wife.

I warmly clasp your hand and kiss you, my dear friend. All the best to you.

Your

A. Chekhov

2. Alexander Fyodorov (1868–1949), a writer and playwright.

320. *To Olga Knipper-Chekhova, 22 December 1901, Yalta*

Dearest sweetheart, I've been waiting all day for a telegram about Nemirovich's play, but nothing has come! I suppose this means it was such a riotous success you've all forgotten about me.

I keep forgetting to tell you: if you need any money, ask Nemirovich for whatever you need. Get organized and be a good little housekeeper, my darling. Oh, if only you knew how much I need you, how very, very much! It's no good being without a wife.

The weather is hot in Yalta just now. Masha is thrilled, she is walking round the garden just in a dress; she can't believe there is snow and frost in Moscow at the moment.

I love you. Do you know that?

My health is absolutely fine. They took the compress off yesterday, and tomorrow Altshuller will apply Spanish fly blisters, and that will be that, the end of the treatment. I'm eating a lot now and am really proud of my appetite.

Now, darling heart, keep well and be happy. I hope you are feeling well and in good spirits for the holidays, but spare a thought for your husband once in a while and, if you can, write to him every day.

I kiss you and hug you, there being no opportunity for anything more serious. Will you come in the first week of Lent?

Your

Antonio

You promised your photograph, don't forget.

321. *To Olga Knipper-Chekhova, 29 December 1901, Yalta*

You are such a silly goose, my sweetheart. Never once since our marriage have I reproached you over the theatre; on the contrary I am delighted that you have work to do, that your life has a purpose and that you don't spend your time spouting rubbish like your husband. I didn't write to you about my illness because I'm already better. My temperature is normal, I eat five eggs a day and drink milk, not to speak of lunch, which now we have Masha here is always delicious. Carry on with your work, sweetheart, don't worry about me and above all don't get depressed.

You don't need to subscribe to *The World of Art*,[1] as it's one of the magazines I take. We are having warm weather in Yalta, all the buds are coming out and if this weather goes on another week they will start flowering.

Masha is put out that you are not writing to her.

Here is a photograph of two Boers.

Dr Altshuller is coming to Moscow any day now, and I've been telling him he must have lunch with you. He is coming to Moscow for a conference on Wednesday. Ask Masha (your cook) to tell him when you will be at home, if he should call when you are out.

Are you going to put on [Gorky's] *The Petty Bourgeois*? When? This season or next?

Well, goodbye for now, you poor wee thing, please look after your health! Don't you dare feel down and play Lazarus. Have a good laugh at it all. I hug you and am sad that that is all I can do.

There was no letter from you yesterday. What a lazy old thing you've become! Oh doggie, doggie!

Well, my dear heart, my lovely, glorious wife, I kiss you warmly and hug you close once again. I think of you very, very often, you must do the same of me.

Your

Antonio

---

1. This was the lavishly illustrated modernist arts journal founded in St Petersburg by Sergey Diaghilev (1872–1929) in 1898.

322. To Olga Knipper-Chekhova, 3 January 1902, Yalta

Sweetheart, two letters from you arrived at once today. Thank you! And Mother also got a letter from you. But you shouldn't bewail your fate like that, after all you're not in Moscow just because you feel like it, it's what we both want. And Mother is not angry with you or grumbling about you, not in the slightest.

I had my hair cut this morning! I was in town for the first time after being ill, in spite of the frost (minus 2 degrees), and I had my hair cut and my beard trimmed – this is all in case you should appear. You're very strict after all, one has to look presentable and have good manners.

Masha has taken on another cook. I am not writing at all, not a scrap! Don't be alarmed, everything will be done in time. After all, I've already written eleven volumes, and that's no joke. After I reach the age of forty-five I'll write another twenty volumes. Don't be angry, my sweetheart, my wife! I may not be writing, but I am reading so much that I'll soon become as wise as the wisest Jew.

It's January already, and so the most horrible weather is beginning, windy and cold and muddy, and after that comes February with its fogs. These are the months when the situation of a married man whose wife is absent is especially pitiable. If only you would come at the end of January, as you promised!

Gorky is in a gloomy mood at the moment, he seems not very well. He is coming to stay the night tonight.

Do you feel that I love you, my doggie? Or don't you care either way? But I love you fiercely, as you know. Keep well, my glorious little German wife, my actress, may God care for you and keep your life tranquil, happy and peaceful.

Your husband
Anton

323. *To Olga Knipper-Chekhova, 29 January 1902, Yalta*

On the razzle again, you Saturnalian! Well, that's good, splendid, I love you for it, only don't get yourself overtired.

What a ridiculous idea to award me the Griboyedov Prize [for *Three Sisters*]! The only thing it will do is expose me to yet more of Burenin's carping. In any case I'm too old to need such incentives.

You're only coming for two days? Is that all? That's like giving Tanner[1] a teaspoonful of milk after starving for forty days. It will do nothing but upset us, drive us further apart. Think about it, darling heart, wouldn't it be better to delay your arrival until the end of Lent? Think about it. Coming for just two days is really cruel. If this is Nemirovich's beneficence, thank you most humbly!

If I can wait until the end of February, then I can wait until the end of Lent. The only thing two days will do is wear you out with the journey, and upset me by having to say goodbye to you immediately after getting sick with anticipation of your coming. No, no, no!

Your last letters were very good, my sweetheart, I read them more than once.

I love you, doggie, I can't help it.

Write to me, I'll write back straight away.

Your

Antoine

I give my Saturnalian a big hug.

If you cannot be dissuaded from coming at the end of Shrovetide, then take note that I won't accept less than five days! Five days and six nights.

---

1. Henry Tanner, an American doctor who carried out research into long-term fasting.

324. *To Maria Chekhova, 31 January 1902, Yalta*

Dearest Masha,

Mother is a little unwell. She had an upset stomach all night, Marfusha kept having to take her to the W C. I didn't sleep, or not well anyhow, and woke up coughing blood. Mother is a little easier now, and there's no blood when I cough, so evidently the worst is over.

The sun is shining today, but it rained during the night. The almond tree is trying hard to blossom; the ones in the town are already in bloom. It's almost as if spring is in the air.

Mother got your letter and was very pleased with it. Please send the clover as quickly as you can; the whole garden has been dug and we need something to sow.

Keep well and happy. Write whenever you feel inclined.

I kiss you.

Your

Antoine

325. *To Grigory Rossolimo, 6 February 1902, Yalta*

Dear Grigory Ivanovich,

I sent money to Dr Danilov as well, but got no response. Not a whisper. It looks very much as though something has occurred, something bad. Is there nobody you know in Kaluga, someone perhaps who knows the doctor and could make inquiries on the spot?

I am living in Yalta, where life is as dreary as being in indefinite exile, and from time to time I suffer bouts of indisposition. I coughed up blood once or twice during the winter and had to take to my bed, which interrupted my work and set me back to the beginning again; in a word, it's not been very good.

I was delighted to hear from you even if only on a business matter.

In the spring I plan to be in Moscow, where I have a nice apartment; we have moved from Spiridonovka to the Gonetskaya house in Neglinny Passage.

I warmly clasp your hand and wish you the best of temper and of health.

Your

A. Chekhov

If you hear from Danilov or anything about him, please let me know.

326. *To Olga Knipper-Chekhova, 13 February 1902, Yalta*

Doggie, sweetheart! I won't come down to the jetty to meet you because it will probably be too chilly for me. Don't be alarmed though, I'll meet you in my study, then we'll have supper together and talk for ages.

Yesterday, completely out of the blue, I had a letter from Suvorin, after a silence of three years. He is critical of the theatre but full of praise for you, since I suppose it would be awkward for him to criticize you.

Apparently Ekaterina Pavlovna[1] has already left for Moscow. If there isn't a performance that she can see, at least she can come to a rehearsal and that will give her some idea.

Tell Chlenov that I shall write to him without fail in the next few days. I've nothing much to write about, otherwise I would have written long ago.

Letters seem to be taking five days, not three, to get to Yalta. So you won't get this letter, which I'm sending you on 13 February, until 17 or 18 February. There you are, you see! So I shall write one more letter to you, and then – *basta!* After that, only a little longer to wait until I can enter upon my marital responsibilities.

1. Gorky's wife.

When you get here, please don't say anything about the food. It's a boring subject, especially in Yalta. As soon as Masha went away, everything went back to how it was before she came, and there's nothing to be done about it.

I've been reading Turgenev. Only one eighth or one tenth of what he wrote will survive; in twenty-five to thirty-five years' time all the rest will be mouldering in the archives. Surely there can never have been a time when you liked that *Alarm Clock* artist Chichagov? Oh my, oh my!

Why on earth does Savva Morozov[2] invite those noblemen to his house? They bore everyone to tears, and then sneer at him once they've left as if he were a Yakut. I'd chase the swine off with a big stick.

I have some perfume here, but not much. And a little eau de Cologne.

I kiss my darling, ravishingly beautiful wife, and cannot wait for her to come here. It is overcast today, rather on the cold side, dull, and if it weren't for thinking about you and your soon being here, I believe I'd take to drink.

I embrace my little German.

Your

Antoine

327. To Maria Chekhova, 13 March 1902, Yalta

Dearest Masha,

It's already getting warmer, the rain has stopped, and it's time to start watering the trees. We are all well; Mother and Granny are fasting. I was told on the telephone today that Leonid Sredin is ill; his temperature is above 39. There is an engine outside making a

2. Savva Morozov (1862–1905), textile millionaire and scion of one of Moscow's main merchant families; the principal underwriter of the Moscow Art Theatre.

tremendous din pounding away at the roadway. Munt[1] is now doing all the performances in Petersburg instead of Lilina; this will really rock the theatre's reputation. The sea is as calm as in summer; the cutter has already started going to Gurzuf. The cranes are thriving, they're dancing a lot. Kashtanka is getting very plump.

Keep well and happy. Which week and which day are you coming? Write and let me know. The barometer is falling, but it still doesn't look like rain.

Your

Antoine

328. To Pavel Iordanov, 19 March 1902, Yalta

These are the books I shall shortly be sending to the library:
1) I. Bunin. *Stories* (two copies)
2) Leonid Andreyev. *Stories*. 2nd edition
3) Skitalets. *Stories and Songs* (two copies)
4) Maxim Gorky. *The Philistines* (two copies)
5) Aeschylus. *Prometheus Bound**
6) Sophocles. *Oedipus at Colonnus**
7) Euripides. *Hippolytus**
8) Sophocles. *Oedipus the King**
9) Sophocles. *Antigone**
10) Euripides. *Medea**

* Merezhkovsky's translations published in the 'Knowledge' Society edition.

1. Ekaterina Munt (1875–1954), an actress at the Moscow Art Theatre who played Natasha in *Three Sisters*.

329. *To Vladimir Korolenko, 19 April 1902, Yalta*

Dear Vladimir Galaktionovich,

My wife has arrived from Petersburg with a temperature of 39 degrees; she is very weak and in great pain. She cannot walk, and had to be carried from the steamer ... However, she is feeling a little better now.

I do not propose to pass on the protest letter to Tolstoy. When I spoke to him about Gorky and the Academy, he replied: 'I do not consider myself a member of the Academy' and immediately buried himself in a book. I gave a copy to Gorky, and also read him your letter. I have a feeling that there won't be any meeting at the Academy on 25 May, since all the members will have dispersed at the beginning of the month. I also have a suspicion that Gorky will not be elected a second time; he will be blackballed. I would dearly love to see you to have a talk. I suppose there is no prospect of your coming to Yalta? I shall be here until 5 May. But for the illness of my wife, which I expect to keep her in bed for three weeks or so, I would have come to visit you in Poltava. Or perhaps we could meet after 15 May, in Moscow, or on the Volga, or abroad? Write and let me know.

I warmly clasp your hand and send you my best wishes. Keep well. Your

A. Chekhov

My wife sends you her respects.

330. *To the Editors,* La Revue Blanche, *7 May 1902, Yalta*

A Messieurs les Editeurs de La Revue Blanche

Messieurs,

J'apprends avec plaisir que vous allez publier en français quatre de mes nouvelles: 'Un Meurtre', 'Paysans', 'L'Etudiant' et 'Maîtresse d'école' dans la traduction de Mademoiselle Ducreux.

Cette traduction m'a été soumise et j'ai pu en apprécier les très rares mérites de sobre élégance et de fidélité scrupuleuse.

Je suis heureux de vous envoyer ma pleine et entière approbation.

Veuillez agréer l'assurance de mon profond respect.

Anton Tchekhov

[To the Editors of *La Revue Blanche*:

Sirs,

It is with pleasure that I have learnt of your proposal to publish four of my stories in a French translation by Mlle [Claire] Ducreux: 'Murder', 'Peasants', 'The Student' and 'The Schoolteacher'.

I have been shown this translation and have had the opportunity to appreciate its rare qualities of sober elegance and scrupulous fidelity.

I am happy to send you my full and entire approval.

Please be assured of my profound respect.

Anton Tchekhov]

331. To Maria Chekhova, 29 May 1902, Moscow

Dear Masha,

It is very hot in Moscow, hotter than in Yalta. I like the apartment a lot, it's very nice indeed, except for the garlands with ribbons and the pictures. The visitors are completely wearing me out.

Dr Varnek came yesterday to have a look at Olga, and ordered her to stay in bed in Moscow for three weeks and then go to Franzensbad.[1]

Send on ordinary letters to me just by putting them in the letter box, as I told you, but ask Arseny to take any registered letters back to the post office with a request to forward them to Moscow; he should let them know at the post office that I shall be coming back soon. Only send letters on, keep newspapers and books in Yalta; you can also hold on to parcels there, should there be any.

I'm waiting for a spittoon to be delivered.

1. A spa town in what is now the Czech Republic.

Keep well. I don't think I'll go to Franzensbad, I really don't want to. I'll come back to Yalta.

My respects and greetings to Mamasha and everyone. Vanya has gone to the Unzha.[2] Chlenov has been here.

Your

Antoine

332. To Vladimir Nemirovich-Danchenko, 16 June 1902, Moscow

Dear Vladimir Ivanovich,

For three days Olga has eaten nothing but cream (without bread), four glasses a day, and only now has she got over the feeling of heaviness in the pit of her stomach. Today she is sitting up in a chair and is being allowed some chicken soup. The main thing is that I am now allowed to leave her, and so tomorrow I shall go with Morozov to Perm. I shall be back by 5 July.

Keep well and happy. If you wish, you may telegraph me at the Klubnaya Hotel, Perm. I shall be there on 22, 23 and probably 24 June, and then travel on a bit further upriver by boat. It is now six o'clock in the evening: Olga is going to get dressed, sit in a chair and have something to eat (chicken soup and some port). She has become painfully thin.

Please pass on my respects to Ekaterina Nikolayevna, and do write. I repeat, I shall be back in Moscow on 5 July.

Your

A. Chekhov

2. A tributary of the Volga.

333. To Olga Knipper-Chekhova, 18 June 1902, on board the Kama

My dearest lovely wife Olya, I slept wonderfully well all night in the sleeping car, and now (twelve noon) we are on the Volga. There is quite a wind and it is not very warm, but it is very, very good to be here. I sit on deck all the time and look at the banks. The sun is shining. Morozov has brought along with him two good-natured Germans, an old one and a young one; neither speaks a word of Russian, so I have no choice but to speak German. If you time it right crossing over from one side of the ship to the other, you can stay out of the wind. So, all in all I'm in a splendid, German frame of mind, I'm enjoying travelling in comfort like this, and I'm not coughing nearly as much as I was. I'm not worrying about you, since I know for certain that my doggie is quite well, it can't be otherwise.

Give my respects to Vishnevsky and thank him for me: his temperature is a little on the high side, but he has no need to be anxious or depressed, he's just not used to it.

My best respects to your mama and my best wishes for her peace of mind while staying with us, I hope the bedbugs aren't biting her. My greetings to Zina.

I'll write every day, my sweetheart. Sleep well, and think of your husband. The boat is shaking, it's difficult to write.

I kiss and hug my incomparable wife.

Send me a telegram telling me what Shtraukh said.

Your

Antoine

334. To Konstantin Alexeyev (Stanislavsky), 18 July 1902, Lyubimovka

Dear Konstantin Sergeyevich,

Dr Shtraukh came to Lyubimovka today and found all was well. The only thing he has forbidden Olga to do is travel on rough roads, and generally she must avoid unnecessary movements. But to my great joy he has lifted all restrictions on her taking part in rehearsals; she can start work in the theatre as early as 10 August. She is not allowed to travel to Yalta; I shall go there alone in August, return in the middle of September and then stay in Moscow until December.

I love being at Lyubimovka. April and May took a lot out of me, but now, as if in recompense for what I have been through, so much tranquillity, health, warmth and pleasure has descended on me that I can but spread my arms in grateful acceptance. The weather is wonderful, the river is wonderful, and we eat and sleep in the house like bishops. A thousand thanks to you, from the bottom of my heart. It is a long time since I spent such a summer. I go fishing every day, five times a day, and the fishing is pretty good too (yesterday we had soup made from ruff), and I can't tell you what a pleasure it is just to sit there on the bank. In short, everything is marvellous. The only bad side of it is that I am being very lazy and doing nothing. I still haven't made a start on the play, merely thought about it. I probably won't start it until the end of August.

Olga sends you her greetings and deepest respects, Vishnevsky likewise. Please pass on my respects and greetings to Maria Petrovna and the children. Keep well and cheerful, and build up your strength and energy. I press your hand.

Your

A. Chekhov

Vishnevsky has put on weight.

I've addressed this letter to 'K. Alexeeff', not C[onstantin], it's easier that way.

Olga is sleeping downstairs, Vishnevsky and I upstairs. We get up at eight o'clock, go to bed at 10.30 or eleven o'clock, lunch at one o'clock and have supper at seven o'clock. Egor and Duniasha are very kind and take excellent care of us. Of the neighbours, the most frequent callers are Mika (your nephew) and the artist N. Smirnova, who is painting my portrait.

335. To Olga Knipper-Chekhova, 17 August 1902, Yalta

At last I'm home, dearest heart. The journey was good, there were no incidents, but it was terribly dusty. There were a lot of people I knew on the boat, and the sea was calm. At home everyone was overjoyed to see me, asked after you and gave me a hard time that you weren't with me; but when I gave Masha your letter and she read it, silence descended and my mother went into a gloom . . . Today they handed me your letter to read, I did so and was most embarrassed. Whatever made you upbraid Masha like that? I swear to you on my word of honour that when Masha and Mother asked me to come back home to Yalta, they did not mean just me, but you too. Your letter is very, very unjust. But what the pen has written the axe may not cut out, so let's just leave it there. I say to you again: on my word of honour, Mother and Masha wanted us both to come, not for a moment did they mean me alone; they have both always had the warmest affection and regard for you.

I shall soon come back to Moscow; I don't propose to stay here although it is very nice. The play [*The Cherry Orchard*] won't get written here.

When I got home yesterday evening, all dusty from the journey, I washed myself thoroughly, in accordance with your instructions, including the back of my head, my ears and my chest. I put on my quilted jacket and white waistcoat. I'm now sitting and reading the papers, of which there are a great many, enough for three days.

My mother is begging me to buy a small plot of land near Moscow. But I'm not going to talk to her about it today. I'm in a terrible mood, so I'll wait until tomorrow.

I kiss and embrace you, keep well and look after yourself. Give my respects to Elizaveta Vasilievna.[1] Write as often as you can.

Your A.

336. To Alexander Veselovsky, 25 August 1902, Yalta

Dear Professor Veselovsky,

Last December I was informed that A. M. Peshkov had been elected to honorary membership of the Academy. At the time A. M. Peshkov was in the Crimea, and I hastened to see him in order to be the first to bring him the news of his election and to congratulate him upon it. But not long thereafter it was announced in the press that, following investigations into Peshkov under the terms of Paragraph 1035, his election had been declared invalid. Furthermore, since this announcement clearly stated that it was being made by the Academy of Sciences, and since I am an Honorary Academician, it followed that I must myself be a party to it. The contradiction inherent in being, at one and the same time, the person who offered his sincere congratulations and the person who now declares the election invalid, is one I have been unable to reconcile in my mind, nor can I square such a position with my conscience. Familiarizing myself with the substance of Paragraph 1035 did nothing to help clarify my understanding. After long reflection I feel able to come to only one conclusion, one that I find most painful and regrettable: it is that I must most respectfully request you to make arrangements for me to be divested of the title of Honorary Academician.

In expressing my deep respect I have the honour to remain your most humble servant,

Anton Chekhov

1. Stanislavsky's mother.

337. Olga Knipper-Chekhova, 27 August 1902, Yalta

My darling, my perch, after a long wait I've at last received a letter from you. I'm living very quietly, I don't go into the town much, I talk to visitors and occasionally do a bit of writing. I shan't write a play this year, my heart isn't in it, but if I do come up with something vaguely play-shaped, it will be a one-act farce.

Masha did not give me your letter, I found it in my mother's room, on the table, automatically picked it up and read it – and then realized why Masha was in such low spirits. The letter is terribly rude, and above all unfair; I of course understand the kind of mood you were in when you wrote it, and can therefore interpret it. But your latest letter is somewhat strange, and I don't know what is the matter or what is going on in your head, my darling. You write: 'It was strange for them to expect you to come south when they knew I was ill in bed. It was as much as to say they did not want you to be around me when I was ill . . .' Who said they did not want me around you? When was I expected to go south? Did I not swear on my word of honour when I wrote to you that there was no question of their asking me to come back on my own, without you . . . ? This won't do, my darling, this really won't do; you must try not to be unfair. You need to be spotless with regard to the fairness of your judgements, absolutely spotless, all the more so as you are such a kind person, so very kind and understanding. Forgive my scolding, darling, I shan't do it any more, I am afraid of it.

When Egor presents his bill, please pay my share and I will give you the money in September. These are my plans: I shall stay in Moscow until the beginning of December, then go to Nervi and stay there and in Pisa until Lent, then return home. I've been coughing in Yalta more than I did in beloved Lyubimovka. It's not a particularly bad cough, but still it is there. I'm not drinking anything. Orlenev came to see me today, and Nazimova was here as well. Doroshevich came. I saw Karabchevsky a little while ago.

Did I write to you about *The Seagull*? I sent a pleading letter to Gnedich in Petersburg, imploring him not to put on *The Seagull*. I got his answer this morning: they can't not stage it, because new scenery has been painted, and so on and so on. So I'm in for more criticism.

Don't mention to Masha that I read your letter to her. Or just do as you think best.

Your letters have a chill wind blowing through them, but I still go on pestering you with my endearments and I think about you constantly. I kiss you a billion times and embrace you. My darling, write to me more than once in every five days. I am your husband, after all. Don't part from me so soon, before we've had any proper life together, and before you bear me a little boy or a little girl. When you've had a child you can do just as you like. I kiss you once again.

Your
Antoine

338. To Olga Knipper-Chekhova, 1 September 1902, Yalta

My dear, my own one, again I have a strange letter from you. Again you unload on to my poor old head all kinds of extraordinary things. Who has been telling you that I don't want to return to Moscow, that when I left it was for good and that I don't intend to come back this autumn? In fact I wrote to you, saying in plain Russian that I shall definitely come back in September and stay with you until December. Did I not? You accuse me of insincerity, at the same time forgetting everything I write or say to you. I simply can't think what I should do with my wife, how I am supposed to write to her. You write that you are overcome with trembling when you read my letters, that it is time for us to part, that there is something in all this you don't understand . . . I feel, my darling, that all this muddle has come about not because of me, not because of you, but because of someone else you've been talking to. Someone has implanted in you a lack of trust in what I say and what I do, you've become mistrustful of everything – and there is nothing, absolutely nothing, that I can do to put it right. I'm not going to try to argue you out of it or persuade you otherwise, for I can see it's useless. You write that I can be with you without uttering a word, that I only want you as a pleasant woman to have around, that you are alienated and isolated from me as a person . . . My darling love, you're my wife, please at long last understand that! You are the closest and the dearest person to me, my love for you has been and is boundless, and you describe yourself as a 'pleasant woman', alien and isolated from me . . . Well, so be it, if that's how you feel.

My health is better, but I'm coughing violently. There's no rain, it's hot. Masha is leaving on the 4th and will be in Moscow on the 6th. You write that I should show Masha your letter; thank you for that trust. Incidentally, Masha is most certainly not to blame in any way, and sooner or later you will come to the same conclusion.

I've started reading Naidenov's play.[1] I don't like it. I don't want to read it to the end. Do send me a telegram when you get to Moscow. I'm fed up with writing to you at other people's addresses. Don't forget my fishing rod, wrap it in paper. Be cheerful, don't be down, or at least look cheerful. Sofia Sredina has been to see me, she told me lots of things, none of them terribly interesting; she already knows you have not been well, who stayed with you and who didn't. Old Madame Sredina is already in Moscow.

If you think you would like to drink wine, write and tell me and I'll bring some. Also let me know if you have enough money or if you can manage until I get there. Chaleyeva[2] is living in Alupka; she is in a bad way.

Now let's get down to business.

Write and tell me what you are doing, what roles you are going to be doing again and what new ones you are learning. You're not a lazybones like your husband, are you?

My darling, be my wife, be my friend, write me nice letters, don't spread gloom and despondency, don't torture me. Be the loving, wonderful wife you truly are. I love you more than ever and as a husband have nothing to reproach myself with, please understand that once and for all, my joy, my squiggly one.

1. *The Lodgers*, a play Naidenov had proposed to the Moscow Art Theatre.
2. Varvara Chaleyeva, a Moscow Art Theatre actress.

Goodbye for now, keep well and cheerful. Write to me every day without fail. I kiss you, poppet, and hug you.

Your

A.

339. To Olga Knipper-Chekhova, 10 September 1902, Yalta

Dearest Roly-Poly,

Don't worry about the little Jewish boy,[1] he is already enrolled in the Gymnasium. We have had no rain for ages, and it feels as if there won't be any for a long time. There is no water at all. The air is full of dust that you can't see but that nevertheless, of course, has its effect. I'm feeling much better however; I'm coughing less and already have more of an appetite.

I declined the offer of becoming one of Morozov's shareholders because I have still not been paid the money I am owed, and everything points to my not getting it for a long time, if ever.[2] I don't wish to be a purely nominal shareholder just to have my name on the list. You are an artist of the theatre and receive a lower salary than you deserve, there-fore you could become a shareholder on credit, but I cannot do this.

Are you getting about on foot or in a cab these days? Are you going to any shows? What are you up to, generally? What are you reading? If anyone is coming to Yalta, please get them to bring a spittoon and some spectacles with them.

This year I shall definitely go abroad. For several reasons I cannot spend the winter here.

Did Shtraukh really say it would be all right for you to have children? Now or later? Oh, my darling sweetheart, time is passing!

1. Chekhov had wanted Olga to help intervene on behalf of Abram Bukhstab, who, although a good student, was not initially accepted at the Yalta Gymnasium because he was a Jew. The plan was to ask a well-placed shareholder at the Moscow Art Theatre to pass on a letter to the Minister of Education.
2. Konshin, the purchaser of Melikhovo, was still defaulting on payment.

By the time our child is eighteen months old I am sure to be bald, grey and toothless, and you'll be like your aunt Charlotta.

Oh, if only we could have some rain. It's awful without rain.

I kiss and hug my old lady. Don't be lazy, write to me, take pity on me! When will the building work in the theatre be finished? Write to me, darling.

Your husband, A.

340. To Stepan Petrov (Bishop Sergy), 24 September 1902, Yalta

Your Grace, Right Reverend Bishop,

Very many thanks for remembering me and writing to me. You gave not only me but my mother great joy when she learnt that I had had a letter from you; she was delighted, asked many questions about you and bade me send her deepest respects to you. I'm still in the same place, that is to say Yalta; I live here on account of being considered an invalid. In the summer I was on the Volga and also on the Kama; I visited Perm then stayed for a time near Moscow, but now, alas, I am in Yalta. However, around 15 October I shall go to Moscow, where I may stay until December; and from there I shall go abroad. I have a rather bad cough, but on the whole you could describe my health as pretty fair.

What is the cause of your feeling poorly? Do you know what is wrong – rheumatism perhaps, or something amiss with your lungs? Whatever the case, I very much sympathize with your desire to move to European Russia, and the sooner the better. Penza is a dull, burnt-out sort of a town, government officials hate being sent there and the winters are very severe. If only you could be transferred to the Tauride or Ekaterinoslav province, one or the other! Life is always interesting here, there is plenty of work, and above all it's warm. You and I would see a lot of one another, since I live in the Crimea and often come to Ekaterinoslav province, where, by the way, I was born. Poltava and Chernigov provinces are good. The snow is gone by March in all four of these provinces. And the folk who live in them are good people. If any of those sees should fall vacant, do bear my suggestion in mind and think about coming south.

My brother Misha lives in Petersburg. He is no longer a government official but works in the private sector; he is in charge of the retail book business on the railways. My sister is in Moscow and continues her teaching work. Brother Ivan is a teacher in a municipal school, as he was in the days when we lived in the Korneyev house; however, the school he now teaches in is a much better one, the Alexander II school.

That just about sums it up. If you should chance to be in Moscow, I beg you please to let me know, otherwise we won't see one another until we're seventy years old.

Allow me once again to thank you with all my heart for remembering me and to send you my best wishes, above all for good health. My mother and I ask your blessing. If you do not possess a copy of the first volume of my stories published by Marx (not the Suvorin edition, but the Marx one), let me know and I will send it to you. It consists entirely of humorous stories written at the beginning of the eighties.

I send you my deepest respects and remain your most respectful and devoted

A. Chekhov

341. To Olga Knipper-Chekhova, 2 October 1902, Yalta

My actress, what on earth do you want to hire a carriage for? There are no decent carriages in Moscow; they always make one feel sick. Let's go in an ordinary cab. I shall be in an autumn overcoat, so the fur coat probably won't be necessary. I'll bring a rug and galoshes with me.

Mother left yesterday by the mail coach in order to catch the mail train to Moscow. I didn't cable you because I don't know whether she will manage to get a ticket in Sevastopol. They say the trains are full and tickets bought up two weeks in advance.

It's very bad news that Nemirovich has been vomiting. Or rather it was bad at the time. When you see him, please tell him I'm most concerned for him and wish him a quick recovery.

It's been announced in the newspapers that all tickets on the mail train and the relief train have been sold until 15 October. If this is really the case, what are we going to do? I've written to Sevastopol on the off chance of getting a ticket.

I'm all on my own in the house now. Quite pleasant, really. I did contemplate installing a mistress, but then I thought: it's not long before I leave!

Keep well, my lovely little mongrel doggie. If you come to the station to meet me, just hire a cab to come to the station and keep it to go back again.

Well, I bow right down to your neat little feet and hug you. Think of me, or you'll be beaten. You know how strict I am.

Your

Antoine

Give my respects to my mother and to Masha.

342. To Leopold Sulerzhitsky, 5 November 1902, Moscow

The new theatre is very good indeed; it's spacious, fresh, and there's none of that cheap luxury that hits you in the face. The company performs as it did before, i.e. well. There are no new plays; the only one they did was not a success. Meyerhold's absence is not noticeable; he has been replaced in *Three Sisters* by Kachalov, who is outstanding in the role. The remaining plays (for example, *Lonely Lives*) have not been put on yet. The loss of Sanin, however, who had such a success[1] in Petersburg, is noticeable. The prices have remained the same as in the theatre the company occupied last year. The production of *Uncle Vanya* is wonderful.

My mother is in Petersburg, my sister is not painting, my wife has recovered her health, Vishnevsky comes by every day. Yesterday my wife went to hear Olenina D'Alheim,[2] who is a truly remarkable

1. Gorky's *The Petty Bourgeois*.
2. Maria Olenina D'Alheim (1869–1970), a singer who founded a series of famous recitals in Moscow called The House of Song.

singer. I am not allowed to go anywhere, I stayed at home for fear of catching cold. I probably won't go abroad, but will return to Yalta in December. Are you receiving *Russian Word*, which is being sent to you? Write and let me know. In any case, what you really should do is buy a little plot of land nearer to Moscow, where you could work, grow flowers and vegetables, and write short stories in the wintertime. You can either buy the land or take it on a sixty- or ninety-year lease. The main thing is that it should be not too far from Moscow. Yesterday Suvorin, Menshikov and Peshkov all came to see me; I've usually got a whole crowd of visitors. I shall try to send you photographs of the actors. Are you treating patients? You really shouldn't do that; it's best to send them to the doctor. Send me the title of the article you mentioned. May the heavenly angels watch over you.

Your

A. Chekhov

343. To Olga Knipper-Chekhova, 30 November 1902, Yalta

My joy and my sweetheart, I arrived in Yalta yesterday evening. The journey was good, the carriage was fairly empty, only four people in it; I drank tea and ate soup and all the food you gave me for the journey. The further south we got the colder it became; by the time we reached Sevastopol there was frost and snow. I took the steamer to Yalta and the sea was calm; I dined on board and had a conversation with a general about Sakhalin. It was cold in Yalta, and snowing. I am now sitting at my desk writing to you, my peerless wife, feeling cold in my bones; it's colder in Yalta than in Moscow. I'll be looking forward to getting your letters from tomorrow on. Write to me, darling heart, I beg you, as I shall soon start to feel miserable in the cold and the silence here.

Mother arrived safely, although she came by coach and horse. I found everything in place and in good order at home, even though Arseny and Granny had used my cherished apples, which I was keeping until December (they don't ripen until then), for the sauerkraut.

Everyone was overjoyed at the news that you will be bringing a dachshund with you. We badly need a dog here. Wouldn't the dachshund like to come with Masha at Christmas? Give this some thought.

Don't be miserable, light of my life, work hard, go everywhere and get as much sleep as you can. How I want you to be bright and healthy! This last visit has made you dearer to me than ever. My love for you is stronger than before.

It's very boring going to bed and getting up without you; it seems all wrong somehow. You have spoilt me.

Altshuller is coming here today and I will give him your wallet. I kiss you countless times, my darling doggie, and hug you too. Georges has come.[1] Keep well, and write to me.

Your

A.

You put so many shirts in my suitcase! Why so many? There's a huge pile of them in the wardrobe now.

Pass on my respects to your mama and thank her for the sweets. I send her my very best wishes. Deep bows to Uncle Karl, Uncle Sasha, Volodya and Ella as well.

344. To Sergey Diaghilev, 30 December 1902, Yalta

Dear Sergey Pavlovich,

I now have [the issue of] *The World of Art* containing the article about *The Seagull*, and have read the article – many thanks. After reading it right through, I once again felt moved to write a play, and shall probably do so after January.

Your letter mentions our conversation about a serious religious movement in Russia. Actually, we were talking about a movement among the intelligentsia generally, not just in Russia. I can't say anything about Russia, where the intelligentsia is still only playing at

1. Chekhov's cousin Georgy Chekhov.

religion, mostly from not having enough to do. One could say that the educated elements in our society have moved away from religion and indeed are moving further and further from it, whatever people may say and however many philosophical-religious societies spring up. I offer no opinion as to whether this is a good or a bad thing; all I will say is that the religious impulse of which you write is one thing, and contemporary culture taken as a whole is another, and it is quite wrong to assume that the latter is in any way a consequence of the former. The culture of today represents the initial stage of work towards a great future; work which will perhaps continue for tens of thousands of years, whose goal is that mankind may, at least in the distant future, know the truth about a real god: that is, not simply make guesses or seek to find him in Dostoyevsky, but know him clearly, as clearly as knowing that two and two make four. The culture of today is just the start of this work, while the religious movement we were talking about is a remnant, practically the final manifestation, of something that has already died or is in the process of dying. However, this is a long story, too long to be completely covered in a letter.

When you see Mr Filosofov,[1] please convey to him my profound gratitude. I send you my best wishes for all good fortune in the New Year.

Your devoted
A. Chekhov

345. To Olga Knipper-Chekhova, 1 January 1903, Yalta

A Happy New Year and all good fortune to you, my darling actress, my wife! I wish you all your heart's desires and all you deserve, but most of all I wish you to have a little half-German who would rummage through your drawers and smudge the ink on my desk, much to your delight.

1. Dmitry Filosofov (1872–1940), a literary critic and member of Diaghilev's *The World of Art* group, based in St Petersburg.

Bravo for having such a good time at the wedding.[1] It's a shame, of course, that I wasn't there; I would have enjoyed watching you and might have taken a turn on the floor myself.

I received a lot of letters today, from Suvorin and from Nemirovich among others. The latter sent me a list of plays your theatre plans to stage. No one play in particular jumps off the page, but they are all good. *The Fruits of Enlightenment* and *A Month in the Country* demand to be done so that you will have them in the repertoire.[2] They are both good, literary plays.

Masha saw in the New Year at Tatarinova's, and I stayed home. Tatarinova sent me a magnificent cactus plant: *epiphyllum trunetatum*. A light rain has been falling since morning.

Write to me, my dear one, console me with your letters. My health is excellent. My tooth has been fixed, so that's one more I get to keep. In short, everything is more or less all right.

I'm no good without a wife; it's like sleeping on a cold stove that long ago went out. Bunin and Naidenov are the current heroes of Odessa; they are being carried shoulder-high there.

I'm being called to drink tea. Keep well and happy, my actress, God be with you. I kiss, embrace and bless you, and pinch your back, just below the neck.

Your

A.

346. To Alexey Suvorin, 14 January 1903, Yalta

I'm not well, I have pleurisy with a temperature of 38 degrees, and I've been like that for most of the holiday season. But don't tell Misha, in fact don't tell anyone, as I'm sure I shall soon be better.

I received your letter, thank you. I will probably get the play

1. Elena (Ella) Bartels had just married Olga Knipper's brother Vladimir (Volodya), who abandoned his career as a lawyer to become an opera singer at the Bolshoi Theatre under the name Nardov.
2. Plays by Tolstoy and Turgenev, respectively, written in 1889–90 and 1850.

tomorrow. I'm leading the most idle existence, not doing anything – not from choice, however. The only thing I do is read.

Keep well, all best wishes for the New Year. I warmly press your hand.

Your

A. Chekhov

In your letter you refer to a large number of new newspapers that are now allowed in Petersburg. The only new one I take is *The New Way*: I read the first issue and have only this to say: I formerly considered the Religious-Philosophical Society a more serious and profound body than I do now.[1]

347. To Konstantin Alexeyev (Stanislavsky), 5 February 1903, Yalta

Dear Konstantin Sergeyevich,

Yesterday I received the *Seagull* medal. I am profoundly, infinitely, grateful to you. I have already attached a chain to it, and shall wear this cherished, elegant little object and think of you.

I have been poorly for a time, but have got through it and my health is now better. If I am not presently working as I should be, the fault lies in the cold (it is no warmer than 11 degrees in my study), in the lack of people and, probably, in my laziness, which last was born in 1859, that is to say the year before I was. All the same, I do intend to sit down properly with the play after 20 February, and finish it by

1. This society was set up by the writer Dmitry Merezhkovsky and others in 1901 to help close what seemed an unbridgeable divide between the Church and the mainly secular intelligentsia, and coincided with a religious revival at the beginning of the twentieth century. Obtaining official permission from the government to hold meetings was no small matter, and although the sensational changes forecast did not materialize, the meetings (attended by many decadent writers of the St Petersburg literary elite) were temporarily banned on the eve of the 1905 Revolution. See also letter 344.

20 March. It is all complete in my head. Its title is *The Cherry Orchard*; it has four acts, in the first of which flowering cherry trees are seen through the windows, an entire garden of white. And the women will be in white dresses. In a word, Vishnevsky will be laughing a lot, but nobody, of course, will know why.

It is snowing. My deepest respects to Maria Petrovna, I warmly press and kiss her hand. It is very good news that she is back on stage; that must mean that all is now well with her.

Be well, cheerful, happy and do not forget your warmly devoted

A. Chekhov

348. To Maria Chekhova, 1 March 1903, Yalta

Dearest Masha,

When you go to buy seeds, don't forget to get some giant hemp. Spring is upon us; I have already received and sown lots of good stuff from Sukhumi. It rains almost every day, so the ground is moist and the plants feel very happy. Arseny has already sown grass for the lawn here and there.

The camellia is in flower. I don't go into town much, I've been staying at home. Sredin has been taken quite seriously ill; Tatarinova's son's temperature is normal, which means it's nonsense to imagine he has tuberculosis.

Mother is well and fasting for Lent; her teeth are giving her a bad time. Wishing you health and happiness,

Your

Anton

Arseny asks if you will buy some edging shears and shears for the lawn.

349. *To Olga Knipper-Chekhova, 4 March 1903, Yalta*

My dearest sweetheart, there is a great celebration in Yalta because a Cubat Frères[1] shop has opened here, the genuine Cubat from Petersburg. Tomorrow I shall go and have a look at what they have and write and tell you; perhaps we will no longer have to rely on getting delicacies from Moscow.

You gave me a good telling off for not having finished the play, and are threatening to take me in hand. Please do take me in hand, that's a threat I very much like the sound of; having you take me in your hands is the only thing I want, but as far as the play is concerned you have no doubt forgotten that long ago, in the days of Noah, I announced to all and sundry that I would be getting down to the play at the end of February and the beginning of March. My laziness has nothing to do with it. After all, I'm not exactly my own worst enemy, and if I had the strength I would have written not one but twenty-five plays. Anyhow, I'm glad there isn't a play, because it means you can rest instead of having to rehearse. The amount of work you do is absurd, it's slavery by any standard!

It is quite cool here, but pleasant all the same. I haven't finally made up my mind about next winter, but I can't say I have especially high hopes of it. For now, the only thing I can say is that I will stay in Moscow until December (especially if you mend my fur coat), and after that I will probably have to go abroad, to the Riviera or to Nervi, until, say, around 15 February, and then back to Yalta. It means we will have to be apart for much of the time, but it can't be helped!! Cudgel my brains as I may, I can't think of any way round it. If you were to get pregnant, then I could bring you with me to Yalta in February. Would you like that, my sweet? What do you think? I'd happily spend the winter anywhere, even in Arkhangelsk, if only it meant you could produce a little one.

Are you going to Petersburg? Yes or no?

At all events, tomorrow I'll go to Cubat for a sniff of European

---

1. An exclusive food shop and also a restaurant in St Petersburg.

civilization. Are you moving to the new apartment? What floor is it on? If it's very high up it will take me half an hour to get there, but that doesn't matter, I don't have anything to do in Moscow anyway.

Bathrooms are all very well, but, as for me, I'd rather go and steam in the bathhouse any day. It's a shame about the apartment in the Gonetskaya house; it was so near the bathhouse.[2]

Well, my darling old girl, I give you a big hug, and when I've done that I'll leap round the room and then kiss your neck and your back, and tweak your nose, my dearest sweetheart.

Your

A.

350. To Olga Knipper-Chekhova, 15 April 1903, Yalta

My incomparable sweetheart, my silly old darling, you are wrong to be angry with me for not writing. In the first place, you yourself wrote to me that you were going away from Moscow at the start of Passion Week, and in the second place, I write to you all the time. In any case, why write if we are soon, very soon, going to see one another, if I shall soon be pinching you from behind and doing other such things? I've already booked the ticket; I leave on the 22nd and will be in Moscow on the 24th. The moment I arrive I'm going to the bathhouse. I'll bring you the sheets.

Why do you always play into the hands of *New Times*? Why pick *The Lower Depths*[1] [to open with] when you know it will be a flop? Oh, what a bad piece of planning that was. I am not at all happy about your trip to Petersburg. I don't really want to write a play for your theatre, mainly because there aren't any older women in the company. That means it will be you who will be cast as an older woman, but I have another role for you. Besides, you already played an older woman in *The Seagull*.

2. The Sanduny, founded by the actor Sandunov – the most famous bathhouse in Moscow.

1. Written by Gorky in 1902.

Well, we had a little rain yesterday. In general spring has been nice here, but a little chilly and boring.

Dr Bogdanovich has died here in Yalta. Did you know him?

Touring to Odessa and Kiev is a good idea. I'll come with you. There will be huge box office receipts in Odessa, and it would be enjoyable to spend some time in Kiev and welcome the spring there.

Why don't you put on *The Petty Bourgeois*? It was a success in Petersburg.

I'll send you just one more letter and one telegram, and then it won't be long before we meet. I'm as swarthy as an Arab. It's lovely in the garden, I sit in it all day and have become horribly sunburnt. Have you seen Modest Tchaikovsky? Have you seen Suvorin? Does Misha come to the theatre? Well, you can answer all these questions when I get to Moscow, my loyal and loving spouse.

I kiss you right on the snout, and clap you on the back.

Your

Old Blackface

351. To Maria Chekhova, 23 May 1903, Moscow

Dearest Masha,

We are still in Moscow. The doctors are advising me not to go to Switzerland; they say it would be better for me at a dacha. I have an appointment to see Ostroumov[1] tomorrow: he will go through all his tapping and listening routine, and then make a final decision. If we don't go abroad we shall probably go to Yakunchikova's dacha at Nara.

I spent yesterday with the Maklakovs at Dergaikovo.

It's very hot and stuffy here.

Please give Sinani three of the books by Moskvich,[2] the ones on

1. Professor Alexey Ostroumov (1844–?1908), a doctor and clinician who ran the Moscow University surgical clinic from 1880 to 1903. He had treated Chekhov in 1897.
2. Grigory Moskvich, a writer of travel guides and tour operator in the Caucasus.

the Crimea, St Petersburg and the Volga. Moskvich himself, whom I've seen, asked for this to be done.

I want to remind you: be careful walking in the part of the garden where the pump is, because the wooden beams have already begun to rot: tell them to put a plank down there.

Give my respects to Mama and Lyolya, and also Polya, Maryushka and Arseny. I press your hand, stay well.

Your

A.

352. To Alexey Suvorin, 17 June 1903, Naro-Fominskoye

Preserve us, O ye heavenly cherubim! Yesterday all of a sudden a letter was delivered to me with twenty addresses on it and liberally sprinkled with postmarks, as though it had come all the way from Australia; I open it, and what do I see? It turns out to be from you, posted on 23 May to New Jerusalem! I haven't been there at all; I did go for one day to Zvenigorod district to see Maklakov, and I mentioned to Vasya and probably Misha that I was going to New Jerusalem because this happens to be the nearest place to Maklakov's. So if it has taken such a long time for you to get a reply, it's not my fault.

I only spent a few hours in Petersburg, but I did see Marx. Our conversation was not particularly specific; in his Germanic way he offered me 5,000 towards my medical treatment, which I refused, and then he gave me about 50 kilos of his publications, which I accepted, and after that we parted, having decided to meet again in August and have a talk then, and in the meantime to think matters over.

I did not tell Misha anything about Marx, so anything he may have said to you is purely his own speculation. But once again there has been something of a change in my personal circumstances. I went to see Prof. Ostroumov, and, after examining me thoroughly, he tore me off a strip. He told me that my health is extremely poor, that I am suffering from emphysema and pleurisy, and so on and so forth. He ordered me to spend the winter not in the Crimea but in the north, near Moscow. Naturally I am pleased about this, but where, pray, am I now to find a dacha for the winter? It has to be in the Moscow area and one in which I won't freeze to death or have to put up with other inconveniences. Whatever the case, I shall start looking and will write to you when I've found one.

Please send me the next issues of the newspaper;[1] I have already packed up the previous ones in a parcel and given it to Vasya to pass back to you. My address is: Naro-Fominskoye, Moscow Province. I'll let you know in good time should there be any change of address.

There is a fine river here at the dacha, but no one to go fishing with.

Lavrov, the publisher of *Russian Thought*, is very ill (nephritis and angina pectoris), and is making shift to ensure that his magazine doesn't end up in the hands of his heirs. Apparently he has already managed to do this; the magazine has been sold and its future is secure. Goltsev remains in charge and they even invited me to become editor of the literature section . . .

So, I am going to be based in the Moscow area for the winter; Ostroumov will not let me go abroad. ('You,' he said, 'are an invalid.') I'm not used to it and am bound to freeze to death. Stay well and safe; I send you and all your family my best wishes. If I receive the next issues of the newspaper, I'll return them to you in the same way, in a parcel I'll give to Vasya.

Your

A. Chekhov

It is a great step forward that floggings and head-shavings have been abolished.[2]

1. Suvorin had been sending Chekhov clandestinely some publications banned in Russia.
2. On 15 June 1903 a law had been passed banning harsh corporal punishment of exiles; also forbidden was chaining to wheelbarrows, the shaving of heads and punishment with the lash or rod.

353. To Sergey Pavlovich Diaghilev, 12 July 1903, Yalta

Dear Sergey Pavlovich,

I am rather late in replying to your letter, as I received it not in Naro-Fominskoye but in Yalta, where I arrived a few days ago and will probably stay until the autumn. After reading your letter I thought it over for a long time, but while your proposal or invitation is greatly tempting, I must in the end answer it in a way neither of us would wish.

I cannot become an editor of *The World of Art*, because I cannot live in Petersburg, and the magazine is not going to move to Moscow just on my account. One can't edit a magazine by post or telegram, and I see no point in being an editor in name only. That is the first matter. The second is that, just as a picture can be painted by only one artist and a speech can be made by only one orator, a journal can have only one editor. Of course I am no critic, and no doubt would not make a very good job of editing a criticism section, but also how could I possibly coexist under the same roof with Dmitry Merezhkovsky, a confirmed and evangelical believer, while I long ago allowed my own belief to dissipate to such an extent that now I can only regard with bewilderment an educated man who is also religious? I have the greatest respect and admiration for Dmitry Sergeyevich as a person and as a writer, but were we ever to be harnessed to the same cart we should find ourselves pulling it in different directions. However this may be, and whether or not I have the wrong approach to this matter, I have always believed, and still do, that only one person can edit a magazine, and as far as *The World of Art* is concerned that person can only be you. Such is my opinion, and I think I am not likely to alter it.

Please do not be angry with me, dear Sergey Pavlovich; I believe that if you were to continue editing the journal for another five years you would come to agree with me. A journal, like a poem or a painting, must be the product of a single mind and reflect a single will. That is how it has always been up until now in *The World of Art*, and to that it owes its value. It should be maintained.

I send you my best wishes and warmly clasp your hand. It is quite cool in Yalta at the moment, or at least not too warm, and I am in fine fettle.

With my deep respects,

Your

A. Chekhov

354. To Konstantin Alexeyev (Stanislavsky), 28 July 1903, Yalta

Dear Konstantin Sergeyevich,

I am very, very sorry that you did not come to Yalta just now; the weather here is exceptionally, entrancingly, good; nothing could be better. There has been rain throughout the summer, and now it is hot, but not dry and dusty, and everything is green.

My play is not yet finished; it's moving forward very sluggishly, which may be explained partly by my laziness, partly by the wonderful weather, and partly by the difficulty of the subject. As soon as it is finished, or even before, I will write to you or, better, send you a telegram. Your own part has turned out pretty well, although I can't really judge since I don't generally derive many insights from reading plays.

Olga is well, she goes swimming every day and fusses over me. My sister is also well; both thank you for your regards and send theirs to you. Yesterday I saw Mikhailovsky-Garin, the engineer–writer who is to build the Crimean railway; he tells me he intends to write a play.

I am in good health. Please pass on my respects and greetings to Maria Petrovna and the children, and also to Elizaveta Vasilievna. I warmly clasp your hand, and wish you good health and the best of everything.

Your

A. Chekhov

I don't propose to read my play to you, since I am not a good reader; I shall simply give it to you to read – when, that is, it is finished.

355. To Alexander Chekhov, 15 August 1903, Yalta

Quousque tandem taces? Quousque tandem, frater, abutere patientia nostra?
Sum in Jalta.
Frater bonus
Antonius
Scribendum est.

[How long, finally, dost thou propose to keep silence? How long, finally, brother, dost thou propose to abuse our patience?
I am in Yalta.
Your good brother
Antonius
It is time to write.]

356. To Olga Knipper-Chekhova, 19 September 1903, Yalta

Dearest sweetheart, my coltish little doggie, how was your journey? How did your stay in Sevastopol with the man with the ginger moustache[1] go? Was everything all right?

I wasn't well when I got back from the steamer; now I've no appetite, my stomach feels dull and stupid, I don't feel like walking and my head aches. What has brought all this on, I don't know. But needless to say, the worst of it is your going away; it takes ages for me to get used to your not being here.

If you haven't yet got around to sending the parcel to Yalta, would you please add some leggings: I shall soon be needing them.

I read in the newspapers today that *The Cherry Orchard* will be produced in December. If so, it is very good news and I approve, only

---

1. Alexander Shaposhnikov, a banker in Sevastopol.

the play should be premièred at the beginning of the month, not at the end. I shall work on it tomorrow.

Nina Korsh and her daughter had lunch with us yesterday. I'm slightly concerned that you only took 75 roubles from me, not 100. That means I owe you 25 roubles, my dearest sweetheart.

Write to me, my dear, my love, now you know for certain how much I love you.

I'll write to you again tomorrow, but for now you should rest, talk to everyone, unpack your trunks. Give my regards to all our friends; don't leave anyone out. Write and tell me how *Julius Caesar* is going; have you heard anything about it? How is Vishnevsky?

I hug you and kiss the palms of your hands. God be with you.

Your

A.

I have a feeling my handwriting has got smaller. Has it?
Today I shall be laying out the cards for patience *solo*.

357. To Konstantin Alexeyev (Stanislavsky), 30 October 1903, Yalta

Dear Konstantin Sergeyevich,

Thank you very much for your letter, and also for the telegram. Letters are all the more treasured by me now, first because I am sitting here all on my own, and second because I sent you my play three weeks ago and received your letter only yesterday; had it not been for my wife I would have known nothing at all and would have been imagining all manner of things that crept into my brain. When I was creating the role of Lopakhin, it was your acting I had in mind. But if for some reason it does not appeal to you, take Gayev. It is true that Lopakhin is a merchant, but he is in every sense of the word a decent man; he must be presented as a wholly dignified, intelligent individual, not remotely petty or capricious, and it seemed to me that this role, which is central to the play, would be a brilliant one for you. If you take Gayev, give Vishnevsky the part of Lopakhin. He won't make Lopakhin an artistic character, but he won't demean him either. Luzhsky would turn him into a cold outsider, Leonidov a coarse little kulak. When you cast this role, keep in mind that Varya has loved Lopakhin; she is a serious and religious young woman and would not have loved a coarse little kulak.

I very much want to come to Moscow, but I don't know if I shall be able to get away from here. The weather is getting cold and I seldom leave the house; I've got out of the way of being in the fresh air, and my cough is bad. It's not Moscow I'm afraid of, it's having to sit around in Sevastopol from two o'clock until eight o'clock, not to mention putting up with some extremely boring company.

Write and tell me which role you decide to take. My wife wrote that Moskvin would like to play Epikhodov. That seems a very good idea to me; the play could only benefit from it.

My best respects and greetings to Maria Petrovna, I wish her and all your family the very best. Keep well and in good spirits yourself.

I haven't yet seen *The Lower Depths, The Pillars of Society* or *Julius Caesar*. I should so much like to.

Your

A. Chekhov

I'm not sure where you are living at present, so am sending this letter to the theatre.

358. To Olga Knipper-Chekhova, 29 November 1903, Yalta

Dearest little colt, I don't know what to do or what to think. People are obstinately not summoning me to Moscow, and it's obvious they don't want me to come. I wish you would write and tell me frankly why this is so, what is the reason, and then I won't waste any more time but will go abroad. If only you knew how boringly the rain drums on the roof, and how badly I want to set eyes on my wife. Do I even have a wife? Where is she?

I shall not write any more; you must do as you please, Madame. I've nothing to write about and no reason to.

If I get a telegram today I'll bring you some sweet wine; if I don't, you'll get a big fat nothing.

I must tell you again, Schnap isn't right.[1] You need a mangy dog like the one you saw that time, or something like it. You can do without a dog altogether if necessary.

I embrace you.

A.

359. To Alexander Pleshcheyev, 5 or 6 December 1903, Moscow

I would be very happy to see you so that we could have a good talk and remember old times.

I am usually at home between ten o'clock and half past twelve, and after that in the Art Theatre for rehearsal until four o'clock, then home again and once more to the Art Theatre for the performance at eight o'clock. I haven't seen any of the [other] plays but am now determined to do so. I haven't seen *The Lower Depths*, nor *Julius Caesar* nor *The Pillars of Society*, and I haven't been to the Maly Theatre either. Let's try to meet. Either come to my house, or let me know when I can find you in. I warmly clasp your hand. Keep well.

Your

A. Chekhov

360. To Olga Knipper-Chekhova, 17 February 1904, Sevastopol

Hello, my incomparable little horse! I'm writing this to you sitting on the steamer, which is due to sail in about three hours. So far the

1. Olga wanted to audition her black dachshund for the role of Charlotta's dog in *The Cherry Orchard*.

journey has been good, everything is fine. Nastya[1] is here on board with Schnap; he feels quite at home and is very sweet. On the train he also behaved as if he were at home, he barked at the conductors and amused everybody; I very much enjoyed having him around, and now he is sitting on deck with his hind legs stretched out behind him. He has obviously forgotten all about Moscow already, though it pains me to say so. Well, my darling little horse, I look forward to your letters. You must know I can't live without your letters. Either write to me every day or divorce me; there's nothing in between.

I can hear Schnap barking at someone up above. I expect some of the passengers are playing with him; I'd better go and see.

So everything is fine, thank the Lord. Can't have better than that. With luck it won't be too rough.

I kiss my boss and hug her a million times. Write and tell me every single detail, don't skimp on ink, my dear, good, glorious, talented actress; may God be with you, I love you very much.

Your

A.

361. To Olga Knipper-Chekhova, 1 April 1904, Yalta

Hello my darling! Write and tell me when you are going to Moscow. I need to know, because I want to arrive at the same time as you.

It is wonderful weather today, but everyone is in a black mood because of the telegrams.[1] There is nothing new; everything is as before. I had my hair cut and washed at the barber's today, and thought of you. If you see anything of interest in the newspapers, please cut it out with scissors and send it to me. I get *Russia*, and also *New Times*, but none of the other Petersburg papers.

1. Anastasia Komarova was a maid in the Chekhovs' house in Yalta.
1. The Russo-Japanese war had commenced in February 1904 and on 31 March newspapers carried the story of the sinking of the flagship *Petropavlovsk* together with Admiral Makarov, the artist Vereshchagin and most of her crew.

I can imagine how you are all feeling. Well, my darling little doggie, I embrace you, sleep well.

Your

A.

362. To Olga Knipper-Chekhova, 17 April 1904, Yalta

Hello, my dearest chaffinch! No letter from you again today, but never mind, I won't get offended or lose heart as we shall be seeing each other very, very soon now. I sent the reviews to the Hotel Dresden, but some of them seem to have fallen by the wayside. It was a pretty big bundle.

As soon as we are together we must put our heads together and decide the question of the dacha. I suppose we shall have to settle on the one in Tsaritsyno. True, it is a bit damp, but it is very near Moscow, the connections are good and when you were there you felt at home, not as if you were staying in someone else's house. We'll have to fix up your room as sumptuously and cosily as possible, so that you will come to love it.

It's rather cold here in Yalta, and raining.

I have another problem here as well: my bowels are out of order and I don't seem to have any way of controlling them, either by medicines or by diet.

Korovin the artist,[1] who is a passionate angler, has been teaching me a special way to catch fish without using bait; it's the English way and it is marvellous except that you need a good river like Alexeyev [Stanislavsky] has in Lyubimovka. I'm going to order a rowing boat from Petersburg. But again I can't start on that before I get to Moscow.

Your lovely little sow with the three piglets on her back sends you greetings. Schnap has for some reason taken to jumping up and barking at Nastya when she calls him cross-eyed.

1. Konstantin Korovin (1861–1939), a painter and set designer for the Mamontov Private Opera Company and later the Bolshoi Theatre in Moscow.

Is Maria Petrovna still ill? If she has come to Petersburg, please pass on my respects to her. The same to the whole company and to Chumina.

I'm finding it so hard to breathe!

Why was there no performance on 13 April? Was somebody ill, or were you all just exhausted?

I'll continue sending you letters for a few more days, and then I'll stop in order to start getting ready for the journey. How boring to have to sit in Sevastopol from two o'clock until half past eight! Where can I park myself? At Shaposhnikov's? Dearest!

There's nothing new, everything is as it was. I hug you, my lovely actress, and take you by the chin to kiss you.

Your

A.

363. To Maria Chekhova, 23 April 1904, Yalta

Dear Masha,

I'm leaving Yalta on 1 May and shall arrive in Moscow on the morning of the 3rd. It's all decided. I had wanted to leave earlier, but can't because I'm having some dental treatment.

Everything here is fine, as usual. Nastya is walking about with an exercise book learning her part,[1] the cook is singing, they produce hot meals but I'm not eating anything except soup because my stomach is still upset, and so on and so on. Schnap goes to the market every day, Tuzik gets cross, Sharik feels himself to be socially inferior and wags his tail shyly.[2]

Mother is well. The weather is cold and not very pleasant. Stay well and cheerful.

Your

Anton

1. Chekhov's maid took part in amateur theatrical productions and later became a professional actress.
2. The mongrel dogs who were part of the menagerie in Chekhov's house in Yalta.

364. To Vasily Sobolevsky, 13 May 1904, Moscow

Dear Vasily Mikhailovich,

I have been in Moscow for some time, but have not been to see you because I have been unwell and unable to leave my bed. I am suffering from catarrh of the bowels and pleurisy, accompanied by a high temperature.

I send you my best wishes! Keep well and happy!

I embrace you warmly.

Your

A. Chekhov

365. To Isaak Altshuller, 26 May 1904, Moscow

Dear Isaak Naumovich,

I have been in bed, day and night, ever since getting to Moscow, and have not once been able to get up and dress. Therefore, of course, I have not succeeded in doing what you asked of me with regard to Khmelev.[1] Even if I had been fit, I doubt whether I would have been able to do anything. Khmelev is very busy these days, and it is not easy to get to see him.

The diarrhoea has stopped, but now I am suffering from constipation. I got some kind of infection the day before yesterday; my temperature goes up after dinner and then I don't sleep all night. My cough is a bit better. I am going abroad on 3 June, to the Black Forest, and I'll be in Yalta in August.

Oh, those enemas – they completely knocked me out! I'm allowed coffee, which I enjoy very much, but eggs and soft bread are forbidden.

I warmly clasp your hand. I'm now lying on the couch and,

---

1. Chekhov had got to know Nikolay Khmelev in the 1890s, when he was living in Melikhovo. Khmelev was head of the Serpukhov *zemstvo*, and in 1895 became president of the Economics Office of the Moscow gubernatorial *zemstvo*.

having nothing better to do, spend my time cursing Ostroumov and Shchurovsky.[2] This is a most enjoyable occupation.

Your

A. Chekhov

Last night was the first time I had a proper night's sleep.

366. To Maria Chekhova, 8 June 1904, Berlin

Dearest Masha,

We are leaving Berlin today for a long stay at a place near the Swiss border, where it will probably be very boring and very hot. This is the address: Herrn Anton Tshechow, Badenweiler, Germany – that is how my name appears on my books here, so I presume that is how you should write it. It's rather cold in Berlin, but nice all the same. The worst thing here, and it hits you in the face right away, is the way the women dress. There is an atrocious lack of taste; nowhere else do people dress so hideously and so utterly without taste. I have not seen a single handsome woman, nor one who has not decked herself out in the most ridiculous looking ribbons. Now I understand why German women in Moscow find it so hard to acquire any vestige of taste. On the other hand, life is very comfortable in Berlin, the food is good, prices are reasonable, the horses are well fed, as are the dogs which they harness to little carts here, the streets are clean and there is a general sense of order.

Ekaterina Pavlovna [Peshkova] is passing through Berlin; her children have contracted measles and she is in despair. I saw her yesterday.

My legs have stopped hurting, I'm eating splendidly, sleeping well and going for drives around Berlin. The only problem is my shortness of breath. I bought a summer suit and some hunting jackets today, that kind of thing. They are much cheaper than in Moscow.

Now that you have my address, please write to me and send letters

---

2. Vladimir Shchurovsky (1852–?), a specialist in internal medicine, professor at Moscow University.

on. You can put several in one envelope and send it by registered post. Only send those which look as though they might be important.

Greetings to Mamasha and Vanya. Live happily and don't be down. I warmly clasp your hand and kiss you.

Your

A.

367. To Vasily Sobolevsky, 12 June 1904, Badenweiler

Dear Vasily Mikhailovich,

Very many thanks for *The Russian Gazette*, which I have been receiving here since the day I arrived and which warms me like the sun; I read it each morning with immense pleasure. And still more grateful thanks and profound respects for introducing me to Grigory Iollos.[1] He is a wonderful person, exceptionally interesting, kindness itself and infinitely obliging. I spent three days in Berlin, and was conscious of Iollos's solicitous care throughout those three days. Unfortunately my legs were not functioning properly and, especially the first day or two, I was not feeling at all well, so I could not place myself wholly at his disposal even for a couple of hours. I am sure he would have shown me many interesting things in Berlin. I formed the impression that he has a very modest opinion of himself, and does not realize the success his 'Letters from Berlin' enjoy in Moscow and indeed throughout Russia.

My health is improving in leaps and bounds. My legs have not been painful for some time now, it is as if they had never given me any problems, and I'm eating, not much but with a good appetite; now there remains only the breathlessness from the emphysema and a general weakness caused by the weight I lost while I was ill. I am under the care of a good doctor here, who is intelligent and

1. Grigory Iollos (1859–1907), the Berlin correspondent of *The Russian Gazette* who translated Chekhov's plays into German.

knowledgeable. This is Dr Schwoerer, married to our Zhivago from Moscow.[2]

Badenweiler is a most unusual spa town, but I have yet to understand exactly what is so unusual about it. It is very green, you feel the mountains close by, the weather is very warm, most of the houses and hotels are detached buildings surrounded by trees. I am staying in a small pension standing in its own grounds, which gets an enormous amount of sun (until seven o'clock in the evening) and has a superb garden. We pay 16 marks a day for the two of us (room, lunch, supper and coffee). The food is good and plentiful, extremely so. But I can just imagine how crushingly dull life here must be most of the time! It has been raining since early morning, incidentally, so I am sitting in my room listening to the wind howling above and below the roofs.

Either the Germans have entirely lost whatever taste they once had, or they never had any: German women dress in the vilest possible taste, and the men also. I did not see a single good-looking woman in Berlin, nor one who had not made herself hideous by the clothes she arrayed herself in. But the way they run their country is exemplary; they attain heights far beyond anything we can aspire to.

Have I already bored you with my prattling? Allow me to thank you once again most warmly, for the newspaper, for [the introduction to] Iollos, and for your visits to me in Moscow, which were so welcome and so enjoyable. I shall not forget your kindness to me. Keep well and happy, and may God send you a warm summer. It's cold in Berlin, by the way. I embrace you warmly and press your hand.

Your

A. Chekhov

---

2. Elizaveta Zhivago was Russian. Dr Schwoerer's best friend was married to her sister.

368. To Maria Chekhova, 26 June 1904, Badenweiler

Dearest Masha,

Everything is fine, except that it is very monotonous and therefore boring: one day is much like another. There has been a change in the weather; it has become very hot so I've had to change my jacket for a shirt. My health is improving all the time, I'm getting stronger and eating enough. I'd like to go on from here to Lake Como and spend a while there; the Italian Lakes are famous for their beauty, and one can live there cheaply and comfortably. I had a letter from Georges today, which touched me very much. I haven't had many letters from you, only two so far. I wrote to you from Berlin, didn't you get it?

Even the nights are warm here. We sleep with the windows open inside the shutters. Incidentally I am sleeping very well, just as I used to, so evidently things are really improving for me as far as my health is concerned. Greetings to Mamasha, Vanya, Georges, Granny and all our community. I'll write again soon. I kiss you and wish you every kind of blessing.

Your
Anton

369. To Grigory Rossolimo, 28 June 1904, Badenweiler

Dear Grigory Ivanovich, I want to ask you a favour. One evening a little while ago you were telling me about your travels to Mount Athos with L. L. Tolstoy[1] . . . Did you go from Marseilles to Odessa? With Austrian Lloyd? If so, please for the love of God seize your pen at once and write and tell me on which day and at what hour the steamer sails from Marseilles, how many days is the voyage to Odessa, what time of day or night the steamer gets to Odessa, is it comfortable on board, that is could there be a separate cabin for me and my wife,

1. Tolstoy's son Lev Lvovich (1869–1945).

is there a decent restaurant, is it clean . . . were you generally happy with everything? What I require above all is peace and quiet, and everything necessary for a man who is very short of breath. I beg you to write! Let me know also how much the tickets cost.

Every day recently I have had a high temperature, but today everything is fine, I feel quite well, especially when I don't walk, I mean I don't feel breathless. The breathlessness is very hard, it just makes you want to cry for help, and sometimes I feel very depressed. I've lost altogether 15 pounds in weight.

The heat here is unbearable, it just makes you want to cry aloud for help, and I have no light clothes here, I'm dressed as though for Sweden. They say it's very hot everywhere, at least in the south.

So, I wait impatiently for your reply. Forgive me, my dear fellow, for troubling you, don't be angry, and perhaps some day I shall have the chance to repay you, I comfort myself with this thought . . . How desperately boring this German spa town of Badenweiler is!

I firmly clasp your hand, send you a deep bow and my greetings to your wife. Be well and happy.

Your

A. Chekhov

370. To Maria Chekhova, 28 June 1904, Badenweiler

Dearest Masha,

The heat has become very fierce here. It has taken me by surprise, because the only clothes I have with me are winter ones, so I'm suffocating and long to get away from here. But where to? I wanted to go to Italy, to Como, but everyone has gone from there because of the heat. There is a heatwave covering the whole of southern Europe. Then I thought of taking a boat from Trieste to Odessa, but I don't know whether that is possible now, in June–July. Could Georges make some inquiries, to find out what boats there are? Is the timetable convenient? Do they involve long stopovers, is the food good, and so on and so on? It would be an absolutely ideal trip for me, if the boat is a good one and not an old tub. Georges would be doing me a very great service if he could send me a telegram, *at my expense*. The telegram should read like this: 'Badenweiler Tschechow. Bien. 16. Vendredi.' This means: *bien* – the boat is a good one. *16* – the number of days the voyage takes. *Vendredi* – the day the boat sails from Trieste. Of course, this is merely the form the telegram should take, if the boat leaves on a Thursday, *Vendredi* won't quite fit the bill.

If it's a bit hot it won't matter too much; I'll have a flannel suit by then. I must admit I would be a little nervous of going by train. I would suffocate in a carriage just now, especially as I am finding it so hard to breathe, and the slightest thing exacerbates it. Moreover, there are no through sleeping cars from Vienna to Odessa, so it would not be very comfortable. Also, the train would get me home earlier than I need to be, and I don't feel I have had enough of a holiday yet.

It's so terribly hot you keep wanting to take your clothes off. I don't know what to do. Olga has gone to Freiburg to order me a flannel suit; Badenweiler has no tailor or shoemaker. She took the suit Duchard made for me as a pattern.

The food here is excellent, but I'm not getting on with it very well; my stomach keeps getting upset. I'm not allowed to eat the local butter. Apparently my stomach is irretrievably damaged, and nothing will help it except fasting, i.e. eating nothing at all, and – *basta*. The only remedy for the breathlessness is not to move.

There is no such thing as a well-dressed German woman. Their lack of taste induces deep despondency.

Well, keep in good health and spirits, greetings to Mamasha, Vanya, Georges, Granny and everyone. Write. I kiss you and press your hand.

Your

A.

[Anton Chekhov died in Badenweiler on 2 July 1904 (old style)]

Index

The biographical note in the List of Correspondents
is in bold